AS THE BEACON TURNS

J.M. Coutts

Note for Librarians: a cataloguing record for this book that includes Dewey Decimal Classification and US Library of Congress numbers is available from the Library and Archives of Canada. The complete cataloguing record can be obtained from their online database at:
www.collectionscanada.ca/amicus/index-e.html
ISBN 1-4120-4423-5
Printed in Victoria, BC, Canada

TRAFFORD

Offices in Canada, USA, Ireland, UK and Spain
This book was published *on-demand* in cooperation with Trafford Publishing. On-demand publishing is a unique process and service of making a book available for retail sale to the public taking advantage of on-demand manufacturing and Internet marketing. On-demand publishing includes promotions, retail sales, manufacturing, order fulfilment, accounting and collecting royalties on behalf of the author.
Book sales for North America and international:
Trafford Publishing, 6E–2333 Government St.,
Victoria, BC v8t 4p4 CANADA
phone 250 383 6864 (toll-free 1 888 232 4444)
fax 250 383 6804; email to orders@trafford.com
Book sales in Europe:
Trafford Publishing (uk) Limited, 9 Park End Street, 2nd Floor
Oxford, UK oxi 1hh UNITED KINGDOM
phone 44 (0)1865 722 113 (local rate 0845 230 9601)
facsimile 44 (0)1865 722 868; info.uk@trafford.com
Order online at:
www.trafford.com/robots/04-2231.html

10 9 8 7

There is no higher honor
Than to be given
The responsibility to
Care for another
Human being.

Richard K. Schachern
April 13, 1953 - May 5, 2003

INTRODUCTION

Imagine spending half of your life working a job that you loved. And, imagine that this job offered the chance to be like a white knight, coming to the rescue of damsels (young and old) in distress. That you were welcomed like the cavalry, arriving to save the day or at least to make a horrible day seem less dreadful. Then, to make things interesting, imagine this job allowed you to work briefly along side the police and or detectives on a crime scene, assist physicians and nurses, firemen and other rescue personnel.

The things you'd see and learn, and gosh, the stories you could tell, leaving the victim's name out to protect the innocent of course, would be vast; not to say that there wouldn't be drawbacks or challenges with this job. If it were easy, everyone would do it and then it would lose its enamoring appeal. But still you stuck it out and now you feel an effervescent stirring to write some of these experiences down. Where do you start? Can I really do it, you ask yourself?

Then, in a simple phone conversation after a friend reads a short journal that you've jotted down, he asks, " Have you ever thought about writing?" That's all it took for the cork that had been suppressing your imagination and all the words describing your job and life experiences to finally, break free. And so to Pastor Greg, Mt. Zion's music director, the emancipator of said "cork," to Nancy Hussey, who spent an incredible amount of time editing and all of the people who made this book possible in one way or another, I offer much thanks. Enjoy this story, it holds many shared experiences of the job and life we still treasure.

For those who weren't there, hop up, put on your seat belt, flip on the emergency lights, turn the siren knob to yelp and get ready for an adventure that began in the fall of 1975. As The Beacon Turns is a book that was originally written in the minds of those who experienced the world of EMS, emergency medical service, during its earlier days in the mid 1970's when the door of this profession read, "NO girls allowed! Keep out!" It is based on true events and real people who pioneered the profession long before the title of hero was awarded. For these young men and one young woman, who somehow braved working with these cowboys, it is a career in the making; one that they loved so much they would have done it for free and practically did.

Filled with real emergency calls and unbelievable antics of comic relief, the book As The Beacon Turns uncovers a true depiction of this journey in an unprecedented way. Toned down to a PG-13 rating, the book reveals the vast variations of personalities and the backgrounds of the people who throughout the course of living out these events, echoed the words, "Someone should write a book!"

This wonderful tale that was written with a refreshing spirit and a bit of sass, begins with a young woman named Angela Naomi Gates, the daughter of missionaries, raised by her aunt and uncle on a farm in Michigan, then introduces many other characters and partners. You'll meet one such partner, Dan, whose pride and joy is his Captain America van, who is a connoisseur of women's legs and a huge fan of Muppets? You will also have the dubious pleasure of encountering a street dweller known as Cat Man. Then before you know it you'll be riding in the front seat or in the patient compartment of an ambulance and will see how it feels to deliver a baby, what's needed to treat a multiple casualty patient and what to do in many other situations.

Learn what went on in the heart and mind of these emergency responders. What did they do in their spare time and how did they interact with area municipalities and the staff at surrounding medical facilities? The answers to these questions and more will be understood once you've finished reading, As The Beacon Turns.

CONTENTS

CHAPTER I

NOT BY CHOICE

Choice is something we have, but often don't exercise correctly. While we are gifted with the freedom to make our own choices, it isn't always a welcome benefit; for making the right choice can be laborious and untimely. Sometimes we fail, or perhaps refuse to see, that it's during those difficult times when faith prevails and our Creator, while holding the blue print of our lives in His hands, stands near offering wisdom and patience to help us while making our choice. So often we lack an understanding of the options at hand and try to comprehend them with a mortal and sometimes selfish mentality. We may feel compelled to move in to help God speed things along, in order to have the issues in our lives turn out closer to the way we think they should be, as we try to read ahead in the great book of life.

Then, as we sit in the residue regretting our rush, we discover that our bad or reckless choice has robbed us of the joy or blessing we might have experienced. Life suddenly seems abraded and our journey here short. Like anything else, we never seem to appreciate what we have until it's gone or in jeopardy. Most importantly, we must realize to deliberately choose to miss out on this wonder or waste it, would be a tremendously bad choice, for you only get one chance. And it's so exciting to see what each new day will bring, as the dawn provides the light in which to do the unwrapping. In making our choices, no matter what weight of importance that it then might hold, it is wise to remember that, "our life is a gift from God; what we do with that life is our gift to God ....therefore choose life, that both thou and thy seed may live."

Choose life. Two simple words that said so much as they etched their meaning, deep into the heart of a young girl while helping to form the foundation of her life. After all, Angela Naomi Gates came from a bloodline, of mercy-minded people who commonly shared such guided words. Her grandmother, aunt and uncle used them primarily. Still, to her, their words fell short in comparison to the cherished words on the yellowed pages from her parents; letters sent from the mission fields that she had reread many times. Now as an adult, life tugged at her to make her own mark in the world; and no matter the size of the token, she felt ready. Unfortunately however, she was beginning to discover that college registration had become more complicated then in previous years. At least the fall of 1975 seemed proof of that; from the display of near frenzied desperation that resulted in just two days of enrollment. No, it was not an adolescent folly of cramming as many people into the counselor's office as possible like one would a small car or phone booth but instead and more seriously, the counselor's office was full of students, nervously searching through their copy of the college catalog. And clearly to most, the strong scent of perspiration and anxieties increased, as alternate classes were being picked over. Dulled with disappointment, Angela's heart and feet felt heavy as she walked out of the counselor's congested office. Now what was she going to do? The nursing program was full. She had waited too long. Who would have thought the classes would fill so quickly? "If only I had pre-registered," she moaned to herself. With her prerequisites already completed, she knew her options were limited.

Angela had always been a person of determination. Even the death of her parents, after a time, proved to be something that strengthened her. She wasn't one to let the work she had invested slip away or become a disappointment to her family. Picking up the college catalog, she began to feel a challenge in her dilemma. "I need to think of an alternate plan, one that will keep me active in college and in the medical field. If I don't, I could very well lose any future financial help from Grandma's estate."

Angela's grandma had been a nurse herself and wanted so much for her daughter Nancy to follow in her footsteps. Instead, Nancy chose music and married a minister. Grandma never thought her daughter made a bad choice; it was just that her dream would not be fulfilled. Then her hope was revived when her only granddaughter, Angela, expressed her desire to be a nurse. A trust fund was set up. Now Angela was starting her third year at Lancemen County Community College.

The initial sick feeling eased as she walked over to a nearby bench along the wall and sat down. "God, show me the rhyme or reason for this," she softly prayed while opening the catalog. Again her eyes searched every corner and dot in the booklet. "There must be some kind of class that would still line up with my major. Hmm, Emergency Medical Technology—what was that?" she wondered. "I don't remember seeing that offered before. It must be an add-on to the nursing program; maybe Emergency Room nursing." She dog-eared the page, then rose and walked toward the registration desk. Scanning the clerks, she approached the one who seemed least busy, then reached out and touched the arm of her target.

"Excuse me," she said, trying to be polite but speaking loud enough to be heard over the commotion. "Could you tell me a little about this EMT class?"

"You must see the instructor himself and set up an interview," snapped the unfriendly clerk at the desk. The day had already been tediously long and was becoming even more chaotic. And clearly, while standing in the midst of it all, the stress expressed by the clerk was equally felt by everyone in the counselor's office as students and office personnel gradually became louder. Anne, as her friends called her, didn't want to vex the clerk. As it was, the poor woman's hair was sticking out on both sides. Throughout the morning she apparently had slid her pencil repeatedly into her hair, missing the crease behind each ear.

"Go down the hall to the last door on the right and ask for Raymond Dewit," she continued. "He is the instructor and he will have to answer your questions. You can't get into the program without his approval," the clerk abruptly barked, as if to shoo Anne away.

Well this day was not at all going in the direction that Anne had hoped or thought it would. Puzzled by her experience, she organized her papers, shouldered her purse, then started down the hall. "What was that all about? My grades are fine," she grumbled to herself. "I have a 3.9 average. Why do I have to be approved? This is crazy. All I want to do, is to go to school and be a nurse." In no time she reached the room that the clerk directed her to and noticed the door was half open. After knocking on it, while slowly pushing it open the rest of the way, she softly called, "Hello." The room was poorly lit. Peering in, she noticed an old wooden desk, a chair and a bookcase. Then, once her eyes acclimated to the light, several large boxes of papers and books set about with no apparent order, came into view. The smell of old dust was in the air. Suddenly, the sound of boxes being tossed from behind another door of an adjacent room caught her attention. She called out again, a little louder, "Hello." The shuffling noise stopped; then a tall man with a faded tan stepped from behind the door.

"Can I help you?" he asked. His thin dark hair adhered to the perspiration on his forehead creating a comical but scary appearance to the grimace on his face. His words were polite but posed, revealing his true posture.

"I'm sorry to interrupt," she said. Her voice quivered as she fought the urge to giggle. She understood that it would not behoove her to be so amused with this man's look of toil, but as he stood panting in front of her, a cartoon-like image of him rock climbing in a windstorm suddenly raced across her mind. "You're obviously very busy," she said, biting her lip. "I'm looking for Raymond Dewit." He stared at her for a moment. A rush of air escaped from his nares. Then after dragging his fingers through his hair to pull it back in place, he took a hankie from his pant's back pocket and wiped the sweat from his face before sitting behind the only desk in the room.

"I'm Raymond Dewit," he answered in an irritated tone. "How can I help you?"

Wishing she'd been more straight-faced, she cleared her throat. "Well, I'd like to ask about the EMT Program."

"What specifically do you want to know?" he asked. Leaning back in his chair, he folded his arms across his chest as if dreading the conversation he knew was coming.

"Well, like what kind of subjects are covered? Is it part of the nursing program?" she calmly inquired. She sensed the tension building as she studied his face. A look of arrogance replaced the earlier one of contempt.

"Are you in the nursing program now?" he asked.

"I've completed my prerequisites and my interview with Mrs.Collins. This semester's nursing program is full and I thought this class might be useful."

"Well, the Basic Emergency Medical Technology class is the first level of the Paramedic Program. It precedes the Advanced EMT class. Together, along with some of the nursing classes, they make up the Paramedic Program and include all that is required for state licensure. Do you have a list of the classes you've already completed?"

Pulling a folded piece of paper from her purse, she handed him the sheet from the counselor's office. Baring a scowl, he unfolded the paper, then began carefully reading it, while tapping a pencil on his untidy desk. It was hard to understand why this was becoming so difficult. All she wanted to do was to sign up for a class, not mortgage a house.

"You seem to have all the prerequisite classes and your grades are certainly adequate," he said, as if the words were bitter tasting. "I can't stop you from taking the class. I can only give you advice. This class is for firemen and ambulance personnel, none of which are women. The pre-hospital setting can be very gruesome, not to mention the demand for physical strength. I advise you to wait for an opening in the nursing program."

As Anne stood in front of his desk listening to his disapproving and degrading words, she could feel a flush of anger come over her face. It seemed to her that he almost hoped she would burst into tears and run out of the room, never to darken his door again. But she had no intention of giving in to that. And at the same time, she did not want to respond out of anger. She knew she'd have to choose her words carefully.

"Mr. Dewit, I would like to at least try the class. If I can't do the work, I'll drop out of the program. I think that this would be very beneficial to me as a nursing student. As a nurse I need to be exposed to both the hospital and the pre-hospital settings. I don't want to impose in an area that I'm not welcome. My only goal is to get an education and to do my best in whatever I'm involved. I'm not afraid of hard work or a challenge. I'll try to stay out of everyone's way."

"All right," he responded ruefully, "but don't expect to get a job in this field. No one will hire you. And—if you think you are going to find a husband or a boyfriend by taking this class, you're making a big mistake. Take this paper to the counseling department," he said, while signing his name adversely. "Give it to Mr. Sage. The class will be held every Tuesday and Thursday, six to ten in the evening beginning next Tuesday. Also, you'll need to sign up for an infield clinical." He paused and woefully watched the piece of paper slip from his fingers, into Angela's. "You still have time to think it over and find something besides this class," he recoiled. "The program was designed for men, so I honestly don't see where you have much of a choice."

CHAPTER 2

THE DEVIL'S BIDDING

"Good grief," Anne softly groaned. "Now what have I gotten myself into?" While mentally reviewing her conversation with Mr. Dewit, she suddenly realized that she still knew very little about the EMT class. Did she pursue it because she was really interested or was it what Papa called, the devil's bidding?

Ever since she was young and barely able to reach the gate latch, she possessed this inherent stubbornness to do the exact opposite of what she was told. She truly wanted to do what was right, but saying no to Angela was like waving a red flag in front of a bull. Even though she was warned many times not to go outside of the gate, as soon as she got outdoors she would head pell-mell straight for the latch. Papa gave credit to his sister for Anne's strong determination, claiming no punishment would dissuade her or break her spirit.

Whatever it was that made her so intent on entering the EMT program didn't matter much now; it was too late to turn back. After sliding the consent form from Mr. Dewit into her purse, she started back down the hall toward the counseling department. In her absence the students had formed a long snakelike line that wound its way out of the office and into the lobby. While looking for a familiar face, she took her place in line, then glanced at the clock that was set in the brick wall. Her stomach complained quietly as the noon hour approached; but after a few seconds the grumbling eased, allowing her mind to drift back to her childhood. Anne was normally very level headed, but it wasn't unusual for a daydream to beckon her into another time and place. Knowing how her mind worked, she subconsciously kept pace with the others as the line moved ahead.

Anne was seven years old when she and her two younger brothers, James and Noah, went to live with her Aunt Ruth and Uncle Henry. They owned an eighty acre farm in Summerville, Michigan. Henry David and Ruth Katherine Gates were also the proud parents of three rascally boys—Jacob, Aaron and Peter, who were very happy to share not only their rooms with their cousins, but also some of the chores. Being the only girl, except Aunt Ruth of course, Anne was able to have her own room. It was small but decorated in a way that felt cozy and private. It was just the perfect place to find refuge from five active and taunting boys when Aunt Ruth was too busy to sit and talk.

Since birth, they had visited the farm many times with Mama and Papa. On occasion they even stayed the night, if their parents' missionary work and journey became lengthy. In no time, they felt very comfortable in the barns and often helped milk the cows and feed the chickens. They were pretty young then and rarely spent much time exploring the woods that took up nearly ten acres of the farm. However after their fosterage into the family that gradually changed. As they grew older, little by little, more and more playful and investigative hours were enjoyed under the tall trees. Uncle Henry often warned the bigger boys of the different dangers to beware of with the little ones. While Aunt Ruth carried on about dirty clothes and how she thought Anne should find more "lady like" things to do than to tramp through the woods with a bunch of raggedy looking boys. Anne smiled to herself while recalling the early years on the farm and a certain day when she learned that "no" was sometimes a good thing to consider.

June was a busy time to live on a farm and the ideal time to collect morel mushrooms. Anne, her brothers, and cousins each carried their own basket as they started toward the woods. The air was sweet with the scent of young flowers pushing their way through the grass that had been weighed down by winter's snow. The sun was warm. The air still felt damp from last night's rain, but then it was still early afternoon.

Anne's basket was scarcely full. Deciding she might have better luck away from the boys, she wandered off, staying within voice range. She liked being far away from the boys, but not too far. She didn't feel as at home in the woods as they seemed to; of course, they had lived near the woods all their lives. After taking a few steps, she heard a sound that stopped her in her tracks. There it was again. Something nearby was stirring in the brush. It wasn't the boys; it sounded smaller and lighter. She was curious, but afraid to look. From the corner of her eye she saw movement. She readied a scream, then stopped as the creature came into full view. It was small, black and white with a soft "kitten" like appearance. Recognizing the animal from a book she read, she remembered its name was "Flower." As she approached the gentle looking critter, she heard a whishing sound as the most hideous odor shot toward her. A fierce, burning sensation ripped into her eyes. Instantly, tears came streaming to dissolve the acrid discharge and restore her vision. Gasping for fresh air, she felt like a fish on shore; only she needed air as badly as a fish needed water. Her only desire was just to breathe.

Not far off the boys began picking up the pungent, unmistakable scent. Jacob, Anne's oldest cousin, was the first to realize her dilemma. She heard him running toward her as he yelled "Skunk!" Feeling relieved in thinking that help was finally on its way, she began breathing easier. The searing in her eyes was even starting to ease. But Jacob, instead of helping or consoling her as she expected, began laughing boisterously. Then she heard him clearly, almost joyfully, announce, "Anne just got sprayed by a skunk!" It got worse. She felt duped. Soon all the boys, even her own two brothers, joined in the mirthfulness.

This was all Anne could stand. She was trying so hard to be strong and not to cry like a "big baby." With all control gone, she started sobbing. It wasn't long before Uncle Henry who had been working out in the field heard the rowdiness. As he grew closer, the aroma pierced the lining of his nasal cavity. Then he saw the boys laughing and Anne crying. It was pretty easy to figure out what happened. "Jacob," he yelled, "stop laughing and take Anne up to the barn."

"But Dad, she'll scare off the animals," he said snickering.

"Come with me, Anne," Uncle Henry said, ignoring Jacob's bantering. "Jacob, you go ahead and bring down that big tub from over the feed," he ordered while they walked slowly toward the barn.

"You mean the one that we wash the baby pigs in for the fair?" Jacob asked, still trying to find humor in Anne's misfortune. Uncle Henry was starting to lose his patience.

"Boy, you'd better do as you're told and leave this girl alone. She doesn't need you heckling her." Looking at the smaller boys he continued, "Aaron you boys go get your mother and tell her to bring some tomato juice and shampoo out to the barn." Anne was so glad Uncle Henry was there. She felt like a beaten settler when the cavalry finally arrived.

"Oh my—oh my," Aunt Ruth repeated as they all met in the barn. Then she quickly went to work deodorizing Anne and the surrounding air. The boys brought in several jars of tomato juice from the cellar. "Thank you very much. Now you boys can get started on your chores. We would like a little privacy," Aunt Ruth said, hurrying them out of the barn. Uncle Henry brought in the hose to fill the tub.

"Good thing we hooked up the hot water or you'd be taking a cold bath," he laughed, trying to ease Anne's distress. Then as he began filling the tub he turned to her and gently said, "I know you don't want to hear this but I warned you not to touch or get close to anything you weren't sure of; you remind me of your Aunt Kate. She was as stubborn as a mule; only a mule generally has a good reason. A mule won't move if he's loaded too heavy or if he thinks there's danger ahead."

"All right, Henry," Aunt Ruth quietly interrupted. "I think Anne understands without all of that. We need to get her into the tub. I'm sure she would like to get this over as quickly as possible. After all, I have work to do in the house. So if you would—please go into the house and in the linen closet downstairs and bring out one of those big beach towels."

"Anything to help," he responded, winking at Anne.

Aunt Ruth was such a comfort. Anne couldn't think of anything better than to spend the rest of the day in the house with her—away from the critters—but mostly, away from those rascally boys. Boys always found the oddest things to find humor in, she thought. After a few minutes Uncle Henry returned with the towel as Aunt Ruth had asked. He was good to her and worked very hard. While sitting in the tub of tomato juice and water, Anne wondered as Uncle Henry walked out of the barn, if he been a big tease like Jacob when he was younger.

It took several treatments with the tomato juice before Anne's hair could be shampooed. Uncle Henry thought it was best just to burn the clothes and he wasted no time doing it. It was nearly time to start supper. Now that Anne was back to normal, she stayed right by Aunt Ruth and helped clean the mushrooms that began the day's catastrophe. Dinner tasted wonderful. The quietness in the air was pleasing considering the day's excitement. Jacob attempted to joke about the day's event but stopped with a stern look from Uncle Henry. Later in the evening Anne ventured out near the porch with the boys to catch fireflies. It was a perfect end to an exhaustive day. Bedtime came.

Uncle Henry entered Anne's room and sat on the white wicker rocking chair next to her bed. "I hope you're not mad at the boys and me for teasing about the skunk earlier today," he began, as he tucked her in bed. "I warn the boys and you of things, not because I like being bossy, but because I love you and don't want to see harm come to you. I know your mother read the Bible to you. Do you remember the part about the Ten Commandments?" he asked.

Anne nodded, "Yes," as she softly answered.

"Well, God gave the children of Israel the Commandments sort of like a guide to follow because He loved them. He knew that if they abided by His laws, they would live life a little easier and would be safer. It's the same thing that I do. I know this has been a hard thing for you to go through but I hope you will remember what I'm saying. As far as the boys teasing you, well, after a few days it won't be as funny to them. When you're all grown you'll all have a good laugh with it. There will be other stories to add to this one." He got up, leaned over, and kissed her on her forehead. "Good night, Anne," he said with a smile.

"Good night," she said.

Thinking back to that night and Uncle Henry's words, Anne knew he had been right about everything he'd said. As predicted, throughout the fifteen years that followed many more stories were told; all in good humor of course. To tell them any other way might be cruel. It would just be another avenue, to do the devil's bidding.

CHAPTER 3

FATE

"Well, Miss Gates, I see you've returned. Have you decided on another class?" asked the clerk at the registration desk. Anne jumped. The sharpness in the woman's voice startled her after being so engrossed in her mental excursion. Then the sound of muffled giggles from the other students standing behind her spawned a feeling of embarrassment. As her dreamy state slowly withered, she likening herself to Alice in Wonderland while stepping back through the looking glass. Realizing she'd been daydreaming, she quickly began fumbling through her purse for the paper from Mr. Dewit.

"Good grief," she mumbled to herself. The seconds of searching seemed like hours. "Oh, there it is," she smiled. "Mr. Dewit gave me his approval to sign up for the EMT class. He said, this paper should go to Mr. Sage." The clerk's impatient scorn as she took the folded note from Anne's fingers was puzzling. Was the woman upset because Mr. Dewit had allowed her into the class, or was she upset because this extra step had interrupted the flow of things in an already too busy day? What ever the reason was it didn't matter, Anne was raised to be polite and polite she would be.

The clerk unfolded the note, then set it on the counter to study. Her eyes moved back and forth as she twisted her mouth from side to side. Anne stood in front of the desk and smiled self-consciously. As she watched and waited, the strong sensation of curious eyes behind her increased. The note Mr. Dewit scrawled out was just a few lines followed by his signature, not a novel, she thought. At last—the clerk seemed satisfied that the hand writing really was Mr. Dewit's and quickly jotted down the cash due on a receipt. "It's your money," she grumbled under her breath. Anne opened her wallet to pull out the one-hundred and ten dollars to pay for the four credit class—happily.

Finally! Anne thought to herself. This whole ordeal is almost over. All I have to do now is to go to the bookstore and buy the books. Increasing her pace as she walked from the office then through the lobby, she approached the glass exit door. Stepping outside, a gentle cool breeze brushed against her skin invoking a quiet chuckle as the image of the skunk and her desperate need for fresh air returned. Wasting no time, she focused ahead in the direction of the book store. As she walked briskly in the bright sunlight, it almost seemed like a new day. She felt her love for the out of doors tugging for more than a moment's regard, reminding her of a child that persistently tugs at their parent's sleeve. Graciously she gave in and walked over to a wooden bench that sat on the lawn near the cement walk. Standing behind the bench she looked over the campus grounds and the grove that surrounded it, like a sea-loving sailor in a crow's nest. A soft but heartfelt sigh escaped, releasing all the tension created by the morning's activities. Clearly Indian summer had disguised the early days of fall with a summer aura. The leaves on the trees still had a fresh healthy green appearance and the annuals that had been planted in the spring were thick and bright with color. The warmth of the sun and the sweetness of the air seemed to transcend, after being pent up in the counselor's office. God's artistic concinnity was pleasing and rejuvenating.

It only took a few minutes in the bookstore for her to find the required books and to pay for them. As she started toward the exit that led to the brick patio, she heard a familiar voice. "Anne, wait up." It was Roger Milky. He and Anne had been lab partners in a Microbiology class. While working on several projects during the semester they had become good friends. She spent many hours studying with Roger at his home. His wife, Tracy was a great cook. After dinner, she would put on a pot of coffee, sit at the table, and read parenting books while they studied. At the time Tracy was in her sixth month of pregnancy. Anne recalled the birth announcement she received about a year ago, heralding the news of their baby boy. They had chosen the name Daniel. When Anne read the announcement she chuckled, remembering Roger's desire to name the baby after his childhood hero, Daniel Boone. Of course he never told Tracy that. She would never have given in to it. Roger just told her it was his favorite uncle's name. After Tracy found out that Roger never had an uncle Daniel, he had to confess his real reason for wanting the name for his son, to which Tracy laughed. Roger was indeed one of a kind. Without him, Tracy would be lost.

"Oh my gosh—Roger!" Anne cheered. "I thought you moved back to Ohio or something. I called your house after the baby was born but the phone was disconnected."

"Well, we did move back to Ohio for a while. The baby got sick and Tracy wanted to be near her mother. It gave us a chance to get our finances in better shape so I could go back to school." He pulled his wallet from his back pocket as he talked and slid out a well protected packet of pictures from under a brown leather flap. Some of the photos he proudly displayed were of Tracy and the baby, but most of them were just of the baby.

After going through the usual, "Oh what a cutie," Anne asked giggling, "So where's his coon skin cap?"

Roger chuckled, "I bought one, but Tracy wouldn't let him wear it. Just before we left to get his pictures taken, I tried it on him—it looked great! Of course, I waited until she wasn't looking, but she caught me sneaking it in to the photographer's studio. Part of the raccoon tail fell out of my jacket pocket and gave me away—so she sent me back out to the car to wait." They laughed while reminiscing the fun times the three of them had, during the Microbiology days.

"So what classes are you taking now? Are you still going to be a Science teacher?" she asked chuckling. A flash of the many stories Tracy told, spun through her mind; but the one that stood out was when Roger almost destroyed their kitchen while building a simulated rocket sequencer; and how he almost burned down the garage with some science experiments he found in an old book.

"For the safety of my son I thought I'd better put that on hold for a while. I started working for Mercy Medical Service this summer. I have an Ambulance Attendant License now and I'm all set to start the paramedic program. Maybe, I'll see you at the hospital. Maybe we can meet for lunch sometime. You are still going for your nursing degree, aren't you?" Anne had never been good about hiding her feelings; so as he spoke, the gradual change in her facial expression was easy to detect. He wondered what could have happened to cause the previously happy grin to turned into this lip biting, moping ellipsis. Then he watched her open the plastic bag with the college logo and pull out her newly purchased books, which he recognized immediately.

"You're kidding me!" he bolted. "How did you get into the class?" Anne raised her eyebrows as if to say, excuse me? " Not to say that you can't be in there," he continued. " It's just that it's…"

"For men only?" she interjected. "Roger, I can't believe you. The truth of the matter is, I'm only taking the class for the experience; and because I waited too long to sign up for the nursing program, it's already full."

Roger smiled, as he pulled his books out of his canvas bag. "Well, it looks like we're going to be classmates again."

Anne was pleased that he wasn't upset and that he was willing to be study partners again; even if she was a girl. Then a playful smile took over. "Well, if it makes it any easier, you can act like you don't know me. I didn't plan this ya know—it just happened." Sensing a feeling of awkwardness as she put her books back into the bag, Roger spoke up. "I didn't mean...."

"It's okay Rog. I've gotten the same response from everyone today." After adjusting her purse strap, she started walking backwards toward the parking lot. "You've made my day Rog—It'll be great, being together in class again. Tell Tracy I said hi. I really have to get home. It's been a long day and I still have to break the news to my family."

"Wait!" Roger called back. "How did you get into the class?"

"Fate—I guess." Then she turned and hurried toward her car.

"Fate indeed," she whispered while driving toward the entrance to the main highway. How great it was to see Roger again. With him in her class it might not be so bad being the only girl. Hopefully she wouldn't be. She didn't want to stand out like a sore thumb. And how great it would be to see Tracy and little Daniel. There would be so much to tell when she got home. She had about an hour's drive depending on the traffic. If her lead foot didn't get her into trouble she would be home by three o'clock. Her Aunt had scolded her more than once about speeding. "If you want the protection of Angels with you while you're driving," she would say reprovingly, "you need to slow down. Speeding is breaking the law, and angels don't break the law." While recalling her Aunt's wise advice, she eased her foot off the accelerator. There was no reason to "tempt fate" as they say. The drive home was pleasant and it seemed that in no time she was safely home.

CHAPTER 4

A BITTER PILL

The challenges we are faced with, unwillingly at times, should be recognized as the mold creating our very character; for those same challenges bring strength and wisdom. While the challenges quite often arrive with some displeasure, the trick of surviving such perplexities and seeing each one as a friend, is sometimes in itself a challenge; but truly not impossible.

Anne experienced the pain of death at an early age. While she, her younger brothers, and cousins ran playfully through the tall stalks of corn, a letter came to the farm telling of her parents' and oldest brother's tragic death. She remembered her grandma telling her that the greatest gift God ever gave was love. It only made sense that losing it would bring the greatest pain; but she found that over time, with the continued love from other family members, the healing became easier. Then when it came time to lay Gramma to rest, again, those precious words echoed in her mind.

Aunt Ruth and Uncle Henry were left in charge of the estate; even so, the financial support continued as if grandma had been there. When Anne explained the situation at the counselor's office to them, they agreed to allow the estate money to be used to pay for her EMT class. But just as she anticipated, the late night drive home was their main concern. Winter would be upon them soon, bringing the snow and icy road conditions. Anne was twenty-three years old and quite mature for her age. Still, a girl being out alone that time of night in bad weather made them feel uncomfortable. She remembered how slick the roads got last winter and suggested calling the Johnstones to ask about possibly renting a room throughout the term of the EMT Program.

The Johnstones were old friends of the family. They moved to Oakland Hills, just outside of Lancemen, several years ago. Freida was a strong German woman. Ted was from the hills of Tennessee. They were in their sixties and had one daughter who lived out of state. As Anne hung up the phone with Mrs. Johnstone, she smiled. The arrangements were complete and the winter night drive would be much shorter now, plus the quiet home of Ted and Freida Johnstone, would be the perfect environment in which to study.

It was Tuesday afternoon. After helping Mr. Johnstone with some light yard work, Anne decided she should go in and get ready for her first EMT class and the early dinner she and Tracy arranged beforehand. Tracy called her on Saturday and was very excited that she and Roger had run into each other and insisted they get together for dinner. The class was scheduled to end at ten o'clock. Depending on the time that she lasted the first night, if they didn't run her out for being a girl, she'd return to the Johnstone's.

Seeing Tracy again and the baby for the first time was great. With so much to catch up on during dinner, the hour just seemed to fly. Suddenly it was time to go to class and the butterflies in Anne's stomach began to flutter. The jittery feeling sort of surprised her. After all, she'd been going to school most of her life. But today it felt odd—as if it was her first day ever. She knew once she got into class and got settled the unrest would end. Plus, Roger would be there for moral support.

Anne pulled into the LCC parking lot and found a space to park, turned off her car, gathered her books and took a deep breath. "Here goes, Lord, stay close," she whispered. The fluttering continued as she walked through the parking lot. Maybe it felt strange to her because her other classes had always been during the day. She looked at her schedule again. Good grief, she thought to herself, I know where the class is—it's my only class. I've looked at that schedule as if it were ten classes. I'm not a stranger to the campus. She chuckled to herself as she remembered the biblical story of Daniel in the lions' den. "He made it," she told herself, "and so will you."

EMT I was to be held in the same classroom as her previous anatomy class. Walking into the room she looked for a couple of seats. The room was large with six levels that set in a half circle formation. Anne went up five or six steps and found a seat for Roger and herself. He had to drive Tracy and the baby home before he could come to class. She heard a couple of guys talking and laughing. Their conversation was somewhat loud and from what she could hear she determined they were both firemen. Other students, all of which were male, straggled in. Roger was one of the stragglers. He saw Anne and took a seat beside her.

"You don't have to sit here if you don't want to, you know," she said smiling.

"I know," he said jokingly, "I'll probably be shunned after they see me sitting with you. My son probably won't be allowed into any of the all male schools for fear that he'll bring some female along with him. But since we're friends, I guess I'll chance it."

Roger knew almost everyone who came in. A few of them yelled "Hey, Rog" from across the room, while others came over to talk or just to say, "Hi," at which point he introduced Anne. The class was filling up. Then two very large girls walked into the room. They didn't appear obese, but rather each had a build like that of a linebacker on a football team. A few comments could be heard as they came in and jokes about them being on the varsity team. Anne felt uncomfortable for them and hoped no one would make jest of her for being in the class. Mr. Dewit entered the room and the joking stopped. Everyone took their seat.

"I trust everyone has their books with them and has at least looked at the pictures," he started. "If you don't have Emergency Care and Transportation of the Sick and Injured by the AAOS, and Brady's Emergency Care, you'll need to have them by next week. We have a lot to cover, so I think we should get started. As you can see by the syllabus, we have over twenty different subjects that we will be covering. We'll be using our books and practical application as our tools of learning. This is a thirty week, two semester class or program if you will. This is the second class for Basic Emergency Medical Technology in this area. So, as you can see this is a new and well overdue program. I trust everyone in this class will do his or her best to make it a success. The State is watching us to see how well we do. They're using us as a gauge to see how effective the program is in creating what is projected to be a new Profession in Emergency Care. You are giving birth so to speak. Although I've never experienced it personally," he smiled. " I understand it can be painful. Hopefully, by working together we can make this easy and as pain free as possible. Also, tonight we will be switching part of next week's class. We'll be working on Patient Handling tonight and we'll be studying Medical Legal next week. Now I would like everyone to turn to page two hundred and sixteen which is also chapter fifty in your orange book."

As Mr. Dewit spoke, Anne thought how different he seemed from the day she had met him in his office. He seemed very likable. She was beginning to understand the importance of the class to him and why he had been rude at their first meeting. With Anne and the two other girls in the class it might not go as smoothly as maybe the first class went. Could that be why he decided to go right to the section where patient lifting came into play in the first class? The other two girls certainly looked like they would have no problem lifting anyone. Although Anne had lived and worked on the farm since she was seven years old and was expected to help out with the heavier chores at times, she couldn't help being concerned with what would take place next.

They were two hours into the class and it was time to take a twenty minute break. "Relax," Roger said, sensing Anne's nervousness, "I'll be your partner. You're stronger than you think. I bet you did your share of cow tipping while up on the old farm," he teased.

Anne laughed, "I was just there as an observer."

"Oh yea, right, I almost believe that," he gibed, rolling his brown eyes.

It was in their earlier Microbiology class that Anne first began sharing her outlandish experiences growing up at home with the five boys. She made the adventures with them sound more like comedies. Practical jokes and scampishness seemed to be something of the norm, some of which probably explained the glint in her bright blue eyes and her quick wit.

The break ended as the students were called back into the classroom to begin that night's practical portion of the lesson. After reviewing the information in the book, they were to work with their partner to develop good lifting skills with one and two person lifts. Mr. Dewit described the techniques that were to be used, then asked students to volunteer to act as patients. Suddenly, the classroom was filled with groans. Anne looked around. On the other side of the room a very large student who looked to be in his mid twenties stood up. He seemed pleased with the attention that was demonstrated and began bowing. His face beamed with joy as he thanked everyone as if he had just finished an act in a play.

"Sit down, Cubby, nobody wants to pick up your rotund body," jeered a dark haired student sitting behind him. His voice was noticeably deep and smooth, with the tonal qualities heard on a late night radio program. Roger told Anne that his name was Roman Anderson. Roman worked on the road and was a dispatcher at Mercy. His nickname was Captain Midnight. Once the laughter and moaning quieted down and Cubby accomplished what appeared to be his goal of making himself an object of sport, Mr. Dewit continued, "Thank you Cubby—but I think we should start out with someone smaller on the first night."

"Just trying to help," Cubby offered before sitting down.

Anne watched as Mr. Dewit's demeanor became more serious. With a sternness, he looked around the room to assign a group of students to act as patients. He picked out a couple firemen that she had heard talking earlier before the class started. Then he glanced over toward the two girls and noticed they had paired up as partners. "You girls split up and work with one of the guys," he called out. As they looked around for a student to work with, Cubby wasted no time in volunteering. Still bearing his broad grin, he approached one of the girls and took her hand to shake it, as he introduced himself. He seemed jolly, as if nothing could break that ever present smile. His cheeks were rounded and rosy, with a porcelain like appearance. The girl smiled in return introducing herself as Charlene and her friend as Diane.

By the end of the two semester program, everyone had gotten a chance to get to know each other and almost everyone had become friends—even with the girls. Charlene and Diane explained that they hoped to work for a volunteer service in a rural area near their homes. Anne explained that she was just there for the experience and planned to go on into the nursing program. Once that was out of the way, the atmosphere became less tense and their presence more agreeable.

The infield clinicals were productive. A total of forty hours in the hospital emergency room offered much to observe. The students were allowed to walk or push patients in a wheel chair back to a room and take vitals. They also learned to chart a medical history and how to assess the patient's condition. Anne found it interesting to watch the way the staff dealt with the cases that came in to the emergency room. The more serious cases were done quickly and efficiently. The thing that intrigued her most was how it became an almost mechanical process. It seemed that certain symptoms the patient exhibited set off flags which then set the desired treatment in motion. There was no big discussion. Everyone knew his or her part. When the job was over, it was business as usual and they went on to the next case. Adaptability was an important part of the caring and handling of each patient. Unfortunately, due to a lack of time, there was little room for mothering—at least that's what Anne told herself, as some of the nursing staff seemed a bit callous.

Each staff member reacted differently to the EMT students. Some of the physicians liked the idea of the program and supported it, some did not. Some of the nurses, Anne noticed, were helpful only after they found out that she was a future nursing student. With the EMT and Paramedic programs being so new, they weren't sure where it would lead. After all, hospitals were always looking for ways to cut costs. Because of that, an uncertainty of their own job security took seed and the unfriendliness grew. But in general, it was a great experience and the majority of the hospital staff was helpful.

The Ambulance clinical was a whole different operation. The guys were serious when they needed to be and although their skill level was still developing, the administration of the care was professionally done. It was in their blood. But the seriousness quite often ended when the call ended. As soon as they returned to their station, the business like setting that was witnessed earlier almost always transformed and or erupted into a playful atmosphere. They were high-spirited. Anne felt as if she were home on the farm, growing up with the five boys in her family again. Some of the guys she had scheduled her ride time with were also in her EMT class or had graduated from the first class. Roger watched and listened each time she rode when he was there, feeling responsible for her safety. He was concerned that the guys would try to take advantage of this unworldly young lass. "Roger, you don't have to worry," Anne reassured him. "They aren't the least bit interested in me; I'm too much like the sister type, not the girlfriend type. I'm just here for the patient care in a pre-hospital setting, nothing more."

"Anne—you don't know these guys like I do. They're interested in anyone who even looks half way decent in a skirt. They don't care whose sister it is, as long as it isn't theirs. They're smooth talkers and I just want you to be careful," he went on earnestly. Then a grin broke through the seriousness. "Not to mention that Tracy would kill me if anything happened to you while you were here."

"Oh, so it's Tracy yelling at you and not your buddies being with me that concerns you," she chuckled. "Sure, blame the woman," she went on. "You men have been putting the blame on women since Adam and Eve were in the garden. The first thing Adam said when God asked him about eating the apple was, 'The woman you gave to be with me gave me of the tree and I ate.' Roger, I am flattered and blessed to have such a good friend, but I'm fine, really. They aren't interested in me anyway. I've already taken care of that."

"How did you do that?" he asked.

"I told them that my parents were missionaries, that I sing in the choir at church and I'm a fill-in Sunday school teacher. Most guys don't want a girl that won't kiss on a first date much less anything else. It's always a good deterrent. Anyway—they've given me good evaluations, and so far have been very respectful."

"Well, they seem to like you all right," Roger agreed. "They think you have a special talent for this. You seem comfortable talking to people and have a calmness about you." He chuckled then continued. "Plus—you apparently have the right amount of feistiness to survive."

"Feistiness?" she laughed.

"Oh—yeah," he grinned, while nodding his head in agreement. "And, you're surprisingly stronger than what they expected. Probably from all of that cow tipping," he said chuckling.

"Okay—enough with the cow tipping," she smiled. Looking at her watch, she began yawning. "Well, my time's up and you know the rules about girls being here later than eleven o'clock. As soon as someone signs me out, I can go home. I need to get busy studying for our final. It's next week ya know," she said as a reminder.

"Well then, I'll see you Tuesday, on D-day," he said. Anne heard the phone ring in the dispatch center, then Roman bellowing Roger's name for a call.

"Come on, we got a man down. If it's old Ned drunk again, you get to ride in back with him," Roman said, as he got into the driver's seat of the ambulance.

"No way, Roman!" Roger replied dashing to the rig. "I've been in the back with him the last three times."

They were off. Anne watched as the emergency lights came on and the rig turned from the garage exit onto the road. She was glad that Roger didn't schedule any of her ride times with him. He said he wanted her to do it on her own so that no one could say she had special treatment or biased evaluations. And she was glad if it was old Ned, that he'd at least waited to fall down when her ride time was over. It was an eye opener and a surprise to her that a man could smell worse than the animals on the farm in Summerville—but yes, old Ned did.

It was D-day as Roger called it. They were all at their desks, pencils in hand, books on the floor, with the test paper face down listening to the instructions. The test would take about an hour. It would be graded, then sent to the State Capital in Lansing. The students would receive their results in a couple of weeks along with a State License if they passed the test with eighty percent or better. When he finished speaking, Mr. Dewit gave the okay. Quickly and quietly, they all turned the test paper over and began. A half hour or so had passed when to Anne's surprise Mr. Dewit left the room. Within a short time of his absence she noticed some of the students were turning over papers that were lying on the floor next to them. She watched as they glanced down, before filling in their test. Some of them stretched as to not make what they were doing so obvious. Some were just blatant. Mr. Dewit will be coming back at any time, she thought. I can't believe they would risk being disqualified after all the hours they put into clinicals and class work. Just then Mr. Dewit walked in. Anne fixed her eyes on her own test as she finished the last few questions. After reviewing her answer sheet, she got up and turned her papers in to Mr. Dewit. Roger watched as she walked back to her seat to pick up her purse and books from the floor. The look on her face must have expressed her discountenance. When she bent over to collect her things, she heard him whisper, "Wait for me outside."

Leaning on the bricked enclosure surrounding the walkway outside, she fidgeted with the papers in her folder. Her mind raced with disgust and disbelief as she mulled over what she had just seen. Soberly she watched as other students left the building, discussing the answers they put on the exam, comparing the answers to questions they remembered. Roger walked out and came up to where she was standing.

"I know what you are going to say, Anne," he started. "It's a prearranged thing. The guys you saw cheating work for municipalities. The program is new and they need a certain number of people to pass in order to get started. They run three or more on a unit. There are more guys that pass on their own, then those who don't. They are careful not to put the aided ones out together. I know that doesn't sound right but that's how it is."

Her face evinced her disappointment. "'He catches the wise in their own craftiness'; what they are doing is wrong and it will catch up to them—and at whose expense? If I understand this correctly, what you're telling me is that politics takes precedence over patient care?" she distressfully asked.

"I'm sorry, Anne," Roger said with a somber but matter of fact tone. "That's just the way it is. We don't like it either—but we just have to let it go. You can't change it. How does that Serenity Prayer go?"

Anne in a soft and disheartened voice responded, "This is not about serenity, Roger—it's about ethics, about integrity, about people's lives. Everyone who is in on this charade needs prayer and not for serenity. They all have to be accountable for this, at some point in their lives. This is what you call a bitter pill. It does nothing but leave a bad taste and it doesn't cure the problem."

"Anne, I'm not saying I agree with it. I just don't know how to change it. Maybe you should pray for a better way, without those guys or me losing our jobs."

"I'll do that," Anne agreed, with a wispy smile. "It's certainly better than a bitter pill."

CHAPTER 5

TEN—FOUR

Almost three weeks had passed since Anne completed her final exam in the Basic EMT Program. She had enjoyed staying with the Johnstones throughout the term of the class, they were pleasant and easy to live with; but now she was happy to be back home on the farm, especially with the end of spring approaching. Planting was in full swing. Even as a child she had loved working in the rich dark earth. It fascinated her to see newly planted seed come to life in the form of vegetation; so much so, that she even studied botany in high school as a science elective. Oddly enough, it wasn't until then that she learned she really didn't have a green thumb. Uncle Henry and boys only let her believe she was a farmer. They, in fact, were the ones with the special gift of bringing about a bountiful harvest. Even so, she still enjoyed tending the crops. However, the first planting in spring had always been special to her; for it was then, in the beginning of that season, that they all gathered together as a family and stood facing the freshly tilled soil, that Uncle Henry christened with a loud proclamation—"Let the field be joyful and all that is in it."

"Freida called last night," Aunt Ruth shared over breakfast. "Katie had her baby yesterday." The Johnstone's daughter, Katie, had been like an older sister to Anne while growing up. Now that she was married and lived out of state, they rarely saw each other.

"How's she doing?" Anne asked excitedly.

"Not too good I'm afraid. Seems she had some sort of complication and will have to stay off her feet for a while. The baby is fine. I think she said he weighed nine pounds and was twenty-one inches long. His name is Nathan Robert. They're going down to stay with Katie until she's back on her feet. They called to see if you could go and house sit while they were away. Anne, they bragged how helpful you were when you stayed with them—how you kept the snow shoveled and all," she urged, after seeing a disquietness come over Anne.

"You know I'll go," Anne said, trying not to sound disappointed. "They were great letting me stay with them and I'm grateful. It's just that, well, I haven't been home long and I missed you and Uncle Henry."

"I know, honey but they need help and we can't let any of the boys go. They're strong and Henry needs them to be here. He's getting older now and I can see it's catching up to him. Some days he just tires so easily. It will only be for a month or so—maybe not even that long."

"Okay, okay," Anne said giving in with a smile. "How soon do they want me?"

"You can wait until Monday if you like. Thank you, dear. It will mean so much to them. Now you go on outside and enjoy yourself; I'll clean up these dishes," she coaxed.

Aunt Ruth had been a fine motherly substitute to Anne and her younger brothers. She made the death of her parents easier to get through by reinforcing the importance of their missionary journeys. Even before their death, it had been a treat to stay with the family while her parents were away; but Anne never expected it would become her permanent home.

Following her Aunt's suggestion, she strolled out onto the porch and proceeded down the steps toward the corral. The sheep's bleating grew as she approached, sounding like babies calling their maa maa. They had always been her favorite of the farm animals. Knowing their love for clover, she crossed the grassy yard, than stopped and reached down to pull up a handful, tapping it against her pant leg to loosen the dirt from the roots.

Sixteen years had past since the dreaded news came of her parents' and oldest brother's death. It hardly seemed possible. While the numbness and disbelief no longer existed, it was a day she would never forget. Everyone said she was the image of her mother as a small girl. Her high cheek bones, burnished hair and big almond shaped blue eyes were still pleasing reminders to her of her mother's face. Of course there were pictures, but her most prized possession was the doll brought back from overseas. Nearing the corral fence, her mind resketched the image of her first permanent night on the farm. It seemed odd to her that, although not haunting, the picture still remained clear after so many years.

She remembered sitting on the bed in her room, quietly rocking and cradling the doll from her mother—and then the bright sun that pushed its light through the sheer lace drapes, stenciling its pattern across the room, as if trying to cheer her or ease her distress. Normally on such a beautiful afternoon the sun would have joined her, as she chased small farm animals or clouds; but not that day, for her dark and lonely aching would not allow it. Then she remembered her aunt coming into her room and sitting on the bed next to her.

Aunt Ruth wore her hair in a low pony tail then, usually tied back with a small plain scarf. The ends naturally curled up and were offset by dancing red highlights that since have faded. She remembered the tender way her aunt held her, and the softness in her voice as she sat on the bed. "Not everyone understands the call or sacrifices of the missions—but your parents did. It's hard, of course, losing people you love. Your mother and I were very close. We went to high school together, you know. She liked your Uncle Henry and I liked your dad. But they both saw it different and things got switched. We ended up married to each other's first choice. It seems God had it planned out all along. Your mother took right away to the mission fields and I have always felt at home working in the fields of our farm. The Bible says the devil comes to steal, kill and destroy. But God has plans for us that the devil doesn't know. God takes the calamity the devil makes and turns it into good. I will miss your parents very much, but at the same time I feel blessed. You see, I've gained a daughter that I thought I'd never have."

Anne had always admired her aunt. Not many women could take in three children with the joy and love that she displayed. It's funny how life takes turns and directions that we would never pick for ourselves, she thought. Leaning over the corral fence to pet one of the lambs, she sighed. "There's just so much we don't understand. And it's strange to me, but it's during those unsure moments that I can almost feel the big hand of God turning the page. And I think—that the only thing that brings true comfort—is knowing that His big hand is there. It's like being a young bird in the nest—only you are a child, in the palm of God's hand."

After spending a few minutes feeding the sheep, she wandered toward the barn, then spotted the mail truck down the road. She had been counting the days and watching the mail for her EMT test results. A fluttering in her stomach tumbled and leaped as she approached the mailbox. Taking a deep breath, she opened the door. There it was, the envelope from the State of Michigan, Department of Public Health, Division of EMS. Should she open it now or wait for Aunt Ruth and Uncle Henry? The question raced in her mind. Her curiosity was too great. Wasting no time, she slid her index finger through the top of the envelope, tearing it open. Then, as she pulled the letter out, she remembered Mr. Dewit said the State would also be sending the License along with the letter. Holding the envelope up to the sunlight she blew into it, but it did not make it any less empty. Her heart sank. "There is no way I could have failed," she anguished as she unfolded the letter and read it out loud.

"Dear Miss Gates: you HAVE passed the Basic Emergency Medical Technology examination that you took on March 27th. Your score was 96% on the written portion and 94% on the practical examinations. You have exceeded the required amount needed, and should receive your License BY MAIL IN TWO WEEKS. Congratulations. Jonathan Boyd, Chief of EMS."

A feeling of elation and relief shot through her. Passing with a good score was important, to keep up her grade point. Her desire was still for the nursing program; but she couldn't explain this strange euphoria, and the more than normal excitement about passing the EMT exams. Being a stretcher jockey was not her cup of tea and she certainly was not welcome there—everyone made that very clear. "Well, I guess I'm just very happy that I passed, that's all," she told herself. "I can't wait to tell Aunt Ruth and Uncle Henry." After hastily collecting the rest of the mail out of the mail box, she ran up the long gravel driveway toward the house.

"You passed!" Aunt Ruth cheered as Anne came in through the kitchen door.

"How did you know?"

"By the look on your face, child; it's glowing like a string of Christmas lights. I'm happy for you—though I'm not surprised. You're a smart girl."

"Thank you, Aunt Ruth," Anne quietly said as she hugged her and kissed her on her cheek. "I have to call Roger and see if he got his results," she continued, bouncing back into an excited tone.

"I'm glad you were here long enough to get your letter," Aunt Ruth said, remembering that Anne would be leaving in a few days. "That look on your face, was a joy to see."

Smiling, Anne walked into the family room and picked up the phone that was sitting on the desk. She dialed Roger's number. The phone rang several times with no answer. Hanging up, she dialed the number for Mercy Medical Service. Maybe he's at work, she thought. She knew the number by heart. While doing her clinicals, the crew passed out ink pens and phone stickers with the number printed on them. She also helped Roman dispatch during the slower times when they weren't on a call.

"Mercy Medical," came a familiar voice.

"Roman," Anne declared, "what a pleasant surprise—I thought you were nocturnal."

"Oh, it's little Angela," Roman retorted, using a purposed radio voice, rolling the letters of her name as he said it. "How's Kansas and Auntie Em?" he jokingly asked, referring to the farm.

"It's Aunt Ruth, and she's fine, everyone is fine. How long have you been on days?"

"Oh, they let me out of the cave a week ago when they fired Barfbag. Merve didn't like all the sleazebag women he was bringing around. They got into a big argument and Merve canned him. No great loss," he went on, sounding like an old crone.

"Well, he is one of the owners. I can see why he would want a respectable image." She paused for a second, remembering why she called, "Hey, is Roger around?"

"No. He and Cubby lit out of here a few minutes ago on cloud nine."

"Cubby? Cubby works there now?"

"Yep, the Cubster and Rog are in the Projects on an assault as we speak. He just got off the phone with Tracy before that. So far, everyone here passed the State exam. How about you? You aced it no doubt," he said answering his own question.

"No, I'm not that smart. I got a ninety-six percent on the written and ninety-four percent on the practical."

"Braggart," he teased. "You know guys don't like women that are smarter than them." She heard another phone line ring. "Hold on a minute," he said quickly putting her on hold before she could speak. She waited a few minutes then heard him back on the line, dispatching a call to a crew on the road. The call was for a car accident on a well-known four-lane highway, just outside of Lancemen. Because the lanes were narrow on this road, it was difficult to judge the space between you as the driver and the oncoming cars; plus, too often the drivers chose their own speed limit, as if it were the autobahn. Due to the large number of accidents on the highway, which was named Dixie, the crews often referred to it as Deadly Dixie.

"Anne, you there?" he abruptly asked. "Hey listen, Merve's having a cookout at his place next Saturday at thirteen hundred for all of us graduates. It's okay, you're invited. See you later." A click of the phone, then the dial tone spilled from the receiver as quickly as his words. "What was that?" she whispered. "He hung up before I could say a word." She sat dazed for a moment staring at the receiver as if it could explain his rapid conversation, before setting it back in place. Walking toward the kitchen door to go outside, she wondered if Roman just volunteered her presence at the cookout. It just didn't seem characteristic of Merve. "Well anyway, I'm sure it will be fun," she said to herself. "But just to be on the safe side—maybe I should take something special as a dish to pass—just in case Merve didn't really invite me."

"Merve—I could use some help in here," Roman called out. The County was breaking loose. It always seemed to happen in spurts; then after a few hours, the dust and the commotion would settle. Finally, the phone lines quit ringing. Suddenly, Roman remembered his conversation with Anne regarding the cookout and thought he best announce his extended invitation.

"But, she doesn't work here," Merve said, sounding a little miffed at Roman's flash report.

"She could," Roman said, then continued with what seemed to be a pre-planned speech. "We need a midnight dispatcher. She knows the basic routine and how to answer the phones. She can read a map, and she learns fast."

"Are you finished?" Merve asked, interrupting as he went on talking. His voice was becoming louder, like a crescendo in a music piece. "There's one problem that you seem to have overlooked," he continued. "The word, SHE. I'm telling you, if you let one in—the next thing you know there's hot rollers in the bathroom and those stupid little rugs they put everywhere to trip over. I just fired John for having women in here. I can't have that stuff going on here. I'm trying to run a business!"

"Anne is nothing like those sleazebags that John was dragging in here," Roman said, continuing with his case. "She's smart and everyone gets along with her. Just try it on a trial basis until you can get someone else in full time. With the ERA going the way it is, you're going to have to hire one of them sooner or later. You might as well set yourself up with someone you already know—that way there are no surprises."

Merve stood up and began walking toward the door. Stopping in front of it he turned around trying to hide his expression of defeat. "Fine," he barked. "Just remember that she's your responsibility—and she needs to be here for Monday night."

"Well, don't you think that I should see if she even wants the job first?" Roman asked, surprised that he agreed so quickly.

"I figured you probably already took care of that too, when you asked her to the cookout. Do yourself a favor, Roman," he added, grinning. "Make sure that she brings some of those homemade canned pears with her on Saturday."

Confidently smiling with a face of a winning politician, Roman called out to Merve as he left the room, "Don't worry, she can handle it. I wouldn't have suggested it, if I didn't think so."

Anne was in total disbelief when Roman called her with the proposal. "Roman you're not going to believe this—but I'm coming into Lancemen Monday morning, to house sit for the Johnstones while they're out of town. I was just telling my Aunt that I was going to have to get a job part time while I was there." She paused, then with a tinge of uncertainty in her voice she asked, "Do you really think I can do it?" Roman was glad she was interested, especially since he had been so boldly confident.

"If I didn't think so I wouldn't have stuck my neck out. Merve wants you in here on Monday. The shift starts at twenty-three hundred. Come in around twenty-one hundred so we can go over things. I'll work with you for a few hours to help get you settled. You already know the basics and I'll leave you my home phone number in case a tornado hits. But don't call unless you have to—my wife gets crazy when women call in the middle of the night," he warned, lightheartedly.

"Okay," Anne agreed.

"I believe that response should have been ten-four," he joked, satisfied with the arrangement.

"Ten-four," she laughed, trying to create a professional tone to her voice. "Hey, by the way—did you know my birthday is October, fourth? Get it? Ten-four. No, really, it is. Anyway—I'll see you on Monday, Roman. And thanks."

CHAPTER 6

LET THE GAMES BEGIN

"Unit One, you're responding code three, to 987 Whitting for a baby not breathing. Whitting runs south off of Henna, one street east of East Boulevard. The call came in through Lancemen Fire. Your incident number is 046 at 00:48."

"Ten-four," replied the voice coming through the speaker on the dispatch console. Three weeks had passed since Anne first began manning the ship. Dispatching mid-nights was fairly easy for the most part. There were times when it got crazy busy. But usually, those times were short lived. You could only send as many ambulances out on calls as you had available. Even with the shared coverage from a nearby ambulance service, periodically there were shortages of ambulances in relation to the call volume. Of course emergency calls took top priority over non-emergency calls; but it was hard to pull a crew off a non-emergency call, once their stretcher was already loaded. It was a big responsibility servicing such a vast area; but Anne enjoyed the challenge, for it gave her an idea of what was needed in order to provide quality emergency care to the citizens of one of the largest and richest counties in the state.

Until she personally became involved in the EMS businesses, she'd never really given it much thought. No one in her family ever needed an ambulance. The mere thought of that was frightening; yet, here she was. Even though it was all very new to her, she felt proud to be a part of this group. Most of Lancemen County's emergency transportation was divided between two privately owned ambulance companies. Townsdale EMS covered the southern sector of the county, while Mercy Medical Service covered the larger more rural northern areas. Here the growing population of over a hundred thousand was spread over eight different townships, six communities, and two cities. The largest of the two cities was the City of Lancemen. It contained the highest number of residents in the north end and had a known diversity of population that was also divided into areas by compass points. The west side was made up largely of elegant homes in a village, graced by the superb architecture and carpentry of the Forties. While the Victorian and English Tudor styled estates stood well cared for on equally manicured lawns, they were in sharp contrast to the houses in other sections of the City where the economic and urbane decay had taken its toll.

In the post war era, Lancemen had been the place to live. The car industry was booming then and kept employment peaked. Then things changed when some of the factories relocated. Families that had money to move, did. Those who didn't, remained. Over time, a sense of despair took over and street drugs became a market that erroneously brought money back into the city. With the drug world came a violence that not only ended in death for the users and the dealers, but it also took the lives of children and other innocent victims.

"Unit Four, you're responding to 16 Elm for a shooting. Police and Fire are en route. Stage at the corner of Fifth and Elm with Fire until the scene is secure. Your incident number is 048. The time of call is 01:23."

"Ten-four," came a sleepy sounding voice. The crews worked forty-eight hour shifts. They would sometimes pull as many as forty calls during that time span. Due to the haphazard sleep they acquired, even a call for a shooting was scarcely enough at times to get the adrenaline flowing; at least until they arrived on the scene.

"Unit Four, arrival with Fire," came a more alert sounding voice. "PD just cleared us in."

"Ten- four," Anne calmly returned, as she punched the dispatch card. Only a few minutes passed when the crew called en route to LOH. Most of the time they went to the hospital of the patient's choice, but in an emergency situation they transported to the hospital that was closest to their location. Anne recognized Dan's voice.

"Be advised," he added, "if you have another unit available, you might want to keep them on the air. I don't think this is over yet."

"Ten-four," she answered.

"Unit One, on the air and clear of Lancemen General. We copied Unit Four and are en route to LOH to lend them a hand."

"Ten-four. Make sure you stay one man on the air please, so I can get you for a call, if I need to."

"You're not getting nervous are you?" Rick asked with a chuckle as he sensed a slight quiver in her voice.

"I just don't trust you guys," she halfheartedly joked, "you have a way of doing these disappearing acts."

"Okay, we'll keep an ear open," he said amused with Anne's humor. "We're out at LOH, with one man on the air." Rick had a boyish charm. He was tall, with straight blonde hair. His laughing brown eyes and magnetic smile amplified his youthful appearance. He had a fun tricksy way, that Anne enjoyed. Though she knew she was naive in many ways, she felt good about how quickly she was catching on to the crew's personalities.

The phones were finally quiet; at least for now. Her mind drifted back to a few Saturdays ago, when the EMT Graduates were at Merve's house for a cookout. Merve had a good sized, four bedroom home on the lake. When she arrived, some of the guys were water skiing. Even though the air temperature was warm, the water was icy cold. That of course, didn't stop them from braving the water in wet suits. After fixing herself a plate of food, she sat at the picnic table with the not so daring or stupid as they watched the skiers compete in a game. Little to her surprise, the object of the game was to see who could ski closest to the dock without hitting it. Sometimes they just seemed so crazy. But then maybe it wasn't craziness. Maybe it was this job, forcing them to face life and death at every angle, that created this need or an interest to challenge life's boundaries.

The phone rang, lighting up the Lancemen PD line. "Mercy Medical." After listening to their dispatcher's request, she replied, "I'll have a unit there in a few minutes. They're coming from LOH." She hung up the phone and called the hospital on the direct line.

"Lancemen Osteopathic Hospital," the ER clerk replied. Anne asked to speak to the crew. She could hear the commotion of the busy ER as Rick came to the phone.

"All right you found us. Are we going back to 16 Elm?" he asked.

"Yea, PD just called. They want you to do a body removal from there to the Medical Examiner's office. You're all I have left. The Lakeveiw Unit is out covering at Liz and Huron and I can't send the Commission Car out on a non-emergency call," she explained.

"No problem, the guy Dan brought in is dead, too."

Their line of work had made death very matter of fact and common place. While doing her clinical rides, Anne learned that death had a feel and a smell all its own. In spite of the effort to provide the patient the best chance at survival, many times an unfavorable outcome was intuit, just by the feel and smell alone.

After clearing Unit Two back to their station in Lakeview, she cleared the Commission Car to return to the crew member's home. Unit One had just cleared the ME's office, and Unit Four was heading back to Station One. Not only did the main station, Station One, house the garage and offices, it also housed the dispatch center and the crew's quarters.

With the pause in the morning's activity and everyone nearly in their place, she sighed. Then she heard Unit Four announce their approach over the radio and turned her chair around to push the button on the panel to open the door. Before she realized it, her chair caught the gun that was propped against the wall. It startled her a little as it fell to the floor. "That stupid gun is always in the way," she said, quieting herself. The gun was a large old Tommy Machine gun that didn't work. Rick brought it in one night to scare off anyone who might see Anne sitting alone in the dispatch center. The center was in plain view to anyone who walked by the full length glass door in the outer office. The glass was thick and would be hard to break, but the garage door was automatic and closed slowly. Sneaking in under it while the crew drove away would be easy, if the crew didn't have time to watch the door close.

Anne heard the crews coming into the garage. She knew she heard more than just two voices. The Commission Car must have come in with Unit Four, she thought. Unit One couldn't possibly have made it back from the ME's office so fast—or could they? The garage could hold ten ambulances, if they had them. It had a wash bay and a dozen or so large oxygen bottles to refill the smaller tanks. Occasionally rats would wander in, often leaving faster than they came.

As she turned to push the button to close the door, she jumped at the sound of a package of firecrackers set off in the garage.

"Here we go again," she mumbled to herself, remembering that it was only last week that Chris was blown off the ladder he was climbing to catch Mike, who was crouched on the drop ceiling over the crews quarters. After Mike yelled, "Incoming," he threw the lit firecracker to warn Chris to back off. But Chris was already coming up the ladder and the firecracker landed down his shirt. Not only did it knock him off the ladder and burn the hairs off his chest, but it left him with a second degree burn the size of a fist.

She heard them laughing and felt somewhat relieved that it was only firecrackers and not gun fire. Then just as she eased back in her chair, the door between the garage and the sitting room flew open, slamming against the wall. Startled, she glanced into the sitting room through the small window that was set in the dividing wall next to her. Shaking her head, she laughed at the frog hand puppet that suddenly appeared in the window. "Hi yah. Hi yah. Hi yah baby," came the puppeteer's gruff voice. Again, the door flew open. This time she heard a familiar cry in an imitated falsetto pitch, "Oh nooooo, Mr. Bill. Not that!" Seconds later, a small male doll flew into the air of the sitting room. To her surprise, the firecrackers that had been stuffed inside it detonated with a loudness that was equal to an M-80. Sawdust from the doll exploded and propelled into the air like a rocket, before falling like confetti.

"Oh man," Rick said as he burst out laughing. Seconds later he and his frog puppet disappeared, as he darted into the front office. Firecrackers were exploding one after another as the crews threw them with half-guarded aim, like children playing war. Anne closed the window in the wall next to her and got up from her chair to shut the door. "Great," she muttered. "It's three o'clock in the morning. The rest of the county's sleeping—but not here—we've got the War of the Worlds going on, less than two feet away."

Without warning, the dispatch door behind her pushed opened. She got up and turned to warn whoever was coming in to get out, when suddenly something strange appeared in front of her and exploded. Pieces of flesh and inner parts went flying. Most of the debris covered her face and the front of her shirt. Even though she was frightened by the deafening blast, a meager scream was all that squeaked out. It all happened so quickly that it was hard to recall any clear details of the event. And with the ringing in her ears?—oh—the ringing in her ears! Amidst it all, she stood wondering—did she really see, what she thought she had? As the fogginess lifted, she realized, yes! It really was a frog that she saw with a firecracker in its mouth.

The amphibious mask was already beginning to harden. Reaching up to touch her face she heard Dan let out a frightened shriek. "Ahhh! What the..." In an attempt to calm himself as well as Anne, he tried to soften his voice. She could feel a trembling in his hands as he tried to hold hers down.

"Anne, don't touch your face." The quiver in his voice told her that something was wrong. Dan had always been so calm in emergency situations. This was a side of him she had never seen.

"We got an emergency in here!" he bellowed. The ringing in her ears increased. She strained to make out the voices of Rick and Chris as they came running into the room. Her eyelids felt sticky and weighed down. By tipping her head back a little and forcing them to open, she could peer from the two slits she created. Seeing the small clumps of tissue on her shirt, she could only guess that her face looked worse. Squinting at her hands, she saw blood and remembered touching her face. That blood can't be mine, she mentally reassured herself; after all, I'm not in any pain. Gradually she was able to make out some of their conversation.

"Come on, Anne," she heard Dan gently say, as he led her toward the garage. In an attempt to keep calm, she tried counting his footsteps. Then panic took over again as he loudly asked, "Who threw that frog at her?"

"I put the frog on the floor near the closet. It must have jumped up in front of her." Rick answered. He had such a sorrowful sound in his voice. Slowly they made their way to the ambulance that Chris had ready to go.

"Bob and I will stay here until Roman comes in. I'm going to call him right now," Chris said. "All right," Rick replied. "We're going to LOH. Don't say anything to Roger until we find out how things go."

"Don't worry, I'll give you time to pack first," Chris answered. They understood the dry humor was his way of dealing with a difficult situation; this however, was more than a difficult situation. Without a doubt, it was a bad deal for Anne—but even worse, if Merve got wind of it, they'd all be packing.

Rick tried to comfort Anne as much as he could. His heart must be racing, she thought. If I could only tell him, that I don't think I'm hurt—just covered with frog. Her face felt completely dry and hard as a rock. The only words she could mutter sounded like the Tin Man on the Wizard of Oz when he first asked Dorothy for the oil can.

Within minutes they were backing into the ambulance bay entrance. They made her stay on the stretcher as they rolled it into the ER and then into the prepared room. Dan gave a pre-advisement to the hospital on the VHF radio while they were en route, just as they did with their other patients. Mary was the nurse with Dr. Brett who watched as they came in the door. The staff remembered Anne from her clinicals. At first they were angry when Rick explained the series of the incident. Although Anne couldn't hear them very well she felt the tension and wished she could speak. Finally, her hearing slowly improved and she was able to recognize Mary's voice as she helped her undress and slip on a hospital gown. Dr. Brett came in and examined her; first one ear than the other. While peering through the otoscope, she faintly heard him say that her ear drums and canals looked slightly swollen but otherwise were healthy. He used a tongue depressor and a warm wet cloth to wipe off the goo. "Oh, that feels so good," Anne said, relieved to hear her own voice. Mary finished wiping off Anne's hands and face as they talked about the near-war episode. Dr.

Brett listened as he reexamined Anne's face. He determined that she was surprisingly in better shape than he first thought and applied a few Steri Strips to a couple superficial lacerations on her cheek.

"Okay, that's better" he began. "Now, let's see if we can't get some of that poor, disintegrated creature out of your hair. How do you feel?"

"Better," she smiled. "At least I can move my face and the ringing in my ears isn't as bad as it was."

"So now, tell me again—you actually saw a frog in front of you with a firecracker sticking out of his mouth?"

"Yes sir," she replied shyly. "It—a—actually sort of looked more like a little cigar. I know that sounds silly, Dr. Brett, but it all happened so quick; and I know Rick never expected it to jump up in front of me."

"Well that's how accidents happen," he smiled. "Where did he get the idea to do such a crazy thing, is what I want to know."

"From the TV, I guess. They like to watch all these different comedy shows. Some of them they can even cite, by wrote."

"Cite by wrote? My grandfather used to use that expression."

Mary came in with a fine tooth comb. "Normally we use these, to comb out head lice. Hopefully we can get most of that stuff out of your hair until you get home and get a shower." Working the comb through Anne's hair she began prattling schemes to get even with the guys. Laughing at her suggestions, Anne joined in with a few ideas of her own. Then the orderly, Steve, brought her a scrub top to put on in place of the frog covered shirt and a cup of coffee. "What a night!" she said, sipping the cup. "What time is it anyway?"

"It's four-thirty," Steve answered. "I think I saw an ambulance backing into the bay a few minutes ago. It must be Rick and Dan returning from that call they went on."

"So which scheme are you going to use?" Mary coaxed.

"None," Anne replied. "They've been through enough already. I know you'll think it's crazy, but growing up, my brothers and cousins played worse pranks than this."

Dan and Rick came into the room. By the expressions on their face, they came in expecting to see a monster and were thrilled to see a clean, washed face with a few small cuts.

"Oh—thank God," Dan sighed.

"Man," Rick said in relief, "I thought I blew your face off. I am so glad I didn't—guess maybe now, I can go home and unpack."

Mary got up and walked toward the door. "You'd still be packing if it were me, I'll tell yah. You'd better be grateful Anne is taking this so well—cause I sure wouldn't." Her curt remark made it difficult to tell if she was really angry or just teasing. Dr. Brett sat on the wheeled stool in the room and half-smiled. Clearly he shared Mary's words—even though he understood the intended playfulness of the war-game that got out of hand.

"Take it easy, Anne, you're free to go. You boys find something else to do in your spare time," he added, as he watched them walk toward the bay door.

"Thanks, Doc. Don't worry, we're cured," they said, waving.

Rick put his arm around Anne's neck and rubbed the top of her head lightly with his knuckles as he quietly asked, "Are you mad at me?"

"I should be," she said grinning. After carefully getting into the back of the ambulance she slid across the bench seat toward the front. "Just be glad I'm not a vindictive person," she continued. "Those nurses had all kinds of juicy ideas to get even; and as long as you guys keep me out of your games, you will never have to worry about them."

"Sounds good to me. I'm too tired to play any more games tonight anyway," Dan said, picking up the radio mike. "Unit Four clear of LOH, en route to Station One."

"Copy that Unit Four—how's she looking?"

"We're one up, looking good," he added happily.

"Very good, let me know when you're getting close."

Anne knew that both Dan and Rick had the next forty-eight hours off, and that when they returned for their next shift, they'd be well rested. She was also quite certain that as soon as time allowed—the games would—and without hesitation, once again, begin.

CHAPTER 7

COMMISSIONED

The emerging sunrise filtered through the full glass door and embellished the outer office wall with a warm and welcome glow. Anne leaned back in the dispatch chair, looked at her watch, then smiled. The skin on her cheek where the Steri Strips adhered pulled slightly; a reminder of the morning's activities. "Less than an hour to go," she whispered. Taking the magnifying glass from the hook next to the map, she aimed it toward the light that filtered through the glass door and created a rainbow effect. Amused by this, she guided the image over Shirley's desk and up the paneled wall. The game ended after a few minutes. Bored with her source of entertainment, she returned the magnifying glass to the hook, then searched for something else that might occupy the last few minutes of her shift.

Suddenly, the red knob on the console drew her attention. Its normal purpose was to wake the crews by activating a light inside a red beacon nailed to the paneled wall in the bunk room where they slept. Attached to the wall next to it, was a plectron that would bellow out an irritating tone to ensure their wakefulness. While contemplating its effect, an image resembling slapstick humor strolled through her mind. She could easily imagine the crews crawling from their bunks with sleepy squinting eyes and clumsy unawake hands as each one grabbed for their pants, shirts and boots. Without question the drill would be far more entertaining to her; and the retaliation to the act, seeming like a thing of vengeance to them, was far more than she intended. Weighing it all out, she supposed setting off the plectron probably wasn't a good idea. After all, her desire was just for something to pass the time.

She was tired and eager to go home to her room at the Johnstones. Her face felt sore and itchy where the Steri Strips were, but she was grateful it wasn't worse. Well, it's almost time for Merve to walk in the door, she thought, as she got up to make a fresh pot of coffee. The calls that took place during her shift were logged. The garbage had been emptied and the floors were mopped. As she poured coffee into a cup, she heard the sound of keys in the door and poured a second cup for Merve.

"Morning" he said, as he walked in. After putting his keys in his office, he walked over to the makeshift counter in the sitting room. "Ahh, coffee," he sighed, as the pleasing fragrance filled the room. His first savory sip brought a mellowing that cast the contentment of a purring kitten. Then his eyes were drawn to the Streri Strips on her cheek. "What happened to your face?" Taking on the appearance of a hound dog with a scent, he crinkled his nose while scanning the room. A sudden flush came over her, as she quickly tried to think of an explanation. Merve was very familiar with the crews and their antics; well, most of them. She didn't want to say anything to get them in trouble. Her mind raced for a response, but nothing came. She felt pressured. She needed more time to think of a good answer. All her normal thinking capabilities seemed blocked. Then, to her wonder, the words just spilled out of her mouth.

"I cut myself shaving." Her face reflected the surprise of her own words, as they echoed in her mind. She couldn't believe she had said such a ridiculous thing. There was no way Merve was going to buy that.

"You cut—yourself shaving," he echoed softly, raising his eyebrows, puzzled by her behavior. "You're not very good at this, are you?" he asked. Then, sensing her embarrassment, he added, "Never mind, I don't think I really want to know." Anne could hear the crews in the bunk room stirring at the sound of their voices. Choking back her shame, she was relieved to see Roman open the glass door and walk into the outer office.

"Morning," he said, noticing them standing next to the counter. After hanging his jacket on the back of the chair in the dispatch center, he walked into the sitting room and reached for a cup of coffee. Looking at Anne, he very calmly asked, "Cut yourself shaving?" Encumbered by a stumbling sensation, she quickly looked down. Without giving him an answer, she picked up her cup and went into the dispatch center.

Merve studied Roman's face, surmising he knew what happened. The strong, sulfuric odor that still lingered suggested the return of unsupervised fireworks. His concern for their safety was greater then his curiosity. And, while he hoped for an explanation, he wasn't surprised when it didn't come. The redness in his face grew with his impatience. Then he bellowed an announcement loud enough for the crews in the nearby bunk room to hear. "All I know—is this place smells like firecrackers again!" Initially, an extreme irritation rang out as he spoke. Then his tone softened as he continued, voicing the heart of a scolding father, rather than the mind of an angry boss. "I would think that you people would have more sense than to play with something that can blow your fingers off. I don't want to leave here every night wondering which one of my employees is going to get hurt. We are in a medical profession here. If you want to engage in explosives, go work at an armory!"

Roman heard the phone ringing in the dispatch center. "Excuse me, Merve, I need to get that. I got it, Anne," he called out, quickly slipping past her. His face expressed relief, as if to say, saved by the bell. "Mercy Medical," he answered. Grabbing the scratch pad of paper on the console, he picked up the pen next to it and jotted down the information from the Lakeview police dispatcher for an injured party. Then he pushed the direct line for his crew at the Lakeview station, while scanning the big county map on the wall. A groggy striding voice answered, displeased with the interruption of sleep.

"Yeah?"

"On the road for a code, my friend."

"All right."

While waiting, Roman rechecked the street location. He sighed. The time duration that passed before they called on the air seemed much longer than the actual three minutes. After relaying the information, he listened for their confirmation of the address, then turned toward Anne and in a low voice asked, "What did Merve say to you?"

"He asked me what happened to my face," she answered in a near whisper, while reaching into the closet for her sweater. A piece of the frog's leg that they missed while cleaning caught her eye. She bent over and picked up the flesh as if it were nothing more than a scrap of paper and put it in the trash. "I couldn't think of anything to say. Before I could stop myself, the words just fell out of my mouth. I told him that I cut myself shaving."

"No really—what did you tell him?" Roman asked skeptically.

"That's really what I told him," she answered in a soft, anxious voice. "I couldn't believe it when you came in and asked the same thing. It's kind of scary to think that I'm starting to think like you guys. Well—it's been a long night and I could really use some sleep. See you at eleven," she concluded. With her sweater draped over her arm, she took her keys from her purse, then walked toward the glass door. Roman called out after her, softly boasting, "I told Merve you could handle it. Can I call'em, or can I call'em?"

Anne greeted the fresh new day as she walked across the narrow, paved street. Overhead, she noticed the gray, opaque clouds that confirmed the threat of rain, predicted for early afternoon. Chattering from the birds echoed contentiously between the buildings. She looked up at the eaves where they were building their nests. City noises seem to project such a despairing feel, she thought. Even the birds sound like they're in hubbub. Standing next to her car, unlocking the door, she looked up as Unit Two pulled into the parking lot. Roger was driving. He unrolled his window as he pulled up next to where she was standing and stopped.

"Hey—it's frog woman. Or should I call you the bearded lady." By his comment, she knew he had already talked to Roman. She walked toward the ambulance, shaking her head, trying not to laugh; giving in to that would only encourage him. His snickering made it clear; he was already entertained by his own humor.

"I thought you were on a call in Lakeview," she said, trying to force his composure.

"We got canceled. Since we were already up, we decided to come in and pick up the clean linen. We were right in front of Mickey D's too, when Roman shut us down. I almost pulled in to grab some breakfast, but this QT (a term the crews sometimes used to describe anyone in a car with white hair) was coming the other way. You know how they always call in and complain that we coded to the restaurant—so I just came here to see how messed up you were."

"Thanks for caring," she laughed.

"So I hear the nurses are pretty impressed with your sportsmanship."

"I'm not so sure I would call it sportsmanship," she said smiling. "I walk by faith not by sight. Things aren't always the way they seem. I think Rick just got caught up in the excitement of the war-game. You guys have a strange sense of humor. It must just come with the job."

Mike Peterson joined in the trifling from the passenger seat. He was known as a big contributor to the sequel of the company's tomfoolery. But the firecracker incident with Chris had slowed him down. Although Chris displayed no sign of revenge, Mike still felt it best to give him a cooling off period. Since then, he'd been laying low and working with Roger temporarily at the Lakeview station. Then, after hearing of last night's adventure, his cutup nature was re-stirred and common sense went to the wayside, as he began the planning stages of the next escapade.

"Hey, we thought of some good ways to get even," he jumped in. "You only have a couple more weeks until they move the dispatch center into the new building. So, you better make your move now."

Anne looked puzzled. "A couple of weeks? I didn't hear anything about that." Roger knew by her expression and comment that Merve had said nothing about the changes that were soon to take place. These were changes she would need to know about, if she were to continue working as a midnight dispatcher.

Over the past year Mercy Medical and Townsdale EMS had been assisting each other with call volume coverage. During that time the company's owners often talked about combining the two dispatch centers. Now, to Roger's dislike, he realized he would have to be the one to bring the news to Anne. He watched her expression while explaining the new operation, hoping to be somewhat tactful. It wasn't long before she understood; there was no place for her in the plan.

"Well, maybe they don't think I have enough experience or knowledge of the county to dispatch full time for both companies. After all, this job was just a temporary spot until they trained someone else. Plus, I'll be going back to college in the fall." It sounded like she was trying to convince herself more than Roger. Maybe she was. She really liked her job as a dispatcher and working with the guys made her feel at home. Then, after pausing for a second, a renewed peace was heard in her voice. "Anyway, I'm not going to worry about it. Worrying is just borrowed troubled and it never changed anything. I trust God has it under control."

Roger was the first to confess that the only time he ever saw the inside of a church was on Easter or Christmas; and, that while he didn't always understand the scripture when Anne referred to it, he still liked to hear it. He thought she had a way of bringing it to life. Many times he'd heard her say, that God was the source of her strength—the cornerstone of her life. Her Christian upbringing was steadfast. Throughout her life the biblical teachings were golden, like the gilt-edged pages sealed on God's holy word.

"Okay, he said, smiling, we're going back to Lakeview. Our relief should be coming in soon. I'm off for the next couple of days—give me a call. And get some sleep; you look terrible."

"Thank you," she said, as she waved and smiled.

Although the crew's language and actions were somewhat coarse, Anne was still drawn to them. Her Aunt always taught her to look at a person's heart. "The crust doesn't always give way, to the sweetness of the bread," she often said. Many times the guys acted like young steeds away from the public eye, but they took on the appearance of a pacer when duty called. She found herself studying them unwittingly while doing her clinical rides. The contrast amazed her. Their rapid response in an emergency did not impede their compassion or assertiveness. And while their humor served as a useful tool to ease the patient's fear, it also served as a stress reliever for them as well. They were just good at what they did, and they did it for very little money. A monetary reward was obviously not all that they were seeking. Instead, the self gratification of a good Samaritan was their trophy.

Almost two weeks had passed since the smoking frog massacre incident. Occasionally, a piece of the poor thing was found in the dispatch radio equipment, resulting in scornful looks from Merve and a considerable slowdown to the crew's shenanigans. Roman chuckled but was serious when he told them, "We better put a hold on the fireworks. If one more goes off—I think Merve's the one who's going to explode."

Anne's job as a dispatcher would end in a few days. Merve finally gave her the news of the merge and changes earlier that night. Realizing her leaving had created a shared, sullen ambiance among her fellow workers, he tried his best to explain his decision.

"It's not that you haven't done a good job here," he told her firmly. "It's just that you don't have enough time in on the radio. There's nowhere else I can put you. Shirley doesn't need any help in the office—and seeing that you're a girl, I can't put you on the road. That's out of the question."

Shirley was the only other female that worked at Mercy Medical. She helped Anne with the log at the end of her shift and was always there to lend an ear.

"I heard the news," she said, after Merve walked into the other room. "I don't know how you feel about leaving this job, but I bet it's an experience you'll not soon forget." They both laughed.

"No, I can honestly say that I won't," Anne replied. "I have to admit—I wasn't too sure about the job when I first came here, but I'm going to miss it."

"You're just a glutton for punishment, you are," Shirley chuckled. Her crisp dark eyes sparkled under the tight curled bangs that framed her round face. "You'll have to come by and see us in the new place. Don't let this make you a stranger." She paused while collecting and putting order to the papers on her desk. "Well, I need to get busy on payroll, or these guys will be looking to lynch me. I'll see you in the morning."

Anne was fond of Shirley. She was a short, middle aged lady of Irish decent who worked for Merve since the company started three years ago. Time and experience made her wise to the crew's capers and habits. Each time they tried to pull something over on her, she would declare like clockwork, in her Irish brogue, "These lads will have to get up pretty early in the morning to fool me." She was alert to be sure, and didn't miss much. Even with Anne's camouflaged expression, she could clearly see she was sad to be leaving.

Anne was half way through her last shift. The night was just dragging. It was the slowest night she'd experienced yet. The crews were in the bunk room watching TV or sleeping. Even the monitors for the Fire and Police departments were quiet.

"C.C. at your front door," came a voice that broke the silence on the radio. Anne reached for the garage door button. She recognized Chris' voice. The Commission Car hadn't turned a wheel all night.

"What's going on?" he asked, as he walked into the dispatch center.

"Not much," she replied. "I've never seen it this quiet. I'm glad that no one is sick or hurt, but I keep hoping the phone will ring, just to keep me from falling asleep." Chris sat in the chair next to her. He turned on the metal desk lamp that was attached to the dispatch console, then leaned back and began playing with the rolodex.

"So, this is your last night I hear. What are you going to do the rest of the summer for work?" he asked, as if he had some plan working in his mind.

"Well, the Johnstones are back home again, so I'm free to go back to Summerville and finish the summer up there. I'm going to miss you guys, but I'm grateful that I had the opportunity to work here."

Chris sighed, unsure if he should speak his mind. "I know Merve probably told you there was no way he would let you work on the road; but there is a way that you can, if you want. You could work with me—on the Commission Car. I won't have a partner for a few weeks. Bob's on vacation. I run the car out of my house, so Merve will never see you. I'll drive and do all the talking on the radio. We can both do patient care on the scene. You can do the rest of it on the way to the hospital. Once you've pulled the calls, he'll have to pay you. You don't need a real uniform; you can just wear dark blue pants. Mike told me he would let you borrow one of his shirts. You might never get another chance to do this. So what do you think?"

Anne laughed, amused that he had said so much so fast and that it seemed so well rehearsed. "What I think is—you sound like the devil, trying to get Eve to eat the apple off the forbidden tree. After he filled her head up with a bunch of half truths, she ended up losing just about everything." Chris was not surprised at all with her response.

"Why does everything that comes out of your mouth have to sound like a bible story? Do you want to work on the road or not? This is probably going to be your only chance."

Well there it was, she thought. Chris was right. This probably was going to be her only chance to use her Basic EMT license. Then there was Merve. He had made it clear he didn't want her working the road. And this was his company. Why did Chris even come in here? I could have walked out of here in a couple of hours and been glad for the experience. Now what am I going to do. If I say no, I will hate myself for passing up this opportunity. If I say yes, I will hate myself for going against Merve. She pondered the situation for a few seconds, sipping a cup of coffee.

Chris began playing with the lamp on the console. He turned it on, then off, then back and forth again. "Why is it always so dark in here?" he asked, as he flicked the light on for the final time. Anne was deep in thought, seeming unaware of his question or of the duel of light versus dark. Leaning on the desk of the console, she turned her head toward Chris.

"What do you think Merve would do if he found out that I went against what he said?"

"I knew that would be your hang-up," Chris said, then continued; "This is my honest answer and not a con-job statement. I think once Merve saw that you could do the job, he'd be okay with it. He might be mad at first but he'd calm down. A female is going to come in here someday and do this job. It's going to happen, and it won't really matter what Merve thinks. I'd like to see it be you. The choice is yours. You can give me your answer in the morning. I get up for my real job at six. You have my number. If I don't hear from you, I'll take it as a no. No hard feelings. I understand you have principles to live by." Listening to Chris made her smile. She knew she'd been right about him. Somewhere under that big person was a big heart.

"Is your wife going to be at the house?" she asked.

"I already talked to Debbie. She's fine with it. She said you could sleep downstairs in Beth's room."

Anne scratched her head and sighed as she looked over at Chris. "Okay. When do I start?"

Chris smiled as he stood up. It was clear he was pleased, but at the same time was trying to emit a serious air, as if he just closed a big business deal.

"It's Monday now. I'll give you a few days to get things in order. Why don't you come over Friday about eighteen hundred and we'll get you settled." He paused as he stood in the doorway. "It really isn't much, but everyone has to start somewhere. Consider yourself commissioned to work on the Commission Car." He walked out of the room and down the hall. When he got to the bunk room, he stopped and opened the door.

"She said yes. She starts Friday. If Merve hears about it before that, she'll never get another chance. So keep it to yourself."

"Okay," the crew's voices chorused. Then one of them called out, as the others followed suit, "Night, Chris. Night, Anne. Night, John boy."

Anne closed the garage door behind Chris' rig as he drove away. "Well that's something I never expected," she said softly to herself. "I've been commissioned to work the Commission Car. I hope and pray Merve won't be too upset; and, that he doesn't mind paying me my commission."

CHAPTER 8

LIFE IN THE FAST LANE

The tepid water felt good against Anne's face as she stood in the shower getting ready for her first shift with Chris on the Commission Car. Her mind reeled with wonder and anticipation of the night to come. Scores of signs and symptoms buzzed through her head, while she mentally reviewed possible scenarios of calls she might encounter. Providing the best patient care was her desire; hopefully, she could do so without her knees rattling so loud as to give away her novice stature.

Tonight would be a different experience than her clinical rides; not only because she and Chris alone would be responsible for the patient care, but also because she had done all of her scheduled rides solely during the daylight hours. Until tonight, the calls she dispatched during midnight's was the only confirmation she had of the stories told to her of the darkness that brought out a whole different world of people and patients. And, while tonight she'd be a first hand witness to these things, she felt as intrigued as she did nervous; for she knew it would test not only her medical abilities, but also her ability to stomach the job as well. Soon she would find out for herself just what she was made of; would she be a man or a mouse?

Standing in front of the mirror on the back of the bedroom door, she scanned her outfit. The neatly pressed uniform shirt she borrowed and her navy slacks seemed to fit well together. She finished scrunching her dark curly hair, then applied a small amount of make-up. After tying her shoes and rechecking her wallet for her EMT License, she smiled nervously. With one last look at her clothes in the foyer mirror, she quietly reassured herself, "I think I have everything. Guess I'm as ready as I'll ever be."

For the time being she completely forgot about Merve and how upset he might be when he found out that she was working on the road. From the moment Chris approached her with the idea, Anne understood Chris was right. She knew that Merve didn't have anything against her personally; he just had a doubter's mind. Some people are doubters and some people are doers she thought, as she imagined his ancestors skeptically watching the flight of the Kitty Hawk, or maybe even scoffing as Alan Shepard took his first step onto the moon's surface. It wasn't that she needed to prove anything; it was greater than that. What ever this unexplainable stirring was, it was set deep and bold within her. She knew this was something she couldn't pass up. The door of opportunity had opened. If she didn't enter, she'd regret it forever.

The Johnstones had gone out for the evening with friends, leaving Anne alone in the house with her rambling thoughts. After rechecking the front door to make sure it was locked, she looked at her watch. She still had plenty of time to get to Chris' house. Carrying a light overnight bag with some toiletries and her purse, she started down the front porch steps. The busy sounds of the Birch Hill neighborhood were very different, from that of the farm. The laughter of children playing, combined with the din of rush hour traffic from a nearby highway took a little effort to get used to. She waved at Mrs. Lawrence who lived across the street as she walked toward her gray Duster and got in. What a city girl I'm becoming, she thought, taking the directions to Chris' house out of her purse. Neighbors in Summerville always take time to speak to each other. They don't just wave and drive off.

While driving west on M-51, she noticed the sun looked like a glowing red ball in the sky. Soon it would enter a decrescent phase and appear to be drawn toward the earth. As a child, she remembered thinking that the sun would set fire to the highest branches of the trees. Then she watched as it quietly slipped past, only to create a tapestry of dawn oceans away. While enjoying the early stages of the blazing sunset she remembered an old adage, which she was fairly certain was adapted from the book of Matthew; Red sky at morning, sailor take warning. Red sky at night, sailor's delight.

The sweltering day was beginning to take its bow. A slightly cooler breeze came through the open car window. She felt the beads of sweat that had been running down her face start to dry. Checking the address and directions again on the small clipping of paper, she realized she was almost at Chris' house. There it was, behind the fire station just like he said.

Pulling into the driveway she was greeted by Chris' daughters who escorted her into the front room. Chris' wife, Debbie, was in the kitchen putting the finishing touches on dinner. She showed Anne into the finished basement and to Beth's bedroom. "Hopefully you'll be able to grab a nap," she offered smiling. "When Chris first started working the road, he sometimes slept all night. That rarely happens now—of course you can't make any money if you're sleeping."

Chris walked in the back door near the kitchen. Beth scurried up the stairs. "She's here daddy. She's going to sleep in my room."

"I know Beth. You're pretty nice to give up your bed."

"Mom said I had to—but I don't mind. I hope Erin doesn't push me out of her bed."

"Erin's only two—you're five. How can she push you out of bed?"

"She does daddy, you just don't know."

"Well I'll talk to her, how's that?" he gently chuckled. Satisfied with the offer, Beth walked over and began setting the table.

Anne was asked to eat dinner with the family. As they ate, Chris reviewed the operation of the Commission Car.

"I have a hand held, two-way radio. We'll receive our calls from the dispatcher with that, when we aren't in the ambulance. The dispatcher will only give us emergency calls. We don't do transfers to nursing homes or body removals. We are paid per patient. The amount is different. We get twelve dollars if we don't collect the money for the bill at the hospital, fifteen if we do. The idea is to get as many patients into the ambulance as we can. The scene of a car accident is like a tree waiting to be picked. If you can talk even a bystander into going to the hospital, by all means do it. That's what they get for gawking. To some people, it really is a traumatic thing to see. For them, talking to medical staff at the hospital is good shock therapy, so to speak. Fire scenes are also good for multiple patients. Everybody thinks they smelled something toxic. They all need to get checked for smoke inhalation, or carbon monoxide poisoning. Who's to say they haven't been exposed to it? If you don't offer them treatment or transportation—you're doing them a disservice. Of course, they don't have to go by ambulance if they don't want to. But we do have oxygen and can start treating them before they get to the hospital. We are here to provide a service. We charge for oxygen, bandaging, back boarding and splinting. If you try to give them a break on the bill by not charging for the equipment or services that we do, you will be taking money out of your pocket and mine. I am twenty-six years old. I have a wife and three kids. I'm working two jobs, if you get my drift. I have confidence that you can handle this. I'm not asking you to do anything underhanded, so get that idea out of your head. This is all on the up and up. You know most of this already. If you have any questions don't hesitate to ask," he explicated.

Dinner was nearly finished. Anne was awed at the quietness and order of the children while they ate. Most children within their active ages weren't that well behaved. They spoke quietly and only to their mother during dinner, as to not interrupt Chris as he spoke. He got up and picked up the phone to call the dispatcher. "I'll let Tom know that we're in service," he said.

Tom was a young supervisor, with an aggressive aptitude. The first time Anne met him he was dispatching. She remembered his foreshadowing ability as he would announce the type of calls the crews would encounter that day. Sure enough, a plane crash and a boating accident occurred just as he predicted. She recalled his astonished expression as he and the crews talked about his premonition. She understood that it was more than likely, just a fluke that the incidences transpired as Tom foretold. Still she knew, "There is death and life in the power of the tongue."

Chris was on and off the phone in what seemed like seconds. "We got a motorcycle PI at Maple and Middle Lake. You ready?" he asked, looking at Anne while picking up his tote bag and radio. She was familiar with the term, and knew that PI was an abbreviation for a personal injury accident. Most of the words they used in the medical field, were shortened to initials or symbols. Grabbing her purse, she thanked Debbie for dinner and followed Chris out the front door to the ambulance.

After buckling her seat belt, she picked up the pad of paper on the doghouse console, then wrote down the information that Tom gave them over the unit radio. Chris looked in the side mirror to make sure the emergency lights were on as he pulled out of his driveway and drove toward the main road. Even though his house was just a few houses from the main road, she wondered how his neighbors felt about him running the ambulance out of his home. "They don't mind. I'm good friends with my neighbors," was his answer, when she asked.

They had to drive several miles to the scene. Once on the main road Chris increased his speed. This was Anne's first time in the front seat of the unit, while on a code three. Having a front row seat gave everything a new perspective. The vehicles they passed seemed so close, and their speed gave the feeling of traveling in hyper-space. It was very different than riding in the back of the ambulance, like she had done during her clinicals. Surprisingly, even with the siren screaming as they approached, some of the other drivers weren't even aware they were coming. Chris used the three different tones on the siren but some cars still didn't pull over. He would have to get practically on top of them before they paid any attention. It made Anne nervous. It was hard to tell if they were going to pull over, or just stop dead in front of them. Chris didn't wait long before he pulled into the oncoming lane and drove around them. Increasing his speed again, it seemed he was trying to make up for the time he lost while waiting for the car to pull over. He stopped at every intersection where the red light faced him. After he was sure the other traffic had stopped and had seen the ambulance, he continued through. Each time he had to stop or slow down, it seemed that he would go faster again to gain time. They had two more miles to go. Anne felt her fingers tighten on the edge of the seat. Chris looked over at her and laughed.

"Your knuckles are white. If you don't let go of that seat you aren't going to be able to feel your fingers." Embarrassed at his comment, she slowly let go of the seat.

"Guess I'm a little nervous," she replied, rubbing her fingers.

"I guess—you'll get used to it. We're just about there," he said smiling. Coming over the last hill before Maple Road, they saw the emergency lights from the police and the on-call fire department vehicles that lit up the intersection ahead.

Chris picked up the radio mic and announced their arrival. Grateful they had stopped, Anne opened her door and stepped out onto the pavement. Her legs felt like rubber, causing her to stumble slightly. After managing a few steps to the side of the ambulance, she opened the side doors and pulled out the orange box that contained most of their first aid equipment. Struggling to walk, she quickly stomped then shuffled her feet. The strength in her legs and hands felt almost normal as she neared the patient, who was laying on the grassy corner near the intersection. Setting the box down, she tried to overhear the firemen's report to Chris of the patient's injuries.

She heard him say that he was a twenty year old male with pain in his neck and lower back. He did not lose consciousness. He was reported to have been wearing a helmet that she noticed was cracked as it hung from the handlebar of the motorcycle. Because of the heat of the day, he had been wearing only shorts and a tee shirt. There wasn't any sign of injury to his face or chest; however, he had multiple abrasions to his arms, legs and back from sliding across the pavement. The most obvious injury was to his lower left leg. Just below the knee and again near the ankle, it was deformed and twisted. It didn't take an X-ray to determine that his leg was fractured. Fortunately it was a closed fracture, so the risk of infection was minimized.

"My name's Anne," she said, introducing herself. "My partner's name is Chris. We are going to be doing a few things here to check you out before we get you packaged up and take you to the hospital. What's your name?"

"Steve," he winced, displaying the pain he felt.

"Well, Steve, your left leg appears to be broken—hopefully the pain will ease once we splint it," she offered as a reassurance. "While we're getting the equipment ready to do that, I'm going to check you out from head to toe. I want you to tell me if you have any pain when I touch each area."

"Okay," he agreed.

"Do you take any medicine on a regular basis, have any medical problems, or have any allergies to medication?"

"No," he answered, to all three questions.

Kneeling next to him, Anne began her head to toe survey by palpating his head, then rapidly moved on to his neck, then back, chest, abdomen and hip area while Chris and the firemen collected the back boarding and splinting equipment. While making mental notes of Steve's answers, she gently squeezed and pushed on his lower extremities. He denied any pain in his right leg and could move it easily. Then she had him squeeze her hands to determine if he had equal grip strength. He denied having any numbness or tingling in his hands or feet. Even with the grossly deformed fracture of his left leg, he still had sensation to his foot, but was unable to wiggle his toes. Before applying the splint, she felt the area on the top of his foot for a pedal pulse. After finding the site, she marked the spot with her ink pen. Once the splint was in place, she rechecked the pulse at the marked area. A foam cervical collar was placed around his neck. He was gently rolled as a unit onto the back board with the help of the firemen. Backboard straps were fed through the holes in the board and clamped to secure him in place. His head was taped down over a set of rolled towels to prevent his neck and head from moving. While the packaging of Steve took place, Chris wrapped the blood pressure cuff around his arm.

"One hundred and ten, over sixty," he announced. "His pulse is ninety and regular. His respiration rate is eighteen—lung sounds are clear," he concluded, handing the stethoscope back to Anne. Next, they lifted Steve onto the stretcher and rolled it toward, then into the ambulance. He agreed to go to Lancemen Osteopathic Hospital, which was the closest hospital to the scene. Even though his vital signs were stable at the time, the severity of his left leg fracture was a concern. With a possible twenty or thirty minute non-emergency travel time, Chris thought it best to use the lights and siren during the transport to the hospital.

The ride was rough and a bit of a challenge to Anne, as she attempted to recheck Steve's vitals en route. Finally, after the third try, she was able to hear his blood pressure. Chris backed the unit into the ambulance parking area. After wheeling Steve into an room that was reserved for him, Anne gave her report of Steve's condition to the nurse. The nurse's name was Pat.

"When did you start working out in the field?" she asked.

"Well, this was my first call, actually," Anne answered in a low voice hoping that Steve didn't hear her. She wanted him to feel as if an experienced EMT had been helping him instead of a rookie.

"Well good for you. You did a good job," Pat replied cheerfully.

Chris came into the room with the bill for the ambulance in his hand.

"We got another call. The stretcher's made up and in the rig," he said urging Anne out. Then he turned to their patient. "Steve, you don't happen to have ninety-five dollars on you, do you? That's what your bill comes to."

Steve seemed surprised that he was asking for the money now.

"No. I'm sorry—I don't usually carry that much money on me." He paused for a moment, gritting his teeth while Pat inserted the needle to start the IV. "Can't you send me a bill?" he asked.

"Sure—take it easy," Chris answered. Slipping the bill back into the clipboard, he turned and rushed out for the next call. It was clear that Steve was in pain; and he knew that if the man didn't have the money, there was no sense in pressing the issue.

Anne was in the ambulance waiting for Chris.

"I would have gotten the information but I didn't think you wanted me to use the radio," she said, as if asking permission.

"Better not—we're doing good so far. I don't want to mess this up," he said, picking up the radio mic. "Unit six on the air."

Anne had her pen in hand, ready to write down the information for their next call. The dispatcher relayed that they were to respond code three for an assault. The address of the incident was a few miles away in a party store parking lot in downtown Lancemen. The injuries of the victim were unknown.

Chris turned the siren off as they approached the scene. Then, easing his foot from the gas pedal, he noticed there were two Lancemen police cruisers and a fire engine sitting in the middle of the party store parking lot. Turning onto the black top, he looked for a place to park, then pulled into an open space between the two police cars and stopped. A man who apparently was in custody, was sitting in the back of the police car parked next to them. Nodding in the direction of the presumed prisoner, Chris wryly stated. "That guy looks like he's having a good day." Drawn by his remark, Anne stared briefly. By the way the man's head was cocked and pushed against the window, it was difficult to tell if he was asleep, passed out, or dead. She got out of the rig and opened the side door to pull out the orange box. Looking toward the fire truck she noticed an older black male sitting on the bumper, and assumed that he was the patient. The right side of his face was covered with blood. One of the firemen introduced the patient, Grayson Williams, to Chris before giving him a report on the situation and Mr. Williams' injuries. Anne walked over to the back of the fire truck carrying the orange box, then set it on the ground.

"This is Anne," Chris said to Mr. Williams. "She's my partner and needs to take a look at your head so we can see how bad you're hurt."

Mr. Williams looked up at Anne and smiled with a dirt smudged, bloody face. His rumpled and stained clothing hung on his thin frame, almost begging to be pulled off and washed before finding refuge in the nearest rag bag. She quickly surmised from his present state that he was not a rich man nor was he well cared for; but even with all of that, the saddest aberrant that immediately drew her attention was his teeth. Underneath his swollen and bruised lips were four protruding incisors that were spaced apart, two on the bottom and two on the top; all of which were different colors. As she stood next to him feeling bad, she tried to keep focused on finding his injuries rather than taking in an account of his appearance. Then suddenly as he spoke, the sour odor of chokeberries and alcohol rose up and nearly took her breathe away. Turning her head as inconspicuously as she could, she took in a deep breath of fresh air while grabbing several gauze sponges from the orange box on the ground beside her. Trying to return the smile he so willing offered, she gently dabbed the sponges over the top of his head.

"Tank you young lady. My head's just abut kil'in me." Reaching into his pocket, he pulled out a bottle that was smeared with blood, then swished the liquid around inside as he proudly held it up to show her the apparent reward of his efforts. "It took me two days of hunt'n empties—to get enough money—for this here bottle of Mad Dog. Then, for some reason—and I don't know why—that man hit me in the head with a brick or sompton. I don't know even him. And I ain't got no money." After a brief glance, he brought it to his lips. Just as Anne started to remove the gauze from his head to examine the damage by the assailant, the bottle caught her eye.

"I don't think you need any more of that, Mr. Williams," she said, taking the glass container and handing it to Chris. She continued examining the cut, to make sure it was clean. The bleeding was minimal now, even though the two inch laceration was deep. It ran from the right side of the hair line toward the left and stopped at the top of his head. He smiled and sat very patiently while she poked and prodded.

"Well, Mr. Williams, I don't know why he hit you either. You seem like a nice man. But you have a bad cut on your head and you need to go to the hospital to get it sewn up."

"Anything you say, young lady, jus so you know, I ain't got no money to pay no amblance bill today." Anne was amused by his dialect.

"Well maybe they can set you up with a payment plan or something. I'm not sure how they do that. Maybe we need to consult my financial advisor," she said while motioning toward Chris. The firemen chuckled at her remark. They knew the importance to Chris of collecting the money whenever possible. Anne understood it too; it was part of his lively-hood and she really wasn't trying to make light of it.

"You know, Mr. Williams, my boss is going to make us wash and wax every ambulance to earn our keep if you don't pay your bill," Chris quipped.

"Oh, I'll pay all right—just not today. I don wont—this young lady—to have to wash and wax—no amblance." As he spoke, his level of consciousness seemed to gradually decrease, resulting in a more noticeable pattern of slurred speech as well as a pronounced delay in his verbal and coordinational response. It was hard to tell if it was from the alcohol or from the head injury. After helping him on to the stretcher, they rolled it toward the back doors of the rig, then hoisted it up into the patient compartment. Because they were a short distance from the hospital, it only took a few minutes for them to arrive. Before Anne knew it, Chris was already backing into the ambulance bay at Lancemen Osteopathic. The vitals she had taken while they were driving to the hospital were written on a piece of paper and tucked in her shirt pocket. She gave it to the nurse, while reciting her report. By the time she finished, Mr. Williams was asleep, waking only to the sound of his name. Chris had the stretcher put back together and was standing by the nurses station when Anne walked out of the room. He and Dr. Brett were discussing their previous patient Steve's injuries, when they were called out for their next run.

The nature given by their dispatcher for this response was for a man down—a regular. Anne remembered the crews referred to this type of patient as a frequent flier, because he used the ambulance service so often.

Lancemen had a handful of people who abused the system. Usually they were intoxicated when they called. Some were just lonely, or hadn't eaten a good meal in a number of days. The hospitals were good about feeding them. What else could they do? This man had passed out after drinking too much and collapsed on the sidewalk. He was breathing and his vitals were within normal ranges. His clothes were heavily soiled with grime and urine, and they smelled as if he hadn't changed them in months. Chris handed Anne a pair of sterile gloves to put on while she tended to him. Because the gloves were expensive, they used them only for extreme situations. Adjusting the fingers of the glove, she heard someone in the crowd that had gathered refer to the patient as a ne'er do-well. There was little compassion for the many indigent living on the streets of Lancemen. After transporting him to Lancemen General, they left to go to a private residence. This call was outside of Lancemen in Birch Hills. It was for a woman complaining of chest pain. After taking the woman's vitals, they put her on four liters of oxygen via a nasal cannula, then set her on the stretcher and took her to St. Luke's Hospital in the south end of Lancemen.

They found the emergency room at St. Luke's to be just as busy as the rest of the hospitals in Lancemen. While walking toward the ambulance, they could easily tell that their pace had slowed down since the beginning of their shift. Chris remarked at how busy the night had been for everyone. They had been listening to the other crews throughout the night, as they heard call after call come over the unit and handheld radios. It seemed that most of the calls were in some way alcohol related. Anne remembered seeing the word spirits on a sign in a window of a bar they passed by frequently and began sharing her thoughts with Chris.

"Did you notice the sign at The Water Hole with the word spirits on it? I can't help wondering what kind of spirit people think they are getting when they're served there. From what I've seen tonight, I'd say it's a spirit of destruction." She thought of how it ate away at every organ in the body, consuming the life of the person who consumed it. Then the image of a call they went on just a few short hours before reentered her mind and turned her stomach. She recalled the painful and frightened screams of two young children in the doorway, as their drunken father dragged his wife down the front steps of their home. She remembered trying to comfort the sobbing woman and her children, as the police forced the man into the patrol car. How many relationships she wondered had lost their value because of the spirit. It was clear to her that alcohol hampered so many people, just in that night alone; yet so many were drawn to it, seemingly as if it were life sustaining. "Why can't they see what's happening?" she asked. Her tone of voice was of concern, rather than a judgmental nature. It was obvious to Chris that Anne had led a sheltered life. Even so, she must have seen people with drinking problems before. He was sure even Summerville had bars.

"Welcome to the other side of the world," he spouted, in response to Anne's revelation. "You'll see how lucky, or as you say, blessed you are. Some of these people have spent most of their lives on the street. They don't know any other way. All they want, is that feeling of being comfortably numb. It's a handed down disease to some of them. The rest drink as a crutch, or to hide from who they really are." Just as he finished speaking, the dispatcher's voice came over the radio.

"Unit four, I need you for a code three at 120 North Ellen." Chris picked up the mic.

"We're on the way. What's the nature?"

"I don't know, I couldn't understand what she was saying."

Anne wrote down the time and incident number, then buckled her seat belt. Because Chris knew the city of Lancemen so well, she rarely had to look up the streets on the map. Within minutes they had pulled up to an apartment complex. Chris explained that the complex housed residents on a semi-independent living program. Most of them were elderly. Some were handicapped.

Anne slid the orange box across the floor at the side doors, picked it up, then placed it on the stretcher. Then she and Chris walked quickly with the stretcher beside them, rolling it into the building and toward the elevator. While waiting, she rechecked the address on the slip of paper. "Apartment number 215," she offered. Standing in front of the door, Chris knocked on it, then checked to see if it was locked. A feeble woman's voice answered, but her words were garbled. Chris rapped on the door again. Slowly the voice came closer, then stopped. They listened for a few seconds. Then the lock released with a click, and the door jarred open. A dim light from within softly glimmered through the small crack. They expected to hear the woman's voice but instead there was silence. Chris moved the door back enough to peer in.

"She's laying on the floor behind the door," he groaned. Pushing against it, he was able to widen the gap enough for Anne to fit through. Once she was inside, she moved the woman far enough from the door, so that he could enter. They helped her to her feet after she told them she wasn't hurt. Her gait was very unstable. An empty bottle of vodka explained the strong odor of alcohol. Chris asked her name and the reason for calling the ambulance.

"My naaame is Marrtha Spenncer and I want—yoou to go—and get my husssband from tha Elk's Club. Hee must b hurt, or he'd been here, by now," she said, running her words together.

"Martha, have you been drinking?" Chris asked, although he already knew the answer.

"Jus oone glass," came her slurred response.

"What—a sixteen ounce tumbler?" Chris wasn't normally harsh, but it was evident that he was losing his patience. It had been a long night. The two EMTs had smelled so much alcohol during its duration, that Chris joked earlier about getting a contact buzz. Now they had to somehow—help Martha. Anne hoped they could find her husband, so he could come and tend to his wife, who was just as full of worry as she was vodka.

"Do you have the phone number for the Elk's Club?" she asked. Martha pointed to a scrap piece of paper near the phone with a few numbers scrawled on it. The apartment was in total disarray. Dirty dishes were throughout the two rooms they could see. Papers and clothes were scattered across the floor and furniture. The tiled and carpeted floor was stained and well worn. A malodor introduced a stale sourness to Anne's senses, as she picked up the sticky phone to call the Elk's Club.

"Elk's Club," came a loud but polite man's voice.

"Hello. My name is Anne. I'm an EMT for Mercy Ambulance. I'm looking for William Spencer. Is he there?" The man who answered the phone talked in such a loud voice, Anne had to pull the receiver away from her ear each time he spoke. It wasn't that the noise in the background was so loud that he needed to speak over it—it was more like he was just hard of hearing.

"Is Martha all right?"

"She's just not feeling well and is concerned that her husband might be hurt and wanted us to find him. Is he there by chance?"

"Yes he's here. He's just about to leave to go home. Tell Martha he should be there in about twenty minutes. She's been calling here all night. I can't believe she called you people," the man offered in a disgusted tone.

"Is he there?" Chris asked. Anne nodded her head yes. "Tell him we can't stay here; she's not hurt or sick." Anne relayed the information to the man on the phone, then hung up.

"He said he would be here in twenty minutes."

"Oh goood," Martha said as she slid down in the chair. "Yoou don have t stay. Thhhannks a millllion ffffor calllin." Her speech was almost unintelligible. Anne found her way into the bathroom and picked up a slightly soiled, dry washcloth. After running the water in the sink until it was warm, she moistened it. Then she took the cloth to Martha. While pulling the saliva covered hair out of the corner of Martha's mouth she began gently wiping her face.

"Here, Martha, let's clean your face up before your husband gets home." Martha's face was streaked with tears and mascara. Her bright red lipstick smeared over the heavily applied rouge, filling in the deep lines and wrinkles in her face.

"Oh thhhank yooou," Martha slurred, feeling the warm refreshing cloth on her face. "You're welcome," Anne replied, smiling. "I've been in a few situations myself, where a warm, wet washcloth felt…"

"Like da beee's kneee's?" Martha asked, before Anne could finish her sentence.

"Yep—like the bee's knee's," she agreed.

Knowing Martha would be asleep before her husband got home, Chris and Anne propped her up in the chair so she wouldn't fall or aspirate her own vomit should she become ill before her husband got there. While walking with their equipment toward the elevator, Chris noticed the concerned expression on Anne's face.

"She'll be all right. He'll be here before we get half way down the street."

Anne looked at him, pushing the elevator button, then softly responded, "I was just remembering a scripture from Proverbs. It goes— 'A man's spirit will endure sickness; but a broken spirit who can bear?' That woman is a broken woman. It's as if she is trying to heal her broken spirit with another. She's got the right idea, just the wrong spirit."

It was almost 5:00 a.m., when things finally quieted down. Chris thought it might be safe to head back to his house. Hopefully, they could get a couple hours of sleep. It seemed impossible to Anne that Chris could function so well, knowing his schedule.

"How are you able to work two jobs with so little sleep?"

He answered, yawning, "A man has to do what a man has to do. I've got a system. I get more sleep than you think. Although I admit sometimes it doesn't feel like it." Rolling the window up he continued, "Debbie said she was going to leave the night light on for you, so you could see your way downstairs. I'm ready to call it a night. See you in the morning."

Anne looked around. "I think it's already morning," she replied, teasingly.

"Well, you know what I mean." As they walked toward the house, Chris whispered to Anne, "You did okay for a rookie." Smiling, she walked into the house and went downstairs.

It had been a busy night. Even though she was tired, a feeling of excitement lingered as she thought about each call they went on. Looking back, she was surprised at how comfortable she felt with her patients. She was glad that Chris was pleased with her performance. I'm not going to get too sure of myself, she thought. I still have a lot to learn, but I hope not tonight. I'm exhausted.

The next couple of weeks flew by for Anne. The more she worked as an EMT on the road, the more she liked it. Some of the patients weren't the nicest, or the cleanest. Some of the lifting was difficult. Most of the time, it was something she truly enjoyed. Chris was encouraging and even some of the staunchest, old fashioned firemen seemed to be softening up to the idea of her being out there. At first they would stand by and watch as she struggled lifting a heavy patient. Then, even Harold, who strongly opposed her working on the road, had a change of heart. "You're all right, kid," he boasted. "If you need any help, you just ask your buddy, Harold."

Everything had gone better than she thought. It made her wonder about which direction to take. Was nursing still the right course? Or could, and should it wait? The Paramedic Program would be starting in the fall. If she took the paramedic classes now, she reasoned, she could still work the road. It will be hard to do, but that's how the other students did it. Working as a paramedic would be a great experience for a future nurse, and it would look good on a resume. She wasted no time in sharing her thoughts with Chris and Dan, who thought the idea was great. Now, she hoped to convince Merve. That wasn't going to be easy.

Merve finally found out that she had been working the road behind his back, and as expected, was not happy. He was more upset with Chris and was somehow convinced that Dan was in on it—so it was Chris and Dan that he called into his office on Saturday morning. Anne was also called in but was told to wait outside his office. She could hear him yelling at Chris. Then she heard something hit the wall. She stood up and looked at Tom who was sitting with Rick in the dispatch center. They both raised their eyebrows at each other, smiling. They seemed as calm as could be. Anne sat back down, rocking slightly in her seat. She felt terrible. "I should be in there taking the heat, not Dan and Chris," she said, quietly. Again something hit the wall. She squeezed her hands together.

"Ooo, that was a good one," Rick said to Tom. They both looked at each other again with raised eyebrows.

"It's not funny, you guys," she fretfully stated.

"Relax Anne," Rick snickered. "That's just the tape dispenser. Merve's just releasing his frustrations. He's not really mad til he throws the type-writer."

"Well I sure hope that doesn't happen." Nervousness and a feeling of guilt was clearly written on her face. It sounded to her as if something would come through the wall at any time.

"It's okay," Tom added. "We've got three quarter inch plywood under the paneling."

The door opened. Chris and Dan walked out. Merve closed the door behind them. Anne nervously stood up again, wiping her sweaty hands across her khaki slacks.

"Sorry, you guys. I really feel bad that he got so angry."

"Oh, that was just the tape dispenser hitting the wall. He isn't really mad until he throws the typewriter," Chris said, smiling. "We've sort of learned to judge his level of frustration by what he throws." As they walked toward the sitting room, he continued. "Well I'm sorry, Anne; I tried to keep you as my partner but it didn't work out." After listening to the yelling and banging, Anne wasn't at all surprised with the news.

"It's okay. At least I had the opportunity to get my feet wet. I'm grateful for everything, really." She felt relieved that they weren't upset and that Merve hadn't screamed at her; but most of all—that he didn't throw the typewriter.

"No problem," Chris said as he began walking down the hall. Then he stopped and reached into his pocket. "Oh, I almost forgot. This is for you." He gave Anne the paper that he pulled from his pocket.

"What is it?" she asked as she opened it.

"It's a purchase order for uniforms. You aren't going to be my partner; you're going to be Dan's," he said, grinning.

"Does Merve know about this?" she asked in disbelief.

"Of course he does," Dan offered. "It's his signature on the bottom. You don't think we would do anything sneaky do you?" he chuckled. "Of course there are some drawbacks," he continued. "You'll have to work forty eight on, forty eight off; which means you'll have to work some Sundays—unless you switch days with someone. I'm picky about who I work with, so don't put me with some bonehead. You'll have to clear it with me first, before you make the switch. Plus, you'll have to work at the Lakeview station opposite of Roger. So you aren't going to see him much, except in the mornings. He's going to be your relief. But, the good news is—you get to work with me!" Anne stood staring at the purchase order, while Dan listed the terms.

She was still a bit stunned. Her face had the expression of a child that just opened a gift that she thought Santa would never bring.

"Is this real, or are you joking?" she asked.

"It's real," Chris assured her. "I wouldn't let him kid around with something like this. Well, I don't know about you guys," he said, while rubbing his slightly rounded belly, "but I'm hungry. Let's go get something to eat." Anne put the paper in her purse and walked toward the glass door.

"Lunch is on me, you guys. That's the least I can do," she said grinning.

"We'll take that," Dan replied. "You're off to a good start, partner. We're going to have a great time. It will be you—me—and life in the fast lane."

CHAPTER 9

BACK HOME

While packing a few clothes for a weekend sojourn to Summerville, Anne gave a brief description of her new full-time position to Mrs. Johnstone. She was pleased to finally have the opportunity to share her news; for many times they were like ships passing, with neither one docking for long. Ever since Mr. Johnstone's retirement a year ago, they had become active travelers, taking advantage of Anne's presence to watch over the house. But her schedule was so busy between college and work, that most of their communications ending up as notes left on the kitchen table, or as a rare phone call in which they made connection by happenstance.

Now, in what seemed like stolen moments, Mrs. Johnstone proudly admired Anne's uniform as she held it up in front of her. Anne, however, was losing her stir of excitement. Suddenly, while listening to her own words detailing the job, she realized she had overlooked a few conditions of the operation that might be of concern to her Aunt and Uncle. A tinge of uncertainty crept in, leading her to search Mrs. Johnstone's face for a clue as to how they might respond. "You have a beautiful day for your drive, Anne," was all Mrs. Johnstone cheerfully offered, while hugging her. Earnestly and secretly Anne studied her manner and movements; but no hint of disapproval appeared on the face that radiated with pride as she stood in front of her, nor did her smile wane as she stood on the front stoop waving to Anne, as she backed down the driveway.

Pulling onto the main road, Anne smiled at her own foolishness; "I'm just over reacting," she reassured herself. "I'm sure they'll understand, once I explain it to them." A few seconds of refereeing the situation passed, then a calm claimed the victory, as she gratefully slid her new Amy Grant cassette into the player. Turning up the volume, she listened while adjusting the bass, then began singing along. It seemed odd to her that this felt more like a business trip rather than just going home. Maybe her room in Lancemen had become a surrogate home; filling-in for the farm in Summerville. After pondering the situation, she decided the sentiment would return, once her feet touched the soil that had belonged to the Gate's for so many years.

She was less than five miles from Summerville, when she passed a speed limit sign that read fifty miles per hour. "That's a turtle's pace," she whispered to herself, "in comparison to the sprinting speed of my mind lately." With so many changes transpiring since last fall, she had to admit there were times when it was a bit overwhelming. It wasn't that she was a stranger to change, it was just that her prudent nature normally resisted it. So when she found herself yielding to the fortuitous whirlwind that breezed in, altering her course and ushering her into a job that Mr. Dewit avowed she would never be welcome, she firmly believed that it must be an act of God's will. What else would explain her working with a group of men so opposite her, without even a second thought. Certainly, her life had developed into a sequence of circumstances, with each unplanned adventure becoming a piece of the puzzle, finding its own connection.

Mentally summarizing the series of events throughout her life, she likened their passage to a moonlit garden labyrinth. She envisioned the towering garden with high hedges, as it created a maze of paths. The woods on her Uncle's farm gave thought of the earthy aroma that flowed from the garden's foliage walls. She could almost feel the strength of the vines, as they embraced the leaf covered branches, creating an understanding for the periodic pruning that was needed to maintain their fruitfulness and healthy growth. Then she realized that the only source of illumination granting direction came from the heavenly light above, as it revealed only a portion of the path with each step. To walk beyond that she knew, proved a walk of faith.

Her reverie vanished, when the hand carved wooden sign ahead grabbed her attention. "Welcome to Summerville," she read aloud. Driving past it and into town, she turned on to Elm street where she recognized Wilson's drug store and a few other long ago established businesses. It was pleasing and comforting to see that the small town with a population of about two thousand residents showed little change. "Some things shouldn't," she happily whispered. Minutes later she turned onto the dirt road that led to the farm. Each time she traveled this road while growing up, she always thought it looked like a painting; no matter what the season. For the trees that lined both sides of the road were a natural canvas, providing the medium for God's artistic hand. In the spring when the new buds glistened in the morning sun, they appeared like tiny beads. Then, when the buds unfolded in the summer, the stretched out leaves created a canopy effect. Fall, with its cooler temperatures, transformed the leaves into a burst of color bringing about a breathtaking spectacle. And finally, when winter brought its chilling winds she felt a warmth inside, as the silhouetted branches appeared to be holding hands in front of a blushing sky.

Pulling onto the gravel driveway she stopped at the barn shaped mailbox her cousin Jacob built in wood shop, and gathered the mail. Continuing up the driveway, she parked next to his red pickup, and noticed Uncle Henry and her brother James walking from the barn toward the house. They waved as she got out of her car. "Well, the farm sure smells the same," she said quietly to her self, as the fresh horse and cow manure stimulated the olfactory mucosa of her nasal cavity. Without realizing, she must have crinkled her nose. Both Uncle Henry and James laughed. "Been a while since ya had your sinuses cleaned out?" Uncle Henry called from across the yard. As they came closer, the fragrance of the barn came with them. It was in the fibers of their clothes, smeared on their skin and peppered throughout their hair. But that didn't stop James from giving Anne a hug hello, being very careful to wipe a small amount of dirt on her arm, with the joy of a pestering brother.

"Thank you, James," Anne chuckled.

"I'll wait until after I'm a little fresher," Uncle Henry said, laughing at James' show of affection.

All three walked onto the back porch and into the kitchen. Anne stopped in the doorway and deeply inhaled, as Aunt Ruth's simmering blueberry jam filtered through the screen door and filled her now cleaned sinuses.

"What an aromatic blessing," she sighed.

"Anne!" Aunt Ruth cheered. "I thought I heard voices out there but we didn't expect you until dinner time. I was hoping to have this jam done before you got here, so we'd have time to sit and catch up on things," she went on excitedly, wiping her hands on her apron.

"Aunt Ruth," Anne scolded with a smile. In one motion, she turned and set her things on the floor and the mail on the counter. "I'm a family member, not a guest." Hugging her Aunt, she continued, "I'll go and put my clothes away and then come down and help you. Working in the kitchen has never stopped us from talking." As soon as the words were out of her mouth, she realized she had let herself wide open for her brother James to jump in; which he did predictably, without hesitation.

"That's for sure; you two talk more than anybody I know, except for Mrs. Chatterbox, I mean Chatterton," he said, amused at his own humor. Uncle Henry chuckled while finishing his lemonade. Satisfied that Anne was home and seemingly well, he and James returned to the barn. Anne went upstairs to put her things in her room. In spite of the distant aroma of the barn, she could smell the fresh linen on her bed when she walked in. The room had been dusted and newly cut wildflowers stood in a vase on her desk. Everything else was just as she left it. She thought about the talks she and her Aunt shared while working in the kitchen. It made the kitchen seem like their special place.

After setting her overnight bag next to the white wicker chair, she hung her dress in the closet, then started back down stairs to pick up where they left off. Aunt Ruth must know every noise in this house, she thought, after hearing her named called as soon as her foot touched the bottom step.

"Anne, we might not have enough lids for these smaller jars. Would you mind running up to Dandy's to pick up two or three boxes?" Walking into the kitchen toward the sink, Anne stood next to her Aunt and watched as she washed the jars. Realizing she was close, Aunt Ruth lowered her voice to its normal volume. "Not that we'll need that many, I just don't want to run out."

"Sure," Anne cheerfully replied. "My room looks great." Reaching to open the screen door she turned and watched her Aunt, admiring her as she stood at the sink while the steam from the water rose above her. "I'll be right back."

The feel of home had returned. She felt joy at being there and was happy at the chance to go into town to take in some familiar sights. While feeling for her car keys in her purse, she stood on the porch and glanced over the farm. "Uncle Henry and the boys sure have worked hard at keeping this place going," she quietly sighed. A sense of pride welled up within her as she slipped into her car and headed to town toward Dandy's.

Dandy's was the biggest store in the area and carried almost everything the larger stores carried. Anne had worked there while she was in high school, as did many of the high school students. Pulling into the parking lot, she was surprised to see that the building had been slightly updated. The fresh coat of gray paint over the brick storefront, gave it a modernized appearance. Business must be good, she thought, making her second trip through the parking lot before finding an empty space. After putting her keys in her purse, she shut the door without pushing the lock down. It seemed strange to leave her car unlocked. That was something the city folk would never do. While walking through the parking lot, she recognized neighbors and friends who had lived in town for years. Brief memories of her youth came with each remembered face. As she approached the automatic doors, they opened and gave way to a shiny new tiled floor. Looking around she noticed the shelves and aisle locators were the same, except they were repainted with the same gray paint as the front of the store.

Then she spotted Mrs. Chatterton in the office near the last register. Anne knew that if she saw her she would want to talk. James was right about Mrs. Chatterton. She was a talker. She had managed Dandy's for twelve years and was a wonderful lady, but she was a talker. Once she started, she was hard to get away from. Quickly, Anne began engineering a plan, hoping just to get home with the lids. Maybe I can slip down the first aisle without being seen, she schemed. Rats! It was too late, she groaned to herself, after hearing a familiar voice, loudly calling her name. "Anne." It was Becky Ritter, a girl she had gone to high school with, pushing a basket of groceries toward the checkout line. "Finally came home, aye?" she asked, with a bit of a smirk. Becky was one of those people who thought TV Soap operas were real stories about her own life, and everyone she knew. Only the names and faces were changed. Feeling an urgency to complete her mission, Anne tried to cut her conversation short, without being rude.

"Just for the weekend. I'm still going to college and still work in Lancemen. I can't talk right now, Becky. Aunt Ruth is doing up a batch of jam and needs more lids. It's nice to see you though," she hurriedly said. Turning to go down the nearest aisle she looked to see if Becky had followed.

"Bye, Anne," Becky called, while watching her escape.

"That was close. Now—lids, lids, where are the lids?" Anne murmured, while scanning the shelves.

"Two aisles over, near the top, on the left hand side." The voice she heard was a welcome and well known delight. It was her best friend, since the sixth grade, Jenny Stolewicker.

"Jenny!" Anne cried happily.

"I heard Becky call your name. She's so loud. I'm sure everyone in the whole store, knows you're home now." Anne noticed a somberness, unlike Jenny, as she spoke. She knew this was not the place for a personal conversation and decided to let it go for now. Instead, she jokingly repeated an old saying that had belonged to Becky since Jr. High School.

"Telephone, telegraph or tell Becky. Some things never change," she smiled. "Hey listen, I really need to get these lids home, and I still have to get past Mrs. Chatterton. Why don't you come over tonight? Dinner's at six thirty. We've got so much to get caught up on," she coaxed.

"More than you think," Jenny said. Lifting her work apron, she revealed her rounded, enlarged belly. By the sad expression in her eyes, it was obviously not a planned pregnancy. "I could use a friend right now. Thanks, Anne."

"You look great, Jenny," Anne said, forcing a smile while hugging her troubled friend. Trying not to reflect her stumbling feeling of surprise, she reached up and took a couple boxes of lids off the shelf. With a silly expression she added, "Almost forgot the lids. See you in a little while."

Anne hurried home. She couldn't believe it! Aunt Ruth never mentioned Jenny was pregnant. Jenny's last letter came while she was away at college in Marquette. "I thought she quit writing because she was busy with school. Poor Jenny," she thought. It grieved Anne's heart to see her friend so distraught. She pulled into the driveway, then walked into the back door.

"I'm home," she announced. "I tried to hurry." Methodically she hung her purse on the coat rack and set the bag of lids on the counter. Noticing that Aunt Ruth was already filling the boiled hot jars with the sweet thickened fruit, she walked over to the sink and began washing her hands. "I got past Mrs. Chatterton and talked to Becky Ritter for a second. Then I ran into Jenny. She was working at Dandy's. I invited her over for dinner. I hope you don't mind."

"Not at all. How's she feeling?" Aunt Ruth asked, watching Anne's face to see her reaction to Jenny's situation.

"She looks good to me. I always thought Jenny was too thin." Working in an assembly line fashion, they began putting the boiled lids onto the hot filled jars. Then they lightly screwed on the jar rings. After a few minutes of silence, Anne continued speaking, "I just wish this was something she could be happy about; why didn't she tell me before now?"

Aunt Ruth sensed Anne's disappointment. Of course she was saddened by Jenny's misfortune. The girls used to sit for hours looking at bridal magazines while growing up, planning their own weddings. They anticipated one day becoming each other's maid of honor. They had always been so close. What seemed to disappoint Anne most was that Jenny hadn't confided in her before now.

"It was probably too hard for her to tell you, Anne," Aunt Ruth began. "A lot of things go through a person's mind at a time like this. Maybe she thought you would be disappointed, hurt, or even mad at her. Jenny and you have always watched over each other. Maybe she thought you would say something to Derrick."

"Derrick Reynolds is the father?" Anne interrupted. "Well this is all starting to make sense now. Jenny's been crazy over Derrick since Jr. High. I warned her about him."

"You should give Jenny a chance to answer for herself, Anne. Remember, it takes two," Aunt Ruth said in a calming voice. Aunt Ruth was right. Jenny was the one with the answers to her questions. She would just have to wait for Jenny.

The canning was out of the way and dinner was ready to come out of the oven. Uncle Henry and the boys were coming in to wash before sitting down at the table. Jenny drove into the driveway as Uncle Henry entered through the back door. He turned when he saw her. "Well as I live and breath, is that Jenny Stolewicker I see?" he asked teasingly, as she walked toward the house. "You look good, Jenny. I always thought you were too skinny. How you feeling, girl? I'd give you a hug but I don't think you'd enjoy it much right now. I've been out in the barn all day, rebuilding stalls."

"I can tell you've been doing something out there," she teased back, crinkling her nose.

"Well, come on in," he chuckled. "I'm sure you already know Anne's home 'til Monday. There's not much that gets missed in this town," he cynically grinned.

"Don't I know that," she softly retorted.

Jenny helped Anne set the table as the guys came in one by one from the washroom. Everyone sat and bowed their heads as Uncle Henry said grace. As soon as the food was passed, Anne's brothers, James and Noah, joined her cousin Aaron in a debate about baseball. The major issue of debate was who was going to win the World Series. Noah's favorite team was the Cincinnati Reds.

"How can anyone beat a team with great players like Johnny Bench, Tony Perez, Joe Morgan and George Foster," he rallied. Aaron was a true blue fan of the Philadelphia Phillies and Mike Schmidt, who he bragged earlier that year set a modern National League record by hitting four consecutive home runs in a single game.

"Not to mention," he continued, Anne grinned as she watched the mound of mashed potatoes grow with the excitement of the re-count of the game that took place in Chicago, "He drove in a total of nine runs. His final homer broke the fifteen-fifteen tie. Not only is he the greatest third baseman that ever lived, but he's a great batter, too." The debate became louder as each one tried to make his point, with neither side really listening to the other. Finally, Uncle Henry broke in.

"You boys can take this outside, while you're bringing in the animals for the night. Aaron, put some of those taters back. The dinner table is not the place to build a pitcher's mound. Now, if you don't mind, I'd like to enjoy my dinner in peace and talk to my two adopted daughters." Anne and Jenny smiled at hearing the nickname Uncle Henry used while they were growing up. Jenny was glad she came over for dinner. Being part of the Gates' family again was just what she needed.

When everyone had finished eating, the girls helped Aunt Ruth clean up the kitchen. Afterwards, Jenny and Anne walked out to the picnic table that sat under the large elm tree in the back yard. The cool breeze of the early evening was a welcome relief. The kitchen had become a near oven itself, after all the canning and baking was done.

"Your Aunt's still a great cook," Jenny said. Reaching back, she eased herself onto the picnic table's bench. "Being here tonight almost feels like we're twelve again. Life was so easy," she sighed.

The sun was setting. As the dark drew near, an echo of the boys' voices bounced off it, then blended with the lowing of the cattle that slowly moved across the field, as they led the animals to the barn. Anne thought this was the ideal time to get to the core of Jenny's predicament without any interruptions, and sat next to her while trying to form the words to begin.

"Well, Aunt Ruth didn't say much," Anne softly opened, "but she did say that Derrick Reynolds was the father." Jenny laughed quietly at her shrewdness.

"Boy, you're not wasting any time. All right. All right," she gave in, reserving a smile. "I think the last time I wrote to you, I was still at Northern. That was just before I knew I was pregnant." Jenny started slowly, as if searching for the words. "I'd been home a month before that for the weekend. I spent most of that time with Derrick. He was home on leave from the service."

"The Foreign Legion, I hope," Anne jumped in.

"Do you want to hear this?" Jenny asked, chuckling at her remark. Her mood became more serious as she added, "I wish this was a romantic story, like Graustarck, but it's not."

"Sorry, Jen, I know this isn't easy," Anne whispered.

"He left on Monday morning, then a month later returned home again," Jenny began, recalling the series of her tale. "This time he was getting ready for the Philippines, and was on a two day pass. I told him I was pregnant. At first he said it wasn't his." Sensing Anne's anger, she patted her knee to calm her, hoping to prevent any more interruptions as she went on. "He knew that I hadn't been with anyone before him. It was my first and only time. He told me the name of a place that did abortions and said he would pay the two hundred dollars. I found out later he knew the cost, because he'd gotten Maggie Rite pregnant the year before."

"And Holly Mitchell and Diane Murphy before that," Anne quietly but sternly interposed.

Jenny's sad expression revealed her surprise and undoubting shame. She knew Derrick was beguiling. Unfortunately for her, it was his sugar coated wily charm that allured her. Anne ached as she read Jenny's heart. It was clear, the words she believed to be old news came as a slashing saber. She rued ever saying them, and searched for a comforting replacement; but soon realized that anything she said now would sound hollow. There were no human words worthy enough to offer her friend of so many years. With all sincerity, she spoke the tired words that seemed of little value, "I'm so sorry Jen, I'll try and keep quiet." A few tears ran down Jenny's face, then became lost in the thick blond hair that draped over her shoulder. After taking a deep breath, she continued.

"Well, I never thought I would even think about having an abortion, but I have to admit I did. I mean, I'd never been in a spot like this before. Anne, you can't just blame Derrick—I was very willing the night we were together. Afterwards, I felt so dirty. Then I found out I was pregnant, and all I could only think about was how hurt my parents would be. They didn't deserve me bringing this kind of shame to them. Derrick kept telling me the whole thing could be avoided by having the abortion. Still, I knew there must be a better answer. I cried and prayed. I begged God for forgiveness and direction. I felt so alone. The next day I gave the money back to Derrick. He was really angry that I decided against the abortion; but I knew I couldn't cover one sin up with another. I had to take responsibility for my mistake. Somehow I knew God would help me though this. Then I kept hearing this scripture over and over in my spirit, 'In whom we have redemption in his blood, even the forgiveness of sins, according to the riches of his grace.' I finally told my parents. My mother cried for a few days. My father wouldn't talk to me. I wanted so much to call you but I felt so ashamed." Jenny dabbed the tears on her face with the hem of her oversized shirt, while Anne gently rubbed her shoulder. Reclaiming her composure, she smiled. "A few weeks later, my mother got a letter from Helen Greenly. Do you remember the Greenlys? My parents used to play pinochle with them on Friday nights. They have a daughter named Melody. She graduated with Jacob," Jenny purposed, trying to refresh Anne's memory.

"Wasn't Helen married to that guy who smoked those nasty cigars and ate all the cookies? And they had that big ugly dog, that always had saliva hanging out of his mouth?"

"No, that was my Uncle Fred and Aunt Ellen," Jenny chuckled, trying to right Anne's confusion. "The Greenlys lived on North Oak in that pale yellow Cape Cod. They moved to California just before we graduated. Anyway, to make a long story short, Melody and her husband, Larry, are going to adopt the baby. I'm going to be flying out to California a month before my due date and have the baby out there," she concluded.

Anne rose up and softly smiled. "Through dry times and mighty storms, He meets us where we are. Isn't it just like God to take our messes and turn them into a blessing? His grace is so amazing." She paused while soaking in all Jenny had said, then reached out and touched her arm. "So how are you doing through all of this?" she asked. "This has been a great ordeal, I'm sure. You said you asked for God's forgiveness; but Jen, I'm not so sure you've forgiven yourself. You just don't look like you—I mean besides the obvious. Forgiving yourself is not a selfish thing. It's as much of life's birthing process, as your labor will be. It's a hard thing to go through, but the outcome is worth it." Jenny smiled at Anne.

"You've always been so grown up for your age."

"Well I've had to forgive myself of a few things, too. It's not the easiest thing to do."

Jenny stood, using the table to push herself off the bench, then joined Anne as they walked toward her car. Periodically a whinny or moo could be heard coming from the barn, overriding the soft croaking that echoed from the pond beyond the corral. The clear country sky made the stars appear brighter, giving way for the North Star to set its landmark to find the Big Dipper. After thinking about Anne's comment Jenny asked, "What in the world did you ever do that made it so hard to forgive yourself? I've known you most of my life, Anne. Other than getting back at the boys for their tricks, you never got into any trouble."

"I've never told anyone this before; so, you have to keep it to yourself," Anne began, feeling a little embarrassed. "A few days before the ninth grade Sadie Hawkins dance, I stole a can of hair spray from Wilson's drug store." Jenny's face was stark in disbelief.

"You did what?" she asked, laughing. "Angela Naomi Gates. I can't wait to hear this!" she declared.

"Well I'm not proud," Anne confessed. "Money was tight that year and the farm didn't do as well as we hoped. I was in Wilson's reading the latest edition of Teen magazine. Walking past the hair spray on my way out, it kind of bothered me that we couldn't afford it. After I stood there staring at it for a few minutes, I looked around, and then hid it in my purse."

"You didn't!" Jenny burst in.

"All right. Fair is fair," Anne chuckled. "I butted in when you were unveiling your tale of woe." She paused, looking at the ground as she leaned against Jenny's car. While running her foot in a half circle in the dirt, she continued. "I don't know if Mr. Wilson saw me taking it, or putting it back the next day; but I know he saw me. A week later when Aunt Ruth came home from shopping, she said she had stopped at Wilson's; and that Mr. Wilson gave her a can of hair spray—for free. He told her he knew we were going through tough times and with three daughters of his own, he understood some things were important, even if they were considered luxuries. I can't even begin to tell you how I felt. I took the can of hair spray back. I knew how hurt Aunt Ruth and Uncle Henry would feel if they found out what I did, especially since they couldn't afford it. And I knew stealing was wrong. Mr. Wilson was behind the counter when I walked back into the store. As soon as he saw me walk in, he came around to greet me. I told him everything, but of course he already knew. He told me he forgave me but the hardest thing would be, for me to forgive myself. Then he told me something, I'll never forget. 'Forgiveness has many doors and they all swing both ways.' So you see, Jen, a shiny apple, a blue eyed boy, and a can of hair spray are all pleasing to the eye; but they can become cunning tools leading to our falling, if we allow Satan to drive the nail. You're not alone in this; we all make mistakes."

Jenny reached over and hugged Anne. Smiling, a tear escaped from her eye and ran down her cheek. "I have missed you so much, sister."

"Me too, Jen," she said, returning a smile. "See you in the morning at church." Watching as Jenny backed out of the driveway, she waved, grateful for the time with her dearest friend.

As she stood on the porch in the overflowing light from the kitchen, Anne could hear the voices of her aunt and uncle in soft conversation. Skipping up the steps, she walked into the back door. Seeing them sitting at the table together brought a contentment.

"Would you like some tea?" Aunt Ruth offered.

"No thanks, I'm fine."

"I'm glad you and Jenny got together," Uncle Henry said, sipping his tea in between sentences. "It's been hard enough for that girl, and this town hasn't made it any easier." Anne walked over and put her arm around her aunt's neck.

"The only reason I ran into Jenny is because Aunt Ruth sent me to pick up jar lids we didn't even need. There's four or five boxes already in with the canning stuff," she said giggling.

"I just didn't want to run out, that's all," Aunt Ruth groveled, embarrassed that she'd been caught.

"Good night," Anne said grinning, as she headed toward the stairs.

"Good night," her aunt and uncle returned.

Church was a real treat for Anne. It gave her an opportunity to talk to people she hadn't see in awhile. The choir she once sang in, before moving to Lancemen, harmonized beautifully singing her favorite version of "Amazing Grace." Then Pastor Thomas came to the altar to deliver his message. After praying, he asked everyone to turn to Hosea, chapter three, starting with verse one. The sanctuary was quiet, except for the rustling of the pages from the bibles. Anne remembered one of the young men in the church saying that the sound they made was one of his favorite things. To him it sounded like rain. While thumbing through her Bible, she mentally hummed a song she remembered of the Holy Spirit raining down.

Anne was familiar with this book and was able to find it quickly. She recalled it gave an account of a man named Hosea, who at God's command married a harlot named Gomer. After the birth of two sons and a daughter, Gomer fell back into her former life, and left her husband. Following God's instructions, Hosea went searching for her, to love her and to bring her home, in spite of her wrong doing. Upon finding her, he bought her back for fifteen pieces of silver and sixteen bushels of barley. Remembering God's words, he told her that she needed to be faithful to him. Unconditionally, he was faithful to her.

Then, Pastor Thomas read sciptures from another minor prophet in the book of Jonah. In the verses he selected, God told Jonah to go to the city of Nineveh; for the people who lived there were wicked and needed to hear His word. Instead, Jonah boarded a ship in Joppa. He chose to disobey God, because he knew if the people heard God's word, they would divert from their wickedness; and God being merciful, would forgive them. Clearly, Jonah possessed an unforgiving spirit and wanted them to be punished. It took a raging storm, and three days and nights in the belly of a big fish, for him to take God's word to heart. But through it all, God kept Jonah safe and forgave him.

"We become that way at times," he offered. "Instead of helping the people we see fall around us, we let them drop into a pit. Then we stand, as Job's tormentors, debasing them for their failures, instead of showing mercy."

Then he went on to Luke, chapter seven, verse forty-seven and spoke more on forgiveness and mercy, which was the theme of his sermon. He preached on righteousness and measured it against self-righteousness. After quoting Thomas Adams, who said, "Self-righteousness is the devil's masterpiece to make us think well of ourselves," he left them with food for thought. "We need to be more like Hosea and our Father who welcomes the prodigal son. Who is without sin? We need to show mercy and compassion to others." He concluded by reminding us of God's mercy and compassion, then prayed, "Let thy mercy, O Lord, be upon us, according as we hope in thee." It was a good sermon, delivered in the gifted style of a Godly man.

A big dinner followed, as always. Anne's older cousin Jacob who had a home built on the other side of the farm, brought his wife and children over to take part in the day's activities. Everyone filled in around the table. Jenny, being an adopted member of the family, came with her parents. In addition to the room filling with the smell of good food, it also became a pleasant potpourri of chatter; including the day's sermon, how the young children had grown, crops and, of course, baseball. Once dinner was over and the dishes were washed, the boys began choosing up teams for a friendly game. The day passed quickly. Before long, it was time to tend to the animals for the night and say good-bye to kin and company.

Jenny and Anne had made plans to meet for lunch early Monday afternoon, before Anne drove back to Lancemen. While showering and packing her things before going down for breakfast, Anne recalled events of the weekend visit that just seemed to fly.

"There never seems to be enough time," she said, while carrying her things downstairs. "Well, you don't have to rush off," Aunt Ruth replied.

"I have to be to work by six. Since it's my first day in a full time slot, I want to get there a little early."

"Anne, why didn't you say anything about this before?"

"I guess I just got side tracked with Jenny's situation and seeing everyone else," she answered while pouring a glass of juice. Aunt Ruth set a plate of eggs and toast on the table for Anne, then sat down. Holding a cup of coffee that had cooled while cooking Anne's breakfast, she sipped the lukewarm liquid.

"Well, you have time now. I can listen over breakfast," she insisted.

Anne said a quick grace. After sipping her juice, she began the presentation of her new position. "Well, you remember I dispatched midnight's for a while. Afterwards, I had an opportunity to work on the Commission Car with Chris, out of his house. Then Dan needed a partner. So he and Chris went to my boss, Merve, and asked him to put me on full time. Well, he said okay, so my first shift is tonight, at six." Anne knew what she offered was just a synopsis. But there was no sense in upsetting Aunt Ruth with tales of firecrackers and having a Tommy machine gun setting next to her, to scare off intruders. What she revealed was true, and to the point.

"Well, what is your job exactly? How many hours a week will you have to work? How much money will you make? Anne, I'm not wanting to pry. You just seem to be leaving so much out," Aunt Ruth said, in her wise and loving way.

"All right," Anne sighed. "We work forty-eight hours on and have forty-eight hours off. I'll be working out of the Lakeview station. I'm not allowed to drive the ambulance. I don't really care about that. Dan's a good driver."

"Where will you sleep? What about your meals?" her Aunt probed.

"The station has a stove; so we can cook in, or we can eat out. There's a room to watch TV and a room for the crews to sleep; that's where I'll be sleeping." Anne knew there was no reason to try to camouflage the answer. To do that would only bring more concern to her Aunt, who by her expression, was already troubled. "Now Aunt Ruth, it isn't like that. We can separate the room with a blanket. It's like me being here with the boys. The guys I work with treat me like their sister. I really like the work we do, and everything has just fallen into place. It seems like a ministry to me. There's so many hurting people. I don't mean just from their injuries. Some of them are afraid and unsure. They need someone who's compassionate to calm them. It feels so natural to me. I know the living arrangements aren't the best. But I truly believe this is a good thing. Aunt Ruth please, just trust me," she said feeling like a lawyer giving a closing statement.

The juice she was sipping while nervously studying her Aunt's stunned appearance felt more like a small orange, as she swallowed hard to force it down. Aunt Ruth didn't move or change her expression for what seemed to be at least ten minutes. Then to Anne's surprise, her Aunt began grinning while still in a state of wonderment or perhaps amusement at the delivery of her job requirements. Within what really was just seconds, Aunt Ruth's puzzled countenance eased. In a nonchalant manor she stood up, and turned her back toward Anne. Reaching for the coffee pot, she poured herself another cup before turning around, collected and as straight-faced as she could be.

"Well, it sounds to me like you're pretty set in this thing. I've always trusted you. There's no reason to change now. Just promise me you'll be careful." Pausing, she looked at the ceiling, then gently rubbed her teeth over her bottom lip, trying to hide an almost sad expression, before continuing. "Anne, I would never want you to feel that you have to keep anything from us—good or bad; but it might not be a good idea to mention any of this to Uncle Henry when you say good-bye. He's got a lot on his mind already with this farm. Let's wait and see how it works out first."

"Thank you, Aunt Ruth. I'll go say good-bye as soon as I put my things in the car," Anne said, hugging her Aunt. With the good-byes done and the car loaded, she headed into town. After having lunch with Jenny, she would drive back home to Lancemen.

Home, she thought, isn't just a building, but it's a place where love and friendship dwells. It's a place of your beginning; a legacy to hold dear and carry with you, as you go on to build your own home. And a family is not only a bloodline but a life line, that grows with each new life that's touched with love, making home a bigger place. Thinking back to her childhood, she had always liked having a big family; and she liked being back home.

CHAPTER 10

DAN THE MAN

(A Legend in His Own Mind) The value of time is in direct relation to the activity surrounding its mean. Comparatively, a child anticipating Santa's arrival or a person anxiously waiting for an ambulance both endure time, as seconds seem like hours. A couple enjoying a walk on a sandy beach, as twilight paints the orchid sky, might wish for the moment to never end and for time to stand still. But time is time no matter what; and its worth only varies according to the need.

Anne played with these thoughts while waiting outside the locked Lakeview station. Somehow, getting the numbers for the combination lock was overlooked. Glancing at her watch, she realized she still had a little more than half an hour before her shift began. She was eager to get started. "Well I guess I can go across the street to the party store and buy a bottle of root beer," she decided. "That will pass some of the time, anyway." While standing at the edge of the road waiting for a car to pass, she noticed a pay phone in the parking lot next to the party store. Maybe I should call the dispatcher and let him know I'm here, she thought. I bet someone there will know the combination for the door. Approaching the phone, she checked the change in her pants pocket, then dropped a dime into the slot before dialing the number.

"Hi, Tom. This is Anne. I'm next to the station in Lakeview, but I don't know the combination for the door—do you?"

"Not off the top of my head. It's been a while since I've worked out there. Roger and Cubby left LOH a few minutes ago. I'd ask them now, but I don't think they want to broadcast the numbers over the air," he chuckled.

"Nah, that's okay. I'll just go back to my car and wait."

"Oh, that's right. This is your first real shift. You're in early. Well my phone line's ringing. Talk to you later."

The party store was small. Canned goods, dusty boxes of cereal and instant foods were crammed tight on the aisle shelves, in an attempt to make up for a lack of space. Anne noticed a young man who seemed mentally slow, counting empty pop bottles in the back room near the coolers. Although she had watched him only momentarily while taking a bottle from the cooler shelf, he caught her glance and smiled as their eyes met. "I like root beer too," he said quietly. Returning to his previous task, he again concentrated on counting the bottles whispering each number to himself.

The sun beat down on the roof of her car as Anne sat looking at the now empty pop bottle. Her patience were running out. "What in the world could be taking them so long?" she wondered. "It must have been at least a half an hour since they left LOH." Then the sound of tires on the gravel driveway caused her to look in the rear view mirror. At last, the ambulance rolled in and parked under the car port. Dan drove in seconds later, parking his Captain America van in the driveway next to her car. The van was his pride and joy. It was a customized piece of work, painted sky-blue, with a red and white stripe angled on each side. A Captain America shield was centered on the hood and complimented the light bar displayed on the roof, bringing pride to any fireman. It was as much for recreation as it was for transportation. The back seats had been removed to make room for a makeshift bed. Black shag like, fake fur covered almost everything behind the driver's seat. It had a real wooden floor and a small lamp that sat on the refrigerator next to Dan's favorite stuffed Muppet characters. It was the kind of vehicle that would give any father nightmares to see his daughter ride off in, for a date.

Anne rolled up the window and opened her car door. Stepping out onto the parking lot, she folded the front seat down and nearly disappeared while grabbing her belongings from the back seat. Reappearing like a juggler preparing to perform, she took the pillow and stuffed it under her left arm. Next she slung the overnight bag over her shoulder. Then, while tightly gripping the sleeping bag under her right arm, she pushed the car door closed with her foot. Moving toward the carport, she faced the glaring summer sun. In a glance before turning away, she caught a peek of Dan and Roger sitting in the shade, on the bumper of the ambulance. Instinctively, she tried to raise her hands to shield her eyes; but her encumbered state, instead, forced her to close them tightly, leaving her to blindly search for a replacement guide. As the acuteness of her ears took over, she discovered that the hum from the dripping air conditioner, that partly hung out of the back cinder block wall, grew louder as she neared the station. Using it as an aid, she slowly continued walking. After inching a few more steps, she stopped cold. A sudden burst of laughter bounding from the area of the ambulance bumper had drowned out her sonar and brought a feeling of embarrassment. She couldn't help but imagine she must look like a minute eyed old mule, loaded down for a mining expedition.

"What, are you moving in or coming to work?" Dan asked.

Anne was very used to the crew's light hearted teasing, and laughed after realizing how silly she must look. Following his voice, she took the last few steps, then stood in the shade of the carport.

"Well, I wasn't sure what I would need, so I just brought everything," she answered.

"I guess," Roger jumped in. "You didn't bring any of those stupid little rugs, that women put everywhere, did you?"

"Darn, I knew I was forgetting something."

"Just ignore them, Anne," Cubby chimed in, as he joined the group. "You should see all the junk they bring."

After repositioning her sleeping bag, she walked into the station and scanned it from the door way. It was a one bedroom structure. Perhaps at one time it had been a small business. In any case, it didn't fare well. The dark paneled walls were splintered in places and scratched in others. The drop ceiling in the main living area seemed fairly new. At least there were fewer cobwebs where the newer ceiling was. The decor was right out of "Tree House and Garden." Sheets in need of laundering covered the windows and were draped over the sofa and recliner.

Feeling somewhat apprehensive, she ventured in to see what other rooms the bungalow offered. Entering a room she thought was the kitchen, she saw an older avocado green stove. It sat next to the sink and a single set of white metal cupboards. Beside that, and on the other side of the bedroom doorway, was a couple of homemade wooden pantries. The doors on the pantries had to be lifted while being swung open to keep them from dragging across the dirty tiled floor, but none the less they worked.

"Come on, I'll give you a tour," Dan cheerfully offered.

It amazed Anne how this building seemed to be like a palace to them, when it really needed to be condemned. She guessed it was a sanctuary of sorts, a place where they could totally be themselves, and she was invited to be part of this event. It was an honor of trust to be the first girl to share this; but as she looked around, she hoped this honor would take place after some cleaning was done. She knew she would have to use some tact in her approach. The last thing she wanted to do was insult them. She would have to find a way to clean the station without changing too much of the character of their place of solace.

"Well, where should I put my things?" she asked, trying to be gracious.

Dan pointed in the direction of the bedroom.

"My bed is under the window. You can sleep by the phone. You're probably a lighter sleeper then I am. And, I wouldn't put my things on the floor if I were you. The mice might chew it up."

"Or carry it off," Roger inserted.

"Mice?" she asked.

Cubby heard the concern in her voice, and briefly studied her facial expression. Her raised eyebrows and a slightly drawn mouth confirmed his suspicions. Her face always seemed to give her away. He chuckled to himself thinking, she would never be a good liar, or a successful gambler.

"You know they're just mess'n with ya, Anne. I haven't seen a mouse in here for a couple of months." He watched her reaction and knew by her increased uncertainty, that his attempt to be reassuring fell short.

Smiling somewhat nervously, she walked into the bedroom and set her things on the bed.

"There's sheets in the bottom of the supply cabinet," Roger offered. "They aren't exactly folded, but they're clean."

Anne turned around. The three of them were standing as if they weren't sure what to do next. "Thanks," she chuckled, untying her sleeping bag, "I can probably figure everything out. This place isn't that big that I'll get lost. You guys fret worse then my Aunt Kate."

Dan's initial expression of hurt feelings turned into a grin as he walked toward the living room, imitating Cookie Monster's voice.

"Well—me just trying to help. Geez, that's gratitude for you." Dan was a big fan of the Muppet characters and could imitate every one of them. Cookie Monster and Fozie Bear were clearly his favorites.

While making her bed, Anne could hear Roger and Cubby giving a recount of the calls they had responded to during their shift. They were very descriptive while giving details to what others would find to be gruesome. But she had learned as early as her first clinical shift, that the gruesome things were not viewed as such by the people working in EMS. Those were the good calls; the ones that challenged your ability to move quickly and effectively. Accidentally getting the patient's blood on your clothes or skin wasn't upsetting. It was worn more like a badge or a vestment, bringing a sense of pride. It reinforced the feeling of self gratification in thinking that your being there somehow made a difference.

Dan restocked the ambulance with needed supplies. After checking the emergency lights and siren, he called out to Anne.

"How long does it take you to make a bed, for crying out loud. I'd like to go and get dinner before we get too busy, ya know."

"Well, I'm not a mind reader. Let's go."

"Girl, am I going to have to tell you everything?"

"Just until I figure out your idiosyncrasies," she chuckled, climbing into the ambulance.

"Yea—well I'll tell you everything you need to know over dinner," he gently retorted while buckling his seat belt. Looking at Anne they both smiled, as if they were opponents shaking hands before a match. It seemed at that moment it was understood; the verbal Ping Pong game was on. Living on the farm with the boys made Anne a worthy challenge for Dan. And she, of course, felt right at home, knowing it was all in sport.

Pulling into the plaza near The Family Diner, Dan parked the rig at the side of the building near the door. It was their usual parking place. The crews had eaten there so often, that they were nearly honorary members.

"What's so funny?" Anne quietly asked, hearing Dan laugh as they walked through the restaurant.

"Didn't you notice everyone staring at you when you walked in?"

"Why would they do that?" she asked, while looking around.

"Because you're a girl."

"So what. I've been a girl all my life," she quietly asserted, taking a seat in the back booth.

"But you're wearing a uniform now," Dan noted, as he sat down opposite her.

Anne was a little uncomfortable as she realized she was the focal point. She almost hoped for a call, so they could leave. It surprised her that her uniform and position were such a curious thing. After a short time, the patrons returned to their food and conversations.

The waitress came over and set a couple of glasses of water on their table. Then quickly, while taking her ticket pad and pen out of her apron pocket, she listed the daily specials. Without waiting for Dan's order, she began writing and dictating his usual.

"Two country steaks, fries, corn, salad with French dressing and a large cola. And for you young lady—what can I get for you?" The waitress, perhaps in her mid-forties, didn't seem mean, but she had a very authoritative, no-nonsense way about her. Her steel gray eyes and tight lips added to her firm demeanor. Anne felt pressured to respond and hurried to give her order, as she rapidly scanned the menu.

"The baked chicken special, please, and a small glass of iced tea."

"Oh, did you hear that, Dan? She said please. Maybe she can teach you guys some manners."

"I have manners," he chuckled. Picking up his spoon, he began playing with his silverware and napkin. Looking up, he continued talking. "Sheeze, Vera. Is there a secret oath you women take at puberty or something? Seems like you no sooner get together, and you've got this gaggle geese, sisterhood thing goin."

"United we stand," she grinned. Content she had gotten Dan's goat, she walked toward the ice dispenser to fix their drinks.

The restaurant was busy for its size. At best it could serve fifty people comfortably. It seemed a good number of patrons were regular customers. Although Vera looked to be the oldest of three waitresses working that night, she certainly was not the slowest. Her tables were waited on and bused quickly, leaving her ample time to stand behind the counter and enjoy her coffee and cigarettes. While glancing over the at the juke box, Anne noticed that the cook came out periodically to talk and joke with people he knew. His sleeves were rolled up revealing a tattoo on each of his well toned forearms. Peeking out from beneath his white chef's hat, a few fine strands of dark blond hair sparsely lay against his shiny forehead. Feeling her eyes upon him, he looked over toward their booth.

"Hey, Dan," he bellowed, loud enough to be heard over the other chatter. "Got yourself a new partner, I see. She looks a lot better than Jim. Probably smells better too."

Anne could feel her face turning red after being spotlighted again. Even so, she smiled at the cook to show her appreciation for what she thought was supposed to be a compliment. Vera empathized with Anne, realizing her self-conscious state and began scolding him, while trying to get him to hurry their orders. Anne sipped her iced tea and wished for a place to hide. Dan chuckled along with the others; that was until he became aware of her eyes glaring at him from across the table.

"What! I was laughing at Charlie, not you!" Glancing back at the wrangling couple, he snickered, "Boy, Vera's really giving him the what for. You'd think they were married by the way they act." Dan was good-natured and full of expression. He rarely held anything back. His laughter was inviting, risible; causing almost everyone within hearing distance to join in with at least a smile. He was the kind of person that would be hard to stay angry with; not that he would care anyway. "Life's too short to sweat the small stuff," was an expression he often used.

Vera brought their food quickly. The waitresses and the cook had learned if the crews needed to leave for a call, their food would go to waste. Therefore, their orders generally took top priority. "The food looks great," Anne offered, while cutting into the golden brown chicken breast. After Dan sprinkled salt and pepper on his fries, he began disclosing a brief report of their favorite eatery. "Charlie," he said, "learned to cook while in prison." Anne watched Charlie while Dan talked, and noticed him smiling as he took Vera's pecking in stride. She appreciated Vera coming to her defense; but still she couldn't help feeling bad for poor Charlie. Even though he was out of prison, he still had a warden.

"He's good to the crews," Dan boasted. "Most of the time he'll heap an extra portion of food on our plates. When business is slow, he'll sit and listen to our war stories. He's a good guy." Taking a break, he sipped his cola, then added more steak sauce to his cut portions of meat. "So, how's the farm?" he asked scooping a forkful of corn.

"Good," Anne answered. "I got to see my friend Jenny. We've been like sisters since sixth grade. We sort of lost touch for a while, after she went to Northern—so it was great running into her."

"Oh yeh? What does she look like?"

"She's blonde. But you can forget it, Dan. She's my best friend."

"So what are you saying?"

"It doesn't matter anyway—she accidentally got pregnanat. You wouldn't be interested."

"Whoa. You can't blame me, I never met the girl. And how do you get accidentally pregnant anyway?" he sneered. Without waiting for an answer, he pointed his empty fork in her direction. "See how you women are? It's always an accident for you. So what do you think—we plan it?"

"No. Guys are just pushier," she scoffed defensively.

"I don't think so!" he quietly announced, sliding a piece of steak into his mouth.

"All right. All right. This is a pointless debate," she chuckled conceding. "Let's talk about something else."

"That's probably a good idea. I'm starting to lose my appetite."

Anne laughed out loud, doubting his comment held any truth. "Sorry," she offered. Clearing her throat she tried forcing a more serious side to the conversation. "So, what did you do over the weekend?"

Dan was happy she'd suggested finding a new topic and began telling her about the fire call he responded to the day before. It had been in the

Court House in the town of Independence. While summarizing the battling event, he went on, in controlled excitement, about two and four inch hoses. The detailed description of the kind of attack they used to contain and then kill the fire had Anne lost in a deluge of fire lingo. Listening carefully she tried not to interrupt, even though she was familiar with less than half of the terms he used. She remembered how upset her brothers would get when she asked too many questions during their, would be chronicles. Listening seemed like the best thing to do, to keep the momentum going; understanding the terms would come later. For the past four years Dan worked part time as a volunteer fireman. He liked fighting fires much more than working in EMS. He mentioned many times that he hoped the CETA Program he was involved in would secure a full-time position for him on the fire department.

Even though Dan did most of the talking, he finished eating long before Anne.

"Are you going to play with that food or eat it?" he asked chuckling. "If we get busy, you're gonna wish you'd eaten a little faster. Who knows when we're gonna get our next meal?"

Anne tried gulping a few more bites but had to stop. Charlie had put so much food on her plate. There was no way she could keep up with Dan's eating speed. Pushing her plate aside, she leaned back in the booth's seat and patted her belly.

"I'm so full. I can't eat another bite."

The phone rang as they got up to pay their bills and leave. It was their dispatcher, calling them for an emergency run.

"Just in time," Dan said, while giving Anne money to pay his bill. "I'll go get the information."

Upon reaching the ambulance, he opened the door then he reached over to pick up the mic. After jotting down the incident number and site of the call, he acknowledged the dispatcher. They were to respond to a baseball diamond at the high school, not far from their station. There was a reported player down with a possible broken ankle. Within minutes they pulled onto the grassy field where a group of players stood along side the patient. Anne walked over carrying the orange box of first aid supplies, and set it on the ground near by. The group of men stepped aside to give them room to work. She noticed the ground was damp from the early evening's dew.

"Did you slip on the grass or did someone run into you?" she asked while taking a pair of scissors out of the box. He moaned and rocked slightly while supporting the injured leg with both hands under his thigh.

His knee was bent, causing the injured and greatly deformed ankle to dangle in the air.

"I slipped—on the grass," he groaned, holding his breath with every other word. "I heard it snap—when it twisted. It hurts less—if I hold it in the air. There's less—pressure."

Anne listened carefully as he spoke. Because his breathing pattern was so sporadic his speech was sometimes difficult to understand. She watched how he supported his leg and realized it was the position of comfort. Splinting the ankle and finding a new position of comfort might increase the pain temporarily, but it had to be done. After carefully cutting off his shoe and sock, she checked the top of his foot for a pulse. Then she gave a quick squeeze to his toenail beds, to determine adequate blood circulation. Even though the foot was extremely pale in color, the patient had good sensation and could wiggle his toes. The fracture or dislocation was closed, but the bone was pushing at the skin from the inside. Any moving of the ankle would have to be done gingerly, to prevent the bone tearing through the skin. While mentally formulating her plan, she remembered the rule for certain fractures; splint them where they lie.

Even though the patient was obviously in pain, he tried his best to maintain a macho like image, while Anne worked at splinting his leg. She talked to him and explained everything they were going to do. Thinking a board splint would not suit her need, she carefully wrapped a pillow around the foot and ankle. Then she placed an ice pack onto a piece of gauze and gently laid it across the injured area. Dan secured it all with a couple of triangular bandages while Anne held it in place. Dan took the patient's blood pressure after they moved him onto the stretcher.

"I can get the rest of the vitals on the way to the hospital," Anne said, looking at Dan.

He nodded in agreement, then asked the other players to help them load the patient into the ambulance. Because the ground was damp, muddy and uneven in places, a four person carry of the stretcher seemed safer. The players were happy to help, and wished their friend well. One of them offered to meet him at the hospital; after the game. After all, it would take time for the hospital to get the patient registered and for x-rays to be taken. He might as well finish the game first and then come up.

After arriving at the hospital, Anne reported the patient's condition to the nurse assigned to him. Dan wrote the bill, then joked around with a few of the nurses. Anne cleaned the back of the rig, then set the stretcher up for the next call. She went to check on their patient before leaving, but was told that he was already on his way to the x-ray department. They cleared the hospital and headed back to their station in Lakeview.

The Lakeview station was by far, less busier than Lancemen had been. Other than the minor auto accident they came across on the way back to their station, the rest of the night was quiet. That was, except for Dan's reboant laughter, while watching a late night TV show. Then there was the shuffling of his slipper-clad feet across the floor.

"Will you please pick up your feet?" she called out from the bedroom.

"Sorry. Am I keeping you awake?"

She knew from the chuckle in his voice that he wasn't the least bit sorry. And now that she was wide awake, it seemed fruitless to try and get any sleep. Sitting on the edge of the bed, she called out.

"Well, I might as well get up and clean the station!"

Dan seemed pleased he was no longer the only one awake; and wasted no time in quickly taking advantage of the opportunity for conversation.

"What's wrong with the station?" he asked, as he walked into the bedroom.

Here was her chance. She had planned to be tactful, but now honesty seemed like the better approach. "Dan, I don't know how to say this without hurting your feelings; but if the township came in and inspected this place, they wouldn't know whether to condemn it, or set up a lab. I've never seen so many different types of mold in a refrigerator before. There are mushrooms growing along the base of the shower. The shower walls are grossly yellowed with rust. The bathroom sink is crusted with old tooth paste, and I can't even begin to describe that toilet."

"And your point is? Don't beat around the bush. I know the bathroom's nasty, but the rest of the station isn't that bad. It just has—a lived in look." He knew he was facing a losing battle. Nothing he could say, nor any expression of displeasure he made, was going to convince her that the station was even close to being acceptable to a girl.

"All right, all right. I'll quiet down. Just don't start cleaning tonight. There'll be dust flying everywhere and then I won't be able to get any sleep."

"Good," Anne smiled. "It's agreed. You let me sleep and I'll let you sleep."

After breakfast they headed to the nearest hardware store for cleaning supplies. On the way back to the station, Anne talked Dan into stopping at a garage sale. She thought the new lamp and drapes she bought would brighten up the station; but after showing her treasures to Dan, she could tell he wasn't as excited as she was. "Just don't get too carried away," he sneered. "I'm not going to make stopping at garage sales a habit."

Fortunately, regarding calls at least, the day had been slow. The only time the phone rang was when Roman called to see how Anne liked working at the Lakeview station.

"Other than needing a little cleaning, it's not too bad," she answered.

"Ha!" came Roman's victorious laugh through the receiver. "That place is a dump. I knew you'd never stay there without cleaning it." He paused. Without covering the mouthpiece of the phone he yelled out to Rick. "Hey Stockwell—I got Anne on the phone. You owe me a ten spot, buddy." Then he confessed he and Rick had a bet going. His bet was that Anne would clean the station. Rick's bet was, she would take one look at it, and opt to sleep in her car. Anne laughed while listening to the wager.

"My car was looking pretty tempting for a while," she admitted. "But the station looks pretty good now. I've been cleaning ever since we got back this morning. We even stopped at a garage sale down the street and picked up a few things," she added proudly.

Roman chuckled, "You went to a garage sale in the ambulance? That's a first. Hey, what about Dan's Ms October—is it still over his bed?"

"Yes, and the calendar from Lovejoy's Funeral Home, is still on the wall by the desk." Gloating about winning the bet, he remarked how glad he was that she made only a few changes while cleaning the station. Even if it was a dump, the last thing he wanted to see was lace curtains or plastic flowers in every room. After offering as much acknowledgment as he felt her progress deserved, he hung up.

Sitting on the sofa, Dan watched the late afternoon Muppet show, while Anne put the vacuum cleaner away. Her playful nature couldn't resist goofing around with him, as she slid one end of the vacuum cleaner hose over the unfinished wall that divided the station. After putting the other end up to her mouth, she talked through it, pretending to be a Muppet character. "Hi, Dan. I'm Snuffleuffigus." Hearing Dan laugh at her gesture, she put the hose down and came around the wall to see his expression. As she made the bend and began to speak, Dan burst into a bounding laughter.

"What is so funny?" she asked.

"Go and look at your face," he chortled. She walked into the bathroom and stood in front of the mirror. The vacuum cleaner hose had left a large, thick, brown ring around her mouth. She laughed, then reached for her toiletry bag that was sitting on the back of the sink. Applying cleansing cream to a wet washcloth, she began the task of removing the goo. Dan giggled when he walked into the bathroom. Whether he was there to be a witness to give an accurate re-count of the incident or just to enjoy every moment of the joke gone sour, she wasn't sure. As she rubbed and worked at the brown ring, panic took over her passive smile. The brown grease smeared, but did not come off. Dan roared. His laughter echoed off the walls in the tiny bathroom.

"Try using some soap," he stammered. His comment jarred the remembrance of a can of hand solvent she'd seen, during her cleaning spree. The solvent was for removing auto grease and oil. She looked in the vanity under the sink, then joyfully declared, "Thank God, there it is!" Using her fingernail clippers, she pried the can open, then smeared the paste like gel over the brown smudge. Her mirrored image reflected the pale yellow paste over her scrubbed red skin, as it emphasized her bright blue eyes. At that point, she was beyond caring about how ridiculous she looked. Her only hope was that the paste would dissolve the dilemma quickly, before a call came in. Through all of this, Dan's contagious laugher and comments left no doubt that he was amused.

"Stop laughing! This isn't funny," she said, trying to restrain her own laughter. Dan left the room snickering, holding his stomach and wiping the tears from his eyes. "It really—isn't that funny," she whispered irksomely to herself. Dan was twenty-two years old and still possessed the sense of humor of a nine year old boy; the kind of humor that brings one to simulate the sounds of gas escaping the human body. But Dan wasn't alone. For some reason, that type of humor was hard to leave behind. Late night sitcom writers exploited it, and many comedies often used it in some form. And after living with five boys, she had learned the best way to respond to it, was just to say nothing. Criticism and/or comments only encouraged them to heighten the volume or odor of their supposed talent; which they often rated, especially when it was a "good one".

The direct phone line rang. Anne rushed to clean the last bit of gunk from her face. Dan put his uniform shirt on over his tee shirt, as he announced they had a non-emergency call.

"Come on, Anne. Time to take Gramma to the hospital." She hurried into the day room, patting her overly scrubbed, red face with a towel. The brown had finally come off. The non-emergency run allowed her a few extra minutes, before they had to be on the air. That's all she needed to cover up the redness with a little make-up. The soft beige foundation nicely transformed a raw looking complexion into a healthy glowing one. The incident had been concealed and forgotten, at least for now.

Dan gave her a brief synopsis of their call and what to expect, as they got into the ambulance and started down the road. It was at a nearby nursing home named Myles. Their patient reportedly had fallen and cut her head. Also, the same hospital that was accepting their patient, had another patient waiting to go back to Myles. Dan said they called this the nursing home shuffle. While driving, he explained that the nursing home was run by nuns. It was clean and the residents seemed well cared for. Most of them sat secured in wheel chairs in the hall during the day. If they could see each other, they seemed to feel less alone.

As they wheeled the stretcher past the kitchen of the nursing home, an aroma like Sunday dinner filled the air. Then while passing the activity board, Anne noticed a schedule of crafts and events. She learned from the aide that led them to their patient's room that not all the residents were nuns or even Catholic. They were all paying customers and equally cared for. The nurse who worked the station near their patient's room, however, was a nun and was addressed as Sister Martha.

While walking with them to the patient's room, Sister Martha gave them a report of her injuries, then handed them the transfer paper for the hospital. Affectionately, she shared that the patient, Sister Gracey, had been a nun for fifty-two years—until she became senile. As they entered her room, the woman sitting in the bedside chair turned toward them, after hearing her name. Her green eyes were dull and her skin somewhat pasty. She had a full head of gray hair with wisps of blood on one side. It was arranged neatly in a bun at the back of her head, and although it was smartly done up, it looked odd and out of balance in relation to her small frame. As they laid Sister Gracey on the stretcher, they carefully adjusted the pillow to accommodate the bun, and the dressing that was professionally wrapped over the right side of her forehead. Sister Gracey was eighty-two, pleasant and seemed mentally sharp for the most part. That was until she mentioned her mother would be worried, not knowing where she was going. On the way to St. Luke's, she had to repeatedly be reassured that everything was taken care of.

After arriving at the hospital, Anne gave the report to the nurse while getting a blanket to cover Sister Gracey. Dan got the stretcher ready for the next patient that was going back to the nursing home. He was a ninety year old man who had been transported to St. Luke's earlier for a replacement of his feeding tube. He was a crabby old fella, who yelled and fussed about everything. First he was hot and then he was cold. The stretcher was too hard, then the roads were too bumpy. No matter what Anne did to make him comfortable while returning to Myles, he grumbled.

As they drove through Lancemen, she glanced down at her watch and then out the front window, to see the sunset in its final stage. Traffic was thinning, as the normal business time of day was done. It was Tuesday, and half of their first shift was behind them. Telegraph was the next main road just up ahead. It divided Lancemen from Lakeview. Just a few more miles and they would be pulling up to the nursing home. She scanned the transfer paper given to her at St. Luke's, while filling in the billing information. Throughout the entire ride the ninety year old man named Elmer Dawson wiggled and cursed. She could feel her patience wearing thin as she tried calming and covering Elmer repeatedly. While growing up she had been told she had the patience of Job. She chuckled to herself, as she recalled the statement and thought—that's only because Job had never met Mr. Dawson. She wondered how the nurses and nuns tolerated his cursing. Then she wondered if his crabbiness was because he couldn't eat, as he was being tube fed. Covering him with the blanket again, she felt somewhat ashamed as she grew more tired with the constant babbling of their patient.

Finally, they backed into the nursing home's ambulance parking area. Elmer began yelling at Dan as they rolled the stretcher out of the ambulance.

"Quiet, you old fart," Dan softly muttered. Anne was a little surprised at his boldness; but she was pretty sure that Dan meant no disrespect and that Mr. Dawson didn't hear him. As they neared the nurse's station, the staff heard Elmer's yammering. One of the aids came and directed them to his room.

"Now Elmer, you just hush," she said, turning the crank to raise his bed. "He hates being moved around," she said in his defense. Cradling him in the plastic litter pole stretcher, they placed him onto his bed while the aide held his hands. "Some days he's so sweet and other days he goes off like this. He'll be fine tomorrow," she said, as she gently brushed her hand against his face.

Dan looked at Anne and asked her if she was ready. She nodded, then he unsnapped the pole stretcher. After pulling the zipper head off, he spread the poles apart causing the zipper to separate. They removed each side of the plastic stretcher and laid it back onto the main wheeled cot. Now Mr. Dawson was able to lie on his bed, without any more jostling. He was glad to be back in his room. After spouting off a few more orders, he closed his eyes and drifted off to sleep. Anne admired the aide. She seemed so poised and had a knack for handling difficult older gentlemen.

While loading the cot into the unit, they discussed their dinner plans. It was getting too late to go to the usual diner. Pizza sounded good. On the way to Don's pizzeria, Dan announced he wanted to make a quick stop at the drugstore first. Anne heard him but was deep in thought. After weighing her care of Mr. Dawson against the aide's, she felt compelled to share her thoughts out loud.

"That aide was a lot more patient then I was. She's got a special gift for handling old people. I wonder how long she's worked there?" Stopped at a red light, Dan half listened while ogling the girl sitting in the car next to them.

"My. My. My," he grinned, as she pulled away. Dan was a leg man to be sure, and summer was his favorite time of the year. Anne was used to his girl watching. That's one thing the crews all had in common. Smiling and shaking her head, she went on.

"I finished a three year ministry program last spring…"

"You're a minister?" he interrupted, surprised as if she had held back a big secret.

"No. There are different types of ministries. There are youth ministries, music ministries, jail ministries—. And then there are people who go into the mission fields, like my parents did. The program I attended was more like an in-depth Bible Study. Anyway, the one thing that was brought up over and over was—that if you wanted to be a good leader, you had to first be a good servant. A good leader has to have a servant's heart. Martin Luther King, for instance, had a servant's heart, and he was a great leader. A good leader doesn't push or demand. A good leader serves his people. That aide at Myles, for example, has a servant's heart."

"What about you? Do you have a servant's heart?" The tone in his voice suggested that the gears in his mind were whirling.

"Why?" she asked. Pulling into the plaza parking lot, he stopped in front of the drugstore.

"Because, I'm in need of a servant. I need you to do me a favor."

"What kind of favor," she chuckled, suspecting an ulterior motive.

"I want you to go into the drugstore and buy me this month's issue of Playboy." Anne thought he was joking, but his face was so serious.

"You're kidding," she paused, waiting for his response. After studying his face in silence, she reasoned, "Dan, I can't go in there and buy a magazine like that. How's that gonna look?"

"Well how's it gonna look if I buy it? There's an article I want to read, okay?"

Anne laughed, "I might be naive, but I didn't just get off the boat. There's more than just a moral issue here; as you so astutely pointed out yesterday—I'm a girl. I have no interest in looking at nude women."

"I don't want it for you to look at. I want it for me." As he spoke, he remembered his comment about wanting to read an article. He was caught. "Sweety, please. Just this once? Didn't I take you to the garage sale yesterday? Do me this one favor and I won't tell anyone about the vacuum cleaner hose."

Anne's laughter became louder. She could believe he would use such a thing for leverage.

"What has that got to do with it?" Again she waited for a response, and again there was silence. "So that's how you're going to play this. Okay. Okay. I can see this is going to go nowhere. Fine. I'm starving. I will do this—this one time—and this one time only."

"Thank you Sweety," he said, as he handed her the money. Grumbling and sneering, she took the money as she unbuckled her seat belt. She opened her door then stepped out onto the parking lot. She knew she had given in way too easy. This was not an act of a servant's heart. Nor was she doing this out of the goodness of her heart. She could almost hear two little voices quarreling back and forth, like in the cartoons: a devil on one shoulder and an angel on the other. She tried to justify it by telling herself it was just a magazine. Why should she care if Dan actually read the articles or looked at the pictures. The truth was, she was hungry—and it just seemed fruitless to debate it anymore. It was quicker just to buy what he wanted and be done with it.

She walked into the store and looked for the magazines. Although she knew most stores kept that type of reading material behind the counter, she thought she would check the magazine section first. Hopefully, she wouldn't have to actually ask for it. While scanning the tiered rack, her face became flushed. It wasn't anywhere in sight. How ridiculous, she thought. It's not here, and staring at the rack isn't going to make it magically appear. I might as well get this over with. Walking toward the counter she noticed a woman and two children nearby. Deciding to wait until they paid for their items, she stopped in the candy aisle. Picking up a couple of chocolate bars, she pretended to look for a certain brand. "I should have just told Dan to buy his own Playboy," she muttered to herself. "I am such a marshmallow. If I don't toughen up, these guys are going to walk all over me."

After making sure no one else was near, she picked up a couple of packs of gum, then nonchalantly walked to the counter. She saw an older man and a woman in her mid-twenties, perhaps, working behind it, unpacking boxes of cigarettes. Nervously looking around, she laid the gum on the counter top. The man noticed her and reached over and picked up the gum. Then after ringing it up he asked, "Will there be anything else?" Anne stammered slightly, as the flush returned to her face.

"Yes, I would also like this month's issue of Playboy please." An uncomfortable tenseness filled the space around them, as he turned around to take the requested periodical from the rack behind him. After sliding it into a brown paper bag he gave her the total and asked if she wanted to keep the gum out.

"Yes, please, the magazine's for my partner." Her honesty slipped out. Both the man and the girl turned around and looked out the window toward the ambulance, where Dan sat waiting. By the sulky expression on his face, Anne realized he had seen them peering out. Picking up the bag and her gum, she took the receipt from the man's fingers. Unplanned poetic justice has its sweet rewards, she thought, giggling to herself.

"You didn't have to tell them it was for me," he complained, as she got back into the unit.

"Sorry, it just slipped," she grinned. Dan was sullen for a few minutes, while driving to the pizzeria. Then his easy going nature took over and he silently conceded. After all, Anne had been a good sport about getting him his magazine, much to her dislike.

The fragrance of hot bread, smothered with sauce and pepperoni, filled the front compartment of the rig as they drove to the station. Dan hurried. By now they were both so hungry that the aroma from their dinner had made their mouths water. Getting back to the station and eating the pizza before a call came in was the only thing on their minds. Anne wasted no time finding the paper plates, once they arrived. Dan flipped through the TV stations before sitting down to eat. They had pulled two calls so far that day—and two at the beginning of their shift yesterday. As Anne sat down with a slice of pizza, it suddenly occurred to her how long and drawn out the twenty-four hour shift had seemed. "These forty-eight hour shifts are going to take some getting used to," she said. After wiping her mouth with her napkin, she continued. "You never know what's going to happen, from one minute to the next."

Hoping to rest her pizza stuffed belly, she walked outside. The stars dulled by the city lights were scattered across the summer sky. Traffic on the main road muffled the sound of any crickets that might be nearby, while the air conditioner hummed and dripped competing with the chatter from the TV that echoed under the carport. Standing in the driveway, she noticed a steady flow of patrons at the party store next to the station.

While it was profitable to the proprietor she thought, it gave little hope of a quiet night, for she knew that some of them were buying alcohol and that some of them would not consume it in moderation. Walking over to her car she checked the doors to make sure they were locked. Then while sitting on the hood of her gray Duster, she leaned over to brush the dirt from her shoes; a residual token of the gravel driveway.

Just yesterday, smiling benignly, she remembered sitting in nearly the same spot playing with thoughts of time, as she eagerly waited to begin her first shift. Inarguably since then, time had made good use of itself while allowing a great deal of activity to fit within its short frame. Assisting to clarify in what she suspected during her preview while working the Commission Car, she now held no doubt that this lifestyle in which she was embarking was very different; for everything seemed to rest entirely on chance. There was no set schedule for meals or sleep. A shower, or even the expected bathroom visits to fulfill normal bodily functions, she now realized would often be hopeful luxuries. Clearly, the only thing job wise that you had to rely on was your partner; and her partner was Dan. She chuckled to herself as she reviewed his part in the events of the first half of the shift. He certainly was a character. His fun loving, whimsical nature was as enjoyable as it was scary. Yet in spite of Dan's craziness, and her being a first hand witness to the crew's antics that sometimes got out of control, she still felt safe. Was it the hedge of protection her aunt had prayed for? Or, was it the crew's brotherly, protective way? Perhaps it was both. Without question, Dan was a little wilder than the others. For a moment she pondered and debated whether he was worse than, or equal to the combination of all the boys in her family. At any rate, he was still her partner. While savoring her thoughts, she jumped at the interruption of a bell that rang on the outside wall of the station. She knew it was connected to the direct phone line inside and slid off the hood of the car. Dan opened the door and called out her name. Before he realized it, she was almost standing in front of him. "Oh, there you are. We have to go in to cover the city. And just when I was getting interested in this movie too," he frowned. Smiling as he talked, she mentally reviewed her previous evaluation of him. Suddenly, a look of wonderment graced his face. Suspecting she had played a trick on him, he walked over to his van. Laughing quietly, she hopped up into the ambulance. After watching him examine the tires and windows, she called back to him through the opened passenger door.

"I would never touch your pride and joy. The price of doing such a thing would be far too dear."

"Yeah? Then why were you smiling?" he asked, suspiciously.

"I was just wondering if I was going to like having you as my partner."

"And?"

In a broad, teasing grin, she answered, "You're the man! Dan, the man. And I fear—a legend in your own mind."

CHAPTER 11

Ɛᴖ ᴄ꒛

A LEGEND ON THE MOVE

Summer's solstice had passed with Autumn's equinox bringing warm days and cool nights. The station chores were done. A friendly, gentle breeze came through the open back door of the kitchen, softening the music from Dan's radio as he washed his van in the driveway. Anne sat on the sofa at the Lakeview station, reading the newspaper. It was a little past noon and a good time to relax before hitting the books, she thought. While leaning back and putting her sock covered feet on the coffee table, she finished reading the comics, then turned to the front page.

Her stomach churned, as she read over the headlines. More news of a hijacked TWA 727, at LaGuardia Airport brought concern that terrorist activity was on the rise. She remembered that it was just last year that the Fraunces Tavern in New York was bombed. It was clear, from reading about the hijacking and other articles, that the widespread feeling of lost innocence and instability was shared by many. It seemed this unrest had grown over the previous two years, as secret governmental issues unfolded. After Watergate and the resigning of President Nixon, the Country seemed in a great distrustful state. "I'll never tell you a lie," was the promise Democrat candidate Jimmy Carter made as he tried to allure skeptical voters. Knowing this former Georgia governor would face many obstacles, including a high trade deficit and unsettled issues from the Vietnam War, the Country hoped for a change.

Change comes in due season, every farmer knows that, and as Anne read the paper she sensed a season of a different nature in the air. Then her thoughts drifted to a passage from the book of Daniel. "And He changes the times and the seasons; He removes kings and raises up kings; He gives wisdom to the wise and knowledge to those who have understanding. He reveals deep and secret things; He knows what is in the darkness, and the light dwells with Him." Hoping to ease the swimming events in her mind, she closed her eyes, resting her head against the poorly stuffed, worn sofa.

Dan came into the station to get a cola and to watch TV. He rarely did anything quiet. Standing in front of the frig, he lifted the tab on the pop can and took a loud drink. He expected Anne to respond; then he noticed she was nearly asleep. Picking up the end of the sofa, he bellowed out a roar, like a cave dweller. Startled, she grabbed at the cushion that was partly sewn to the back of the ragged sofa, to keep from falling. It held for a few seconds, then ripped, sending her spilling onto the tiled floor with most of the padding and fabric still clutched in her hand. Once Dan realized she was unharmed, he broke into his usual guffawish laughter.

"You jerk," she said, in a half angry, half chucking tone. "I could have split my head open."

"You were sleeping. You don't have time to sleep. You have homework to do. Unless you have those drugs and EKG rhythms written on the inside of your eyelids, you better get cracking on those books, Ms. Paramedic." Anne put the stuffing on the arm of the sofa, as she stood to her feet, then brushed off her uniform pants. Next to her, on the floor was the rest of the cushion.

"I'll get to it as soon as I fix the couch. Look what you made me do."

"I didn't tell you to grab onto that ripped up, old thing."

Feeling an urge to even the score, Anne picked up the pillow from the sofa and threw it at Dan as hard as she could. That was all it took—and the chase was on. Leaving no gap of time open, she bolted. Dan was hot on her tail and closing in as they ran from room to room and leaped from bed to bed. In an attempt to slow her pursuer, she picked up blankets, sheets and towels, throwing them behind her as she went. Each time she thought she had gotten him she laughed. Dan returned the same, each time he freed himself from the article of entanglement. She ran from the day room toward the kitchen. She didn't want to run outside. The last time she did that, during the game of cat and mouse, Dan locked her outside for over an hour, while he watched TV and laughed, ignoring her pleas to come in. Running into the bathroom was no good. That's how the lock on the door got broke. The tables were turned then. That time, she had piled up both box springs and mattresses against the bathroom door trying to trap Dan in. It ended with him ramming the door from the inside, sending everything flying into the kitchen cabinets.

Panting, she turned around. He wasn't there. Slowly and cautiously she crept into the kitchen. Maybe she lost him, she thought—or maybe, hopefully he just got tired and stopped. Then suddenly out of nowhere it seemed, there he was, standing right in front of her holding a huge glass of water. "Dan—no!" she yelled. Darting past him, she rushed through the back door with the water hitting the ground at her heels. Seconds later, the back door slammed shut. "Great!" she groaned. Leaning over she put her hands on her knees, to try and catch her breath. She hoped for a call. Unless Dan took pity on her, and she knew that was unlikely, getting a call was the only way she was going to get back inside. Walking toward the carport, she wiped the sweat from her face onto the sleeve of her T-shirt. "That's what I get for trying to get even," she grumbled. "I should have been studying instead of all this stupidness." Then, she noticed a couple of kids walking down the side street, carrying books, staring at her as they went by. People must think we're nuts, she thought. Seeing them reminded her of her own books inside the station, and she knew she had to somehow persuade Dan to open the door. Coming up with a good reason, or a suitable bribe to get in wouldn't be easy. Then she remembered his birthday was a few days after hers. Allowing that occasion to lead her plan of action, she quietly checked to see if the door was unlocked. "Darn," she whispered. The knob was secure. After rapping her knuckles against the gray metal door, she waited and listened for a response; but none came.

"Dan, I know you can hear me. Let me in. I give up." The door didn't budge. "Come on, Dan—please? I need to study for my test." She stood in front of the sheet covered window next to the door, earnestly listening, hoping to hear more than the sound of the TV from inside the station. She quietly waited for an answer before continuing. "Okay. If you let me in, I'll make you the Cookie Monster costume for Halloween like you wanted."

"Really? You promise?" he asked, as he slowly opened the door.

"I promise. I'll be going home for my birthday. I'll have Aunt Ruth help me. She's good at that kind of thing. Truce, okay? I have to quit playing around now and study."

"You should have been studying instead of sleeping, anyway. I was just trying to help; and what thanks do I get? A pillow in the face." Anne laughed at his tale of woe as she walked over to the desk and set up her books and papers.

"Don't even try to sound like a martyr," she jokingly sneered. "Nobility is not your forte." Picking up the sadly tattered cushion, Dan tried to put it back in place. "You ripped this off—I think you should at least make an attempt to fix it."

Looking at the tired, decrepit piece of furniture, she walked over to the supply cabinet, and took a roll of three inch cloth tape from the shelf. After ripping off a strip that was long enough to match and overlap the width of the cushion, she stretched it across the top ridge of the sofa, and secured it in place. Then she added a couple of pieces of tape for good measure, and covered the whole sofa with a clean sheet.

"How's that?" she asked, satisfied with her mending job. Dan watched as she made the repair, pleased with her ingenuity.

"What we really need is some new furniture," he grumbled. "But Merve's too much of a tight wad to spring for it. His excuse is, we don't take care of what we got."

Anne laughed, "Gee, I wonder where he got that idea?" Just as she put the tape back on the shelf, the phone rang. She began putting her uniform shirt on. Dan hung up the phone.

"Do we have a call?" she asked.

"No. That was Tom, calling me, to call Emma. The phone was off the hook for over an hour. I told him it was your fault. You know how women are always on the phone." Anne was so pleased it was not an emergency call, she totally ignored Dan's quip. Hoping to steal a few hours of study time before a call came in, she sat at the desk focusing her attention on the cardiac rhythms, in the book entitled, Rapid Interpretations of EKGs.

The months she'd spent working on the road over the summer, presented her with enough information to evaluate the direction and choice of classes she would take during the Fall semester. With that, she thoughtfully and prayerfully gave in to tabling the Nursing Program, at least for now. Timing was everything; and it was clear to her the day she walked into the Counselor's office to sign up for the Paramedic Program, that there never was going to be a better time. The only way you could get in was by having previous road experience as an EMT and by working in the field at the time of enrollment, in some capacity. Mr. Dewit, apparently heard she'd been hired by Mercy Ambulance. At least to her that explained his friendly greeting, when she walked into his office for her admission slip. The enrollment went smoothly. It made last year's battle with the stressed clerk, waiting in the long lines and Mr. Dewit's disagreeable way seem like a bad dream.

The classes consisted of two, four hour meetings. One class covered the pharmacology of the drugs used in the field. The other discussed the use of the drugs in relation to cardiac dysrhythmias and other life threatening emergencies for adult and pediatric patients. Most of the information seemed to be over their heads initially, but little by little their understanding grew. There was so much to remember. Each drug had an indication, contraindication, side effect, method of administration, dose, and expected result. The cardiac drugs worked hand in hand with knowing the correct interpretation of the EKG presented on the carried cardiac monitor. But the rhythm wasn't always the determining factor. The patient's vitals played a major role. The one thing that was expressed over and over was: treat the patient, not the rhythm. If the patient did not display symptoms warranting the accompanying medication, don't give it!

Intravenous therapy and intramuscular injection were taught using a dummy arm designed for IV instruction and by injecting oranges with fluid from a syringe. After a while, some of the students felt comfortable with the instructor and they began sneaking in small bottles of vodka to use as a substitute for the water they'd been injecting into the oranges. The instructor, of course, felt it inappropriate and acted quickly to return the party like atmosphere into a classroom setting.

Dan and Rick showed no interest in becoming Paramedics. Dan's call to fight the fiery foe was clear, while Rick expressed dreams of squealing tires at the Indy 500. The foundation of their aspirations was not built on this newly developing future of the emergency field. That was understandable. The job was, by far, not one of the highest paying careers. Combined, the EMT and the Paramedic Program accounted for two full years of intense college classes, plus over two hundred hours of infield and hospital clinical time. Once that was completed, the State Licensed Paramedic would be earning a little more than the guy flipping hamburgers at a fast food restaurant.

Still, the business of emergency medicine had come a long way since the frontier days of 1920, when Julian Stanley Wise started the first volunteer rescue service. Years of perfecting rescue breathing and trauma systems created new programs and interest in this avenue of aiding the sick and injured. Then the "Emergency" show, which premiered in December of 1971, caught the attention of many and inspired children of all ages. A few years later in 1974, President Ford signed the EMS Systems Act. Finally, in 1975 the American Medical Association recommended that EMS be recognized as a specialty and the National Association of Emergency Medical Technicians was formed. With such strides being made over the past five years, the future of the paramedic looked bright.

But it was not the called gifting or desire for everyone. And unfortunately, while the future of the paramedic appeared bright to many, it brought a feeling of darkness to others. The older firefighters, who were within a few years of retirement, did not welcome the transition. Then there were the mom and pop funeral homes that still ran a private ambulance service out of their chapel; they had no desire to get involved in the Paramedic Program as it was too costly and truly, it held a mixed bag of occupational variances.

Adapt or be left behind, was the answer the physicians had who were working on this star, waiting in the wings. They had high hopes as they worked on the development of its Standard Operation Procedures, and were anxious to see this angel of mercy fly. The season was changing. Even though it brought conflict and contrast, its purpose would be fulfilled.

Two hours had past since Anne first sat at the desk to study for next week's test. Her stomach grumbled. Then, realizing the daylight in the station had dimmed, she reached for the lamp switch. "I can't believe we've been here all this time and haven't had a single call. Maybe I should check the phone," she yawned. The Lakeview station was much slower than Lancemen had been; sometimes too slow. There were times she would pick up the direct line, just to make sure the phone still worked. The dispatchers at the receiving end generally teased her for her impatience and offered different things to do each time she called. Stretching, she stiffly pushed herself up. The wooden chair she had been perched upon seemed to have compressed her buttocks and legs into stone. A needle like sensation slowly made its way through her lower extremities, as the circulation returned. She had been so absorbed in her books, that it wasn't until she stood that she noticed Dan's musical snoring drifting from the mended sofa. It reminded her of a song. She giggled to herself as the soothing grazioso rhythm was interrupted with short bursts of staccato like nasal jolts, returning to and repeating the unplanned measures.

She missed having a regular study partner. With Roger working opposite shifts, it was hard to get together. They tried meeting at the station during their normal scheduled hours, but that generally proved to be a hit or miss waste of time. She always thought herself to be a good student. Still, any help was more than welcome. Understanding her frustration, Roger and his new partner, Jerry, tried to come in early before their shift change to study with her.

Jerry was an ex-postal worker and had initially worked part-time for Mercy Ambulance. After working one or two shifts a month, he decided it was not enough. Once the EMS bug bit him, he was hooked. As soon as a full-time position opened up, he took it without hesitation, trading in his mail truck for an ambulance. He had a keen sense of humor and was a welcome addition as a full-time employee. "Ratio and proportion, ratio and proportion," he repeated when the three of them went over the IV piggyback drip rates of the drugs they were learning. The understanding of EKG rhythms, and mathematics of the drug doses seemed so easy for him. He related well to Anne's way of thinking, as he made up stories creating characters to represent the activity of the drug and its effected organ. She enjoyed the stories because they helped cement the information she needed to remember. Dan enjoyed the animated tales too; although he would have preferred a different subject, he listened all the same.

Commitment and good work ethics were part of Anne's upbringing. She often heard Uncle Henry say, "Anything worth having, is worth working for." Having a Paramedic License had become her heart's desire and she was willing to work for it. Her determination was not without sacrifice, however; as suddenly, time took full rein. Between work, classes, and hours of studying, free time had become a precious jewel. It was something valued and hard to find. So with that in mind, she often saved the gem to spend a rare weekend home, or to go to church, and infrequently, even to enjoy a near nil social life. As it was, calls from her friends in the youth group often turned into a list of messages collected by Mrs. Johnstone, which then led to rare stolen interims that were spent sipping coffee at a nearby cafe.

Anne's visit home for her twenty-fifth birthday was a welcome break from books and tests. News of her friend Jenny's delivery of a healthy baby girl and a new start at a college out west, added a special touch. Aunt Ruth was a great help in getting her started on Dan's Cookie Monster costume. They were able to find the perfect, artificial blue fur for the head, body and arms. To save on time and cost they decided Dan could wear the costume tucked inside a pair of overalls. The only thing left to do was to make the eyes and attach them.

As Anne sat at the kitchen table in the station, she felt a flutter of excitement. Dan's promised gift was just about finished. On her lap were two white socks. Each one had a black circle hand sewn onto it, to look like eyes. At least that's what she was hoping for. They would be the final touch of the costume. After sliding the socks over the largest Styrofoam balls she could find, she looked at the transformed creation. She was delighted. The eyes looked so much like the stuffed character's she'd used as the model, that it made her giggle. Smiling, she picked up the blue fur head from the table to get a complete picture. Then a noise at the window next to her drew her attention. She could hear the dry fallen leaves slap against the glass pane, as they gave into whirling winds. Lifting the sheet draping, she watched as they danced across the frosted lawns like little eddies. Then the glowing harvest moon caught her eye. Dark opaque clouds seemed to greet, then pass before the moon, as if exchanging a friendly salutation. The phone ran. Dan sprang from the sofa in a startled state, then dashed for the phone.

"Let's go," he announced. "Mr. Willard's in another diabetic coma." Anne turned off the sewing machine, grabbed her navy uniform coat, zipped up her black combat boots and headed for the door. They had just been to the Willard's home a few hours earlier, to bring him back from his scheduled radiation appointment at St. Luke's cancer center.

Mr. Willard had lung cancer. He lived at home with his wife, Sally and their dog, Duke. The only time he left was to go the hospital for his treatments three times a week and for emergencies, usually when his blood sugar dropped. It was hard for his wife to regulate his sugar with his cancer compounding the problem. Even though he was on oxygen at home, he still smoked a pack of cigarettes every day. "Live by the sword; die by the sword," was his response when he first caught a glimpse of Anne gazing in wonder at the mound of spent cigarette butts in the ash tray on the night stand next to his bed. "I don't blame anyone but myself," he continued. "I only wish I had quit years ago, when it could have made a difference. I don't suppose it matters much now. If only my poor wife didn't have to go through this again. Her first husband died from cancer too, ya know."

That was months ago, and since then Mr. Willard had become noticeably weaker. Lately, each time they left his home to make his radiation appointment, he would look back and say good-bye to his house as if he didn't expect to return. They both made it a point to reassure him they were going to wait at the center as usual, then bring him back home after his treatment. Occasionally Dan teased that if he wanted to stop for a burger and a beer, they would. Sometimes after hearing the kindness in their voices, his thin face would draw upward with an attempted smile. Then his skeleton like arm would reach out from under the blanket to pat the hand of whoever was closest to him.

Now, as they raced to his house with lights and siren, Anne remembered the last words he spoke when they wheeled him up his sidewalk, just a few short hours ago.

"Pray God takes me soon honey, this is too hard for my wife."

"I will," she answered, in quite agreement. Pulling into the driveway, her mixed emotions danced like the whirling leaves on the lawn. She saw Mrs. Willard waiting at the front doorway. Her exhausted expression gave in to tearful relief, when they parked and jumped out of the rig. Within minutes they had Mr. Willard loaded on the stretcher and were en route to

St. Luke's. Because of the unconscious state he was in now, Anne couldn't give him any of the tube, oral glucose they carried, for fear he would choke. She always felt so helpless on calls like these. There was little else to do, except take vitals, give him oxygen, watch his airway, and make him comfortable.

The traffic gave way to the lights and siren, allowing them to arrive at St. Luke's in record time. As they wheeled Mr. Willard's stricken body into the emergency room, Dr. Corpuz noticed the concern on Anne's face. He was familiar with their patient's medical history, and heard the radio report. Following them into the reserved room, he ordered an IV and a glucose test.

Mr. Willard's blood sugar was lower than normal and barely registered on the glucometer. The IV was difficult to start due to his past medical history and the many tries over the years to obtain an IV. Once the D5W was infusing well, a 50 cc syringe of glucose was given as fast as the syrupy concentrate would allow. His eyes fluttered, then opened slowly. Anne sighed in silent relief. Even though she sympathized with Mr. Willard's desire for a quick passing from this earth, it was still hard to let go.

She walked out of the room to complete the billing form, with Dr. Corpuz right behind her. Dr. Carlito Corpuz was Filipino. He had earned an accomplished reputation as a surgeon, before changing his direction to work as an ER physician. His strong accent made his English sometimes hard to understand. He was a very good doctor, with a known intolerance to unethical patient care.

"Anne," he began, as he touched her arm to get her attention, "I know you were upset when Mr. Willard came in. The man has cancer. You spend more time with him than your other patients; but you cannot let yourself get attached to him. We try and give care to patients as if they were family—but they are not our family. I like you. You do a good job. If you do not learn to separate yourself from these people, you will not last long in this field. You will be no good to anyone." He looked down for a moment and paused. "The man wants to go find peace—the same as you someday. His time is soon. Now—go out there," he continued, invoking his hard-shelled demeanor; "and don't bring back any drunks. I'm sick of drunks. I'm a doctor, not a baby-sitter."

"I'll do my best, Dr. Corpuz." He was such a funny little man, she thought.

Geri, one of the ER nurses who was standing close enough to hear their conversation, smiled as they made eye contact. "He's more of a softy than he wants to admit—but he gave you good advice."

Anne walked out to the registration desk. Dan was next to the clerk, filling out the billing form.

"There you are. Do I have to do my job and your job too?" he teased.

"I just wanted to make sure Mr. Willard was all right."

"Don't go getting mushy on me. What are you going to do when he croaks? The man says good-bye to his house every time he leaves, for crying out loud."

"Leave her alone, Dan," Dorothy, the registration clerk, interrupted in Anne's defense. "It's nice to hear that somebody cares about these people."

"I care—but a lot of people die out there. She's going to have to learn to get over it." Anne knew Dan well enough by now to know he was no more hard-boiled than Dr. Corpuz. Maybe, she thought, the image of coldness was just a shield of protection, a sign of repressiveness. For sadly, death is not the beginning of a gentle heavenly journey for some people; but indeed a journey we all must take as a conclusion to life on earth. Although she had experienced death's sting as a child, it did not end her life; it just changed its course. Nor did it stop her from becoming fond of Mr. Willard. Standing behind Dorothy, next to the Xerox machine, she remembered an old Jewish saying, "The only truly dead, are those who have been forgotten." She hoped she would remember Mr. Willard in years to come, if even just in a whisper.

The drive back to Lakeview was quiet. Dan had gotten used to, and even enjoyed Anne's chippery, talkative nature. So to him, the vocal idleness was unwelcome as it made him feel uneasy. He tried to think of something to say to spark a conversation, but nothing came to mind. Then he searched through every radio station to find the Oldies or the Motown sound she liked. After surfing through the dial a couple of times unsuccessfully, he became disheartened and finally just turned it off. At last he thought of something to break the silence. While Anne gazed out the passenger window, he slyly reached over and grabbed the end of her lap belt. Jerking down, he tightened it across her hips and abdomen, leaving little room to breathe.

"Aaa! What did you do that for?" she howled. Dan's contagious laughter jutted in, preventing her from maintaining her miffed expression. She was all too familiar, with his impish ways. If he wasn't lifting up the end of her bed when she was asleep, causing her head to slide into the wall, he was piling his box spring and mattress, complete with pillow, sheet and blanket on top of her. When he tired of that, he developed an art for throwing darts. One morning she found herself waking to the sound of darts hitting the wall just above her head. He almost always waited until she was asleep before he launched his attack. Using a nickname, initially offered as an atonement for a prank gone awry, he generally graced her with a sing-song warning of, "Oh Sweetie," or an enthusiastic battle cry. Finally, to her rejoicing, the dart throwing ended when one of the darts stuck in the phone receiver while she was talking to her Aunt Ruth.

Just as they neared the road to the station, the dispatcher's voice came over the radio.

"Unit Four, what's your location?"

"We're coming up to the station."

"Good. You're right on top of a PI on Dixie Highway. It was reported as a head-on auto accident, with unknown injuries."

Flipping on the emergency lights, Dan flew passed their station and in minutes had turned right onto Dixie. Just up ahead, they spotted the accident in the center of the road. They noticed that neither the police nor the fire department were on the scene yet. As they neared, the only head-lights they saw were those of the dying vehicles involved as they flickered dimly in the night, creating an eerie, morose feeling. Anne wasted no time in removing her over tightened seat-belt. Adrenalin surged through her as she stepped out of the slow, but still moving ambulance. The smell of radiator fluid and hot oil filled the air, as steam rose above the smashed engines. Making her way around the twisted metal, she met Dan, who quickly over-viewed the scene while checking the wreckage for possible gas leaks.

"I'll check out the black car," she stated, while carefully stepping over pieces of torn bumper and shattered glass on the road. As she approached the black Camaro that had severe front end damage, she cringed as a cry of pain came from the patient sitting in the driver's seat. A silence followed. Then, while trying to open the car door, the cry again pierced through the chilling night air and echoed off the buildings and trees, spaced a good distance from the road. The wail was loud and unnerving, as it muffled the sirens of the responding Lakeveiw fire department. Encouraged by the sound of life, no matter how ghastly, Anne wasted no time with the jammed driver's door, and hurried to the passenger's side to gain access to the patient.

As Dan approached the nearly demolished station wagon several feet away, he could hear the sobs of a woman in near hysteria from the driver's side. There was a man standing next to her door trying to calm her. The man seemed shaken, but relieved when Dan put his hand on his shoulder.

"Boy, am I ever glad you got here so quick. That guy in the other car is really messed up. I couldn't get his door open. It looks like the whole dashboard is crushing his legs. I've been trying to calm her down," he said pointing to the woman in the station wagon, "but I'm not having much luck. I saw the whole accident. Man, I couldn't believe my eyes. I dropped my buddy off at the gas station to use the pay phone to call for help, then came right back. I hope I did the right thing." The man rambled while Dan tried to reassure the woman. After a few minutes, he was finally able to calm her enough to answer his questions. As he was listening, he noticed the front passenger's side of the station wagon was completely pushed back against the seat and had created a pocket around her. The windshield was shattered and bowed outward in front of her face. In spite of the damage to her car, in-between sobs, she insisted she was not hurt. There was no question in his mind—she had a guardian angel that night.

As they continued examining each patient, the air brakes on the fire truck hissed, then popped, while coming to a stop behind the smashed wreckage. A police car arrived seconds later with its blue and white flashing lights, blending in with the other emergency vehicles transient bursts of illumination, that bounced against the thin, chilly air.

The scene jumped into action, as each well-trained man knew his role and responded quickly. As soon as the officer on the fire engine finished over-viewing the scene and collecting needed information from Dan, he began giving orders to his men. The engineer stayed with the fire truck as he engaged the pump that charged the booster line, just in case a fire broke out. Two of the other firemen pulled the hydraulic power pack and "jaws of life" from a compartment on the fire truck. A volunteer fireman that pulled up on the scene raised the hood on the torn cars to clip the battery cables, while another grabbed the cribbing boards to stabilize the car during the extrication of the patient.

Dan walked the woman and the bystander over to the police car for questioning; then joined the others in helping Anne with the trapped victim. He carried a yellow plastic blanket under his arm and handed it to Anne as he leaned into the passenger's side of the black car.

"How you doing?" he asked. His playful nature was set aside for the time being.

"I'm glad those guys got here so fast," she answered, in relief. "We need to get him out of here. His legs are caught under the dash. His feet are wedged between the pedals and the floorboard. He can feel me touching his legs in the places where I can reach, but without a flashlight I can't tell much else."

"Okay. Cover him up with this blanket. They're going to pop the door off. I'll go get my flashlight." The fireman pulled the cord to start the gas motor on the power pack. It grabbed, then rumbled as it idled, sounding like a lawn mower.

"Kenny," she said, talking loud enough to be heard, "I need to cover you up with this blanket. The firemen are here now. They're going to take the door off so that we can get you out. Did you hear me?"

"Yeah," came a weary voice. "Lady—my legs hurt so bad—please get me out of here."

"We are going to get you out Kenny. Now, you're going to hear some loud popping noises, and the window might break; but I've got you covered, and I'm going to stay with you the whole time, okay?" Anne talked to him, while holding the blanket over Kenny and herself, like a tent. The plastic kept most of the flying glass and small particles of debris from hitting them; beyond that, it was of little protection. Even though the air under the blanket got stagnant with the smell of blood, it was good at keeping their body heat in. Kenny groaned whenever they repositioned the jaws. Each time the fireman squeezed the trigger, the tips of the hydraulic tool spread, forcing the metal of the car to fold back as if it were a pop can. In no time, the door pins popped and the door was removed. The crisp, night air filtered under the blanket from the driver's side. Reaching around to hold Kenny up, Anne reassured him again.

"It won't be long now, Kenny. Just a few more minutes."

She heard Dan and a fireman she recognized as Bruce Hall talking, but couldn't clearly make out what they were saying. There were too many other voices and noises in the background. Then she heard him call out to one of his men, "I'm ready for the ram!" The edge of the yellow blanket lifted. It was Dan, coming back around next to her with the flashlight. Bruce had already made a cut at the front of the posts with the cutters. Now he worked at placing the hydraulic ram in the door opening. The officer gave the signal and the displacement of the dash began. Kenny yelled as the pressure eased off his knees, leaving his feet still pinned.

"Kenny, it's okay. You're almost out," she said.

Dan grunted while kneeling with one leg on the driver's seat next to Anne, trying to bend far enough to see Kenny's legs under the pushed and crumpled dashboard.

"I think I can move the pedals myself. Hold on." Dan stretched with one hand toward the floor, holding the flashlight with the other. Bruce worked from the other side to help Dan. Another fireman brought the stretcher, with a backboard and cervical collar. Anne felt Dan pull the broken pieces away while she quietly talked to Kenny, who by now was shaking due to shock and or the cool night air.

"That's it. Let's get him out!" Dan announced. Bruce handed Anne the cervical collar while two of the firemen slid the backboard under Kenny's buttocks. Once the collar was in place around his neck, Kenny was turned and eased onto the backboard, head first. Anne continued to support him from inside the car. Dan helped raise his legs.

"Stop! Wait a minute," Anne called out. "He has plastic from the dash embedded in his knees." The firemen held the backboard partly braced on the stretcher, as she quickly picked the broken bits of plastic from the deep lacerations above and below his knees. When she was done, they finished sliding him onto the backboard, then strapped him in place.

"How you doing, Kenny? You still with me?" she asked, as they wheeled him toward the ambulance. She was anxious to see what his blood pressure was.

Once inside the well-lit unit, she quickly reviewed questions of his injuries and medical history, while taking the blood pressure cuff out of the cabinet. She noticed the cut across his forehead was deeper than it had looked while sitting in the smashed and dimly lit vehicle. The blood on his face was dry, matting his copper red hair to his tanned, freckled skin. He looked younger than the date of birth his driver's license stated. His answers came slower with each question. Looking at her watch, she guessed they had been on the scene for about twenty-five minutes. With all that had to be done, that seemed right; but now she was ready to go.

Dan came up to the back of the unit and opened the doors. Anne looked over from the bench where she was sitting next to her patient. The policeman who had been reviewing the scene, stood beside Dan. A scowl revealed his anger, as he placed a ticket in Kenny's wallet.

"Can he hear me?" he asked, in a controlled but peevish tone.

"I think so," she answered.

"Kenny," he said in a loud stern voice. "I've got good news and bad news, my friend—so listen up. The good news is—you didn't kill that woman you hit. The bad news is—we found your horde of drugs in the hole you cut out under your seat pad." He waited for a response. Kenny didn't move. "I'll see you at the hospital," he said in an irritated tone. "Where are you taking him?"

"LOH?" Anne answered, looking at Dan for confirmation. Dan nodded his head.

"All right, I'll be right behind you." The doors were shut and they were on their way. Anne tried a couple of times to get Kenny to respond to her without even as much as an eye twitch. She wondered; was he not answering her because of his injuries, or because of drugs he might have used? Or was he just afraid? She felt herself becoming somewhat protective of him, while sitting in the car. After all, he was her patient. As they backed into the ambulance entrance at the hospital, Doctor Corpuz's advice echoed in her mind. She knew she shouldn't let her emotions take control. Kenny was not her family; and his reckless behavior could have killed someone.

Anne was tired and ready for a good night's sleep. She could see the station's lights as they drove past the pond, near the nature center. Even Dan was quiet.

"Unit Four, prepare to code. Let me know when you're ready to copy," came Roman's voice over the dispatch radio.

"Go ahead, for Unit Four," Dan answered.

"You're responding to a PI accident on Sashabaw, in the curves. It must be your night for trauma."

"I guess," Dan replied, while flipping on the emergency lights.

Again, the red and white reluctant tunnel lamps bounced off the trees and buildings, alternating with the rotating discs in the light bar and the domed beacons on the hood. They were almost hypnotic against the fine mist that sifted from the dark clouds, now shielding the moon's glow. The siren offered a warning as Dan switched tones, from yelp, to wail, to hi-lo. A chill surged through Anne, as she remembered the last call they responded to in the same location.

Less than two weeks had passed since a seventeen year old boy with his girlfriend flipped and rolled through the last curve of the winding road, before crashing into the stone wall. That fatal accident in the curves of Sashabaw was becoming a familiar sight. Its steep slope was deceiving, as it flowed into the half dozen or so curves, near the lake front. The pattern continued, bordered by a wooded area, ending its unwary path in front of a five foot high, stone wall. The straightest and lowest point rested just north of a party store.

"Clear right," Anne announced, after checking her side of the intersection.

"I hope this isn't going to be a repeat of our last call out there," Dan said, as he pushed down on the accelerator.

By the array of emergency lights ahead of them, Anne guessed the accident was within a few hundred feet.

"Unit four arrival," she said, while squeezing the black button on the mic. Peering through the windshield, she scanned the scene. Dan slowed, then stopped the ambulance next to a white sedan that had crashed into the stone wall. Unbuckling her seat-belt, Anne noticed it was the only car involved. Dan got out and walked toward the smashed vehicle. In the few seconds that it took her to get past the front of the rig, he already had the sedan's passenger door opened and was crouched next to the woman in the front seat, assessing her injuries.

This was so out of character for him, she thought, as she came closer. He had always been more than happy to let her do most of the patient care while he went for the equipment. As she peeked in around him at the passenger's side, she chuckled to herself. Once she got a good look at the patient, it all made sense. She watched as Dan carried on so professionally, while talking to the very attractive blonde woman. He was doing such a good job, that outside of his motive, she felt proud. Standing behind him, she held the passenger door open, then pushed it back to give him more room. Touching his shoulder, she hesitated before interrupting.

"Do you need anything?"

"Yeah—For you to get in here," he answered, backing out. His face was pale. He looked like he'd seen a ghost.

"You all right?"

"Oh, Lord, have mercy," he uttered. Trudging toward the ambulance, he seemed almost woozy.

What got into him? she wondered. Taking his place in the car, she leaned over the woman and in a soft, calm voice introduced herself.

"Hi, my name is Anne. I'm afraid I'm going to have to ask you a few questions, that you may have already answered before we move you," she said, looking into the patient's frightened green eyes.

"The only place that I'm hurt is my right foot and ankle," the patient offered. "I could see that my husband was going to hit the wall, so I stiffened up and pushed down, like I was braking."

"Okay—I'm sure right now, more than anything, you'd like to get out of there. And, as soon as I take a look at your foot and ask you a few quick questions while I'm doing that, we'll get you moving. What's your name?"

"Nadeen"

"Okay, Nadeen—just to double check—you're having no discomfort in your neck or back, is that right?"

"Not from the accident. We weren't going that fast. Bill was slowing down to turn into the party store. I think I'm just sore from tensing up." Anne listened, while touching and gently pushing on each vital area, starting from Nadeen's head, working toward her feet. The side lights from the ambulance offered enough light to see down to the patient's knees. Her light sage green dress matched her eyes perfectly, and were striking enough to catch Anne's attention and become a fleeting distraction. A volunteer fireman who had been in the car with Dan leaned over the driver's seat with a flashlight.

"That's where Dan stopped," he said, trying to hide his grin. Anne looked further, toward the patient's feet. She couldn't help notice that Nadeen had well shaped, bronze-toned legs that were artfully positioned, as if she were a model posing for a shoot. Anne continued the head to toe survey, as the fireman moved closer, directing the flashlight's beam onto the patient's ankles, giving Anne a better look at the injury. Dan's ghastly expression was now understood. At the end of the beautiful set of legs, the right ankle folded sideways and had a wide tear in the skin, revealing the end of the tibia and part of the fibula. The hinge joint had split apart, pulling both bones away from the talus of the foot. It wasn't anything they hadn't seen before, but to a leg man like Dan, it was too much to handle.

The fireman helped Anne while she supported the deformed ankle. They turned Nadeen in her seat and helped her on to her good foot. She was able to stand long enough for them to pivot her before sitting her on to the stretcher. Once the pillow splint was in place, they loaded the patient and began the transport to Lancemen Osteopathic Hospital. Nadeen's vitals were within normal ranges en route, and the bleeding had stopped. Anne noticed Dan periodically looking back from the rear view mirror. She had to admit she was a little amused with his reaction. Chuckling to herself she noticed his color had improved, but his somber expression was unchanged. She new he would never forget this call.

The tables had turned while driving back to the station. Dan was speechless. The seat-belt trick wasn't going to be enough to spark a conversation this time. He just wasn't in the mood for chatter. Oh well, I'll give it a try, she thought, while slyly reaching over for the end of his lap belt. Grabbing hold, she pulled down as hard as she could, before realizing it wasn't buckled. Her elbow flew back toward the back of her seat, cracking loudly against the Data Carrier Unit that was attached to the wall behind her seat.

"Aah," she yelled, dropping the strap and rubbing her elbow. Dan looked at her for a few seconds, realizing her failed attempt. Then he broke into a peel of laughter that echoed in the small area of the front cab.

"You didn't have to go and do that to try and cheer me up. I would have come around eventually," he snorted.

"I didn't hit my elbow on purpose. And certainly not to entertain you," she grunted, still rubbing her arm, while looking to determine the damage.

It was three in the morning and she was wide awake. Between the calls, the coffee at the hospital, and now whacking her arm, sleep would not come easily. After arriving at the station, Dan sat in front of the TV in his tee shirt, shorts and slippers, flipping through the late night channels before finally getting up and going to bed. Anne sat at the table, sewing the last eye on to Cookie Monster while softly singing some of her favorite hymns to herself. Smiling, she pulled the needle through the cloth, to tie off the last stitch. A sense of satisfaction came over her, as she carefully held up the finished project. Seconds later, a feeling of drowsiness began to set in as she slipped a hard hat inside the costume's head. The hat, she discovered earlier, provided support in keeping the costume in place, and the eyes from shifting. Elated, and even a little enchanted, she folded Cookie's arms onto his chest and put her sewing things away. Walking into the bedroom, she could hear Dan's song-like breathing from the other side of the room as she slipped into bed. Methodically, as she had done throughout her life, she pulled her quilt up around her neck. Folding the sheet, just so it would overlap on to the quilt, she tucked it under her chin. "Just a few hours of sleep, Lord," was the last thing she remembered in a whispered prayer of hope, before sleep took its claim.

It was not a real surprise to Anne, that the morning began with Cookie Monster looming over her as she lazily awoke to Dan's imitation of the character's voice, barking through the mouth piece.

"You want a Cookie?"

"Maybe later. What time is it?"

"Oh, me don't know. Cookie don't have a watch." It was amazing how real the costume looked. The size of everything seemed true to form. And—Dan definitely had the voice down pat. While trying to get her eyes to focus, she reached for her watch on the kitchen chair next to her bed.

"It's eight o'clock, Cookie. Time for me to get up and take a shower, so we can go get some breakfast. I'm starving."

"Me, too."

Dan was more than thrilled with his birthday gift. Anne could hear him talking to his girlfriend Emma's two children over the phone from inside the bathroom. Their shift ended at six that evening. It would be a long ten hours for Dan, yet gratifying to her as she listened to the excitement in his conversation. He was great with the kids, and the costume would make him even more endearing to them. But the tonic twist was even grander and more perfect than that; for it allowed the child side of him to come out and be enhanced, rather than ridiculed. It polished the armor of this ongoing legend. Whether he was the legend just in his own mind ... or theirs ... he didn't care. And if this costume of blue fur and Styrofoam eyes could enrich the epic, then what did it matter? He was a legend none the less; a legend on the move.

CHAPTER 12

MAGNETISM OF THE CRAZED KIND

Insanity, schizophrenia, psychotic behavior and so on, have been a curious thing since the characteristics of such disorders were first noticed by others functioning in a seemingly normal environment. Since that time, a variety of theories have been named as contributors and causes by psychoanalysts. While theoretical approaches, such as Freudian, Jungian and Kleinian have offered some forms of psycho-dynamic treatment, since the late 19th century modern day analysts do not completely agree. Their ideas and techniques suggest different avenues of determinants and treatments.

Some theorize it is a learned malfunction due to the surroundings of those who are affected, calling them a product of their environment. Others blame the moon in relation to the ocean's tide, comparing it to the amount of water in the human body. Health experts consider low blood sugar a front runner, followed by and including, diet, chemical imbalances, lack of oxygen during birth, genetic responses, and the result of drug and chemical misuse. While the Latin phrase, Avoir le diable au corps, have a devil, gives reason to believe that demon possession is the cause of one's stark madness.

Even though Anne had studied these principles, right now they were the farthest thing from her mind. Her only thought, as she struggled to hold the arm of her female patient, was to keep control. It was obvious the woman suffered from some kind of an extreme mental disturbance, as she behaved more like an animal than a human. From the time they entered her hospital room, fifteen miles east of Lancemen, the woman named

Catherine, ranted loudly. She seemed unaware of the purpose of her own movements, as she pulled and jerked at her hospital gown.

After listening to a brief report from the nurse, Dan took a couple of rolls of three inch wide gauze from his pants pocket. One by one he tied the patient's legs and wrists to the stretcher, while the security guard unlocked the hospital's leather restraints.

"Sweetie! You need—to hold—her still," he quietly growled, while repositioning the enraged woman's wrist against the rail of the stretcher. Anne sighed. She knew the importance of keeping a firm grip. There had been many times at home when the farm animals had to be held in place, but never before had she seen a human behave so erratic.

While discreetly watching Dan to determine the degree of his frustration, she noticed tiny beads of perspiration gently rolling down his forehead. Some glistened in the dim light, as they fell on the tiled floor; others disappeared in the blond bristles of his neatly trimmed goatee. His hands moved quickly as he unrolled and overlapped the gauze, in a figure eight motion, in an effort to anchor Catherine's flailing arm. Then as her fever gradually died, she relaxed, panting as if in labor. Taking advantage of the temporary stillness, he worked quickly hoping to have enough time to finish tying one arm, before moving on to the other.

The guard slid the key into the second restraint. Anne tightly gripped the resting arm. "Ready?" he asked, looking into her eyes to ensure they were working together.

"Ready" she answered. As soon as the restraint eased off the limb, it rocketed straight up, resembling a bull leaving the gate at a rodeo. Again, Anne pushed the arm along side the stretcher bar, this time kneeling on it for added security.

"She's—so strong! This is harder than getting a heifer to stud," she quietly groaned. Outside of a grin, Dan offered no response to Anne's comment. He was very used to her old timers' sayings; after all, he'd heard them enough over the past year. But to the hospital staff, her words were very out of character, for they only saw Anne's gracious manner, modestly tinted with a gentle tomboyishness. Until that moment, they probably never imagined she'd worked with large farm animals. Reacting out of reflex, their stiff professional faces soon gave in to the unexpected remark, as they burst into sputtering snickers. Their behavior reminded Dan of young school girls with the giggles, as they tried to collect themselves. The guard's upper body quivered as he turned his head to hide his laughter, while the nurse quickly resumed the task of packing the patient's clothes. Realizing their amusement, Dan found it a perfect opportunity to taunt the farm girl, now turned EMT. "Do we have to talk about that right now?" he jeered, pretending to be disgusted. But Anne was so focused on controlling the arm, seeming to have the strength of Atlas, that she heard none of Dan's trifling, nor was she aware of the staff's jollity.

Suddenly, Catherine's claw-like hand swept in front of Dan's face, and brushed across his eyebrows. "That was too close," he sighed, pulling away. Placing his hands on his hips, he stood up and arched his back. The soreness from being bent over in a hovering position eased, as he moved around the stretcher to begin tying Catherine's legs. The struggle continued, but to Anne's relief, she noticed it was losing its vigor. She wasn't afraid really; she just wasn't totally at ease with the thought of being alone in the back of the ambulance with a raving mad woman, while en route to the state hospital.

The security guard collected the leather restraints and put them back into the muslin bag, while Dan rechecked the gauze for snugness. The nurse handed the paperwork to Anne, then pulled the straps on the stretcher a little tighter, while offering a goodwill warning. "Watch her, she bites. She got one of my aides good yesterday."

Anne nodded, "I'll be careful." Dan picked up the bag of clothes as they followed the guard toward the freight elevator.

Just as they wheeled the stretcher around the corner at the end of the hall, Catherine seemed to regain a second wind. Picking up where she left off, she began tugging at the cloth shackles, while whipping her head back and forth. Foam had started to build up around her lips, as obscenities spewed from her mouth. "We always use the freight elevator, for patients like this," the guard announced. "It's not a good thing for the visitors to see."

Keeping a quick and steady pace, they worked their way though the hospital, toward the ambulance entrance. The bright spring sun filtered through the large tinted windows as they entered the last hall. Wheeling the stretcher outside, Catherine looked around as if waking from a dream, seeming to realize for the first time that she was restrained.

"Robert! Oh, Robert," she called, looking at Dan, "Why have you done this to me?"

"I think she's talking to you, Dan," Anne teased, bouncing her eyebrows a couple of times.

"Shut Up!" Catherine growled, glaring at Anne. "It's her. That's why you've done this. She can't do for you what I can. You know that Robert!" Anne was startled by her angry statement. Dan was flattered and entertained.

"Ooo, this could get interesting," he cheered.

"Please—don't make this any worse," Anne appealed, climbing in the back of the ambulance. Sitting next to Catherine, she watched her movements carefully. The woman's behavior was impetuous, appearing to be like a tethered, Tasmanian devil. Trying not to draw the haggard woman's attention, she read over the transfer paper that she held on her lap, with one eye on the paper and one on the patient, making sure she remained securely tied. Each time the woman noticed Anne's eyes in her direction, she spewed threats of how she intended to kill her, as well as the Pope, and all the Catholics. Anne tried winning her with kindness from the beginning of the call, but failed severely. She tried small talk, asking Catherine about the Raggedy Ann doll that was in the bag with her belongings. In response, the woman began yelling at her using inappropriate words in broken sentences. Her language was vulgar and filthy, some of which Anne could not believe she was saying. While looking through the woman's paperwork, she noticed a date of birth typed on the petition, indicating that Catherine was close to the age her mother would have been.

The clothes in the bag belonging to the woman fell on the floor as they turned a corner. Anne bent over to pick them up and felt the woman's fingernails grabbing at her pant leg. Carefully she slid away from her, as she re-bagged the clothes. The suit jacket and skirt among Catherine's things were costly, something an executive might wear. Anne wondered as she laid the blouse on top of the other clothes, what made Catherine turn into this erratic, crazed person, now tied in four point restraints on her way to a state mental institution.

The Book of Matthew, chapter eight entered her mind. She recalled there were two men who were possessed by fierce demons, but were freed after the demons entered a herd of swine and ran into the sea and drowned. She wished that if there was a demon in this woman, it would be cast out and drowned as well.

Even though she felt comfortable that the restraints were secure, it was hard not to be somewhat uneasy with Catherine's jagged, irrational movements. She clearly had a strong hatred for Anne; but she loved Dan, thinking him to be Robert Redford and herself to be Barbra Streisand. Her ranting flipped back and forth from "killing the Pope," to the growing delusion of Anne coming between the romancing stars. Each rebound increased the hostility in the mordacious woman as she sputtered, then gnashed her teeth with such force Anne worried they would break. It surprised her how easy it was for her to get caught up in the delirium, even though she knew Catherine had no idea what she was saying. Dan looks nothing like Robert Redford, she thought, and this lady sure doesn't look like Barbra Streisand. But at least the Pope and the Catholics are safe for now.

Pools of sweat formed in the creases of Catherine's neck. Her face became a brighter red each time she strained to raise her head. The veins in her forehead stood out as she pushed with all her might against the gauze restraints. Her frosted hair was matted with perspiration and saliva. The foam on her lips had crusted over, causing her words to slur a little more, as she glared at Anne and yelled, "You're with them aren't you? I know what you do at night." Dan had been listening, and periodically watched the patient compartment from the rearview mirror. "Oh, Sweetie, is there something you want to tell me?" he jested. Catherine's voice changed the instant she heard Dan speak. It was artificially sweet, almost eerie.

"Robert. Robert. I knew you wouldn't leave me." The sexual description that followed was detailed and spoken with force. It was more than Anne wanted to hear; it was repulsive and embarrassing, even to Dan.

While fumbling with the air conditioning switch, he nervously laughed, "Did it just get hot in here? Maybe I should turn on the air."

"Maybe—you should just drive a little faster, so we can get this over with," Anne suggested, feeling vexed.

"Getting a little testy are we? You're just jealous, cause she doesn't love you."

"Yeah, okay, you're right Dan," she faintly replied. Looking out the back window she tried to get her bearings. Relieved at how close they were, she gave one last attempt to quiet Catherine. Gently touching her shoulder, she noticed the gauze held up surprisingly well; but with all the struggling, it had scrunched together and created a constriction, that caused her patient's hands to swell.

"Catherine, we're here. Try to relax. You've got yourself all lathered up, and your hands are beet red from pulling against the gauze."

"Shut up! Why are you talking to me?" she screamed.

"Well—I don't know. Guess I was just trying to be nice," Anne wearily sighed.

The unit slowed to a stop. Dan came around to open the back doors. Taking the bag of clothes from Anne, he chuckled at seeing how drawn she looked. "Well, are we having fun yet?" he asked, as she jumped out. With an insincere smile, she reached for the lower stretcher bar. After nodding to Dan that she was ready, they rolled the stretcher out and set it on the ground. Dan squeezed the release handle as they lifted it to its highest level. Then he began pushing the head of the stretcher in the direction of the front doors that were in the alcove of the main entrance. While walking to the side of it, he was careful to stay an arm's length, keeping his distance from Catherine. "Robert," she called softly.

Now it was Anne's turn to have a little fun. "I think you should at least give her a kiss, Robert," she called back, from the foot of the stretcher.

"Not on your life. I'd be afraid to get that close, after hearing what she said. She could seriously hurt me."

Catherine's pleas for Robert lasted for a short time, as she wiggled and twisted. Then for the first time since they crossed paths during the past hour, she became completely quiet. Standing atop of the ramp, Dan peered through the eight-by-ten, glass and wire layered window, that was set into the thick double doors. After noticing an empty hallway, he pushed the buzzer to gain entrance. A warm spring breeze gently tossed Anne's hair, as she scanned the tall Gothic style buildings. Their strong, slender, vertical piers and pointed arches seemed to emit a mysterious aura. She wondered how many mentally disturbed patients had been housed there since the center was first built, nearly a hundred and thirty years ago.

While admiring the grandeur of their design, she thought of the sea of stories she'd heard of Eider Valley. Each time they transferred a patient there, or met with another crew who had been there, Anne usually heard, yet another Eider Valley tale. The buildings were set up like a small city, on a grassy, one mile square area of land. It housed many patients that entered, but never seemed to leave. A line from a song, "Hotel California," flowed through her mind, whenever she listened to the crew's stories. She usually tried to discount most of what they said; still, it was hard not to wonder. The echo that was created when the doors slammed shut while walking from section to section, did have a permanent-like sound; and it even made her feel a little uneasy at times.

Although they admitted they had never seen them, the guys often talked about the chambers in the basement of the older buildings, where the dangerously mad patients were kept chained and shackled to the walls. They claimed they'd heard groans at night that echoed off the buildings, painting a picture so vivid, that Anne's first night there she all but expected Egor to answer the door when they buzzed to enter. Since that time, she had transported more than a dozen patients there and decided their tales came more from their childhood days of watching Frankenstein movies with Sir Graves Ghastly on Saturday afternoon, than from Eider Valley itself.

"Yes?" came the voice from the speaker next to the buzzer.

"Mercy Ambulance," Dan answered, pushing the button on the intercom. The door buzzed and unlocked. "Sheesh. It's about time.

I'd packed a lunch if I knew it would take that long to answer," he half jokingly snarled. Gripping the door handle, he pulled back on the thick, solid door.

After entering the foyer, they stopped in front of the admitting office and handed the paperwork to the clerk, standing behind the Dutch door. "What's she got in the bag?" she asked. Before they could answer, Catherine came back to life, yelling in a fit of rage.

"It's not yours! It's not yours!" she screamed repeatedly over and over, twisting and jerking every part of her body. Neither Dan nor Anne could hear the directions the clerk gave, so she wrote on a piece of paper—med four, women's section. She motioned for a guard to come and take them, then handed him the patient's bag.

A staff member always took the crews to the floor, in order to unlock and re-lock each door they went through. The guys joked that it was really because they were your only real assurance to get out, since one crazy wouldn't bother another. And, since you couldn't tell the players without a program anyway, it was best to stay close to them.

The doors slammed shut and echoed in their usual eerie way, as they went through each corridor. Neither Dan nor Anne made any attempt to talk as they waited for the elevator, for fear that their voices would set their patient off in a different direction. Catherine's loud rambling continued, but now had become more of a monotone hum—that was until they entered the elevator. Once within the tiny walls of the cubical, her gibbering bounced off the acoustic surroundings and would have been deafening if her pitch were any higher. Clearly, by the crew's and the guard's facial expression, her dissonance made the ride to the fourth floor, seem much longer than it actually was. After exiting the elevator, they waited in front of a large wooden door, while the guard unlocked it. He opened the door slowly, as if expecting someone to be there, then pushed a woman back while calling her by name. Once inside the "C" area, they wheeled the stretcher down the hall, which was full of a number of patients that roamed in and out of their rooms. A couple of them found Dan interesting, but were intercepted by the staff working the floor.

The guard continued to lead the way in the direction of another staff member, who was just ahead of them unlocking the door of Catherine's room. Looking around, Anne became curious as she noticed that each door had a ten inch square, steel mesh screen set at face level. Stepping back as the door swung open, she studied the small patient room with maize, cinder block size ceramic tile, that covered the floor and walls from top to bottom. The only window, was about three feet tall with a smaller pattern of mesh screening in front of the glass pane. There was no furniture in the room and no sink. A hole in the floor, covered with a drain, was to serve as a substitute toilet. A bare, but clean looking mattress was on the floor near the drain.

Once inside the room, they lowered the stretcher. Dan unsnapped the pouch that held his Band-Aid scissors. The guard walked over and shut the door. "Make sure you still got those when you leave," he said.

"There's no reason to explain that one," Dan jokingly retorted. "Those women looked like they wanted a piece of me. You get me out of here safely—that's all I want."

"Oh, they like men," the female staff member offered. "Other than the guards and doctors that work here, they don't get to see many men."

She talked while helping Anne and the guard hold Catherine down, as Dan cut away the gauze restraints. Within minutes Catherine was free to roam within her room. After quickly pushing the stretcher into the hall, the door was locked, leaving the enraged woman alone. Her squalling, although muffled by the thickness of the walls, could be heard the distance of the hall.

Expressing a soft sigh of relief, they pushed the stretcher onto the elevator and stood next to the guard, as the doors shut. The elevator jerked slightly as the tired sounding motor grumbled, then gave in, easing into a delightful hum, as they were lowered to the main floor. "At last," Anne thought, "this bad dream is almost over." The instant she walked through the thick oak doors and out onto the ramp, the warm sun touched her face, releasing a smile. "Oh joyous freedom," she whispered to herself. Being outside had always brought her contentment. She couldn't imagine living, or even working in a place that was so confining. While pulling the stretcher toward the ambulance, she turned around and walked backwards, to face Dan.

"If I never go on a call like that again, it will be too soon. That poor lady. I wonder what in the world made her snap. I noticed the clothes in her bag were nice. They looked like business clothes," she concluded. Standing next to the rig, she quietly looked at Dan as if waiting for pearls of wisdom, that might explain the reason for Catherine's madness.

"That's what happens when you women try to make it in a man's world. It's just too much for you to handle."

"Oh, please." Anne laughed sneeringly. "I should have expected that." She opened the passenger door, then reached under the seat for a spray can of disinfectant. "If it wasn't for us women, you'd be the one cleaning the stretcher." Climbing into the back of the ambulance, she took a pair of sterile gloves from the top cabinet, then grabbed a towel from a lower one. The odor that developed part way to Eider Valley was confirmed when Catherine slid off the stretcher, while in her room. She seemed to have lost control of her bodily functions, as well as her mind. "I wonder," Anne began thoughtfully, while spraying the stretcher, pausing briefly to watch the disinfectant turn into a rising foam, "Why did they name this place Eider Valley? Did they name it after a person, or were there a lot of ducks here at one time?" Dan was leaning against the back bumper, holding the blanket and pillow, listening and gazing at her as if she'd lost her mind.

"Ducks?" he asked sharply.

"Eider," she explained, laughing at his expression, "is a kind of a duck. They use its down to fill comforters."

"Oh well—like I should know that," Dan sarcastically responded. "Maybe—they named it that because everyone in here is daffy."

Laughing, Anne unfolded the paper sheet and began making up the stretcher.

"I don't think they see it like we do, Dan. Anyway, if you ever need a date, you know where to find one."

"That's almost funny," he sneered. "Like I would have a problem getting a date."

After securing the pillow onto the stretcher, Dan helped Anne load it into the unit, then shut the doors. While driving toward the main road, he waited for the radio traffic to clear before picking up the mic.

"So tell me," he asked bantering. "How hard is it to get a heifer to stud?" Anne looked at him puzzled, wondering where he was coming from. A few seconds passed. Her mental recovery seemed vague at first, but then she recalled the comment. "I don't really know. Our cows are Holsteins, and our neighbor has Angus and Herefords. Our cows are too big for the heifers to support the weight while they're being ridden. Uncle Henry and the boys sometimes took the seasoned ones to the Martin's barn, but mostly now, they just have the inseminator come out. Aunt Ruth won't let me around the barn until the cows are settled. I guess I just use that expression, because I hear the boys say it. I've seen the chickens do it though."

"I'm almost afraid to ask," Dan went on reluctantly, "but I'll bite. How do chickens do it?"

"Well there's not much to say, really," she replied, chuckling at his curious yet cynical expression. "The rooster hops on the chicken and rides her, while she runs around squawking, and flapping her wings. When it's over, he plucks a feather off her back, then holds it in his beak. Then with his feathers all ruffled up, he prances around the yard, still holding on to the feather, like he's really done something. My Aunt Kate was over once, helping me feed the chickens and said, Ain't that just like a man." With that, Dan's enthusiasm suddenly became sour, as Anne began giggling at his expense.

"Oh, now I see how you are. You ought to be ashamed—is this the kind of stuff you teach your Sunday school class?" he protested at the set up.

Pleased that her volley had played so well, she laughed while making a mark on the dashboard as if keeping score. "It was a joke Dan. See how you are? You can dish it out—but you can't take it," she softly chuckled as Dan picked up the mic.

"Radio, from Unit four."

"Unit four, go ahead; this is radio," Roman cheerfully responded.

"We're clear of Eider Valley."

"It's about time; I thought maybe they were going to keep you."

"Maybe next time they'll just keep my partner."

"Now—now kids, play nice. You're clear to your area."

Dan seemed pleased with his comment—as if he'd scored a touchdown, taking the lead at the end of the third quarter. He liked getting the last word in and delivering the final jolt of the ribbing. Watching his gloatish behavior, Anne chuckled. She was all too familiar with his mindset, growing up with the fun loving, competitive egos of her brothers and cousins. It seemed the same sibling-like sparring had carried over to Dan. He was, after all, like family to her. He offered a feeling of protection, then turned around and taunted her on a whim. Whenever he needed advice on nylons or clothes for his girlfriend, Emma, Anne was the one he would go to. Anytime she went home for a visit, she always saved something for Dan from Aunt Ruth's kitchen. They had learned to work so well together, that little conversation was needed. In some cases, that was ideal. As the temperature rose throughout the summer, so did the amount of calls they pulled each time they went into Lancemen. There were times when a precarious situation was made safer by just moving without chatter. Then there were times when it just didn't matter.

"Unit Four, you'll be the second car in. You'll be backing up Unit one, at 385 Benson. PD and Fire's on the way for an overdose, reported to be combative."

"Copy, on the way," Anne replied, hanging up the mic.

Benson Street was just outside of downtown Lancemen. As they neared the neighborhood, Dan turned off the siren to avoid attracting attention. Even though the summer was young, it had seemed long and torrid. Offering no mercy, the midday sun blazed across the brown, dried grass. Heat waves rising above the paved roads and sidewalks held the appearance of water at a distance. Equally fiery temperaments seemed constant, as the number of assaults and homicides rose in response to the misery of the undying heat.

"Man," Dan uttered in amazement, as they pulled up to the scene. "Half the city's here. If you see me scrambling, girl, you'd better be on my tail."

"I know the routine, I'll be all right," she offered as an assurance, restraining her own apprehension.

Squeezing the unit between two fire trucks, Dan parked behind Unit One. Mentally counting the police cars as she got out, Anne opened the side doors to grab the orange trauma box.

"Maybe you should leave that here—it'll be one less thing to think about," Dan suggested, as the commotion from the given address spilled out into the street. "We'll just take the stretcher and leave it outside, near the porch," he soberly stated, swinging the back doors open. Anne responded without hesitation, sliding the box back in place on the inlaid floor. After pushing the cot up over the curb onto the lawn, they lowered it half way, then left it in the small yard. Bystanders, with folded arms and nearly expressionless faces, emitted a feeling of boredom, or perhaps disgust. Anne wondered while scanning the crowd—how many times had they seen a similar spectacle, and how many hours had passed since today's event began, before help was called?

Dan sprinted up the steps. Just as his boot touched the lip of the porch, the screen door flew open. Rick stopped and stood in front of him, stunned that he was there. His face was flushed, with strings of wet blonde hair stuck to it. He sighed, brushing his hand over his forehead, trying to catch his breath.

"Good, you're here. We need more gauze—and the stretcher. I don't know what this guy took—but there's eight of us sitting on him—and he's tossing us around like were nothing. We can't even get his arms together to cuff him. So were just going to hog-tie him to the stretcher."

After hearing a portion of Rick's hurried report, Anne dashed to the unit. Sliding the cabinet door open, she stuffed her pants' pockets with rolls of gauze. Quick-paced, she returned to the porch and followed Dan and Rick in, as they carried the stretcher into the house.

The front room felt like a sauna, and smelled like a locker room. Arms and bodies moved with determination to pin down and harness the giant sized man, who was face down on the stained carpet floor. He was well over six feet tall, Anne thought, as he easily stretched past the length of the couch next to him. Pulling the gauze from her pockets, she held her hands out, keeping a couple of rolls for herself. Wasting no time, she joined the others in an unmatched wrestling meet, with the opponent seemingly ahead.

Sitting with all of her weight on the patient's thighs, she pushed his calves against the floor. The overdosed patient, bucked and jolted in a desperate act to free himself. Shouted instructions from the family to the patient were loud and magnified as they bounced off the commands of the emergency personnel.

"Jesse! Hold still! They jus trying to hep you, now. You lisen to me, I'm yor mamma."

"Push down on his shoulder, so he can't move his arm!" came another voice.

Sweat dripped from every fireman and EMT onto Jesse as he rolled on the dirty floor. Hoping to get a firmer grip, Anne grabbed a wadded shirt from the floor to wipe her hands. Within seconds, a sensation of tiny hairs moved up her right arm. Glancing down in a quick startled sweep, she scraped her hand across Jesse's pant leg to rid herself of the cock-roaches that crawled up her arm and scurried across the floor from under and inside the shirt. Then a partially restrained foot kicked back toward her drawing her attention as she repositioned her grip on his legs. The chaos continued as the patient's large hand slipped from a fireman's grip catching him across the face. Blood ran from his nose. Jesse's mother noticed the incident and quickly came to her son's defense.

"Please don't hurt my boy. He ain't in his right mind," she pleaded.

"We're not trying to hurt him. We know it's the drugs," the fireman answered, exasperated. "It's too blessed hot, and were tired of fighting with him."

"That's it," Rick announced. "Let's just all grab him," he said nodding to include the male family members, "and put him on the stretcher. Once he's there, we need about four people to sit on him, so the rest of us can tie him down." Grabbing the patient by his pant legs, belt, or any other part of him that could be grasped, the army of people that were crammed into the tiny front room heaved Jesse onto the stretcher. Anne started to lean on his lower legs, but then a fireman she knew as Darall pulled her back. "You're doing a good job, honey—you just ain't got enough weight to hold him down," he said, squeezing in past her. Then she heard the handcuffs click. Within minutes, with the help of the family and a corporate boost of internal adrenaline, the fight was over. Once the stretcher had cleared the doorway, she slipped passed the others, dashed out to the ambulance and jumped in.

As they approached, she could see Jesse was strapped and tied face down. His hands were cuffed in front of him, forcing his elbows to point outward in a wing-like position. With his size, and the few inches of distance between the stretcher and the cabinets, she knew his arms would be smashed; and, because everyone was so tired and upset, they wouldn't care. As Rick and Mike loaded the stretcher into the rig, Anne reached down to lift his elbows, so they would clear the wall. Just as the stretcher locked into place, she saw Jesse's big hands bolt toward her, as he grabbed her wrists.

"Let go! Jesse," she called out. Rick looked up.

"Jesse, let go!" he bellowed. Noticing Jesse's fingernails had dug streaks down Anne's arms, he jumped in the unit, pulling his flashlight from its holder. Rapping the butt of it across the huge handcuffed talons with one hand, he used his other to pry Anne free. Mike jumped in as Jesse bounced around. Finally, Anne was able to pull away.

"They're beat'n him! They're beat'n him," A woman screamed from the front seat. Dan was next to her, with the radio mic in his hand.

"Will you shut up! I'm trying to talk here," he yelled, trying to get the woman to sit still and put her seat belt on. Once the commotion in the back of the unit was tolerable, Rick turned Anne's arms over to exam them.

"You all right?" he asked, half concerned, half angry.

Anne sighed, "Sorry, I was just going to move his arms out of the way," she confessed.

"You dope," he smiled. "Stay away from him. We'll be right behind you," he said, while sliding toward the back door. "If he grabs you again—yell for Dan to stop." Anne was a little shaken, but glad Rick didn't make her switch and ride with Mike to the hospital. The last thing she wanted was for them to think she couldn't handle the job. Sitting back on the small bench behind the driver's seat, she rested, looking at her arms. Jesse's nails had broken the skin, but the bleeding was minimal. She watched him bounce all the way to St. Luke's while listening to Dan, who had his hands full with Jesse's sister. The entire time he tried talking on the radio to the dispatcher and then to the hospital, she yelled, as he repeatedly told her to "Quiet down," and "Shut up."

Anne leaned back, turning her head in Dan's direction, "Didn't we just do this about a month ago?"

"Yeah, you seem to be a magnet for this stuff," he answered, while backing into the hospital's garage. Jesse fought and bounced on the stretcher, until it literally pounced on its wheels as they rolled him into the ER, past the clerk's desk. Walking in front of the waiting room, Anne noticed the faces behind the window staring at the wild man tied to their cot. Following the nurse and two security guards, they went into a room, with Dr. Corpuz right behind.

"All right. What is this man's story? What did he take?"

"No one knows, other than some kind of street drug," Anne answered, taking her watch out of her pocket. "His family said he showed up about three hours ago now, after being gone for a week. His mother said he seemed okay, then he went nuts and started tearing up the house.

They watched Dr. Corpuz as he tried to examine the patient. Jesse was anything but cooperative. He tried getting his arms out from under himself, but the security guards moved in to stop him. Then he snapped at Dr. Corpuz with his teeth as if he was a mad dog. Putting his stethoscope back into his lab coat, it was clear Dr. Corpuz had no patience for Jesse.

"Were the police on the scene?"

"Yea. They're outside. They followed us here," Dan grunted while trying to hold the stretcher down.

"Good. They can have him back. I can't treat this man and I don't have time for this. Get him out of my emergency room."

The security guards escorted them back toward the garage. Again, patients and their families stared as Jesse rolled past them. His sister and mother stood in front of the clerk's desk.

"Where you taking him?" his mother asked, with her face full of worry.

"I'm sorry, Mrs. Murphy, Anne replied, as they rushed by. He's too wild. The doctor can't get close enough to treat him. He's going to have to go jail, to ride this out."

Two of the police officers waiting in the garage stood next to the patrol car as they approached.

"I knew this was going to be a wasted trip," one of them groaned. "Okay, cut him loose," Officer Martinez barked, then ordered... "You guys are going to slide him onto the back seat from one side, while I pull him through from the other." After hearing the plan, they stood by the stretcher, taking position next to the back door of the patrol car. Martinez crawled through and knelt on the seat. Dan and Anne worked at cutting the gauze, while Rick and Mike held him in place and waited for their cue to unbuckle the stretcher straps. Officer Jordan and a hospital guard tipped the stretcher leaning it at an angle toward the seat. Martinez grabbed the chain on the handcuffs and watched, as the last strap was released. Grabbing Jesse's belt, Dan and Mike slid him into the patrol car, while Martinez pulled him onto the seat. Then he backed out quickly, shutting the door. Rick tried shutting the opposite door, but met the resistance of Jesse's feet against it. They watched for Jesse to pull his legs back to kick, then piled together, pushing against the door as it locked.

"Did you have the doc look at your arms yet?" Jordan asked Anne.

"Not yet. I thought I'd just scrub them with a surgical brush and put an antiseptic on them."

"You know you can press charges if you want. It'd probably be a good idea. Who knows what's wrong with that guy. It'll help keep better tabs on him, if nothing else."

"It could get me hurt, too," she partially jested.

"You'll be fine," he said confidently. "We'd go to court with you. I'll talk to Tom. Is he on tonight?" he asked. Getting into the front seat of the patrol car he shut the door, then rolled down the window. "Don't worry, I'll take care of it."

Anne stood next to Dan, as the police drove away with Jesse kicking at the steamed up windows.

"He did get you pretty good, Anne. It might be worth taking their advice," Rick offered as he walked outside to his ambulance.

"If it's such a good idea, why do I have this knot in my stomach?" she softly asked Dan.

"You're probably just hungry. Let's go to Charlie's and see what his special is."

Anne laughed, "Do you have a tape worm? Let me wash my arms first, okay? It'll just take a minute."

"Well hurry up then. I'm hungry. I worked up an appetite on that call."

"You had an appetite before that call," she halfheartedly joked.

More than a few weeks had passed since they ran on Jesse. Anne's arms had healed; and as she sat alone in the courtroom across from his sister and others, she wished she had followed her own instinct. She remembered Dan missed lunch that day. Instead of going to Charlie's, they ended up at the police station, so pictures could be taken of her arms. Martinez and Jordan both reassured her they'd come to court; but as Anne looked around the courtroom, all she saw was the sneering faces of Jesse's people.

"Excuse me, miss, are you Angela Naomi Gates?" a short, thin, black man asked.

After a brief hesitation, she answered. "Yes, sir."

"Could you come out into the hall, for a minute, please?" He seemed nice enough, she thought, and there were a lot of people around. Picking up her purse from the bench, she politely responded.

"Sure."

She felt Jesse's sister's eyes on her, as she got up and followed the man. After passing through the doors, he walked into the hall and sat down on a bench along the window.

"I should probably introduce myself," he started. "I'm Henry J. Telston. I'm Jesse's lawyer. I have a favor to ask and it might sound strange coming from me, but it will make my life easier." Anne watched his face intently for the most part, but occasionally was drawn away, when a police officer resembling Martinez or Jordan walked by. Realizing he did not have her full attention he asked, "Is there something I can help you with?"

"There are two police officers that said they'd be here. I was just wondering why they aren't here."

"This is just the arraignment, Miss Gates. They aren't expected to show for this."

"Oh, I didn't know that."

"Well, I can see you're a little nervous—and I can understand why. Jesse's sister is pretty good at givin' the evil eye, which is sort of why I asked you to come out here. I've been asked to represent Jesse, not only in this case but a string of others. I almost can't keep up. He goes from one thing to another. I know that has nothing to do with you, but what I would like—is for you to drop the charges against him." He studied Anne's face as he spoke. Her confused expression came as no surprise. "What's this old guy up to you're wondering. Well I'm not up to anything, really. I just want to get Jesse somewhere, where he can get some help before he goes too far. This case has thrown a monkey wrench into my plan. These are difficult people to deal with, as I'm sure you've seen. I'm very sorry Jesse hurt you, and that's why I want to get him off the street—before he hurts someone else. I know what I'm saying sounds backwards, but trust me, Miss Gates, you don't want to get involved with these people."

"Mr. Telston, it wasn't my idea to press charges against Jesse. I did it as a favor to Officer Martinez and Jordan. I'm working in a field where I wasn't welcome at first. Everyone has been great though, really. I was just following what I thought was expected of me. There's a lot of politics out here. I just didn't want to rock the boat."

"Now that's funny," he laughed, full bellied. "Young lady, maybe you don't realize it—but you've already rocked the boat, just by being out there." Placing his hand on hers, which she cradled in her lap, he continued. "You're right. There's a lot of politics. Well, you lasted this long—you must hold your own pretty good." Reaching into his jacket pocket, he pulled out a pen and a piece of paper. "Here's my number," he said while jotting. "If you ever need a good honest lawyer, call me." Anne took the paper and slipped it into her purse. They both stood, then shook hands. "Keep up the good work, young lady." Smiling at his remark, Anne turned and walked toward the stairs.

"Well, hallelujah," she whispered, scurrying down the courthouse steps. "Lord, get me out of here safe and sound, and I'll be eternally grateful." The main lobby had emptied considerably since she first entered it two hours ago. As she reached for the inside foyer door, she felt someone come up behind her. Turning, she immediately recognized Jesse's sister.

"You talk too much, you know dat? I'm gonna member you girl." If there was anything Anne had learned from working near Lancemen—it was show no fear. Looking as if totally unaffected by the comment, she turned and walked out the door.

After spending the rest of her two days off in Summerville, she pulled into the station parking lot. From the amount of cars, it looked like they were having a party. Gathering her overnight and book bag, she made her way to the door.

"Hey, what's going on? I am scheduled to be here, right?" she asked, setting her bags on the desk.

"Of course, Rick cheerfully answered. I just came to see what happened in court the other day. You didn't chicken out did you?"

"No. I went. Why?" she asked suspiciously.

"Cause we took your buddy Jesse, to the hospital again."

"You did? What for?"

"His sister shot him. Six times. Apparently, they let him out of jail on bond or something, and he got high again. This time he went after her, and she shot him. So—what happened in court?"

"After I reported in, I went into the courtroom and waited for an hour and a half—while Jesse's sister and her people glared at me. Martinez and Jordan never showed. Finally, Jesse's lawyer came up and asked to speak to me out in the hall. He said it was just the arraignment so Martinez and Jordan didn't have to show. Then he asked me to drop the charges against Jesse."

"You're kidding me. You didn't do it, did you?"

"Of course she did," Dan jumped in. "Look at her."

"I think you're forgetting it wasn't my idea in the first place," she said firmly. "No one else made any attempt to say a word to me, outside of Jesse's lawyer and his sister. He gave me a way out, and I was more than happy to take it." Rick, Dan, Roger and Jerry, all sat quietly while listening to her explanation. Rick suppressed his grin as long as he could; her answer really came as no surprise.

"Well all right then. Guess I got what I came for. They're waiting for me in Lanceman," he said, strolling toward the door. "See ya, chicken," he added, stopping to rub his hand across Anne's hair.

"Thank you," she responded, trying to re-fix her hair with her fingers.

"Have a good shift," Roger offered, with Jerry leaving behind him. They shut the door with no more being said, until they passed by the window. Then a clucking sound echoed from under the carport canopy.

"I am not a chicken," she declared.

"Oh, they're just kidding," Dan said, laying on the sofa, putting his hands under his head. "They probably wouldn't have even gone to court. Anyway, I got some good news and some bad news. Which do you want first?"

"Good grief, now what? Okay, give me the good news."

"I got hired full time at Independence Fire. This is our last shift together."

"That is good news for you. I'm excited for you, Dan, really; but who am I going to work with?"

"Well, that's the bad news. You're going to work here with Roman until the end of the summer. Then, they're moving you to the Lancemen station. I don't know who you're going to work with there, yet. But I feel sorry for him."

"What's that supposed to mean? I thought you liked working with me."

"I do. You're a good partner, Sweetie—but you're a magnet for crazy calls. It'll be worse in Lancemen. Half those people are already crazy and you're drawn to them. That's all I'm saying. You've got an overactive, magnetic resonance or something—a magnetism—a magnetism of the crazed kind.

CHAPTER 13

OF WISDOM AND LOVE

Mercy Medical Service and life were just not the same without Dan. Yes, his dream to be a full-time fireman had come true, and yes, Anne was sincerely happy for him; but still, she couldn't help feel a little sad that he left. It wasn't that her new partner Roman lacked EMT skills or that he didn't have a sense of humor; he did. He just wasn't as lighthearted as Dan, and he certainly wasn't as good at playing verbal ping pong.

While driving to Summerville for her cousin's birthday, Anne remembered a conversation she'd had on her last visit home with Aunt Ruth, who suggested that Dan was like her favorite cat, Mouser. Not a cat on the farm could catch a mouse or scare off the birds from the berry bushes better than Mouser. Anne understood it wasn't like she'd never see Dan again. There was a good chance she'd run into him on a call in Independence. But truly, a good cat and a good partner were hard things to find. And even though Roman couldn't take Dan's place, Aunt Ruth was sure Anne would find something unique about him as well.

Aunt Ruth always has a sweet way of pointing out the obvious, Anne thought, "and my mind—always has a way of staying busy," she quietly complained to herself. Realizing she'd been daydreaming, she looked around to get her bearings. "Just five miles or so, and I'll be coming up to Summerville's boundary line," she said, readjusting the radio station. In seconds her ears picked up on a familiar Amy Grant tune, and she began singing along. Then, as the song ended, her mind eased again into a wandering state, as she drove past stores and other landmarks that gave a down home feeling. "If people are from Summerville—they're referred to as folks; if they're from anywhere else, then they're just people," she thought out loud, as the subliming attitude of each group crowded her mind. She had learned a lot about different ethnic backgrounds since she began working in Lancemen. Then she recalled a Spanish friend she had in high school. One day her friend, Maria, tried out for the cheer-leading squad, but was turned down. Maria thought it was because she "wasn't white enough." Anne remembered thinking that Maria's comment sounded so odd. She never thought of her friend as being any color— she was just her friend. Actually, she liked Maria's bronze toned skin, and even tried tanning with a quick tanning product once. But, instead of a glowing tan like Maria, she ended up with orange streaks. She chuckled while thinking of the end result, and of the flies that the suntan lotion attracted while laying in the back yard of the farm. "The only tan lines I ever had were in the form of a farmer's tan," she laughed.

Suddenly, she heard a strange noise and turned the car radio off. The front of the car swerved slightly to the right, causing a sinking sensation in her heart. The dull flapping sound could only be one thing—a flat tire. "Great! I let Aaron borrow my spare the last time I was home," she sighed, scolding herself, as she pulled over to the side of the road. "I was supposed to replace it—but I forgot. Well, at least I'm not too far from the gas station," she continued murmuring, while reaching for her purse. After looking in the rearview mirror, she slipped out of the driver's door. "I hope Al filled his pop machine. A cold root beer, sure sounds good right about now." She had a habit of prattling to herself when things went awry. Somehow, it seemed to have a way of easing the stress of a situation. The boys always teased her about it, but she didn't care.

"Good. There's Armstrong's," she said, walking down the shoulder of the road. Quietly she laughed to herself, thinking of when Armstrong's was called triple A service, after the owner, Albert Archibald Armstrong. Albert senior changed the name several years ago, saying he didn't want folks coming in to pay their car insurance. No one ever did, of course, but once he got something stuck in his head, it was best to let it be.

As she neared the gas station, she gazed over the field that butted against the edge of the road. Occasionally the breeze from a passing car drew up the dust from the shoulder and whipped it against her legs. Outside of that, there wasn't much air movement. But the temperature was pleasant, and certainly a welcome change from the blistering heat of early summer. With August at its midway point, signs of fall would soon begin. Anne always looked forward to the onset of each new season, and fall was her favorite. It was a time of harvest, when the toiling work of the previous months all came together. She loved the crisp air and often commented that it held so many scents, you could almost taste it. After days of canning and filling the cellar with fruit for the winter, she liked walking through the barn to smell the fresh stacked hay. Knowing that winter's bitter winds would be quick to follow, she relished all that she could, for as long as she could. But for now, winter was still some months off and she just wanted to enjoy the day that was before her. Maybe that's why she felt no hurry in her pace, even though she only had a few hundred feet to go.

Counting the change in her purse, she approached the pop machine, just as Al Jr. stepped out of the station.

"Hey, Anne," he broadly smiled. "I heard you were coming home for Pete's birthday. Where's your car?" His arms held several cans of oil that he rearranged as he talked.

"Down the road about a mile; I picked up a nail or something. And unfortunately, I loaned my spare to Aaron on my last visit home."

"Well, let me finish up with this oil change and I'll go take a look at it. Maybe it just needs a plug."

"Thanks, Junior. Can I use the phone to call home?"

"Sure. It's on the wall behind the counter, same place it's been for the last twenty years. Oh, and there's root beer in the cooler. The pop machine's broke." Turning around, he walked toward a shiny green Mach I that was parked under the oak tree next to the garage.

Entering the gas station, she noticed the new addition was finally finished, and that each bay was full of activity. Hoping to block the sound of the pounding pinging and air compressed tools that bounced off the walls and cases of oil, she shyly closed the door between the garage and the office. Picking up the phone, she looked for a rag to wipe off the grease before dialing.

"Hello."

"Well hello, cousin, happy birthday. I'm on my way. I'm at Armstrong's. As soon as Junior fixes my flat tire, I'll be there."

"It's Anne. She's got a flat. She's at Amstrong's." Anne paused and listened, trying to make out who he was talking to. "Aaron wants to know if you got a spare. If not, he still has your old one and we can bring it up. Never mind, he says we're coming up any way. See you in a few."

"Why do people always hang up before I have a chance to say good-bye," she sighed. Walking outside toward the cooler, she swished though the icy water until she spotted a root beer. After flipping the top off, she brought the chilled bottle to her lips and allowed the sweet sarsaparilla flavored beverage to quench her thirst. Noticing that Junior was lowering the hood of the Mustang, she strolled over to let him know that the guys were on the way.

"I can still go down and take a look, if you want, Anne. Just because you wouldn't go with me to the seventh grade Sadie Hawkins dance—doesn't mean I have any hard feelings," he teased.

"Junior, you never asked me—and you don't like to dance anyway," she chuckled. "Pete hung up before I could say anything. I think Aaron's bringing my spare."

"Suit yourself," he smiled. "Just remember, I offered."

Anne watched as he picked up the oil pan filled with empty cans, then reached to help him with his tools. "I'll get them," he insisted. "You'll get your hands all greasy."

As they walked toward the garage, a brief comfortable silence that sometimes occurs between long time friends fell unnoticed. Stirred by the movement, as she took a sip from the brown glass bottle, he spoke up. "That root beer looks pretty good. Think I'll get myself a bottle."

"While walking up here, I hoped you'd have some."

"Do you still talk to yourself," he asked, chuckling.

"Sometimes. Hey—did you read about Elvis?" she asked, knowing he must have a least heard the news. "I couldn't believe it when I read the headlines yesterday. It just seems like some people will always be around. You never think about them dying. August 16th will be a day people will remember for a long time," she offered, then paused before asking, "I wonder what caused his death?"

"Disco music", he said, matter-of-factly.

She giggled, surprised by his unexpected response. "Junior, stop it. The poor man died, and you're making fun."

"I'm not making fun," he shyly smiled. After stopping to toss the oil cans into a tall, plastic drum, he wiped his hands on the towel that was partially tucked in his back pocket. "You said you wondered what caused his death. And I answered—Disco."

"Yeah, well don't let Becky Ritter hear you say that. I'm sure she'd think you were making fun. I've never seen anyone so crazy about a person she never met."

Stepping over to the cooler, Junior reached in, as an older blue sedan pulled into the gas station driveway.

"There's your knights, coming to your rescue. You still have the chance to have a real mechanic take a look at that tire," he grinned.

"Well believe it or not, I've actually seen them change a tire before—and they did okay." The sedan pulled up and stopped near the concrete island by the air hose. Pete yelled out from the passenger window, "Hey Anne, how far down's the car?"

Walking toward the sedan she answered, "About a mile—and no, I didn't drive on the rim. As soon as it lost air, I pulled over."

"Good, at least you remembered something we taught you," Aaron grinned.

Junior walked over to join in the conversation. "If you boys decide you need any help from a real mechanic, I'll be here." Anne chuckled, as the male-ego bantering continued. Then she interrupted, knowing that the mention of food would help speed things along and get her tire fixed quickly.

"Sorry you have to change a tire on your birthday, Pete. I bet Aunt Ruth cooked you a special meal—and baked her famous, chocolate cake."

"Well get in, Cous, so we can get going," he grumbled teasingly. "Women. Seems I spend half my life waiting on'em. Hey Junior, you're welcome to come over for some cake when you're done here."

"I'd like to, but by the time I leave, you buzzards will be fighting over the last crumb. But thanks for the invite."

"Okay—see ya later," the guys said, simultaneously, as they pulled away.

Within minutes Aaron spotted Anne's car, spun around in the middle of the road and pulled up behind it. They laughed at his unexpected driving stunt, as each of them piped in with a comment and the nickname of Mario. In no time he had the hub cap off and had loosened the lug nuts from the flattened tire. Pete finished jacking up the car, then stood and watched while Aaron pulled the tire off the peg screws.

Anne leaned against the sedan while finishing her root beer, and gazed at the lazy blue sky. Occasionally, masses of white cumulus clouds gently floated over, offering an easiness to the day. Letting her head gently fall back, she closed her eyes. A shadow moved across the ground, and drew her attention upward as it briefly blocked the sun's light. Studying the passing form, she decided its shape resembled a bowl of popcorn. Then, as it drifted a little farther, it appeared almost like a gaggle of geese; some with their wings ready for flight, and some with their heads submerged in water. Sweetly, she recalled her childhood and the summer afternoons spent lying in the meadow amid the wildflowers. She remembered more than once she'd been drawn away from her chores by the white cottony firmament, set up to entertain a child's imagination. She took the last sip of her soda while watching the clouds fade into the distance and a new group drift into view. By late afternoon, the clouds will increase in number and size, she thought; and by evening they'll take on the flatness of stratus clouds.

Farmers depend so much on climate conditions. Over the years, Uncle Henry taught Anne and the boys to watch and learn the weather signs that nature provided. Leaves on the tree, with their underside up, indicated rain, as did an increased number of house flies. In fall they checked the thickness of the nests built by the animals in the woods and watched to see the amount of food they stored. Certain types of insects that collected on the barn and in the hay, gave clues for an expected harsh winter. "God created these creatures with an instinct of survival," Uncle Henry spoke up, nearly every winter. "Any man who doesn't prepare for the snow or rain, has less sense than a bug." There were so many different signals that the farmers watched for, from the earth, the sky and inhabiting creatures, that sometimes Anne wondered if they had Indian Scouts for relatives.

Suddenly, her ears picked up on the roar of a car, coming up from the south in the distance. She couldn't make out the model, but could see the orange and black vehicle was moving very fast.

"Who's that?" she asked, trying to get Pete's attention.

"Chuck Guthrie," he answered slowly, staring with a stillness, as the Roadrunner approached with warp speed. "Man, he's flying. Aaron—get up and move away from the car." Just as he finished speaking, the orange and black car flew past them in a blur and spun out of control. Then it began rolling over and continued several times, until it crashed into a telephone pole that snapped at the base like a toothpick.

"Oh, Lord!" Anne cried. "I can't believe he did that! Quick—go to Armstrong's and get some help," she directed, then started running toward the car.

"Wait, what are you doing?" Pete asked, trying to grasp all that had happened.

"I'm going to check him out", she answered. Her tone was urgent and sure.

Aaron hurried to his sedan and jumped in. "Go with her Pete. I'll be right back."

Pete raced to the car to help Anne, wrestling with mixed feelings throughout the short distance. He wanted to help. But mostly he wanted Chuck to be fine; not only for Chuck's sake, but also because he didn't deal very well with blood. Every year, when everyone sat around the barn cleaning their rifles for deer hunting, Pete just sat and watched. As much as he wanted to join the others, he just couldn't stomach it. He felt his heart race, as he said a silent prayer. Feeling ashamed for his selfishness, he whispered, "Sorry, Lord, I just don't think I'm going to be of much help if I'm throwing up." Losing sight of his cousin, he called out nervously, "Anne."

"I'm over here," she answered. He followed her voice and saw her standing in the field, nearly fifty-five feet from the twisted wreckage. Then to his relief, he saw Aaron and Junior as they pulled up behind Anne's car. They dashed from the sedan to the field where Anne stood, looking down at the body that had been thrown from the car, before hitting the pole.

"He's dead," she said, with an authority that left little question.

"I called the police," Junior offered. "They should be here any time."

"Aren't you supposed to do CPR or something?" Pete asked from a few feet away, still trying to digest the situation.

"I'm sorry, Pete, but his neck's broke. After feeling for a pulse, I pulled his jaw forward to open his airway, but his whole head came with it. His cervical spine is snapped in the middle, just like that pole," she soberly answered. She had become so accustomed to the street language used by the guys she worked with, that she didn't even think about what she was saying until she noticed his color wane.

"Maybe I should go finish with the tire," he suggested, embarrassed by his squeamishness.

As he walked away, the breeze picked up slightly, lifting the hair off the deceased boy's forehead. Anne and the others stood by waiting for the police. In the distance, the winding sound of a Federal Q siren could be heard.

"Here comes the ambulance, slash—hearse," Aaron announced. Sadly, he walked away from the body toward the road to report their findings.

"Better wait until PD gets here before we move him," Anne said to Junior, who agreed while studying her face. The Sheriff Deputy pulled up behind the old Cadillac style ambulance, and met Aaron and the attendants as they all walked out through the field.

"That's the Guthrie kid, alright, one of the attendants spoke up. "He just got his license back after smashing into a bunch of cars in the teacher's parking lot the last day school, three years ago. I knew we'd run him some day—but not this soon."

"Did anybody move the body?" the deputy asked.

"Just enough to check for a pulse and airway," Anne answered. "He's pretty much in the same position as when I got to him."

"Are you a nurse?" the deputy asked, reaching for his portable radio.

"No sir, I'm a paramedic. I work as a full-time EMT in Lancemen County."

"Dispatch, this is six-fifty—I need the ME out here and traffic investigation."

"Ten four."

"Now who all was here—and where were you when this took place?" he continued, while pulling out a pad of paper, looking at Anne.

"I was leaning against the white sedan, while my cousins were changing the tire on my car—the Duster."

"Okay, I'll need your names and a description of what you saw."

Watching the attendant cover the body with a blanket, Junior broke in, "Excuse me officer, but I just came to help out. I didn't see the accident. If you don't mind, I'll go and help Pete finish with Anne's tire. I can walk back to the gas station. It's just up the road from here."

"That's fine, just leave me your name, and you can go."

"If I get back to the station before you leave, Anne, I'll call the house and let your aunt know where you are."

"Oh my gosh, I forgot about Aunt Ruth. Thanks for your help, Junior."

"No problem. I just wish we could have done more," he said, turning away.

After answering the deputy's questions, Aaron and Anne walked through the field toward the paved road. As they approached the shoulder, they noticed the traffic team who arrived a few minutes earlier, had the road blocked off, and that one of the men from the team, was talking with Pete. It looked like he and Junior had finished changing the tire and that Junior had already gone back to the station.

"Poor Pete," Anne sympathized. "He won't forget this birthday for a while."

The ride back to the farm was quiet at first. Aaron and Pete were busy with their own thoughts. Then Aaron slowly become aware of Pete's puzzled expression.

"You okay, Pete?" Aaron asked.

"Yeah. I'm doing okay. I just can't help wondering why he was driving so fast."

"He always drove that fast," Aaron said, tooting the horn while passing the gas station. "He almost didn't graduate, after smashing into the cars in the teacher's parking lot. Good thing it was the last day. Mr. Delanie was hot after Chuck took out the front end of his new station wagon—just a few days before his family vacation. Chuck was quiet, and he didn't have many friends. It was like he didn't want anyone hanging around. So we just left him alone." Pete turned around to make sure Anne was still behind them in her car.

Pulling into the driveway, they spotted Uncle Henry standing on the porch—waiting.

"Junior called," he said, as they got out of their cars. "It's a shame about that boy, but I'm glad you're all safe. I don't know if you still have much of an appetite, but dinner's ready."

He seemed a little tense as he spoke, but they understood. The call from Junior about the accident probably gave him a start, and with the added pressure of the increasing cost of running the farm already on his mind, he actually hid his concerns very well. He was a hard worker and a good farmer, but it seemed lately no matter what he did, he struggled to make ends meet. There had been meetings with the American Agriculture Movement and talks of rallies and strikes. But the only thing that he knew for sure, was that the farm had been in the Gates' family for generations, and God willing, he wasn't about to lose it now.

Grace was said with an added prayer for the Guthrie family. Then the plates and bowls were passed. Talk of the accident would not be considered table talk, and with the paleness of Pete's complexion, Aaron decided instead to offer a progress report in hopes to ease Uncle Henry's mind.

"James and I are almost ready to combine the oats," he offered, buttering a roll. "Noah and Jacob are clearing a place for the baled straw when it's time. And Pete's doing a great job with the new watering systems. We've always been able to keep this farm steady in rough times. We know you and Mom are concerned, Dad—but we're going to make it. What is it you always said, 'Worrying is borrowed trouble'...."

"All right now, you're going to have your mother all teary eyed," Uncle Henry interrupted. "Each one of you has been working along side me since you were little and I know you can all see what's going on—but I'm not frettin as much as I am thinking and talking to God. And just so you know, after weeks and weeks—I've pretty much got it down to a science as to how much thinking and how much talking I need to do."

"Oh, do you now?" Aunt Ruth smiled.

"That's a fact."

"Anne," she asked, "Would you mind refilling the bowl with some of those green beans while I go and get the cake? I wouldn't want your Uncle Henry to have to do his thinking and talking on an empty stomach."

The boys, who really were young men, chuckled at Aunt Ruth's teasing.

"Hey," Anne asked, "Did you hear they're talking about passing a law to raise the minimum wage from $2.30 to $3.35 an hour by 1981? Too bad we only get paid nineteen out of the twenty-four hours we work."

"You're kidding," Pete said, "You mean you don't get paid for the whole time you're there?"

"Only if you don't get a chance to sleep during your shift. They figure five hours is sleep time, and they don't pay you for that."

"Oh, Anne, before I forget," Aunt Ruth jumped in, while lighting the candles on Pete's cake. "We got a letter from Jenny yesterday. There's a separate letter for you. Says she lost your Lancemen address. It's on the desk in the den. Make sure you read it before you go back to the city." Then turning with a grin toward Pete, she asked, "Ready everyone?"

With voices that sounded nothing like a choir of angels, they all cheerfully sang happy birthday. After blowing out the candles, the normal applause followed. The cake was cut and served with Aunt Ruth's home made ice cream, which she only made for family birthdays. Pete smiled while opening his presents. None of them was extravagant, but each one was appreciated. The party ended and the chore of cleaning the kitchen began.

Once the last clean dish was back in place, Anne felt she finally had time to sit and read Jenny's letter. As she started to walk into the den, she heard a car pull into the driveway and stop.

"It's a police car," Aunt Ruth nervously said. "He must have more questions about the accident." Walking toward the screen door, she pushed it open as the officer came up the steps of the porch.

"Mrs. Gates?" he asked.

"Yes."

"I'm sorry to bother you, but I have a few more questions about the accident that some of your family witnessed earlier—then I'll be on my way."

"Certainly, come on in," she answered. Anne walked back into the kitchen. "I think you may have already met my niece."

"Yes, I interviewed her at the scene. Angela, did you or your cousins know Chuck Guthrie very well?"

"Not really. Aaron went to high school with him, but I don't remember him ever mentioning his name before today," she said, politely.

"Well, the reason that I'm asking is because the accident investigator mentioned that the tire tracks looked like the car was heading straight for the sedan—but at the last minute turned away. I talked to Albert Armstrong Jr. on the way here and he seemed puzzled as to why Chuck

Guthrie would want to hurt any of you. It wouldn't change anything as far as the accident is concerned. I was just hoping you might be able to shine some light on this mystery."

"I can honestly say that I'm puzzled too. I've never seen Chuck before today."

"That's fine. You've pretty much confirmed what Mr. Armstrong said. Thanks for your time."

"You're welcome. Sorry, I couldn't be of more help."

"How strange," Aunt Ruth commented, as the deputy left.

"I'm sure it's just a coincidence," Anne suggested, folding the letter she'd gotten from the den. "I'm going to take Jenny's letter and read it later, Aunt Ruth. It will be dark in an hour or so, and I need to get home and review for the ACLS course that starts tomorrow. The test is in a few days and I have to pass it or I'll never get a chance to work as a paramedic."

"Another test? I thought now that you had your Paramedic license, you were done."

"ACLS stands for, advanced cardiac life support. It's a certification that all the emergency room doc's, nurses and paramedics have to have, in addition to whatever licensure they hold. Once I pass it, I'll have to renew it every two years in order to keep up on any changes. It will be good to have it already behind me when I start back into the nursing program."

"I'm glad to hear you still plan to do that, Anne. I'd feel better if you were in the hospital, where it's a little safer."

"I'm fine Aunt Ruth. You just keep praying for that hedge of protection around me," she smiled. "It sure seemed to work today—and I'm grateful. Well, I'm going out to say good-bye. I'll call when I get home," she concluded, hugging her Aunt.

"All right, dear. Tell the Johnstones we said hello when you see them; and have Harriet give me a call to let me know how she liked the recipe for the dumplings that I sent. Good luck on your test. I love you."

"I love you too. Bye."

While walking out to the barn to say good-by, Anne remembered Dan saying that she was a magnet for strange events. "I'm sure it's just a fluke," she said, trying to put the thought aside. Leaning down to grab a fistful of grass, she entered the barn and stopped in front of Daisy's stall, the horse she sometimes rode. "Hey, girl. They being good to you?"

"She scraped her leg a few days ago. That's why she's in here," Pete offered as he came around the corner after hearing Anne's voice. "Hey Anne—I was thinking about going to Chuck Guthrie's funeral. I thought it would be nice if some of us went, seeing that Aaron said he didn't have many friends; just to pay respect—you know."

"I think that's a good idea, Pete."

"Thing is," he started, as his face flushed with embarrassment, "What if they have an open casket? What if his face is messed up? I can handle it when I'm taking care of the animals after they've gotten hurt. But other than that—it's weird; when I see blood—it turns my stomach."

"It was a little hard for me too at first, Pete," she said. "But once I focused on the fact that I was there because someone looked to me for help—I tried to become the help they needed. The guys that I work with are very good EMTs; but there are times when even they get a little shook. Of course they try to hide it. The one thing that I've noticed is no matter how bad someone looks to someone else, to a mother it's different. To her, the injured person is always beautiful. If you go to the funeral—and I think his family would appreciate it—just try to remember one thing. This is the last time they are ever going to see their son, brother, or whatever the case is, on this earth. And to his mother he is as precious and as beautiful to her, as the day he was born. Don't spoil it for her. Just let her be glad that you came respectfully, to show sympathy for their loss. Once she understands why you're there—then focus on that, and not on how he appears to you. You'll be fine. I'm proud of you for wanting to go."

"Man, you sound just like my mom."

"I wonder why," she laughed. "I've been listening to her most of my life. She has so many words of wisdom and love." Reaching over to hug him, she smiled. "Happy birthday, cousin. I have to go home and study for yet, another test."

"See ya, Anne. Oh, thanks for the gloves, they're great. Hopefully, I won't lose them before winter. And um, Anne? I just wanted to say—you were pretty professional out there. I hardly knew you were the same kid cousin I grew up with. I was even kind'a proud of you. Thanks for not laughing at what we just talked about."

"You don't laugh at people that you love, Pete. Not when it comes to something like that. You came for advice and I tried to answer you honestly, from my heart. I guess you got more than gloves for your birthday," she smiled. "You also got my version of your mom's words—of wisdom and love."

CHAPTER 14

LIFE GOES ON

Feeling like the rabbit from Alice in Wonderland, Anne hurried through the hospital's parking lot toward the street along side of its administration center. "Of all mornings to wake up late," she grumbled, raising her home-made calico purse from her side. Unsnapping the linen flap on the outer pouch, she brought it around, then peeked in, making sure the sharpened number two pencil was still there. Satisfied with a glimpse of yellow, she dropped in her keys, then snapped it shut. Being spurred by her race with time, she increased her speed as she walked, while repositioning her purse against her hip and adjusting its shoulder strap. In seconds, she had gone through each step as if planned, without pause or fumble, before sliding into the briskest stride her short legs could muster.

She had only gotten a few yards, it seemed, when the sound of an oncoming car caught her attention. Disappointed with the forced loss of momentum, she slowed down to a jog until she reached the curb then stopped. Releasing an earnest sigh, she impatiently waited on the older beige auto that steadily approached. With one foot abutting the curb in an eager stance, she subconsciously began drumming her fingers against her thigh, as she gazed at the hospital business entrance on the other side of the street, now just twenty or so feet away. Watching as the foyer door opened, she instantly recognized the hospital security guard as he stepped out, and began waving to draw his attention. Then, after realizing that the gesture was unnoticed, she decided to call out. Unfortunately, she was hampered by a soft timbred voice that normally didn't carry well. And now that the car, with its gentle rumbling, was nearly in front of her, she knew the odds of him hearing her were slim to nil. Still, she decided it was worth a try. Taking a deep breath, she pushed as hard as she could from her diaphragm, hoping that he just might hear as she yelled, "Hey Murphy!" But in spite of the honest effort, her words sadly seemed to spurt out and disappear. They just weren't strong enough to even faintly prick his ears or cause an urge to look around; so with that, she began to jump up and down a few times, while waving.

Suddenly, the sight of Anne's flailing arms finally caught his attention, reminding him of someone signaling from a deserted island. Amused by her comical behavior, he laughed, while bracing the door open with his foot. "Hey, Anne!" he called out, adjusting the tray held tight in his hands. "Say, aren't you supposed to be taking a test? You better hurry up. They're about to start. The girls've already cleared the coffee and donuts away. I've got the leftovers here for me and the boys," he graciously declared.

The engine noise from the faded beige car muffled his report as it passed between them, mixing with the music from a Mahalia Jackson tape and a splash of chattering from the two older black females within, dressed in their Sunday best. Drawn by the familiar tune, Anne struggled to read his lips, while enjoying a sprig of the church service she would miss that day. As soon as the street was clear, she scurried across, sprang up the steps and gave a shy cheer of success, while entering through the foyer door being held for her.

"They're on a different floor than you were on yesterday," the guard offered, using his head to point in the direction of the elevator. "You need to go to the third floor. They're in the conference center, first room on the right. Here, take a donut for later," he urged, holding out the tray.

"Thanks, Murphy," she said, picking up one of the plain fried cakes as she slipped by. "I missed breakfast."

"Good luck," he called out.

Unsnapping her purse, she quickly peeked in and laid the soft fragrant treasure onto a folded tissue, as she approached the elevator. After pushing the white plastic arrow, she checked her wrist for the time, then began tapping her foot, as she whispered, "Praise God, I still have ten minutes before the test starts." Nervously watching the numbers over the elevator door, she got ready to enter.

This was the last day of the ACLS course. In an effort to lower the number of premature cardiovascular deaths, the Lancemen County Medical Control Board enthusiastically accepted the program as a "from this day forth" practice and wasted no time in setting up the classes. They had determined that all hospital nursing personnel, physicians, and paramedics working within the county were henceforth, required to be certified in Advanced Cardiac Life Support, in addition to whatever licensure they currently held.

The two day ACLS course contained the standards that the National Conference on CPR and ECC developed in 1973. Their set of Standard Operating Procedures for treatment of sudden death were thoroughly reviewed during the first eight hour class, as well as rhythms associated with heart attack damage, airway control and oxygenation, defibrillation, synchronized cardioversion, and the pharmacological treatment for each rhythm.

The elevator indicator toned, announcing its arrival. Anne stepped closer in anticipation. She knew the treatment for cardiac disturbances hadn't changed much since she took her State Paramedic exam a few months ago; in that she had an advantage. Still, taking a test, no matter how prepared, always brought on a feeling of anxiousness.

Entering the elevator, she turned and pushed the button for the third floor while mentally dancing with the list of cardiac algorithms. After selecting one, she began reciting the treatment for the slow heart rhythm, known as bradycardia audibly to herself. "If the heart rate is fifty or below and the patient's blood pressure is low, or if premature beats are seen on the cardiac monitor, you should give the patient 0.5 milligrams of atropine IV. You can repeat the dose every five minutes if necessary, up to 2 milligrams, or until the heart rate increases to sixty or above, or until the systolic blood pressure is ninety or above. If no improvement is noticed, start an isopro-terenol drip of 1 milligram into 250 milliliters of D5W, which will produce a concentration of 4 micrograms per milliliter. Then infuse it piggy-backed with the IV already started by titration, at 2 to 20 micrograms a minute," she continued without pausing, as the elevator stopped at the third floor. "By that time, you should be arriving at the hospital with the patient who will need a pacemaker if he or she still shows no sign of improvement. And by that time I'll be relieved to be there, I'm sure," she murmured, walking into the conference room.

Taking a seat next to Roger, she took her pencil out of her purse.

"Nice that you could join us," he teased, seeing her somewhat ruffled state. "You missed the continental breakfast. I was beginning to think you chickened out."

"No, I woke up late. Then Pete called, with news from the home front. I'll tell you about it after the test," she replied, gently scratching the right side her head with the tip of her pencil.

Looking around the room, she recognized most of the people sitting at the tables that stretched end to end in several rows. Some were paramedics from Mercy Medical, but most of them were firemen, nurses, and physicians. And seemingly at that moment, they all appeared to be equal; for no gender or level of profession separated them. They were all waiting with pencil in hand, to take the same test.

While waiting on the instructor to pass out the written portion of the exam, Anne read over the syllabus that was handed out on the first day. Looking at the time slots listed, she noticed a short, half-hour break was scheduled to follow, offering a bit of a breather before the station testing began.

The most feared station by everyone was the Mega Code. In this station, the instructor displayed different selected cardiac rhythms on a simulator, while announcing changes in the would be patient's condition and vital signs. It was set up like a mock cardiac arrest scene, where the testee, working alone, was expected to orate all treatments, including drug and oxygen therapy, for each offered situation. The instructors, known to show no mercy as they went through the entire regimen, did so, knowing this information could make the difference between life and death. After all, that's why they were there—there would be no room for mistakes.

"Talk about mental exhaustion," Anne whispered to Roger, as she stepped out of the room after completing her Mega Code.

"How'd ya do?"

"I passed; but my mind froze for a second on some of those drip rate concentrations. The pressure is different in here than it is out in the field somehow. It was the same way when I took my State Board exam. Fortunately for me, I had an evaluator with a heart. He saw how nervous I was after I started babbling and sent me to get a cup of coffee. When I came back and restarted, I did fine. I remember the instructor laughed when he asked me, 'Why didn't you do that the first time?' That guy was a godsend, for sure."

"Well, take a breath and relax, the worst is over. I still have to do my airway management station. What do you have left?"

"Nothing. I'm done. Guess I'll go outside for a few minutes and get some air while I wait on you stragglers," she teased.

"Oh, lucky you," he grinned. Strolling toward the elevator, they noticed a group of classmates waiting to get on. "What'd you say we take the stairs. I don't feel like waiting."

"No problem," she replied, as she entered the stairwell. Grabbing onto the hand rail, she noticed an echo while stepping down onto the first couple of steps. The urge was too great to resist. Instantly, in response she gave in to a toe tapping dance on the metal grid riser, likening an old

Shirley Temple movie. As the resounding metallic tone from her shoes slapped against the steps, then bounced off the cement walls, Roger gibed, "I think you missed your calling."

Smiling, she continuing down the stairs, then paused at the second floor. "Here ya go, Rog. I'll see you back upstairs at one-thirty, when they hand out the test scores."

"Okay, Grace Kelly," he quipped. "I'll see ya later."

Anne apparently wasn't alone with the idea of spending a few moments under the early afternoon sun. Pushing the outside foyer door open, she took care as to not bump a small group of nurses sitting on the steps, each lighting a cigarette. Being outside helped her put time back into perspective, as she remembered she was scheduled to be at the Lakeview station later that day to start her forty-eight hour shift with Roman. Hopefully there would be time for lunch once they were dismissed. The mere thought of food produced a growling in her stomach, as she approached the wooden bench set on the stone patio. She felt a little embarrassed by the quiet demonstration of her missed breakfast. Then she remembered the donut Murphy gave her earlier. Bringing her purse around in front of her, she unsnapped it, then pulled the still intact treat from its nest of folded Kleenex. Taking a bite, she leaned against the brick wall as one of the nurses spoke up.

"Hey—don't you work for Mercy?"

Anne smiled, then nodded while trying to swallow a mouth full of donut before answering. "I work out of the Lakeview station."

"I thought so. They don't have many girls working there, do they?"

"No. I'm the only one so far."

"Well that could be heaven, or that could be hell. So how do you think you did on the test?"

Humored by her comment Anne smiled cordially, then answered. "Outside of the Mega Code, the test wasn't too bad. But I just got my Paramedic license a few months ago, so that helped. What'd you think of the test?"

"What I think is—is that half of the test is a waste of our time. Sticking a tube down a patient's throat is a respiratory therapist's job. We don't intubate and we never will, unless they're planning on paying us a respiratory therapist's wage on top of ours. Sh..o..o..t, girl!"

"She did just fine," one of the other nurses jumped in, chuckling at the abrasive response of her fellow worker. "Rhonda's just venting."

Anne smiled, relieved that she wasn't the real target being fired upon. "I'm not mad at you girl," Rhonda explained apologetically.

"Anne. My name is Anne," she volunteered, walking closer with her hand extended.

"Well Anne, you're new to this business, so maybe you don't know how the medical field works," the nurse returned the offer, shaking Anne's hand. "And I'm not saying it doesn't have its rewards. But it seems like somebody is always pushing for more. It's hard enough to keep up with the patient load as it is, plus all the other changes we have to keep up with. It's always one thing after another. That's all I'm saying."

"Well, I guess I'll have to deal with it as it comes. I'm in too deep to back out now," Anne smiled appeasingly.

"Now, don't let her make you think she doesn't like her job, Anne. She's a good nurse. By the way, I'm Vickie, this is Joan and the blond bombshell is Liz," she said, as each one stood to reenter the building. "It's just that this course was sprung on us, and we're all a little tired after working our midnight shift. But," she taunted, "the bright side of it is, if we ever get tired of nursing we can always become respiratory therapists—right Rhonda?"

"Hey, don't get me started again," Rhonda jokingly returned.

Walking into the cool air conditioned foyer brought an instant aware-ness as to how warm the afternoon had become. Roger met Anne at the stair doorway.

"I was just coming to get you."

"We were chatting about the test and sort of lost track of time."

"Yeah? Well, I say we get our grades and get out of here. I'm hungry and tired of being cooped up."

"My sentiments exactly," Anne joyously approved.

The certificates were passed out, with each of the testee's name typed on the front and a space provided for a signature on the back. After signing her card, Anne proudly slid it into her wallet next to her Paramedic license and joined the others, as the class filtered out of the hospital office building, making traffic on the side street wait as they crossed. Nothing was going to stop them from leaving, or slow them down in any way. Anne agreed to meet Roger, Jerry and some of the others at Neat Eats for a quick lunch. Food and a nap before starting her shift were the only things that seemed important now. Keeping a close eye on the time while eating her garden salad, minus the onions, Anne listened to the others talk about the test. Actually, and as general with every subject, the test shared the stage with each noted anatomical feature of every young female nurse and physician involved in the course. Although she had pretty much learned to tune out what she didn't want to hear, sometimes she found herself chuckling along with the comments too funny to ignore. She knew the guys took pleasure in using colorful adjectives and analogies to see her response. Just a blush of her face was usually enough to satisfy them. And then, there were times they would go on until she shook her head and laughed, while telling them how stupid they were.

"Man, did you check out that blond nurse with the twin mountains?" Pierce, a Lanceman fireman asked. "She reminded me of my last trip to Colorado."

"Her name is Liz," Anne offered, pleased that he had not yet embarrassed her.

"You know her?" he unexpectedly asked. "Annie. Annie, you've been holding out. That chick's hot! Man, I'd crawl through glass just to sniff her bicycle seat."

"Her bicycle seat?" Anne disgustingly asked. "Why would you want to sniff her bi….."

"All right. All right. That's more then I want to hear," Roger jumped in. "Trust me Anne, you don't want to know."

"So—are you going to introduce her to me?," Pierce continued, watching a flush spread over her face.

"No," she chided. "I just met her for the first time today. And even if I did know her, I sure wouldn't introduce her to you, after that comment."

"It's just a saying," he laughed, looking for support from his fellow amigos.

"You're on you're own," Jerry piped in, chuckling. "Personally, I thought that little redhead, Pat, was good looking. In fact, I've already got her number," he said, waving the slip of paper he pulled from his top pocket.

"You dog," Pierce enviously kidded.

"I can't believe you guys," Anne half teasingly spoke up. "We just completed a ACLS course, and you act like you just went to an auction."

"We were serious when we had to be. Then it was time for pleasure. Anne, haven't you learned that by now? Business before pleasure. We get the job done, then it's our time," Pierce cheered.

Anne glanced at Roger to see what comment he might offer. "Don't look at me. I'm married," he chuckled. Seeing her discomfort, he added. "They got you good this time, didn't they Anne?"

"Yea. Yea," she replied, bright red, feeling duped. "You just wait. There's going to be a time when you're going to need my help, and I'm going to make you sweat it out."

"But you're just such a good sport. We just can't help ourselves," Pierce teased, picking up her check. "Here, since you were so nice, I'll pay for lunch. How's that for a peace offering?"

"It's a start," she retorted, as they all stood to leave. Smiling, she left a tip, then walked to the door. "I'll see you guys later. I'm going home to try and catch a short nap before work tonight."

"Bye," they chorused, from the cash register line.

Anne felt refreshed after her brief rest, as she pulled on to the gravel driveway of the Lakeview station. Mechanically, she pulled her overnight and sleeping bag from the back seat. Walking toward the station door, she noticed Roman's car was the only one in the driveway. Maybe they were short staffed because of the ACLS course. Still, I can't imagine they'd down the rig, she curiously reflected, knowing that Merve would never allow that.

"Afternoon Anne," Roman greeted, as she entered the station. "How was ACLS?"

"Tiring, but we all passed."

"What a surprise. How could I have expected anything less?" came a jolt of unexpected sarcasm. Standing in front of the supply cabinet he began slamming boxes within the cabinet as he searched for unfound equipment. "What! Am I the only person who orders supplies around here?"

"Roman. You don't have to yell. Maybe they just haven't brought them out yet. Jerry told me during lunch, he ordered them last night."

"I bet—he did. He comes in here with this blue print plan on how to correctly order supplies, as if he was the company's financial advisor or something."

"Come on, Roman. There's no reason to act like that. He's not trying to make anyone look bad. It's a good plan. If anyone would welcome it, I'd think it'd be you. You're always complaining about overstock in the cabinet," she encouraged, setting her overnight bag on the sofa.

"Oh, so now we have miss goodie two shoes, throwing down with the debaser of women. Maybe you're not as pure as you pretend to be."

"Roman! What in the world's gotten into you? I've never seen you act like this before. Are you all right?"

"Yes—I'm all right!" he grunted, closing the cabinet door, empty handed. "Geez, quit looking at me like that. Okay—maybe my blood sugar's just low. What'd ya say we go to Charlie's."

"Sure. I'd be happy to. Just let me call in, and put my stuff on my bed. I'll make it up later."

Roman was anything but himself. Even after eating, he still seemed out of sorts. Anne watched as he reached into his shirt pocket and pulled out a small plastic bag of pills.

"Is your back hurting you again?" she asked with concern. Picking up a glass of water, he slid a small blue tablet into his mouth then washed it down.

"Yeah, as a matter of fact it is," he rumbled, annoyed by her question, "I helped my father-in-law move a bathtub into a two story house yesterday. Look, I don't feel like talking right now. As soon as this pain pill kicks in I'll be okay," he said, grabbing his check.

Without another word, Anne unbuttoned the pocket on her uniform shirt, then reached in and pulled out a small wad of one dollar bills. Counting out enough money to cover her meal, she picked up her check. Placing a tip for the waitress next to her glass, she got up and brushed the crumbs from her lap. Walking behind Roman she felt like the silent observer, puzzled at his behavior and wondered whether the medication he took for his back pain would effect his driving at a high rate of speed, in the event of a call.

He seemed to mellow over the next quiet few hours. And to Anne's relief while watching "Charlie's Angles," he made his usual comments as to what babes the stars were. Finally, he seemed like himself as they joked and talked, as if their earlier tiff never took place. Normally she would have been eager for a run. She enjoyed the challenge of the call, even if they weren't always true emergencies. But the calmness after ACLS was welcome, as well as the return of Roman's normal disposition.

This was the perfect time to catch up on a long overdue letter to Jenny, she thought as she sat at the kitchen table, waiting for the eleven o'clock news. She missed reading through the newspaper while at ACLS, and even though a large portion of the news wasn't good, she still liked keeping up on current events. Ted Bundy was still on the loose after his second Aspen jail break in December. New York, however, had their serial killer behind bars. The notorious ".44 Caliber killer", the "Son of Sam," was to be arraigned in a few days. "What a summer they've had," she commented to Roman, who was almost asleep on the sofa. "With the heat, the brown outs and looting," she went on softly, seeing the heaviness in his eyes.

"Makes you almost feel at home," he mumbled, displaying that he was still listening.

"All except the brown outs," she jokingly replied.

The newscaster went on to tell of the death of Julius Henry Marx, better known and loved by the world as "Groucho." He had passed away August 19th, at the ripe old age of 86; just a few days after the King of Rock and Roll was found deceased. Then, the anchor person relayed that the Republican Party was reported by a Gallup poll to have only 20 percent of the US voters' support, the lowest representation in 40 years.

"Who cares," Roman spoke up brashly. "Who's Gallop, anyway," he continued while sitting up, swinging his legs around, and setting his bare feet on the tiled floor. "I'm going to bed. Hopefully, I won't see you till morning, nothing personal. We've had such a slow day, I frankly don't think that's going to happen—but still, one can hope."

"Okay then. I'll see you whenever," Anne answered, getting up from the lounge chair to turn the TV off.

Well—he was right about their day together being slow, she thought. But the entire day had actually seemed much longer and busier to her. What seemed like a day to Roman, was really just a little more than five hours into their shift. Five hours hardly makes up a day, she thought, while brushing her teeth. Roman had been so moody lately, she knew he would not want to banter about time, even if it was just in fun. As she crawled into bed and looked across the room at Roman sleeping in his bed, she remembered how much fun he used to be, and wondered what changed him. There were times, more often lately, that he and his wife argued on the phone. He certainly wasn't as easy going like he used to be, but what concerned her more than anything, was the little blue pills. Roman, she decided, would be first on her prayer list as she turned out the light and settled in.

Even as a small child, each night after saying her formal prayers, as she called them, she would lie in bed and silently talk to God, as a friend talks to a friend. She truly understood that God was more than a high and lofty spirit watching over His children from a distance. For she felt Him in her very soul, dwelling within the secret place of her heart of hearts. Through every hour He was there, and tonight was no different. Once her concerns for Roman were laid out before Him, she drifted off to sleep.

Suddenly, the sound of a car hitting a telephone pole or a tree just outside woke Roman and her from a sound sleep, as they both sat up in a bolt.

"What was that?" she asked.

"I don't know, but it sounded close. Better get up and get dressed, I've got a bad feeling."

No sooner had he finished his sentence, when the phone rang. Grabbing his clothes, he rushed to the bathroom.

"We heard the crash, where are we going ?" Anne asked, tucking her navy shirt into her gray uniform pants. "He said it's on Dixie highway, by the carpet store," she called to Roman, while hanging up the phone.

After quickly slipping into her shoes, she tied each one, using the bed for support.

"That's at least two miles from here—and we heard it like it was next door? This is not going to be good," Roman said, grabbing the keys from the hook near the door.

Pulling out of the carport, he reached up and switched on the emergency lights. The dial on the radio glowed in the dark, grabbing Anne's attention. One-thirty, she thought, as they past the duck hatchery. It seemed much later. Approaching the railroad tracks, she felt like she was riding with Starsky and Hutch. Turning onto Dixie, they could see a single set of emergency lights ahead. Nearing the scene, she tried to mentally prepare herself for her duties as a Basic EMT.

"Let me know what you have, as soon as you can," came the dispatcher's voice. "I've got Life One standing-by if you need them."

"Ten four," Roman answered. Pulling up to the scene, he drove past the fire engine that had stopped north of the involved vehicles and carefully made his way around a light blue Fairlane that had severe front end damage. Then they noticed a shiny black Firebird just about a hundred feet away. Stopping on the opposite side of the car, they both stared in awe. Nothing could have prepared them for the cataclysmic enigma that their brain attempted to digest and their eyes saw in reality; for the Firebird was completely gutted. To their disbelief, the entire seating area and roof of the car was gone; neat and clean, as if it were never part of the car. Not a scratch was seen on the front or the back. The golden bird painted on the hood, was unmarred. Eerily, the headlights powered by the still running engine, shown brightly while offering a direction of the ejected passengers. Shining against the steep grassy hill below the railroad tracks, the incandescent beams revealed two supine, motionless bodies. Trying to bring herself back into a thinking mode, Anne called to Roman as she trotted toward the fireman who was standing beside the Fairlane. "I'll go and see what Brent's got, so we'll know if we need the Life Unit." Hearing her statement, Roman nodded while stepping over the debris in the road, as he made his way toward the two bodies on the hill.

Touching the fireman's shoulder as he backed out, Anne asked, "What do we got, Brent?"

"This guy's still alive—barely. Looks like he's got a massive head injury. She's dead," he said. Then he pointed in the direction of the front passenger, slumped against the window. Glancing at Brent's face and then at the two victims in the car, Anne noticed that his skin color was almost as pasty as theirs. "Looks like she flew right into the dash, belly first," he added. "I think she's pregnant, Anne. What do you think we should do with her?" Overhearing the end of Brent's report, Roman stepped around the car and announced that the two people on the hill were dead and that he had called for the Life Unit for the only surviving victim in the Fairlane.

"What about her?" Brent persistently asked, while holding the man's head and neck still.

"I thought you said she was dead?" Roman called back, as he opened the ambulance door.

"She is. But maybe we can save the baby!"

"I don't think we could do anything to save this baby, Brent," Anne sadly offered, standing next to the female patient. "She looks like she's at least, eight months along and her belly feels like Jell-O. Women that are this far in their pregnancy usually have a very firm tummy. I doubt she was even seat belted. With the speed and impact between these two cars, I bet the amniotic sac and uterus exploded on impact. We better just forget the baby and concentrate on keeping him alive," she answered. Swallowing a sick feeling, in order to maintain her expected professional role, she walked toward the driver side of the car.

Roman carried a backboard and straps, while walking toward the demolished blue auto. Handing Anne the foam cervical collar he had tucked under his arm, he began to captain his crew. "Okay, let's get him ready. Anne, once you have the collar in place, dress the head lacerations. I brought you some four-by-fours and gauze," he said, pulling a couple rolls and packaged sterile pads from his pocket. "I need to go talk to the cop. I'll be right back."

Taking the equipment from Roman's hand she noticed him reaching for his shirt pocket as he turned to walk away. Brent continued to hold the semiconscious victim's neck still, while she secured the Velcro piece of the collar in place. The large clots that had started to form over the deep cuts across his face helped to control the bleeding as she encircled his head with the rolled gauze, taping it in place. Roman came behind her with the backboard and began sliding it underneath the groaning patient. Then out of nowhere it seemed, a woman's voice interrupted the extrication.

"I'm a nurse. I can help. What's wrong with your patient?" she asked in a tone that suggested she was taking charge.

"Thanks," Roman barked, not conceding control, "but our Life Unit's seconds away." Supporting the patient's upper body, Anne and Brent lowered him onto the long backboard. Roman held the head of the board until Brent came out from the back seat area and took a corner. The Life Unit was in sight.

"You people are doing it wrong. Listen to his airway. He needs to be suctioned," the nurse bellowed.

"Thanks for the suggestion, Ms. nurse, but I think we can handle it. We have all the airway equipment we need in the ambulance and can intubate the patient, which is more than you can do," Roman roared, as the crew from the paramedic rig pulled up and jumped out. Jack, one of the paramedics, brought the stretcher and rolled it under the backboard while listening to Roman's report. The nurse stormed off, flushed, throwing out threats of informing her hospital's Chief of Staff Physician of their ill treatment.

"Is she talking about ill treatment to her, or the patient?" Jack chuckled, seeing an equally red glow on Roman's face.

"She doesn't know what she's talking about," he jeered, as they rolled the stretcher toward the Life Unit.

The doors of the ambulance were open as they came around to the back, revealing a hulk like figure, that partially blocked the light from the patient compartment. Jack's partner, Rick, had to lean over while working in the back of the unit, due to his size. Standing in the doorway while gripping the intubation equipment in his large hands, he looked just like a giant crouched in a child's toy car. But in spite of his height of six foot four inches, he was thin enough to move around well within the confined space. Behind him, a pre-spiked IV bag of Lactated Ringers hung from a latch hook on the wall, on the patient side beneath the ceiling. The color coated EKG leads were snapped onto the electrodes and lying on the bench seat ready for placement. In the background, the gentle humming of the suction unit could be heard drawing air.

"Let's rock and roll," he said curtailing a smile, while not abandoning the need to move quickly in an effort to save the man's life. They knew the importance of time. And while precious minutes had already slipped away during the extrication, they hoped to regain some of that by starting the same treatment the ER would initiate, only they could begin the treatment now. Anne watched as they worked like clockwork. In seconds, the patient's breathing was being assisted through an ET tube and the IV of Lactated Ringers was running wide open. Jack jumped out of the back and scooted around to the driver's side. Then they were off—lights bouncing off the night sky, buildings and trees, the same way they had before, when she and Dan responded to an accident in the same area a few months ago.

Anne stood and watched as they drove away. "Come on," Roman sighed. "We still have work to do here. Get out the folding cot and grab the metal hooks. We'll load the guy from the hill, onto the bench seat.

Then we'll put the woman he was with onto the folding cot and hang that from the ceiling. The other woman from the Fairlane can go on the stretcher. They all still have to go down to the hospital to be pronounced dead officially, before the ME sees them."

The petrified faces of the deceased persons lying on the hill were that of terrible fear. Standing between them on the grassy bank, Anne surveyed the ghastly, hollow masks of death that marked the impending doom they witnessed in their final moments of life.

"In all the years that you've been around this, Roman," knowing he had worked at a funeral home before coming into EMS, "have you ever seen expressions frozen on someone's face like this?" Anne asked, in a sorrowful tone, partially, trying to make sense of the accident and partially trying to seek comfort in Roman's expertise. "These people saw the accident coming," she continued, while helping to roll the man's body onto the backboard, before sliding him onto the bench seat. "It looks like the blue car drove right through the Firebird. It must have been airborne!"

"I'm sure once the cops are done with their investigation, we'll know soon enough."

"I feel bad for their families," she continued, stirred by the tragedy.

"You're not going to start crying, are you?" Roman snapped. "If you want to boo hoo over every dead body we see, you can find someone else to work with...."

"I'm not boo hooing," Anne butted in, surprised by his jab, "I just made a statement. They're dead, and I'm sure that there are people who are going to be sad, at the very least. I am just empathizing with their families, that's all."

Roman pretended to ignore her explanation while looking for the fireman. Anne knew he heard every word she said, but decided that this was not the place to push the issue; it was best to let it be.

After strapping the second stiffened body onto the portable cot, Roman looked over as Brent walked past talking with the accident investigator. "Hey, Brent, come on over here and help us hang this cot from the ceiling hooks, so we can load the other two." The tone in his voice was that of controlled resentment. This was not by any means, Roman's normal disposition. She and Roman had always gotten along so well. Now he acted as if he hated being around her.

As Brent made his way through the weedy hill, Anne fought the compelling desire to ask Roman about the pill she was sure he took when they first arrived on the scene. He just started taking the pain pills a few weeks ago when he strained some muscles. He wasn't a drug addict. He drank vodka sometimes, she knew, and remembered that once he drank too much at a wedding before coming in to dispatch mid-nights. After he passed out, the other guys just rolled the chair he was in out of the way and filled in so Merve wouldn't know. Other than that, he just took an aspirin occasionally for a headache. So why now, the sudden dependency on the pills?

Once the last hook was securely holding the hanging cot in place, Anne made her way to the back of the rig and jumped out. Without a word, she helped Roman unload the stretcher as they steered toward the other bodies. Brent continued to help, while studying Roman's sedate mood.

"You all right, Roman?" he asked. "I know this isn't pleasant, man, but I know you've seen worse."

"I'm just tired and my back's sore."

"Why don't you have one of the doc's take a look at you while you're at the hospital?"

"Yeah, maybe I will," he answered in a discounting way, lifting the last corpse into the rig.

After shutting the back doors, Anne walked around to the passenger side, got in and started to buckle her seat belt. Roman opened the driver's door and grabbed the steering wheel to use it like a winch to bring himself up.

"Why are you sitting up in the front?" he asked stoically. "You're supposed to ride in the back with the patients."

"Roman, they're dead… they don't need me back there," she responded miffed, and puzzled by his question. Seeing that his stance was unmoved, she undid her seat belt in protest. "Fine! I'll sit on the seat in the sectional with my feet in the back, but that's it. There's nowhere else to sit back there anyway," she spouted, while climbing over the seat in the middle of the sectional that divided the front and rear compartments.

With her back to Roman and both feet on the floor, she once again glanced over the victims and wondered who made the wrong and perilous move. Although they were covered, the jiggling belly of the woman from the Fairlane was still just as clear as the mental picture of the other two's horrified expressions. As she looked out of the side window in an effort to release the image from her mind, she offered up a silent prayer for each of their families.

"I'm not trying to be hard on you, Anne," Roman spoke up, in a gentle tone, "I just want you to understand what you're getting into. Anyway, this is stupid. Taking dead people to the hospital never made sense to me. They aren't going to do anything but say the obvious. Then the ME will have to come and take them to do an autopsy. I don't understand why he just doesn't come to the scene and take them. You know the company only gets twenty-five dollars for each removal we do. We do it as a favor for the funeral homes and the ME's office. Politics. But hopefully, now that the Life Units are starting up, we'll eventually dump this part of the job onto someone else. I think that once Merve sees all the money he could be making on emergencies, instead of tying up his units up on these twenty-five dollar removals, he'll back out. He's a smart businessman, and he's tactful."

Anne recognized the change in Roman's manner as he spoke. While backing into the ambulance entrance, she decided this had to stop. She had to find a way to talk to him about the pills and his mood swings. And she had to get it across to him that she wasn't a rookie anymore. She'd worked with Chris and Dan on some pretty good calls. There was no reason why she, or anyone else for that matter, should have to sit in the back of the ambulance with a deceased person.

Standing as they stopped, she walked between the bodies toward the back doors, then opened them. Dr. Frank stood on the bay's deck and stared at the bodies, even though he had been notified they were coming in.

"They're all dead? Do the police know what happened yet?" he asked, astounded by the deaths of so many, from one single auto accident. Studying his surprised and saddened posture, Anne felt relieved and grateful that she was not alone in her earlier pitiful statement. For this was a man who she knew had seen his share of surreal and tragic cases throughout his many years as an emergency room physician. Yet he clearly and unapologetically voiced his compassion, rather than just dismiss them as mere dead bodies, as Roman suggested she do. I know Roman is trying to create an emotional environment that I can work in, she thought, as they pulled the body of the pregnant woman out of the back of the ambulance. But these were people—not the skin shed from a snake, or any other thing meant to be discarded as if no longer worthy of thought or love. It was clear, as she watched the reaction of the ER staff, that apathy was certainly no more the answer than caring to the point of mental upheaval. She knew there must be a happy medium where she could be sympathetic of each patient's situation, and yet, still hold them distant enough to remain professional. In time, she decided, she would find that place. Or maybe she was all ready there.

After unloading the other two victims, Anne stood upright in the back of the ambulance, unhooking the metal cot that supported the last casualty. She remembered how Rick had to lean over, in order to work in the patient compartment. Breaking the silence of her own deep thought, she looked at the helpful orderly as he gripped the opposite end of the metal frame and nonchalantly announced, "I guess there are some advantages to being short." Smiling at her remark, he took a few steps backwards as they lowered the female corpse onto the hospital stretcher, that was set up behind him.

The ambulance bay, sat in an alcove on the east side of the hospital. For the most part, it offered protection from inclement conditions, but it wasn't wind proof. It wasn't unusual for a brisk huff of wind to whirl through, leaving spent cigarette butts and other litterish type objects from the nearby sidewalk, in small neat piles tucked in the corners of the hospital's brick wall. As Anne stooped down to place her end of the cot onto the waiting stretcher, a sudden gust whipped into the wind drawn bay. Then another yet stronger gust whistled in, catching the paper sheet that was draped across the victim's body and sent it sailing into the air. In response, the orderly squeezed his eyes shut to protect them from the flying dirt. Then as soon as the wind died down, he blinked a few times to rinse away any dust particles, only to find himself looking into the stone face of the corpse before him, still etched in gruesome fright. Gaped in near revolt, he froze momentarily.

"Oh geeze! How fast were they driving?"

"I don't know if it was speed or what caused it," Anne replied, "but obviously, somebody messed up. It was the bizarrest thing I've ever seen, that's for sure."

Finally, the unhappy task was finished, and only the cleaning remained. Anne sprayed disinfectant over the stretcher and folding cot while Roman wiped down the bench seat and walls in the patient area. After putting the metal cot and hooks away, she helped him load the stretcher. Walking back through the ER, Roman tossed the used towels in the hospital's soiled linen tub, then joined Anne in the nurses lounge for one last refill of coffee. Sipping her cup as they left the hospital, Anne followed Roman through the ER doors out to the ambulance bay.

"How'd the other guy do? Did Dr. Frank say?" she asked.

"He said he didn't think he was going to make it. He's still in surgery."

"I wonder were the Life Unit is. They did a good job."

"Yeah, they worked quick," Roman said, perched on his seat, feeling for his seat belt, "but it didn't matter. Not this time anyway. Well, the sun will be up soon. How about breakfast?"

"Sure. I'm not really hungry, but toast and coffee sounds good."

"Unit Four is finally clear," Roman said, holding the mic near his mouth.

"Good," the dispatcher returned, in a tone that said breakfast was on hold. "You're right on top of a call on Pelton."

"Go ahead." Roman replied.

"You're responding to 392 Pelton, for a woman in labor. LFD's on the way. Your incident number is 960, at 03: 47."

After returning the mic to its holder, Roman reached into his shirt pocket and pulled out an empty plastic baggy. Releasing a snort, he stuffed the bag back into his pocket and pulled out a pack of cigarettes. Anne watched in silence from the corner of her eye, as he put a cigarette to his lips then rolled his thumb over the lighter wheel. She knew they were only minutes away from the call address. There was no time to talk. After pulling up behind the Lanceman fire truck, they stopped. She got out and opened the side doors then grabbed the handle of the orange box. Walking into the front door of the given address, they listened for voices to follow. The squawk of a fire radio led them down the hall to an open door of a small apartment in the back of the unkempt building. As they entered the front room, the strong odor of dust, mold, mildew and everything else unwashed, hit them like a slap in the face. Then they saw the firemen surrounding a woman who was lying on the sofa. Her legs were spread apart, and her knees bent, to accommodate the birth of the child whose coming was imminent.

Pierce was with the group of fireman on the scene. Looking up, when Roman and Anne entered the room, he picked up the obstetric kit and handed it to her. "Boy, am I glad you're here. I don't know nothin bout birthin babies," he feebly joked as the sweat rolled down his face. Anne opened the kit, then the package of sterile gloves while firing off questions of the woman's prenatal history.

"Is this her first pregnancy? How far apart are her contractions? Did her water break?"

"I don't know. She won't talk," Pierce said. "She's had this glazed stare on her face ever since we got here. I think she's high on something."

Tucking the sheet from the OB pack underneath the patient's buttocks, Anne was puzzled by the dark substance smeared on the patient's inner thigh. Then immediately a bulge of the vaginal opening gave proof that the baby was coming now, and that nothing else mattered. She expected the crowning to present the top of the baby's head, but instead it revealed a little round bottom pushing through. "She's breeched," she softly announced, somewhat disturbed, while gently pushing her right hand against the perineum. Supporting the infants buttocks as it slid out onto her left hand, she realized the dark substance was stool from the baby and that it should have been her first clue to the breech birth.

Throughout the whole ordeal, the mother showed absolutely no reaction or awareness of the delivery. One by one, the baby's legs dropped onto Anne's hand; first the left leg then the right. Soon the torso, arms and shoulders cleared the pelvic opening. Everything was going slow and smooth; but still Anne's stomach was in knots. After feeling around the neck for the umbilical cord, an increased anxiousness stirred within, as she noticed the baby's head was not making any progress in the delivery. The urge to help and gently tug on the body, as they did with the animals on the farm, was growing. But she quickly erased that thought from her mind. Then the infant became limp, and she knew that she and the baby were in trouble. She could feel the sweat streaming down her face as she gulped hard, then sighed. Cradling the body of the infant on her right arm, she slid a couple of fingers into the pelvic opening, to find it's mouth to provide an airway. Sweet Jesus, she silently prayed, please help us with this baby. I don't want to see death's face again tonight. Roman watched her from behind, instructing the woman to push. Pierce wasted no time calling the hospital for suggestions. The room swelled with tension and perspiration in the few minutes that they were actually there; though it seemed like hours.

"The doc says to make an airway with your fingers," Pierce cried out from the other side of the room, cupping his hand over the receiver.

"She all ready did that," Roman called back. "It seems like it worked—at least the baby's not flaccid, anymore."

The sweat burned Anne's eyes, as another bead rolled down her face. She felt exasperated. "Ask them—What should I do next?" she sighed.

Without waiting for an answer, Roman reached down and grabbed each side of the woman's hips and pulled her closer to the edge of the sofa. Her legs dropped further apart, and in an instant the baby's head was expelled.

"Praise God!" Anne cheered, cradling the baby as he took his first honest breath. Roman applied the clamps to the cord, then cut between them. Anne picked up the suction bulb from the pack, squeezed it flat to eject the air, then slid the tip into the infant's tiny mouth. A frown took over the pale little face, forcing a crimson glow to replace it. Simultaneously, it united with the most joyous sound that could pour from this little one who cried out as if angry, while relief and smiles filled the room.

"You have a little boy," Pierce told the mother of the child, who looked at him without reflection. "And I'd say he's ticked," he laughed, as if unaffected by her aberrancy. "You did all right, Anne. You seemed a little nervous when his head was stuck, but other than that, you were pretty steady."

"You're just still trying to make up for yesterday. I have never been so scared in my life," she grinned unashamed. "Roman's the one who's the hero here."

Pushing the stretcher next to the sofa to bring the mother over, Roman offered her an easy and genuine smile. "No—you're wrong, Annie. I have to give the credit to my days of adolescence—and Mary Lou. We spent a lot of time on the sofa in their cottage."

"Well, I think we can probably let that remain an obvious, pleasant memory if you don't mind," Anne suggested. The firemen laughed, humored by her comment.

"Do you want to move her over, or wait for the placenta to deliver?" Pierce asked.

"That could take twenty minutes or so. It's more for her comfort anyway and she doesn't seem to even be here. The baby looks good now, but he could have aspirated some of that gunk. I say we just go. LOH is just up the road," Anne replied.

"Sounds good to me. I sure don't want to hang around here if I don't have to."

Anne held the baby while Pierce and the others helped Roman put the mother on the stretcher, then load her into the ambulance. She talked to the mother while en route to the hospital and noticed no change in her mental status. "Your mama is sure going to be surprised to see you, little one," she sadly whispered, holding an oxygen tubing in front of the infant face.

St. Luke's was a just few minutes farther away than LOH, and since they specialized in babies, Roman suggested they go there instead. The nurses oohed and aahed as they wheeled the mother and baby through the doors. In a short time they realized the mother was out of it. "Oh, he's going to have a great life," one of them said, "poor baby." Once they finished touching each tiny toe and finger, Anne and Roman proceeded to wheel the stretcher to labor and delivery for the yet to come placenta.

"You know you'll have to come back and sign the birth certificate, don't you?" the nurse on the floor advised.

"Anne can do that," Roman offered. "She was the one wearing the catcher's mitt."

"Well whoever you decide, you'll have to go to the records department tomorrow."

Anne threw the bloody paper sheet away, then washed her hands. The warm water and soap was refreshing, as its clean aroma greeted the hairs in her nose. Boy, a hot shower would sure feel nice, she thought. Her mind began to drift, then she sensed Roman walking up behind her.

"Save some water for the fish," he joked. "I'd like to wash my hands too." She smiled, then grabbed a handful of paper towel. "Sorry," she said, wiping her hands. Turning around, she noticed that Roman had already made the stretcher. He even put a clean pillow case on the pillow. How different he seemed, she thought. He was in one of the best moods she'd seen in weeks. She knew he was out of the blue tablets. Maybe he picked up something at the patient's house. They never did find out what she was on for sure. No! She told herself, Roman would never stoop to that.

"Well since you all ready took a bath while hogging the sink, what do you say we stop by the station so you can change out of those nasty, rather pungent clothes, and try for breakfast again," he suggested, while drying his hands.

"I'm for that," she cheered. Wheeling the stretcher out of the labor department toward the elevator she looked back at her partner. "You know, Roman, we can both put our names on the birth certificate. After all, you were the one who got his head to slide out."

"No," he said, entering the elevator, "I wouldn't feel right about taking the credit without putting Mary Lou's name there too. I don't want to confuse the kid. By our names, he'll see that a couple of EMTs helped bring him into the world. And then he'll see Mary Lou's and wonder what in the world did she have to do with it. No, it's better if just you sign it," he concluded. They walked down the hallway on the main floor, past the ER toward the garage.

"What did you think they'll do with the baby?" Anne asked, her words slightly echoing off the bare garage walls, as they loaded the stretcher.

"They'll either call social services, or give the baby back to her," he answered, while taking his cigarettes out of his pocket. After tapping the bottom of the pack against the palm of his hand he pulled one out, then held it between his teeth while flicking the lighter. The smoke from the burning paper and tobacco stung the membranes of Anne's nares as it drifted in front of her.

"Just so you know, Ms. Angela from Kansas," he started, using her pet name as he always did when teasing her about her farm life, "I'm done with the pills. I've been taking them longer than what you think, and after watching that poor excuse for a mother today, I decided, no more. I don't want to end up like her—or any of these other dirt bags we run on," he said, turning his head while exhaling his last drag, before throwing the half smoked cigarette on the garage floor. Grabbing the steering wheel of the ambulance he pulled himself up and got in. "I know I've been a jerk lately, and just between me and you, my old lady's about to kick me out. I'm gonna talk to Merve about taking some time off. He's pretty cool about this stuff. I don't want to lose my job or my wife. I'll tell the guys myself... otherwise rumors will be flying. And you know how their imaginations work," he chuckled, as the weight of saying it out loud somehow offered light to the dim tunnel.

"What a roller coaster ride you've been on, Roman," she said, studying his face. His bloodshot eyes peered over the drab skin, that was normally well toned and clean shaven. "I know that I'm naive about a lot that goes on out here, and I don't know how hopeful, or hopeless you feel. But I remember reading once, that life begins on the other side of despair," she said, while they drove back to their area. "Sort of like, when we were struggling to help that baby. I was almost ready to just pick up and go to the hospital—even if I had to kneel with my fingers in the baby's mouth the whole way. Talk about despair. But as soon as he let out that sweet cry, all hopelessness was gone. It even took some of the gloominess of the deaths from that car accident away. I will always remember this day, and the strong character of that baby. He hung in there. In fact, if I had any say in it, I would give him a name to reflect his character. My friend Jenny and I used to go through books and pick out all the names of the children we planned to have, while mapping out ours lives. I always liked the name of Carroll Erin, for a boy."

Roman immediately turned toward her and grinned. "No man is going to let you name his son Carroll."

Laughing, she explained, "Carroll is a Gaelic name. It means "champion and steadfast." Both of those describe that baby. It didn't matter what else was going on—that baby was waiting to meet the world. And thanks to Mary Lou," she grinned, "and a little prayer, meet the world he did. His coming into the world has already made an impact on both of our lives, though in a different way. Who knows, maybe his mother will turn her life around. Or maybe he'll be adopted out. I remember our Pastor saying that a baby is a demonstration of God's opinion that life should go on. Last spring at home, when all the calves and colts where being born, I remembered what he said. It made sense, that God planned all that happened at

Calvary in the spring. What better demonstration could He give, that life should go on than to offer it eternally? Being part of that birth today was great—once it was over," she chuckled. "Yes sir, Carroll Erin, has already proved himself worthy and that in spite of many things, life goes on."

CHAPTER 15

ഇറ

GROWING PAINS

James Riddle Hoffa, was born on Valentines Day in 1913. He was a grade school drop out, who as a teenager in the 1930s, began building the Teamsters union practically alone. His rough and stalwart negotiating techniques made some view him as a union hero, while others believed him to be a criminal, and alleged that he was linked to organized crime. In 1967, he was sentenced to serve 13 years in federal prison for tampering and mishandling the Teamster's union pension. After serving a mere fraction of his sentence, it was commuted by President Nixon and he was set free on December 24, 1971. Three years later, he announced his plans to regain some of the control of the union he had built; although then it was being run by his adversary Frank Fitzsimmons. On July 30, 1975, it became clear that his plans were not to someone's liking, for on that day he disappeared from the parking lot of the well-to-do restaurant, Machus Red Fox, in Bloomfield Township and never returned to his Lake Orion home.

Anthony Giacalone, believed to be a captain of organized crime from Detroit, was supposed to meet Jimmy that day, leading many to speculate that the Mafia had a hand in his vanishing. In no time, rumors flew as to where his remains could be found. It was said in jest that he was a pillar in his community about the same time that the Renaissance Center in Detroit was being built, suggesting that he was part of the cement work.

A variety of strong emotions drew from just speaking the name of Jimmy Hoffa, as if by definition; for it was always associated with the word, union. Even in his absence, his deep seeded creation continued and was evident in some of the recruiting characteristics of his local. Some saw it as a necessary evil, so to speak; while others held to a different, less aggressive approach. As a result, an invisible line rapidly formed dividing the two modes, so strong in position and sensitivity that it resembled the passion that poured out of the Northern and Southern States more than a hundred years earlier.

Although different in magnitude by far, Lancemen County was also divided between the north and the south, at least as far as the private ambulance service went. Townsdale EMS remained in the southern sector of the county with Mercy Medical Service still covering the northern portion. Even though the boundaries of response for the two companies hadn't changed, the population within both areas clearly had experienced a growth spurt. The most evident shift was seen in the northern end of the county, for without question the rural appearance and the small farm life style, was fading.

From the moment the two companies merged they were run as sisters, established under one umbrella. Unfortunately, as it sometimes goes with families, they soon discovered that they had discrepancies that brought strife. Initially, only sentiments of sibling rivalry emerged as the employees realized that each company's medics, had their own way of running a medical and their own way of working with the area municipalities. Then, as the union began making its way into the world of EMS, the border that divided the two sisters became as wide as the Great Wall of China. Early on, Jimmy Hoffa's Teamsters approached the employees to join their union; but Townsdale decided instead to go with MATA, Michigan Ambulance Technician Association. Whereas Mercy Medical Service, following many harsh discussions that piqued the employees, decided to form their own association. There was no question about it, the employees at the two companies had different ideals. Mercy's employees were happy to work toward changes, slow but sure; while Townsdale's people had a more aggressive tenet and were now willing to risk it all in a wild cat strike.

Anne and her new partner, Buster Johnson, pulled up and parked next to the garage at St. Luke's.

"Unit Two arrival," Anne advised, keying the radio mic.

"Give me a TX, ASAP," Tom's voice returned through the radio speaker.

"Well, Buster, what do you think? Should I go and sign the birth certificate, or call first?" she asked.

"You go ahead and go down to records. I'll call and see what Tom wants," he offered.

"Thanks—I'd hoped you'd say that. I'll try to hurry."

Roman was given the few weeks off he'd asked for and since it was almost time to rotate the crews anyway, Anne started working out of the Lanceman station early. Her new partner, who recently switched from working at Townsdale EMS to Mercy, would just be temporary until Roman returned. Buster had worked as an EMT for about a year and so far he had been fun to work with. Anne liked his sense of humor and effortless laugh that demonstrated his enjoyment of life. He was a baseball enthusiast, and while she herself didn't know much about the game, she always liked playing it at home with the boys. With them, all she had to do was just swing the bat toward the ball and if she hit it, they would tell her when to run or when to stay in place. She wasn't interested so much in the rules or the competition of the sport; she just liked having fun. Still, the little information she remembered was enough for a common interest conversation with her new partner.

Content with her completed task, Anne strolled back into the hospital's ER and headed for the nurse's lounge. Opening the door, she found Buster somberly drinking a cup of coffee.

"You look like you just lost your best friend. What did Tom have to say?" she asked.

"I don't know if my move up here was a good or bad idea. Townsdale's going on strike. They called the company at noon today to tell them. Tonight at midnight—they're all walking off."

"You're kidding. What's going to happen to the people who need an ambulance in their area?"

"They're going to get us. Tom said the company will pay anyone who goes down there double time."

"How's everybody feel about that?"

"He said most of the guys up here want the money. But I'm stuck in the middle. What am I supposed to do now? Those guys are still my friends. I don't want to scab against them!"

"Well, I could use the money for sure, but you and I are partners and if you don't want to go down there...."

"Let's just play it by ear," he sighed. "Did you sign the certificate?"

"Yeah. They liked the name I picked out and said they'd write it in, as his name. Whoever adopts him, of course, can change it if they want."

"What about his mother?"

"She died of a drug overdose, just a few hours after they arrived here."

"Well this day is just one ray of sunshine after another. They'll probably have to dry that kid out before someone adopts him. Hopefully, he'll do all right; unless he gets stuck with some couple who makes him eat crap, like beets and brussels sprouts."

"I like beets."

"Yeah, well do me a favor and don't eat them in front of me," he grinned. Setting his Styrofoam cup on the counter, he picked up the coffee pot for a refill. The coffee looked as dark as ink as he poured it from the stained metal pot. "Just what I needed," he said, bringing the cup up to his face, taking in the strong aroma of the dark steamy Java. "Cowboy coffee. Coffee that's been on the range all day." Without hesitation he brought the cup to his lips and drew-in a large gulp. The coffee was apparently hotter than expected, from the wincing face he made while painfully swallowing the hot liquid. "Wow! The first cup wasn't that hot. Well, I guess we can't hide in here forever. Better get out there and see what's going on."

A squeal erupted from the hand held radio. "Unit Two, are you clear? I have a code three on Nevada Street for a seizure."

"Ten four for Unit Two. We're on the way out," Buster answered.

Dawn, one of the ER nurses, entered the lounge. "You guys got a call?" she asked.

"Yeah, for a seizure, just a few streets away," Anne replied. "We'll probably be back."

Taking the side streets, Buster headed toward Nevada Lane. Anne began reading the numbers on the houses, then stopped after noticing a woman up ahead, jumping up and down while waving her arms.

"Bet it's up there," she smiled.

"I can already tell," he groaned. "As soon as we pull up, she's going to start yelling—what took you so long?"

"Most people up here are just glad to have the help," Anne replied. "It's like we're the cavalry or something."

After stopping in front of the house, Anne got out of the rig and grabbed the orange box from the side compartment. Buster took one of the small oxygen cylinders and followed Anne toward the olive green bungalow. They entered through the back door near the kitchen. "Hello," Buster called out. "Mercy Ambulance." Instantly, Anne noticed a scorched odor drawing her attention to a pot that had boiled itself dry on the stove. It seemed almost angry to her, for being left unattended as it spewed its last few drops of liquid onto the hot burner. Without hesitation, she reached over to turn the knob to the off position then moved the empty pot to the back burner, with a near-by potholder. A woman jaded in appearance, dashed into the room.

"Oh god I got so scared, I forgot about our lunch," she said. Her voice quivered as she spoke. "It's been months since my son had a seizure. He's in here."

Without delay, they followed the woman across the dull but clean, tiled kitchen floor into the living room. A young child about two years old, laid motionless on the sofa. They drew closer to examine him. Suddenly, he arched his back and became rigid. Then, each extremity gave in to an uncontrolled tonic, clonic jerking. Tears streamed down the woman's face. Anne moved closer to the child to keep him from falling off the sofa. Buster reached into the orange box for a bite block. The child's teeth were clenched tight. Normally, they tried to insert the soft Styrofoam block into the seizing patient's mouth to keep him from biting him tongue. They had learned as far back as their first aid class that the story of a patient swallowing his or her tongue was just a myth, unless, of course, the patient bit off part of it while convulsing. Supporting the child to prevent injury, they watched as the seizure eased.

"He feels hot." Anne said, wiping the saliva from the corner of his mouth with a gauze square. "How long has he been running a temp?"

"Not long. I gave him a couple of baby aspirin about a half hour ago."

Buster held the oxygen mask in front of the child's face. "Is he on medication for his seizures?"

"No. He had a couple of seizures before—when he was sick with the flu. They did some tests on him, but never did say what was wrong. It scares me to death. Sometimes he looks like he's not even breathing."

"Well, it's normal for a seizure patient to stop breathing for thirty seconds or so," Anne explained. Taking the lightweight blanket from the back of the sofa, she scooped the child up into her arms. "But then," she continued, "they start breathing again on their own. That's why we put them on oxygen; to replenish what they lose during the seizure. We really need to try to break this temp. If you get a container of cool—not cold water—and a wash cloth that we can take to the hospital, I'll work at bringing his fever down on the way."

"Oh," the mother said, puzzled. "I always use ice to cool him down. Is that wrong?"

"Well, if he cools down too fast, then he'll start to shiver. That's the body's way of warming itself, when it feels cold, and that would just make him hotter. Cooling him down gradually is better."

"I see. I'll be right back with the water."

"What hospital do you want us to take him to?" Buster asked, assuming the mother wanted the child transported.

"Oh, St Luke's. That's where his doctor is." Anne took the damp cool cloth from the pan of water and tucked it under the child's armpits. Holding him securely in her arms, she walked toward the back door. A half worried, half at peace mother quickly searched for her purse and keys. In seconds she was behind the crew.

"I get to ride with him—don't I?" she asked.

Buster set the pan of water on the bench seat of the rig. "Sure, but you have to ride up in the front. Anne will stay with him. Don't worry—you can still see him. The insurance company only allows patients and staff to ride in the back," he explained, sounding like a stewardess giving preflight instructions.

Readjusting the young bundle in her arms, with Buster's help Anne stepped up into the ambulance. Then, after placing him on the stretcher, she noticed his eyes flutter, as he strained to get his bearings. In seconds, the exhaustion from the activity of the febrile convulsion took over, and he willingly gave in to sleep. During the short trip to the hospital, she learned the child's name was Andy. Loosening the rest of his clothes, she dipped the cloth back into the water, then squeezed as much out as she could before draping it over his legs. Throughout the transport, she half listened as the dispatch radio barked out one call after the other. Tom's voice was bringing its usual magic of turning a quite easy day into controlled chaos.

Hours had passed since young Andy's midday seizure. Auto accidents, strokes, a possible broken arm at a play ground, a factory worker with chest pain and a couple of nursing home transfers had filled the day up to and even past dinner. Throughout the day, Anne and Buster crossed the path of other road crews who were just as busy. They chuckled and groaned while all voicing the same cry—get Tom off the radio! Dinner ended up being a burger and fries from a drive-through restaurant, crammed in between two back to back nursing home transfers and a body removal. Now as the wiped out twosome entered the station, they entertained visions of a quiet night.... Tom had gone home.

"I cannot believe that one person can sit down behind a radio console and have the same crazy effect, every single time! Where did you guys get him from?" Buster asked, in playful reproach.

"He was already here when I arrived," Anne chuckled. Tired and worn, she unlaced her shoes while leaning against the arm of the sofa. "Hey, it's after midnight. I wonder if Townsdale went on strike like they said."

"I don't know, and right now I don't care. I'm going to bed. Do you sleep on the top or the bottom bunk?"

"It doesn't matter, I guess. We didn't have bunk beds at the Lakeview station."

"In that case—you get the top," he said yawning.

Anne finished brushing her teeth, then turned off the bathroom light. Looking into the dark living room, she stepped forward then stopped just beyond the doorway. Remembering that there was a black sofa to the left of the bathroom, she began running her hand against the paneled wall, feeling for the it's vinyl covering to get her bearings. Once she located the piece of furniture, she stood still for a moment and waited. Either her eyes would acclimate to the dark, or the headlights of a passing car would pierce through the pressed yellow windows and help light her way to the bunk room. Because the Lancemen station sat on the main road that cornered a side street, droves of traffic passed in front and along side it on a regular basis, even during the early morning hours. Before Merve purchased the building to use as the crew's quarters, it was a gas station. Its garage area had three bays that were perfect for parking the ambulances. The bay at the end was used as a wash bay and was separated from the other two by a large tarp that hung from a steel pole. On the back wall, outside of the garage area, a shed had been added to house the small and large oxygen tanks. Within the living quarters there was one small bedroom with two sets of bunk beds to accommodate the two sets of crews, both Basic EMTs. A large closet at the back of the windowless bedroom contained a shelf with supplies and a painted brown refrigerator. They worked forty-eight hours then were off forty-eight hours, with the pattern repeating. The start time had changed from the initial, six in the evening, to seven am. The company was growing.

Turning to enter the bunk room, Anne heard the sound of two ambulance doors shutting one right after the other. Laughter followed, echoing outside between the eaves of the station and the bay doors. Rick burst into the bay area, as he opened the paneled glass door.

"Oh here's where the sandbaggers are holding out," he jokingly announced. His sudden loud voice interrupted the sleeping respirations that drifted from the bunk room. Then after a cough and a stirring of sheets, the rhythmic breathing picked up where it left off.

"Must be nice to be in bed already," Mike Peterson jealously gibed.

"Where have you guys been?" Anne asked.

"Getting the tires on the rig replaced," Rick answered, mater of factually. Sitting on the low counter that stretched across the front wall of the living area, he bent over to unzip his black combat boots.

"What happened to your tires?"

"Someone sliced them."

"You're kidding!" she replied.

"Oh. You guys missed it!" he began, his face beaming with excitement. "We took dinner down to the midnight dispatcher—and while we were there, this guy from Townsdale slit our tires. Harvey, from Bloomfield PD was sitting right next to him in his patrol car doing some paperwork when the guy did it! Harv said, when he saw the guy he just jerked his door open and used it to knock him to the ground, then cuffed him. Why anyone would try to sneak that close to a cop car with the cop in it, is beyond me. What was he thinking, ya know? So now they've got security hiding in the bushes, just in case some of the others come back."

"And—they got Gooch," Mike piped in, laughing. "One of Lancemen's finest officers, keeping watch over our units in the city. You know how crazy Gooch is. Man—he's like Superman, Wyatt Earp and the Fly, all rolled into one. He'll be on those guys like white on rice."

"How stupid," Rick continued. "A two dollar and ninety cent an hour job ain't worth going to jail for. I'd quit and get a different job before I'd go to jail."

"They took that guy to jail?"

"No, they took him to the circus," Mike laughed, teasing her naivety. "He just told you, Harvey cuffed him."

"Shut up," she giggled, embarrassed. "Who was he?"

"Bob the jailbird Banford. I don't think you know him. Anyway, they want us to park the rigs inside for a while. Where's your keys? I'll back your rig in for you," Mike offered. No sooner had the words left his lips, when the phone rang. "Maybe not. You guys are up next," he laughed.

Yawning, Rick answered the phone. "County Morgue." He listened, said a few okays, then good-bye. "Ooh, it's your lucky night sister," he began, snickering. "You just won the prize. You and Buster are going to be up for a while. You get to take a stiff over to Dover's Funeral Home from the Pine Street Apartments. You'll be up all night waiting for someone at Dover's to answer the door. Mike and I fell asleep in their driveway the last time we were there."

Anne wished he was joking, but something in the pit of her stomach told her he wasn't. Buster, awakened by their loud chatter, came out of the room rubbing his eyes.

"What time is it?" he asked, hoping it would be closer to dawn than it was.

"One thirty-five and ten seconds. Beep," Mike taunted. He unbuttoning his shirt, then threw it on the sofa. "You and Ms. Anne are on your way to Dover's—and it's our turn for some shuteye."

"We'll see, Mickey," Buster retorted. "I heard you from the bunk room. We got the same, slow, don't want to get up in the middle of the night kind of people at some of the funeral homes down in the south end too. I'll bet we're back here in an hour."

"Good Luck," Rick chuckled. Carrying his boots tucked under his arm, he closed the door to the bunk room to block the light before hopping into bed.

Talk about a bad feeling, Anne thought, while getting into the passenger side of the rig. Buster may be new to this end of the county, but he sure wasn't a stranger to EMS. He had something up his sleeve, but what?

They had been to the Pine Street Apartments so many times, even Buster knew their location by heart. Anne wrote down the incident number, using the map light as they drove non-emergency to the address of the deceased party. The five floor apartment building was in a dirty run down area of Lancemen. The elevator seldom ran. It was small anyway. The stretcher only fit in there if they raised the head and lowered the front bar. Depending on how long the person had been deceased and whether rigor mortis had set in, he or she may be too rigid to sit up. In that case, they would have to carry them down all five flights.

The City of Lanceman was just one of twenty, initial small villages established in the early 1800's that made up Lancemen County. Its first permanent settlers came from Mount Clement with two ox-teams, cutting their way through the woods and swamps. It's recorded that in April of 1840, a fire broke out and destroyed everything in the downtown area on both sides of Saginaw and Pine Street, including the barns and outhouses. The citizens wasted no time in rebuilding the town. Most of those same buildings, with their meticulous detailing and time laden effort of scrolling architecture, still remain standing in the downtown area. The Pine Street Apartments were also once regarded as high grade in their hay day. But due to many years of neglect, their beauty waned sadly into an eroded state of needed repair. Only the tarnished chandeliers that were too high to steal or break, remained intact.

"Unit Two arrival," Buster sleepily uttered. Jerking his door open with more effort than usual, he pushed himself off the driver's seat then walked to the back of the rig where he stood eyeing the Victorian brick building. One single light bulb shining over the door entrance offered little to guide their steps. The wattage seemed so low that it may as well have been a candle. He noticed that there were three or four apartments with lamps on. But the stingy glow that they emitted through windows with miss-sized drapes or bare screening that presented an occasional silhouette, was of little help. The street lights weren't much better. Most of those were either burned out or broken out by boys with rocks or drunks with guns. Voices echoed through the dense morning air. He looked at his watch. It was a little past 0200 hours. He opened the back doors of the rig; then together they rolled out the stretcher while the sound of hushed babies cried and dogs barked to warn nearby strangers. "These old buildings give me the creeps," he stated. "Lets get this over with so we can get back to bed."

"Up here," came a deep voice from one of the lit, second story windows.

Anne noticed the badge on the man's shirt as he turned to the others in the room, then heard him announce, "Mercy's here."

"I wonder if the elevator works," she said, thinking out loud.

Using his foot, Buster pushed a cat laying on the front stoop out of the way in order to open the front door. "Move—kitty kitty."

Lifting the handle, he leaned against the thick oak door. It squeaked as it opened. After entering the large octagon shaped foyer, they rolled the stretcher toward the elevator. Dried leaves caught in the breeze each time the door opened crunched under its wheels. The design of the black and white tiled floor and the molding on the walls made Anne think of an old 1940's movie. She slid the elevator's metal gate to one side. "It must work. The last time I was here they had the gate tied closed. I hope the person fits."

"Oh they'll fit," Buster answered with great certainty.

The elevator jerked, then hummed as it moved upward. When it stopped, he pulled back the gate, then rolled the stretcher down the hall toward the room with the open door.

"This was an expected death," the policeman began, assuming they knew the routine. "The family and ME have already been notified. The family wants him taken to Dover's Funeral Home. The ME told me he'd advise Dover's. The rest is up to you folks. Mr. Earnest Welsh," he continued, "was a cancer patient. He was eighty six years old at the time of his death. We talked to his daughter a few minutes ago. She said he was very independent, even though he was nearing his last stages of cancer. She said her father called her yesterday and complained of a headache but nothing more. About an hour ago, some of the neighbors in the apartment building smelled a foul odor coming from his apartment. They broke down the door before we got here and found him undressed and curled up on the floor next to his bed." He pointed in the direction of the bedroom, then walked over to the body and lifted the cover sheet. "Looks like he's been down awhile—probably since yesterday. I'd guess, he died not too long after he talked to his daughter."

Anne and Buster leaned over to pick up the body of the small framed man. His fetal position and stiffness made it easy to pick up him up and place him on the waiting stretcher. Even with the open windows, the foul odor of his body secretions and dead flesh were noticeably strong. Anne attentively covered Mr. Welsh with the paper sheet while listening to Buster and the police discuss what Uncle Henry referred to as small talk. They started out talking about the weather, then the City of Lancemen, then baseball and then Detroit's last year Rookie of the year, Mark Fidrych. They marveled and chuckled at his antics, stats and his lanky, goofy appearance, until the time of morning and the reason they were there was nearly forgotten. A screech from the police radio asking the status of the officers brought them back to duty.

"Okay—we'll see you on the next one," Buster said as they left. Rolling the stretcher in a sitting position toward the elevator, he smiled at Anne. "Those guys were pretty cool. I think I might like it up here after all."

Anne yawned as they drove around to the back entrance of Dover's Funeral Home; flowers and the deceased always went around back. "You have to ring the door bell for them to let us in," she said, as they stopped. "It looks dark. The ME was called so long ago, they probably went back to bed."

"Yeah, well I'm not waiting all night for them to get up," he said opening his door.

After unhooking the stretcher, they rolled it out while Buster squeezed the handle to release the locked wheels. Standing in the moonlight next to the sign that read "deliveries," Anne pushed the button for the doorbell. They waited impatiently for several minutes, with no indication that anyone even knew they were there. Anne remembered Buster's comment to Mike just before leaving the station. "Well, it looks like we might be here for a while, unless you're planning on taking Mr. Welsh back to the station with you." Smiling at her own humor, she rang the bell a second then a third time. Seeing the scowl grow on Buster's face, she offered "You know I didn't mean that as a jab—it was a just a joke. I'm just as tired as you are."

A few more minutes passed in silence. Buster sighed then walked over to the ambulance. After opening the passenger door he picked up the radio mic. Anne strained to hear, but he was too far away to clearly make out what was being said. Then she heard the keying of the mic and the dispatcher's voice in return. When Buster finished, he walked back to the stretcher without a word and stood next to Mr. Welsh who was partly uncovered. Suddenly, an eerie feeling surged through Anne when she realized the breeze had blown the sheet off the dead man's face. She couldn't help but notice that his eyes appeared to be in a fixed gaze, as if he was watching the clouds drift over the crescent moon. Trying to shake the "willies," a term her brother James used to describe the feelings you sometimes get after watching a scary movie, she pulled the sheet back over the deceased man's face. Again, they waited quietly. Buster glanced at his watch; Anne wondered what his conversation with the dispatcher had been and, of course, what his plan of action was. She didn't want to ask too many questions. After all they just started working together. It takes time, to learn how someone works. But now her curiosity was starting to get the best of her.

She watched as Buster walked across the driveway toward the grassy yard; his plan, whatever it was, started to unfold. With purpose in every movement, he bent down and took one of the metal scalloped backed lawn chairs, dragged it across the concrete drive, then set it next to Mr. Welsh. "Let's lower the stretcher," he said, with authority.

"What are we go'na do?" she asked, suspiciously.

"We've waited long enough. I even had the dispatcher call them. We're going to put Mr. Welsh in the chair. When they decide they're ready for him—they can come out and get him."

"You aren't serious," she nervously laughed. "You can't leave a naked dead man in a chair unattended!"

"He won't be naked, I'll cover him with the sheet."

"Buster, you know what I mean," she whispered, appalled and some- what amused by his answer to their dilemma.

"All right, what do you suggest we do," he desperately sighed. "It's going on three o'clock in the morning and we still have another twenty four hours to work, once this day is through. I want to get some sleep, and these people won't answer the door!"

"Okay. You can leave him in the chair—but we have to make sure he's not naked," she finally agreed. At this point she was too tired and exasper- ated to think of another solution. They lowered the stretcher and gently picked up the frozen like corpse and set him in the chair. Trying different positions, they finally leaned him slightly to the side so that he wouldn't fall onto the ground. Anne took the sheet and wrapped and tucked it until she was satisfied that it wouldn't blow away. Buster reached up and began unknotting his neck tie, then slipped it around Mr. Welsh's neck. Anne was beyond asking any more questions, so she stood and just watched as he very carefully adjusted the tie making sure it hung straight and even.

"There," he proudly boasted. "He's not naked. Let's go home."

Shaking her head and too worn to argue, she muffled a smile while walking to the ambulance. She knew this is not something that she'd share with her grand-kids.

Again, Buster picked up the mic. "Radio, this is Unit Two. Can you go to Blue?" Blue was a secondary frequency that the crews could use to relay information to the dispatcher that wasn't appropriate for the main, Gray frequency.

"On Blue."

"Yeah—we're clearing Dover's. You might want to call them back and let them know that they have a delivery at the back door, sitting in the lawn chair."

"Ten four."

Anne was surprised that the dispatcher Mark, acknowledged him so easily. It was as if the information Buster relayed didn't even faze him. Hopefully, she thought, the people at Dover's will come out and get Mr. Welsh before the neighbors see him, or before a stray dog drags him away.

A week had passed and the bite marks had healed from the chewing they took from Merve about leaving Mr. Welsh outside. With the strike still going on and equipment coming up missing or being ruined, he had more important things than the incident at Dover's to worry about. Anne and Buster began their last shift before Roman's return on Monday. At the beginning of their shift, each new crew was expected to get a report from the off going crew, wash and fuel their rig and resupply its cabinets. Anne and Buster took great care and pride as they finished towel drying their freshly washed ambulance. Even the chrome of the siren that sat on top of the unit's roof glistened in the bright morning sun.

"Ooee, look at that baby shine," Buster bragged.

Mike and Rick stood outside of the bay next to him and Anne, whipping and buffing their ambulance. "You won't say that when we're done," Mike laughed, rubbing a little harder with each retort. "You'll need your shades to shield your eyes—from the glare of this buggy."

Anne giggled, amused by their bantering. Guys always seemed to have to have this rivalry thing going. Who's rig shined the brightest, whose was the cleanest, whose tires were the blackest, were only a few of the items included in the ambulance competition.

She checked the small oxygen bottles in the rig. One was full and one was nearly empty. Cradling the near empty bottle in her arms, she walked around to the oxygen shed behind the bays. While supporting the small tank in her arms she maneuvered her hands free, to work through the combination lock on the door. Within seconds of her lifting the lock from the latch, the door swung open and without warning, a large tank fell against her. Startled, she tried pushing it back; but it happened too quick and unexpected for her to set any kind of decent footing. Plus, with the weight of the other tanks all chained together, it was more than she could hold. Falling onto the paved parking lot, she was able to land beside the tank rather than underneath it. Then the other large tanks followed and fell against each other, producing a loud echoing clang, while a hiss of air escaped from the small tank cradled tight in her arms.

"Let it go! Let it go! You trying to blow us up?" Mike bellowed, as they ran to see what caused the thunderous racket. Releasing the near empty bottle, she laid it on the pavement and let it roll into the grass. Brushing off her pants, she stood as Buster helped her the rest of the way.

"You all right?" he asked.

Rick looked at the chain, then at the hooks in the shed. "Somebody set this up. The chain's been cut. That could have been bad if one of the stems for the regulator broke off. It would have been like a rocket taking off."

"You don't think those guys from Townsdale did this, do you?" Anne asked, blotting a small amount of blood from an abrasion on her elbow with her hand.

"I don't know. But we better keep a closer eye on things, just in case," Rick said sternly.

"I don't think they meant to hurt anyone," Buster said, in defense of his old work buddies.

"Yeah? Well whatever you call it, I think they're getting a little carried away," Rick barked. "This kind'a crap's not funny."

After rolling and lifting the large tanks back into place, they re-locked the door with a key lock they found on a shelf in one of the bays. Outside of being nearly squished or blown up by an oxygen tank, it had been a pretty quiet morning Anne thought, as they left their favorite Coney place after breakfast. Turning onto Saginaw they headed south toward the main street. A woman stepped out from between two parked cars and waved, then started blowing kisses. She was short with straight thin hair, was slightly over weight and bared a big toothless grin as they passed. Anne smiled and waved in return.

"Who was that!" Buster asked, repulsed.

Laughing, Anne answered, "That's Barbara Valentine. She's harmless. Roman and I ran on her a couple of weeks ago. She acted like she'd fainted. Then when the firemen got there, she started grabbing at them and tried to kiss them. Roman says she's lived in this city her whole life. She was born at Eider Valley and has been a ward of the state ever since. This city has a number of people who are housed through state programs. I remember when I first started working down here, I saw a man standing on a corner of a main road arguing with himself as if there were two people. After a while, it didn't seem so odd." Then she pointed to a man that was pushing a wheeled trash can down the main street. He was a small scruffy looking character, who had a large American flag attached to the right side of the can and tied to the handle bar. "That's Bob. They call him Lancemen Bob. Then there's a man who dresses up like an American Indian that hitchhikes all over. Roman said he's run on him a couple of times during the summer for heat exhaustion. He said most of the time he has lice. A few weeks ago I saw this huge scary looking thing, dressed in a purple cape who stood about seven foot tall pushing a grocery cart with a cat riding in the kiddy seat..."

"All right, you had me up to there. You're making this stuff up, aren't you."

"No. As God is my witness—I really saw him," she smiled, knowing that it was all a little too strange to believe. "They call him the Cat Man. I guess he was this big high school basketball star that got messed up on LSD. They had to lock him up for awhile and now he just walks around with all of his worldly possessions in the grocery cart, with that cat keeping him company."

"You won't be offended if I check out your story, will you?"

She laughed as they pulled into the gas station. "Not at all."

Buster stopped at the pump then went inside to have the attendant turn it on. As he walked out, another station attendant came out behind him and cupped his hand to peek into the back windows. He watched while pumping the gas, trying to figure out what the guy was doing. Finally, he gave in and looked at Anne through the open driver's window and asked, "What's he looking for?"

"A body. Sometimes some of the guys come and fuel up while they're doing a removal."

"You people are so weird," he chuckled.

"Oh—And this comes from a man—who leaves a deceased person, in a lawn chair, at three o'clock in the morning?"

"That was different," he smiled, trying to hide his guilt.

"Sure it was," she grinned.

"Unit Two, come in Unit Two," came the dispatcher's voice.

"Unit Two, go ahead. We're at the pumps."

"Copy a code three. You will be responding to 560 Beaker for an unknown injury. Your incident number is 078 at 10:16."

Buster went in to sign for the fuel, while Anne wrote down the information. Then she looked for the street on the map. Returning, Buster hopped into the rig and reached for his seat belt while she gave him the directions to the address.

"Go two streets up and then you're going to turn right. Now, go down three more streets, then turn onto Beaker," she instructed.

Pulling onto their street, they could see the lights of a PD unit up ahead.

After stopping behind the patrol car, Anne grabbed the orange box and handed the oxygen bottle to Buster, as they hurried to the given address. Skipping up the steps of the small concrete porch, they entered the front door.

"We're back here," one of the officers announced from a back bedroom.

"Well—I hear them, but I sure don't see them," Buster said in a low tone.

Looking around, they stopped for a second to find a path to take through the piled high knickknacks that touched the ceiling. "Are we in a house, or a novelty shop?" Buster quietly asked the officer who met them.

"It's a fire trap. She says she just collects this junk. She's back here. Wait'll you see this."

Lifting the orange box over and around hanging macramé planters with mirror inserts, each loaded with an array of salt and pepper shakers, Anne made her way through the front room. When she got to the hallway she was able to lower the box while taking a few steps to the end bedroom to join the others.

"Oh, my dear girl," the middle aged woman sitting on the bed sympathetically groaned. "For heaven sake's; all of these big strong men, and you have to carry that box?"

"It's okay. Now what's going on with you," Anne smiled.

The woman sighed shyly. In response to Anne's question, she slowly pulled back the blanket and sheet to reveal her side. Anne looked in surprise as she noticed the large amount of blood and the many, many small particles of fatty tissue peppered over the bedding. But even more than that, she couldn't get over the size of the hole at the woman's side, giving the appearance of an explosion from the inside out.

"Excuse me ma'am—I don't think I caught your name."

"It's Meredith. I know this must look terrible, but it really doesn't hurt."

"Meredith, how long ago did this happen? I mean," Anne stammered, lost for words that would describe the torn tissue professionally. "It looks like you—blew up." Then, realizing she should be doing something besides staring, she reached into the orange box and took a handful of non adhesive dressings and another handful of four by four gauze squares. While wrapping the wound that was the size of a grapefruit, she listened to Meredith's story.

"I've had this thing growing on my side for some time—but it never bothered me, so I didn't bother it. Then this morning, while I was getting up—it burst open. It doesn't hurt, like I said; but I didn't know what else to do besides call you people."

"When was the last time you saw a doctor?" Anne asked, while taking a roll of gauze from Buster, to wrap around and hold the dressings in place.

"Oh I saw my doctor a few weeks ago, when I got my flu shot."

"Your flu shot?" Anne reeled in disbelief. Gentling her voice, she continued. "Meredith, I don't mean to be rude; but I'm having a hard time understanding why you were worried about getting the flu, but you weren't worried about this big thing growing on your side."

Anne turned to take the last roll of gauze from Buster. "I've seen this before," he quietly offered. Seeing Anne's questioning expression, he continued. "During my clinicals at the hospital, this lady came in with the same thing on her abdomen. It's just a big cyst or non malignant tumor of some kind."

"Really? Well, Meredith," she gratefully sighed. "You've shown me something new today. I'm sure it looks worse than it is—but then that's the way most things are. How' bout we put a clean gown on you and get you to the hospital."

"I think I'd like that."

On the way to the hospital, Anne thought about all the bizarre things she had seen during the short time she'd been working as a Basic EMT. While she wasn't exactly thrilled with all of the oddities—there was truly something intriguing about this strange world and its challenges. And while it was out of the question for right now, she hoped Merve would eventually let her work as a Paramedic. Clearly, the company was experiencing growing pains. She understood that. But that didn't ease the personal need that she felt to grow; nor did it lessen the desperate hunger to advance in her career. Still, she understood that even in the waiting there's stretching and molding. Rushing through things sometimes causes you to miss out on something grand, or maybe, to pass up a step that would make the next experience less painful. No, she decided while leaning over to take another blood pressure, it was just better to sit and learn. There was still much to do while enduring her growing pains.

CHAPTER 16

~~~~∞∞~~~~

THE PROMISE

"Jesus stood on the coast of Judea beyond the Jordan and spoke to the great multitudes in the presence of his disciples and the Pharisees, who also came to test Him, saying, 'It is easier for a camel to go through the eye of a needle, than for a rich man to enter the kingdom of God.'" A man's pride has always been, and will always be his downfall; for a man's pride will cause him to worship the works of his own hands, and his riches will appear great. He will put those things above God and worship them in place of God.

The Townsdale employees had fallen into the same mind set. Their pride and anger had become so great, that the strike could never be settled in any manner acceptable to both parties. So as they entered the third week of the dispute, Glen, the company's main owner, fired all of his employees. Throughout the strike, there had been a few who decided not to walk. Those employees were rehired immediately while the others had to reapply, giving the company the opportunity to pick and choose who they wanted to rehire based on their past performance. Once the dust settled, a number of paramedic slots would be open. Roman returned at the end of it all, and was initially offered a position with Rick at the Lakeview Station. But Merve felt because of the weeks it would take to hire the needed replacements and work out the schedule adjustments, he should remain with Anne, at least for now. Buster decided to go into dispatch and take a full time position, hoping it would lead to a supervisory advancement. Tom had placed his foot on the executive ladder and moved up to Chief of Paramedics. The strike had brought about many changes that forced the company to move ahead a little quicker then they planned. But everyone seemed up to the challenge and worked well together.

Roman laughed, after hearing the highlighted excerpts of Anne's two week tour without him. "He put his tie around the dead guy's neck? Oh, that's rich."

"Well, at least it was a new tie. It was kind of a nice thing, don't you think?"

"No, I don't. Anne—you don't go home to Kansas and tell your family about this stuff, do you?"

"I did at first; but then they all looked at me like there was something wrong with what I was saying. Guess I've grown used to this way of life. It seems normal to me now. My Aunt Ruth says she worried that I'm becoming callous and worldly."

"Worldly? What does that mean?"

"Uncaring… following the way of the world, instead of the way of God. Unless you've been brought up in a Christian home, you might not understand. Sort of like this job. There are just some things about it that you can't understand until you see it and smell it and experience the outcome. Since I've been in this field, I've realized how much I take my upbringing for granted. The world out here is very different."

"You're right about that. I did a lot of thinking while I was gone, and I decided that I'm going to go work with my brother-in-law in the spring. It's just time that I move on with my life."

Anne studied Roman's face as he spoke. He looked rested, yet he carried a resolute air. She knew the divorce rate was high in this business. Between the long hours, low pay and just not being able to go home and talk about your day like other people did just added to what some considered to be stress. She agreed that it was tiring at times, but she didn't think too much about the stress. There was something new everyday, and she liked that.

"Unit Two, come in for a baby not breathing."

Her heart raced. "Unit Two, go ahead."

"You're responding to 364 Whitting. The cross street is Central. The incident number is 257, at 13:46."

Well, maybe there is a little stress, she told herself, while writing down the information. She was glad that Roman knew the City of Lancemen so well and that they were able to save time by taking the back streets. After slowly nearing the address, they stopped in front of the house. Anne opened her door and started to get out, when Roman grabbed her sleeve.

"Wait," he called out.

She looked at the front door of the house and stared. The big figure in the purple cape that she had seen out in the streets, now approached them carrying something wrapped in an old soiled jacket.

"Help me! My baby quit breathing," he uttered, unfolding the collar and lapel of the tweed wrapping. Fear gripped his face, as he looked down. Anne looked into the bundle and began to take it, but then stopped. She didn't know what to say, or what to do. It wasn't a baby—but a very dead—beagle dog.

"I'm sorry, but we can't do anything for your dog. He's been gone a long time—and we don't treat animals."

Roman leaned over her shoulder. "Oh for crying out loud."

"But he's part human," the strangest man Anne had ever seen, pleaded. "Can't you give him some oxygen or something?" She felt helpless. She wanted to calm the man standing in front of her; but then there was Roman sitting behind her, breathing down her neck and she sensed by his huff that he was quickly losing his patience. Positioned sideways in her seat toward the open door, she sadly watched as a tear ran down the tall dark man's dirty cheek.

"I'm sorry—but we don't even have an oxygen mask to fit a dog. It wouldn't help anyway. He's been gone too long," she explained, as gently as she could. She wondered about his cat. Maybe that was dead too. Curiously she stared at him, trying to decide which feature was oddest. Was it his dark hair, wrapped in a rag of some kind with strands of matted clumps sticking out? Or was it his eyeglasses with the black frames that surrounded smeared lens held in place by pink bubble gum? Then, as he brought his dirty hands to scratch his scraggly beard, she noticed specks of something hard and dry caught in its bristles. With each movement, the odor from his clothes that was strong of urine and poor hygiene, sorely whiffed up and hit her square in the face. She felt sorry for him but what more could she say than she already had?

"Shut the door and get in here," Roman barked. "He's crazy. Nothing you say is going to make sense to him. Let's go," he said, as he drove away from the curb. Anne slid back into her seat and quickly shut the door. Looking out the back window, she watched as the Cat Man sadly stood on the curb, clinging to the stiff, dead dog wrapped in the brown tweed jacket.

"Maybe we should call someone."

"Who are we going to call, Anne? He's crazy. It's probably not even his dog. Forget it."

"All right," she sighed, with hands raised in surrender. "I just thought, that maybe—somebody could at least help him bury the dog."

Roman reached into his pocket for a cigarette. Resting it against his lower lip, he picked up his lighter from the cup holder in the dog house. He ran his thumb over its wheel a few times until it produced a flame. As the paper caught fire, it sizzled and gave off an orange glow while blending with the smell of burning tobacco. The scanner, programmed into the unit radio, picked up the tone of the Lancemen Fire Department. They listened for the address. No, it wasn't the Cat Man. It was for an address in the north end of the city. Seconds later, their dispatcher gave them a call for the same address. They were to respond with the fire department for a diabetic.

Lancemen City had its own paramedics. They were a fun loving group. And while Anne didn't care much for their loud, and sometimes vulgar mannerisms, they truly reminded her of cowboys with their rough and tumble ways. Most of them were older and had been firefighters a number of years, with this paramedic thing sprung on them like a bad joke. She chuckled to herself every time she saw Mel Reed carrying one of their medical boxes into a house, for he always spouted the same thing. "A man takes classes for fire fighting to be a fireman—not a paramedic. If I wanted to be a paramedic—I wouldn't have taken classes for fire fighting."

Pulling up behind the fire truck they stopped. There was Mel. Anne chuckled to herself and could almost read his lips. Roman jumped out, joining her at the back of the rig to grab the stretcher. Diabetic calls were pretty much no brainers. Either the patient's blood sugar was high, or it was low. Most of the time it was low. They used sticks that were specific for testing the amount of sugar in the blood. The hard part was starting the IV. Most diabetics seemed to have small or fragile veins. It was best to find a vein that was fairly large in order to push the pre loaded syringe of thick glucose into it. Within seconds of doing so, the near comatose patient would flutter his or her eyes and wake up as if it were a miracle. Then off to the hospital they would go to have their insulin regulated, if indeed that was the cause.

The remainder of the day held its normal type calls. Slip and falls, assaults, chest pains, minor auto accidents, children with arms stuck in places they shouldn't have been in the first place, and of course nursing home transfers. The only thing that seemed odd was, that no matter which hospital they went to throughout the day, they all had been plagued with the same thing. Multiple calls from the Cat Man. He was desperately persistant. While Roman was standing in the ER of Lancemen General after dropping a patient off, he overheard one of the nurses wearily explaining to someone on the phone that the hospital didn't treat dogs.

"Is that loon still calling for someone to save that dead dog?" he asked.

"It's like the fifth or sixth time," Emily, one of the ER nurses, said. "Has he been calling the other hospitals too?"

"Everyone of them. Anne and I went to his house earlier this afternoon. That dog's been dead for days."

"Well then, why didn't you just bury the thing. At least then he wouldn't be driving us nuts."

Anne looked at Roman, smiled and raised her eyebrows.

"Not a word, missy," he warned, catching her silent gibe. Standing by the nurse's station, he could feel the scorn of the nurses who saw Anne's scolding expression. Giving in for the sake of peace, he walked over to the phone, grumbling to himself. He called information and asked for the number of the Social Services department, then sat down and punched in the numbers. He introduced himself to the party on the other end, then explained he was looking for Burke Waterman's case worker. Burke Waterman? Anne mentally repeated. Was that the Cat Man's real name? Roman never let on that he knew his real name. He waited, then began giving the person on the other end of the phone an accurate and concerned sounding description of their visit with the man in the cape.

"Thank you very much," he concluded seriously, while restraining a grin. "There you go, ladies," he said standing. "The case worker said he would go over to the house on Whitting and take care of the dog problem."

"Thank heavens," Emily cried.

"Not—a word, missy," he repeated his warning to Anne, as he walked toward the door. She smiled, for she knew by the smirk that he held in secret, that he really felt good about making the phone call. All was well.

"I guess we're leaving," Anne chuckled. "See you later."

"See ya, Anne. Hey, try and keep those guys in line, would ya?" Ingress, an older but tough little nurse, called out.

That wasn't always easy, Anne thought. They had their own way, for sure. And while in some aspects she was accepted as one of the boys, there was a very clear difference. The way they thought and reacted to situations was just a mere part of it. Merve's biggest complaint about women was that "they thought with their heart and not with their brain." To Anne, that seemed to be exactly the right way. After all, you can tell your brain to do anything; and it might obey for a while. But if your heart isn't in it, eventually the brain will lose out. The right and true answers almost always came from the heart.

Roman and Anne's last few weeks as partners had ended. Max Haley, a new paramedic hire, was scheduled to work with Anne. He was enthusiastic and didn't mind the fact that she was to be his teacher. She had been a Basic EMT for nearly two years now and was sure of her job and duties. Still, giving her the position of teaching him came as a surprise, especially since she was expected as part of the training, to teach Max how to drive the ambulance. Being a girl, she had no driving status herself and would have to teach him everything from the passenger's seat.

"Okay," she began. Reaching over to the set of switches in the ceiling panel above the driver's seat, she pointed at then demonstrated each rocker switch. "Here's the switch for the emergency lights. You have primary and secondary positions. Primary, of course, uses all of the emergency lights. This is the switch for the light bar on the top of the rig." Flipping the switch on and off, she continued. "Here are the side lights and these two switches that say left and right are for the white tunnel lights. We always turn our head lights on when we're driving in an emergency and when we're driving non-emergency with a patient on board." Max watched as she moved her hand to a dial on a control box for the siren. "There are three different tones for the siren. Yelp, wail, and hi-low. You can change them with the knob on the box, or turn the knob to F H—Free Hand and change the tones by tapping the center of the steering wheel. PA—is for the other mic. When that mic is keyed, you can talk to people outside of the ambulance or you can make neat sounds like horses trotting." She continued the demonstration by tapping her fingers against the mic. "Or cutting wood," she proceeded, running the mic up and down on her uniform pants.

Max smiled. "You're being a pretty good sport about this."

"You mean because I can't drive the rig myself? I don't really care about that. But I do think it's a little insulting that the reason they won't let me drive is because they think women are bad drivers. I used to tell myself that it was because Merve thought of me as his daughter and was just trying to protect me. But I know that's not really it. Driving to me is not worth making a big fuss. I like the patient care part better anyway. What can I say?" she smiled in return.

Max was short, not much taller then Anne's five foot two frame. He had a full head of thin light auburn hair, and a beard that made its way down his neck to match. He reminded her of the Vernors gnome, even down to the mischievous twinkle in his eyes. As they talked, an unfamiliar car pulled into the station parking lot. An average size man with dark curly hair in about his late twenties got out and walked toward their ambulance.

"Hi, my name is Robbie Thomson. I'm one of the new supervisors. You must be Anne," he smiled. "And you're?" he inquired, putting his hand out to shake Max's hand.

"Max Haley. Anne was just giving me a driving lesson."

"Why are you sitting in the passenger seat?" he asked Anne, puzzled.

"Because I'm not allowed to drive," she answered, somewhat embarrassed.

"You're kidding," he laughed. "But you, can teach him? I'll be back."

"What do you think he's going to do?" Anne asked out loud, while watching him get back into his car to drive away.

"Make some changes, would be my guess," Max chuckled, being entertained by it all.

"Unit Two, prepare to code."

Anne recognized Buster's voice. "Here we go. Unit Two's ready," she said, after picking up the radio mic. As she wrote down the information Max scanned the map. Looking up, she noticed a puzzlement in his expression. After a quick explanation of how that particular map worked, they were off. They started slowly out onto the main road with the siren blaring and lights flashing. Everything would imply that they were on an emergency call, except for the speed that Max was driving.

Anne grinned as she spoke, hoping not to make him feel bad. "You can drive a little faster if you want. After all, this is an emergency call."

"You think so?" Max replied, chuckling, feeling a little awkward. Pushing the accelerator down, they picked up speed. Following Anne's directions, he turned onto a dead end street. The call was for a woman having difficulty breathing.

"You can pull up behind the Lancemen fire truck," she suggested.

"How'd I do?"

"Not bad, once we got out of second gear," she teased, jumping back into a teaching mode. "We don't need any of our equipment on this one. Lancemen has their own paramedics. We just help them and transport the patient. They're kind of a rough bunch on the outside. But they do their best to help people out. Their real forte is fighting fires. They like eating smoke and slaying the fire dragon, as they say. To hear them talk, it's like play time for them."

Leaving the stretcher outside, they entered the small wooden house. They couldn't go much farther than just inside the front door. The living room was tiny and full, as the firemen from the rescue squad and the engine crew filled the room. The patient sat in a recliner chair, gripping its arms to hold herself up. Her breathing was labored. She fought to take little puffs of air through pursed lips. Her chest heaved in response and the veins in her neck stood out. Sweat dripped from her face onto her swollen feet that barely touched the unfinished wooden floor. One of firemen set up the oxygen tank and adjusted the liter flow, while another knelt beside her and wrapped a tourniquet around her arm just above the elbow. He looked for a vein to start an IV but the lighting in the house was so dim that he had his coworkers turn on every light source in the room. It was still not enough. Two of the lamps had burned out bulbs, so a couple of the other firemen looked through kitchen cabinets and closets for fresh replacements. The woman seemed to be improving with the O2 therapy through the non-rebreather mask. Her husband watched the activity, silently frowning before he finally spoke up, "If you tell me what you're looking for, I'll find it for you."

"Light bulbs. Do you have any more light bulbs?"

"Yes—But they're not in the kitchen," his tone clearly displayed his disgust, "they're in the hall closet." Anne knew they were just trying to do their part to help the patient. But she couldn't help giggle a little to herself, as the engine guys dressed in their turnout gear moved around with the grace of a bull in a china shop, knocking over items in the house with the edge of their coats. Then suddenly, the lamp they so desperately wanted to use to offer more light to start the IV came apart in one of the firemen's hands. But in spite of all that, the medic was able to establish the IV and after calling the hospital on the apcor radio, he gave her forty milligrams of the diuretic from their drug box.

They had done all they could do for now. Mel looked over at Anne. Sweat rolled down the side of his face. She could almost read his mind. He was not having a good time; she knew that. "We're ready for the stretcher, little girl," he said smiling. He sensed Anne's amusement. She turned to go out to bring the stretcher in, with Max following her. The expression on his face spoke volumes and almost made her laugh out loud. Controlling the urge, she leaned toward him and whispered, "We'll talk later."

After moving some of the furniture to make room for the wheeled cot, a couple of the firemen stepped outside. Max squeezed the corner handle to lower the stretcher half way, to keep the wheels from dragging over the porch steps before he and Anne lifted it up, to carry it into the house. After rolling the cot next to the patient, Anne raised the head to a fowler's position, so the woman could sit up and breathe easier. Then, while helping her to her feet so she could pivot then sit on the cot, they noticed not only by the odor but also by the brown smear on the vinyl chair, that the woman had lost control of her bowels. Mel, who was standing next to Anne, rarely ever held anything back—and today was no exception. In his normally loud and gruff tone he unthinkingly blurted out, "Pee Yoo." The room caved-in to snickers as each person, except the patient and her husband of course, awkwardly found humor in his remark. If it had been anyone but the boys from Lancemen, a scene like that would not fly. They were cowboys doing their best to provide the best medical care they could, with as much poise as possible and none of the Doc's ever expected anything more.

Quickly, they covered the patient with the paper sheet and gently laid the O2 bottle between her legs, then snapped the cot straps in place. Anne backed up, pulling the stretcher toward the door. She had pretty much concurred the art of walking backward down the stairs while carrying the stretcher. She knew to keep the wheels from hitting the steps and not to let the cot wobble. Without fail, anytime the stretcher wobbled the patient instinctually reached out to grab onto something to prevent or ease the feeling of falling.

Mel spoke up as Anne neared the doorway. "Wait a minute little girl. Let me behind you and back you down the stairs," he offered. A second set of eyes was always helpful and a normal safety precaution. Once he slipped past her he lifted his hands to give her support. By the giggles from the firemen around her, she could tell that something was going on, but what? She turned her head before moving back and saw Mel looking straight ahead at her buttocks, unsure of where to put his hands to help guild her down the steps. A second later, apparently, he had decided and cupped his hands under each of Anne's back cheeks. Trying not to let things look any worse to the family than it already had, she bit her lip while quietly growling just loud enough for Mel to hear, "You're a dead man when this is over." Totally unthreatened, he grinned. Anne carefully began backing down each step, with Mel advising her as to which step she was on and how many steps were left. Now with both feet firmly on the ground, he let go. From the small group of neighbors who had gathered outside, Anne heard an older lady comment about how nice the fireman was who helped her down the steps.

Mel heard it too and grinned, "See, I was just being nice."

"So you say," she retorted. "I still owe you."

Anne sat next to Mel on the bench seat of the ambulance, taking the patient's blood pressure while on the way to the hospital. She wanted to be mad at him, but couldn't. His gesture probably was, just an effort of aid and not one of purposed disrespect. She realized her being there was sometimes awkward for them. And finding humor in whatever the situation was that made them uncomfortable, was their way of dealing with it. After relaying the patient's vitals to Mel to write on his report, she said nothing more. When the call was finished, she stood outside of the ambulance entrance making up the stretcher for the next call. Mel walked out of the hospital, talking with a couple of the other firemen from his station. Noticing Anne, he called out, "Hey no hard feelings, aye little girl?"

Anne softly smiled. It was as close to an apology as she could expect. "Maybe the next time you can just grab onto my belt. Without—giving me a wedgy?" she suggested.

"I'll see what I can do," he grinned. Walking toward the fire truck, he continued his conversation with his fellow firefighters.

Max understood after just a few hours of his employment, that this was not a normal job. The Paramedic field was still like a baby taking its first steps. And like most babies, they needed a helping hand. At 16:00 there was a company meeting scheduled at a newly leased building, near Lancemen Osteopathic Hospital. The crews were told that the meeting was to brief them on present and up and coming changes. All those who were not working on the road were expected to be there. As the meeting started, Tom introduced Robbie Thomson, the new Road Supervisor. Then he discussed a few station and equipment modifications. The HLRs, better known as the thumpers, were coming off the rigs due to the problems they'd experienced. The HLR's were CPR machines that were set up on the center of the victim's chest to do cardiac compressions. They had straps to secure them in place and would free up the EMT's hands to do other tasks during a cardiac arrest. The problem was that if they weren't set up just right or if the ride to the hospital was over rough terrain, the piston doing the cardiac compression would walk up the patient's chest and stop at the throat.

The Commission Cars were next on the agenda. The time and need for them had expired. Therefore, from this day and until further notice, a rig would be set up to run out of the main fire station in Bedford. Because the car was being subsidized by the west end townships, it would pull calls in that area only. As he continued talking, Doctor Big Dave Malley entered the meeting room at the station. Dr. Malley worked in the ER at Mercy's base hospital, Lancemen Osteopathic. He also was on the County Medical Control Board and was the company's Medical Director.

"Sorry I'm late," he began, after Tom turned the floor over to him. "First of all, I just want to say that you're all doing a great job out there. I mean that. The Paramedic Program was a risk at first. When we initially introduced it, we were met with some resistance. But you've all worked hard and the skepticism has eased greatly. And—so now that you're becoming professionals—I want to introduce you to a run form that we've come up with." Smiling, he handed a stack of forms to Robbie and Tom to pass out. "This form is going to replace the scraps of paper that you've been leaving with my nurses. Now the form is pretty much self explanatory but I'd like to go over it—just to satisfy myself that it's clear to you. Fair enough?" After reading over the form Mike raised his hand. "Yes Mike," Dr. Malley said.

"Yeah—what are we supposed to put where it says—impression? Good PI?" Mike asked jokingly. Laughter from the group followed, easing the somewhat fidgety atmosphere.

"Now see—that's why I wanted to go over it. Good PI. That's funny, Mike," Big Dave smiled. Then he started from the top of the three paged NCR papered form, and worked his way down. Lifting a copy of the drug form, also on NCR paper, he showed them what was to be filled out each time they used the drug box and explained the procedure for restocking the box. Doctor Malley was well respected and liked by the EMT's and paramedics. He was a patient teacher to those who wanted to learn. He had a good sense of humor and was encouraging. He made it a point to never talk over the crew's heads, and always treated them as professionals.

Listening to him talk about the new drugs and ideas that they had in mind for the paramedics made Anne that much more anxious to use her paramedic license. She looked around the room at the guys as they laughed and intently listened. For the first time, she felt cheated. Of course she didn't want her thoughts to be known, so she looked down at the different forms and papers handed out, like she was studying them, until the feeling passed. Looking up, she caught Robbie watching her. She wished Roger had made the meeting. He was always good at pulling her through the rough spots. Finally the meeting was over and she stood up to leave. As she followed the others out, Robbie came up behind her. "Don't worry, you'll get your chance soon enough."

Weeks passed and still Anne heard nothing more from Robbie. Gradually over time, the spoken words seemed like a mare's nest and then they were forgotten. Her life as a Basic EMT and Max's teacher would have to be enough. It was mid October. She and Dan made a point to get together to celebrate their birthdays. Cookie Monster was a year old now. It was hard to believe that a year had come and gone since she sat and sewed the eyes on the costume at the Lakeview station. Once in a while she would run into Dan at a hospital or while on a call in Independence. He was very happy as a firefighter and had hopes of moving up in rank.

Zipping up her jacket, Anne headed out the station door toward the rig. A call came in for a house fire. The Lancemen Fire Department was already on the scene. Stepping outside, she could smell the smoke right away. "It must be close by," she told Max. Seconds later they spotted a glow in the evening sky. Anne jumped in the rig and grabbed the mic. Max flipped on the emergency lights and pulled onto the main street like a pro. Anne quickly wrote the information down, then tossed the pad of paper in the dog house compartment. They could see the dark grey clouds mounting up ahead. This was a fully engulfed structure fire for sure. A fireman's dream—and everyone else's nightmare.

"Don't drive over the hose," she warned Max, pointing to the four inch line on the ground as they arrived on the scene; then added, "Nothing makes these guys madder than running over their hose." Jumping out of the rig she noticed the fire department had a number of charged lines stretched from fire trucks and hydrants. Then she spotted the white helmet of the chief and walked toward him.

"Hey, Anne," Pierce yelled from the engine. She looked up and saw him motioning for her to come over.

"I'll be right back," she called to Max. Pierce was several feet away. Between the roar of the fire, squelching radios and firefighters calling out to each other, she knew she'd have to get closer to hear him. It had been a month or so since they delivered the breached baby. She hadn't seen him since then but that wasn't unusual.

"We got a report that there's some kids in there," he yelled from the pump panel. "It ain't gonna be pretty. So get ready." She looked around for Max. A strobe light bounced off his face. He was just a few feet away.

"Max," she said touching his arm. "We need to set up the stretcher with burn sheets and bottles of sterile water. Pierce says they might have some kids in there." The words almost echoed into the night air, bouncing off clouds of smoke that were just as eerie as they were electrifying. Then she heard Pierce yell, "Here they come."

A Firefighter she knew as Deon quickly walked toward them caring a small steaming body and laid it into Max's arms. Anne ran to the rig and ripped open the burn sheet wrapper. Unfolding the sterile sheet, she opened it onto the stretcher, then grabbed a couple of bottles of sterile water. Max handed the child up to her as she stood in the patient compartment. Once he was sure she was ready, he dashed around to the driver's seat. By the time they reached Lancemen Osteopathic, Anne had the child wrapped in the sheet and soaked down. The burns on the child's face were severe enough that Anne had to hold the oxygen mask in front of it, rather than use the elastic straps. The child was a little girl, who looked to be about four years old. Her skin was literally charred in places on her legs. She made no sound, but was breathing. They had no name or medical history to give the hospital. There wasn't time to ask. After hearing Max's radio report, the hospital phoned the burn center and requested a helicopter for the child's transport to the University Hospital. They would do what they could until it arrived. Anne and Max headed back to the scene. Pierce said kids. This was only one. Hopefully, there'd be no more.

A candle in a Halloween Pumpkin was said to have started the blaze that took the lives of three children, their mother and possibly the girl at the hospital. Anne and Max laid yellow plastic sheets on the ground as a temporary morgue until the ME arrived. Wrapped and covered, the victims laid side by side under a tree in the front yard of their home. How horribly sad, Anne thought while tucking the yellow sheet around the last small body. The crew stayed on the scene another hour while the fire department worked to contain the fire to prevent its spread to nearby homes. Some of the firemen needed oxygen due to their "taking in" too much smoke. A couple of them needed wet cloths placed on burned skin, where the fire had burned through old turnout gear and gloves. While treating their needs, Anne looked at their faces. This fire was not a time of play—or not a firemen's dream. Even to them, it was a nightmare.

Sitting on the bumper of the fire engine, Anne watched the firemen somberly roll up the wet hose. The ME had come and gone. A county removal service came for the bodies. Only the basement of the house remained. There was a mood present that she'd never felt before. There was no laughing or loud talking by these cowboys. They worked and spoke quietly. Mel stepped over the hose as he neared the engine where Anne sat and grabbed a can of soda from a cooler. After flipping up the face shield on his helmet, he slipped the yellow air pack from his back, then laid it on the ground. Sitting next to Anne on the engine bumper, he pulled off the tab from the can and took a drink.

"How's your wrist?" she asked, referring to a minor burn she had treated.

"It's all right. How about you, little girl. You and your partner hanging in there?"

"He seems like he's doing okay. He's over there talking to a couple of your guys."

"How bout you?" he asked.

"Okay," she said forcing a smile.

"Personally, I don't think women belong around this crap, but you stuck it out and you were helpful. You're a pretty good sport—I must say."

"Thanks. I've developed a whole new respect for you tonight, myself."

He laughed. "Is that what I just said?" Nodding his head, he thought for a second. "Yeah, I suppose it is. Well, I got work to do. See ya, little girl."

It takes days for the smell of a house fire and burned flesh to leave the hairs of your nose. It doesn't matter how many showers you take, or nose sprays you use, it's still there. The gruesome images last longer, but fade over time. They received word from the burn center that the child made it. She had a long recovery ahead of her, but when she was ready an Aunt from Boston would take her home. It was a rough call, and Anne looked forward to having a few days off. She knew from the way the guys talked, they drank a little heavier after a call like that. She supposed it helped to numb their emotions, as they tried to wash the images of the victims away. At one time, her refuge had been her home in Summerville. But even the comforting words that Aunt Ruth offered didn't help. No, each person had to find their own way to dissolve the sights and smells of such a tragedy. She found her place to work things through came from a pew while reading through the pages of a book she'd held dear, nearly all her life.

Sunday morning was a blessing to Anne in more ways than she expected. After greeting friends from her young adult group, she took a seat. Mr. Staten, who ran the nursery with his wife came up behind her before the service started and asked her to help out with the three year olds. This was the last thing in the world that she wanted to do, but to save a long explanation about the house fire she just smiled and got up to follow him. Within minutes of setting her things down on a table in the room, the children started to file in. Most of them begged their mothers not to leave them for the first few seconds, but once they saw the toy box and building blocks, they dried their tears.

Danielle walked in clinging to her mother's arm. She was a pretty little girl. She was slender and tall for her age. Her mother reassured her that she'd be fine, just as she did every Sunday. Standing as if she wasn't sure of Anne, Danielle clutched her picture Bible for children, tight in her hands. Still bashful and leery, she walked to the coat closet, crawled in and found a seat on the floor.

"Danielle," Anne began, smiling. "Why don't you come over here to the table and show me your Bible." Slowly, Danielle stepped out. Looking at Anne, she opened the book to the first page and began telling her of the events on each page, according to the picture. To Anne's surprise this child of three, knew the Bible better than a lot of adults she knew. Moving deeper into the book, Danielle studied a page with a man looking into heaven at angels.

"Oh," Anne said softly, pointing to the picture. "That's Jacob. And that's the ladder he saw in a dream. See the angels going up and down the ladder?" Danielle nodded. "Danielle, did you ever have a dream?" she asked.

With a serious voice and well thought out expression, Danielle looked into Anne's eyes and answered, "No. I've never even had the chicken poxes."

Endeared and humored by the sweet honest response, Anne fought with the urge to burst out loud laughing. She knew it would embarrass Danielle and send her back into the closet. Certainly that was not what she wanted to do. Smiling, Anne suddenly understood why she was there. Life—she realized, is what brings you through death. There was never a promise given that hardships or tragedies wouldn't come. Only a promise that you would not have to go through them alone. She was very glad for Danielle, an instrument of the promise. And as she looked at the pages in this child's book, she remembered she wasn't alone.

CHAPTER 17

THE GIRLS

In 1911, Walter Flanders and family moved into the great stone mansion he built on Green Lake. The large piece of property he acquired, a collection of a half dozen farms or so, had a fine garage with an immense iron turntable that housed the only car for miles around, a Flanders Twenty. The homestead contained an impressive dovecote that held hundreds of exotic birds imported from foreign countries. And not far off, a large barn stood stocked with the finest Holstein cattle and thousands of chickens. Once a year he gave a festive barn party for his friends and neighbors, with favors for the ladies, stogies for the gents and a sumptuous repast for all who came. Eventually as time passed, the days of merriment became banal to Walt, and in the early twenties he sold out to the Aviation Country Club. Then after the bank crash, the club closed and was later bought by the Lochaven Club.

Anne sat on the bench seat of the ambulance while listening to the detailed account of history from the eighty-seven year old woman that she and Max were transporting from the hospital, to the Resthaven Nursing Home. It amazed her how much the woman could remember and the sharpness of every recollection. From the moment she began reciting her story, her face beamed; and with every re-count, a wrinkle seemed to fade. It was as if she was still there enjoying the gala activities of the country club, painting a picture so real that Anne could almost picture Mrs. James Donnelly, their patient, dancing with her husband, Jim. She described herself as wearing a pastel pink satin dress, just above her ankles, with velvet trim. She wore long white gloves that reached above her elbows, with a ring or two over the fingers of the gloves. Her hair was drawn up and tucked under a sweet little hat that was arranged in the latest ornamental flare of lace and feathers.

"And Jim," she said smiling." Oh you would have liked Jim. He was so handsome. Yes he was. He was the cat's meow, for sure."

The woman continued as if she had just uncapped a bottle of fine perfume. She had so much to share. Anne wondered as she spoke, was she always this talkative or was her return to the county club, now the Resthaven, the spark to her chatter. Then she touched Anne's hand to draw her attention and began speaking in a near whisper, as if confessing a secret.

"I was seven years old, the first time I ever got drunk. It was on an old jug of cider my sister Madeline found," she said slightly louder. "My father loved cider. In the fall we would make several trips to the Franklin Cider Mill." She chuckled, then continued. "When my mother found us pie eyed, she thought we had gotten into the whiskey bottle that my father kept for medicinal purposes. We were just about to meet with the hickory switch, when Madeline slurred out the word, cider. It was the only thing that saved us."

Anne laughed. "Well, Mrs. Donnelly, we've arrived at the Resthaven. I'm sure it won't be exactly how you remember it. They probably had to change a few things to accommodate the patients who stay here now. But I'm sure there will be a lot of things to stir your memory, just the same."

Anne had been at The Resthaven several times before. It was enormous and grand as it sat on a hill top overlooking the spacious acreage, shaded by tall oaks. She always suspected a place like this would have a wonderful history. And after hearing Mrs. Donnelly's stories, she knew she would never see it the same again. As they slowly approached the circle drive, she gazed across the lawn. She could almost envision previous club members dressed in white linen, playing croquette on a lazy summer afternoon. Now just a few feet from the entrance, Anne tucked the blanket up around her patient's neck. Max stopped the ambulance, then came around to the back doors to help unload the stretcher. Guiding the head of the wheeled cot, Anne stepped onto the brick floor of the large open veranda. Several white wooden rockers moved slightly in the wind beckoning anyone nearby to sit and enjoy the view. Placed just below eye level, flower boxes filled with summer's annuals sat on a stone wall that bordered the portico, adding color to its beauty. Strong stone columns stood from floor to the ceiling at each corner for support. Their rustic appeal mixed well with the smooth white columns at the yard entrance. The hint of Greek architecture seemed to add comfort to the country charm.

As they rolled past the large windows, framed with leaded glass, they heard the sound of a player piano. Mrs. Donnelly's face lit up even brighter than before. Max opened the double doors, then grabbed the foot of the stretcher and pulled it up the short ramp into the main entrance, which was also the living room. Mrs. Donnelly gazed up at the cathedral ceiling and the prism chandeliers and smiled.

"Welcome back, Mrs. Donnelly," the Director of Nurses graciously greeted. "I understand you are familiar with the Resthaven." Mrs. Donnelly looked around. The huge stone fireplace was empty. No fire rose to warm the room. Where she had once danced with Jim, men and women now walked behind walkers or waited in wheelchairs to be moved.

"Well, it isn't exactly like I remembered, but I'm sure it will be fine," she said, forcing a smile.

"We'll do our best to make you comfortable," a nurse pleasantly offered, as she led Anne and Max to the patient's new room.

There was no elevator. Every resident not staying on the main floor had to be carried up stairs. The crews knew the staircase well, and often felt it easier to leave the wheeled cot at the base of the steps and carry the residents up on the vinyl, pole stretcher. The staircase was about six foot wide with a beautiful cherry wood banister. The first set of carpeted steps met a landing, graced by a large stained glass window. Mrs. Donnelly's room was on the second floor. The wallpaper and drapes struggled to maintain the feel of the years gone by, but the disappointment in her face clearly said this wasn't the same place she fancied.

"Here's your room," Anne cheerfully said, as they laid her on her bed. "Now I know this might not be just as you remember, but like I said, they had to make some changes. I bet when you were here last, that fireplace downstairs had a big crackling fire. But some of those nice old people in the wheelchairs down there don't have a mind as sharp as you and they might just roll into it. And that wouldn't be good."

"Oh I know dear," she said, patting Anne's hand. "I guess I expected too much. I'm only going to be here for a while anyway. Either I'll leave when I'm better and live with my daughter, or I'll go home to heaven and be with Jim. Either way I'll be happy. Now you don't worry about me, I'll be fine. You've both been very nice to spend so much time listening to me go on like I did. Thank you very much. If you come back, stop by and say hello."

"You know," Max began teasing, "if you get really bored—they've got this big slide like a shoot, that they use in an emergency for a quick escape.

I bet a couple of you youngsters, could get together and have some fun going down that thing."

Mrs. Donnelly chuckled, "Well, I'll keep that in mind. Thanks for the tip."

The sun had moved slightly since they first entered the old Flanders Mansion. Standing in the shade of a towering oak, the late October breeze felt cooler than before. Anne zipped her jacket, then reached into the ambulance for a sheet pack. Max folded the blanket to help prepare the stretcher for their next call.

"Man, that was a bummer," he said smiling. "Did you see her face when she saw those old people in the wheelchairs?" Anne knew the smile wasn't one of pleasure but rather of awkwardness. There are no books written on how you were expected to respond or feel as a professional at a time like that; nor were there any lessons taught in their classes as to the proper edict of patient emotions. They were taught not to make faces and say things like—gross, or man look at that. The reason for that was clear. But this woman had invited them into her past as she bubbled over in excitement, while sharing something very dear to her. And the crew listened to her joy—gladly. But then the joy is always the easy part. It's the disappointment and sadness that makes you fumble inside.

"I think she'll be all right. Maybe she felt young again telling that story, knowing she was coming back. Maybe she thought—or hoped, Jim would be there. I remember after my parents died, I used to set my mind up to think that they were going walk in the door any time to pick us up from my Aunt and Uncle's farm. After a while those thoughts gave in to other things in my life. It's good that she still has her daughter. I think at that age, it would be scary to be alone."

Anne didn't mind the nursing home transfers, even though some of the elderly patients were not aware mentally of what was going on. Sometimes they would yell for no reason that you knew of, or slap you, or try to bite your arms, hands, or even your clothes. Once in a while they might urinate or defecate on the way to the receiving facility. The guys hated those calls, not that she was particularly fond of them. Then there was the gomer dust, as they called it; the dry dead skin from the patient, that got onto your uniform and worked its way into the very fibers each time you handled or moved the aged. They had a variety of nicknames and acronyms for nursing homes and patients. Wrinkle ranch and gomer home were just a few. The word gomer was adopted from a book one of them read that stood for—Get Out of My Emergency Room.

And sometimes, depending on the amount of care that was evident in their patient's condition, they would change the initials of the facility involved. For example, Lancemen Nursing Center, LNC, would be changed to Lancemen No Care. It was a well known fact amongst the crews and hospital staff that if you wanted to know which nursing home provided the best or the worst care, just ask the people who cared for the residents—outside of the facility.

It was devil's night. A week had passed since they responded to the house fire, started by the Halloween candle. So far this day had been quiet; but then it was only a little past seven in the evening, and it was still early. The phone rang.

"You guys are up next. Answer the phone," Mike hollered from the garage. Max got up from the sofa where he'd been reading and picked up the receiver. Anne came out of the bathroom and listened to his conversation to determine whether they did indeed have a call.

"We have an unresponsive male," Max said, as he sat down to tie his shoes. Mike opened the bay door for them as they got into their ambulance. The address was not far off; and it seemed like the emergency lights barely had enough time to even warm up, before they pulled up to the house.

"Looks like we beat the fire department," Anne said, grabbing the orange box. Max followed as she made her way up the old wooden steps onto the porch. A grey haired black woman came and flipped on the outside light, then pushed the ripped, screen door open. "He's back here," she said. The house was a squalid mess in both appearance and odor; and no doubt the heat from the furnace, that must have been set to at least eighty something, only helped to intensify the stench. Walking through the dimly lit hall, Anne noticed a number of cockroaches crawling up the wall and motioned to Max. The woman led them into a room, where a half naked elderly black man lay supine on a very worn, bare dirty mattress. The only thing between him and the ticking was a plastic table cloth that was scrunched beneath him.

"He's been like this for days," she announced, as if she was bothered by him being there. "I can't get him to eat or nothin, and I ain't got no time to fuss over this man. I want you to take him to Lancemen General."

Anne walked over to the bed to see if he would respond to her.

"He don't talk none. He hasn't for a long time, since his stroke."

"What medication does he take?" Anne asked, picking up the prescription bottle on the night stand next to the bed. Max waited with pen in hand to write down the medication name, when she suddenly dropped the bottle.

"Oh," the woman laughed, "she afraid of the bugs."

"I don't have bugs in my house," Anne replied with disgust, shaking her hand to make sure there were no more of the roaches crawling on her. "Let's just get him out of here."

Picking up the orange box of equipment, they made their way toward the door to get the stretcher from the rig. The woman walked ahead of them, seemingly still amused by Anne's reaction. "I's don't kills them anymore," she haughtily barked. "I's just make a paste out of their bodies—and puts it on my jaw when it ails me."

Max grinned while standing at the back of the rig. "She's a dandy. I got a couple of buddies I could introduce her to. So, ah—where's the fire department?"

"They've probably been here before, and opted not to come. Not that I blame them. Have you ever heard anything so nasty? I feel like I've got bugs crawling all over me," she said shaking off the imaginary insects.

Without another word, they carried the stretcher up the steps and onto the porch. After entering through the front door, they quickly rolled it down the hall and stopped in front of the ill man's room. It only took a couple of times before they realized the stretcher was too long to make the turn. It just wasn't going to fit, even after setting the top half in a sitting position. The pole stretcher was also too difficult to maneuver, so they grabbed the paper sheet from the cot and wrapped it around the patient, to protect their clothes. Max sat him up, then reached under his arms, while Anne grabbed his legs. They carried him to the hall and placed him onto the stretcher, still with little response noticed in his level of consciousness. After covering him up the rest of the way they headed for the door. The woman waited in the front room with the patient's insurance slip in her hand.

"Here's his card," she said handing it to Max. "He got Medicaid."

As soon as Anne was in the patient compartment, she shut the doors and uncovered the man. Roaches ran to hide from the light. She stomped on every one she saw. Max called ahead to the hospital. After the nurses made a rapid assessment, they took him to the decontamination room so the man could be showered.

Max filled out one of the new run forms, while Anne scoured the back of the unit. After hearing the description of the house that Max gave, the nurses decided to have Social Services check out the residence before the man went back; which wouldn't be for a while. Just in their initial survey alone they could tell that he was severely dehydrated. Then, as luck would have it, they got a call in the ER from their dispatcher, to go back to the same residence. This time for a man with asthma who was short of breath.

"This is going to be another scoop and run Maxie, "Anne sighed, buckling her seat beat.

And scoop and run they did. Even with having to carry this patient down from the second story, they made it to Lancemen General in record time.

"So runs the round of life from hour to hour," Anne silently spoke to herself remembering the words of Tennyson, as she once again scoured the back of the rig. Her mind drifted to her early teen years, when she and Jenny would lie on a quilt in the hayloft at home, reading book after book until they were called for chores. But the daydream was short. Hearing a cough, she turned her head and she saw Max standing at the back of the rig grinning like the little gnome he likened, waiting to share his news.

"I am not going back to that house," Anne sternly stated.

"Oh no… It's better than that. We get to do a removal," he announced, knowing how she had tired of the body removal business. "Well hey, what are your buddies doing? Maybe we can dump it on to them."

"Rick and Mike? They're on a PI north of Lancemen. They went on a hanging before that; but it turned out to be a Halloween dummy someone strung up in a tree. I guess they thought it would be funny. And people think we're sick?"

"Well, I say we scoop and run. We're getting pretty good at that."

"Where's the body?"

"Buster said it was here. He said you knew where the cooler was."

"All too well I'm afraid," she groaned. "The hospital morgue is on the other side of the parking lot. You need to turn this buggy around, so that we aren't wheeling the body across it. It looks tacky when you do that. Did Buster give you the person's name?" Max pulled a slip of paper from his pocket.

"Herman Cann," he read.

"Herman can what?" she snapped.

"That's his name. Herman Cann. Look here, sister, don't get testy with me," he teased, realizing her displeasure. "This wasn't my idea."

Anne understood from his comment and the grumbling she felt within her, that maybe she was just letting this whole thing get to her. After all, removals were easy. You didn't have to take vitals or sit and carry on a conversation when you didn't feel like it—and they never complained. What could be simpler?

After wheeling the stretcher into the refrigerated room, they began reading over the toe tags. "Here he is," Max called out. "He's still on a backboard."

"Well, I don't feel like trying to get him off it right now. Just leave him on it. The people at the funeral home can take care of it. I know, I know. I'm getting a little crabby. See—you haven't been here long enough to know just how old this gets. I became an EMT and then a paramedic to help people, so they wouldn't end up like this. I understand it still happens; we aren't God, but I must say—I like living, breathing people a lot better than cold, not breathing people."

Throughout the trip to the funeral home Anne continued to plead her case. "Tom's brother worked here for a short time before going to Colorado. Once, he and I took this guy to a funeral home that didn't have an elevator. The deceased guy was on a backboard, just like this guy, but only it wasn't ours. Anyway, we got to the place and carried this guy who was very heavy, dead weight, no pun intended, stretcher and all, down the stairs and then into the room that the mortician requested. Then we rolled the body next to this stainless steel table and unbuckled the stretcher straps. We picked up the board to move the body over, but it wouldn't go. We figured we must be caught on something, so we pulled the sheet back that was over him. But we weren't caught on anything! The man had a death grip on the side rails of the stretcher with both hands. Mark had to literally pry the man's hands off the rails. And—he had a grin on his face." Max smiled suspiciously. "I'm not making any of this stuff up," she assured him. "You can ask Tom. Mark's eyes were as big as saucers when he told him about it."

Turning the corner, they were about five miles from their destination. Suddenly, they heard a banging sound coming from the back of the ambulance. Anne turned and looked in the back. Max looked in the rear view mirror. "What is it?" he asked.

"It's just the stretcher hitting the bench seat. It must have broken away from the stretcher bar." Max pulled over to the side of the road. He looked at Anne as if he was waiting for her to get out and re-lock the stretcher in place.

"I'm not going out there. You guys are supposed to be the brave ones. You all think that women can't do anything, until it's something that you don't want to do. No sir. You just go right ahead and be brave. I'll wait right here."

At this point it was clear, this whole thing had certainly set Anne in a mood. Max almost felt it was safer to face the loose, rolling around dead man than to argue with her. After zipping up his jacket, he opened his door and got out. In seconds he opened the back door. Anne turned and watched as he grabbed the foot of the stretcher and pushed it against the locking mechanism on the stretcher bar. He pulled it a couple of times to make sure it was secure, then came around to the front of the rig. Hopping back onto his seat, he put the gear shift in drive and once again they were off. "Oh man, this is a little too close to Halloween for this kinda stuff to be happening," he nervously grinned.

Luckily, the remainder of that call was uneventful and the weeks that followed were pretty much routine. Then to Anne's surprise, the week before Thanksgiving, she was given permission to drive. At first, she could handle only non-emergency calls, which was fine with her. Taking this thing one step at a time was probably best anyway, especially with the snowfall. She remembered watching, when Dan drove in the snow on an emergency call and noticed that he generally went just fast enough for the back of the ambulance to start fishtailing; then he would ease off a small amount and continue down the road. She knew you had to have a feel for the rig. It wasn't at all like driving a car. That much she'd learned from riding as a passenger.

Anne spent Thanksgiving at home in Summerville. She was careful to watch that her conversations didn't include much of her work experiences. Even though she and the other crews often reviewed and discussed their calls while eating at the restaurants they frequented, she understood by the other patrons sitting around them that left, that Uncle Henry probably wouldn't consider it to be table talk. While mentally reviewing some of dialogues about brain matter and such, she decided that he probably was right.

Max's holiday plans consisted of taking part in the annual Thanksgiving Day bash at the Gonzo Mansion, as they called it. The very large old home that he shared with his buddies and two brother's was built back in the 1800's. It sat near a main road, about ten miles east of Lancemen. From the stories he told, she was surprised that their neighbors were so tolerant of the activities that occurred there. But then maybe the useful trades they all possessed, like carpentry and roofing, provided the tool on which to build peace.

The shortest day of the year was upon them. White Christmas lights were strung in every tree that lined the streets of downtown Lancemen. In front of the Courthouse, a large pine tree covered in multicolored lights softly reflected a warm glow in the sparkling snow. The city was quite. It almost seemed like everyone was bedded in for a long winter's nap. Only the crunching of the snow beneath the tires of the ambulance could be heard as they drove toward the station. Anne flipped through the radio dial looking for Christmas songs. The last verse of God Rest Ye Merry Gentlemen came through the speaker. She began singing, prodding Max to join her.

Smiling he said, "You don't what me to sing."

It was nearly midnight. Normally the crews would have welcomed a lull in the action. Sleep and a hot meal were like gold to them. But tonight for some reason, they felt as restless as children on Christmas Eve. As Max pulled up into the station parking lot, it became clear that they were not alone in their desire for activity. Jack and his partner Big Rick, who worked out of Lakeview on Life Five, were out front throwing snowballs at Mike and Rick Stockwell. Suddenly, the ambulance windshield was covered with snow as a barrage of packed balls slammed against it. After the first round, the battering stopped. Taking a chance, Anne rolled her window part way down. A snowball burst against the top rim, with a portion of it hitting the inside wall of the driver's compartment. Scurrying to the back of the rig, she raced to lock the doors before the snow warriors could attack from the rear. Max had to fight to get the doors in the front compartment locked. But finally after some effort, he and Anne were safe. Rick and Mike stood outside of their windows laughing. They had put up a pretty good fight for as cold as they were.

"Hey," Anne said, through the tiny space she dared offer from her window. "What do you say we go Christmas caroling?"

"How are we going to do that?" Mike asked.

"Over the PA. We can follow each other, like a convoy. It'll be fun."

Jack, Big Rick, Rick and Mike stood next to the ambulance and deliberated for a second. The night had been quiet. They weren't that far out of their area. Why not—it was Christmas. After brushing the snow off their clothes, each of them got into their own ambulance. Rick flipped on their emergency lights. "Christmas lights," he called out from his window. Similarly, they all followed suite and turned on their lights, while listening to hear which song the other unit sang from the PA, so they'd all be together. Like three ducks in a row, they slowly drove around the four and a half mile stretch of road that encircled Lancemen for nearly forty-five minutes. Cars that drove passed them honked and waved. Some yelled Merry Christmas.

Finally, driving in circles lost its appeal, so instead they decided to sing Christmas carols for the city's firemen at the main station. One by one, they lined up at the back of the building and faced the bunk room windows on the second floor. It was obvious, as they began singing the first measure that they weren't any better at planning than they were at singing, for they all began voicing a different song before quickly switching to Jingle Bells in unison. Almost immediately, sleepy unhappy faces appeared at the windows. Yawns began and tired hands raised up to rub squinting eyes. Mel and Pierce stood along side a number of other firemen they knew; all were dressed in tee shirts and long johns with pillow pressed hair, that stood up. Slowly, a few of them offered expressions of wonder. Clearly, however, it was not the same kind of wonder that the angels in Bethlehem inspired; but rather a wonder of—what are you doing? And sadly enough to the joyous singers, the firemen weren't the only ones unmoved by the jubilant message of good tidings and cheer. For out of the corner of her eye, Anne noticed a man and woman standing next to the ambulance in their bathrobes and boots. Slowly, she rolled down her window.

"I know you mean well," the woman started, "but we have young children who are trying to sleep."

"Sorry," Anne replied. "I guess we didn't realize how loud we were." Max reached up and turned off the emergency lights. Anne, disappointed that their festive mood had not been better received, hung up the PA mic. Like pups with their tails between their legs they headed back to the station. Jack and Big Rick drove past and waved as they continued west, toward Lakeview. Anne looked down at the radio dial. It was almost three in the morning.

"Well, what are we going to do now?"

"Try to get some sleep, I guess," Max answered.

The New Year began as most, with pie crust promises and resolutions for the future. Max caught on to things quickly and Anne figured he would move on to a paramedic car on the next rotation. A new group of students came from the college to do their field clinicals. This time, there were a few girls hoping to make it through the program. While talking about the class with one of the students, Anne learned that Mr. Dewit was looking for past student graduates to help teach during the practical lessons. Merve apparently thought she did well enough to teach, she thought. What could Mr. Dewit say? She was used to hearing no, so what did she have to lose? The next morning after a shower and quick nap, she went to the college. To her surprise, Mr. Dewit welcomed her like the prodigal child who had come home. Of course the fact that her time was voluntary, might have had something to do with it but still Anne liked the idea of helping the students before they came out to the road.

Life in Lancemen seemed to be moving along at its normal pace. In contrast however, the winter months in Summerville were usually quiet. But it gave Uncle Henry time to work through his plan for the spring crops, and to think of new ways to save money. Even though it was still too early to tell if last December's strike would bring any relief. He said he didn't have time to wait for other people to make a move; he had a farm to run. Roger and his wife took the boys out to the farm a few times for a sleigh ride. The boys of course, had a great time and their visit sparked a welcome gladness. Aunt Ruth made Tracy promise to bring them back in the spring to meet the new, fuzzy and fluffy babies. Roger and Uncle Henry always enjoyed each other's company. Roger took to the farm like he was born there. He always remarked to Anne about what a strong man Uncle Henry was.

"Yes, he's as strong as a bull—and just as bullheaded," she responded, with no more to be said, for she knew it was a family trait that she herself sometimes exercised.

It was February 22nd, 1978; just two days after the horrifying story broke, reporting that a derailed train carrying liquid propane had exploded, killing fifteen people as it leveled two blocks of Waverly, Tennessee's business area. And, it was only a week since every news paper headline clamored in bold print that Leon Spinks had become the new Heavyweight champion, over Muhammad Ali. Although it didn't make the papers, back home in the somewhat calmer city of Lancemen, news of Merve and Glen switching from Dodge to Ford ambulances flowed throughout the ranks. One by one the rigs were replaced; and oddly enough, the make of the ambulances wasn't discussed nearly as much as the new paint design. Previously, Townsdale's ambulances were red, white and blue, while Mercy's had been maize and white. The new design kept the white background, but added a navy and maize stripe, with each color representing both companies. The owners stayed with the original names for now, but there was talk that eventually they would be called Paramed Incorporated. At first the new, freshly painted ambulances were a little hard to get used to, but after a while Anne thought they were the prettiest around.

Spring had finally arrived and was welcomed by everyone who was tired of heavy coats and snow shovels. The girls, along with the other students that had been riding their EMT clinicals, finished the program and graduated. Now that the semester had ended, Anne was no longer needed at the college; however, an extra hand was always welcome on the farm, so a lot of her days off were spent in Summerville. Max, as she predicted, was going on to a paramedic car in a few weeks, which meant she'd have a new partner to break in on her next shift. Even though she was happy for Max, she felt somewhat disheartened to know that she had been side stepped again, and wondered if Robbie's words would ever come through for her.

John, her new partner, was waiting at the bay door of the station when she pulled up. He was pleasant looking enough, and had a bit of a waddle when he walked into the garage, which she attributed to his mild plumpness. She couldn't quite pin it down exactly, but something about him reminded her of Jackie Gleason. He enjoyed books of the Antarctic, stories of the Iditarod and westerns. While he was quieter than the others, she often found him to be easy going with a good sense of humor. That, she truly understood, was a necessary characteristic to survive. John's orientation went easier, now that she could actually drive non-emergency and emergency calls, herself. And at no extra charge, she also included a brief demonstration of the Lancemen shuffle, a dance created for the homes with cockroaches. "If you keep your feet moving, they can't crawl up your legs," she suggested.

It seemed like time had zoomed by. John and Anne were starting their fourth week together. Their rig was washed and stocked and both crews were jammed into the small bedroom, making up the bunks.

"You have to watch out, John," she warned. "Sometimes they come back to the station after you've left and short sheet your bed."

"Yeah—but we quit short sheeting Anne's bed. She's so short, she could never tell," Rick laughed. "What fun is that?" Then they heard a tapping on the front door. Rick went out to see who it was, and noticed someone in uniform standing outside. "Hi—Can I help you?"

"Yeah, my name is Randy. Mr. Thomson told me to come here for an orientation ride. I just got hired."

"Sure, come on in. Let me just call down there and see what he wants us to do."

Randy stepped into the station and shyly stood in the doorway, waiting for directions. Rick picked up the direct line and was put on hold to wait for Robbie. "Hey Randy," he said grinning. "Close the door, man, or you'll let the bums in."

Randy wasn't sure if he was serious or kidding but responded quickly all the same. "Oh sure—sorry," he said, turning to close the door.

Anne and John came from the bunk room to introduce themselves after hearing part of the conversation, while Rick continued to wait for Robbie to come to the phone.

Smiling, Randy whispered while shaking their hands, "I'm a little nervous."

"Oh, well you'll like it here," John said, in an easy calming voice. "I've been here about a month, and I feel right at home." In the background, they could hear Rick inform Robbie that Randy had arrived. Rick appeared to be listening to what sounded like instructions, at least that's what they presumed from the okays he repeated. Then his conversation ended.

"Robbie said you're supposed to ride with me and Mike for a few days until Mike goes out to Lakeview. And apparently, we're going to start rotating our shifts. Robbie said he'll stop by to explain it later after he meets with the Association. And Anne—in a couple weeks you'll no longer be our token female. They just hired two more women. They'll be working out of here, opposite of you. Merve wants to give it a try and see what happens. Townsdale had a couple girls down there for a while, and it's worked out so far. Well—come on Randy. I'll show you where to put your things."

Anne stood a little dazed. The news of her staying on a Basic car really came as no surprise—but did she hear right, about the girls? She knew they would have to hire another girl someday, but now they hired two! She began wondering if the girls were from the class she'd been working with. A couple of them did exceptionally well. Then suddenly, a funny feeling came over her as she remembered that some of the female students demonstrated more interest in talking to the guys, than taking a patient's blood pressure. Well whoever they are, she finally told herself, I'm sure we'll get along just fine.

The day picked up and they got so busy that Anne forgot all about Mike and the girls. Their first run was with Mr. Deadman. He was a very sweet man in his mid-thirties that was mentally slow. When they first arrived at his home, he was shaking because he thought that he had accidentally overdosed on two Tums. Anne took the wrapper and read it to him, explaining that he had taken the correct amount and that he would be fine. "Oh thank you," he said, nearly in tears. "I was so scared."

Next, they ran on an asthma patient. After that, they responded to a pedestrian versus car accident at a main intersection in the north end of the city. Then within a few minutes of transporting that patient to Lancemen Osteopathic, they were given the information for a hospital to nursing home transfer. By now they were very hungry and as soon as they cleared the nursing home, they tried grabbing lunch at a drive through hamburger joint. But before they even had a chance to unwrap the burger, they were sent on an assault, then a seizure, and after that, a shooting. When they cleared the hospital from the shooting, they were called to an address they knew by heart, at the Rosin's house. Charlie and Flossie Rosin were a black married couple who drank throughout the day. The crews had never seen them sober - so they didn't know what their normal relationship was like. Anne had been at the address a number of times herself and always for the same reason, an injury resulting from an argument. Certainly today she suspected it would be no different.

As Anne and John entered the house, they saw Charlie sitting on the sofa, with Tory, one of the fire department paramedics, wrapping his legs with gauze. Blood was everywhere. Flossie was in another room, being detained by the Lancemen Police. She apparently took to cuttin on Charlie's legs during the usual argument. In spite of the many stitches that lay before him, he was still worried that they might take her away.

"Where's Flossie?" he repeated, while peering into the back room. "I just - wan'ta see her."

"She's talking to the police, Charlie," Tory said. "She ain't going nowhere, so relax."

Charlie couldn't wait any longer and began hollering from the sofa. "Flossie! Flossie! Girl—why'd you do this to me? Don't you knows—I love you?"

"She knows that, Charlie. You guys have to quit hurting each other; and, you both need to quit drinking that Mad Dog. You get too crazy."

"I knows it. I just don wants them to take Flossie to that place—like last time."

"Well if they do—it will only be for a day or so. You'll need a few days to rest, anyway."

Anne watched the way Tory handled Mr. Rosin and thought he did very well. A good number of Lancemen's residents, were blacks from down south. They had a vernacular language all their own and were generally very respectful to those who came to help them when ever they were sick or hurt. For the most part they were good people who worked hard at making the best of life.

As the amount of calls in the City of Lancemen increased during the day, by nightfall it had become clear to the crews and firemen that the State checks must have be sent out. While most of the recipients of the checks probably used the them for the intended purpose, the EMS workers quite often met with those who didn't within twenty-four hours of their arrival. An emergency call placed by such a recipient, who was sort of standing next to a pay phone outside one of the bars in town, was always the same. Someone too drunk to walk home, pretending to be hurt or passed out or as they would say, "I fell out." Leo Gomez was a regular transport, and one that the police tried to avoid; not that they were afraid of him in any way. It was just that many times when he called for a ride to the hospital, he often got into a scuffle with the police on the scene and ended going to the hospital for a different reason then his initial complaint. The doctors dreaded him coming in; for they knew before the night was over they would have to call in security.

Then there was Emmo Pippins, a popular fellow from across the straights, who bought booze for everyone on check day. He was mellow in character by far next to Leo and was very dependable. Like clock work, you could count on running on him every three weeks; and every three weeks it was the same scenario. You would enter the residence, stepping over several others passed out on the floor, and then help Emmo to his feet. As he inched his way across the floor dragging his baggy jeans that were soaked with urine and watery stool, he left a sludge trail as he went. He literally lived on a sofa at a friend's house. The only time he got off was when they called EMS to pick him up. For the entire three weeks he drank from a large jug, ate nothing, urinated and defecated right on the sofa in the same clothes.

But the regulars weren't all men; not by any stretch. Lancemen had a variety of women who equally abused the service. Once Anne and her partner were called to a school parking lot for "a party down." When they pulled up they saw a well known female patient, Victoria McFay, sitting on the pavement while leaning up against a fireman's legs, passed out as cold as could be. Anne shook her head and snickered when she got out of the rig. While waiting for the ambulance, the other firemen in the group occupied themselves by tossing Victoria's wig around like it was a hot potato. Jokingly they called her "Queen Victoria" as they helped Anne and her partner put the anesthetized patient on their cot. She knew they weren't trying to be cruel. It was just that the whole drunken regular thing became very tiresome day after day and it was something that you had to experience day after day to understand. The hospital and EMS workers had a mental list of the frequent fliers and watched as the list grew. Sometimes it would reach a plateau and then sometimes it would shrink when one or two died off.

Anne and John were exhausted. While on the way to yet another non emergency call, they drove past their station. As they neared, Anne wished they were pulling in, rather than driving by. Then something caught her eye. She took a second look and motioned to John to slow down. They couldn't believe their eyes. All of the station's furniture sat outside in the parking lot in front of the door. It wasn't tossed as if they had been evicted, but set up like you would set it up in your home. The lamps were on and the TV was playing the eleven o'clock news. Anne watched briefly, as James Christy's photos of Pluto flashed across the screen.

"Well, at least we know it wasn't Rick and Mike. They've been as busy as we've been. It must have been one of the outlying stations. See that's why they call them the vacation stations. Who else would have time to do that?"

After finishing up the call, they headed toward the station and hoped the bums hadn't taken over. It was after two in the morning when they finally got the furniture moved back inside and things back together. "At last," Anne whispered as she crawled up on the top bunk. Lying still, she tried to unwind. What a day, she thought. Then she heard John talking. But there wasn't anyone else in the room—she knew that. Unless maybe she'd drifted off to sleep, and the other crew came in without her knowing. Forcing her sleepy eyes to focus, she stared at their beds. No, they weren't there. Leaning over her bunk, she looked under to see who in the world he was talking to. She chuckled to herself then watched a second longer to be sure. But there was no uncertainty about it. He was definitely talking in his sleep, just as clear as if the person was next to him. Laying back on her bed, she asked herself, "Should I wake him?" Maybe that wasn't a good idea, she thought. They had a guy who worked there for a short while who had been in the Vietnam War. He was very nice when he was awake, but it only took a couple of times before they learned to wake him from his sleep at a distance. Soon, the weight of her own eyelids tugged harder. Finally she gave in and decided to just to let him sleep.

The phone rang. She must have drifted off. It rang again. Feeling as if in a fog, she tried forcing herself to wake up. Then she heard John say as clear as a bell, "Well, gotta go. Talk to ya later." Then she felt the bed move as he got up from the bottom bunk. Leaning on her elbows, she watched as he walked with a sway like Jackie Gleason to answer the phone. "Hello," he said as bright eyed as if they had slept for hours. "Hey Anne," he called out. "We got a run."

Quickly she crawled to the foot of the bed, then climbed down the bunk boards like a ladder. While pulling her uniform shirt over her tee shirt, she mentally replayed the scene. Oh my gosh, she thought,—that's the funniest thing I've ever seen. Then without restraint, she burst into laughter.

"What's so funny?" John asked, totally puzzled.

While scurrying to the rig, she spilled the story that brought her such hilarity. "Unit Two on the air," she chuckled.

"Unit Two you've just been canceled. Sounds like - maybe that was probably a good thing," the dispatcher remarked.

"I'll give you a TX," she said.

"Now don't go calling Mark and telling him this nonsense, or anybody else. I do not talk in my sleep."

"Yes you do, John—I heard you loud and clear. All right. You can claim anything you want, but I really did hear you—just like I said," she snickered. The next morning she shared the story with the other crew, but no one else seemed to find the same humor in it as she did. Guess you had to be there, she finally concluded.

It had been a few weeks since Mike left to work at Lakeview and Randy was quickly settling in. One thing for sure, it didn't take long for his shyness to ease. This Irish lad with red hair and freckles looked every bit like the boy next door. But after spending time with this bunch of guys, the real Randy came through.

"Boy, you sure can't tell a book by its cover," Anne teased. "I thought you were as wholesome as apple pie…"

"I am," he bragged. Then the others at the station chorused, "Right!"

Finally the day came, a day of initial mixed feelings for Anne. The girls Merve hired had worked their first forty-eight hour shift and she was coming in to relieve them. To her delight, they were the same girls from the class she had worked with.

"Morning, Anne," Linda chuckled, when she walked in the station door. "You didn't tell us it was going to be like this."

"Yeah? Well, so what do you think?"

"Oh I think you know me and Denny well enough by now. These boys aren't going to keep us down. We're going to get along—just fine." Anne knew by her comment that Linda perceived the job as a great challenge mixed with the bonus of fun. Moreover, she was pretty sure, by the twinkle in her eye that things were about to be dealt with, more on an even keel; not that Anne had ever let the guys walk over her. If nothing else, it would be interesting to see what was to come. No doubt, the boys would see it as—there goes the neighborhood. But personally, she was happy to say—here come the girls.

CHAPTER 18

AMERICAN GRAFFITI (EMS STYLE)

Jeremiah Johnson led the ideal life, according to Anne's partner John. He dreamed of having a cabin far away from the civilized world, with no running water, electricity, or furnace. He talked of his squaw wife who would serve him his meals, then sit at his side until he finished eating, to which Anne often remarked, "Oh brother."

The forty-eight hour shifts the crews worked were long and sometimes grueling, unless of course, the crew worked out of an outlying, AKA vacation station. From the stories Anne had heard, the Bedford station was almost like a rest home, at times. The amount of calls there, were by far, less than the amount of calls in relation to those pulled in Lancemen; leaving many enjoyable hours for fishing and barbeques. But it didn't really matter if the forty-eight hours were spent at the station flipping hamburgers, or in the front cab of the ambulance, sooner or later the amount of time each crew member spent with each other, eroded past polite conversations allowing surrender to more personal and interesting conversations. Because they had to know their partner's whereabouts at all times, they had to act almost as a shadow, which wasn't always easy. Yet over time, as they learned each other's traits along with their good and bad habits, that intrusion became less of a task. Nonetheless, the challenge was different for each person for clearly, and for different reasons, the guys saw things differently then did Anne. But after just a short period of time, by their comments, Anne could easily recite most of the guys favorite foods, best liked TV shows, music preference, movie and star choices, sports team pick, and saving best for last, which anatomical area of the female body was most appreciated.

John wasn't usually as bold or open with his feelings regarding the ladies, at least not in front of Anne. He seemed a little shy, or even more private, actually. So, when he began sharing an experience he had at a friend's wedding, she was a little surprised. They were sitting at a cover point when he nervously began revealing his memorable event. After folding the sports section of the newspaper in half, he set it on his lap. The windows were rolled down and the dispatch radio at a comfortable volume. Once he orally skimmed over the nuptial rites at St. Mary's church, where the wedding took place, he quickly jumped on to the reception. It was there that he met Nancy, a young woman who he described as, "the prettiest he'd ever seen." Then he proudly told how he asked her to dance and that she graciously stood and walked with him to the dance floor. Anne listened quietly as he went on like a school girl, giggling to herself while wondering, where the squaw would fit in.

"She was wearing this dress that sort of floated when she walked," he went on. "It was a nice dark pink color. She said it was mauve. We danced and talked until the reception was over. Then she gave me her phone number. I just can't believe—she danced and talked with me."

Anne laughed, amused by his modesty. "You're so funny. Why wouldn't she want to talk to you, John? You have a great sense of humor, you're smart and fun to be around."

"Yeah, but I sure don't look like Robert Redford."

"There is nothing wrong with the way you look. If she wanted to be with Robert Redford she would have been with Robert Redford. But she wasn't… she was with you."

"That's only because he wasn't there."

"Oh stop it—So, tell me. Did you make her sit at your feet while you ate?" she teased.

"Well, not yet. We have to go out on a couple of dates first," he jokingly replied, to save face. He never thought that his boastful words of his cabin life with a squaw would return so soon to haunt him.

A gush of warm summer air came into the open window and pushed against the morning paper that Anne held in her hands. For a moment it appeared like a head sail on a tiny boat caught by a great wind, out on the open sea. Then after a few forceful movements with her hands she was able to fold the newspaper to the crossword puzzle section. Rare as it was, they'd been sitting in the parking lot of the Lakeview Kmart for over an hour. That was pretty much the norm for an ALS rig; but not for a Basic car. Realizing their fortune, they gratefully savored and enjoyed the break, for they both knew it would be short lived. With her shoes off and her feet propped up on the dash, Anne leaned over the paper and diligently worked the puzzle. Drawn by the intense silence of her partner, she looked over at John who sat with his mind reeling deep in thought between joy and confusion. She smiled while thinking back to a few times when she herself gave in to the whirling butterflies of love's woes.

"So, how long do you think I should wait before I call her?" he finally asked, after a pondering pause. "You know—you're a girl. I thought you might know about this stuff."

"Well, what did you say when she gave you her number?"

"I said I'd give her a call in a couple of days."

"Well then, give her a call in a couple of days," Anne replied, while penciling in another answer to her puzzle.

"But isn't there a time period that I'm supposed to wait, so she doesn't think I'm too anxious?"

"John," she said, in a voice that smiled. "What do you want to do?" Setting her pencil against the paper she scanned his eyes. "Do you want to call her—or do you want to wait?"

"I want to call her; but I don't want to scare her off."

"It sounds to me like she liked being with you. If you told her you would call her in a couple of days, then you should stick to your word and call her. I don't know why people feel like they have to play a bunch of games when they start dating.—Do you want her to like you, or someone else?"

"I want her to like me, of course."

"Then be yourself—and let her like you, and not some fake person. You're better than anyone you could make up anyway. I don't know why you're so worried. If she didn't like you she wouldn't have spent so much time with you. Right?"

"I guess. I just don't want to mess this up. She's so nice and so pretty," he said smiling, as if he were looking at her photo. Then his expression changed from delight to worry. "Hey, do me a favor. Don't say anything to the guys—You know they can be like dogs about some things."

Anne looked back, amused by his comment. "Relax, John. You're letting this make you an old man. And I wouldn't fret too much about the guys. Some of them really are dogs—but most just act like dogs because they think it's expected, not that women are any different. Some people are hustlers and others are just sheep. Either way, it's sad that anyone would feel a need to run a scam in order to succeed. There's a lot to say about integrity. At least that's what I think. Anyway, what's a five letter word for mountain-climber's aid?"

"Piton."

"That fits! All right—thank you, Jeremiah."

While pressing the pencil against the paper to form the letters, her ears picked up the fire department's tone over the dispatch radio.

"There goes Lakeveiw," she advised, tucking the newspaper behind her seat. The tone repeated, followed by their dispatcher's information. Knowing they were the closest unit, she jotted down the address onto a pad of paper. John turned up the radio and headed for the parking lot exit.

"Unit Two, get ready to code." Hearing the words that opened the gate, they were off.

John was a good driver. Anne felt safe with him behind the wheel. He didn't fly up and tail someone's car until they pulled over. Instead, he approached at a steady increasing speed that gave them a chance to move to the right and stop. Anne learned by watching her seasoned partners and by her own experience that driving the ambulance on an emergency call required not only concentration, but constant preplanning of an escape route. Too often the vehicles they approached would stop suddenly in front of them, or turn in the wrong direction without warning; while others seemed oblivious to their presence, in spite of the siren behind them.

Seven miles from their initial starting point, and they were finally nearing the address of the call. Lakeview's dispatcher had put it out as abdominal pain. As they turned onto the requested street, they saw the fire trucks parked up ahead. Pulling up to the address they realized the trucks had blocked the driveway, so they had to park in the street. Anne opened the back doors and unhooked the stretcher. After scanning the front lawn they decided their only access to reach the front door was to go down a small ditch, then through the yard.

"I don't know why these guys can't leave the driveway open. Every time we run with them, we have to apologize to the patient for the rough ride across their grass," John softly protested.

After leaving the wheeled cot on the front walk, they entered the house to see if this was the best entrance and whether or not the patient even wanted the ambulance. Over a course of time, they discovered that sometimes family members just panicked, when the patient didn't really want or need to go to the hospital. So rather than track up their house, they often left the stretcher outside when weather permitted, until they were sure of the circumstances.

The Lieutenant from the fire department greeted them as they walked in the door. "Hi, John, Anne," he began. "We have a forty-two year old male with a history of kidney stones, complaining of abdominal pain. He thinks he's passing another stone. We've got LOH on the apcor trying to get him something for the pain, so we can get him out of here. This guy can't sit, stand, or lay down without thrashing all over. We finally got the IV started. Talk about a moving target. He's in the family room in the back with my guys," he concluded, as they walked through the house.

Anne noticed the foyer had a narrow passage. Then she studied a couple of sharp turns as they went from the living room into the kitchen. Walking past the big overstuffed sofa next to the doorway of the living room, she scratched her head. Then she spied an island in the kitchen that would make it difficult to maneuver the stretcher around. One of the volunteers with the department caught her eyeing the layout of the house, searching for a better way to come in.

"We can use the sliding patio doors," he offered. "There's a paved path that goes beside the garage next to the driveway. If you want to stay and help these guys out, we'll bring in the stretcher."

"Thanks, Henry," she replied, then walked closer to the inner circle of the scene and stood next to John. She watched as one of the paramedics removed two small vials from the middle shelf of the beige drug box. Then he took out a syringe and an alcohol swab. Turning to one of the other paramedics on the department he asked again, in a low tone, to quietly confirm the dose the hospital requested. "Hey, Dave. Fifty of demerol and fifty of vistaril. Does it matter which one I draw up first?"

"I don't think so. The doc didn't say."

Anne understood that because they were a new ALS department, they wouldn't have all the answers. So to her, it seemed like a fair question. At least he was willing to ask. She watched quietly for a few seconds while he studied the glass vials. She was aware of the rivalry between the fire department paramedics and the paramedics of the private EMS companies. And it was for that reason she hesitated to make a suggestion. Anything could be taken wrong and she didn't want to step on any sensitive toes. But then, at the same time, she could see that the patient was in horrendous pain. And in light of that she finally spoke up, as tactfully and softly as she could.

"The demerol vial has a rubber top that creates sort of a vacuum. You have to exchange the same amount of liquid that you take, with air from the syringe. So if you want to draw up one cc of demerol, you have to first put in that same amount of air. Then, after you pop off the glass tip from the vistaril where it's scored, draw it up in the same syringe. Don't squirt any of the demerol into the vistaril when you draw it up. And make sure the needle tip stays in the liquid or you will draw up air instead. You don't want any air in the syringe." She was relieved to see that he followed her instructions without resentment. After rubbing the area with an alcohol swab he gave the patient the analgesic mix IM in his right buttocks. Giving it IV was not suggested as it caused a burning sensation at the IV site. Within a few minutes the man seemed to tolerate the pain well enough to lie on the stretcher. En route to the hospital, the paramedic and Anne worked together watching the patient's vitals and respirations.

"When did you get your medic's license?" he asked.

"About a year ago."

"I just wondered. I haven't seen you working an ALS car." By her expression, he understood and thought it best to drop the conversation. "Hey, well thanks for the help anyway."

The patient's vitals remained stable during the rest of the quiet transport. After they turned his care over to the ER staff, Anne went out to the alcove in the ambulance parking area to make up the cot. First she tucked the bottom sheet under the poles of the vinyl stretcher. Then she took the pillow and fluffed it up and placed it at the head between the poles. Taking a clean towel, she draped it over the pillow, folded it in half, then pushed the ends under the pole stretcher. She worked without thinking about her task, as she had done it more times than she could remember. Instead, her mind was consumed in self pity as the dilemma with her unused paramedic license ate at her.

"Hey, Anne."

She jumped, startled by the voice that pierced through her mental churning. "Hey, Robbie. How are you? Are you stationed out of here today?" she asked cheerfully, trying to camouflage her true feelings.

"Yeah. Jerry's up on the floor talking to one of the nurses. Did you guys bring in that guy with the kidney stone?"

"Yeah."

"How'd fire do?"

"They did all right. They needed a little help with the pain meds but other than that they did fine."

"And who helped them with that?"

"I did."

"Oh, I see. Well that explains the sour face."

"It's just so frustrating. The fire departments trust me. Any cardiac arrest that we go on with Lancemen, and I get to do the intubation. I help out Lakeview. I taught Max to drive, and I show everyone else the ropes that comes in. They all move ahead, and I stay on a basic car. Why doesn't Merve trust me?"

"It isn't that Merve doesn't trust you. If he didn't trust you, you wouldn't even be here. That other girl that worked here before you came—What was her name? I only know her by her supposed porn name—Hot Sleaza."

"It was—Lisa." Anne chuckled, after hearing his sad attempt to growl her name.

"Yeah, that's it. Anyway, from what I heard, she did a lot of damage in just a few weeks. By the time she left here, Merve just about lost all hope for a contract with the fire departments in the west end of the county. Their wives did not like having her around. Merve's just being cautious." Leaning over, Robbie helped her load the stretcher into the rig as he talked. "Hiring the other girls is going to put you in a good spot to go ALS. He'll do that, before he ever puts two girls together. I bet by fall you'll be working out of Lakeview. At least that's my plan."

"That'd be great; but, I'd rather he moved me because he wanted me there—instead of having no other choice."

"Oh, he always has a choice. Like I said, if he didn't trust you, you wouldn't be here. Just hang in there, kid. It's just a matter of riding out the waves. Anyway—the real reason that I came out was to ask you about tonight's volleyball game at the station. What time does it start?"

"Rick told Mike sometime around eight o'clock. Don't you remember?" she asked. "Mike's coming in to finish Randy's shift. Randy and Tom's brother are going for a weekend rock climbing trip."

"Oh. I didn't think Mike was coming in until eleven or so. But it makes sense that he'd come in early for the game. Well okay—guess I'd better get back in there and find Jerry. See you tonight."

The two empty bays at the station were wide, but they were not quite wide enough to make the sixty by thirty feet recommended size for a regulation volleyball court. However, the homemade volleyball constructed from a plastic bleach bottle, stuffed with towels and held together with cloth tape, was nearly regulation in size; it just lacked the needed bounce for a suitable serve. Truthfully, the only thing even close to being correct as far as the required equipment of the game invented by William G. Morgan in 1895, was the net and one of the poles. The other pole was a long handled shovel stuck into a bucket of sand. But those kinds of things were just mere formalities. To watch the enthusiasm of the crews as they played would give the idea that in their minds they were in a well-lit gym with all the officials present.

"It's your serve," Rick called out to Jerry as they rotated clockwise. If the ball, bleach bottle, was hit on the plastic side, you could get it to go a respectable distance. They all knew the importance of tucking in their thumb while making a fist to serve the ball, to prevent serious injury. It seemed over a course of time each player had been careless with that, but only once. And even worse than that, was to be in the way of the ball after it was spiked. That was nearly suicidal. Dead weight, plus the power of an aggressive spike was without a doubt, perilous.

It was the start of their second game. The match consisted of the best two out of three games. Rick was the loudest voice of his team. Chris stopped by to play after running into one of the crews while working at the hospital. Anne, Linda and Mike joined them on one team. On the other side of the net were Jerry, Robbie, Denny, John, Randy and one of the nurses from LOH, Karen. It was common for off duty crews to stop in if they were in the area, as there was something always going on if the crews were at the station. Equally as common, was for the local police officers to stop in, some more regularly than others.

Sweat ran down Chris' face. Standing to serve, he flipped the ball to the plastic side. "Six, seven," he called out. His hand came up under the ball and hit it hard enough for it to go over the net. The ball returned, then Mike tapped it to Anne. The game continued, then broke for a pause after a police car pulled up and parked a couple feet away from the bay door.

"Hey, it's Officer Terrence Clark," Rick announced. "Good, we need another player."

"Hey, Terry," Mike hollered from the other side of the bay.

"Boy, you don't call a man with a gun Terry, if his name is Terrence. You call him by his given name," he lightly retorted.

"Yeah Mike, what's wrong with you," Anne spoke up in Officer Clark's defense. The joking and bantering was an ongoing thing between the crews, the police and fire department personnel of Lancemen. They had all spent a portion of the wee hours after normal people are fast asleep, chasing each other through back alleys with balloons filled with water and eggs to toss and tag their opponent's vehicle. The egg fight incident ended quickly, however, after it nearly ruined the paint job on one of the patrol cars. There were certain things that the officer's captains just didn't find amusing.

"Come on," Chris said tossing the ball into the air. "We need another player."

"Man, it's the middle of my shift. I don't want to get all sweaty."

"Come on, Officer Clark," Linda said, trying to appeal to him by using his professional name. "If you were chasing a bad guy you'd get sweaty. Plus, this is more fun. We'll finish this game off, then you can help us out with the next one."

Terrence stood and watched as the game resumed. By his comments it was easy to see that he was itching to play. First, he removed his hat, then he began unbuttoning his shirt. By the time they finished the game, he had his gun belt off and uniform shirt neatly folded and draped over an empty cardboard box in the corner.

"All right. The games are even up," Jerry declared.

Terrence took his place next to Chris dressed in just a white tee shirt and his uniform slacks. It was Anne's turn to serve. Carefully, she moved the ball to find the flat side of the plastic bottle. Her hand came under the ball, but it didn't quite make it to the net. Instead it hit Chris' shoulder. They all laughed, except Chris of course.

"What are you doing? Over the net, Anne. Over the net!"

Still giggling after an insincere "sorry," she re-positioned herself to serve again. Chris turned around this time to watch where the ball was headed. It went over the net, and the volley began. Terrence was at a disadvantage with his smooth soled work shoes. He slipped a couple of times and nearly fell once. Every sport game they played was like a war to the guys. They were serious. They jumped and slammed into each other with a mighty vigor. At last the game ended. The score was twelve for Rick's team. Fifteen for Jerry's. A grand spike by Randy brought the winning point and victory to Jerry's team.

You would have thought it was an Olympic Game, by the excited roars that echoed in the bays. They were pumped. The fervor soon spilled out into the parking lot. Keeping the doors shut during the game helped to keep the noise from moving out onto the street. But the heat and smell of sweat had become unbearable, so they opened the bays doors to welcome the evening summer breeze. Anne went into the station to grab a cold root beer from the refrigerator that was in the back closet. When she came out she stood and watched, gaping at the circus that erupted in her very brief absence. Chris had taken the round blue light cover off the bar on the top of Terrence's patrol car and held it over his head while he walked in circles making siren sounds. The nurse had his cap and gun belt on and was pretending to shoot bad guys. Randy and Denny rode around in the parking lot in Randy's jeep in circles around both of them, laughing wildly, while Terrence's face grew more grim. Jerry and Robbie stood by the bay doors laughing with the others. How could you not? Then Robbie remembered his supervisory duty and came to Terrence's aid.

In moments, the car and Terrence were put back together. Randy and Karen were saying good-bye and Denny had joined the others. All was well and quiet once more in Lancemen. Terrence had been a good sport with it all and waved as he got back into his patrol car before turning onto the main road in front of the station. Suddenly, Chris had a feeling of someone's eyes on them. He was drawn to their only residential neighbor's house across the street. He watched as a man sitting next to the neighbor got up and walked to a undercover patrol car. The man's face was hard to make out in the dark but it looked familiar. As he neared the car and came under the street light, his face was easily recognized as Captain Henderson from Lancemen PD.

"Well, that's not good. I think Terrence's captain just got into that car. I wonder how long he was sitting there? We need to find Terrence and warn him."

"Are you serious?" Anne asked. "Poor Terrence—if that man sat and watched all of that?"

"Hey, Anne," John called out, as he walked toward their rig. "Come on, we got a call."

While driving to the address of Bill's bar, where a fight had taken place, they discussed the dilemma they had gotten their friend into. It didn't matter if they acted crazy at the station. It was their performance on the scene of a call that was important to them. That was their time to be serious. Merve knew how the guys got at times. They were just having fun. But Terrence held a position that required a little more maturity. He was an Officer of the Law. And for that night, he was an officer that seemed to have disappeared.

By midnight, they learned that Terrence had been suspended without pay for three weeks and was assigned to a road position for five years, with no chance of advancement during that time. They all felt bad for him, but there wasn't anything they could do at this point. He was wrong to take off his uniform shirt and gun belt. Still they felt without a doubt, that the three ring circus in the parking lot is what tightened the noose around his neck. They were glad that his punishment wasn't any worse. At least he didn't lose his job. And hopefully, the water balloon battles in the alleys with the police wouldn't end because of this. Their antics were usually harmless. They were just a vent. Didn't the man across the street understand that?

Morning came as expected. The sun was bright and already emitting enough heat, mixed with humidity, to bring a sweat to Anne's brow as she and John washed the ambulance. Between the warm breeze and the sun, her hair was almost dry from the shower she'd taken earlier, before the guys got up. With only one bathroom and four people, sometimes they had to wait their turn. She hated being in the shower when a call came in. It was hard to rinse a head full of shampoo out, dry off and get dressed in three minutes. That was the allowed response time to the ambulance at night for an emergency call. During the day it was one minute from the station or hospital to the rig.

Anne stood on the floor of the passenger side and reached around through the open door to dry the windshield of the ambulance. Two cars pulled onto the parking lot. One was Tom's. Her first thought was that the captain called and complained to Merve and they were all in big trouble. John finished drying the front beacon on the hood of the rig, then walked over to Anne as she stepped onto the ground. Their beds were made and they had hoped to get breakfast before the calls started rolling in, but now that might be changing. Tom walked over to the other car that pulled up and parked next his. The driver got out and walked with Tom to where they stood. Anne was surprised when they recognized him as one of the students who rode his clinicals with her during the EMT class.

"Morning," Tom began. "This is Rod. He's a new hire. He's going to take Mike's place. I need Mike out at the Lakeview station to work with Chuck. There'll be some other changes later. I'll let you know."

"Hi Rod," John said, offering his hand.

"Hi again, Rod," Anne said smiling. "You did a couple of ride a longs with Max and me."

"Well—why don't you show him where to put his things," Tom suggested. "Rod, they can fill you in on how things go around here, and if you have any other questions you can ask me or Robbie."

To their relief, Tom said nothing about Terrence. Anne and John exchanged smiles as she took Rod in to show him the bunk room. Mike was already packing his overnight bag when they walked in. He said he already knew he was going back out to the Lakeview station. And by his expression, she could tell he knew something else, but what? Between that and Tom's words, her mind was in a quandary. Robbie had led her to think that she would be next to go out to Lakeview. But now Mike was going out there. Was that still a possibility? She knew she'd never work out at the Bedford station. Not after Lisa. Trying to clear her mind, she concentrated on her tour of the station.

"John and I sleep on this side. John's bed is on the bottom, and he talks in his sleep—just so you know. These are your beds," she said, straightening the blanket on the top bunk. "Rick usually sleeps up here."

Rod seemed satisfied with the arrangements as he slid his overnight bag under the bottom bunk. While still bent over, he pushed on the pillow to test its softness, then sat on the bed. Looking up at Anne he ran his hand over the blanket, then suddenly he fell back, crashing onto the floor as the mattress broke away from the rail. Hearing the commotion, Rick entered the room. Rod looked like a turtle trying to right itself as Anne pulled on his arm to help him up.

"Oh my gosh, are you all right?" she asked.

Rick burst out laughing. "Hi. I'm Rick. I think you've just been initiated into our little group." Then he turned to see if Mike's car was still in the parking lot. "Nope, he's gone—like Gethro going for viddles. That dog," he laughed. "Set'n up the new guy. I wonder how him and Chuck are going to get along. Ole Mickey just loves.. to torment Chuck."

"They have a million pranks," Anne said looking at Rod. "And there is no stopping them." Leaning over, she started pulling the three inch cloth tape from the box bed support that held the mattress suspended until the unsuspecting victim sat down. "If you're not a Good Joe about it, you're worse off. Then they peg you as an easy target. My suggestion is—just don't encourage them."

"Oh, don't listen to her. We're not that bad," Rick chuckled.

Rod looked in the closet for the bunk support slats. "It sounds like a fun place to work to me. That's why I applied here. Trauma, fun, what else could you ask for? Well, they're not in the closet. Where else would he put them?"

The phone rang. "We'll take it," Rick offered, picking up the receiver. He listened for a second, then hung up. "We'll both take it. Come on, we got a bad one, just south of St. Luke's."

Hopping up onto the driver's seat, Anne buckled her seat belt. John was right behind her and picked up the pad of paper to write out the incident number and time of call. She flipped on the emergency lights, then pulled out onto the main road right behind Rick and Rod. They knew that the fire department responding with them was still basic. They wouldn't be running ALS for a few months yet. Fortunately, St. Luke's was nearby and LOH just down the street. The township police department requested at least three ambulances respond. They reported four cars were involved, with at least that many patients and one obvious K. The crews knew the K was a deceased victim. The Dead On the Scene, DOS, must have been very obvious. They didn't usually make a statement like that unless it was.

Anne looked in her side mirror and saw their Life Unit from LOH not far behind them. The scene was just ahead. Following the directions from one of the officers, she parked the rig next to a flipped over station wagon. The unrestrained female driver had been thrown out and hit a small tree head on. The fire department was already doing the assessment and had applied the cervical collar. When Anne approached, she found the young woman was unconscious with a very large head laceration across her forehead, right down to the skull. After gently lifting a small branch from under the flap, she quickly wrapped it with a surgapad and a roll of gauze, handed to her by the fireman at her side. John brought the backboard, straps and stretcher. One of the firemen carried a small boy over that had been in their patient's vehicle. He had been protected by a car seat and suffered a tiny scrape on his leg but otherwise seemed unhurt. Anne left the firemen and John to finish packaging the woman and took the child over to the ambulance. He was screaming. She wanted to get him away from seeing the woman who they assumed was his mother in such a horrifying state.

"Shh, little guy. It's okay. We're going to take your mommy to the doctor's." Remembering that the fireman told her the car seat was stuck in the smashed car, she brought the boy around to the front passenger seat of their rig and set him there. She checked him over again while trying to calm him. "Shh, its okay. As soon as we get to the hospital we'll call someone in your family to come and get you." She realized he probably wasn't listening to a word she said, but hoped by using a soothing tone he would respond. It was hard to keep his attention with so much going on around them. Within a few feet, one of the policemen was trying to direct the near grid-locked traffic, while yelling at the gawking drivers that passed. Then the wreckers tried to make their way in to clear out the smashed cars. Behind and on each side of her, she heard the crews and some firemen yelling out directions and requests for equipment as they worked together to prepare the patients for transport.

She watched as John and the firemen pushed the stretcher toward the rig. Moving the child deeper back into the seat, she buckled him in, then shut the door.

"John—what hospital are we going to?"

"We're going up to St. Lukes. The Life car already called LOH and had them notify St. Lukes for us—and the other basic rig. We're splitting up the hospitals—so that we don't bombard one hospital with all the patients."

"That's a good idea. So how's she doing?"

"She's still unconscious. Let's go."

The police stopped traffic and watched as Anne backed up the ambulance to turn around. The hospital was just a few miles away. Once there, she carried the child in while the hospital security guard helped John unload the stretcher. Rick and Rod were right behind them. The hospital was prepared due to the call from LOH. As they came into the ER, the staff quickly directed them into the saved rooms. Rick and Rod ended up with one patient with minor injuries which was hard to believe with the noted amount of damage to the door she was sitting near. Bloomfield PD came in shortly after with the unconscious female patient's purse. Anne and one of the ER clerks searched through her wallet for her ID and a phone number to call the family. Meanwhile, the hospital social worker came for the child until they arrived.

Anne sat on the bench seat of the rig for a minute before sweeping the patient compartment floor with a whisk broom. Those calls were the ones that drained you. The adrenaline just rushed through every vein and vessel as you moved as quickly and efficiently as you could. There was no time for tunnel vision. You needed to be aware of what was going on in front of you, as well as around you.

"What a way to start the day," John said, coming up to the back of the rig.

Leaning against the bumper, he turned halfway so that he could see her as he talked. Grasping the clipboard in his hands, he took his ink pen from his shirt pocket to write in the information he needed. "So, help me out here—how deep and long was that laceration on her head before you wrapped it?"

"Well, I could see a good portion of her skull. The flap was about five or six inches long, at least."

Listening as he wrote, he listed the description of the patient's injuries that she saw. After adding his own comments, he finished filling in the run form, then walked back into the hospital to leave them a copy for their records.

It had been an interesting first day for Rod. Once they left the hospital, many other calls filled their day and the crews never saw each other until late evening. When they finally met for dinner, Rod began talking about the calls he and Rick had responded to. To hear him talk you would have thought he was a veteran fitting in like a silk glove. While sitting at the table at Neat Eats, he sipped a glass of water and told of his meeting of Barbara Valentine and another regular patient—who was often just plain mean—Mr. War Feather. At least that was the Indian name that he adopted. His real name was Edward Zembo.

Then the group talked about the multiple car crash that started their day. Each one offering an update on the patient or patients they transported. The patient Rod and Rick transported, they said, seemed initially to have only minor injuries, but ended up with a ruptured spleen and a craked rib. Later they ran into the surgeon who told them, that she came through the surgery and was doing fine. The fifty-year-old male that the Life Car transported had a confirmed pelvic fracture. He was listed in serious condition. Returning to the hospital troughout the day while transporting new patients to the same facility as they did previous patients, gave the crews a chance to check on their progress if the information was available.

"So, John how'd your lady do?" Rick asked.

"She was still unconscious when Anne and I went back. They were getting ready to ship her down for a CAT scan at MTI. The kid's dad came and got him. Good thing Anne was there to watch him."

Anne stopped chewing her food, then swallowed. She looked at John and the others, who agreed with his statement so easily. Her face became flushed with contempt, and finally she just had to let go.

"Hold up. Time out," she said, clearly miffed by his comment. "I didn't take the kid because I was the most qualified to baby-sit him. I took him because I was the driver and you were the attendant. You were going to be in the back with her, and you were going to be the one to give the report to the hospital. This boy, girl thing has to stop right now. I can't work on an ALS car because some nasty girl came and slept around—but you guys do it and it's okay. And it's okay that I taught Max to drive from the passenger seat. Why? Well—because everyone knows that women can't drive very good. Now how stupid is that? My paramedic license doesn't say girl paramedic, it just says—paramedic. I worked just as hard as everyone else in that class, but they pass me by. Why? I'll tell you why. Because of that nasty girl—and because I'm a good baby sitter. That's why."

"Now, Anne, I didn't mean anything by that. Everyone knows you're good at your job and I like working with you," John jumped in, trying to calm her down.

"No." Rick reasoned calmly. "It's not that. She's upset because Mike went out to work at the Lakeveiw station. That was supposed to be her spot. There's no secrets around here, Anne. Everyone knows everyone else's business. You know that. Have some faith."

"Faith? Now tell me why is it—that when someone claims to be a Christian, and I do—that other people who have never even cracked open a Bible—always seem to know how the Christian is supposed to live their life. If I make a comment about something that I see, it's not considered an opinion, it's a judgment. If I get upset about a wrongful prejudice—then I have no faith. It seems like a contradiction to me. Like we have two different sets of standards."

"Doesn't the Bible have contradictions?" Rod asked.

"No. It contains paradoxes and parables," she said standing up, tired by the conversation.

"Where are you going?" John asked.

"I'm going to pay my bill. I'm not mad at you guys. I'm just frustrated. Maybe I should have stayed in Nursing School. Maybe God's trying to tell me something here. If I don't get on an ALS car in the next few months, then maybe I'll just go back to school. I don't know. I just don't know."

Weeks passed. Little by little, Denny and Linda took turns rotating over to Anne's shift with their partners as the opposite crew. Anne welcomed the female company. She learned that Denny was just a nickname. Because most Americans slaughtered her Ukrainian given name of Olha, she picked an American name. Anne enjoyed listening to her stories about the Ukrainian lifestyle which included ethnic foods and fashion. But most appreciated and entertaining was a saying that Denny used often when she was at her wits end with the guys. The expression, Hovory do hory, meant—talk to the mountain. This was something that brought spiritual meaning to Anne. But Denny explained that the women in the Ukraine would use it when trying to discipline stubborn children. It was an American equivalent to "talking to the wall." Anne tried borrowing the expression, but it didn't seem to have the same effect as when Olha said it. Maybe it was something in the accent or the correct usage of the words that made the difference, she surmised. Try as she might, Anne's interpretation sounded more like, Da hovo lay, doe hovo lay. But Denny's good natured spirit and burst of laughter gave quick understanding that she wasn't offended by the unintended hack job of her native language.

Linda and Anne had become friends as well. It was always fun for Anne when Linda worked at the same station. So many times the guys unintentionally set themselves up for a man slamming verses women slamming contest, of which Linda was the champion debater. Linda welcomed the chance to retaliate when a lark was directed toward her. Shaving cream in her shoes in the middle of the night as she slipped them on for a call was just such a provocation. "Oh you boys don't know who you're messing with," was a common retort after a successful prank.

Outside of the calls, it was hard to believe that this was actually a job. Truly, they played as hard as they worked. Each activity fed the other and both were exhausting at times.

Anne arrived at the station at the start of her shift. Robbie pulled in right behind her. "Morning," he said, as he got out of his car.

"Morning." she smiled.

"Well, I've got some news for you that's long overdue. Merve agreed and assured me that on the fall schedule, you'd have a place at the Lakeview station. I even made him write it down and I made you a copy. Here you go," he said handing her a sheet of paper.

She looked at it. It was Merve's handwriting all right. "On an ALS car, right?"

"Yes," he chuckled. "On an ALS car. Well, I've got to go to the office. See you later."

Anne stood looking at the paper, flipping over and back again before picking up her overnight bag.

"See, I told you to have faith," Rick said, when she shared her news.

"'Faith,' my friend, 'is the substance of things hoped for, the evidence of things not seen.' I had hope and faith. Though I have to admit, I was beginning to wonder if I was hoping for the right thing."

Rod and Rick planned to meet with John and Anne for coffee and dessert to celebrate with her later in the evening; but the calls were non-stop. Instead, a shooting in the south end of Lanceman, then a heart attack that developed into a cardiac arrest in the north end, kept John and Anne busy for the most of the evening. In fact, the only highlight in Anne's evening was when she ran into Officer Terrence Clark at the hospital following the shooting. She found him near the ER nurse's station after the shooting, writing out his report.

"Hey, Terrence. How you doing? Boy, do we miss you," she smiled.

He looked around to see if any of his fellow officers was watching before he spoke. "You guys keep away from me. You're nothing but trouble. I almost lost my job."

"Yeah, we heard," she said in a soft voice, realizing he was nervous about being seen with her. "Sorry. They were just having a little fun. Who would have ever thought that the chief of police and our neighbor were related."

"It's not funny," he quietly growled.

"I'm not laughing at you, Terrance. And don't worry, I won't be a thorn in your side much longer," she jested. "It won't be long and I'll be leaving Lancemen."

"Oh yeah. Where you going?"

"I'm supposed to start working out of the Lakeveiw station in a couple of weeks—on an ALS car."

"No kidden. Merve is finally going to let you try your wings eh? Well good for you, Anne. I'm happy for ya. I mean that."

Anne spotted one of Officer Clark's fellow co-workers walking by. She picked up her clipboard and pretended to be writing out a report while standing next to Terrence, hoping he wouldn't get yelled at for talking to her. She was sure he couldn't possibly get in trouble if it was business. Looking down at the clipboard, she waited for the other officer who she didn't recognize to pass, before finishing her conversation and saying good-bye.

John and Anne pulled into the station parking lot a little after 1:00 a.m. She had just finished brushing her teeth when she heard Rick and Rod enter the station through the garage door. Rod walked into the bathroom and stood next to her.

"Do you need to get in here?" she asked.

"No. I need you to do me a favor," he said, in a low secretive voice. He was up to something; there was no question about that—But what? Another game, she thought. Oh, how she had come, to dislike these games. It seemed like throughout her whole life, or at least since she began living on the farm with her cousins—there was always one boyish prank after another.

"What now?" she peevishly whispered.

"Now, come on. This is going to be funny. I've got it all set up. I borrowed an IV bag from one of the ALS cars. I've got the bag and the tubing strung over the drop ceiling, right over Rick's bed. All you have to do is reach up over your bed and turn the dial. I've got it hanging down just enough for you to see it. It will get his bed a little wet, that's all. What do you say?"

"No. He's going to think this was my idea and then he's going to try and get back at me."

"Come on, Anne. If you do this, I promise I'll never ask you to do another trick."

"Oh—I hate you," she sneered. "Okay. But this is the last time. And you better tell him the truth when it's over."

"I will. I promise."

Anne walked into the bunk room and began crawling up the end of the bed like a ladder.

"What'da you guys got cooking?" John asked suspiciously. "I heard you in the bathroom, pss, pss, pss, talking like a big pow wow."

"Nothing. I was just telling Anne that we saw Terrence today," Rod spoke up, after a few seconds of silence.

Anne knew he was lying through his teeth, but she decided to go along with it; especially since she and John had seen him too. At least it was something that was believable.

"Yeah, John and I saw him at General," she began. "He told me that us white people all act alike. He said we remind him of that movie, American Graffiti."

"He said that? Well, you guys do. You're all crazy. I'm the only normal person around here," John said, chuckling.

As he talked, Anne slowly reached up and felt for the dial on the IV tubing. There it was. Running her thumb up the plastic wheel, she opened it all the way. In just a few weeks from now she told herself, I'll be doing this for real—and for a real reason, instead of these stupid games. Looking for a more comfortable position she rolled over. That's funny, she thought. Rick's bed should be getting wet by now. Reaching down to pull the sheet up more around her neck, she suddenly realized that it was *her* bed that was getting wet. In fact, it was very wet.

"You—dogs."

The acknowledgment they had waited for was there. They all burst into roaring laughter. Even her own partner John who was aware of the trickery that lay before her, said nothing to dissuade the event.

"We didn't want you to forget us. It's just a little going away present," Rick laughed.

Crawling down from the bed, Anne tried to hold back her own laughter. "And to think—of all the nice things that I say about you guys when you're not around."

"Yeah, I can imagine," John sputtered.

Anne reached for the light switched and turned on the overhead light, while enjoying the protest from everyone in the room. "Too bad. Cover your eyes. I can't remake my bed in the dark."

She came back with clean dry towels and sheets to lay over the wet area of her bed.

"Will you hurry up. People are trying to sleep," Rod teased.

"Oh—I owe you mister. You just wait."

"You know," Rick said, with a reserved bit of laughter. "I think Terrence is right. Sometimes it is kind of like that movie American Graffiti around here. But we just have a different technique. Around here it's American Graffiti—EMS style."

CHAPTER 19

THE STORYTELLERS

Anne always went home to Summerville in September to help with the harvest canning, to prepare for winter. She remembered while growing up when some of the students were excused from school during the potato harvest to help their families pick potatoes. During her last phone conversation with Aunt Ruth, her aunt mentioned that she noticed while picking berries that the animals in the woods were already starting to prepare for winter. It looked like it might be a bad one so they decided to store up extra for themselves, just in case.

Dill, sweet, and bread and butter pickles were done up in late summer. The tomatoes would be the first to be canned in early fall. Aunt Ruth insisted on peeling each tomato before turning them into sauce for chili, pasta and then catsup. All of the normal vegetables were also canned, but Anne thought that the kitchen smelled best while doing up the jams and fruit. The simmering cinnamon apples and pears that filled the kitchen with their heavenly aroma were her favorites, in addition to the spiced grape jam, gingered rhubarb jelly, blueberry marmalade, apple butter, and pumpkin butter. In the years before, some of the vegetables and berries were frozen. But this year they would can everything except the meat, to save space in the freezers for that. Extra grain, feed and hay would be stored for the stronger animals that could make it through the tough winter, and those best for breeding would not be butchered. It was a way of life for them. She remembered when a friend from the city visited the farm. For some reason, her friend liked the cows the best. Months later when she ran into Anne, she asked how Bessie was doing, to which Anne replied, "Oh, she was delicious." After seeing the horrified look on her friend's face, she smiled. "Diane, that's why we raise them, they're not pets. They don't have the ability to reason, like a dog or a horse, at least that I've ever seen. We treat them very well until its time to butcher them and even that's done as painlessly to the animal as possible. Uncle Henry is not a cruel man. He's a farmer, just trying to feed his family. The animals and the produce that we sell, bring in the money to keep the farm going. We are not rich. I can assure you of that. But I can't think of a better place I'd rather grow up."

While working with Aunt Ruth in the steamy, fragrant kitchen, Anne let her in on a few selected activities at Mercy. She told her that when she returned to the city, she'd be starting her first ALS shift. Feeling somewhat ashamed, she confessed that she had wondered if it would ever happen, or if she was aimed in the wrong direction. "Then," she continued, "Rick asked me where my faith was. He's certainly heard me talk about it enough. It wasn't until I heard his question that I realized I had set my shield of faith down, and let the enemy in. I was walking by sight, and not getting far. My self pity had blinded me. I felt convicted, but my pride wouldn't allow me to admit it to him. I knew then, it was exactly what I needed to hear."

"God doesn't wear a Timex, Anne. He works on His time not on ours... and I'm sure He's never late. Don't be too hard on yourself. You're human. We all fall from time to time. God understands that." Anne smiled. Aunt Ruth was always there to make sense of things. She had been as a harbor to her, grounded within the beacon of God's light.

The drive to the Lakeview station from her family's farm was restful. She felt that she was becoming less of the naive farm girl she once was. The past few years had forced her to grow up quickly. Even her aunt had noticed a maturing in her, and said she was very much like her mother had been. Maybe she'd picked up her mother's torch as a missionary, in a way. She knew that what she had seen over the past few years was more than anyone should ever see in a life time; and yet she understood she had just touched the surface. But it had not discouraged her in any way. Instead, she possessed a willingness to meet the future head on, without hesitation. It was an inherent desire to go beyond the norm to help another person make it through this race called life. Only now on an ALS rig, they would be better equipped to make a difference in the outcome.

The Lakeview station was like going home to Anne. After all, it was her first full time station. It would seem odd to be there without Dan or Roman. But still, it a was a welcome sight to behold as she parked in the gravel driveway once again. For the next four months Anne's partner would be Chuck. At least, that's what everyone there called him. His given name was actually Michael Jay. But they decided that with Mike, sometimes called Mickey, it would be less confusing for the time being to call him Chuck.

Anyway, Michael jumped at the chance to be called Chuck, after his hero Chuck Yeager, the famous pilot of the X-1, Glamorous Glennis, that broke the sound barrier on October 14, 1947. Chuck often went on about Yeager's day in history, and how his plane was carried aloft in the belly of a large four engine B-29 before being dropped out like a bomb at 25,000 feet. "At the end of the flight," he said, "it was recorded that the plane had reached a 1.07 Mach air speed, which marked the beginning of the era of the supersonic age." Then he bragged that Yeager received the Harmon International Trophy, and swore that someday he'd be a pilot himself.

Anne's partner, Chuck, came from a well to do family in Marysville. He was raised in a staunch Catholic home and even had a cousin named Albino Luciani, who was the Cardinal Patriarch of Venice before becoming Pope John I, that same month. He had a vast knowledge about cars, boats and planes, plus he knew all about the radios and frequencies that were needed to communicate with most of them. Anne sat and listened with awe as he rattled on as if he expected that she comprehended every word he uttered. No one, she thought, could possibly remember and actually understand all of that. But Chuck did.

He was a good paramedic and partner. He had a number of characteristics that she enjoyed but her favorite was that his vocabulary contained more than four letters words, and he did not limit them to the letter "F". That was one of her biggest protests with some of the guys. She understood how Holden Caulfield, from the book "The Catcher in the Rye," felt as he walked through the stairway of his brother's school where the walls were desecrated with profanity. From the way he described his feelings about removing it from all the walls in the world, to him it must have seemed like the "Task of Sisyphus." To her, it was pure language laziness—and she hated it.

Loaded down with her overnight bag, sleeping bag and pillow, Anne entered the station. To her delight, Roger was sitting on the sofa waiting for her.

"Hey, welcome aboard. You finally made it," he cheered.

"Thank you. Thank you," she bowed. "Who's out in the rig? I saw someone, but their back was turned to me and I couldn't tell without setting my stuff down."

"It's Chuck. He counts every Band-Aid, every four by four and so on. Nothing goes unnoticed with him. He brought the boxes and Life Pack in for you to check out. I told him I'd go over everything with you."

"Great! Let me set my stuff down in the bedroom." Looking around, she noticed that the station hadn't changed a bit.

"Okay," he said when she returned. "This is just a review for you I know, but we're going to go over it like you've never seen any of it before. That way I won't forget anything—Ready?" he asked.

"Ready," she smiled.

He set the plastic storage unit on the coffee table, undid the latch then pulled it open. "This," he said, "is an ALS box. It's identical to the BLS box, but carries more equipment. It's orange in color as you can see; and, at least I think, it's shaped like a doctor's bag, but is twice as big. First of all, in the morning when you begin your shift, you'll have to check the larynoscope blades in the intubation kit every day, to make sure the light at the tip comes on, or you won't be able to see into the patient's pharynx. There are spare batteries and bulbs in the supply cabinet. Here are the endotracheal tubes. They range in sizes between 2.5 to 9.0. The ones for the pediatrics below 5.5 don't have a ballooned cuff. The adult sizes do. This is your IV pack. It has everything you need to start an IV on your patient. The IV tubing's in the cardboard box. We generally use the 10 cc, macro setups. There are two IV needles, one 20 gage and one 18 gage. We also keep a four by four, an alcohol swab, a betadine swab, tape and a Band-Aid in the kit that's wrapped up in a chux, which is held together with a tourniquet. I'm sure you remember from doing your ALS clinicals, that we place the chux under the patient's arm before starting the IV.

There are three different bags of IV solution. Lactated Ringers, D5W, and 9% Normal Saline. The airway and oxygen equipment, bite blocks, ammonia inhalants and bandaging equipment is the same as what you're used to. We set the B/P cuff and the stethoscope on top of all the bottom stuff because it gets used on every call. Your electrodes and defibrillation gel are on the top shelf here," he said, pointing. "You really just need to look it over to get yourself reacquainted.

Now for the drug box," he continued, as he traded places with the white and orange box next to him on the floor. "There is a list of drugs that we carry in the back of the clipboard, plus every shelf is labeled. You just have to check it out to make sure everything is there and not broken or crystallized. During the winter months, some of the drugs like the lasix crystallizes easily. When it's cold we keep the boxes in the station. You have to also make sure your narcotics are there. And check the expiration dates on the drugs as you go along, to make sure they're safe to use. The big pre loaded stuff like the dextrose and sodium bicarbonate are in the bottom.

Sometimes the boxes they come in are the same color, so you have to watch out for that. There are some alcohol swabs and syringes in the second row tray on this side," he said, sliding it out.

"It looks like a fishing tackle box," she said, playing along as if a first time observer.

"It is a fishing tackle box," he answered with a grin. "In fact, a few months ago, and I won't mention any names, a crew from an outlying station walked into a patient's house with their fishing equipment, instead of medical equipment. The volunteer on the fire department they were with, picked up on it and quietly went back to the rig and exchanged the boxes. The patient never knew," he chuckled. "But, you aren't going to have time to do any fishing out of this station." Smiling, he took a sip from a ceramic cup, then picked up the white briefcase sized Life Pack from the sofa, then continued. "Now for the fun toy. This is the heart monitor, synchronized cardioverter and the defibrillator. This lightweight beauty splits apart, if you like. One side is the monitor side, the other is the defibrillator. These are the patient cables, or patient leads," he said, uncoiling the grey plastic coated wire that branched off into three wires, three fourths of the way up. "And this is where you insert the cables," he said, holding the plug in front of the receiving socket. "Make sure the pins line up." Then he held the other end of the patient leads and separated the three color coated wires. "The electrodes snap onto the ends here," he said, then continued. "White is negative, black or green is ground, and red of course is positive." Then, he pointed to and pushed each button and knob on the case, indicating their purpose. "Here's on, off and synchronize." Sliding the defibrillator paddles out, he continued. "Now, you can also do a quick look, by just setting the paddles on the patient's chest to get a reading before you even hook up the patient cables. If the patient's heart goes into the famous but deadly rhythm of ventricular fibrillation, before you shock him or her, check and make sure that the setting isn't in the sync mode. Then you charge the paddles here," he said, pointing to the two black buttons on each paddle. "Wait for the whining sound to stop, then push the two red buttons at the same time to deliver the 200 or 300 joules, or whatever you have the dial set at. Make sure that there isn't too much of the defib gel on the paddles, or you will slide across the patient's chest, or maybe get an arc of electricity between them. That's not good. Paddle placement is important. Some people just have a bony chest so it's hard. But if the paddles aren't on right, you'll know it right away from the smell of singed chest hair and burnt skin. But above everything else, say clear... loud enough for everyone near the patient to hear, and make sure that no one else is touching the patient. Max and I saw this volunteer get slammed against the wall who didn't realize his knee was touching the guy we were shocking."

Periodically as he talked, he'd set down whatever equipment he was reviewing and exchange it for the cup of instant cocoa that he'd been nursing since Anne first walked in the door, twenty minutes or so ago. "Now," he went on, "the batteries in the Life Pack develop a memory. If you or the crew before you had a busy shift, you'll still have to discharge them several times into the discharger before they can be recharged." Charging the paddles to demonstrate, he held them onto the side plates of the discharger, then released the stored energy. Each time he pushed the buttons to charge the capacitor with energy, he would wait until the whining stopped before releasing the energy into the specialized plates resulting in only a click, giving a false impression of the power Anne knew the paddles really held. He did that a couple of times, then walked with the defibrillator unit over to the fish aquarium.

"What are you doing?" she asked.

Without a word, he placed the paddles on each side of the glass, then released the charged energy. The water rippled and the fish stopped swimming.

"Roger! I can't believe you just did that."

"Oh, we do it all the time. It doesn't kill the fish. They just don't swim as straight anymore. But they're fine." He finished discharging the paddles into the discharger, then set the batteries in to be recharged. Just as he set an extra stored pair of batteries into the Life Pack, the fish started to move. "See, they're fine," he said sprinkling a pinch of fish food on top of the water.   Chuck walked in and went to the supply cabinet. "Hey Anne. Are Roger and you about done?"

"Almost. I see Roger's science experiments haven't changed much," she grinned.

Chuck laughed. "Oh, you mean the fish? Yeah, we do that all the time. We haven't lost one yet. And they never complain. Plus, we feed them good. Well, as soon as I put this stuff away, maybe we can catch some breakfast. We told Charlie at the diner that you were coming out. He's looking forward to seeing you. I think he likes you. He says you got spunk."

"No. He just likes to embarrass me."

The phone rang. Roger walked in the bedroom, then picked up the hot line. "Hello. Okay, I'll tell them." Anne quickly put the equipment back into the boxes as he spoke. "You got a PI up on Highland. Actually, there's two. The other one's in Clear Lake, about four miles west. He's got Mike and Big Rick on the way there from LOH. Their call came in first. They got a jump on ya," he concluded, while helping them throw the boxes in the rig. "Have fun. And buckle up."

Chuck flipped on the emergency lights and pulled right onto the street in front of the station. Turning left at the next light they flew past the Lakeview police station, past the cemetery near the court house and on to the next traffic light at a main intersection. The light was red for them. He stopped the rig. A few cars continued through, while the rest slowed or came to a screeching stop.

"Clear right," Anne advised.

Quickly he proceeded through the intersection, then turned right onto Highland Road. The accident was just four miles from there.

"Life Four," they heard Mike calling over the dispatch radio. "We stopped and checked out your scene. You got one critical with a doc on the scene, and one minor. We popped in the IV lines. The doc's going to stay with your patient until you arrive. We're going on down to our PI."

"Thanks, Mike. We'll catch up to you later," Chuck calmly replied. "That Mike. He's so crazy."

Within seconds they pulled up and stopped the ambulance next to the demolished vehicles that strew glass and metal debris over all five lanes of a normally busy road.

"Over here. Over here." A woman waved her hand. Anne grabbed the orange box and quickly went in her direction. Chuck was there just seconds before her.

"This woman's a doctor at LOH. She'll ride with you if you want," he advised. "She says our patient has multiple injuries—but mostly she's concerned about her airway. I'll go get the stretcher. You can tube her on the way. If you can't get it—let Dr. Sudgen try." Anne knelt down next to the patient to assess the rest of her injuries. She had a deep laceration across her forehead. Her right arm was broken. Then Anne noticed some discoloration at the center of her sternum. Chuck rolled up with the stretcher and lowered it all the way to the lowest level. The patient was still breathing but her respirations were slowing. Quickly they slid the backboard underneath her with the help of the doctor and firemen who were available. The doctor applied the cervical collar while Anne reevaluated her chest and abdomen. Chuck and the fireman hooked the cot straps in place. Then a couple of firemen helped wheel the patient to the ambulance and loaded her in, while Anne grabbed the intubation kit and selected the correct tube size.

They locked the cot in place right in front of her, as she sat in the seat at the head of the stretcher. Her hand shook as she smeared the size 7.0

ET tube in her right hand with the lubricating jelly. Picking up the laryngoscope handle with her left hand, she unfolded the already snapped on medium length, straight metal blade. The light at the end came on. She was set. Gently, she pulled the patient's jaw up, just enough to see down into her oral pharynx. The airway was clear. There was no vomit or any other object present. Using the blade to sweep the patient's tongue to the side, she found the epiglottis, then lifted the blade straight up. Instantly, the veed white vocal cords came into view at the glottic opening. She waited a second for the patient to inhale, then made her move. The tube slid easily between the vocal cords, into the trachea. She sighed a big sigh of relief. The vapor from the patient's own decreasing respirations, could be seen in the tube. After attaching the Ambu bag to the tube connector, she gave the bag a squeeze, then filled the tube's cuff inlet with 10 cc of air from a syringe. Next, she hooked the oxygen tubing from the wall connector to the bag and began assisting the patient's breathing. The doctor had already placed the EKG cables on the patient's chest, while Anne was involved in controlling the patient's airway. Picking up her stethoscope she listened to the patient's lungs to ensure the tube was correctly placed. She smiled. "You're in." Anne then proceeded to tape down the tube.

She had concentrated so hard on intubating her patient, that she almost forgot they were moving. The IV solution was still running at a rapid drip rate. The doctor took another set of vitals, while Anne squeezed the bag in time with the patient's own respirations.

"I already called LOH," Chuck yelled back. "I hope you got the tube. I told them you did."

"We got it," Anne yelled back.

"Good job. The basic car came for the other patient from the pickup truck. Just so you know. We'll be at the hospital in about three minutes."

Three minutes was not enough time to set up and start a second IV, so Anne finished overviewing the patient's other injuries with the help of the doctor.

"We make a good team, Anne. You did a nice job with that tube."

"Thanks. This was my first real ALS call. I always seem to start out with the doozies," she smiled.

"I never would have guessed."

The patient's EKG was somewhat fast, with a rate of one hundred and four, but otherwise appeared normal en route. Her blood pressure was holding steady at ninety-eight systolic for a while, and then she started to rapidly crash right outside the ER doors. As soon as the ambulance stopped, the hospital security guard opened the doors. A few of the docs and nurses were on the dock waiting. They walked next to the stretcher as she was being wheeled in, while gathering more information from Anne and the doctor who rode along. "Was she wearing a seat belt? What did the steering wheel look like? Did she spider the windshield with her head?" were a few of the questions that Dr. Malley asked while he and his staff worked fast and orderly; but it was too late. In spite of how quickly they worked to support her airway, draw blood for her labs, x-ray her spine, and other treatments, the "time of condition reversal" had expired. Due to the fact that she was not wearing a seat belt and with the speed she was driving, she apparently flew straight on into the steering wheel. They guessed that it was the impact of her chest against the wheel, that tore her aorta. The actual cause of death was hemorrhage due to the rupture.

Anne was glad that the guy in the pickup truck ended up as a treat and release patient. Initially, it was suspected that he had an fractured ankle. But the x-rays were negative and it turned out to be just a bad sprain. Chuck sensed that she felt bad about the woman dying. The patient looked like she was only in her mid-thirties.

"Good job on the tube," he stated, matter of factly. "Patients that are still breathing are sometimes harder to get. Don't let this bug you. I know it was your first ALS call, but this isn't TV and we aren't Johnny and Roy. It seems like every cardiac arrest that they go on, the patient by some miracle comes back to life, wakes up and shakes their hands. I hate those shows—they're so misleading."

"I know Chuck. I didn't just get off the EMS boat. I know very well how it works, for real. I was just hoping that my first ALS call would be something to tell my grand-kids about—ya know?"

"You all ready have enough to tell your grand-kids about," he laughed.

Each shift that Anne and Chuck worked together throughout the fall months gave them more time to learn about each other's background. She learned that he was born in May on Friday the 13th, 1955 in Port Huron. He attended Catholic schools his whole life until he was a sophomore, at which time he entered into a public school after the Catholic school closed. When he was sixteen, he earned a Red Cross Advanced First Aid card, worked as a lifeguard, swimming instructor, and coached a recreation league swim team until he began working full time in EMS in the area where he lived. He also attended the Red Cross National Aquatic School at Lake Copneconic and was certified as a Water Safety Instructor where he also learned how to run aquatic programs. She found out that he and Mike, Mickey, knew each other for a few years before coming to Mercy and that Mike has always enjoyed tormenting him with tricks. Chuck enjoyed having fun, but he was more serious about things and felt that sometimes Mike went too far. She knew that Mike viewed him as too stiff. And after listening to Chuck, Anne thought that maybe it was his response to the antics that egged Mike on.

But Mike was clearly not the only one that saw Chuck as an easy target. Quite often Big Rick carried on a shower ritual, whenever Mike wasn't at the station by turning off the hot water while Chuck was in the shower. He always waited, of course, until Chuck had time to get good and soapy. Then there was the time when Chuck first began working part time at Mercy—when "firecracker" Rick Stockwell crept ever so carefully through the crawl space over the dropped ceiling, and poured oil that had been drained from an ambulance over Chuck while he was in the shower at the Whitting station. And then once in the dead of winter, they took the largest icicle they could find hanging from the station eaves, and placed it in bed next to Chuck, while he was sound asleep on the sofa bed. Chuck sometimes grimaced at their antics. But, most of the time he took it all in stride and from time to time would even return the volley in equal proportion.

It was early October. A few days had passed since Anne and Dan had lunch together to celebrate their birthdays. Chuck and Anne were sitting at Charlie's for a late afternoon meal with Chuck's new girlfriend, Suzette. She was sweet and very attractive. She had the most unusual color of hazel eyes that Anne had ever seen, and they complimented her shoulder-length, blonde hair nicely. Chuck, like always—had the handheld radio next to him on the table. They had just ordered their food when a call in came in for them. It was for a dirt bike accident about eight miles west of the restaurant, on State Park property. Someone would meet them at the road and take them back. The ALS unit from Bedford was also responding. Suzette said she would stay and wait at Charlie's for them to return.

The Lancemen County Sheriff's Department, had two units parked at the trail entrance when Chuck pulled up and stopped a mile or so inside the State Park. Then, just up a few feet in front of them, a Clear Lake Township fire engine sat with its lights on; as did several other volunteer department vehicles. Even in broad daylight, it looked like Christmas. Then, they saw the dust from their other Life unit coming up over the hill behind them. A man dressed in a red flannel shirt and ragged jeans waited on a dirt bike to show them the way back over the trail to where the accident had taken place. He appeared very shaken, pale and sweaty.

"They're back here—about two miles in. Stay on the path and follow me," he loudly instructed, while revving the engine of his bike. Big Rick and Jack were the first to begin the four wheeling convoy, with Chuck and Anne right behind them. The ground was soft in places. It was mostly a rich copper color and was bare of grass at this point. The path was narrow and the ruts were deep. It was a trail made for bikers and four wheelers, not an ambulance. The hills were becoming steeper and the dips sudden. The stretcher in the back of the rig slammed against the floor as it fought with the bar latch to remain locked in place. With each abrupt jerking move, the boxes slid across the floor between the bench seat and the side doors. Finally, they stopped at a place that was somewhat level and close to the injured bikers.

The deputy on the scene who had been with the bikers, met them as they pulled their equipment then began his report.

"Hi. Okay, what I've got so far is two bikers were flying up over the hill on opposite sides, not realizing the other was there until they hit head on at the top. Both these guys are severely injured. They both have open leg fractures, in addition to an array of other injuries. Some of the firemen over there," he said, pointing to the back side of the hill, "are working on one patient. Then you got a couple of volunteers working on that guy over there," he said, pointing to the crest of the rugged dirt slope. "He looks like the worst to me. Let me know what hospital you're taking them to before you go."

The bikers groaned loudly in pain, as their caretakers worked quickly to find every injury and package them for the trip to the hospital. Anne worked with Chuck and started an IV on their patient. Then while going to the rig for another splint, Rick yelled over for her to bring him an IV setup. All four paramedics worked together until the patients were ready for transport. Somehow, just before they were getting ready to leave, Anne ended up as Rick's partner.

"Anne, I want you to get us out of here. Stay on the path. Don't go into the ruts or slow down, or we'll get stuck for sure."

Anne jumped up onto the driver's seat and adjusted it so she could at least touch the pedals. Rick must have been driving on the way there, she guessed. Chuck and Jack were in front of her, leading the way out. It was so rough that all she could think of was the amount of damage that the bouncing and slamming was doing to the fractures of their patients. She started down another hill. There was a huge dip coming up. She watched as the unit in front of them bounced several times before beginning its climb up the next hill. She hoped that the main entrance was not far off. She felt tense. Her stomach was in knots. She did not want to cause these men any more pain than what was necessary, or worsen their injuries.

"Don't slow down!" she heard Rick yell from the rear compartment. They hit a soft spot—and then the back tires started spraying up mud from behind the rig. "Great! I told you not to slow down, and to stay clear of the ruts. Now we're stuck." She thought she was doing fine until then. The back door opened, then closed. The next thing she knew, Rick was standing in the drop-off, next to the driver's door telling her to move over. Without a word, she obeyed. While crawling over to the passenger seat, she noticed that the volunteer riding with them was now lying across the patient, in order to keep him from bouncing.

"Why didn't you listen! I told you not to slow down or go into the ruts," he barked again softly, trying to control his anger.

"I didn't go into the ruts. And I only slowed down a little, so we wouldn't hit the dip so hard."

"It doesn't matter how hard we hit the dip if we're stuck, now does it?"

It only took a few turns at rocking the rig forward and back, before they were moving again—but that didn't matter. The tongue lashing didn't end until they pulled up to the main entrance of the park, where a dozen or so curious people had gathered. Rick stopped right in front of them, then opened his door to get out.

"I'm going back to take care of the patient. Now—do you think you can handle it?" Without another word he slammed the door. Anne sat for a moment, then moved over to the driver's seat. Between Rick's anger and their patient's condition, she was so befuddled and embarrassed that for a second she'd forgotten the direction of the hospital. She hadn't been remiss; she merely wanted to protect their patient.

Looking to the right, she recovered her bearings. In minutes they were on the main road and en route to Lancemen General. After flipping on the emergency lights, she picked up the mic and called on the way to the hospital. The chagrining state had passed and for now she was concentrating solely on a safe trip. Traffic so far was yielding to them nicely. They were almost half way there when she heard Jack asking the dispatcher to relay the information about both of their patients' condition to Lancemen General. They must not have been able to get through on the apcor radio, she thought. Sometimes they entered into what they called dead zones, which blocked communication to the hospital and then sometimes, distance was a problem. She turned up the volume slightly, so that she could hear Jack's report over the siren. His verbal sketch was concise. Hopefully, it would help the hospital prepare for their patients' arrival.

Weeks had past since they responded to the dirt bike accident. To their surprise, both patients did remarkably well, but still had months of rehab in front of them. Chuck's cousin the Pope, had passed away. His family was devastated, of course, and Chuck said he had never seen his mother so upset. The newspapers were full of the mass suicide of Jim Jones and his followers. In the final count, 911 were dead including more than 200 children. Jogging and a sudden boom for fitness was all the rage. Some burned calories outdoors, while others did so on the floors of discotheques. Either way, most of the participants were dressed to kill in the latest fashionable garb required by the activity at hand—or foot.

It was late November and due to the chilly nights, it had become routine to bring the drug and orange box in at night. Anne sat on the sofa while going through the drug box, as she did in the beginning of every shift. Chuck had worked an extra shift at another station the day before, and was now in the shower getting ready for his shift with her. Because the hot water trick had become very old to him, he waited until both Rick and Mike left before getting into the shower. Thinking it was safe, he went into the bathroom. A few minutes later the front door opened and a cold winter chill blew in. Mike and Big Rick stepped inside, stomping their feet.

"I thought you guys left," Anne said.

"We just went out to warm up our vehicles," Rick replied, slipping his coat off. They stood in the living room, watching TV to pass the time. Then something in the bedroom caught Mike's eye. He walked toward Chuck's bed with an impish smirk, then picked up the can of shaving cream out of his toiletry bag. Shaking the can, he bent over Chuck's neatly pressed uniform that laid on the bed and filled the sleeves, pockets and pant legs with the musk smelling, white foam. Rick laughed. "He is going to kill you," he said, as he watched what Mickey was doing.

"I know—What a great idea, don't you think?"

It was too late. There wasn't much Anne could say or do in Chuck's defense now. She finished with the boxes, then set them down next to the door. Minutes later, Chuck came out of the bathroom in a tee shirt and sweat pants. Suddenly, he realized that the off going crew was still there, and sensed trouble. He walked into the bedroom to get dressed. Within seconds he noticed his freshly dry cleaned navy shirt and grey pants frothing at every opening.

"Mike! I'm going to kill you!"

"Oh, don't be such a big baby. You've still got another uniform in the closet."

"That's for tomorrow! What if I get gack from some patient on my clothes today. What am I supposed to wear tomorrow?"

"Oh, quit your crying. It'll wipe off."

Chuck was fit to be tied. He reached down and picked up the can of shaving cream, then walked over to the uniform in a dry cleaner's bag that was hanging on the hook on the wall, and began filling up the sleeves and pockets, in retaliation to Mike's prank. They all watched straight faced as if he had lost his mind, and never said a word. Then Mike smiled as he walked toward the door to leave. Chuck threw the empty can onto his bed.

"Hey," he called to Mike, disappointed and miffed. "Aren't you going to take your uniform with you?"

Mike cackled. "That's not my uniform—It's Jerry's."

Anne put her head down and tried to suppress her laughter. The turn of events had become so comical, it was hard not to give in. Still, Chuck was her partner and it wouldn't be right to find humor in his ill directed repayment. Rick however, had enjoyed the whole show tremendously and shook in silent laughter. Wiping the tears from his eyes, he finally gained composure, then turned to leave.

"See you later—Chuck. Bye, Anne," he said, as he walked out and closed the door. Nothing more was ever said until Chuck finally settled the score with Mickey a few weeks later. Then once again, Robbie had to play peacemaker between them.

With Anne working out of the Lakeview station and Denny and Linda in Lancemen on the same days, it allowed them to get together on their days off, to meet for breakfast to compare notes. And from time to time they did just that. The three of them also went over to the college to help Mr. Dewit when he needed help with the hand-on practicals, and evaluations of the Basic EMTs. To Anne's surprise one day, Mr. Dewit asked how she felt about setting up an agility test for the Basic EMT class. They would have to use a dummy weighing about a hundred and fifty pounds or so. The student would have to carry and manipulate the dummy over stairs, and lift it from a chair to the stretcher without jarring it too much.

"Sure," she answered happily. "How soon do you need this set up?"

"Oh, anytime within the next couple of weeks would be good. I figure if you three girls set it up, then the guys can't complain it's too hard. I know the three of you can handle it. I've seen you carrying a weighted dumbbell around like it was a small sack of potatoes. I've got some guys here that I'm not so sure about. I think they must spend way too much time watching TV," he chuckled.

Whether or not Mr. Dewit realized it, he had just given her quite a compliment. Giggling to herself while leaving his office, she remembered that three years ago this same man did not want to even give her the time of day, much less allow her into his class. He even told her that she was wasting her time, and that she would never get a job in this field. Now, this same man was asking her to set up part of the teaching and testing in the EMT Program. "Life sure is funny," she thought aloud.

As winter whipped in, Chuck grew more excited about entering into his second snow season with the car he so dearly loved, his 1978 WD Wagon, Subaru. The car was metallic blue, with white steel wagon wheels and all weather tires. It had four wheel drive, tinted glass windows, an AM/FM radio, and extended track seats. He added a brush bar and skid plate as well as fog lamps. He also replaced the high beams with aircraft landing lights. It was ordered in the fall of 1977, but due to the dockworkers strike, it wasn't delivered until January of 1978. The cost of it, brand new, was $4700.00.

Anne sat at the station, waiting for Linda and Denny to pick her up for breakfast before going over to the college. It was nearly time for midwinter break. Looking out of the window, she noticed that they had gotten quite a bit of snow during the night and thought how odd it was, that they didn't get called out for a car crash or some other snow related accident. She was almost ready to wake Chuck to tell him about the snow, knowing that he would be elated, but then she remembered about his car stories. They had all heard his stories so often of how his car sailed through last year's monster snowstorm—that they could have easily recited each one by heart. Anne liked working with Chuck and thought he was a good guy; but still, she just didn't relish the idea of hearing the stories this early in the morning, although somehow she knew she would as soon as he saw the snow.

Big Rick and Mike came into the station to start their shift, with Linda and Denny right behind them, all stomping the snow from their boots on the rug at the door. Each one of them debated about how many inches the weatherman claimed they had accumulated. The station was not that big; so it didn't take long after hearing their voices for Chuck to come out of the bedroom in his sweats, rubbing his eyes.

"Cool! It snowed?" Chuck asked. His face beamed with the excitement of a child at winter's first dusting. "Hey," he started. "Remember the twelve foot high snow drifts along the road in front of Eider Valley last year?

Remember how great my car was? Yep, and I made it all the way from Marysville without any problems," he bragged. Quickly he looked for his keys to go out and let his car warm up before leaving the station.

As soon as he came back in, he began the dreaded stories of the Subaru Wagon.

"Nobody. I say nobody can get that car stuck," he said at the end of a famous, only unto him, tale of his prized auto.

"Anne can," Rick gibed. She knew he was referring to the dirt bike accident they went on during the fall.

"Oh, here we go. Haven't you forgotten about that yet?"

"How could I? Chuck, you were there. Tell me if I'm lying." Looking at Linda and Denny he started to recall the incident. "We got this call at the State Park. When we first pulled up, there's about twenty or so emergency vehicles, and then we see this guy on a dirt bike, that was so pale I thought he was going to faint. He was our guide. We followed him back into this field—ba-haing over the back forty, over hills and dips that were so steep, it was like a dirt roller coaster. And then, there were these ruts on the path that were about a foot deep. We finally get back to the crash site. So then we carry all of our gear up this hill where the deputy said these two bikers crashed head on. When we get up to the top, we find two human pretzels. These guys were so broken up. They had bones sticking out of their arms and legs, broken ribs, punctured lungs, you name it, they had it. Everything was going good. We got the lines started, broken whatever splinted, backboards and C collars on, the whole nine yards. So now it's time to leave. Well—I've got this volunteer in the back who jumped in to help me on the way to the hospital. Then somehow I ended up with Anne—and now she's going to drive us out. Keep in mind that I gave her specific instructions on how to drive. I said stay out of the ruts—and don't slow down. So we get to the bottom of the steepest hill—and what does she do? She slows down. And yes, of course we got stuck. So I had to leave this goober looking guy with one tooth in the back with the patient, while I come up front to get us unstuck and drive us out to the main entrance."

"And then," Anne interjected, "right in front of a crowd of people, he gets out and says, there—now do you think you can handle it from here?"

"I couldn't help it. I was so mad."

Linda laughed. "Yeah, you were only mad because she got you stuck. If you'd been the one to get stuck, it'd been a whole different story. Then it would have been the path's fault or something else."

"See," Rick said, disgustingly. "You women just all stick together, no matter what. There's no point in even talking about it."

Denny and Linda looked at Anne. Then they all smiled in agreement. For some reason that they couldn't explain, to them Rick's final words raised the stakes in Chuck's car versus snow challenge.

"That's right, so be quiet," Denny jested.

"Okay, Chuck, you're on. We're going to take your precious car for a ride and do our best to get it stuck. How much time do we have to work with?"

"I have to leave here in at least an hour and a half," he answered, approving the duel. "But you go right ahead; I'll be here waiting. I know not even you guys can get that car stuck."

If ever there was a sincere effort to bury a car into the snow, it happened that day. They tried every drift and hill piled high with snow and yet it was not enough to embed, impede, hold, or bog down the little blue car. Each one took turns, as they were sure they would be the one to put an end to the stories. But it never happened.

"Now see," Anne jested, "if car companies were smart, they would use stuff like this to sell cars. They could have a man standing next to a car and have him say—my wife tried for three days to get our car stuck in the snow and she's the worst driver I know, and she still couldn't do it. This is a good car."

"Oh yeah, like that would go over," Linda laughed.

Defeated, but still happy with the fun that they had while trying, they went back to the station and gave Chuck back his keys. He was so thrilled that their efforts proved his statements true, that he offered them money to buy their breakfast.

"Hey, Anne," he said, as she headed for the door. "You know Rick was just teasing you when he was telling that story about you getting the rig stuck."

"I know—we've worked a couple of shifts together since then, and we had a good time. He was just trying to get my goat."

"Well that's good to hear," he said, "because I'm taking a couple of shifts off at Christmas, and he's offered to pick them up. I just wanted to make sure it was okay before I told Robbie."

"Oh ya, that's fine. Rick and I are both readers. We like to compare authors and books that we've read. He likes to read out loud, which is nice. And I like being read to."

Linda laughed. "That must be why you like working here so much. I've only been here a few months and I can already attest to the fact that we've got more than our fair share of authors and storytellers around here. There's not a person that works here that doesn't have a story of some sort to tell. I guess our retirement's all set. If we ever get burned out from all this, we can all just sit down and write a book and call it—The Storytellers."

CHAPTER 20

THE GIFT

"One dollar and eighty-seven cents. That was all. And sixty cents of it was in pennies," Rick said, as he began reading aloud. His voice was smooth and deep. Anne knew by the way he studied the words, and paused at all the right spots, that she was in for a treat. O. Henry's short story entitled The Gift of the Magi had always been one of her favorites during the Christmas season. She had seen the black and white version on TV a few times, but having it read to her out loud was even better yet.

Content as a new kitten, she snuggled against the pillow behind her and pulled the quilt up around her neck, the same way she had done whenever her mother or Aunt Ruth read to her at bedtime. This was the first time she or Big Rick had ever spent Christmas away from their families, so they decided to make the best of it. "On went her old brown jacket; on went her old brown hat," he continued. The tone and excitement in his voice clearly followed what the author must have intended; for it was very easy to picture Della, Mrs. James Dillingham Young, the woman he described from the pages of the book. As he neared the end of the story, he leaned closer to the lamp that was attached to the wall over the bed where they sat. Anne knew the story and the words by heart and mentally said them to herself as he finished. "The magi," he read, as he began the last paragraph, "were wise men—wonderfully wise men."

Anne sighed quietly to herself. After taking the last sip of her hot chocolate, she set her mug on the table next to the bed and listened as he read the last words, then softly clapped and cheered.

"Yea. Thank you, Rick. I think I like that story more, each time I hear it."

"It's a classic all right. Now—why don't you get off of my bed and take your quilt with you. I'm roasting."

Chuckling, Anne gathered up her home sewn cover and moved over to her own bed on the other side of the room. "Man, what a crab. You're not supposed to be a crab on Christmas Eve."

"Maybe if I was at home where I belong, I wouldn't be. As soon as I agreed to work for Chuck, I knew I was going to regret it. My favorite cousin is going to be at my house tomorrow along with the rest of the family and I'm stuck here."

"My family's having a big day too, Rick. I wasn't exactly thrilled with working either, but that's the way it is. There's no point crying about it now."

"Yeah? Well, why don't you make us some more hot chocolate and I'll tell a story about my cousin Bob, and why he's my favorite."

"Will you quit being crabby?"

"Maybe."

Smiling, Anne picked up her mug and went into the kitchen to heat up a fresh pan of water. The direct phone line to dispatch rang. She listened as Rick talked to see if they had a call. No, it sounded like just idle chit chat. She remembered Linda said she was going to help answer the phones over the holiday and wondered if it was her. Stirring the instant hot cocoa, she reached for the bag of marshmallows and dropped a few in. Rick chuckled while replacing the receiver as she walked back into the bunk room, carrying the steamy mugs.

"That was just a welfare check. Things must be slow. Okay," he said, as she set his cocoa on the table next to him. "Here's the story of my cousin Bob. I was sixteen at the time of this story and like most sixteen year olds, had little confidence. I had just gotten my driver's license, was seriously starting to get into girls and attended high school at Lancemen Catholic. I played basketball and was one of the starting members of our team. We were a class C school and ranked in the top ten of the state. Every other week it seemed we were in the newspapers, so as you can imagine—the pressure was great." Pausing he picked up the mug and took a sip. Licking the melted marshmallow from his lips he put the mug back on the table, then continued. "We were fourteen and zero, undefeated. March Madness had begun. I played great in the district games, but I stunk in the regional, stunk in the quarter finals—but we still won and qualified to go to the semifinals. A week before the semifinals I was so nervous that I started acting crazy. I couldn't eat or sleep; I got down to 165 pounds, and I'm six four so you can imagine how I looked. My poor mother was worried sick. Well, I don't know if she called him or if he just came over, but my cousin Bob showed up a few days before the semi's and asked me if I wanted to go for a ride. So I did. We drove down and cruised Woodward, and of course stopped at Ted's for a burger and fries. We talked some I guess, but really all I remember was that I just felt so much more relaxed with him there. Okay---so now it was Friday. Our coach had everything organized. We were told what to wear and what hotel we'd be staying at so that we wouldn't be at the same hotel as the other teams and so on. Plus we knew that there were all kinds of college coaches there watching.

Now, the team we were playing against had this kid named Jeff----he was the cousin to a girl who went to our school. This guy was good. As you probably know from living with guys, they always put the best defensive player on the best offensive player. Well, Jeff was right in my face the whole game. Everything he threw up went in. He scored thirty-two points of which twenty-eight was while I was guarding him during the first half. I couldn't believe the zone this guy was in. So of course they pulled me out. My sister, who was pregnant, was there and went into false labor, but she and my mother thought it was real labor. Thank God my cousin Bob was there with a clear head. He was an ex-Marine and a cop. I don't know if I mentioned that before. Anyway we lost. I was almost glad. I was so tired and fatigued—that I don't know how I could have even mustered enough strength to play another game." Chuckling, he picked up his mug, then swallowed a large gulp of cocoa, as if the memory of the game brought on a tired thirst. "Man, I was spent. The MHAA, Michigan High School Athletic Association, gave us complimentary tickets to watch the finals, which meant that we got to watch the team that beat us play another team. So there I was, sitting in a folding chair at the end of the aisle, nodding off to sleep, while everyone was yelling and cheering around me." Again he chuckled in self amusement. "Well the next thing I knew, my cousin Bob was trying to help me back into my seat. Apparently I fell asleep and toppled over—chair and all—sideways right into the aisle. How embarrassing. But Bob played it off so well that I don't think anyone noticed for longer than a few minutes. What a great guy."

Anne smiled. She always enjoyed hearing tales of the guys' past, as it unfolded a little more of who they truly were. "You know," she began, "last year during Christmas, the crews got to switch areas to spend time with their families, if they lived close by. Maybe tomorrow, if we aren't too busy, we could drop in on your family for a few minutes."

"That might make it worse. Then I wouldn't want to leave."

"It's up to you. Whatever you want to do," she said, yawning.

Rick reached up and turned off the lamp. The cold winter wind whistled outside and pushed against the poorly insulated walls of the station. The furnace hummed quietly as Anne drifted off to sleep, with visions of a restful night dancing through her head.

The direct phone line rang. Rick threw the bedding back and stood to get his bearing. The phone had given him such a start, that he had to think for a second to remember where he was. After taking a few steps, he reached for the receiver while hitting his leg against the table. Anne jumped out of bed, grabbed her uniform and staggered into the bathroom. She didn't even wait to see if it was a call. The phone only rang in the middle of the night for one reason. She knew if she waited, there wouldn't be enough time for a quick trip to the facilities before dressing and dashing out to the cold rig. Looking at her watch, she realized it was later than she thought. It was nearly six thirty in the morning. Christmas Morning. "Hurry up," she heard Rick announce. "I need to get in there, too." Pulling her pants over her long johns, she grabbed her shirt and boots. Rick was standing at the door, dancing from foot to foot when she stepped out.

"The rig's warming up. I already got the information," he said, shutting the bathroom door.

Anne slipped into her boots while buttoning her shirt and scooting across the living room tile. Sliding one sleeve into her coat, she headed out the door. In seconds Rick was behind her, and they were on the way. Again she looked at her watch. Four minutes had passed since the phone rang. From a dead sleep into the cold. It wasn't bad—still she knew three minutes was expected for an emergency call.

The heat was just starting to flow from the vents when they pulled onto the scene of an unresponsive party in Independence. Dan greeted them as they trotted through the snow near the front walk of the residence.

"Merry Christmas, Sweetie" he grinned. "You guys aren't going to need all that equipment," he said in a hushed tone. "We've got an elderly female, with no vitals, found by her family in the bathroom. It looks like she's been there a few hours. The family's talking with one of the deputies in the kitchen," he continued, stepping onto the porch. "The deceased is upstairs."

Entering the house, they followed Dan up the staircase, left of the foyer. The wooden steps were well worn and seemed to give slightly as they trotted up to the top riser. Turning to the right, they went down a short hallway and stopped in front of a small bathroom. Anne set the orange box down on the hall floor and slipped past Ralph, one of the firemen, who was standing in front of the sink writing down the patient's medications, as he took each one from the medicine cabinet. The patient was sitting on the toilet leaning against the wall. Anne stood in front of her. She noticed that the area of her face that was against the wall seemed more discolored—almost as if burned. Looking down, she saw a heat register set in the floor between the wall and the toilet.

"We closed the register as soon as we got here," Dan offered. "Looks like she was cooking pretty good for a couple of hours."

"Sheeze. What a thing to wake up to," Rick said quietly, after making sure none of the family was within hearing distance. "Gramma—simmering on the pot."

"No kidding," Dan chuckled. "I guess it was kind of an expected death from what the family said. She's been sick for a long time. Looks like she's got her own drug store here."

Anne had been hooking up the cardiac monitor while they talked. They were all so used to this type of scene that it seemed perfectly normal to discuss it with ease.

"It's straight line, of course. Do you want to call the hospital—or do you want me to do it?" she asked.

"I might as well do it. I've got the clipboard and the apcor."

"Here's a list of her meds," Ralph said, handing it to Rick who was standing in the doorway.

"Thanks. I'll go down and get her medical history from the family and see what they want us to do."

As he turned to leave, the deputy met him in the hall. "I've got all that information right here. The family wants you to take her to Emerson's Funeral Home," he said. "Let me know which hospital and doc you talk to for the pronouncement time, so I can let the Medical Examiner know."

Well, it certainly wasn't how they had hoped to spend Christmas morning; but then again it could have been worse, Rick thought, as they stood in the garage of the funeral home waiting for the mortician to let them out. Anne walked down the row of flowers left by families and friends of those who had lost a loved one. Many times, over the last couple of years she had picked through the unclaimed flowers to take the healthiest ones back to the station. The guys teased and called her a grave robber. The flowers would just be thrown out or taken to a nearby nursing home if she didn't take them. The people who ran the funeral homes didn't care one way or another.

"Sorry I took so long. Anne—aren't you going to take any of the flowers?"

"Not today, Mr. Emerson. Thanks anyway."

"Well here's a tip. Have lunch somewhere on me."

"Thanks. Merry Christmas," Rick said.

"Merry Christmas," Mr. Emerson replied.

Rick never even looked at the money the mortician slipped into his hand until they got out into the rig. "Man, he gave us ten bucks. Now, if we can only find someplace that's open we can get something to eat. I'm starved."

"Well I didn't think anything would be open, so I brought in eggs and sausage to fry up and homemade coffee cake. It's all back at the station."

"Really," he teased. "Well in that case, I take back all the means things I said about you."

"At least until next time," she laughed.

Rick showered while Anne made breakfast. He offered to wash dishes afterward but she made him promise to leave the water alone until she finished her shower; which he did. The world seemed at peace as happiness filtered from the TV. Commentators explained each float in the Christmas Parade and other programs with church choirs and Christmas stories filled the rest of the morning and part of the earlier afternoon. Rick and Anne each had called home to wish everyone Merry Christmas. Neither one of them, of course, mentioned their first and only call of the day—at least so far.

The brisk awakening that started their day soon took its toll. By mid afternoon, heavy eyelids drew each of them into a drowsy state which ended again with the phone on the wall in the bedroom ringing. A cancer patient who was initially staying at a nursing facility had gone home to spend Christmas with his family. Then, somewhere between opening the gifts and sitting down for dinner, he took a turn for the worse. While the family didn't feel it was an emergency, they still asked that the crew respond without delay and without lights or siren. The residence that they were called to was several miles north of their station on a back road. After arriving they made a quick evaluation of the patient, then went out to get the stretcher. While reassuring the family, they bundled the patient from head to toe, then started outdoors toward the ambulance. The snow was quite deep causing Anne to struggle while pulling the stretcher through the knee high, niveous fleece. With each step, more and more of the soft icy crystals packed its way into her boots, causing them to become heavier. Then, as she backed into a drift, she lost her footing and disappeared.

"Anne," Rick called. "Where did you go?" He chuckled.

"Right here," she answered, pulling herself back up. Somewhat embarrassed, she laughed. "My boots are full of snow. I can't move."

"Well, empty them out or something," he snickered. "The family's probably watching from the window."

Glancing sideways she noticed a lower point in the drift and trudged toward it. The wind began to pick up, voiding the warmth that the sun emitted. Suddenly a gust whisked across her face as they slowly worked their way through the snow. Laughing, she blinked her eyes, then feebly blew back at the wind in an effort to clear the tiny cold particles from her eyelashes that blocked her view. Finally they were at the back of the rig, loading the patient.

"That was the littlest house I've ever seen. I had to duck under every doorway," Rick smiled, while lifting the opposite side of the stretcher as Anne. Their height was so vastly different that she had to stand on tip toes, while he had to crouch in order to lift the cot into the rig. That was the hardest part of the two of them working together. "For a second," he added, while chuckling, "I thought we were at the house of an elf—being Christmas and all."

The other calls that they responded on throughout the day were spaced a few hours apart. Then, just as they were leaving a restaurant they found open for dinner, a code three came in for an auto accident. The scene of the PI was actually just outside of their response area, which told them that the crew for that area must be on another call, and that things were picking up. The sun was setting and the roads were starting to ice over with the temperature change. The back of the rig fishtailed as they coded south toward a small college campus that shared the grounds with a Catholic priesthood seminary. Up ahead on the winding road across from a lake, they saw the blue flashing lights of a police car and began to slow down. Then as they neared the scene, a pale green pickup truck that crashed head on into a tree, came into view. It was the only vehicle they noticed involved in the accident. During the winter season it was common for a gale wind to whip up over the road off the lake and cause hazardous driving conditions near the seminary. But up until now, no one had ever hit the tree that sat back from the road behind the iron fence.

Stepping out onto the shoulder of the road, Anne headed for the pickup. Rick noticed another potential patient in the back of the patrol car and went in that direction. After opening the door he leaned over the back seat.

"Hi. My name is Rick," he began. "Were you in the pickup?"

"Yaw—I vus," came the slurred words in a Swedish accent.

"Well—are you hurt?" he asked. The man's head wobbled as he tried to focus on a suitable answer. His flaccid body tilted, besotted by the alcohol that now reeked from his breath and clothing. Clearly, there was no question of his intoxicated state. He was three sheets in the wind; perhaps even to the point that his sheets could be described as thread worn.

"My leg—it hurts," the answer slowly sputtered. "But don't vorry about that now—phew—ve are in sooo much trouble."

"Okay, well we'll worry about that later. What's your name."

"Olav."

"Listen, Olav, there's not much room in there. Apparently you walked over here—do you think you can walk over to the ambulance so that I can take a better look at you?"

"I—vil try."

Rick helped the man to his feet, then aided him as he stumbled toward the rig. They stopped and stood next to the ambulance while Rick opened the side doors. Anne was already inside with her patient, who seemed equally as intoxicated.

"And you're sure you aren't hurt?" Rick heard Anne ask her patient, as he boosted Olav up into the back compartment.

"Lief, are you fine?" Olav asked, while falling onto the bench seat, next to Anne.

"What's this guy's name?" Anne asked Rick.

"His name is Olav. He says his leg hurts."

"Oh—but it's not—that bad," he mumbled. "Lief—veee are in so muuch trouble. Dey vill send us back—ven they see vat ve did."

"Olav," Anne spoke up, pointing to the small padded bench behind the driver's seat. "Why don't you sit over there on that seat, so we can take a look at your leg."

"Vat ever—you saaay. I have already—caused too much….." he garbled, while stumbling and weaving the two or three steps it took to stand and turn himself around before flopping onto the seat, behind where Rick was now sitting.

"Good grief," Anne sighed, shaking her head and grinning at Rick. "Olav—do you want me to look at your leg?"

His head hung over in front of him and bobbed. He didn't answer. "Are the police done with them?" she asked Rick.

"Yeah. He said they're students here at the seminary. We better take them to St. Luke's then, I guess."

"Lief—we're going to take you to St. Luke's—is that okay with you? Lief buddy—are you with me?" she asked smirking.

"Yaw—yaw—I'm here."

"So—if you guys are seminary students—where did you get the truck?"

"Ve took it—from the garrrrage. I don't thinnnk—dey vill lettt—us graaaduuaate."

Rick stopped at a red light, then looked back at the group, chuckling. The two exchange students were so comical looking it was almost too funny for words.

"Let me get this straight," Anne began, "just so that I give the right story to the hospital. You guys took the truck from the garage. Had you already been drinking—or did you take it to buy the alcohol?"

"Ve broke into the—comm-uuunion vine."

"Lief—Okay. You broke into the communion wine—got drunk—took the seminary truck from the garage—and then crashed it into a tree. Is that how it went?"

"Ohhhh—Olav is right—dey vill sennnd us back home."

Just then, a loud, strange gurgling sound started erupting from Olav. His head jerked up and he began vomiting. Not just in front of him, but it projected from his mouth and splashed against the side doors, and ran down into the wheel well. Quickly, she stood to reach for a large basin for Olav to throw up into; but it only splashed out and ran down the sides of the yellow plastic container. Then Lief tipped over and slid down onto the bench seat.

"Is he doing what I think he's doing?" Rick asked, turning around at another stop light. "It's a good thing we're almost there. Guess we'll be out of service for a while, cleaning up this mess. Merry Christmas, Anne," he chuckled.

It would have been easier in warm weather. Then they could have just hosed the rig down. Instead they had to wash everything with the doors closed so that the vomit wouldn't freeze, while wiping the back compartment down. Finally, they cleared the hospital and headed back for the station. Rick was behind the wheel again. Usually they would alternate every other call. But Anne didn't feel like driving, so Rick gladly took the driver's seat. They were just a mile or so from the hospital, when Anne noticed a car in her side mirror getting very close to the side of the ambulance.

"That guy almost hit us," she said, trying to get Rick's attention.

"What guy?"

"There's a guy weaving back and forth in the lane next to us. He almost hit the side of the ambulance," she answered.

"Oh ya—I see him."

"Here he comes again!" No sooner had the words left her mouth, when they felt the car crash into the back corner of the rig.

"He got us! And there he goes," Rick continued, watching the car blend into the other traffic on the four lane road that ran in front of St. Luke's. "Man—is this day weird or what?" Pulling over to the side of a nearby street, he reached for the radio mic. "Radio, from Life Four."

"Car calling?"

"This is Life Four, radio."

"Life Four, go ahead."

"Yeah, we just got hit. We lost the other driver in traffic."

"Well, that's not good. Are you hurt?"

"Yeah—I mean no, just a little shook up."

"Where are you?"

"We're about a hundred miles west of Saginaw, on the Boulevard." There was a noticeable pause from the dispatcher. Rick and Anne both started laughing, after realizing what he'd said. "I mean—a hundred feet."

"I was just going to say—that would put you just outside of the state capital. Well, is the rig driveable?"

"Yeah," Rick chuckled. "As soon as I get my bearing we'll head back to the station."

"Very good. Give me a TX when you get there."

"Vew ," he joked in a Swedish accent. "Vhat a day. You wait until I see Chuck. I'm going to kill him. This stuff should be happening to him—not me. This day reminds me of a day that I had this past summer when I was working with Jerry."

Anne sat back in her seat. Another one of Rick's stories was about to begin. They were always fun to listen to, and relaxing to him.

"See—we were working out of the Bedford fire station and frequented this little diner called Henry Hooligan's Fish and Chips. And there was this really cute waitress there that everyone called Kitten. She was twenty years old, talked too much, had sandy blonde hair, and was about 125 pounds. Well anyway, over the summer I got to know her pretty good. She liked to kiss. And she had this way about her that made me feel like I was a M - A- N, man," he chuckled. "Well, she asked if she could ride with us on a call—just to see what it was like. So we started out on this basic transfer from a nursing home with this old guy who was dehydrated, covered with gomer dust, and had hair sticking out of his ears. He was very lucid when we first picked him up but for some unknown reason, he coded. He took his first step on the pathway from life to death. I checked for a pulse. There was none. So I pulled the resuscitator bag out of the orange box, and taught Kitten how to do CPR. She put the heal of her hand on the guy's chest just like I showed her. Her shoulders were straight—she was a natural. Her finger position and the depth of her compressions were perfect. I counted out the rhythm while starting the IV. Jerry had already pulled over to help hook the guy up to the monitor and set up my drugs. I gave the patient one milligram of atropine—and he came back completely. His sensorium was intact and everything was just like it was when we first picked him up. When she saw what happened, she became this living nerve end. She was ecstatic—a jangle of nerves. You helped to save his life, I told her. The old guy did fine the rest of the way to the hospital. She thanked me later," he smiled, bouncing his eyebrows. "After that call, we had this naked—nine month pregnant lady—who went nuts and was running around outside, yelling obscenities at the cops. We had to corral her with a blanket.

After that," he chuckled, "we responded to an injured party. Man, you should have seen the front seat of this car, where the accidental blood letting took place. It was everywhere—on the dashboard, the seat, up on the inside fabric of the roof. It was unbelievable. So we followed the trail into the house and found this girl about sixteen or so sitting at the kitchen table, mad as a hornet, pouting with her arms folded across her chest. Then this big guy came walking down the hallway—proud as punch that his boy had been with this girl—bragging, as he directed us into the bathroom down the hall. The whole scene was so bizarre I almost started laughing. Jerry went down to take care of his boy, while I talked to the girl to see what happened. At first she wouldn't say a word. So the kid's dad spoke up." Rick's face flushed, then he shook with laughter while recalling the event. "This guy," he continued, "looked like Baby Huey back from Hee Haw—salute! His big hairy belly hung over his pants like a muffin over the pan. His shirt was covered with food crumbs and splatterings—plus, it was too small. I could barely make out what he was saying, so the girl finally confessed that her braces got caught on her boyfriend's business. He apparently freaked when the two became one. When he tried to pull away the braces remained attached. Apparently, he hadn't been circumcised and her braces nicked a small artery or vein on the foreskin. As you can imagine, the call into the hospital on that one was a hoot. And after that—we went to back up another unit that lost control while pulling up to the scene of this PI over on Wilson Boulevard. When we got there, their rig was down in a ditch near the lake, headlights pointing up towards the heavens or sky or whatever. They couldn't move. Don't worry boys, I told them—we'll help you out. Their patient, it turned out, was a felon who was wanted in seven states, that crashed into a pole after a police chase. When we first pulled up, his girlfriend was in the back of the police car and he was standing outside of his van in his boxers, with his pants around his ankles. It was so funny. It seemed like every call we went on that night—people were losing their drawers—or something close to it."

"Really. So whatever happened to that girl—Kitten?"

"She quit her job at Henry's and started taking classes to go to medical school."

"Well good for her. Sounds like she made out the best out of all of them."

"Oh—she did," he smiled.

"You know what I mean."

They chatted back and forth the rest of the way to the station, comparing war stories. What an odd way to make a living she thought to herself. Then she thought about Kitten and how that one call changed the course of her life, as if her helping to save the patient's life brought a new dimension to her own life. Life—it's so odd; wonderfully odd. Yes. It is wonderful—and odd—and grand. Certainly, only the wise could be sage enough to understand that and see it for the gift that it is. For the gifts of the magi and of the couple in O. Henry's story weren't really the gifts; but rather it was the love and the sacrifice of the givers. Truly that alone is the treasure. Truly that, is the gift.

CHAPTER 21

FULL CIRCLE

Suicidal ideations. Anne had often read those words on a court petition while transporting a patient to a psych facility. Generally, those patients had a history of some sort of mental disorder and were medicated for chronic depression or schizophrenia. But today as she stood looking into the eyes of a smiling young man in the graduation photo hanging on the wall, she wondered what in the world compelled him to fall into this sad state of self destruction? Did he breakup with his girlfriend? There would be other girls to date; didn't he realize? The note that he left gave no clue of reason to those outside of his life. It merely read, I'm sorry. Love Benny.

She turned to look at the tiny monkey that stood in the cage on the floor of the front room as the chattering grew too loud to ignore. "Hush now, little Muncho," she softly uttered, after noticing his name on a metal tag tied over the cage door. A sheriff deputy came from the back hall of the residence, sliding his hand held radio back into its holder on his belt.

"I've got the ME and a detective on the way," he said. "At this point we aren't sure he was the one who pulled the trigger and wrote the note. It's a good possibility he did. But still, it would have been a stretch with the angle of the rifle and the length of his arms." Motioning to the monkey as Anne knelt in front of the cage, he added. "I wish that little guy could talk."

"It sounds like he's trying to say something," she replied touching the top of the cage. The monkey reached up and moved her fingers as if he expected something to be there.

"Or—maybe he's just hungry."

"How long are you going to need us to hang around?" Alex, Anne's new partner, asked. "Just so that I can let our dispatcher know."

"The neighbor said his sister goes to LCC and his mother started a new job a few weeks ago. She didn't know where. We're trying to find his sister. If she isn't here in a half hour or so, we'll cut you loose. There's no reason to call the hospital for a pronouncement time. We'll let the ME handle it," he concluded while walking toward the door.

Alex watched Anne run her fingers over the side of the cage, stopping from time to time to let the monkey grab hold. "It looks like we might be here for awhile. I'll go out and radio dispatch—while you play with your little friend," he said smiling.

For a new person, she thought, he carried himself quite well; and he was quick. Without hesitation, he wasted no time once he realized he had a valid reason to go out and get some fresh air. Throughout the world of EMS, at least their end, it was well slated and quickly understood that anyone who could not stomach the job would be labeled as a whimp, or worse, they'd be called a little girl. Then of course there were times when the scene was gruesome enough that it even gave the most tenacious, experienced medic cause to step back. Most of the crews carried a jar of Vicks and a small tube of toothpaste in a small plastic baggy, to which they put a fingertip full of the product in their nose or mouth to mask the smell of a decomposing body or any other unpleasant odor. When a scene was such that even the old timers brought the plastic baggy out—it was agreed that all name calling be set aside.

The screen door slammed shut leaving her alone in the house with the monkey. Slowly, an eeriness came into the front room like a waif, as music from the deceased boy's stereo drifted down the hall toward them. Sitting back in the cage, the monkey held his hands in his lap and looked up with a sweet, yet doleful expression. "I can't tell if you're sad or hungry little guy. Probably both. Well—let me see if I can at least find you something to eat."

Initially, the call came in from the neighbor who heard the gun shot. Apparently she knew the family well enough to know their cars and called Benny's house to see if he was all right. Then after letting the phone ring a number of times with no answer, she called the police. Anne and Alex arrived minutes after the sheriff's department. As soon as the rig stopped, one of the deputies directed them into the back bedroom of the house where Benny's lifeless body was found lying against a bunk bed ladder, held up by the mattress frame of a loft style bed. Clearly, due to the large gun shot wound to his lower chest area and grave amount of lost blood, there was no point in beginning resuscitative measures. His waxen, cyanotic body had already become cold. Beneath him in the shag carpet were pools of coagulated blood; in addition to the crimson splattering on the aluminum foil covered walls and the unmade bedding. A purple glow from the black lights on the floor gave a surreal appearance to the whole scene. Then the music from an album in the background stopped and started again, drawing their attention. The arm of the record player apparently had been set to return to the beginning of the black vinyl disc, to weave over the compressed grooves again and again. The chorused lyrics, "We are the champions," spewed out as Alex and Anne carefully inspected the body; assuring not to disturb even a thread of the clothing. Listening to the words as she worked, Anne knew it was from a song more familiar to other people her age, than it was to herself.

While looking for something to feed the monkey she repeated the words of the song to herself, trying to figure out why Benny would have picked that particular tune. He was so young and had so much ahead of him. While opening the refrigerator, she remembered hearing someone say—that suicide was a permenent solution to a temporary problem. There's no future in it. If only Benny could have hung on another day or a week, maybe whatever it was that was so painful would have passed. Just from her own experiences alone, she'd learned that life's changes often came rapidly and without explanation. Only now, while recalling the events that once seemed agonizingly unbearable to her, she realized that they had since faded and transformed into mere shadows without any real cognizance. The death of her own parents and oldest brother had been one of those things. And then who, without lessening the pain she experienced by losing her family, could ever forget their first broken heart? For her, that devastation happened more than ten years ago; but at the time, she too thought her life was all but over. Since then however, many things had developed and taken root—or flight, most of which she was pleased to have experienced. Certainly there were events she would rather have missed. But then if clay could talk—more than likely it would voice its dislike of each twisting and pulling of the potter's hand. Yet if the process ceased, the work of art would never be; and the lump of clay would always be just a lump of clay and nothing more. She understood that it's during the weak times and struggles of our lives that strength begins; it's then, that a segment of our character is molded.

As the monkey finished the last piece of hot dog that Anne broke off for him, Alex came back inside and announced that Benny's sister was pulling in the driveway. Suddenly, a flash zoomed past the large picture window. The voice of a young woman screaming Benny's name echoed under the eaves. The police grabbed her before she could come in, barring her from her own home, but saving her from the horrid sight that they knew would haunt her forever. Anne hated this part of the job more than anything else. To hear and feel the gut wrenching sorrow from the loved ones who were left behind to deal with the pain passed on by those who could not bear it themselves, was never pleasant. She sighed and looked over at Alex who seemed slightly shaken but not surprised by the sister's response.

"Let's go out and help them," Anne suggested. "She's the reason the cops held us here."

"What in the world do you say to people when this happens?" he asked.

"There's not a whole lot to say. You just try and comfort them and let them lead the conversation. Listen—and be strong for them. Nothing makes sense to them right now. They generally fly through the different stages of death—denial, blame, anger and so on. Well," she sighed, "we better get out there. Ready?"

"I guess."

The neighbor came over and put her arm around Benny's sister. Benny used to cut her grass from time to time she said; and while she didn't seem like a close friend, she was a familiar enough face to ease some of the fear and offered a place of refuge until the girl's mother came home. Watching as they walked across the street to the woman's home, the deputy released Anne and her partner from the scene. Alex sighed while buckling his seat belt. "If I never have to see that again—it will be okay by me."

"Well I wish I could tell you that you won't—but I'd be lying. Unfortunately, if you stay around here long enough—it will only be one of many. It might bounce around in your head for a few days, but then it will find a place to rest and become just another bad call. You kind'a have to have thick skin and a soft heart all at the same time. But really—the good calls outweigh the bad—you'll see."

Alex and Anne were like frontiersmen in a new area of the county that the company had just taken over; and Anne, once a pioneer, now a senior partner, was showing the new paramedics the ropes just as she had done with the new Basic EMTs. Alex was her first rookie, ALS partner. She had always enjoyed watching the faces of the newbies. It seemed so long ago now that she had been in their shoes. After all, it had been about four years since she first stepped foot in the back of an ambulance, leaving the nursing program behind.

Alex reached for the knob on the FM radio to find something a little more uplifting to direct their minds. Then he sat back in his seat just as the dispatcher's voice came over the unit's speaker announcing the information of another call in the downtown area of Oxthorn. It was for a woman with difficulty breathing. The address was about eight miles away, on the main street in an upstairs flat. After coming to a stop in front of an old brick building, Anne came around from the driver's side and helped Alex carry the equipment up the narrow enclosed flight of stairs.

"We're up here," a voice directed.

Entering the small apartment, they walked over to the double bed in the center of the living room—slash—bedroom, where a woman in her mid forties fought to breath. Alex took her blood pressure while Anne hooked the tubing of an oxygen mask to the portable tank. After sliding the elastic strap of the mask over the patient's head, she snapped the cardiac monitor leads onto the electrode pads. Alex felt for a pulse while Anne placed the pads onto the woman's chest.

"Is the oxygen helping you breath any easier?" she asked. The woman nodded.

"When did you start getting short of breath?" Alex asked. The woman pointed to her watch, indicating that her distress began about two hours ago. Then she picked up her inhaler and shook her head to explain that it didn't help. Alex checked the patient's legs to see if they were swollen while Anne jotted down the rest of her medications. "Is your name Dora?" she asked, looking at the prescription bottle. The woman nodded again. Her breathing seemed less labored. A small group of people in the kitchen could be seen talking close together as if in secret. At first their conversation was quiet but it grew louder and noticeably more tense. The patient stirred nervously and her shortness of breath increased. Sensing the effect of the conversation on their patient, Anne finally spoke up.

"Excuse me," she started. One of the men turned in response. "I know it's probably none of my business—but whatever it is that you're talking about is making Dora worse. Is there something that maybe I can help with?"

The man looked at the others and began speaking as if embarrassed. "We were trying to figure out if we have enough money to pay for the ambulance—so Dora can go to the hospital."

"Well, you don't need any money right now. The company will send you a bill in a week or so. If you don't have the whole amount then—I'm sure they will set up a payment plan with you."

"Really? The ambulance service that ran out of Zegler's Funeral Home made you pay first, or you didn't go."

Anne looked at Alex. She could almost read his mind. That seemed like a pretty tacky way to run a business. But maybe they figured they'd get their money either way, whether the patient rode as a patient—or a corpse.

"Well sir, our company doesn't do it that way. So just put your money away and relax," she said smiling. "Dora, we're going to give you some medication to help you feel better and then take you to the hospital."

While Anne reassured Dora, Alex took the blood pressure cuff off of the patient's arm, put it back into the orange box, then exchanged it for a bag of D5W and the IV tubing. "I'll start the IV and call LOH for the meds. We got about a twenty to twenty-five minute drive, don't we?"

"That's close, depending on traffic," Anne answered, nodding in agreement. The family was so grateful, that the two men helped Anne put the equipment away. Then they carried the stretcher up the stairs, while Alex started the line and radioed the hospital.

Alex caught on to everything so quickly that Anne hardly felt like a training officer. Many of his personality traits were different than her past partners and yet in some ways were the same. Like Chuck, he rarely cursed. And similar to Roman and Dan, he enjoyed mimicking the Blues Brother's and other characters from the TV show, Saturday Night Live, which they all found to be intoxicatingly funny. "I'll have a cool water sandwich on a Sunday go to meeting bun; Bow, bow, bow," was one of his favorite lines. And it always proved to be just as amusing as his unrestrained, light and honest laughter. He was usually jovial and was always—very careful—about eating healthy foods. A donut would never touch his lips. "Empty calories. That's all that is. Nothing but grease, flour and sugar," was his response at the sight of any such item, in any form.

When winter finally broke and the back roads of their assigned area became dry, Anne often followed him in the ambulance while he jogged. Once he reached his preset goal for the day, she'd tap the horn on the steering wheel so he could slow his pace to cool down. After trotting over to the rig, he'd open the passenger door and grab the towel that he had sitting on the seat. While asking about the amount of time that it took him to reach the aimed distance, he'd place his wire framed glasses on the dash, then use the towel to wipe the sweat from his face and neck. Next he'd pick up his sports drink and take a good healthy swig. While returning the glass bottle to the cup holder, he'd put his toothpick back between his teeth. And finally, he'd slide his round spectacles on, while crinkling his nose to force the gold frame to return to its proper place. Unless they got a call in the middle of the excursion, it usually went the same way as if by some sort of rite.

Alex didn't talk in his sleep or snore. To Anne, that was a treat. In fact, the only habit of his that seemed odd at all, was that he always had a tooth pick in his mouth, except of course when he was eating or sleeping. That was especially nice since their station was based out of a small back room in the basement of an old church in the Village of Orion, which they shared with the police department. Within its cinder block walls they had a metal cabinet for supplies, a set of bunk beds, a black and white TV that sat on a folding chair, a lamp and a telephone. The only bathroom in the basement, was right next to their bunk room. It had one toilet and one sink that everyone shared but not everyone cleaned. The two rooms were divided by a couple of unpainted, mudded sheets of drywall that offered visual privacy and nothing more.

All of the department's dispatchers were middle aged women who were small town, yet polite to outsiders. Their midnight dispatcher, Carol, had a deep raspy voice and a smoker's cough that got so bad, sometimes Anne and Alex thought they might have to go out into the phone center and give her oxygen. Then there were a few instances, after Officer Ben Maloney went in to use the bathroom, that they almost brought out the oxygen for themselves. The gaseous sounds and odors that made themselves known during such an episode were not pretty, and without exception induced Alex to joke about the imaginary green fog that escaped from under the bathroom door. While most of his grumblings were muffled by the pillow that he held over his face, the choking and gagging and comments about the paint peeling off the walls, bubbled out clearly each time he lifted the pillow, while pretending to take his last breath. "Sorry guys," Ben volunteered from the bathroom, after hearing Alex's emoted display. "I'd open the window—but it's painted shut."

Initially, there was resentment from the police department toward this newfangled ambulance company who came in and took over, replacing the home town's service. But once they saw the writing on the wall, they welcomed Mercy EMS and all of the new lifesaving techniques provided by this Advance Life Support ambulance service.

Anne looked around at the midmorning haze, while pumping gas into the ambulance. It was going to be a hot and humid one. She didn't need a newspaper to tell her that. It'd be the kind of day that people with emphysema and other pulmonary diseases dreaded.

Alex looked at the dip stick, then slid it back into the tube. "We're full," he said, letting the hood of the rig drop down into place. Taking the clean corner of the paper towel, he wiped the sweat from his forehead. "I've got a bad feeling about this day."

"Yep, the chronic lungers are going to be in trouble for sure, with this humidity," Anne agreed.

"Unit Six," the radio squealed.

"Unit Six is at the pumps—go ahead," Anne answered, speaking into the mic.

"You're responding to downtown Orion—it looks like it's going to fall right across from the movie theater. PD says it's in a flat above the hardware store, for a man complaining of shortness of breath."

"Okay, we've got their unit in sight. They're waving us down," she replied, noticing the black and white patrol car up the street. "Good thing I already signed for the gas," she said, jumping onto the driver's seat. " I didn't hear their siren when they pulled up, did you?"

"Nope. It's a good thing we're close."

Anne pulled up in front of the black and white, then stopped. Coming around to the side doors, she grabbed whatever equipment Alex couldn't and followed him up the stairs next to the hardware store. Upon entering the flat they found two officers kneeling over an unconscious man, preparing to do CPR.

"He was trying to talk to us when he went down. I'm sure glad you guys got here. I've never done CPR on a real person before—just that dummy."

Anne set up the suction unit and began pulling up on the handle to create a vacuum. Using the hard plastic wand she began suctioning the pink frothy sputum that poured out of the patient's mouth.

"Do you think you can do this while I tube him?" she asked Officer Cooper.

"Sure—I guess. What do I have to do?" he agreed apprehensively. Clearly, at that moment he would rather have been crouched behind his patrol car caught up in a shoot out with a bad guy, than to be in that apartment suctioning bloody saliva from an unconscious man.

"The suction unit works like a bicycle pump. Just move the handle up and down while you suction all that gunk out," she said quickly, then handed him the wand. "There's a hole right here," she said, tapping her thumb over it to demonstrate. "Put your thumb over the hole while you pull the wand out of his mouth. That's important, okay?" He nodded. "Do that for a couple a seconds while I get set up, then I'll hyperventilate him with the resusci-bag. This intubation tube will help to create a good airway without blowing all that stuff back into his lungs," she explained while lubricating the selected tube.

While Anne and Officer Cooper worked at establishing an airway, Alex coached Officer Mark Pelton through the chest compressions, freeing him up to start an IV. After taping the IV catheter down, Alex reached for the drug box. Anne placed the EKG electrodes on the patient's chest while Officer Dennis Copper squeezed the bag, pushing air into the patient's lungs through the tube Anne had inserted into the patient's trachea. The monitor showed a very slow dying heart rate.

"I wish he wouldn't have waited so long before calling," Anne said. "We could have done a lot more to help him earlier. He's basically drowning in his own body fluids at this point."

"The lasix is on board," Alex announced.

"He's so bradycardic, that I can't even feel a pulse. Let's give him—point five of atropine and see if that doesn't pick things up. Mark, stay on his chest until we have a pulse."

The officers worked with the ALS crew following their requests without hesitation. Anne contacted their base hospital for further orders. After being on the scene a little more than twenty minutes, they slowly witnessed a dying man with no palpable pulse or blood pressure, initially taking two to three breaths a minute, become a man of savable worth.

"Okay," Anne said, holding the receiver to the apcor radio. "Let's check for pulses."

"I've got a pulse," Alex said, gently pressing his index and middle finger over the patient's carotid artery. "The rate's about sixty."

"LOH, we've got a pulse of about sixty—hold on for a BP."

Alex looked over at her while taking the stethoscope earpieces out of his ears. "BP's a hundred over fifty-eight."

Anne relayed the information, then listened for further orders from the hospital. "Ten four LOH. We'll slow the dopamine drip down and monitor his vitals. We'll re-contact if we have any further problems—other than that we'll see you in about fifteen or twenty minutes."

Throughout the summer, Alex came to realize that Anne had been right. The good calls did outweigh the bad. And throughout the summer, the company as well as the employees took on changes leading them to avenues that would enhance the role of their profession. They no longer did body removals on a regular basis. There would be no more stiffs stopping in for gas while en route to the morgue or naked old men, except for a tie, sitting in lawn chairs waiting for the mortician. They were evolving into real professionals. Even the nurses, little by little, were referring to them less and less as "ambulance drivers" and more often as paramedics. Sometimes, they joked with the nurses they knew and called them bed pan emptiers in retaliation to the title they all loathed. It was a good feeling to be appreciated and respected. But at the same time they knew it was wise not to become too inflated with their new found grace. For there was always someone or something waiting to pop that bubble of egotistic pride.

Once in a while if the morning was slow in the north end of the county, the crews working Lancemen were allowed to meet with the Orion car for breakfast at a point in between the two areas. This was a good way to keep up with actives within the company. And, as long as it didn't affect their response times or create complaints from people sitting around them, Merve usually didn't have a problem with it.

"Do you want to start out with a round of coffee?" the waitress asked.

"They're having coffee—I'd just like some water please," Alex jumped in. "I don't know how you guys can drink that stuff," he grimaced.

"That's because you're still, just a newbie," Linda laughed. "I'll give you a year and you'll be chugging it down like the rest of us."

"I seriously doubt it. You guys should just have permanent IV bags of coffee. Then you'd never have to run out."

"See—that's what I'm saying Alex. You're just a rookie," Linda chuckled, while taking her cup from the hostess.

"So, who wants to go first?" The waitress asked flipping open her pad of meal tickets.

"I'll have your special—over medium," Anne started. Rod waited until they had all placed their orders, then looked at Anne while stirring his coffee.

"Are you going to just sit there and let her talk about your partner like that?" Rod asked.

"I'm sure Alex can take care of himself. He might be a rookie, but he holds his own with no problem."

"Yeah, okay, I'll give him that. I heard the docs at LOH talking about that guy you took in a few days ago—the one in full blown congested heart failure? They had him on a vent for the first day, but now thanks to you, he's already off."

"Really?" Alex remarked. "That was a good call. Those Orion cops were great. They didn't seem like they even wanted to be there at first, but Anne got them doing stuff and then they acted like they were bummed that they couldn't ride along to the hospital," he chuckled.

"Oh yeah—Jack was talking about a cop from Orion named Maloney," Rod started. "He said he and Jerry responded to a call on Bakersfield—when they pulled up on the scene, this Maloney was trying to body slam some guy in the driveway of this woman's house." He paused taking a bite of toast, then continued. "He said this guy was on top of this woman sawing her head off with a hack saw. Maloney tried to stop him—but as soon as the guy saw him coming up the driveway, he started sawing faster—so Maloney body-slammed him to get him off. Jack and Jerry showed up just as Maloney and this guy hit the ground. Maloney's backup wasn't there yet, so they helped wrestle this guy down so Maloney could cuff him."

Alex sat in the booth listening intensely, then pushed his plate back. "Well—I'm certainly glad I don't like ketchup on my eggs. That's the grossest thing I've ever heard. I hope that woman was unconscious before he started hacking her head off."

"It was in the middle of the day. None of her neighbors heard anything, so they think she must have been. Jack gets the same kind of goofy calls that Anne does. It ought to be interesting when they start working together in the fall out of the health care center."

"What health care center?" Anne asked.

"See—I told you she didn't know about it," Rod stated, looking at Linda.

"What's going on now? Why does everybody always know what I'm doing before I do?"

"Robbie said he was going to send a memo to the outlying stations yesterday," Linda said. "I guess he didn't get around to it yet. What a surprise. Anyway, they're supposed to talk about it at the company meeting next week. We don't know all the details yet, either; but LOH is going to be building two new health care centers. One in Oxthorn and one in Bedford. The company's going to have a crew stationed at each one to help the staff when they aren't on calls. Instead of working twenty-four hour shifts, the medics who work there will be working twelve hour shifts. Hey—at least you'll be able to get out of that basement in the church."

"So where am I going to be working?" Alex asked.

"Probably in Lakeview or one of the vacation stations," Rod smiled. "With someone who gets normal calls."

"I thought these were normal calls."

"See, Alex," Linda laughed. "I told you—you're just a rookie. And you still have—so much to learn."

Linda watched as the waitress refilled their cups, then continued. "So, Anne, speaking of odd things, did I tell you the newest Tom Graze story?"

Tom Graze was a Lancemen fireman that was well known for two things. He was very likable and very clumsy. There was a number of stories of lumbering, heavy-footed mishaps that occurred when ever Tom was present. Once he accidentally set off a fire extinguisher in the back of the rescue unit on the way to a medical. Recalling the nonchalant way he stepped over the cloud of foam through the back doors of the module style rescue when they arrived on the scene could still produce a belly chuckle from all who knew him. Then there was the time when he backed the rescue over the orange bio-phone radio that they used to call the hospital. Yet the funniest, but not to him or his captain, of course, was when he attempted to cure a brand new, Texas sized, cast iron skillet, by heating it with oil, then setting it on an open window sill to cool. Unfortunately, the window was on the second story of the fire hall, right over where the captain parked his newly approved vehicle, after months of fighting with the City Council to put it in the budget. There was Tom—waving to greet Captain Hailey as he pulled into the parking space, when he accidentally brushed the edge of the skillet with his hand sending it crashing onto the hood of Hailey's car. The fireman who told the story recalled that the captain sat in the car for almost ten minutes before getting out so that he wouldn't strangle Tom. And then once he got out, he paced in front of the car mumbling about the huge dent in the hood of his shiny new baby.

The handheld radio for Linda and Rod's unit squawked just as she started to share the newest Tom Graze anecdote.

"Wouldn't you know. Well, I'll catch up with you later," Linda said, leaving a tip on the table. "See ya, Alex."

Anne finished her last sip of coffee, then reached for her check. Pulling a small wad of money from her shirt pocket she counted out two dollars then pulled a couple of quarters from her pants pocket for a tip. Alex was already at the register.

Following Alex outside, Anne stopped at the newspaper box in front of the restaurant and inserted a couple of coins into the slot. "What a beautiful day," she said, while removing the daily issue. A squeal erupted from the radio, in Alex's hand.

"Unit Six, come in for a code." They recognized the dispatcher's voice. It was Mark, one of the company's best dispatchers. He attributed his gift of listening to the TV, fire radios, scanners and their own radio system, to the fact that he had "an ear in every orifice."

"You're responding to the corner of Henna and Dome Avenue for a motorcycle PI. PD states there are two down, with injuries."

"Ten four," Anne replied.

Alex had worked on a Basic car for a little more than six months before taking a paramedic position. Now that the company had grow large enough to support this policy, it was nearly etched in stone that all new employees had to have a set time to experience the fundamentals of patient care, before working on their paramedic or driving skills. Which made sense, since eighty percent of the patient care was of a basic nature. If the technician wasn't able to get their basic skills down-pat, their paramedic skills would be poor; thus the rule was instituted.

Alex changed the tones on the siren while approaching the intersection.

"Clear right," Anne advised. "There they are—up on the left, behind the police car."

Alex pulled onto the shoulder of the intersection, then stopped. Anne hopped out and grabbed the orange box from the side doors, then walked over to the male patient closest to her who was laying on the grass, next to the road.

"Hi," she began. "Where are you hurting?"

"Right here, in my groin," he moaned.

Both patients, who looked to be in about their late twenties, were wearing very short cut off jeans that were frayed at the edges, a tee shirt and tennis shoes without socks. They had abrasions from the gravel and pavement, but neither had any apparent fractures and actually looked in good condition considering the mechanism of the injury.

Kneeling next to him she palpated his neck and back. "Does it hurt anywhere along your spine?"

"No."

Moving down toward the area of complaint she picked up the frayed edge of his shorts and moved the inside pocket to get a better look. "Were you riding on the front or the back?" she asked.

"The front. I think I caught myself on the handle bars. We both came straight over the front of the bike. There was a car that stopped in front of me and I locked it up so we wouldn't rear end it."

"Well, I don't see any blood. And your scrotum doesn't look swollen or torn," she offered seriously, unaware that a crowd had gathered near the scene. "What about you?" she questioned the other patient. "Are you still having pain in the same area?"

"Yeah. But it's all right. I don't need you to look."

"Are you sure? You could have ripped something."

"Maybe we should move this inside the rig," Alex interrupted. "We've got quite a crowd brewing."

Anne looked up. "Sure. Sorry. Guess you'd like a little privacy."

Alex placed the backboard on the ground and helped Anne log roll the first patient onto it while keeping the motorcyclist's neck immobile. They worked quickly to package both patients, placing one on the stretcher and the other on the bench seat. Once in the back of the rig, Anne finished her assessment of the second patient.

"It doesn't hurt that bad—I'm okay," he reassured her, as they picked up where they left off. She heard what he was saying but the painful sound in his voice made his statement unconvincing.

"If you don't feel comfortable with me checking you, I won't. I just wanted to make sure you were okay," she conceded.

"Well hey," the first patient spoke up. "You can check me again if you want to."

Alex laughed. "You guys are fine. What do you say we just get going."

"Sounds like a good idea," Anne agreed, feeling slightly embarrassed. Taking the blood pressure cuff off the patient's arm, she hoped he understood she was just trying to do her job.

Throughout the summer, they drove past the health care center being built in Oxthorn to check on the progress. Everything was moving right on schedule. Working forty-eight hours had been rough at first, but Anne got used to it. Then the twenty-four hour shifts came and that was easier, of course, but she didn't know if she'd like working just twelve hours. It would feel odd, not being there at night. But she was willing to take a stab at it. Working right with the nurses and doctors might be fun. Here we go again, she thought, another new adventure.

Jack was older than the rest of the employees. Most of them were in their early to mid twenties. Jack was in his mid thirties, they guessed. But he never let on that he felt any older, and it really wasn't an issue anyway. Plus, it was nice to have someone who had danced or wrestled a little more with life to talk to from time to time. The first thing that Anne learned about Jack was when it came to patient care, he never hurried. He was thorough and compassionate.

"It's for you guys. You got a call," the clerk called over to Anne as she neared the nurse's station. She and Jack had been working out of the health care center for about a month and were settling in fairly well. Anne peeked her head into the room where Jack was doing a patient assessment.

"Jack. We got a call."

"Okay," he answered. "The nurse will be right in to finish," he advised the patient sitting on the exam table.

"You driving or riding?" Anne asked holding up the keys.

"I'll drive, if you don't mind."

"No problem."

"Unit Seven," the voice over the dispatch radio began. "You're on the way to 547 Thomsom Road for an unknown medical, with incident number 872, at 11: 32."

Anne had a pretty good idea of the street's location but scanned the map to be sure. Thomsom Road was a secondary major road about four miles north of the center. There were only a few houses on the road. They were spread a good distance apart with large woodsy fields filling in the rest. The next major town or city north of that was about twenty miles.

"It must be that house coming up," she said.

Jack stopped, then backed into the driveway. Anne stepped out and opened the side doors of the rig. After grabbing the orange medical box, she reached for the oxygen bottle.

"Man—this place is really run down," Jack said, eyeing the uncut grass and fallen shutters. There wasn't a police unit or fire engine on the scene with them. They were alone. The birds chirping outside offered a sign of life; but the house itself and whoever lived there was quiet. The back door was open.

"Hello," Jack called, stepping through the doorway into the house. Anne followed, looking around as they proceeded from a laundry room into the kitchen. The house had objects scattered about that didn't seem to fit the room they were in. There were wood saws on the counter next to crayons. Down a little farther was a small tub of bear grease and some sort of saddle soap. Both had ruts where possibly fingers had scooped through.

"Hello," he called again.

"I'm in here," an elderly voice answered.

They moved toward the voice that was deeper in the kitchen and behind a wall. Standing at the table, was a tiny woman, bent over with age.

"Did you call for an ambulance?" Jack asked.

"Of course I did. Why else would you be here," she snapped.

"Well, what's wrong? Why did you call us?"

Suddenly the woman's expression changed from just being irritated, to being angry at this stupid man that stood before her. "Well, I'm shrinking. Can't you see that?"

"Not really," he apologized. "How tall were you?"

She quickly dismissed his question as if she hadn't heard it, then continued her conversation which slowly became more confusing. She claimed someone was stealing her money and thought that it was the voices that talk to her who were responsible. Then she began showing Jack her bills and asked him to write out her checks so she could pay them. She said she had no family to speak of and no one to come in and take care of things. She couldn't remember her last meal. Her clothes were wrinkled and soiled. It was clear that she hadn't recently bathed. But none of that was worrisome to her. Her biggest and only complaint was that she was shrinking—and soon she'd be gone.

Anne looked around the room while Jack took the woman's blood pressure. Normally, the medic riding in the back took vitals and did the assessment while the other medic charted the medications and medical history of the patient. But Jack seemed to have a way with her, so Anne began looking at the prescription bottles on the kitchen counter to record what their patient might be taking. The bottles were empty and the medication labels were torn off. Then she noticed an envelope next to the empty containers baring the name of the resident addressee. The ink had smeared and bled from a liquid spill, but she could still make out the name, Mrs. Marguerite K. Keaton.

"Is your name Marguerite?" she asked.

"Yes. And don't you call me Maggie! My husband's sister had a dog named Maggie. That was the sorriest excuse for an animal I've ever seen. I tried running that thing over a couple of times—but it was too fast for me." Sensing her irritability Jack quickly reassured her they would only call her by her proper name. Okay, Anne thought, somehow she had to make friends with Marguerite or it was going to be a long ride to the hospital, unless Jack attended. But truly, in all reality, Eider Valley would be a better place to handle their patient with the type of complaints she'd expressed.

Jack was one step ahead of Anne it seemed, or else they were on the same wave length, for the thought of Eider Valley had no more than graced her mind, when Jack announced to her that Marguerite had agreed to be transported there, rather than the hospital. Now all Anne had to do was call their base hospital and inform them of the patient's condition and the destination of choice. Normally that was easy. But how do you tactfully describe the woes of a shrinking woman who hears voices. There were no cakes sitting on a table that said eat me or a vial of potion that said drink me, nor was the patient's name Alice. Anyone of those items would have offered an answer; or more likely would have made the situation harder to relate while keeping a straight face; not that she found the poor woman's dilemma funny. She felt bad for her. Marguerite was definitely in need of help; that went without question.

"LOH, this is Alpha Unit Seven calling with an incident number of 872. We were called to a home in Oxthorn to an unknown medical. Upon our arrival we found an elderly female living alone in her home with the primary complaint of, shrinkage. Her vitals are within normal ranges and she appears in fair condition—however her home is somewhat in disarray and it is unknown as to her last meal. After talking with her for sometime, she's agreed to be transported to Eider Valley for evaluation. Do you copy so far?"

"We copy, Alpha Seven, and concur with the requested destination. Does the patient understand that she will be signing herself in for voluntary commitment?"

"Yes, Dr. Malley, I think she understands. She's already agreed to talk to a professional for help. Also just for the record, she states that she hears voices and feels they are responsible for taking her money. I'd be happy to give you a more complete report via our run form at a later time," she gently offered, hoping the physician would pick up on the delicate nature of the call.

"Very good. In light of that, I will end this transmission so you can proceed with the transport. We will go ahead and give Eider Valley a call, unless you require something further."

"No sir. I think that will about do it. This is Alpha Seven clearing at this time. We will re-contact if the situation changes."

Was it something in Anne's conversation to the hospital? Or perhaps was it something that Jack said—or was it the voices? Only Marguerite knew for sure; or did she. Suddenly, just as they were leaving the house for Eider Valley, she changed her mind and stated that she wasn't going today. She'd decided to go tomorrow instead. There was nothing that Anne or Jack could do or say. She wasn't sickly or malnourished. She didn't appear to be a harm to herself or others. Unless they had a court petition, they had to leave her at home if that's what she wanted. To take her against her will would be kidnapping. They re-contacted the hospital and advised them of the change, to which the hospital agreed to send out a social worker as soon as arrangements could be made. Whatever it was, it really didn't matter now. What did matter was that Marguerite was at home and alone once again with no one to take care of her.

The crews had become team members and fast friends of the staff at the care center. Bonnie, one of the of RN's, had asked to do a ride along shift with Anne and Jack. She was an enthusiastic supporter of the EMS program and without a doubt could handle anything they responded to. Once in a while she'd share stories of her college days and how she and her friends attended and participated in different known protests and demonstrations at other colleges. Sometimes they had no idea what the article of debate even was until they got there. They would just join in and chant whatever the participants chanted. No harm, no foul. It seemed like good clean fun at the time. Currently, in addition to living on a farm with her husband and three boys, she enjoyed taunting the new interns and residents that the hospital sent out to the care center, and, going out with the other nurses to watch "The Rocky Horror Picture Show" at whatever movie theater it was playing; to which one night, Anne agreed to tag along. She was sure it would be a harmless and fun experience. From the way Bonnie and the other nurses talked, it sounded like they went all out each time they attended the show. They took turns dressing the part of the characters in the movie and always brought props like rice, newspapers and toast to join in on the scene and spoke all of the required memorized lines—right on cue. Anne was amazed by how many people like the nurses, followed the movie and brought props. The movie itself would be considered distasteful by the standards of her upbringing and it would never win and Oscar, she thought. It had nothing on Star Wars or M*A*S*H—but she had to admit, watching the audience was entertaining and fun.

Now it was Jack and Anne's turn to play host. While giving Bonnie a quick tour through the rig, they shared their story of Marguerite—the incredible shrinking lady and her promise to go to Eider Valley. Then, sure enough, but not to their amazement, Marguerite's memory was sharper than Anne and Jack had expected. For almost to the minute, twenty-four hours later, she called the dispatcher and said she was ready to go.

The transport started out well, but half way there she changed her mind. She was afraid and began crying, so they turned around. Bonnie and Anne took turns trying to calm the elderly patient, as they both knew that she needed mental help as well as someone to care for her. Jack understood the situation and was patient. Even though they seemed lost at sea and had to ask him to turn around to go back and forth several times, he willingly obliged. Finally after three hours, the boat landed. Linda had been dispatching that day, as she did more and more often, and was not at all happy with having her ALS rig tied up on a three hour call that she expected to last no more than forty-five minutes.

"Give me a TX," was her stern response, after Jack called arrival at the State Mental facility. Once inside he walked over to the pay phone in the foyer leaving Anne and Bonnie to direct the still unsure Marguerite to the waiting room. They listened to Jack as he tried to plead his case with Linda who was now on the other end of the phone not letting him get a word in edgewise. Then their elderly patient made her way toward him and clung on to his shirt as if for dear life, shaking and sobbing.

"Poor Jack," Bonnie chuckled. "One woman yelling at him at one end—and another one hanging on his shirt tail. That man sure has had his fill of women today."

"Oh, he's a good sport about it most of the time. Some of the women we pick up in the ambulance are something else, to say the least. I never knew women acted like they act until I started working here. This job has been quite a learning experience for sure."

"People in general are pretty odd creatures, I'd say. All except for us, of course," Bonnie smiled.

"Of course," Anne chuckled. "Well, I guess I'd better try and rescue Jack from Marguerite. I can at least, do that much. But he's going to have to deal with Linda on his own."

On their way back to the care center Bonnie sat on the bench seat of the rig and went through the cabinets again. She wanted to be prepared—just in case they got the bad one.

"What's the jar of Vicks for?"

"For the calls where the stench is so strong that it would gag a maggot," Anne answered, smiling. She knew the series of questions that would follow. The face of the person asking, always carried the same disenchanted nose wrinkling expression. It was a dead give away that the expected group of questions would immediately ensue. Still, it surprised her that even Bonnie, who had worked midnight's in both a Chicago and Detroit ER, would be as curious as any lay person. On the other hand, a victim of an accident or shooting out on the street, looks quiet different from a victim in the clean controlled setting of an emergency room. It was puzzling to her but it seemed for some reason the environment of the event, somehow played a part on the response of those involved in the care and treatment of the victim. And while Anne knew it was nothing in comparison to a battle field—she knew it was as close as she'd ever want to get.

"Doesn't it bother you to eat in the same place that you work? I mean, I know we eat in the same scrubs that we treat patients in at the hospital, but I don't sit on their bed and eat."

"No," Anne replied, "Eating after a bad call doesn't bother us. In fact, that's when we usually hash things over. Once I ran into a quickie burger place to grab some lunch and this woman stood next to me eyeing me up and down. I tried not to pay attention. I just wanted to get my lunch and get back to the rig. Finally, she stepped real close and asked me in a low quiet disgusted tone, 'How do you eat, after you do what you do?' For a second I felt like Jack the Ripper. I just looked at her and smiled and said, 'Because I'm hungry.'"

A year had passed since Anne and Jack began working at the care center. With the end of summer approaching, the fall schedule had become the hot item of conversation among the employees at Mercy EMS. Anne had decided to go back to the Lakeview station and free up her slot in Oxthorn for Alex, who had become bored with working in Bedford at one of the company's vacation stations. The Bedford area was less populated and while it had an abundant supply of lakes for fishing, you'd have to be a fisherman to enjoy it and Alex wasn't. Plus, the call volume was far less than he was used to while working with Anne. Jack was happy with working at the care center and opted to remain there.

"Well this is our last shift of the schedule together, Jack," Anne announced over breakfast. She watched as he opened the packet of jam to spread on his toast.

"Yep," he chuckled. "And I can't help but wonder if we're going to go out like a lion or a lamb." Anne understood what he meant. They certainly did seem to draw the unusual calls. But it made things interesting and they enjoyed the challenges that accompanied the out of the ordinary events. The restaurant phone rang. Jack looked up, watching the waitress who answered. "Yep, it's for us. I'm glad we're about finished, I have a feeling it's going to be a long twelve hours."

The call was for a woman who had fainted. Arriving on the scene of her home, they walked in and found her laying on the floor of the front room, next to the sofa. She was conscious and alert but was afraid to get up.

"That's fine," Anne reassured her. "You can stay right where you are while we take your blood pressure and check your pulse."

Jack pulled the stethoscope ear plugs out of his ears. "A hundred and eighteen over sixty. Pulse is fifty two. You look a little pale yet, Mrs. Perkins, and your pulse is kinda slow. We'd like to start an IV and take you to the hospital."

She looked over at her husband who was sitting on the love seat on the other side of the room for advice.

"You do what they say, Barb. You about scared me to death, passing out like that."

Anne had all ready set the IV line up and was looking for a vein. They were small and wiggly. She looked on both arms and hands before finally deciding on a small hand vein. Wishing for better veins didn't make them appear, but a small prayer before she started the IV sure wouldn't hurt. After prepping the site over the vein, Anne forewarned Mrs. Perkins.

"You don't have the best veins, so I need you to hold still. We have to do this in one try."

"I will. I don't want you to have to poke me any more than one time."

A twenty two gage needle is a small sized needle for an adult, but it was the biggest size that Anne could use in relation to the size of the patient's veins. The catheter went in easy on the first try. Anne slid the IV tubing into the end of the catheter, then taped it in place. It was running fine so she set it at a keep open rate. Suddenly, Mrs. Perkins began seizing. Her face turned bright purple. The seizure lasted not much more than a few seconds but when it stopped, they noticed the screen on the cardiac monitor showed a classic textbook rhythm known as course ventricular fibrillation. In this condition they understood that the ventricles of the patient's heart were contracting so fast that any perfusion of blood would be ineffective and would result in her death. Instructors often likened the appearance of a heart in this state to a bag of worms.

"We got V-fib on the monitor," Anne whispered to Jack. He wasted no time in grabbing for the intubation equipment as Anne quickly cut off the patient's blouse and bra. Jack positioned the mask of the resusi-bag over the woman's face, then squeezed the bag a couple of times before sliding the stylus into the selected ET tube. Anne lubricated the paddles, then charged up the EKG capacitor. The whine from the defibrillator filled the room, then stopped. After firmly placing each paddle on the patient's chest she looked to be sure no part of her body was touching the patient. "Clear," Anne warned, making sure of Jack's position.

"Clear," he replied, while reaching for the drug box.

Simultaneously, she pushed the buttons on each paddle, releasing the stored energy of 200 joules. The patient jumped as the direct current surged through her limp body. The rhythm on the monitor had changed. Now she was in a ventricular tachycardia. They were making progress. While still in a life threatening rhythm, at least the heart was able to function somewhat near normal. The rate of beats per minute were around two hundred. Again, Anne charged the paddles. This time they were set at 300 joules.

"Clear," she warned.

"Clear," Jack returned.

Again the body of the woman jumped. Anne set the paddles down, then took the pre-loaded syringe of lidocaine from Jack. Using the small IV catheter she had started earlier, she pushed 75 mg of medication through the hub on the IV tubing. The drug, lidocaine, was used to ease the excitability of the heart by raising the threshold. Anne's instructor said to think of it as Superman with a big L on his chest, raising a caved in ceiling off a crowd of people. Again, the rhythm on the monitor changed—from a sinus tachycardia into a normal sinus rhythm.

"Thank God," Anne whispered.

Instantly they remembered Mr. Perkins who was still sitting on the love seat and had been a witness to all the procedures performed on his wife during the past two or three minutes. He was pale and holding his chest.

"She's going to be okay, Mr. Perkins. How are you doing?" Anne asked. He mumbled he was fine but it was clear that he wasn't. This is not good, she thought. Jack also understood the problem with having one critical, cardiac patient and possibly another, with just the two of them there to offer care. He set the resusi-bag down and hooked a non-rebreather oxygen mask to the O2 tank. Mrs. Perkins was breathing on her own now and no longer needed to be intubated or bagged. Jack went to call for another rig and the volunteer fire department, while Anne set up a lidocaine drip. They both watched over the couple, until help arrived.

Back to back cardiac arrest calls weren't common, but when it occurred it really made for a tiring day. There was so much to do and think about and prepare for, not to mention that there was always a grand mess to clean up afterwards. Nonetheless, with the rarity of calls they seemed to attract neither Jack or Anne was surprised when they cleared the hospital from transporting Mrs. Perkins, that another cardiac patient was waiting in the wings.

After pulling up to the given address, they grabbed their equipment and entered the house. The patient's wife directed them into a bedroom where they found two Oxthorn cops standing over the patient who was not breathing. The patient had a history of cancer and had a stoma at the base of his throat. Taking the resusi-bag from the orange box, Anne attached the peds mask and placed it over the hole in the patient's neck. It made a perfect seal. Quickly Jack set up the IV while instructing the officers in the techniques of CPR. Anne set the monitor up in-between assisted respirations. The screen showed an asytole or a straight line rhythm, indicating that there was no heart activity at all. Jack had finished with the IV and started pushing the first line meds. There was no change noticed on the monitor and no palpable pulses. The whole of it seemed pretty hopeless, so Anne went to call the hospital for a pronouncement time. The wife and daughter who were at the home seemed to have disappeared, so other than a medical history of cancer, Anne had little else to report. Picking up the phone, she called LOH which was their base hospital. The report she gave must have sounded very bleak for it didn't take long at all for the physician at the other end to give her a time of death. Then, just as she was getting ready to end the radio call, via land line, she heard Jack calling to her.

"Excuse me, Dr. Dowell—could you hold on for a second? My partner's trying to get my attention." Anne set the receiver down on the kitchen counter, then walked into the bedroom where the patient was.

"He's got pulses," Jack informed her quietly.

"You're kidding. The doc just gave me a pronouncement time."

"Well, now you have to go back and tell him that he's not dead. Look," he said pointing at the man's chest. "You can see his heart beating under his skin between his ribs. He has a blood pressure and spontaneous respirations."

Neither Jack nor Anne expected this kind of response from a presumed deceased party. And he certainly didn't feel any better about it than she did. This man, their patient, had cancer severe enough that he had a stoma and he was basically dead when they got there. They only went through the drug therapy as a formality because of the short time factor. This man was probably on his way to meet his maker, until they butted in.

"Hi, Dr. Dowell? Sorry. It seems like our patient wasn't quite ready to leave us. He has pulses and a blood pressure. His doctor works out of Avon Oaks Hospital and his wife wants him transported there. If you could call them and let them know we're bringing in a post cardiac arrest patient, I would appreciate it."

Jack walked through the automatic doors at Avon Oaks with the restocked drug box and slid it into the cabinet of the ambulance. Looking over at Anne who was making the stretcher, he sighed.

"Well, I just got a good chewing out from the patient's physician. He said he just released our patient from here two days ago and sent him home to die. He was diagnosed with throat and lung cancer five years ago. I've never felt so bad about saving someone's life before."

"Well, Jack, I wrestled with it too—but it seems there is more to the story than we know. It just wasn't his day to go—for whatever reason."

"Guess you're right. Seems we're two for two, kid. What do you say we get back out there and see what the rest of this day has for us."

For the Oxthorn crew, lunch was now a forgotten thing as they headed lights and siren to their next call. The address seemed familiar to Anne—and as soon as she saw the house she remembered she had responded there nearly a year ago for a man having a stroke. Stroke patients were pretty common calls, so normally it wouldn't have stuck out in her mind. But this was a call that she remembered very clearly; not because the patient's condition was all that unusual, for she remembered that everything went smooth and that the patient was very pleasant. The thing that brought about the unforgettable image was that her patient threw up on her—mid sentence—and totally unexpected by either of them. She recalled he said, it was the strawberry milk shake that he drank before the CVA occurred. And she recalled the way that it suddenly spewed from his mouth and ran down her pant leg and into her shoe. While making their way to the front door of the residence, Anne chuckled as she gave a summarized story to Jack, complete with sound effects of the squishing noise her shoe made afterwards.

"Hello," the patient greeted, as they entered the front room. "Hey—you're the girl I threw up on when I had my stroke."

"Yes I am, sir. And we're not going to do that again today, are we?" she laughed.

"I hope not."

"So do I. Your wife said you were complaining about some chest discomfort. Let's hook you up and see what's going on."

After working their patient up they transported him to St. Luke's without event—and without any vomiting. Now just two hours of their shift remained. Lunch came later than their growling stomachs would have preferred, but at least it finally came. Taco's from a Lancemen drive through was better than nothing. They figured they had a pretty good chance of eating if they ate while en route to Oxthorn.

"Unit Seven, prepare to code."

Anne switched on the emergency lights to make their way to the next call. Jack could at least eat on the way; she would have to wait.

"Man, I feel like I've just entered the Twilight Zone," she said, after they turned onto the given street.

"You're just now starting to feel like that?" Jack chuckled.

"I'm serious. Remember that kid that I told you about who shot himself and he had that monkey in the cage? Well, that's his house," she said, pointing. "I remember—because I almost whacked my head on that bird feeder. See it hanging from the tree near the driveway? It looks like a cat's head."

"It reminds me of Marguerite's house, the way it's all run down."

"I wonder what happened to his mother and sister?" she queried out loud.

Entering the house across the street from Benny's old home, they found an older gentleman who had fallen and broken his hip. While packaging him up for the trip to the hospital, Anne's curiosity about Benny and his family finally got the best of her.

"Say, Mr. Garrison," she began. "Did you know that family that lived across the street?"

"Yes."

"Well, we responded to that house about a year ago and I wondered what happened to the girl and her mother."

"They moved up north near the upper peninsula," Mrs. Garrison jumped in. "Benny used to cut our grass sometimes. My daughter was over there that day and brought Genna here to stay until her mother came home. Shame a thing like that happened. No one ever thought he'd do that. His father died in a car crash a year to the day of Benny's suicide. They were very close. Losing a husband and a son almost destroyed his mother. But I hear she married recently. Maybe her new husband will come down and do something with the house. No one has stepped foot in it except the police since that day."

Mr. Garrison was transported as comfortably as possible and arrived at the hospital in stable condition. Nothing more was said about Benny or his family.

"You know, Jack, I was thinking," Anne said, while rolling the passenger side window down. "Did you ever notice how everything seems to go full circle? We always seem to return to where we started out, in some manner. When we come into this world we wear diapers. Before we leave it, there's a good chance that we'll wear diapers. Even with every call we had today—something about it made a complete circle. I haven't quite figured it all out yet, but I'm sure there's a good reason. Maybe it's so we don't lose our way—I don't know."

"Well, when you figure it out let me know. In the mean time, I'll drive us back to Oxthorn. If we make it that far in the circle, I'll be happy."

CHAPTER 22

FAIR WARNING

Walking into the Lakeview station was like returning to a vacation cabin after a ten year absence. At least that's what Anne thought as she stood clutching her overnight bag in the center of the front room. With a wry smile and disheartened eyes she scanned the ceiling and dusty sheets that were sadly cast over the tarnished round curtain rods. Then her attention drifted toward the cobwebs that seemed the size of Canada in the corners of the room, as the smell of sweaty old socks sourly rose and rested on the hairs of her nose. Remembering that Linda and Denny had each worked there a few shifts, she thought maybe they didn't have time to clean or even dust. Or, more than likely—the girls felt little or no inclination to pick up after those boys. Unmistakably, it was still the guys' retreat—and apparently just the way they liked it.

Sighing, she tossed her overnight bag onto the worn, tattered sofa; then leaned over the cardboard box that Aunt Ruth had packed and took out a couple of plates of food that were wrapped with tin foil and a red checkered dishtowel. Turning toward the refrigerator, she heard the front door open, as Jerry stepped in.

"I'd approach that thing with a big stick if I were you," he warned.

She laughed, recalling the first shift she had worked with Dan—and the science projects that made her wonder, if the refrigerator was a breeding ground for his Muppets or Cousin It.

"I thought about it—believe me," she smiled. "Hey, I just got back from the farm and brought you a plate of food from Aunt Ruth's kitchen. I remembered that you're a vegetarian, so there's no meat."

"Well, let's not spoil it by putting it in there. I need to run over to my house anyway. What do you say we wait and put it in my frig."

"Sure. But what about the ambulance?"

"I came in early for Roger. He had to be somewhere by 9:00 and didn't want to get tied up on a late call. I've already gone through the car. If you want—when we get to my house, I'll even cook us up some eggs and toast. Breakfast on the house."

Jerry's three bedroom bungalow was about five miles from the station, near the curves of Sashabaw in the north end of Lakeview. The nice thing about living within the area of your assigned station was that as long as you got on the air quickly and your partner didn't mind, you could hang out at your house and do a load of laundry or any other little chore until a call came in. Some of the crews didn't like staying at someone else's residence in between calls; they preferred to be at quarters and that was fine. But Anne enjoyed picking through and listening to Jerry's enormous record collection on the days that they ran out of his house—at night they stayed at the station.

As soon as they finished eating breakfast, she cleared the table and helped with the dishes. Jerry's house was neat and everything seemed to have its place, which of course to Anne, was an admirable trait. She was also impressed by his intelligence. The only other individual that she personally knew who was as book wise was one of her college instructors, Mr. LaTour. It only took a few sessions of his teaching her pharmacology class for his genteel demeanor to spark her imagination. Like a scene from an old movie, a mental picture graciously unfolded as she fancied him sitting at home in front of a glowing fireplace, wearing a wine colored smoking jacket while engrossed in a book like "The Winds of War," as he slowly and thoughtfully drew his pipe from his mouth. Then he'd speak to his faithful golden retriever Ginger—although really, she wasn't even sure he liked dogs—who lay at his side, keeping watch over her master.

Eventually when Anne and Mr. LaTour, David, became friends, she shyly confessed the image her mind had so vividly painted. As she spoke, he smiled until she'd finished, restraining his high pitched chuckle that usually accompanied a raised brow expression of amusement. And then, with a hushed but earnest voice—he thanked her. Sometimes she wondered if she dreamed it all up, well—because—maybe that was the kind of man she wanted to eventually marry. Not that she was interested in marrying Mr. LaTour or even Jerry as far as that goes. Neither one of them seemed to be in much of a hurry to settle down with a wife and family anyway. And maybe to her—that was one of the things that made them so smart.

"Unit Six," the dispatcher's voice barked over the hand held radio. "I need you on the air for a code."

Anne draped the dish towel over the edge of the kitchen sink, called out to Jerry then dashed out the back door. He was close behind her. The nature of the call, their dispatcher relayed, was for a man down. They'd been called to the same address many times with the Lakeview fire department, who was also responding and would be the ALS providers. She and Jerry would be the transporting unit if one was needed. In less than seven minutes they pulled onto the scene and parked right behind the fire department's rescue. A mixed group of firemen stood on or near the front porch trying to gain access inside the house. Two of the firemen were engineers that came on the pumper. The others were paramedics and of course there was an officer. Any kind of medical or fire scene had to have an officer.

"Where's his dogs?" Jerry asked Captain Douglas Smith who was on the porch closest to the patient's bedroom window.

"He says they're all up north at a show. The doors are all locked. He says he's fine—he just can't get up. Apparently he fell out of bed over an hour ago."

They all knew the patient well. He was a paraplegic who trained Doberman pinschers. Even though he usually kept several dogs at the house, they knew he had a loaded gun under his pillow for protection.

"What's that?" the captain asked, trying to make out the words the patient repeated. "I think he said the kitchen window might be open."

Pat, one of the paramedics, was first to reach the window. Standing on his tiptoes he slid his fingers under the base of the sash and pushed up. The window raised until it was about half way open, then stopped. "Come over here, Anne," he said.

"What," she groaned humorously, knowing by his voice something was up and it wasn't the window.

Smiling, he echoed the inflection in her voice. "What.—Don't you trust me?"

"Should I?"

"Come on, I'm going to boost you up to the window so you can crawl in."

"Why do I have to crawl in?"

"Because you're short."

"Doug's short."

"But he's the captain. You can't push a captain through a window. It's not right."

"Oh for crying out loud—all right."

Chuckling, Pat motioned to Jerry to come over and help. Facing each other they laced their hands together to make a cradle like support for her to stand on so she could open the window. Once there was a large enough area for her to enter, she grabbed hold of the sill, pulled herself up and leaned against it, placing a knee on its base. While sitting on the edge, she used the side frames to help keep her balance, as she swung her feet around. The kitchen table was right in front of the window and allowed her no place to put her legs, so she had to scoot across it—through yesterday's left over scrambled eggs, hash browns and toast. Just as she began lowering her feet onto a chair, one of the trainer's dogs came around the corner and stopped right in front of her.

"I thought you said your dogs were at a show," she called out.

"All except her. She stayed here with me. She's very gentle. She won't hurt you."

"I hope she knows that," Anne grumbled under her breath. As soon as her feet hit the floor she went to open the front door and let the others in. After checking the man to make sure he wasn't hurt, they helped him into his wheelchair then collected their gear to leave.

"So, Anne—where ya been?" Pat asked.

"I've been working out in the Orion area, with Alex and then Jack. We just started a new schedule, so Jerry and I'll be in Lakeview for a while."

"Oh," he chuckled. "The Anne and Jerry show. Well, all right then. We'll be seeing ya around. Hey," he teased, as he hopped up into the rescue. "It was fun pushing you through the window. Nice to see you're still a good sport."

"My pleasure," she smiled.

A new crispness in the evening air came as a messenger that said autumn was near. During this time and in the weeks that followed, Anne spent many hours driving back and forth to the farm in Summerville. The harvest and canning were two events that she had always looked forward to. Then Thanksgiving and Christmas with her family danced in. This year, both holidays came with greater meaning and joy, as her cousin Jacob and his wife Corinne's new baby who was born on Thanksgiving, choreographed each step that marked their first Christmas together. Anne loved holding little Kendall, which meant "from the clear valley or thankful"; but she really didn't care much for the teasing from her Uncle Henry and the others. "That looks like a pretty natural picture, Annie—or—Time's a waste'n, girl. Maybe you need to get yourself a husband so you can have one of those little bundles yourself," were just a few of the phrases of folly they offered—all in fun of course. But she knew without a shadow of doubt, it was nothing to rush into and truly, it was the farthest thing from her mind.

It was December 28, 1979. The Red Wings had played their first game at the Joe Louis Arena in Detroit. Their 3-2 loss was a big topic of discussion among the guys at the fire stations and at Mercy. Jerry, who was raised in Texas, never spent much time ice skating so he and Anne decided to join in the fun by doing donuts in large empty parking lots and by writing their names in the snow with the ambulance.

"Oh—you're good," Anne said, watching out the back window, then turned in her seat to recheck his tire scrawled signature in the side mirror of the passenger door. "Ugh," she continued, moving her arms and hands in an attempt to help direct his maneuvering of the rig. "Watch out, you almost drove over your last R."

"Unit Six," the dispatcher's voice came over the speaker.

"Unit Six," Jerry answered.

"You still at Fort Dix?"

Their first thought was that someone called and complained about them spinning around on the Flea Market parking lot. "Yes," Jerry replied musically, reflecting a tone that said—now what?

"I need you to slide over to the Orion area and cover there for a while. We're starting to get slammed in here."

"Oh, we'd be happy to." After placing the mic back in the clip, he moved the gear shift into drive, then looked over at Anne and laughed. "I wonder if he meant that literally? The sliding part, of course."

Jerry's laugh was more like a cackle than a regular laugh. It carried an inviting sound that beckoned those within hearing distance to join in. He had a charming sense of humor and an entrancing way with women that caused them to flock to be near him. Once, while waiting at the bank in front of a drive through window, two of the tellers working the booth all but yanked each other's hair out, trying to be the one to wait on Jerry. Anne sat in the ambulance watching in total amazement. It's only Jerry, she thought; not that his dark brown eyes, hair and well trimmed beard weren't attractive. He was nice looking. But still to her—he was just Jerry.

"Unit Six—Where are you now? I got a code in Oxthorn at the police station."

"We're about eight miles out, on Lamer—and we're on the way."

Anne reached down on the floor between her and Jerry and picked up the metal clip board. Using her thumb she flipped it open, then took out one of the run forms. After letting the lid drop shut she slid the form under the clip, then took her pen from her shirt pocket. The siren screamed and the emergency lights flashed as the ambulance fish tailed over the snow covered two lane road that was divided by a median. No nature of the call was given. It was an unknown medical of some sort. Knowing the type of the injury or complaint in advance was sometimes helpful, as it gave the medic a chance to mentally formulate a plan of treatment. Anne always liked to fill out as much information on the run form on the way to the call, in order to save time for other things once they arrived on the scene, especially—when Jerry was driving.

"You know," she began, clearing her throat. "Not that I'm in a big hurry to do this right now, or even within the next couple of years—but I thought—maybe someday I'd like to get married and have a couple of kids."

"So is this a proposal?" Jerry laughed.

"No. I just thought I'd let you know. Because in order to take part in either one of those activities and to enjoy them—I'd have to be alive."

Jerry was the fastest driver she'd ever worked with; but yet, he was skillful and competent. Unquestionably, he knew and felt the proportionate dimensions of the rig, for many times he had gracefully squeezed it through incredibly tight spaces in traffic, while moving at a good clip. Snow coding, however, was a little more nerve racking. The back of the rig fishtailing over the snow didn't really bother her; that was pretty much the norm. It was the unplowed shoulders that left the other drivers no space to pull over that created some of the discomfort—and it was usually while approaching them that she closed or half covered her eyes.

As soon as they started to pass through Orion, he eased off the gas then picked up speed again once they were through town. Orion and Oxthorn were both small towns that were initially established over a hundred years ago; both still had some of their original store front buildings on the main drag. The Oxthorn police station was in the center of town, just left of the only stop light. Usually one of the officers or staff stood watch to direct the responding crew toward the best entrance, in relation to their patient; but not this time. The station parking lot looked like a ghost town.

After pulling up alongside the building, Jerry hopped out. Anne squeezed between the two cab seats and cabinets to enter the patient compartment instead of going outside through the passenger door. She grabbed the handle of the orange box and tossed it up on the stretcher to take it inside. Suddenly, a horrifying sight caught her eye as Jerry opened the back doors. He started to say something, then glimpsed at her awestruck stare and turned around.

Behind him, two male figures slowly walked toward them with arms held straight out at their sides, with torn dripping clothes and or flesh, likening mummies or zombies on a Saturday afternoon horror flick.

"Oh my word," Anne whispered.

Jerry quickly pushed the doors open the rest of the way and started walking toward the men. The man closest to him uttered that they had been working on a friend's furnace in his basement, when it flashed. Anne took the orange box from the stretcher and set it on the floor, then grabbed two burn sheets from the cabinet. Just at a glance, it appeared that both men had all the hair on their head and face singed off. After draping the sterile sheets over the bench seat and stretcher, they helped the two seriously burned men up into the rig. The man on the stretcher who said his name was Lee, told Jerry some friends of theirs drove them to the police station. They must not have known the care center was so close, or opted not to go there for whatever reason, but that didn't matter much now. For either way, they would have been transported by ambulance to the hospital.

While cutting off and removing the remaining bits of charred clothing, the crew gathered information as to their patients' medical history and medication allergies. Once they had more of a complete idea of the percentage of skin surface involved and the degree of the burns, they could call the hospital for an order of pain medication. From what they could tell at this point by the deep reddened skin, broken blisters and seeping plasma, most of the burns appeared to be second degree. With proper treatment, that type usually did not require skin grafting as they were partial thickness, rather than full thickness burns.

Anne stood at the head of the stretcher taking several bottles of sterile saline from the upper cabinet to pour over the clean white sheets that covered the patients from chin to ankle. After tearing the plastic seal from each bottle, she slowly poured enough of the water solution to cool the burns and provide at least temporary relief to the pain ridden tissue. Jerry explained everything they were doing while setting up an IV for each victim. This—was going to be tricky. After doing their patient assessment they realized that the burns of each man covered the entire body, with the exception of their feet and ankles where their boots had been. Because of that, they would not be able to start the IVs in the normal sites, as the skin on both of their patients' arms were severely blistered.

Jerry was happy to see that Lee had been wearing high top work boots, as it left an extra inch or two of unburned flesh to work with. Leaning over the stretcher Jerry began running his fingers up and down both of Lee's ankles trying to feel for a vein; not one was visible. Seeming somewhat troubled, he sighed while gently raking his hands through his hair. A second later, an idea apparently came to him as he raised his own foot and set it on the corner of the stretcher. After pulling his pant leg up, he pushed his sock down and quickly studied his own leg to mentally mark the anatomy and position of the veins. Anne caught sight of what he was doing and briefly set her own search for a decent vein aside. Then she remembered learning that the great saphenous was the longest vein in the body and that it ran along side the inner part or medial side of the leg, from the dorsum of the foot to the femoral vein. Somehow and to her amazement—it was that vein on Lee's leg that Jerry was able to push the 18 gage IV catheter in on the first try as if the vein was in plain sight and waving at him.

"I'm impressed," she said quietly. "How about giving me a hand over here."

Jerry turned and started an IV using the same method on Anne's patient. After another quick dousing of sterile water Anne called the hospital while Jerry drove. They had already been on the scene ten minutes or so and knew they had to get their patients moving. Due to the extent of the burns, the hospital had no problem with giving a hefty order of morphine sulfate to Anne for each patient. While en route, she watched their airways and listened for changes in their respirations and voice. Signs of labored breathing and stridor were perilous. Body temperature was also important, as burn patients chill easily. While the cool water was comforting to them, a recheck of skin temperature and warmth of the patient compartment was an ongoing issue.

After the burn victims were inside the hospital ER and the report had been given on each, Anne spent better than twenty minutes in the back of the rig scrubbing it with a deodorizing disinfectant. The smell of a burn patient was one of the hardest to get rid of. From previous experience, they knew it could linger in their clothing and nose hairs for days. After making the stretcher, she went back into the ER to see if Jerry had finished restocking the drug box and to check on their patients. While standing next to the ER work station she glanced around for her partner. Then one of the physicians talking on the phone caught her attention. She listened carefully as he made the arrangements for the admittance of their patients with the burn center that was thirty miles away. They were well known to be the best in the area. As soon as the men were stable and well medicated, the transfer would be set up. Jerry came up behind her carrying the drug box. "You ready?" he asked.

As they neared the ambulance entrance, Jack and Rod entered with an empty stretcher.

"Hey, fancy meeting you guys," Rod kidded. "Did you bring in that call from Oxthorn?"

"Yeah. It was a couple of burn patients. They're probably going to ship them out to the burn center before too long," Anne answered. "Man, you should have seen Jerry's IV technique. That was sweet. He did a blind stick using his own leg as a model. Right in—the first time."

"Yeah—I heard that about him," Jack smiled. Anne shook her head in playful disgust. "What's wrong with you?" he continued. "I meant that he's a good medic."

"Sure you did. It never stops does it? You guys can't even carry on a conversation without bringing sex into it," she retorted.

"Shame on you," he teased. "Your mind's always in the gutter."

"Oh right," she chuckled.

"So that was a good call, ah?" he grinned, satisfied with her returned jest. "Was PD on the scene?"

"We were at their station, but they never came out. Why?"

"Do you remember that call we had, where that cancer patient was trying to go home to meet his maker and we dragged him back?"

"Yeah."

"Well, his doctor wasn't impressed, that's for sure—but PD was. Robbie told me that was the call that changed their whole view on the EMS business. They saw that it worked and apparently liked what they saw. That guy's still alive you know."

"No kidding."

"Hey, Jerry," Rod stepped in. "I ran into your brother—working over here at the Lancemen station."

"Yeah, Bill's been up here a couple of years now. He just got his medic's license. He'll probably be working on a paramedic rig come spring."

"Oh yeah? Well, keep him away from Anne and Jack. You know the kind of calls that they get."

"In that case," he laughed. "What are we doing working with them?"

"Don't pay any attention, Anne," Jack piped in.

"Oh—now that you're involved," she grinned, "it's—don't pay any attention, Anne."

"Touché," Jack said. "We'll catch ya later. We have to take Mr. Taylor back to the nursing home."

Tired and chilled to the bone after a long day in the bitter cold, Anne crawled under her quilt at the station and adjusted the lamp next to her bed. It was Ground Hog Day, 1980. The evening news was full of world wide problems. Talks of the Soviet invasion, the Persian Gulf oil supply, and more corrupt officials within our own government were headliners. In light of that and their busy day, she looked forward to jumping into bed with a good relaxing book. "The Fireside Book of Dog Stories" by James Thurber seemed like a good selection for something pleasant and upbeat. And, in honor of the prairie dog, er ground hog—well close enough—she thought it would be fitting. She had read this book before; actually a number of times. It was a gift from her friend Jenny after the death of a Boarder collie named Solomon, who had lived on the farm for eleven years. Immediately, she turned to the Introduction and began reading.

"Anne—wake up," Jerry said, gently shaking her.

"What do you want?—I didn't hear the phone."

"Get up," he whispered. She must have dozed off, she thought. "I want you to go out to the front room and sleep."

"Leave me alone, Jerry. This is my bed and I'm sleeping here."

She turned over, pulling the quilt up over her face to block the light. Jerry left the bunk room and shut the door. Lying in bed Anne could hear voices in the front room. Jerry's—and a female voice. But that was nothing unusual; the guys often had visitors at the station. She felt around under the covers for her book, then after a brief search she found it and dropped it into her overnight bag on the chair next to the bed. Yawning, she pulled her arms back under the warm quilt and drifted off to sleep.

Awakened by a noise, she laid still and listened while trying to make out the direction and cause. Straining to force off the fuzziness of sleep from her mind, she concentrated on the rhythmic squeaking. Then whispers and groans filled the room. Granted she was naive, but she knew without a doubt what that sound was. She couldn't believe it! How could he be so bold! Right there in the bed next to hers—Jerry and his female friend were having sex! Oh—for crying out loud, she thought. Now what am I supposed to do? How embarrassing! Quietly, while trying not to draw any attention, she pulled the quilt over her face, then slowly moved her head under her pillow to muffle as much of the risqué act as she could. Her mind reeled between who she was more upset with—Jerry or that girl, whoever she was. Then she grew angry with herself for not getting up and going into the front room earlier. But how was she to know he would do this? Somehow—in spite of everything, she finally dozed off.

The phone rang. Jerry answered it. Anne listened. Yes—they had a call. She waited a second longer. His voice was the only one she heard. Maybe she'd been dreaming. Sitting up, she grabbed her shirt and pants off the hook on the wall. After pulling her pants over her long underwear she slid her shirt on and tried doing up the buttons while grabbing for her boots. She zipped them one at a time, then stood and turned toward the door. Suddenly, she became aware of someone in Jerry's bed. It was that girl—naked—holding the sheet up over her breast, smiling as friendly as she could be. Totally without shame she waved, moving her fingers like a fan. Then, in a voice like a piccolo, she happily said, "Hi." Anne instantly felt a scowl pulling at her brow. Then the light from the front room caused her to squint as she walked from the bedroom. Grabbing her purse from the floor, she said nothing. Her silence continued as she scurried past the chair in the front room, picking up her coat on the way toward the door.

"Come on," Jerry called.

Without a word, Anne walked out into the cold and got into the ambulance. Listening to the dispatcher as he gave the street address, she took the scratch pad of paper from the doghouse and wrote down the information.

"Unit Six," the dispatcher called again. "You're canceled. Cancel your run."

Sliding her ink pen back into her shirt pocket Anne quickly attempted to sort through the embroiled feelings she knew would erupt.

"Jerry!" She started out, stern yet controlled. "Don't you ever—do that to me again."

He turned and faced her. Smiling sweetly, seemingly unaffected by her anger, proudly and gently said. "Well you could have joined us if you wanted to."

That—was it! In that instant, Anne felt very strongly torn between Popeye, Thumper's mother and the volcano of Paricutin, which in 1943, buried the entire village of its same name. It was all she could stand; she could not "stands no more". If she had nothing good to say, she should "say nothing at all". But most of all—she knew if the words that she felt at that moment spewed from her mouth—they'd be as hot lava, burning everything in its path.

After a brief and well felt seething, she finally turned and opened the passenger door falling the way of Thumper's mother, while earnestly grumbling "Oh dear Lord, give me strength."

Walking back into the station she tossed her coat on the sofa and headed toward the bathroom. She heard Jerry and his friend softly talking as she washed her hands, then when she came out she noticed that Jerry and the girl were gone. The furnace fan kicked in and blew warm air throughout the station, muffling the soft rumble of the car that ran in the parking lot. She must be going home, Anne thought as she slipped into bed, pulling the quilt up around her neck. Her anger was short lived, it always had been. In no time she dozed off to sleep.

During the next shift that she and Jerry worked, they ran into Robbie at LOH.

"Can I talk to you for a second?" she asked. While her feathers were pretty much back into place, she thought sharing the incident with Robbie might be appropriate—after all, he was a supervisor and maybe she could save Jerry's next female partner the same embarrassment. She began her tale of woe, starting with Jerry coming into the bedroom—waking her to go into the front room—and went on from there. Robbie listened thoughtfully and with concern. Jerry walked over at the end of the story and listened while Anne finished. Robbie looked him in the eye, straight faced and asked, "Did you do that?"

Jerry smiled. There was no remorse and not even as much as an iota of shame when he answered, "Yeah."

Robbie drew in a deep breath and looked at Anne, then looked at Jerry, then exploded into laughter. Raising his arm and hand up toward Jerry, Jerry responded in the same manner with their hands meeting in midair as he high fived him. "All right, you dog. That's the funniest story I've ever heard."

Anne smirked and shook her head. Of course they'd stick together. After working with them all this time, she should have known better. There was just no reason to expect anything different.

"Hey"—Robbie called, as she turned to walk away. "He tried to get you to go in the other room. You had fair warning."

"Whatever," she replied.

Sitting in the rig with her arms folded, the simmering rekindled. Then she told herself that there was no sense in being upset. Basically, at least until she saw Robbie, she was over it. But still, it'd be nice if she could get at least one guy to be on her side. Her old partner Dan came to mind. Now that—was funny! Why in the world would she even think that he would support her in this. After all, he was the one who had invited his girlfriend over to the station and then went home sick without calling her to let her know. The story, according to Tom who had taken Dan's place, was that, he was sound asleep when she arrived. Apparently she'd taken her clothes off and then crawled into bed with Dan. At least she thought it was Dan. Then when she ran her hand under the covers, she startled Tom. When he jumped, she suddenly realized that it wasn't who she thought and loudly announced, "You're not Dan," before leaping out of bed.

Oh—and then there were the confiscated porn flicks she heard about, that Dan and Barfbag borrowed from the local police station—that they ran from a projector onto a sheet hanging over the front window of the station, substituting it for a movie screen. It would have been a good concept, except with the sheet being so thin, the film showed through it and onto the neighbor's roof like a drive-in movie. It was a Lakeview cop, who was driving past the station and came to a screeching halt, that brought it to their attention when he had them step outside to see for themselves.

Truly she understood it was going to be a fruitless endeavor to even pursue this much farther. Even though it didn't seem right to her by any means—they would all claim the same thing, as if by an entente, that she had fair warning. Still, she certainly never dreamed, that was the reason he came in to wake her. No. They were right in one thing and one thing only. She was warned—but to her thinking, it was anything but fair.

CHAPTER 23

A MAN FROM TEXAS

Cardiopulmonary Resuscitation—CPR—is a technique used to artificially circulate oxygenated blood and breath for pulseless, non respirable individuals. It is a method that was first performed in part by God Himself according to Genesis 2:7, "And the Lord God formed man of the dust of the ground, and breathed into his nostrils the breath of life; and man became a living soul." Now, many centuries later in this sophisticated age of technology, this basic lifesaving procedure is still stellar in returning to the brain and other organs of the body the one fundamental thing that they cannot survive without—air.

While this act of breathing life into another person has apparently been sensed or understood as plausible over the years, it was not always performed in the same manner as it is today. For there are a number of documented accounts where men, who were desperate to bring life back to victims who were clinically deceased, rolled them back and forth over a barrel, bounced them tummy side down over the saddle of a horse, used the back-pressure arm-lift method and even tried to inflate the victim's lungs by inserting the tip of a bellows into their mouth.

But in 1960, a new resuscitation training manikin was introduced: Resusci Anne. Her story began around the turn of the century when the body of a young girl was pulled from the River Seine in Paris. The identity of the girl was not established and since her body was absent of any signs of violence or trauma, it was assumed she had taken her own life. It was customary in this situation for a death mask to be made so that her family could identify her later. But, apparently, even death had not erased her delicate beauty and refined angelic smile, for several romantic stories based on this enigma were published and became popular throughout Europe, as well as reproductions of her death mask.

Then, in the 1950's she was "reborn" when a Norwegian toy and doll manufacturer named Asmund S. Laerdal began developing a resuscitating training manikin. Because he wanted students to be willing to learn this lifesaving method, he entrusted the sculptress, Emma Mathiassen, to fashion a face for the life sized model, to create a realistic appearance. The rest is history. Who would have dreamed that the gift and belief of a toy maker could transmute the tragic death of a young girl from Paris into a system of life giving resuscitation?

"Annie, Annie, can you hear me?" Anne said while demonstrating the first step of CPR, known as—shake and shout, listen and feel. Then she looked back at the small group of students who stood watching with embarrassed grins, knowing that they were next and expected to do everything that she was doing, and laughed. "Oh come on. It's not that bad. What if this was your friend or your grandmother? You know—the one who always bakes your favorite cookies. Wouldn't you want to help her?"

"I'm not putting my lips on my grandmother's," one of the teens said. Chuckles from the other students in the group followed.

"Mark, she's not breathing. That's your name, right?" she asked. He nodded. "Please tell me that you're not really going to just let your grandmother lie there, knowing how important time is. Okay, just as a quick review," she smiled, "how much time is there between someone who is clinically, or so so dead—and someone who is biologically, or really dead?"

"Four to six minutes," he rendered sheepishly.

"Very good. So that means if you spend too much time hemming and hawing, you can pretty much kiss gramma and those great cookies goodbye—right?"

"Come on, Mark," one of the girls in the group spoke up. "Your gramma needs you. What if it was me?"

"Then I'm definitely not doing it," he grinned, red-faced.

Anne chuckled. "I know its a little awkward in here. But I'm telling you—if this were real life, it would be very different. You'd be surprised what you can do when its staring you right in the face. And it really, truly—can make a difference between life and death."

The initial behavior by this group was similar to many groups that came through during the ten hour day that was devoted to learning chest compressions and mouth to mouth ventilation. CPR Day at the Dome was a fine tuned instrument of Raymond Dewit's, EMS Coordinator at Lancemen Community College and Anne's EMT instructor. Blue Cross and Blue Shield, The American Red Cross and Laerdal, were just a few of the organizations who had joined this project. Each group provided volunteers, manikins, projectors and whatever else was needed to efficiently set up and run as many CPR stations as possible. Normally the sports arena would have been filled with football fans; but today, thousands who wanted to learn how to save a life would walk through its revolving doors.

Buses loaded with students and teachers were being dropped off at the entrance gates as early as nine o'clock. Some families, residents and even people working nearby were standing at the doors when they opened at eight a.m. Area TV stations brought cameras to televise a midday news segment showing the process of the work stations where hundreds had already sat and watched an hour long film explaining the ABCs of CPR before they even knelt down beside Resusci Anne, the life sized model of the girl from the River Seine.

"The ABCs of CPR are what?" Anne asked the man and his two teenage boys who had just entered her station.

"Airway, breathing and circulation," they chorused.

"Very good. Now who's going to go first?" She waited a few seconds while they looked at each other. "Come on—this poor girl is as blue as my shirt." All of the instructors were asked to wear their career uniforms so that the students could familiarize themselves with the many different partners devoted to helping others on a daily basis.

Embarrassed at his hesitation, the man finally spoke up. "You must really like what you do."

"I do. Very much. You have to, cause you sure don't do it for the money," she chuckled. "So now—back to poor pulseless, non breathing Annie. Who's going to be the first one in the group to help her out?"

Smiling, the man came forward and knelt beside the manikin. "Annie, Annie can you hear me?" When he finished, one by one his sons came forward. Both seemed awkward and shy initially while doing one man CPR. Then as they worked together doing two man compressions and mouth to mouth ventilations, they went through the motions like pros.

"Okay, you guys. Nice job. You just earned your CPR card," she said, handing them a signed slip of paper. "Just go over to any one of the lines at the table and show them this."

She watched briefly as they walked away, thinking that it was such a treat to see the smiles on the faces of those who came, earnestly wanting to make a difference and hoping to help someone who might otherwise have little chance of survival.

Dinner time neared. The last bus load of students had long ago left and the after work stragglers were making their way toward the exit. It was time to pack up the manikins and the rest of the equipment. The day had been long, but it was a great success and already plans were being made for next year. No doubt Mr. Dewit was pleased with the enthusiasm, turnout and fun everyone experienced, not to mention the opportunity it gave to carry out Mr. Laerdal's belief and dream. It would have been great if he could have seen the pride on the faces of each person as they received their own CPR card, as Mr. Dewit had. Thinking back over the day, Anne couldn't remember one time that she looked over at the card table when Raymond wasn't there smiling.

While walking through the parking lot, Anne said good-bye to a few of the nurses she knew as they talked about the freshness of the early spring evening and the glowing sunset. A hot shower was the next thing on her agenda and a good night's sleep. Tomorrow she'd be starting her new schedule bid in Lancemen with Jerry's brother Bill. She'd been spoiled while working in Lakeview, sleeping through most of the nights. That would not be the case in Lancemen, especially now that the fire department had pulled out and were no longer responding on medicals. They had agreed to respond on car accidents where extraction tools were needed but that was it, other than that, they were strictly firemen. Their disagreement over contract talks and the minimal pay differential for working ALS had prompted their decision—and—well they were pretty much just tired of the drunks.

"Freddie! Get up, Freddie," bellowed the voice of a large black woman, who was standing over a man that was spread eagle and face down in the grass before her. Using her foot she nudged his arm while repeating his name. Anne and Bill watched to see if he would respond to her. They had both tried shaking him but he never even flinched. It was midmorning and they were on their second call of the day. A small crowd of the area neighbors had gathered around, drawing the attention of a few firefighters who were driving by and stopped. The man lying in the grass reeked of alcohol and apparently had vomited before falling.

"Did you guys try an ammonia inhalant yet?" One of the firemen asked.

"Yeah," Bill answered. "It didn't even phase him."

"That's cause dat nasty liquor he done drank stinks worse than that thing you put under his nose. He's used to that. That man drinks anything he can find and lots of it. I hear he's nice when he's sober—but I ain't never seen it." Again the women pushed her foot against his arm.

"Let's try picking him up," Anne suggested.

Even out in the fresh air, the stench of his clothes, which he probably hadn't changed in days or weeks, mixed with the vomit and alcohol was sickening. Secretly, Anne took a deep breath before leaning over to help Freddie to his feet. Grabbing one sleeve of his red plaid shirt, she watched as Bill grabbed the other. While slowly pulling him up from the ground, the large woman in the bright flowered dress again began calling the man's name.

"Come on, Freddie—get up. Come on now, you just drunk."

"Come on, Freddie," Bill joined in, smiling at the concerned woman.

The movement and fresh air must have been enough to stimulate some sort of awareness; for within seconds of being lifted like a crane, his eyelids began flickering as he feebly tried to position his legs to stand. The first couple attempts were like a fawn or baby colt trying to support themselves for the first time. Then, as his face gradually came into view, they realized that Freddie had probably been laying in the grass for at least a few hours. The peach colored vomit had dried on his cheeks and was matted in his partially flattened afro hairdo that was also layered with chunks of food, fallen leaves and recently cut lawn clippings, giving the effect of a piece by Picasso.

"Oh man, Freddie—look at chu," came a voice from the crowd, expressing the nauseating disgust each of them felt.

"Oh—Freddie," the large woman said as she took a step back, wrinkling her nose. "You got head cheese."

Immediately, a soft burst of laughter rose from those in the crowd. The firefighters surrendered with Anne and Bill giving in with a chuckle to the contagious humor. It was the first time they had ever heard that expression. As they looked over the scene, they were certain it was the woman's comment that won the amusement and not Freddie's sad situation. Then, two men from the crowd stepped out and walked up to Anne and Bill who stood supporting the drunken patient. Reaching under the wobbling man's arms, they took hold and began leading him toward home.

"He ain't gonna be too happy when he wakes up all the way—that's all I know," the woman said shaking her head.

"Thanks for your help," Anne called out, watching as she strolled away. The woman waved without turning around while the crowd slowly dispersed. Bill leaned over and picked up the orange supply box as they started toward the rig.

"Man, I don't miss getting up in the middle of the night for this stuff—no way." The fireman grinned. "You guys can have it."

Those words echoed in Anne's mind a number of times over the next few weeks. She couldn't decide if the words were a wish or a warning; for the days became so busy, they often seemed to run together. Occasionally she found herself sniffing the sleeves of her uniform shirt, trying to remember if she had taken a shower that day. Throughout the summer most of their shifts were filled with back to back calls. Some days seemed like an overlaid blur, replaced by the darkness of night that came with the speed of a shining black stallion—but not with the grace or beauty. Meals were often quick mouthfuls of hurriedly chewed food from a local drive through restaurant. Car accidents, stabbings, shootings, patients having shortness of breath, chest pain, and of course a multitude of non-emergency transfers, only began the list of calls that seemed endless.

"Unit Six, you're responding to 537 Clovis for an assault. PD said they don't have a squad available to send. Looks like you're on your own. Keep your radio close by."

Bill squeezed the black button against the mic. "Ten four."

The street was well known to anyone working in EMS in the north end of the county. It was one of several within a quarter mile area that was referred to as the projects. The low income based apartments were built to help those in financial despair. But the lack of money for some had brought an even heavier weight as a number of residents living there, looking for a quick way out, resorted to selling drugs.

It was an understood rule that you never went into the projects lit up or running hot with your emergency lights or siren on. That was a sure way to draw attention and bring a very large crowd of bystanders to the scene. In the case of a stabbing or a shooting, that could get ugly; especially if a child became injured in the cross fire. You were smart to get in—do what was needed—and get out. Even while most of the residents county wide were respectful to the EMS personnel, it was not unusual for alcohol and or drugs to turn a reasonable person into an irrational dolt.

"You really need to sit still. I can't get the glass out of your head with you squirming around," Anne repeated. She could tell the man in his mid twenties sitting on the kitchen chair next to her was becoming less and less tolerant of her picking through the large cut in his scalp.

"Man, girl. What are you doing?" he yelled, bolting from the chair. "That hurts!"

"Well, I'm not trying to hurt you. I just need to get that glass out of that cut so I can put a dressing on it. It has to come out. Either I do it—or the hospital can do it. It's up to you. There's no reason to get upset with me.

I'm not the one who hit you on the head with a bottle. I came here to help you. If you don't want my help just say so and I'll leave."

"All right. I'm sorry. You can do it—jus hurry up. I want'a get this over with."

Normally Bill would have chimed in by now offering a comical comment of some sort to ease the discomfort of the situation—but it was three in the morning and they still hadn't had dinner. Or had they? It was so easy to lose track of things like that on the busy days.

"You were a little rough on that guy, weren't you?" Bill teased Anne, as she drove away from the hospital toward the station.

"Oh please! I can't believe the people in this city have nothing better to do than get drunk and beat each other up at three in the morning. If they were in bed sleeping where they're supposed to be, this stuff wouldn't happen. And maybe we could get at least a nap in. I don't know if I'm more tired or hungry."

"Are you going to whine all night?" Bill grinned.

"Maybe—if I want to," Anne smirked, realizing by his comment how crabby she sounded.

She liked working with Bill. He and his brother Jerry were two of the finest paramedics she knew. They both shared a family trait of a gift of gab. Each had a way of bringing comfort and peace of mind to the patients they transported and their family members; not to mention that they both possessed great skills and common sense—well usually. Without question and in spite of the one and only incident with Jerry and the girl at the station, Anne felt it was an honor to work with him.

Jerry was older by a few years. The boys were born in Michigan where their father worked at a gas station and an A&W before moving his family, a wife and three young children, to Texas. Their new home sat on a large piece of land within walking distance to Fort Sam Houston. Their father had been stationed there for a time when he was in the Army Air Corp. Bill said his father did reconnaissance missions when he was in the service and was very fond of what he called spoon'en eggs. Once while he and Anne were sitting in the rig covering in the Lakeview area, Bill told her of how he used to work with his father as a youngster setting up advanced promotions for different circus groups through a booking agent. They made up taps, which were three by five cards that would say things like, Win Win Win, that were to be sold in blocks for fund raisers. They traveled a lot doing this type of work but no matter where they went, his dad would always order pancakes that he spread with butter and ate like a tamale, or spoon'en eggs for breakfast.

The pancakes were pretty much just normal pancakes but his eggs had to be cooked a special way. Sometimes the cook at whatever restaurant they were in would prepare and serve the nearly raw eggs just as he liked them, cooked in an egg pan, not on a grill and served in a bowl. If there was any part of the egg that could be picked up with a fork, they were too done. Bill said he knew exactly what the eggs were supposed to look like and ate his own breakfast accordingly. If his dad was satisfied with the consistency and texture of the yellow and white mixture in the bowl, he could take his time; but if not, he ate quickly. His father was normally a pleasant man but he liked his eggs a certain way and could not stand it if they came to him cold or over cooked. Once she remembered he said, that his father actually poured the eggs onto the floor of the restaurant and ground them into the threads of the carpet with his foot. That was the maddest he ever got. But no matter what, his father always paid for the food.

Anne always liked hearing the guys talk about their lives growing up. They were all so different plus it often explained many of the mannerisms and habits they possessed. She also understood from listening to Bill's stories how truly different he was from Jerry. Many times while listening to the youthful games of bets that were seldom won, and no welshing was allowed, she laughed as her oldest cousin Jacob came to mind. Jacob was always challenging the younger boys to do something daring to which the winner would receive his prized agate; and to the loser—a new and dreadful task awaited.

A short time after Bill, Jerry and their sister Liz moved to Texas, they were offered a choice between a swimming pool and horses—horses won. The very next day, a colt named Joe Hastings was purchased from Fort Sam Houston. Another colt named General also came to live in the small barn behind their house but Joe Hastings was Bill's favorite. He said that Joe hated most kids because they threw rocks at him through a fenced in area where he was kept while at the Fort, but he liked Bill. Every day when Bill came home from school he'd feed and tend to Joe. Two years later he said, while his sister was riding the full grown quarter horse through a mud puddle, he picked up a rock that cut deep into his hoof causing it to bleed profusely. Bill said his dad took off his own tee shirt and wrapped it around Joe's foot until the vet came. Joe wasn't much good to ride after that and gradually became mean.

It was a well-known fact to the boys and Liz that the one thing Joe hated, was to have someone blow air up his nose. This torment to Joe, that Jerry discovered while riding him on a windy day, became the supreme punishment of all punishments for a lost bet. So, of course, when Bill lost his bet to Jerry, he was not at all surprised to find himself standing before Joe. As Bill shared his tale, complete with all the comical reenactment he was known for, Anne thought back to certain events while living on the farm and clearly remembered that to a nine year old boy there was nothing worse than welshing on a bet.

"Okay, Billy boy, it's time to pay the devil," he said, repeating Jerry's statement. Anne recalled the boys at the farm always said, it's time to pay the piper; but she thought paying the devil probably carried more weight and would really make you not want to welsh.

"There I was," he said, holding up his hands as if grabbing on to each side of the horse's head, while recalling the day. Anne watched in amusement. "Face to face with Joe. I was holding on as tight as I could to his cheeks. I took a deep breath, leaned back, looked straight into his nostrils—then let'er rip. I didn't even get all of my breath out when Joe jerked his head free and latched onto my hand with his teeth. Then he started whipping his head back and forth with my thumb still in his mouth. I started yelling—Aah! Aah! Jerry reached up and punched Joe along side the head and he finally let go of my hand. I was sure my thumb was gone—blood was squirting everywhere. But what was worse was—I knew we were really going to get it from my dad. Then Jerry grabbed a rag from somewhere, put it over my hand and started squeezing the cut until it quit bleeding. After he pulled it off, he looked at it and laughed. The cut was just a little puncture wound from one of Joe's teeth—but it felt huge."

The story of Joe Hastings was just one of many. Each one was comical and fully animated—except for the story of their father's death. Bill said his father died from a heart attack in a hotel room when he was forty-eight years old. He received a Veteran's funeral and was buried in San Antonio Texas. Because his father was so young, he felt that the consumption of red meat contributed to his heart condition. To this day, both Bill and Jerry are vegetarians.

The beginning of the next shift was starting. When Anne pulled into the station Bill was outside spraying down the ambulance. One of the firemen she recognized from Lakeview walked over to the back doors of the rig, carrying an armful of supplies. Apparently, he was Bill and Anne's student rider.

"Hey, you guys," she waved.

"Hi, Anne," Jimmy nodded.

Anne set her overnight bag in the bunk room, then walked over to the phone to call in. She noticed a stack of folded paper sheets on the counter and guessed they were for the rig. Bill walked in looking for more towels to dry the ambulance.

"Hey, Billy. Do we need anything else besides the sheets?" she asked.

"I don't think so; I think Jimmy's got everything else in the rig already."

"Okay then, I'll run them out."

Anne set the blue and white paper sheets on the bench seat then jumped up into the ambulance. Jimmy had a large emesis basin neatly filled with four by four gauze dressings, three inch rolls of gauze and tape, oxygen masks and tubing and other miscellaneous items, searching through the cabinets to find where they went.

"Well that's a good way to learn where everything is," she said, smiling. "That way you don't have to scour the shelves looking for stuff when you're in a hurry."

"Well I'd like to take credit for it being my idea, but it wasn't. Bill loaded up the basin and sent me out with it," he smiled.

"Well at least you're honest."

The phone in the station rang. Bill came out and closed the garage door.

"We must have a call," she said, jumping out of the back of the ambulance. The student, Jimmy, moved up to the seat behind the front compartment and hooked his seat belt. Anne sat on the passenger seat and picked up the mic.

"Go ahead, dispatch, we're ready to copy."

"Code three to 67 Green Street for a woman feeling dizzy."

"Ten four," she replied, then slid the mic into the clip. Sensing the comment she knew Bill was about to say, she chuckled while holding up her hand to indicate—stop.

"What?" he grinned, while flipping on the emergency lights.

"I know what you were about to say. What woman isn't dizzy? Or—And that's different, how?"

Bill and Jimmy laughed. "You know," she smiled, directing her sentence toward the patient compartment where Jimmy was sitting, "I'm the one who fills out your evaluation. So I'm the one you should be humoring by not laughing."

"Yes ma'am. Sorry. It won't happen again," he chuckled.

Anne quickly filled in the dispatch information on the run form as they screamed down the main road of Lancemen. "Three more streets. Clarence, Madison then Green. There it is on the right—67 Green. The white house with the blue shutters," she announced.

Jimmy helped carry the equipment in as the three of them approached the house.

"Never stand in front of the door," Bill told him. "Stand off to the side until they open it for you."

As they neared the front of the house, a woman standing inside opened the storm door. "It's me," she said; "I want to go to the hospital."

"Okay," Bill began as they entered. "What's wrong with you that makes you think you need to go?"

"I just don't feel normal. I get shaky and dizzy. I keep thinking someone's here in this house—but there ain't nobody here but me."

"What's your name?" Anne asked.

"Sandra Jetter."

"Okay, Sandra, this is Jimmy and he's working with us today. If you don't mind, we'd like him to take your blood pressure and pulse before we go."

Jimmy slowly walked up to the woman who sat on a kitchen chair in the center of the living room. He noticed that both Bill and Anne spoke to the woman gently and carefully. She told Anne the different medications she took for her moods. After listening to her blood pressure reading, he removed the ear pieces of the stethoscope away, catching the tail end of their conversation which included a short list of psych drugs.

"Sandra, do you feel too dizzy to walk to the ambulance? If you do, we'll be happy to bring in the stretcher."

"I can walk," she answered. "I feel better now—that you're all here. Just let me just go and brush my hair first."

Anne and Bill sensed that the woman wasn't mentally stable. They knew that Jimmy felt the same uncomfortable eerieness. And they knew it was not wise for her to leave their sight to go brush her hair or do anything else.

"I think your hair looks fine, Sandra," Anne spoke up. "But if you want to brush it on the way to the hospital that would be fine. I'll grab your hair brush for you on the way out."

"It's in the bathroom; I'll show you," the woman said, bolting from her chair.

Anne quickly followed her and stood in the doorway of the bathroom, watching as Sandra ran the hair brush very sternly through her hair.

"What do you think, Sandra? It looks pretty good, I'd say."

"I hate my hair!"

"Some days I can't do a thing with mine either—but I really like the way your hair looks. It has a nice shine to it."

The woman seemed content with Anne's compliment. It sounded truthful and Anne had a calmness and confidence about her that most people responded well to. After putting the brush back on the shelf that hung over the toilet, she walked out of the bathroom and headed toward the kitchen door.

"Where are you going now, Sandra?" Bill asked. "I thought you wanted to go to the hospital."

"We have to go out the back door. I lost my key for the front. You have to lock it from the inside."

Jimmy looked at Anne and Bill while shutting the front door. After locking the dead bolt he slid the chain into the slot. Bill was in front of Sandra, waiting at the kitchen door that he held open for her to exit. Anne followed her through the kitchen. They were nearly past the counter by the sink when Sandra suddenly stopped and picked up a very large butcher knife that was laying on the cutting board near the stove. Anne stopped and stood silently behind her. She felt a coldness begin to fall over her like the darkness of winter. Years of working the streets had taught her when to know fear and when not to show it. She watched the woman study the knife, turning it from side to side. Her only thought was—Sandra, quit playing games. Just make your move, so we can get on with this. Then, as quickly and as arbitrarily as she had picked it up, the woman placed the knife back on the cutting board. She began humming and walked toward the kitchen door. Throughout her transport to the hospital, she never said another word. She just smiled and looked out the back window as if she were going on a pleasant Sunday drive.

"Man," Jimmy said to Anne, while placing the blanket on the stretcher. "I thought that woman was going to cut the mole off my face with that knife she picked up. That was something else. Doesn't that scare you, when people do that stuff?"

"I don't know, Jimmy. I guess it depends on how tired I am. That stuff gets old after a while. It's a hard question. I don't remember ever really being afraid of anything—even as a kid. I remember being sad and upset and lots of other things, you know. But I don't think I was ever afraid. My mother told me that God has not given us the spirit of fear. And I always remembered that the angels in the Bible said—"Fear not"—whenever they showed themselves to people here on earth. So I guess I've just held to that. I like the way that sounds—Fear not!" she grinned.

"Unit Six—calling Unit Six. If you can hear me, I need you on the road for a code."

"I'll get the radio. Can you go in and get Bill?"

"Sure thing," Jimmy answered.

Anne scooted to the front of the rig and grabbed the radio mic. "Unit Six, go ahead."

"You've got a woman not breathing at 452 Wilson. Your incident number is 982 at 18:20."

"Copy."

Jimmy and Bill came out of the hospital, lowered the wheels of the stretcher, and tossed it up into the back of the ambulance. Jimmy quickly locked it in place, then jumped inside shutting the back doors behind him.

"What do we have?" Bill asked, hopping up onto the passenger seat.

"A woman not breathing. I've got the run sheet started. The address is 452 Wilson."

"Jimmy, you ready?" Bill asked. "We've got a woman not breathing. Do you want the IV line or the ET tube?"

"The tube, I guess. I don't care. It's up to you guys," he answered with a quiver in his voice.

"Now there's no reason to be nervous," Bill smiled. "The worst thing that can happen is that she'll die."

"Gee thanks," Jimmy said. "That makes me feel a whole lot better."

"Just kiddin'. We'll be right there with you. You'll do fine."

Anne turned on to Wilson. She was glad Jimmy was there. If this turned out to be a cardiac arrest, an extra set of hands would be nice to have to do CPR while the drugs were being pushed and the airway established. An extra set of eyes to monitor the patient's rhythm if something workable developed was also helpful.

"We're in here," a man's voice called out as the crew entered the house.

Bill and Anne walked into the kitchen of the small, older home and saw a woman in a wheelchair slumped over in front of the table. The man, who they assumed was her husband, anxiously stood behind her and watched while Bill checked for a pulse. He was dressed in a clean but slightly tattered blue flannel shirt. His hands looked tired and wrinkled as he wiped a tear that ran over the aged creases of his cheek.

"I'm very sorry, sir; but it appears like she's already gone."

"I's afraid of dat. Oh, I's afraid of dat," he repeated sorrowfully while cradling his face in his hands. "I've been taking care of her for ten years now. Everyday I'd get up and make up a pot of soup and feed her with this here turkey baster. Jus a lit'a bit at a time, so she could swolla. Then I'd wash her up real good—so's she feel nice, ya know."

"Well it certainly looks like she's been well cared for. I'm sure you did everything you could for her, sir."

"I did. I really did."

"I'm just sorry we weren't able to do more."

"Well I guess it wa jus her time. Dat's all. She'd been get'ten more an more tired lately. I should'a saw it comin."

Anne looked around the front room while Bill and the gentleman talked. The house was orderly, at least it appeared like someone was trying to keep things neat. The walls were in great need of paint and newspaper covered the wooden floor. She guessed that it was in an attempt to keep them from getting tracked up, like a rug or carpeting would if he could afford it. She felt bad for him. He seemed very kind. Then a small newspaper clipping framed and hanging on the wall caught her eye. The man that the article was written about was named Benjamin E. Jones. She motioned to Jimmy to come over and take a look.

"That man in the kitchen's a war hero," he whispered.

"Sir, is your name Benjamin E. Jones?" Anne asked.

"Yes ma'am, it is."

"This is quite a nice article about you hanging on the wall. Oh, I'm sorry—I wasn't trying to dismiss what's happened to your wife, Mr. Jones—the article just caught my eye."

"Dat's all right."

"Just so you know," Bill said as he stepped out into the front room to take a look at the article himself, "we're waiting for the police to come and make a report. Whenever there is a death at home, for whatever reason, they have to make a report."

"Dat's fine."

"You're from Marshall, Texas?" Bill smiled. "I grew up just outside of Fort Sam Houston."

"You's from Texas too?" Benjamin beamed. "I knew it! Yes sir! Ya know—You's can always trust a man from Texas—cause he won't lie to ya. An if he does—you's won't know it!"

"That's right," Bill smiled.

Just then a police officer came through the door. Anne gave him a quick report of what they found and introduced him to Mr. Jones.

"It was a pleasure meeting you, sir," Bill said, shaking his hand as they were getting ready to leave. "I wish it had been under better circumstances, of course. But still, it was a pleasure."

"Thank you's all for be'n here. It would'a been a lot harder wit out ya. I appreciate everyting you's did."

While walking back to the ambulance Anne thought of the love and devotion it took for Benjamin E. Jones, the war hero, to take care of his wife for so many years. He never complained, even once while they were there about what he felt he was called to do, or his circumstances or living conditions. To her he was more than a war hero. In addition to that, he was a great man and a great husband; and obviously very proud, to be a man from Texas.

CHAPTER 24

As Irish as Apple Pie

Could it get any colder? Anne wondered while picking up the newspaper from the gray carpeted floor of the ambulance. A predicted eighty degrees below zero with the wind chill factor was a bit more than a breath of winter she thought, it was more like a harsh bite. She laid the folded daily press from Wednesday on her lap then peered through the party store window to search for her hungry partner, Randy. He just wanted to get a few snacks, he said, to enjoy while listening to Garrison Keillor host the radio program, "A Prairie Home Companion." Every Saturday while doing up the dinner dishes at home, she and Aunt Ruth used to listen to the narrated story of Lake Wobegon, the town of 942 residents, "where the women are strong, the men are good looking and all of the children are above average"; a town full of characters very much like her own Summerville. Perhaps that was the reason she always looked forward to hearing the program herself.

Randy was easy to spot. All she had to do was look for a tall guy with red hair. "There he is, in the potato chip aisle," she said to herself. "I hope he buys a small bag. I don't need to eat any more chips." Like most people, it wasn't unusual for her to gain a few pounds over the holidays; but then after Rick jokingly referred to her as buffalo butt a few weeks ago, she began watching her food intake a little closer—just to make sure she got back to her normal 128 pounds by spring.

She glanced at the radio clock in the dashboard and held her watch up to compare them minute to minute. It was 16:59 by both. Then her eyes were drawn toward the western sky and the water color back drop that twilight had painted. The peach glow from the city lights stood out under the pale, magenta hue that washed over the dark clouds and softened the bitterness of the cold outside. Laying her hand on the arm rest, she began studying the landscaped trees with their bare branches that reached up to the striated sky and appeared to be sketched in by a firm steady hand. Suddenly, a gush of blustery wind pushed against the ambulance as she sat studying the workmanship. The rig rocked slightly as it yielded to the whirling flaw that angrily whipped icy crystals of snow across the windshield making a sound like tiny pebbles. Again she became aware of her missing partner and searched the party store window. "If Randy doesn't hurry," she whispered, "he'll miss everything but the last line of the radio show—'And that's the news from Lake Wobegon and that's the end of it.'"

Then a man walking through the parking lot caught her attention. His head was bent and tucked into the hood of his tattered red jacket. She continued to watch him as he staggered down the sidewalk and tried to make out his face. She knew by his clothes that he was one of the street people that they often ran on. His bare hands looked rough and dry as he sorely attempted to grip the front panels of the jacket together. "That's Michael Allen," she said to herself. "He knows the mission has gloves for the needy, and he's certainly needy." Hypothermia was a serious concern this time of year; not only for the street people, but for anyone exposed to the brutal cold for even a short duration.

She felt sorry for him as he struggled against the winter storm. He didn't stop at the railroad tracks next to the party store parking lot, like he would have in the summer or spring. No, the sad shelter of large cardboard sections that were braced against a tree might keep the rusty, metal box spring used by the homeless dry and cozy under normal conditions, but it'd be of little worth against the arctic blast that blew in a week ago. She knew the shelters in the local churches and rescue mission would only take in the street wanderers if they were sober. It was too hard to control the drunken indigents, plus there were children in some of these places.

Sitting in the passenger seat, she shivered in sympathy as the wind howled and pushed against the heated ambulance. "Randy must be buying out the store," she muttered, while moving the heater knob a little more to the right. She expected, when he returned to the rig, he'd complain of how hot it was and say that it felt like a furnace. But she couldn't help it—she just couldn't seem to get warm. Even with her new long underwear, a Christmas gift from Aunt Ruth, that was guaranteed for thirty below, it was bone chilling and teeth chattering.

Leaning back into the seat, she opened the newspaper and held it up in front of her. The bold, black print across the top of the page began the article that described the inauguration of Ronald Regan, the 40th president of the Unites States and George Bush, the vice president. Sliding her sock clad feet from her boots, she rested them against the heater vent in front of her on the dashboard. Her eyes moved down the page and onto the next. The US hostage crisis had ended after 444 days, with the release of 52 US captives who were seized at the US embassy in Teheran. The stock market reported signs of a rebound after a huge drop earlier that month, while the flu epidemic continued to encumber the nation.

She heard a fumbling at the driver's door as a quick fridge breeze raced in and rattled the pages of the newspaper, all but tearing them from her fingers. Lowering it, she watched as Randy stood outside hugging a bag of carefully selected snacks to the breast of his jacket while fighting with the wind. Then the door bounced back against the hinges and nearly knocked him down. Finally, he jumped up on the seat and shut the door.

"Randy, are you all right?" she asked chuckling.

"Man, that wind is cold."

The heat from the vents blew against his face and at first appeared to be a welcome comfort. Then after a few seconds, just as expected, an onslaught of droll grumbling began.

"Good grief, girl, I can hardly breathe in here. You're going to melt my ice cream."

"Oh, quit your bellyaching. I just saw Michael Allen walking towards downtown. I bet he wouldn't complain about the heat. And I know you did not—buy ice cream."

"Sure I did. Don't you like ice cream?"

"Yeah, in July—not January when it's this cold."

"You're such a wimp," he teased, while watching her search through his trove.

"See, there's no ice cream in here," she sheepishly smiled.

"Ice cream? Who would buy ice cream on a day like today?" he jeered.

"Very funny, Randy," she retorted, while pulling out a package of ginger snaps. "Oh lookie lookie, I see cookies. And I like these, too—even if they are store bought."

The dispatch radio keyed. "Unit Six, come in for a code."

"Put them back, sister," he smiled, picking up the radio mic.

Anne let the package of cookies slide back into the bag, then pulled her pen from her pocket and wrote the information for their call on the newspaper.

"A sick party," she said, jotting down the nature of the call, "is sure better than a car crash on a day like today. My fingers are still numb from that PI we had two days ago and it's even colder today."

"Weren't you wearing any gloves?"

"Yes, mother," she smiled. "But they got soaked with blood. Then they stiffened up during the extraction and froze to my fingers. Don't you remember that when we finished the call, I threw them away and bought a new pair?"

"Oh I guess now I do," he said. Looking in the side mirrors, he backed up then turned toward the downtown area.

Because of the extreme frigid temperatures, the crews began developing new adjuncts of patient care which were based more on the lines of survival. They had all pretty much decided that anyone involved in an auto accident would quickly be pulled from the smashed vehicle. Clearly, the present weather conditions did not allow the normal time for the head to toe survey before applying the cervical collar and backboard. Certainly, maintaining a secure C - spine would be attempted; but their main objective would be to move the patient into the heated rig as soon as possible to prevent loss of limb or death from frostbite and or hypothermia. The crews had also learned to dress in layers of clothing, which made it cumbersome to move in and out of the smashed autos and nearly unbearable while inside a private residence or hospital, but they spent so much time out of doors, keeping warm was imperative for them to function.

Anne pointed. "There it is, Randy. The two story gray house on the right—with a parking lot of cars in the driveway." He pulled up next to the curb and stopped. The wind whipped across her face as she got out of the rig and opened the side door where the orange medical box was kept. The flu had been unmerciful, sweeping through almost every household in the county. As a result, nearly every hospital emergency room was full of vomiting, dehydrated patients that were too weak to even support themselves while sitting.

With the handle of the orange box in one hand and the drug box in the other, Anne used her foot to clear a path through the snow on the sidewalk, then from the porch steps, one riser at a time. Because of her short frame she usually had to lift the boxes while carrying them, to keep them from hitting against her upper calves. "Whoa," she said, stepping onto the wooden porch. An icy crust of snow had caused her foot to slide. "Watch your step, Randy," she warned. "The porch is kind'a slick." Guarding each step as he walked, he came up behind her with the clipboard tucked under one arm and an oxygen tank under the other.

After knocking on the storm door she lowered her face into the scarf that was wrapped around her neck. The wind whistled through the pillars of the porch. Now that the sun had completely gone down, a drop in the temperature was more noticeable. Peeking over her scarf, she studied the crusted white blanket, embellished by the street light's glow. A thousand diamonds appeared to be sewn into its fiber. Perhaps it was nature's exchange of beauty for bitterness, she thought. Then the aroma of fried chicken drifted through the cracks of the door and playful screams and the laughter of children bounced from the walls inside the old wooden house.

"Come—on! Did you try the door bell?" Randy asked impatiently.

"Yeah. You heard it. And I even knocked on the door," she answered. "Apparently they didn't hear me."

Seeming as if in one motion, in response to his complaining, she set the drug box down, pulled the storm door open while yanking her glove off with her teeth, then she rapped on the wooden door with her bare knuckles this time. Stepping back, she let the storm door fall back into place. Within seconds a man's voice came toward them, ordering the children to go play in another room. Then the wooden door opened, releasing the light from inside the house, dimly revealing the frosted artistic work that was delicately etched across the panel of glass in the storm door. The man flicked on the porch light, but she still couldn't make out his face.

"Did you call for an ambulance?" she asked.

"Yeah—come on in." He took a step back and yelled up the steps that ran along the wall near the foyer. Virginia! The amblance's here. Hurry up now. I got things to do."

"Maybe we should go up and check her out?" Anne suggested.

"She'cn walk. Virginia—what are you doing?"

"I'm coming. Ain't no need for yelling," the woman's strong voice echoed down the stairway. Anne caught sight of Randy's expression as he watched Virginia who was fully dressed, drag a small suitcase that hit every step on the way down until she reached the bottom. Several adults walked back and forth from room to room talking and laughing, as if they weren't aware of an emergency for which the crew was called, lights and siren. A little girl came from a play area and snatched a cookie from the dining room table. Then a dog who had been laying under it, hidden by a tablecloth, got up and grabbed the cookie, eating it as he ran. They watched as the child instantly became distraught, throwing herself onto the floor while kicking and crying.

"Bernadette! Now you get up off that floor and quit carrying on," Virginia called out, while slowly buttoning up her winter jacket.

"I'll take care of her. You jus go on and get back here. I told you—I got things to do. I don't know why you got that suitcase. That hospital ain't goin'a keep you."

In silence, Randy turned to open the door. Anne picked up Virginia's suitcase with one hand and the orange box with the other. They had no idea why they were transporting the patient at this point, or to which hospital—but they were going all the same. Randy moved down the porch steps in front of Anne. After putting the equipment he had toted away, he stood next to the side door of the rig and waited. Anne escorted their patient, carrying the orange box and the patient's baggage like a bellhop. She noticed that two of the cars in the driveway had the snow cleared off and were probably still warm from an earlier drive. The game was unfortunately a familiar one. Before she even said a word, she knew the answer.

"Virginia, don't you think it would have been cheaper if someone at your house took you to the hospital?"

"I got insurance. I'll give you the card once we get out of da wind."

Virginia, like so many others, totally missed the point of what the word "emergency" meant. Too often the crews responded to houses in the city, coming lights and siren at the caller's request, only to have to stand there and wait for the person to gather his or her things or brush his or her hair before leisurely leaving. But then to the patient's thinking, he was doing what was most beneficial to him. By going to the hospital in the ambulance—a patient could get into a room in the ER faster. It was not only more convenient for him but it was also more cost effective. A taxi took longer and required cash upfront. An ambulance on the other hand was quick and free if you had State issued insurance—and if it responded in an emergency status. Plus, the "ambulance drivers," a most dreaded title, "were so nice—they'd carry your things for you and help you up into the truck."

Not all of the welfare recipients misused the service, of course. But there were enough who did. And the crews knew that it would only be a matter of time before the State would catch on and the folks that really needed the help would be left to suffer for those who had been self serving.

"Don't say a word, Randy," Anne started, while pulling away from Lancemen General, leaving Virginia in the ER. "It could have been worse. We could have had to drag all those kids out to the rig too. Did you see that little girl having the fit over that dog eating her cookie? I never acted like that in my life. I knew better. The seat of my pants would have been warmed up so fast… Spare the rod spoil the child, don't cha know."

"I hear ya. My mom was little, but she carried a big stick. She was quick, too," Randy chuckled. "She kept me and my brother Jeff in line with no problem. And I'm telling you—you did not want to get in trouble at school. That was the worst! Our principle carried a paddle that had holes drilled through it that whistled when the air passed through. Man, did that thing sting! I only got whacked once—I never wanted it again. Then he called my mom—and when my dad got home from work, I got it again."

"I hear ya," she chuckled. "It was the same way at our house. But the world's a changing place, Randy. Nowadays, you've got all these doctors who probably never even had kids, telling people they've never met, how to raise theirs. And the amazing thing is—people just follow like sheep—sort'a like the jelly bean craze. Just because the president likes jelly beans, now it's the big thing and everyone's eatin' them. People who have never been in the service are wearing camouflage jackets. And last week, I saw this girl with her hair teased and brushed straight up. My cousin calls it scary hair. He's right. She looked scared and I was scared. It only takes one person to set a trend—then everybody else follows—even if it's a bad idea or looks stupid."

"Hey, that reminds me," Randy said, digging through his book bag, as if he hadn't heard a word she said. "I almost forgot. I bought these yesterday. They're really good. They're all different flavors," he smiled holding up his found treasure.

She laughed. "Randy—you bought jelly beans?"

"Here, try this one. It tastes like blueberries," he continued. While stopped at a red light, she took the shiny blue confection from the plastic bag and dropped it into her mouth. She chewed it slowly and thoughtfully as Randy impatiently watched.

"It's just one, small jelly bean, Anne," he grinned. "It doesn't take that long to eat it."

"I merely wanted to give you an honest and well thought out opinion," she said, reflecting the voice of a gourmet food analyst. "It doesn't taste exactly like blueberries but it's pretty good."

"See?"

"See nothing," she chuckled.

"We were dropping the green ones in our beer last night," he bragged. "We wanted to see if they'd turn the beer green—but they don't."

"Why do you want to drink green beer?" she asked, pulling up to the station.

"For Saint Patrick's Day, of course. You're going with us, aren't you?"

"Where?"

"To Filthy McNasty's—it's an Irish tavern. It's a good time. Rick sings with Father Pat and his band. You don't have to drink the beer if you don't want to. Shirley usually drinks grapefruit juice when she's there."

"Shirley goes to a bar?"

"It's not a bar—it's an Irish pub."

"Randy, it's still a bar—as much as I would like to hear Rick sing, I can't go."

"Why not? God won't mind—Father Pat will be there."

She laughed. "He's not even a real priest, is he?"

"I'm not sure," Randy chuckled. "All right—so why not?"

"Well, for one thing, I hate the smell of alcohol and I don't want to smell it on my friends. Two, as soon as I step in there, people will start with the hypocrite tongue wagging stuff. 'Oh look, there she goes—off to the bar on one day—and then she goes off to church on Sunday.' Even if I never took a drink—which I wouldn't—it would all be the same. No, it's just a bad idea and I don't really belong there anyway, but thanks for inviting me."

"We could sneak you in—but if you really don't want to go, I guess you don't have to." Smiling, she shook her head indicating she was not willing to change her mind. "Okay, okay," he conceded. "Then just humor me and listen to some of the songs we sing."

"Do I really want to hear these?" she chuckled.

"Ready?" he began without waiting for an answer. "The drums go bang, the cymbals clang, the horns they blow away. McCarthy pumps the old bassoon while I the pipes do play. Henesy Tenesy tootles the flute, the music's something grand, a credit to old Ireland is McNamara's Band."

"Yey." Anne clapped. "That was a fun song. What's that guy's name? Henesy Ten..."

"Tenesy. Henesy Tenesy."

Spring was nearing as well as Saint Patrick's Day; and to Anne's delight, she had learned nearly every Irish song that Randy knew. More and more she wrestled with the idea of joining her friends at Filthy McNasty's for the annual day of celebration, a day that Bill referred to, although he wasn't Irish or very religious, as the holy day. It was nonetheless a special day that began hundreds of years ago in remembrance of Saint Patrick, a great and noble Irishman who encountered horrific obstacles while trying to establish Christianity in Ireland.

If nothing else, learning the songs had been a good history lesson, for she learned that the men who were convicted of crimes in Ireland were sent to Van Dieman's Land, an Australian prison. But the education didn't stop there. The Excise or tax man, she gathered from the lilted tunes, was a favored character who roamed through the potato skin and barley stills that were tucked away in the forest and lowlands, hoping to collect a bottle of the demon rum for himself. The love songs were runes of silken tapestries that brought her childhood friend, Jenny to mind, for Jenny had always been a fan of poetic romance. Then there were the humorously written songs of love-hate relationships. Most of the songs were catchy, light hearted, toe tapping ditties that reflected their experiences of life. But the ballads honoring the men who fought in the battles and wars were dirge like, with the "Easter Rebellion of 1916" among the best remembered and heart wrenching. After hearing the lyrics of "William McBride" with its strong, thought rendering message, Anne couldn't imagine how a song that sad and that unsettling could be sung on Saint Patrick's Day. Or could it? The more she learned, the more she became drawn to the music and passion in which the people of Ireland lived. But still, the celebration of all of this took place in a pub.

"Why can't they have the Saint Patrick's Day party someplace else?"

Randy grinned. "You aren't serious?"

"Well I was hoping. All right—I'll go for a little while—but just to hear Rick sing. And if I start to feel uncomfortable, then I'm leaving and that's that."

"It's not like you think. A lot of the cops, firemen and nurses you know will be there. It's just a good time."

It was Tuesday, March 17. Anne left the Johnstones and drove to Filthy's, feeling a little apprehensive. Then slowly the songs she'd learned crept in, as well as a yearning to hear the tunes and instruments in perhaps a similar atmosphere to that of Ireland. As she pulled into the parking lot she looked around picking out familiar vehicles. It was eight o'clock. The building was smaller than she thought and very plain. A wee bit of the music filtered out, then became loud and party like, when she opened the door.

"Hey, you made it!" Randy cheered. "Come on over here. We saved you a seat. I'll get you a drink. What will it be? They have diet and regular pop."

"Root beer or diet whatever will be fine."

"Don't look so nervous," Shirley chuckled. "There's lots of us teetotalers here. See—I'm drinking grapefruit juice, straight up."

Randy was right; Anne knew nearly everyone there. The music was delightful and seemed to go from one toe-tapping lilt to another. In no time, Bill's girlfriend, Jan, had her doing the Irish jig. Then there was the

Unicorn song in which they positioned their hands to feature each animal in the song. "There were green alligators and long neck geese, humpty back camels and chimpanzees, cats and rats and elephants and sure as you're born, the loveliest of them all was the unicorn." Rick had a smooth baritone voice and Father Pat, who really was Irish, played the fiddle like nothing Anne had ever heard. Then they sang the "Faygo" song and shortly after that, during "The Black Velvet Band," everyone chorused loudly with glasses raised, "And she was," while swaying arm in arm, standing on the chairs around the huge wooden table in the center of the room.

Anne looked at her watch while in the lassie's room. It was eleven thirty. Oh my word, she thought. I never planned to stay this long. I have to go to work tomorrow. She picked up her purse and looked for her keys. The angel key chain that Aunt Ruth gave her the first day she drove a car solo caught her eye. Blinking, she pulled it out then tucked her purse under her arm. The pub was full of smoke. It didn't seem like it was that bad earlier, but suddenly she noticed that her eyes were really stinging.

"Randy," she said tugging on his shirt sleeve. "I'm going now. I need to get some sleep."

"Me too. I'll be leaving soon," he smiled. "Hey, thanks for coming out. I'll see you in the morning, bright eyed and bushy tailed."

"Anne, you leaving?" Shirley asked. "I'll walk out with ya. The smoke's starting to get to me."

As Anne pushed the door open the smoke rushed out into the crisp cool air as if it too was tired of being pent up inside the tiny pub. The stars shined brightly overhead as the waxen moon peeked between the clouds, adding to the pleasantness of being in the open.

"Well, what'd you think?" Shirley asked.

"It was fun. I noticed that some of the songs have the same melody as some of the old church hymns we sing."

"Funny how that happened," she smiled. "But then, it is a gala event in honor of a saint."

"See, now I guess that's where I'm confused. I really just wish they could have it somewhere where there wasn't any alcohol and that people didn't smoke."

Shirley chuckled. "That'll be the day. I could live without the smoke myself, but you'll never be able to persuade anyone to have a Saint Patty's Day party without green beer or ale. It just wouldn't be Irish."

"Well, I know it was my first time celebrating this happy event, but it seemed to me that the people who weren't drinking were having a pretty good time, too." She smiled, then added, "How'd that line from Othello go? 'Oh God, that men should put an enemy in their mouths to steal away their brains!'"

Shirley laughed. "Well, that about says it all. I'll see you in the morning, Anne. My brain and I will talk to you tomorrow."

"Good night, Shirley."

Anne took another sip of her morning coffee, then tapped on the kitchen window before waving to Mr. Johnstone who was out in the back yard filling the bird feeder. His hands were full; a bird house in one hand and a bag of seed in the other. "Have a good day," he called. Mrs. Johnstone was away visiting her daughter. The Johnstones were planning to move into a condo soon. Anne knew this would be the last spring that she would see the crocuses and hyacinths that grew and blossomed along the walkway near the house. Next year, she'd have to enjoy the spring flowers at her own apartment.

"Oh man, am I tired," she yawned, while driving to work. The station was just up ahead. Pulling into a parking space she noticed that Randy was already in the rig checking out the equipment.

"My," she teased, while standing at the side open door. "Aren't we energetic today? How much sleep did you get?"

"Enough," he smiled. "Did we tire you out?"

"I'm a little sore from doing the Irish jig for three hours," she grinned. "And my eyes are still stinging from all the cigarette smoke—but other than that I'm doing good."

"You and your old partner, Dan were quite the dancers, until he fell off the chair," he laughed.

"That was pretty funny."

"So, are you going next year?"

"I don't know," she smiled. "I like the music and the dances are fun, but being in with all that smoke and demon rum—it just doesn't feel right to me. We'll see."

The days passed quickly and grew warmer. St. Patty's Day was now just a remembered night of dancing on chairs with friends in song. Now, it was bluegill season. Growing up with a pack of boys gave you no choice but to understand what that meant. To them it was hours of dropping a single hook in and pulling it out a minute later with a tiny but delicious fighter at the end. It was pails full of pan fish just beckoning to be cleaned and fried—and lots of good fertilizer for Aunt Ruth's flower bed. But keeping the cats out was another story.

"Hey, Rick," Anne greeted when he came into the station. "That's quite a nice fishing vest. How many pockets does it have?"

"Lots. That's why I like it. I was going to take this girl I met blue-gill fishing but we had a late call and our plans got messed up. I'm tired anyway—so now I'm going home to drink a beer, eat a tuna fish sandwich and a bowl of canned soup—and then I'm going to bed. I just stopped in here to use the phone. So what are you doing?"

"Well, I'm working—as you can probably tell from my uniform," she chuckled.

"Funny. You know what I meant."

"I'm waiting for Randy to get out of the shower so we can hopefully go and get something to eat before things get too crazy."

"Man," he began, chuckling. His face held a far off look that carried a past event. "We had the funniest call yesterday. Actually, the call itself wasn't funny but it sure took a turn once we got to the hospital. What time is it?"

"It's almost nine."

"Well, let me make this phone call real quick and then I'll tell you the story. Maybe you won't even think it's funny—but I did. In fact, every time I think of it, it still makes me laugh."

Anne walked over to the coffee pot that sat on the corner shelf. After pouring a cup, she added a couple spoonfuls of sugar and powdered creamer. While stirring the golden brown liquid she walked toward the sofa to wait for Rick's story. She remembered he was a great story teller. His voice had a rich baritone timbre and an equally rich way with words that easily recreated the event, making you feel as if you were there and a part of it from the very moment that it actually took place.

"Okay. You ready?" he began, as he hung up the phone.

She nodded.

"Well, we got this call for a drug overdose. It was in one of those big old houses on Lameer. You know, right where Oakview dead ends. Anyway—when we pulled up, this woman was standing outside on the porch waving her arms and jumping up and down—you know. Then, as we were getting out of the rig, one of the fire department's pumpers with a couple of their guys showed up. So then we all went upstairs to the last bedroom at the end of the hall and found this girl lying on the bed—naked as a jay bird. Now the woman who was outside flagging us down is standing next to me. She said when she came home from work, she found the girl and called us right away. The girl was just renting a room from her and she really didn't know her that well. The only thing that we knew—was that she had snoring respiration's, drool coming out of the corner of her mouth—and that she was naked. There weren't any needle tracks or empty pill bottles, so we started a line on her and checked her sugar. That was fine. She passed the hand drop test and the eyelash touching thing we do, you know, to see if someone is faking. Nope, she was really out of it. So we put her on the stretcher and took her down to LOH. Okay, now we're in the hospital and I'm giving my report to Doctor Dowell. He's listening and as always, is genuinely concerned. The nurse left to get a sheet to cover this girl who looks to be about our age, in her mid twenties—and to call the lab, or whatever else. Well, this girl as I already told you is stark naked."

"For the third time," Anne interrupted.

"And she is just beautiful," he continued, ignoring her quip. "Her skin's like porcelain, she has a flat tummy, muscular legs, nice everything else and flaming red hair; not to mention, that at this point we can tell she's really a red head, if you know what I mean."

"Why are you telling me this?"

"Just bear with me," he smiled. "No pun intended. So she has this nice little tuft of hair, you know where, and we're all standing there staring at her and yet at the same time trying not to; but we're all aware that we're all staring and trying not to. So then this fly comes out of nowhere," he chuckled. "And it lands right on this nice—fiery red tuft of hair. So, Benny, you know that big kind'a goofy orderly they have?"

She nodded. "He's very nice."

"Yes, he is. Now don't interrupt." Refocusing on his story, he began chuckling a little harder as he went on. "Well, so Benny walked over and just sort of waved his hand to shoo the fly away. Which it did. And then, as it's flying off he says, very seriously—'Probably, not the first time'. I thought I would just die. We laughed so hard that my side started to ache. Even Dr. Dowell was laughing and you know he never laughs at anything like that. He's always so professional. But it was so funny the way that he said it, 'Probably not the first time.' Oh my."

Anne sat on the sofa smiling. She was more amused by his expressions than by the story.

"You're not laughing," he said, somewhat disappointed. "Don't you think it's funny?"

"It's all right."

"Well let me tell you again what he said. Are you ready? Here goes.... 'Probably not the first time.'" Chuckling, he waited a second for her to respond with something besides a smile.

"I'm sorry, Rick," she grinned. "It's just not as funny to me as it is to you. But then I wasn't there. Not that I really think it would matter. So anyway, where do you go fishing?"

"Sheeze. I can't believe that you don't think that's funny. To answer your question—I have a pontoon boat that I take out in the morning just to scout out the lake for the beds of where the bluegill are nesting. If you go out there in the morning when they first wake up, and wear a pair of polarized sunglasses, you can see right down into the water. I make a map of where all their beds are in the morning. Then at dusk I go out with my rod and reel, a five gallon bucket and a pocket full of black rubber spiders—and bring'em in. As soon as I catch my twenty-five fish limit, I go home and start cleaning. A fork for scaling and a good knife for the rest is all you need. Do you know what you got when you're done?"

"What?" she asked, chuckling.

"Good eatin, that's what you got. Good eatin."

Randy stepped out of the bathroom. "I thought I heard voices. Hey Rick, are you going to breakfast?"

"Nope. I've got fish and a cold beer waiting. And a pretty funny story too, but that'll have to wait. See you guys later."

"See ya, Rick"

Randy went into the bunk room to grab his duffle bag. Anne turned off the coffee pot and carried the pot into the bathroom to rinse it out. Randy's towels were on the floor and his toothbrush and paste on the sink. Anne laughed to herself while thinking about Rick and the conversation they had just shared. These guys were not only work mates but they were friends and like brothers to her. She remembered that just a few days ago at the hospital cafeteria one of the food servers asked her how it was to work with all of those good looking guys? Her response came immediately and without a second thought. "Do you know any?" The girl behind the food tray laughed. To Anne, it was sort of like when a girl at school had a crush on one of her brothers. It was hard to see what the other person saw, because she had only viewed her brothers and cousins as awkward, goofy, pestering boys. And it didn't seem to be much different here. They were still awkward, goofy, pestering boys—just taller. They were like the boy next door. As American as …. or in Randy's case, as Irish as Apple Pie.

CHAPTER 25

AVIAN WONDERS

OR

(MARIONETTE'S
FUNERAL MARCH)

Anne sat in the back of the rig at St. Luke's writing out the run form for a CPR patient that expired in spite of their efforts. She paused for a second after taking a sip of the orange drink from the nurses lounge, then continued filling in the county form. She had the patient's name, address, medical history and medications filled in—it was the narrative that wasn't finished; or at least it didn't seem finished.

"Okay—I've got it! Arrived to find an eighty-seven year old female at home without vitals. I don't know what else to write," she said. "Old Mrs Fitzgerald was basically dead when we got there—and she's still dead. I always have trouble writing out a big, long story about this stuff."

"Yeah? So go work for a fire department. Then you won't have to write much of anything," her partner, Dale, teased. "Do you remember that lawyer we ran on during our last shift, who fell off his roof while blow drying the tar he just put down, while it was sprinkling? Remember what fire's run form said? Broke arm. That's all they wrote. They didn't put down anything about the distance that he fell, or even mention the electrical jolt he got from the hair dryer. Their entire narrative consisted of—broke arm. Two of the most important days in a person's life is the day they're born and the day they die. Now, if you want to leave some sorry looking run form about that woman on the day she died—that's up to you."

"All right, all right—I get the picture," she chuckled. "I'll write out a nice and complete run form. And just to set the record straight, I certainly did not mean to insinuate that Mrs. Fitzgerald's life or death wasn't worthy of a professionally written form—I just said, I have trouble using a whole bunch of words to say a few things."

"Really," he smiled. "Well you sure couldn't prove that by me. You don't seem to have any trouble using a lot of words when you're yabbering. Why don't you just put some of that talent to use, while writing out your run form?"

"Be quiet," she laughed. "And you know, Dale, you shouldn't be so mean to the firemen. That stuff has a way of coming back to bite you, ya know."

"Oh here we go. Why—do you always have to stick up for those guys?"

"Because they're my friends. And because they don't all write bad run forms."

"Whatever you say, little Ms. hose head groupie."

"Now, now. There's no need for name calling," she smiled.

Dale hired in to Mercy Ambulance back in the winter. He and Anne had partnered up in April, when the new schedule bid started. She found him to be a very skillful conscientious paramedic. And as a plus, he was a clean freak. They worked well together; so much so, that the other crews referred to them as the Dynamic Duo. He liked to rock climb—and all the rest of the things that guys like to do. He was fun and friendly to almost everyone, with the exception of certain firemen and all bossy nurses. He wasn't rude, of course, he just didn't go out of the way to be friendly.

In addition to working at the LOH care centers, the medics also worked in the Emergency Room at the main hospital. Anne took the morning shift when they were not busy on their own calls. That was the shift when the bossy nurses worked, according to Dale, so he preferred to work afternoons. Anne had just taken a patient back to a room to get a set of vitals when one of the nurses peeked her head in.

"Anne—your dispatcher just called. Your partner's on his way."

"Okay, thanks Kathy. Someone will be right in, Mr. Long." Turning around, she tucked the blood pressure cuff back into the holder on the wall, then scurried past the nurses' station and hit the bottom of the wall to open the electric doors. Dale was waiting in the ambulance at the curb, near the patient drop off.

"What do we got?" she asked as she hopped up on the passenger seat.

"A PI on the expressway in Orion. PD's already asking for a second unit and fire's on the way. Linda's dispatching. She sent the Basic car from Borden's Nursing Home—so they all ready got a jump on us."

Anne knew the location of the nursing home very well. It was in Orion, about five miles south of the car accident scene that they were responding to. She reached for her seat belt, then sat back to enjoy the ride. Many emergency calls had passed since her first solo ride with Chris. Now for the most part the zooming and sometimes strategic flights felt comfortable and routine—a white knuckler was rare. As they screamed down the main drag leaving Lancemen, Dale flipped the siren knob from wail, to yelp, to hi-lo. And then every so often, he'd move the knob in-between tones and hold it there for a few seconds. The crews had recently discovered, much to the mechanics' dislike, that if you lined up the siren knob just right, between wail and yelp, you could produce a high pitched, ear piercing tone that moved traffic very well. Unfortunately, it wasn't designed to do that and more times than not, blew out the siren fuse or the entire mechanism. Anne looked out over the hood of the ambulance and watched the lights twirl within the glass domes of the beacons on each side. The tunnel lights around the top of the rig clicked alternately with the overhead light bar as they flashed. She felt the rig lean as they cornered the north bound expressway ramp as if they were on two wheels.

"Way to go, Mario," she teased.

Dale increased his speed, then took the center left lane of the expressway. Drivers on both sides slowed as they passed. Then they noticed the brake lights on the cars a few hundred feet ahead; gawkers they guessed, an indication that the accident wasn't far off. The dispatcher reported the accident to be on the south bound side. Their plan was to use the emergency turn around to join the others who were already on the scene.

"Come on, come on, you people—what are you looking at? Just drive and get out of the way," Dale grumbled. Traffic had slowed greatly. He merged to the left, then took the shoulder. The emergency turn around was about a quarter mile away. Anne pointed at the jackknifed semi that sat twisted in the median. In a glance as they cruised by, she saw Rick Stockwell from the Basic rig standing with a backboard next to the semi's smashed cab. His pale blonde hair stood out, giving way to his identity and allowed her a brief mental flash of the exploding frog incident that occurred a few years ago. Dale slowed down as he came up to the emergency turn around. Traffic on the south bound side had apparently been rerouted by the Lancemen County Sheriff deputies who were working the scene. Shutting down the roadway was a common procedure when accident victims were critical or deceased. Just up ahead, strobe lights on an array of emergency vehicles flashed, shaming the most decorated Christmas tree. It was a sight that the crews had become so accustomed to that it felt like home, not that their homes were chaotic. But the planned steps regarding patient care, an endowment intensified by a controlled surge of adrenaline, had become as second nature to them as skating is to an Olympic gold medalist.

Dale pulled up on the right shoulder of the expressway and stopped behind a deputy's car. In a quick overview of the scene, they saw that the semi's cab had separated from the trailer and had flipped over before coming to rest on the driver's side. A couple volunteer firemen appeared to be peeling back the windshield to extricate the accident victim. To Anne's right she caught sight of a small, two door wagon down in the ravine against a group of trees upside down on its roof. A new Basic employee, Ret Hayward, and a small group of firemen had the patient from the wagon backboarded and on the ground. "I'll take the car over here," she said, pushing her door open.

The weeds in the ravine were tall and thick; but the path of bent grass that the firemen and Ret had already laid made it easier for her as she carefully made her way in their direction. She knew by personal experience after twisting her ankle several months ago, to watch out for ruts in the ground and ripped-off pieces of car parts which could be hidden in the weeds. Tony, one of the volunteer firemen, saw her approaching after she'd walked a few yards and yelled that they were bringing the patient up to her. She looked down at the EMT's surrounding the patient and noticed they were doing CPR. Even from a distance she could see the dark blue color of the patient's face. This is not good, she thought, as she turned around to rush up the hill. After opening the side doors of her rig, she jumped in to spike a couple of IV lines. While running the fluid through the IV tubing of each bag to remove the air, she set up the EKG monitor cables, snapping each end onto an electrode. Suddenly, the back doors opened and one of the volunteers working with Rick came and unhooked the stretcher from the bar.

"The guy from the semi's pretty messed up," he announced. "His left femur and humerus look like they're busted—probably a couple ribs too. They're bringing him over on the board now."

Anne rushed around to the back of the rig to help him pull out the stretcher to get it ready. Seconds later, both patients arrived at the back doors at the same time. Now she was faced with a difficult decision. She'd have to decide which patient to send with the Basic car and which to care for herself, based on which was the most critical and which was most likely to survive. As the senior paramedic over the accident scene, it was her responsibility to make the right choice. She looked at the CPR victim. He was young and had an obvious head injury. But in addition to and more importantly than that, his heart had stopped. She knew that cardiac failure was very unusual for someone his age unless something grave or traumatic caused this acute situation. And from the way that his face, neck and shoulders appeared, with the deep cyanotic telltale vee sign indicating a major rupture to his heart, she was quite sure that this was indeed the tragic case for the young man who was unconscious in front of her.

"He wasn't seat belted, was he?" she asked Ret.

"No. We found him about twenty feet from the car, in the brush."

"Looks like he might have hit his chest on the steering wheel or something," Rick offered.

"Probably ruptured his Aorta," Anne surmised.

Then she glanced at the driver of the semi. Even though he was unconscious, at least he was breathing. Clearly he had a better chance, if they acted quickly. "Dale," she directed, "we'll take the guy with the femur fracture. Ret, you and Rick take the CPR." Immediately everyone assumed their designated roles. Jumping up into the back of the rig, she understood that even though it only took her a minute to make the decision, right or wrong, she'd have to live with it for a lifetime. But that was the kind of challenge that came with working in the field of EMS. There'd be many such choices throughout her career. It was an expected part of the job. The medical training they received in the classroom, a never ending process for sure, was only a small part of their education. Undoubtedly the events occurring in the streets provided another avenue and a tome of lessons. But the mixture of street and book knowledge wasn't enough; in addition, they also had to have a willingness to put themselves out on the line day to day without fear or hesitation.

Dale and Anne understood the value of time and worked quickly to immobilize the multiple fractures and establish an IV before leaving the scene. Sometimes you didn't need an X-ray machine to tell you a bone was broken. Just a deformity or the sound of bone particles rubbing together, know as crepitis, was enough to warrant a splint of some sort. Now they were ready to go. Just as Dale started to squeeze through the cabinets that divided the front and back compartments to get into the driver's seat, the back door opened. It was Ret.

"We're getting ready to leave," he began after clearing his throat. "I've got a couple of the firemen riding in the back with me, to help do compressions and bag our guy. I can't seem to get a good seal with the mask though. The air we're tying to push in seems like it's just coming back. Rick said his neck's broke which I'm sure isn't helping. Anyway," he continued after swallowing hard. "He's already called LOH with both of the patients' info. He just wanted me to let you know." The expression on his face revealed how green he was. He'd only been with the company a little over a week; but the look on his face was not one of fear, it was more like a question of—what have I gotten myself into?

Anne felt sorry for him but couldn't help chuckle to herself, remembering how she felt when she first started working on the road. She was pretty sure that Rick sensed Ret's despair as well, for he could have easily relayed the information that he sent with Ret by radio—car to car. Ret didn't need to bring the news personally at all. It was just Rick's way of giving him a chance to get out and grab a quick breath of fresh air.

"You're just going through the motions, Ret. No one's expecting anything heroic," she offered. He watched as she tried to tear off her patient's tee shirt. "Hey, do you want to use my scissors?"

"Thanks," she said, taking his shiny new scissors from his hand. "I had a pair a minute ago. I don't know where I set them. I'll give yours back to you at the hospital. Okay, Dale, let's go."

Both crews arrived at LOH within fifteen minutes. One crew had a hopeful outcome—and one had an ominous outcome.

After moving their patient to the assigned room designated by the hospital staff, Anne and Dale lifted their patient, Carl by his driver's license, onto the hospital cart.

"This guy's from the semi," she said, starting her report. Doctor Malley listened while he and the ER staff worked rapidly to treat the accident victim. "He's fifty-five years old. The crew on the scene just prior to our arrival reported that the semi came across the median from the north bound lane and hit the station wagon in the south bound lane. Then according to the witnesses, they said the semi turned over and spun back into the median. He was still seat belted in the driver's seat of the cab, which was on its side when they found him. His pupils are slightly unequal." While lifting the bloody dressing that was loosely wrapped she continued. "He has a large laceration across his forehead. He was a little combative at first but as you can see now, he's quiet. He doesn't follow commands, so we don't know the range of motion of his extremities. He hasn't spoken a word, but he moaned when we palpated his left rib cage. He's moving air well, his lung sounds are equal and clear and his abdomen is supple—there was no guarding or tenderness noted during the head to toe survey. His left humerus is deformed just superior to the elbow. His left femur's fractured about mid-shaft. There's a great deal of crepitis under the skin of that leg as well as swelling. We applied the traction splint and put a couple of cold packs over the fracture site before wrapping it. There's a couple of gauze pads under the cold packs to prevent skin burn. His last blood pressure was a hundred and seventy over ninety and his pulse is still eighty-eight. The EKG showed a normal sinus rhythm throughout the transport without any irregularities. I don't know what meds he's on, if any, or allergies. I guess that's it."

"Good job," Doctor Malley said. Leaning over with his pen light, he began showing the difference in the patient's pupil size to the new intern. "Stop back in a couple of hours and we'll let you know how he's doing."

Satisfied with her oral report, Anne stepped out of the room to finish her written report. There was no time on the scene or while en route to record anything other than the patient's vitals signs and his name from his driver's license. She'd have to complete the rest while Dale cleaned the rig. But when she walked into the hallway and saw the stretcher against the wall, she realized that Dale apparently decided to help her by finishing the paperwork himself. Every piece of equipment they brought in with the exception of the clipboard was neatly loaded on the cot just waiting to be put away. He was so funny about the run form. She often teased him that he should be a writer. And sure enough, just as she suspected, as she rolled the stretcher past the nurse's station she saw him sitting at the desk with pen in hand.

Ret had given his report to one of the other physicians and was not far behind her. "Don't look so glum," she said. "The accident wasn't your fault. Having a team of surgeons on the scene wouldn't have changed the outcome of your patient. If you let it get to you, it will eat you up and you'll be of no good to anyone."

"I know. It's not that. It's just that this is my first week doing this job and I've all ready had a slew of people die in front of me. First, I had a house fire with five kids all under the age of five, the grandmother, the dog and a bird. Then we were on a call at one of those car factories up on Edison where these guys were inspecting the cement sewer system. Somebody hit the lift lever by accident and lopped off one of the worker's head and the other guy's leg. The first thing I saw when we ran into the factory was this man running toward me with a lopped off leg in his arms, stuttering as he was trying to tell me where the remainder of these workers were at.

I'll never forget it. Then a few days later we had this guy out in Bedford at some little shop who had been dead for a couple of days. The janitor found him when he came in to clean over the weekend. That was pleasant. And now this! I don't think I'm cut out for this kind of work. I thought it would be different somehow. I wanted to help people who were sick and stuff. But every time I get there—they're already dead. And then," he chuckled, "the other day—when I was sitting in the parking lot of a drug store waiting for Rick and sort of dozing off—this bird flies into the side mirror of the ambulance right next to me. Then he started flapping his wings trying to right himself. I thought he was going to fly right into the rig and peck my eyes out. I'm not kidding. It scared me half to death. As soon as he flew off, I started looking for Alfred Hitchcock. I knew he must be looming in the corner somewhere."

Initially Anne sat sympathetic and silent, listening to Ret as he recalled his dreadful initiation into the field that she thoroughly enjoyed; for she knew it wasn't always so gruesome. But then when he got to the part of the bird at the drug store, she couldn't but help laugh out loud.

"Ret, you poor thing," she chuckled. "I know it gets kind'a rough sometimes. And I have to admit, that bird thing is kind of weird. Just ride it out for a while. It's not a glamorous job and the pay's not that great but it has its rewards."

"We'll see. Hey, by the way—where's my scissors?"

"Didn't I give them back to you?"

"No. Come on, Anne—I just bought those."

"Settle down," she smiled. "If I can't find them, I'll buy you a new pair."

Dale stepped through the doors from the ER entrance into the ambulance bay. "Hey, Ret, how's it going?"

"Other than Anne losing my brand new bandage scissors, I'm okay."

"I told you, I'd buy you a new pair," she grinned.

"Sorry, pal. I'd let you take the pair from our rig but she probably lost those too."

"I did not," she laughed. "They're around here somewhere."

"They're like socks that disappear in the dryer. We must go through a pair of scissors a week," he jeered. "Come on, missy—let's go back to the station. Maybe there's a pair in the supply cabinet. I want to grab my Harry Chapin tape anyway. I heard on the radio this morning that he died in a car crash yesterday in Jericho, New York. I think we should listen to it—as a commemoration."

"Man. You guys are cold," Ret soberly declared. The electric doors opened, then Rick walked out into the bay as he spoke. "Rick, is this right to you? Here we just brought this guy in and now these guys want to go listen to the tape of some dead singer, who just died in a car crash yesterday!"

"So, what's your point," Rick smiled. "You got'ta loosen up Ret. We didn't cause that accident to happen."

"Nope. It's just Newton's Law of Motion," Dan interjected. "Stationary objects stay stationary and objects of motion stay in motion. It's the result of someone not paying attention and kinetic energy—mass times velocity, times two."

"That guy in the semi would be dead too if he wasn't wearing a seat belt," Rick offered. "He looks rough now, but we've seen worse pull through. Personally, I thought it was a good call."

While driving to the station, Anne told Dale of the calls and events that compiled Ret's introduction into the world of EMS. Then as they pulled onto the parking lot and stopped they noticed Robbie's car and another car that they didn't recognize. Dale jumped out and went into the station to get his tape from his duffle bag. Anne waited in the rig. A minute or two had passed when a fluttering sound drew her attention. Turning the radio down, she strained to detect its direction. Dale came out of the station with his tape in hand and hopped back up into the rig.

"What are you looking at?"

"Can't you hear that fluttering?" she asked, still concentrating on finding the source.

Dale sat still for a second. "It sounds like it's coming from the bushes next to the station. Let's check it out."

They both got out of the rig and slowly walked toward the bushes. The fluttering grew louder as they approached. "It's a bird of some kind," Anne whispered. "It looks like it's caught." Carefully she reached her hand through the branches and leaves toward the bird.

"Watch out!" Dale barked, hoping to startle her. "That thing might bite your hand—or peck your eyes out," he giggled.

"Be quiet. You'll scare the bird," Anne snapped playfully.

"Well, I think we found Ret's bird. It looks like it's seizing. Maybe it's got a head injury from hitting its head on the mirror—or maybe it's just been drinking the water from the city's supply."

Anne knew that Dale's pointed wit referred to the large concentration of seizure patients they ran on. It wasn't so much that they all lived in the City of Lancemen or that there was anything really wrong with the water. It was just that a good portion of their repeat seizure patients also had a history of alcoholism, who didn't eat on a regular basis or take their medication. Instead, they just drank.

"Hush," she whispered as she lifted the bird out of the brush. "It's a pigeon."

"Hey! What are you guys doing?" Robbie burst in, after sneaking up behind them.

Anne jumped. "I hate you guys so much," she said, clenching her teeth.

"Annie. Annie. Now is that any way to talk to your boss?" Robbie laughed. "Carol, come on over here and meet a couple of our finest paramedics," he said to the blonde woman standing behind him. "This is Dale Martin and his partner, who you see holding the flopping bird, is Angela Gates. But she goes by Anne. This is Carol, a new employee."

"It looks like your bird's having a seizure," Carol said softly. "Let me go and call our vet. We call him all the time. He's real good about helping over the phone."

"Well, this should be interesting," Dale smiled.

"Just ignore them, Carol," Anne said, bringing the bird into the station.

Robbie shrugged his shoulders jokingly at Dale. "What'd we do?"

Anne stood in the center of the station's living room, once a psychiatrist's office, holding the bird out to protect its wings. This pigeon's been seizing a long time, she thought. I wonder if it will ever be able to fly again.

"The vet said to start an IV and give him some valium," Carol said as she hung up the phone.

"How much valium?" Anne asked.

"I can't remember the exact amount," Carol admitted shyly. "But it can't be much."

"Where in the world do you start an IV on a bird?" Anne asked lifting its wing. "I'm not starting an IV. It would take forever to find a vein. I'll just give it IM."

Robbie and Dale stood on each side of Anne, watching to see her next move.

"Just don't stand there, you guys—go draw up some valium."

"Now don't get testy, mother hen," Dale chuckled. After going into the back room, he came out with a syringe of valium and an alcohol swab from a spare drug box. Anne set the bird on the back counter and held it as still as she could with one hand. Dale handed her the alcohol swab. She looked for a place to wipe the small white square, to prepare the area of injection as she normally would for a human.

"Oh for heaven's sake," she said, wiping between its feathers. Picking the syringe from the counter, she pushed the needle into the breast of the bird thinking that it would be the meatiest part, then squirted about one centimeter in. Within seconds the bird stopped seizing.

"Praise you, Jesus," she sighed.

Smiling, Dale looked at Robbie and asked, "So, how do we fill out the drug form? It has to have a name of the patient, doesn't it?"

"Not this time. Just fill in the words—stock replacement. I'll take the box over to the hospital myself."

"Good job, Anne," Carol offered. "If you want—I'll take the pigeon home with me until he's well enough to fly."

"Thanks, Carol. He does look a little dazed. I don't know if it's from the prolonged seizure activity or from the valium," she smiled.

The wall phone over the desk in the living room rang. Dale answered it.

"Come on, Anne, we have a woman in labor. You're in the back if she's ready to deliver. You know how I hate these calls with women's issues."

She looked at Carol and snidely grinned while washing her hands. "The only time they hate dealing with women's issues is when there's a problem with it. Other than that—it's their favorite subject, if you know what I mean." After grabbing the towel from the bundle off the shelf next to the sink she hurried toward the door while drying her hands. As soon as she stepped outside she called out to Dale, "You might as well drive, Dale. I'll take the back."

The address given by the dispatcher was on the other side of town. It was late afternoon but traffic moved well. Almost every car they passed had yielded to the right and stopped. As they approached the neighborhood of the call address, Anne said each of the street names out loud.

"Oakwood. Elmwood. The next street is Scottwood. We're looking for 384 Scottwood." Dale turned off the siren as they turned onto the residential street.

"It looks like it's going to be the house up on the right—where those people are in the driveway," Dale said as he eased off the gas and started to brake. The rig stopped. Anne jumped out, opened the side door and grabbed the orange box.

She walked toward the man standing next to the passenger side of the parked car and noticed a woman sitting inside. The woman, who was dressed in a fully draped moo moo, moved the folds of fabrics as if she had lost something.

"I think she already delivered," he said. "We tried to get to the hospital—but it looks like we didn't quite make it."

"Better grab the OB kit," Anne called back to Dale.

After setting the medical box down on the driveway next to the car, she pulled out a pair of sterile gloves. "Is this your first baby?" she asked.

"No," the woman answered. "It's our third. I think I felt her fall out. At least I hope it was a her. We already have two boys," she smiled. It was easy to see that the woman was trying to remain calm for her husband's sake who seemed very nervous. Anne quickly unbuttoned the large draped gown from the waist on down. Reaching underneath the fabric, she began a search and rescue mission by feeling from the vaginal area where the umbilical cord began and followed it down until she felt the infant at the other end.

"I found her—hopefully her," she smiled at the woman. Dale opened the OB kit as she lifted the infant toward the dress opening. As soon as the cool air breezed against the baby's skin, a cry rang out.

"It's a little girl, mamma. And she looks just fine," Anne grinned. Then to their surprise after hearing Anne's herald, a clamor of applause rose from a small group of neighbors gathered at the end of the driveway, blending with the baby's first vocal complaint of discomfort. The crew and the couple had all been so occupied with the new life that was tucked warmly in the folds of her mother's dress, that they hadn't even noticed the group until the joyful clapping began. Dale smiled while handing the receiving blanket from the kit to the mother who took it gratefully and wrapped it around her bundle. Anne handed the scalpel to the father and showed him where to cut the umbilical cord.

"Right between those two clamps," she instructed.

He seemed to be so proud to be part of his child's birth. After carefully and nervously cutting the cord, he took the bulb syringe from Anne exchanging it for the scalpel. Seconds later, after following her instructions, he inserted the tip of the bulb into the infant's mouth and nose and suctioned the unwanted mucus like a pro. Dale wrapped up the rest of the OB kit and grabbed the orange box. A neighbor who had been at the end of the driveway helped bring the stretcher next to the car. Anne helped position the mother and baby once they were in the rig. Dale stood at the back doors smiling. It had truly been a good call.

It was early morning, just before dawn. Anne walked through the lobby just outside of the emergency room at St. Luke's to see if the early edition of the newspaper had come out yet. A copy of printed events could be seen behind a clear sheet of Plexiglas in the red metal stand in front of her. She stepped closer to see if it was yesterday's paper or today's latest edition. Bold letters across the headline told of a hotel disaster in Kansas City, Missouri where more than a hundred had died and even more were injured. Dale came up behind her.

"I already bought a paper," he said.

"Oh my word," Anne sighed. "What a terrible accident. How devastating it must be for the families of the people who were killed and hurt. Can you imagine going on a call like that? Where would you even start?"

"It'd be a mess. That's why we go to those mock disasters. Now let's get out of here. I'm beat. Four hours of sleep is not enough for this boy."

"Poor Ret," she continued, while following Dale out to the rig. "If we had something like that happen here—after the week he's had—he'd quit for sure."

"Quit babying him. He's all right."

"I'm sure he is. But you know, not everyone's cut out to do this kind of work. Personally, I can't think of anything else I'd rather do with my life right now—but I know this job has changed me and I know it's made its mark. When I go home to the farm to visit my family, it's very clear that I'm not the same person that I was before I started working here. Even though my family doesn't say anything—I can see it in their eyes."

"How can you be the same person, Anne? You scrape people off the street for a living, for crying out loud. You've seen things over and over that normal people never see. And I'm not saying that you're not normal, so don't even say it."

"But see, that's what I mean," she began to explain. "Remember that girl from the Scouting Explorer group that rode with us when we picked up that guy out in Bedford? The one that was hit by a car while riding his bike? Remember? We pulled him out of a swamp that he flew into next to the road. There probably wasn't a bone in his body that wasn't broken. Anything that could excrete out of a person, did. And I ended up intubating him before we got to the hospital. Boy, did she turn green and then she was as white as a ghost. I thought for a few minutes we were going to lose her, too. I told her to go up front and sit. I didn't have time to take care of him and her too. She said she was all right—and she stuck it out. Then, when we got to the hospital and they pronounced him dead, she kept repeating over and over—he died, he died. It was pretty clear that she did not handle that call well. But to us, it was just a normal call. In fact, it was a great call. Not because someone died or even got hurt, but because there was a lot to do and it was challenging. How normal is that?"

"You're making too much out of this, Anne," he sighed. "You've been doing this longer than me. And you already know the answer. It's what we do. Maybe we are a little different. You, more so than me," he teased. "But everyone is different in some respect. We're all made to do something. We have a purpose—that's what you always say. Well this is our purpose. And we enjoy it because it's what we're good at; not because we like the gore. After a while we don't even notice that—so let it go. Let's just go back to the station and get some sleep."

"All right," she yawned. "I guess maybe I just think too much about things."

"I guess," he replied. While driving to the station, as if deep in thought he added, "You know, it's been a while since you've gone home to the farm. You always get this way when you miss Zigfrid the dog. Who would name their dog Zigfrid anyway? Now that's not normal."

"It's not Zigfrid," she laughed. "It's Ziggy. And you're right, maybe I'll call Aunt Ruth tomorrow and see what they're doing this weekend. Thanks, Dale."

"No problem. Zigfrid—what a stupid name for a dog," he laughed.

Summer was flying by. And before long Anne noticed her days off were filled with a stir of activities. In between chaperoning different camp outings for the youth group at church, she went to cookouts, baby-sat for Tracy and Roger so they could get away, and even went out on an occasional date of her own. So it wasn't until mid August that she was finally able to get away to spend a few days at home in Summerville. Now, while sitting on the same chair that she'd sat on at the dinner table since she was young, she sighed quietly while admiring her family. Aunt Ruth and Uncle Henry both looked wonderful, but the years of hard work on the farm and the fact that they were just getting older was starting to show in their faces. The boys looked more and more like men with each visit. Aaron, the baseball enthusiast, was excited about Ernie Harwell being inducted into the Baseball Hall of Fame. "He received a standing ovation in Cooperstown," he bragged. "He's the one who said, 'Baseball is a tongue-tied kid from Georgia growing up to be an announcer and praising the Lord for showing him the way to Cooperstown.' He's a Christian ya know and sometimes he speaks at the Sunday Morning Baseball Chapel." Anne couldn't imagine Aaron ever leaving the farm he loved so much, but to be a Baseball Chaplain, to him—would be like a dream come true.

Jacob and Corinne's little ones were growing like weeds. And Pete's plan of college to become a veterinarian was finally becoming a reality. He especially enjoyed the story of the seizing pigeon. Then there was Ziggy,

Anne thought, who still had puppy energy. Only now he was about forty pounds heavier and when he came to greet her, he almost knocked her down. Good old faithful Ziggy—he had not forgotten her.

As she looked at each laughing chatting face of her family, she realized individually they all had busy lives, but most of it still revolved in some manner around the farm. Without a doubt, she was sincerely content with the direction that her life had taken, yet it only took the delightful smell of Aunt Ruth's early morning breakfast to remind her of how much she missed waking up in the small bedroom, in her white wicker bed. Then, for the first time while watching her family busy with their routine chores, she felt left out of the farm activities, like a spectator. She understood that it had been her choice to move away. But how did she become a visitor? It was a self-imposed feeling that she did not like—it was one she'd have to change.

Keith Green was becoming one of Anne's favorite Christian music artists. Before leaving the farm, her brother James gave her the tape, "For Him Who Has Ears," as an early birthday present. Sliding the cassette into the player of her car, she turned up the volume and began singing along. Glancing above the horizon, she noticed that the sky was starting to cloud up. Rain had been predicted for early evening and it was greatly needed. She took a sip of root beer from the bottle she bought at the gas station just out side of Summerville then set it back into the cup holder. In another thirty minutes or so she'd be in Lancemen.

It was starting to sprinkle. While reaching to her left to turn on the windshield wipers, she noticed a seagull coming toward her car. "What in the world is he doing out in the middle of nowhere? There's not even a lake near here," she said to herself. Suddenly, the bird smashed into her windshield and for a second, just sort of stuck in place while the windshield wiper scraped over its head. It looked almost like a cartoon image—then it fell off. She pulled over to the side of the road and sat dazed for a second. "What's with these birds," she whispered. After looking in the rear view mirror, she spotted it behind her in the middle of the road. She started to get out of the car to see if the poor thing was even still alive, when a cement truck whisked by and ran it over. "Good grief! Even Carol's vet can't do anything to help that bird. It's flat as a pancake." After re-hooking her seat belt she put the car in drive and pulled back onto the road toward Lancemen. Now that was weird, she thought. Wait'll I tell Ret.

The next morning when Anne woke up it was pouring rain. After her morning shower she got dressed in her uniform, applied her make up, scrunched her hair and grabbed the bright orange rain coat from the hook behind her door. While driving to work, the rain began to let up turning into a slight drizzle. Then by the time she reached the station, normally a fifteen minute drive, it had stopped altogether and the sun came out. She parked her car then picked up her purse. Dale walked out of the station carrying a large emesis basin; a rectangular bowl that was normally used for vomit patients, but instead was full of supplies to restock the rig. She waved then grabbed her duffle bag from the back seat of her car.

"How was your visit home?" he asked.

"It was good. Let me go and call in before I'm marked late—then I'll be right back."

"Bring a bundle of towels with you," he called out.

Dale was sitting on the bench seat in the patient compartment putting simple oxygen masks and non-rebreathers in the cabinet when Anne came out of the station. "Boy I just made it," she said, smiling. "Here's your towels. Where do you want them?"

"Just set them on the jump seat. Looks like you brought the sun with you," he said sweetly. "It was pouring rain a minute ago. Then as soon as you pulled up, it quit raining."

"It seems that way, I guess," she said, scratching her head. "But I'm sure it's just a coincidence." She paused for a second waiting for his rebuttal. Instead, he quietly turned and took a couple of the towels from the seat to put them in the cabinet.

"Why are you being nice to me?" she asked.

"What are you talking about, I'm always nice to you," he grinned.

"Yeah right, sure you are," she replied. Shyly, she moved her hand over and pushed the towels onto the floor.

"See—you start this stuff," he lightheartedly scolded. "And then I'm the bad guy."

She chuckled, then picked up and refolded the towels. "I hope they got some of this rain at home. They sure need it. Oh, I brought you some of Aunt Ruth's fried chicken. We raise the chickens ourselves, you know. Well, they do anyway."

"Oh, feeling a little left out are we?"

"A little," she confessed. "But I'm working through it. What else do we need in the rig?"

"I think we're all set. I got here early so I've already called in the station supplies. They hired a new guy at the supply center down in the main office. He seems pretty cool."

"Oh yeah? What's his name?"

"Ronny. We saw him last week. Remember he was that tall skinny black dude sitting at the table in Robbie's office filling out the app?"

"Oh yeah, Now I remember. And he had that quiet, funny laugh like that cartoon dog on TV."

"Unit Six," the dispatcher's voice barked over the radio. "Unit Six come in for a code."

"You ridden or driven sister?"

"You can drive. I'll go lock up the station. I need to grab my purse anyway," Anne answered before dashing off.

The dispatcher reported the call to be a man complaining of chest pain. The location was north of town in a new subdivision. Even though Dale and Anne knew their way around most of the city, they got a little turned around when they first drove into this unexplored area. The street signs were dark wood with fancy painted letters that made it hard to read unless you were right in front of them. And because the sub was still under construction, some of the houses didn't even have numbers.

"There it is—Silver Birch," Anne said, pointing to the right. "Our address is 145."

Dale pulled onto the new driveway. The house was a two story brick with cream shutters. The sidewalk curved passed a small group of freshly planted bushes. The lawn was bare of grass so they left the stretcher on the sidewalk and entered the house carrying the boxes and oxygen bottle. A concerned looking woman greeted them at the door, then led them upstairs. As they followed her into a large bedroom, she told them that she and her husband called for the ambulance because her father-in-law, who was eighty-two, had complained of having chest pain; but now he was claiming that the pain was gone. Entering the room, they saw a gray haired man sitting in an overstuffed chair in the corner of the room. Another man sat on the bed next to him, gently rubbing the old man's arm.

"How are you doing, sir?" Anne asked.

"I'm doing just fine," he barked. " I don't know what the fuss is all about. I just had a little indigestion, that's all."

"Dad, you said your chest was hurting," the man sitting on the bed spoke up.

"It was. It was just a little indigestion, I said—and that's all it was."

"Well sometimes indigestion might feel like chest pain. I think your family just wants to make sure you're all right," Anne smiled.

"Well I am all right. What's your name?" he asked.

"Anne. I'm a paramedic."

"And what about him?" he asked, pointing at Dale.

"His name is Dale and he's a paramedic too. What's your name?" she asked.

"Ken Bailey. And this is my son, Gerald and his wife, Marilyn. Now that we all know who we are—what happens next?"

Anne glanced at Dale for a second to keep from giggling. Mr. Bailey's crabby disposition was precious and amusing to her. "Well we're here because your family was concerned because of your chest discomfort, which we've already established was just a little indigestion. But since we're already here, why don't you let me take your blood pressure and hook you up to the heart monitor so we can write that down on our report. That way our boss won't think that all we did was stand around and chit chat about how fine you are."

"Well, I guess that would be all right. I certainly don't want to get anybody in trouble."

After reaching into the orange box, Anne grabbed the blood pressure cuff then wrapped it around Mr. Bailey's arm. After inserting the tips of the stethoscope into her ears, she leaned over while squeezing the bulb, to inflate the cuff. Watching the dial, which would give the measured reading of the pressure exerted by the blood on the wall of vessel during the highest pulse wave, she slowly deflated the cuff. Removing the stethoscope tips from her ears she stood up smiling, "One forty six over eighty eight. That's not bad."

"I told you, I was just fine," he snorted. He watched as Anne snapped the electrodes onto the end of the monitor cables. "Now what are you doing?"

"I'm going to put these three sticky pads on your chest in different places so that I can make sure that your ticker is ticking when it's supposed to," she replied.

After pulling off the paper covers from the electrode patch, she placed each pad in the correct position while asking him about recent daily activities that could have contributed to today's incident. "Now before today, have you had any problems? Are you eating good? Are you having any trouble sleeping?"

"Well I don't think I'm having any trouble."

"Dad, yes you are," Marilyn spoke up. "Dad's been living with us for nearly five years now and up until now his health has been fine. I don't know if it's the move into this house a few weeks ago that's done it, but last week he started waking up in the middle of the night. Then he gets up and wanders through the house for hours—and then he sleeps all day. It's like he has his day's and night's switched."

"We're concerned that he's going to hurt himself or maybe even go outside while we're asleep," Gerald added.

"Oh, so your nocturnal," Anne said, teasing Mr. Bailey.

"Nocturnal? What the hell's that?"

Anne chuckled. "It's when you're awake at night and sleep during the day—like an owl. You're like a wise old owl."

Silently, she studied his face as he pushed out his lower lip, digesting what was said. Then he smiled as if the morsel was enjoyable, then asked a question that seemed quite odd and totally unrelated. "Say—how do you get a one armed man out of a tree?"

"I don't know," Anne replied, puzzled at where this was going. "How do you get a one armed man out of a tree?"

"You wave to him," he chuckled. "Say—I believe my chest pain really has gone."

"Dad," the couple chorused.

"Oh, go on. There's no need to fuss. Would you want strangers poking you with needles?"

"Mr. Bailey, I hardly think we're strangers; and really, it would be a good idea if we took you to the hospital so the doctor could look at you. And, even though your EKG and everything else looks good, I should probably start an IV on the way to the hospital, just in case your chest pain returns. What do you say?"

"Well, I guess it'd be all right. But you only get one chance at the IV."

"That's all she'll need," Dale offered. "IV's are her specialty." Looking toward Gerald he continued, "I've finished writing his medical history and medications down. I'll set the containers back on the dresser before we go and bring in the stretcher."

Anne and Mr. Bailey had become fast friends. Growing up she truly adored her grandmother and supposed that was the reason the retirees found favor with her. She often found herself perched on a soap box as their advocate, standing in the gap for the injustices she felt were dealt to them. "These people have worked hard all of their lives—and now in their Golden Years—most of them live in poverty and get the worst medical care," was often part of her speech of vindication. Transferring the elderly back and forth over the years from hospital to nursing home while working for Mercy had opened her eyes to the pitiful treatment some patients received. Some patients from low income nursing homes had cockroaches crawling across their bedding and flies on their faces and on their food as they sat with glazed expression in oversized highchairs left to fend for themselves. Some facilities reeked of urine and stool. Others had the patient's TV or radio chained to the night-stand next to the bed to prevent the staff from stealing the luxuries brought in from outside. But it wasn't just the poorly paid, undereducated staff that was at fault; for many of them shared Anne's thoughts and cared for these people, even though they felt they were alone in their mission. Many times it was the family members that had dropped the responsibility of caring for the patients, sending them to these facilities without so much as even a holiday visit. But Mr. Bailey was fortunate. His family had a place for him and he was mentally strong.

Dinner would have to wait. Anne could almost hear Dale's tummy rumble as they left the hospital and Mr. Bailey for their next call. A young girl at a riding stable in Bedford had fallen from a horse. The person calling in the incident told the dispatcher the girl had briefly lost consciousness but now she was awake. They were unsure of her injuries. Anne jumped up onto the driver's seat and buckled her seat belt. It would take twenty minutes or so to get to Bedford this time of day. They were somewhat familiar with the area of the riding stable and knew it was a good distance. The siren wailed and yelped until they finally turned onto the main road where the riding school sat several hundred feet back. As soon as they pulled through the entrance and down the driveway they saw a couple of the instructors waving and pointing to the gate behind the main building in front of the barn. One of the women approached the ambulance then called out, stating that the patient was on a path just south of the largest corral. She motioned with her arms, then ran in the direction for the crew to follow. Turning off the emergency lights, Anne drove through the corral gate and around several jumps toward a back opening that led to the path where their injured equestrienne was. She noticed a young Bay that was tied to the fence as he whinnied and danced from the right to left.

"He looks pretty guilty," she smiled. "I'll bet he's somehow behind our patient's spill."

She pulled up along side the opposite fence line and stopped. Then the woman who had followed them back came up to the driver's side of the rig.

"She's on the path just on the other side of the fence," she panted. "I'll show you where."

"Okay," Anne replied. "Let us grab a back board and our stretcher."

"We didn't want to move her until you got here," the woman continued. "She seems fine now but she was out for a few minutes and we didn't want to take a chance."

Anne opened the back doors and unlatched the stretcher as she listened. Dale came around with the orange box and helped pull out the cot before grabbing a backboard. Anne jumped up inside the ambulance and pulled a cervical collar from the cabinet. After pushing a roll of three inch tape into her pant's pocket, she tossed a set of towel rolls to Dale. Now they were ready.

They followed the woman a short distance down the path where a group of girls, all about the age of twelve or thirteen, sat next to and around another young girl who was laying flat on her back in the center of the dusty path. Two other women stood a few feet from the group. As soon as they saw Anne and Dale with the stretcher they instructed the girls to get up and make room. Dale introduced himself and began asking the patient, Sarah, questions about her fall. After he'd completed his head to toe survey he placed the cervical collar gently around her neck, then asked for volunteers amongst the girls in the group to help backboard Sarah. Even with the teasing and giggling between Dale and the girls, they all did fine. A couple of them voiced an interest in becoming paramedics like Anne when they grew up. Sarah had no complaints other than a sore rump but the instructor was adamant about having her transported and evaluated at the hospital.

"Is that your Bay?" Anne asked, as they rolled the stretcher toward the ambulance.

"Yeah. His name is Bailey."

"That's funny," she replied. "Our last patient's, last name was Bailey."

"Well if he dumps me again," Sarah smiled, "his name's going to be Alpo."

"Now, Sarah, you know you don't mean that," one of the instructors chuckled. "I'll call your mom and let her know you're on the way to the hospital. She said she'd meet you there. We'll see you next week. I'm sure you'll be fine."

Anne and Dale lifted the stretcher up into the rig.

"Here comes the scary part," he teased. The line he'd picked up from Bill was perfect for medically stable young patients like Sarah. It always brought out a giggle and the same "Don't drop me!" response. Now that Sarah was safely secured in the patient compartment with Dale attending, Anne hopped up onto the driver's seat to begin the trip to Lancemen General. She remembered how heavy the traffic was on the way out to the riding school and opted to take an alternate set of roads back to Lancemen. The direction she'd chosen was a little more winding but it was just as smooth and would probably save time.

Sarah and Dale had quite a conversation going in between him taking her vitals. He had never ridden a horse in his life so he had many questions—and Sarah, without hesitation, seemed to have the answers. After traveling east about six or seven miles, Anne turned up the radio so Sarah could hear the music. They passed by an old barn that marked the boundary line of a large farm and apple orchard where she occasionally stopped. The family that owned the farm grew apples, strawberries, asparagus, corn and pumpkins and sold them roadside, during each crop's season. Suddenly she noticed that the easy country road seemed to have a traffic jam up ahead. After lifting her foot from the gas pedal she slowly came up behind a group of cars that had stopped in front of her. "What in the world?" she wondered aloud. Because the ambulance seats sat up higher than a car's and offered more of a birds-eye view, she was able to see what was going on further up on the road. With that as an advantage, it only took a moment for her to realize what had caused the problem. The farmer's turkeys, which were the biggest she'd ever seen—nearly the size of an ostrich she thought, had gotten loose and were now blocking the entire road. All three of them stood boldly, wing to wing—apparently on a mission or so it seemed, for they were unquestionably steadfast in their decision and would not move.

The woman who sat in the first car facing the feathered barricade tooted her horn, but would not get out. Then a man in the car behind her impatiently emerged flinging his arms in an attempt to shoo the gobbling trio. His plan failed. Angrily, the team drove him back as he scurried to his car and around to the passenger side where he stood tapping on the window to get his young rider's attention. A child in the passenger's seat followed the man's orders, presumably her father, and unlocked the car door. Anne watched, giggling, while he reached into the car, then backed out with a sandwich baggy full of a familiar round cereal. With a friendly smile he dipped his hand into the bag, then the tossed out the tiny round morsels like a farmer feeding his chickens. Obviously, he thought he could lure the turkeys from the road with the dry crunchy treat, but they weren't the least bit interested. Each emotion he felt was clearly etched on his face including the frown as he watched the cereal floating in the air for a few seconds before it dropped to the ground. Frustrated, he got back into his car and laid on the horn until the woman in the first car slowly nudged her way between two of the birds. The man followed so close behind, it was difficult to tell if he was pushing her car or just riding on the bumper.

Now it was Anne's turn. She wondered where the farmer was who owned the turkeys and wondered why he had not come to the rescue of the people who had slowed and stopped. She tried to get Dale's attention to share in the comedy but then decided it would only spark Sarah's curiosity. They had placed her on the backboard to guard her spine and prevent movement in the event there really was an underlying injury. Twisting her neck to see these huge birds would not be beneficial to her, or fair if she could not see them for herself.

As Anne inched closer to the birds she thought about Uncle Henry and knew he'd be pretty impressed with the size of these Toms. Then the largest one in the center took a step back but held his ground while angrily gobbling away. Anne reached over to the siren knob and gave it a quick twist back and forth. Whoop, whoop. Instantly, the turkeys chorused in return—gobble, gobble. Whoop, whoop—gobble, gobble—whoop, whoop. She was so entertained with the duet that she almost forgot about Sarah. Then she heard Dale's voice, and remembered they were supposed to be on their way to the hospital. Slowly and gently she pushed her foot down on the execrator. Little by little she began creeping toward the plumed, gallopavo gang, trying to pass through without ruffling any more feathers than she already had. "Oh, what a hoot that was." she said amusingly to herself.

When they arrived at the hospital, Anne pulled the rig under the canopy in front of the emergency entrance and stopped. Sarah's mother was outside waiting. Her face looked drawn with worry as she held tight to the sweater draped across her arms.

"She's just fine," Anne said. "Come around to the back doors of the rig and see for yourself." By her expression, Anne knew she expected to see a battered and broken child. Instead and to her relief, she saw a smiling giddy youngster strapped to the backboard on the stretcher.

"Sarah, are you all right?"

"Yes, Mom. This is Dale. He and Anne took very good care of me—and now Dale knows everything about horseback riding."

"Why is she on that board?"

"It's just a precaution," Dale answered. "It keeps her back and neck from moving until the doctor clears her of any spinal injury. But she's doing great. Really." He slid down the bench seat, jumped out and stood next to Anne as she unlocked the stretcher to roll it out.

"Ready, Sarah?" he asked.

"Yep," she giggled. "Here comes the scary part!"

Anne's stomach grumbled as she stood outside next to the rig preparing the stretcher for their next call. It was mid afternoon and they hadn't had breakfast or lunch. She wished, just this once, Dale would write his run form out a little faster; but something inside her knew that he wouldn't. He was meticulous about his paperwork to the point that he even saved copies of the good calls, to critique them later. While buckling the pillow down in place with the stretcher strap, she looked up and noticed one of the company's vehicles pull up along side the curb and stop. Ronny, the new supply person, got out and walked toward her.

"Hey, Ronny, how you doing?" she asked.

"I'm doing better now."

She studied his face. "You do look a little frazzled—what happened?"

"Well, I went out to the station in Lakeview to drop off their supplies and pick up their dirty linen. On the way there, I was driving past that pond where they have all those ducks and geese. You know—people are always stopping to feed them."

"The hatchery?"

"Yeah. So anyway, I'm just driving along thinking about stuff—when all of a sudden I ran over something. Well right off I'm thinking, oh my God I just ran over a kid! So I pulled over to the side of the road and got out to look behind me. And then I see all these geese spinning in the middle of the road—and feathers flying everywhere. A whole bunch of em. Just like a bowling strike of geese. Then this lady comes running out from I don't know where and she's crying and yelling at me about running over these geese—like they were her babies or something. I tried to tell her that I didn't do it on purpose, but she wasn't listening to a word I said. I didn't know what she expected me to do. So I just got back in the van—and drove to the station. Your buddies, Jerry and Roger, were there. I told them what happened and they both started laughing. Man, I thought—there goes my job. That lady's going to call and complain and that'll be it. I still got some feathers caught up in the front of the van by the radiator and on the grill."

Anne looked over at the van and saw a couple of feathers sticking out from under the bumper move in the breeze, then flutter loose and float away. She tried not to laugh. It was obvious from the tone in his voice that he was still quite shaken by his experience. "Merve's a pretty cool boss, Ronny. He's not going to fire you over something like that."

"That's what Jerry said, too. Man, that was the weirdest thing. I was standing at the side of the road—just listening for that song that they always play at the beginning of that Alfred Hitchcock show."

"It's called the "Marionette's Funeral March". I took piano lessons for a while. It was one of the songs in my book."

"It was a funeral march, all right. Those geese were some dead ducks, for sure."

"Well I don't know what to say, Ronny," she chuckled. "There seems to be a lot of weird things going on with the birds lately." Instantly, the turkeys came to mind. Surely, under the circumstances, she thought he of all people would be interested in hearing her story of the farmer's mighty trio. So in a brief synopsis, she began sharing the sequence of events that occurred with the turkeys, the sea gull, the pigeon and lastly, Ret's bird—who really, the series of fowl events had actually started with.

"No kidding," he said, shaking his head. "Man, now that's more than just weird. That's down right spooky. What in the world's going on?"

"I'm not sure. It's probably just a coincidence. But then, we may never know. Maybe they're just supposed to be—avian wonders."

CHAPTER 26

THE BIG FALL

Mountain climbing dates back to about 1850. Initially, the systematic sport of climbing began with a British group of men who were aided by professional guides. Since that time, a number of men and women have joined climbing societies or have enrolled in climbing schools to learn what it takes to safely scale the dusty ridges while meeting the crusty challenges of nature.

Anne's partner, Dale, had never gone to a climbing school nor did he express any desire to belong to a society. She never heard him claim any hope to be like any of the great or famous climbers that he read of, nor did he display a hunger to reach the summit of Mount Everest or the Alps. For him, rock climbing was merely a passionate hobby that took seed in him during a maiden expedition with his older brother, Frank, and a few buddies about six years ago. Since then, he said they'd made several trips out west to Wyoming to climb the Grand Teton and Devil's Tower. Clearly, each jaunt he described was full of fun as well as a personal challenge, as each agreeable bead of sweat and sporting burst of laughter blended beneath the majestic skies of the old west. And while intently listening to the impressive events that he shared, Anne's interest in rock climbing grew; but at the same time she was amused, for each grand tale seemed to end with the same set of sentences, to the point that she could easily recite them herself—word for word. "Man, that was such a fun climb. Really, Anne, the ranges in Wyoming are just incredible. Without a doubt, they are one of my favorite places on earth to be."

While Anne knew the area in and around Lancemen County didn't have any mountainous regions, she often heard Dale talk about a place not far to the east called Grand Ledge. He said it was a good place for beginners to learn, as well as a decent place for experienced climbers to keep in shape for the big climbs. Anne remembered him saying that during the spring and fall months it was easier to rock climb because it was cooler. So as the summer ended, she began hinting every now and again how she'd like to take one of the shorter trips to Grand Ledge—just to find out what this love affair with a rope and the uplifted layers of rock was all about. To her, somehow, this new adventure would be a tradeoff for the white water raft trip she missed out on with the church's singles group; even though a few months later she was able to join the same group for a day of sky diving, which she enjoyed very much once her parachute safely opened. Most of the time she blamed the boys on the farm for her appetite for adventurous excursions, though she knew it was more than likely something innate that was passed on from her parents.

"All right. I'll take you," Dale conceded, after about a dozen or so hints. "I'll set up a trip for next week. How about Tuesday?"

"Tuesday will be perfect. And I promise I won't bug you about it anymore."

"Yeah. I almost believe that one," he chuckled.

Tuesday was slow coming for Anne. But she kept her promise. Dale made sure of that, as each curious expression from her was cut off with a good-natured response from him—"Wait until Tuesday."

Anne was delighted when the morning of the great climb finally arrived. They agreed to meet at the station in downtown Lancemen at 11:00. At 10:40 she stood in the parking lot next to her car wearing a pale yellow tee shirt and a pair of the old gray uniform pants that she'd kept from the early days as a Basic EMT before getting her paramedic license. Since then, the company had switched to French blue pants.

The weather couldn't have been any nicer, she thought, looking skyward. The sun peaked in and out of white fluffy clouds while a cool mild breeze gently eased through. Then her attention was drawn to Dale as he pulled onto the parking lot in his little light blue car and parked next to her. She opened the passenger door of his car and got in. His tattered, loose fitting pair of jeans and dingy white tee shirt with a faded logo, seemed fine in comparison to what she had chosen to wear. She was satisfied that she'd dressed appropriately. The only thing that he took the time to look at before they left were her sneakers. He said the sole of her shoes would be important for a good climb.

With that out of the way, he backed up and pulled out onto the main road. Anne decided to save her questions until they got near their destination, as to not tire Dale or make him regret his agreement of the trip. While en route, they stopped for lunch at a drive through hamburger joint, then drove toward his parents' home where he and his brother stored their climbing gear in the garage. After swallowing the last slurp of pop through his straw, Dale set his empty cup in the holder on the floor, then mentioned in an, oh by the way fashion, that he and his father didn't have a very close relationship. Because of that, and also because he was eager to get to the climb—he just wanted to breeze in—get what they needed and breeze out. Anne sensed by his statement that it was a private matter and not open for discussion, so she let it be.

After driving several miles further, Dale flipped the turn signal switch, then pulled onto a driveway in front of a mid-sized ranch with white aluminum siding. An unattached garage sat about twenty feet from the house and had black-eyed Susan mixed with white and purple phlox running along side the wall closest to the house. Anne assumed it was his parents' home. She noticed a man dressed in dark blue work clothes standing in the yard winding up a garden hose. Then she saw a woman leaning against the rail of the back porch, shaking out a rug. The woman reminded Anne of her Aunt Ruth when she set the rug down, dust flying about, to smile and wave. Dale pulled up to the garage and stopped. After getting out of the car, he quickly introduced his mother and father to Anne, then immediately walked toward the garage to gather the equipment they needed for the day's event. Anne instantly felt a thick wall of tension, but smiled politely at his parents before joining Dale in the garage. Fumbling with the awkward feeling left by the icy introduction, she watched him take the colorful nylon rope down from the plastic coated bicycle hooks, along with a couple of canvas bags that held other gear. His movements were just as meticulous and organized, reaching for each well-cared-for piece of equipment, as they were when he cared for the sick and injured at home in Lancemen. With little conversation, Anne took the articles he handed her and placed them on the back seat of his car. Under the circumstances, she thought it was best to ask about the equipment after they reached the base of the rock faces they were to climb.

Once Dale seemed satisfied that he had what he needed, he called out to his mom that he'd see her later. That was it. Then he turned and walked toward the car where Anne stood waiting.

"We're all set," he smiled.

Anne felt a little strange as she buckled her seat belt. This was a side of Dale she'd never seen. Until today, he'd never mentioned that there was any problem between him and his dad. Maybe she was just surprised because she'd always felt that they were not only partners, but friends as well. After all, they had talked about so much since they first started working together, with some of the conversations even leaning toward a more personal nature. So why did he keep this to himself? Well whatever it was, it was a family matter and this was certainly not the time to pry, she thought. If he wanted her to know, he would have said so. After all, it wasn't like he and his dad weren't civil to each other—they just weren't overly friendly.

"Okay, Anne, I don't hate the man," Dale spoke up. Apparently he had sensed her discomfort in the quietness. "We just don't see things eye to eye—that's all. My mom says I'll understand him better when I get older. And that's all I want to say about it."

"You don't owe me an explanation, Dale. I just came here to learn about rock climbing," she smiled.

After he and Anne carried the bags and rope through a small trail not far from their parking place, Dale stood at the base of the rock and looked up at a face covered with a number of oval shaped spurs. "They call this face, Potato Chip," he said.

Anne smiled. "I can see that. It really resembles scattered giant sized chips." Then she watched as he took a multiple strapped piece of gear from the canvas bag that was set on the ground in front of his feet.

"Hey, that looks like a harness."

"That's exactly what they call it. This should fit you. Your legs go through here like this," he said, as he held it up in front of her. Holding her hands just as he had, she took the harness and put it on while he continued to explain that there were several faces of the rock they could climb that ranged in different levels of difficulty. Of course they'd take the easiest one first, so she could get a feel for the rock and her hand and foot holds. She tried to take in all that he said as he continued explaining each piece of equipment. He showed her a device that he said was for belaying. The rope would move smoothly through this while ascending or abseiling. He also showed her an item that he called a karabiner and showed her how the gate on it worked.

"Some karabiners have an open gate and some have a lockable or screw gate," he said, then continued talking while hooking onto the tie-in point of her harness. "Now I'm going to stand on the ground," he grunted, while hooking into an anchor already set into the top of the ledge, "and pull in the slack of the rope as you climb. At the beginning of each climb you say—belay up. There you go sister. Start over there. Just look for the best ledges and cracks of rock to grab hold of and stand on—and climb away."

Anne took a deep breath, then stepped over to the rock face in front of her. After looking it over, she picked a direction to start. "Belay up!"

It seemed pretty easy, she thought. But then this was one of the easiest of the faces to climb. By the end of the day they'd get harder. After all, half the fun was in the challenge.

Dale laughed. "Keep going, Anne. You're doing good. You look just like a monkey."

"A monkey? I'm not sure I like that," she said.

"Keep going, sister, you're almost to the top," he chuckled. "Just reach up and tag the anchor. When you're ready—I'll lower you down."

"Belay up," she announced, as she began her next climb. Throughout the next four faces she pushed on, enjoying every minute of digging her toes and fingertips into the cracks and crevices.

"Come on, Anne, you're almost there."

She looked up at the ridge above her. Just another three feet or so and she could call it a day, but the muscles in her thighs were so tired and sore she wasn't sure she could make it. Taking a deep breath, she stood clinging to the ledge in front of her with streams of sweat running down her face. She tried to concentrate on her breathing. Somehow, she needed to build just enough oomph to climb—a mere three more feet.

"Don't look down. Just lean back into the harness. I've got ya."

There it was—that word don't. Just as soon as he said don't—do stirred within her. She giggled to herself, knowing her stubborn nature. Now she'd have to at least have a glimpse, if not for any other reason but to settle her curiosity as to how far up she'd climbed. Turning her head, she glanced toward Dale. Thirty—maybe forty feet, she guessed. Then she swallowed hard and looked up at the anchor in the top ledge. This was a sport where you really had to trust your equipment and partner. But then that wasn't any different from working out on the highways and byways at home in Lancemen. Out there she trusted both every day of her life—so why should this be any different?

Taking a deep breath, she leaned back into the harness. A cool breeze brushed against her face and dried the salty sweat. Then it passed through her hair and touched her scalp where it was wet. She thought of how frightful she must look, then sighed indifferently as the thought of her appearance eased. It felt good to rest.

"How you doing?" Dale asked. "Are you ready to come down?"

"Not yet. Let me try—just once more. I'm so close."

"All right," he chuckled. "I knew you wouldn't give it up. Swing your body a little to get back on the wall."

Anne felt the rope move as she angled closer to the rocky face. She knew if she couldn't do it this time she'd have to come down—she was about all oomphed out. As she strained and pushed to reach the ledge that was just inches away, she looked for a rocky lip to grab and a place to position her feet. Now like a baby opossum on her mamma, she clung to the wall in front of her. Moving up a little farther, she felt her right foot slide from its hold. If she couldn't find another ridge or crevice for her foot quickly, she'd have to give up and come down. Her left leg just didn't have the strength to keep her supported much longer.

"Darn! I can't find a place to put my foot. All right Dale," she sighed. "Let me down."

"It's all right, Annie. You did better than I thought you'd do."

As soon as her feet touched the ground, her legs started jumping uncontrollably. Dale laughed. "You've got sewing machine legs. That's what they call it. It only lasts for a few minutes. Just lean over and put your hands on your knees. It'll stop."

Still in her harness, she leaned onto her knees. After a few minutes, she let go to see if the condition had passed.

"Did I really do all right?"

"Yeah. You did great! Most people don't climb five faces their first time out."

"Four and a half."

"You were close enough. I think we can say five," he smiled. "How do your legs feel now?"

"Not bad. I think the shaking's about done."

"Good. I'm going to make a quick climb before we go. This time you watch me."

Anne was a little nervous when Dale first began his climb. Her legs seemed okay now, but what if the twitching came back and she messed up? She carefully eyed each step and grip as he ascended, pulling up the slack as he moved. He was quick. The face that he climbed next to where she had left off was like a walk in the park to him. In no time he had reached the top and was back on the ground.

"That's enough. I want to get this stuff back to my folks' house, before it gets too late and my old man has a fit, if he hasn't already left for work. Besides, we still have to drive back to Lancemen."

The ride home was a mixture of tired yawns and excited chattering, on Anne's part at least. She laughed, "Oh my gosh! Do you think I'll be too sore to lift the stretcher tomorrow?"

"Yeah, if you're a sissy," he grinned.

She sat back smiling. Nothing he could say at this point would take away the joy and satisfaction she felt with this newfound sport.

The sun was setting. As they pulled back onto the driveway at Dale's parents' home, his mood remained upbeat. His mother offered to warm up some dinner but he declined. "Some other time," he said. "I still have to get Anne back home." The forced smile on his mom's face could not hide the disappointment that was clearly felt; but at the same time, there was a look of expectancy to the given answer. Anne wondered what in the world could have been so great to cause so much anger between Dale and his dad for it to last this long. But she never asked or said a word—nor did she bring up the subject again, not during the trip home or even while working their shifts together.

"Unit Six, you're responding to 52 West Nebraska for a stabbing. PD's on the scene, reporting two patients."

"Ten-four, for Unit Six," Anne replied. After hanging up the mic, she buckled her seat belt, then jotted down the information on the run sheet. The emergency lights clicked and flashed as she and her partner drove out onto the main road. Looking at her watch, she thought about her family. She guessed they were probably just getting ready to sit down to dinner. And what a feast it would be. Her mouth watered while thinking about Aunt Ruth's pumpkin pies. It was Thanksgiving Day. It was a day to reflect on thankfulness. It was a day of family gatherings. And while others sat with heads bowed saying grace, she and her partner, Bill, Jerry's brother, were on their way to a stabbing in the south end of Lancemen. They were told that the fire department would not be responding. Only the Lancemen police who were already on the scene would be there.

Bill turned the siren off as he pulled up behind the patrol cars in front of the address and stopped. After they grabbed their equipment from the rig, he and Anne dashed toward the wooden steps, of the front porch. One of the officers greeted them at the door with a flashlight. They slid past him through the door while listening to his direction. He told them that their patients were in the front room to the left. As they entered the house a sudden blast of heat from the furnace, mixed with the sickening smell of blood and alcohol, rushed to the hairs of their nose. Then they saw the two men lying on the front room floor. They were both covered with blood. Bill went to one patient and she went to the other. The house was dimly lit. Even with the drapes pulled open, a slight amount of sunlight was all that came in. Lamps that would have offered a luminous glow were now broken on the floor next to tipped over tables resulting from some sort of struggle. Two of the four officers on the scene stood with their flashlights over each victim while the crew examined the injured men and started the IVs to replace the lost blood volume.

Anne's patient was lying unconscious between the wall and a recliner chair. She moved quickly to assess the penetrating wounds that were visible at her present angle. He'd have to be moved for her to complete her survey. After lifting his blood soaked shirt again to get a better look, she grabbed his feet then dragged him a few inches across the carpet. In response to the noticeable injuries, she then grabbed an IV bag of Lactated Ringers and an IV tubing from the box. After tearing off the clear cover from the bag of solution, she inserted the hard plastic tip of the IV line into the bag's port. As soon as insertion was complete, she quickly ran her thumb over the control wheel and watched as the fluid filled the line. After grabbing a large bore catheter from the orange box, she knelt next to the patient to search for a vein. Officer Edward Farley stood next to her, holding the flashlight with one hand and the IV bag in the other.

"Ed, can you move this chair a little more to the left? I'm still having a hard time getting to his arm and I'm already kneeling in blood." Without hesitation, he took the flashlight from his hand and repositioned it under his arm, then grabbed the back of the chair to move it to the side. Awakened by the sudden beam from the flashlight, a dozen or more cockroaches scurried out from underneath the chair and spread out across the shag carpet on the floor. In a knee-jerk response, he reached down with his black gloved hand and began sweeping them away from the patient's arm just as Anne leaned over the prepped IV site with the needle, ready to insert it into the brachial vein. Startled by his quick movement, she sat up. Then, as the vile nocturnal insects came into view, she instantly understood what he was doing. As Ed knocked each of the flat-bodied winged German species of Croton from the patient's arm onto the floor, he quickly exterminated them with his big boot by grinding them into the soiled carpet. While the whole event took only a few seconds, it was more than ample for the extreme distaste for these creatures to rise up in Anne. She wanted to scream, but knew she had to stay focused. While gritting her teeth, she quietly murmured. "I hate these stupid bugs." Then she shoved the sixteen gage catheter into the vein. A flash of blood appeared in the hub—she knew she was in. After advancing the catheter the rest of the way into the vein, she hooked the hub end into the end of the tubing. The patient's skin was too wet with blood and Lord knows what else for the tape to stick, so she took a roll of gauze and held everything in place with that. Much to the nurses dislike, she knew there would probably be a couple of the roaches accidentally wrapped in the gauze as well. She was sure Bill's situation wasn't any better. In a glance she realized he was ready to go. Officer Jimmy Sapellski helped him load that patient onto the stretcher, while Ed helped her get her patient packaged onto the pole stretcher to carry out to the rig. One patient went on the bench seat and the other remained on the cot. The closest hospital was Lancemen General. Anne had no time to call them on the bio-phone. Bill had their dispatcher notify the hospital over the land line and hoped they could be ready with such a short ETA.

Both patients went into the same trauma room. It seemed a little chaotic at first with Bill and Anne both giving their reports at the same time. Both men had multiple stab wounds and had lost a lot of blood. Neither was conscious and both reeked of alcohol. There was no way of knowing their medical history, or prescription medications, or allergies. Anne's patient had stable vital signs—for now. Bill's patient must have taken a hit in a vital organ, possibly the liver, gauged from the deep cut on the right side just below the sternum. Even with the mast pants on and inflated, shock trousers used to push blood from the lower extremities to the body's vital organs, that patient's vitals were dropping quickly. Sherry the Head Nurse, came in and announced that the surgical team would be ready in the OR by the time they got up there. The lab would call up when they had the results and would send the needed blood. Minutes later, the patient was being rolled down the hall with IV bags hanging, oxygen running and the portable EKG monitor tossed on the gurney near his feet.

Anne walked out of the room toward the sink to wash her hands. She looked down at her clothes and then over at Bill who was walking toward her. They were both covered in blood and, guessing by the way it smelled, vomit.

"Did you get a good look inside the rig?" Bill asked, smiling. "Well believe it or not, we faired better. I already told Mark we're out of service until we change clothes and hose down the car."

"Jimmy didn't happen to say who stabbed those guys, did he?"

"Yeah. They stabbed each other. They were fighting over some woman. He said another one of their cruisers took her before we got there. He said she was so ugly she could haunt a house. These guys were so wasted, they probably don't even know what they were doing."

"Maybe they forgot they were supposed to be carving a turkey, not each other. Man—what a way to spend Thanksgiving."

"Family gatherings are so much fun," he chuckled. "Well, come on, let's get over to the station and get done. I've all ready replaced the IV bags.

Sherry said we can drop the run reports off later. I think she just wants us to get these stinky clothes out of her ER."

Anne picked her jacket up from the floor and followed him out to the emergency room exit. "Dale and I had this stabbing in the summer—up on Kenneth, at Rob's bar and grill," she began, relaying the story to Bill. "There was this guy laying on the floor when we got there. He was rolling around, complaining about back pain—mid thoracic. We figured, because there was a fight before he got stabbed, that maybe he'd pulled or tore a muscle. People with spinal injuries don't generally thrash around. There wasn't any blood on his shirt to indicate that he was cut where he was pointing. But we put him on a backboard anyway, as a precaution. When the x-ray came back we couldn't believe it! The blade of the knife was imbedded into this man's back and sat nicely between his lungs and heart. The handle of the knife had apparently broken off during the fight and was still in the hand of the assailant when he ran out of the bar. That guy was lucky that the blade of the knife didn't move."

"No kidding. When I lived in San Antonio, I went to this cantina called Paloma's Place. One day, while I was sitting at a table drinking my beer, these two hombres started arguing. Apparently one of the guys, was messing with the other guy's sister. The next thing I knew—the guy who was seeing the other guy's sister was lying on the floor oozing out whatever blood was left after the fight that took place beforehand. That place looked like a slaughter house by the time they were done. I left before the police got there. That was the most blood I'd ever seen until today. But it shouldn't take too long to get this buggy cleaned up if we hose her down in the garage at station one. I figure if we pull the rig up on those short ramps, it will lift up the front end enough for the water and blood to run out of the back doors and into the drain."

"Sounds like a plan. I'll wipe down the stretcher and the boxes while you do that."

Trauma has a funny way of sparking the interest of those who are not the victims, Anne thought. As soon as they pulled into the station, Rick Stockwell and his partner, Randy, came out to see the back of their rig. She knew that if it had been covered with mud and grass, they might have come out to look—but more than likely they would have gone back to doing what they were doing before. Had it been a moderate amount of blood—they would have come out to look, but may or may not have even stayed to hear the story behind the call that lead to the patient's blood loss. However, a whole lot of blood is different—for it offers a lot more to talk about and automatically gives the story a higher degree of interest.

Now standing in the front of the garage, Rick lifted his arms to guide Bill onto the short ramps like a flag man guiding in a jumbo jet onto the apron. Randy twisted the water valve and picked up the hose from the garage floor. After adding the soap to the bucket, he filled it the rest of the way with water. Rick started wiping down the stretcher while listening to Bill's re-count of the call. Anne watched and listened while wiping the boxes down. She already knew the story, she was there. So instead of staying for the conclusion, she grabbed the scrubs Sherry gave her at the hospital and walked toward the shower. As she stood in the warm clean water, the man who had gone to surgery entered her mind. Hopefully, some good would come out of this senselessness. Then she remembered the words of Von Gesner—"And let there be for every pulse a thanksgiving and for every breath a song".

It was the last day of November. Anne had partnered up with Robbie at the Dome for a concert that would return again the following night, on the first day of December. The two bands that were performing were very well known, even to Anne. Santana was the first group to go out onto the stage. The second group was The Rolling Stones. While driving home after the first night's concert, Anne thought of her conversation with a member of Santana who introduced himself as Alex. He seemed pleasant and didn't seem to mind her asking a few questions about the actual distance that the band could see out over the viewers due to the lighting. And about how he liked working with the other band, The Rolling Stones. Mercy Ambulance had the contract to provide medical care, along with one of the area hospitals during the events at the Dome. The crews generally worked either on the concourse at designated sections or in the first aid area. It was unusual for them to work right on the stage area near the bands. But with the freshness of John Lennon's death in New York City approaching its first year anniversary, the request was made for the crew to be nearby and on the stage.

Anne was intrigued while watching the different personalities and life styles of the groups. She remembered a girl named Debbie, presumed to be Alex's friend, who commented on the crew bringing their cooler up on stage. She smiled, recalling Debbie's expression when she explained that it was not a cooler but a medical box of supplies. Then Anne wondered if the ping pong table would be set up in the back tunnel on the second night like it was on the first.

She enjoyed watching Bill, a member of the Stones, who played against some of the crews as well as a couple of very pretty lady friends. He was the only member of the band that came out of the group's dressing room. But she understood that they probably wanted their privacy and who could blame them. The second night of the concert was much like the first, Anne thought, except it started an hour later than it was scheduled. Still, everyone seemed to have a good time.

The story of Lake Superior with its cold winds of November and the sinking of the SS Edmund Fitzgerald off of White Fish Bay had reached its six year anniversary. But the current news of Natalie Wood's death was still found in nearly every newspaper, as that tragic event occurred less than a week ago. And, as the last few pages of the year approached, Anne looked forward to a new year and warmer weather. She didn't mind the winter so much. It was the dragging of the stretcher and equipment through the snow that got so old. Plus she thought that being outside in a cotton shirt in seventy or eighty degree weather was certainly more pleasant than the layers of clothes needed to survive the colder conditions of Michigan winters.

Finally the estival of summer eased in, bringing the cotton shirts out. And while summers are typically filled with lighter clothes as well as other traditional things like swimming and picnics, this summer would be different for some. It would be the first summer in fifty-four years that the turnstiles at Edgewater Park would be silent. While that would not be earth shaking for some people, it would be disappointing to others. Anne had never been to the amusement park, for Grand River and Seven Mile was quite a hike from Summerville—and it was an expense that could not be spared considering the amount of youngsters in her family. But she remembered hearing Becky Ritter and a few others in her high school talking about the Hall of Mirrors and the roller coaster called The Wild Beast. It sounded like a good time, but she didn't feel horribly bad for missing out. There were many other things that she enjoyed doing, and bike riding was one of them.

Throughout the summer she and her partner, Bill, watched as a construction company laid a bike path that ran from the borderline of Lakeview, all the way out to Bedford Village. The station that they worked out of was just on the inside of the boundary line of Clear Lake Township on the Lakeviw side, making it easy to keep track of the progress of the path as the workers completed each side near the main road. Merve had rented out part of the building to set up a post in response to the increased call volume in that end of the county that was growing with the population. Now Mercy Medical Services had six full time stations in different areas of the county.

Clearly, the company was taking on a newer look as the number of rigs, posts, and employees grew. Collectively, they were known as a very elite group of professionals, not only by the hospital staff throughout the county but also by a good portion of the municipalities they worked with side by side. In addition to the increased number of ambulances, the units had also switched their call titles. Instead of Unit Four or Unit Six, they were Alpha 630, or Bravo 649, depending on whether it was a Basic EMT rig or an advanced, paramedic rig. Plus, they were slowly changing from the Dodge converted vans with the gas engine to Ford diesel vans. Initially, the Ford ambulances took a little getting used to. They were noticeably taller and slower. They would not raise up on two wheels around the curves like the Dodges did, for they seemed top heavy and would flip over if the driver took a corner too fast.

The decision to switch to the diesel rigs was sparked by a near tragic event with John and his partner, Roger. In a recount of the story, John said it began with the two of them sitting at a cover point in front of an old vacant party store. He was reading a tale of the Antarctic to Roger when they both started to smell gas. The odor was strong enough that they got out of the rig to look underneath. To their horror he said raw gas was streaming from under the rig, plus, there were flames dancing over the pooled petroleum on the ground. Immediately, John ran to the pay phone outside of the party store to call the fire department. He had his back to the rig while he nervously dropped his change into the coin slot. The last thing he said he remembered was Roger leaning into the ambulance grabbing their personal items. Suddenly there was a huge flash and an explosion. He bolted to the side of the building to take cover. Then he peeked his head around to see if Roger was within eyesight; but he was nowhere to be found. His stomach turned and fear welled up inside, thinking that Roger had been blown sky high. Then to his rejoicing, he saw Roger peek his head around the opposite side of the store. He said he ran to him to make sure he was all right, as each of them called out the other one's name. Laughing in hindsight he said he almost felt like the people on the commercials that are seen in the meadow running toward the other in slow motion. The next day they learned that it was not an isolated incident, as similar fires were reported in other states. With that, Merve wasted no time in ordering the first diesel ambulance.

It was mid-August and the dog days of summer were at their peak. Bill and Anne had one of the new rigs and enjoyed the air conditioning tremendously, as not all of the older ambulances had such a luxury. One day while driving down Highland Road, they realized that the newly laid bike path, a project that they'd been eyeing for a number of weeks, was finished. The construction crew was gone and the black tarred lane above the curb looked as smooth as silk.

"Okay Billy, when do want to go out for a ride?"

"Let me see when Jan's next day off is and I'll get back to you. She's working at the hospital today. Maybe we'll run into her."

Bill and Jan had been dating for nearly two years. She was a nurse and initially worked out at the Health Care Center in Bedford. Now she worked at the main hospital in LOH's ER.

Anne remembered when Jan first left the Health Care Center and went out to Arizona to work for a doctor to help set up a hair transplanting business. Bill was so upset that she left. "Why did she leave," she remembered him saying. "Man, I would have even married her." Anne could still recall her response to Bill and his reaction when she asked, "Bill, why are you asking me this? You should be telling Jan how you feel, not me." Two weeks later, Jan was home and back with Bill.

"Jan's next day off is Thursday and so is ours. How does Thursday look for a jaunt? We can ride out to that new restaurant in Bedford and have lunch, then ride back. If we start from your place in Lancemen, it'll only be about a fifty mile ride there and back."

Fifty miles! Anne thought. She wasn't thinking about riding no fifty miles! Parachuting from a plane was one thing and rock climbing forty feet up was another—a fifty mile bike ride was a little more exercise than she thought she wanted. But she knew Bill's impelling way. If she didn't go she'd be branded a wimp, not that she really cared. What the heck, she bargained. She was young and strong. It'd probably be fun.

"Okay, Thursday sounds good," she smiled. "We should probably leave my place at least by ten o'clock if you want to be in Bedford by noon—don't you think?"

"Sounds good. I'll let Jan know and we'll be at your place by ten."

Throughout the rest of the shift they didn't talk much about the bike ride, but Anne thought about what she'd wear to stay cool while protecting her skin from being sunburned. She didn't want to carry a purse of course and money stuffed into her pocket might feel bulky after riding a few miles. She could put her money in a bandana and tie it to her handlebar. That way on the way back, if she got too hot and most of her money was paid out for her lunch, she could tie the bandana around her forehead or just use it to wipe the sweat away. Once the plan was set in her head, she began to look forward to Thursday.

The weather forecasted for the day of their big ride was windy, hot and humid with a high of eighty-seven. After getting dressed in a pair of light cotton pants that she rolled up and a short sleeved shirt, Anne ate a bowl of cereal then brushed her teeth. She was out on the sidewalk tying her navy bandana to the handlebar of her ten speed bike when Bill and Jan pulled up. Everyone took a turn in the bathroom, then they were on their way.

The wind pushed against them as they traveled west toward Lakeview but the sun was at their backs. They had gone nearly eight miles before they turned north to stay on the sidewalk. Then they sped over a curved path that ran under the shade of a number of tall oaks, reminding Anne of a "Star Wars" movie. Turning south again, they pedaled past a small airport. These were areas that Bill and Anne had driven past, in the ambulance many times. But now on their bikes, everything seemed to take on a whole different perspective.

Heading west again, Anne came to realize that the worst part of the trip would be the hills in Clear Lake Township. As she approached the first of the really steep hills she moved her hand to the gear switch and pushed the lever to make the ride easier. Jan slowed down enough for Anne to ride next to her. Anne smiled and shook her head. "I can't believe we're doing this. Who's idea was it, anyway?"

Jan smiled back—then at the same time they both laughed out loud, almost singing the answer, "Bill's."

The ice cream stand up ahead had a water fountain outside. After a quick drink they hopped back on their bikes, then continued pedaling. Finally, they were in front of the Appetite Eatery. After chaining the bikes to the wrought iron fence in front of the restaurant, they walked inside and found a seat.

"Man, my gluteus maximus is killing me," Anne grinned. "I never realized how hard that bike seat was until now."

"Well we're half way there—now we just have to ride back," Bill chuckled.

"I can't believe you talked me into this Bill," Jan smiled. "And on the hottest day of the summer! It feels so good in here, I might not go back out."

"I'm with you Jan," Anne laughed. "The first truck, van, wagon, or whatever I see that can haul my bike—I'm flagging it down for a ride. You can call me a wimp—I don't care. As long as I'm not sitting on that bike and sweating like a pig, I'll be happy."

"You wimp," Bill teased.

"Sticks and stones."

Satisfied with a light lunch and a tall glass of ice tea—the rested travelers began their journey home. But it wasn't long before Anne sadly realized that while she honestly thought that sitting on the cushioned restaurant seat instead of the bicycle seat, for even a short time would bring comfort to her aching backside—she soon found that it didn't. And, even though she'd only been teasing Bill about hitching a ride back by boat or train if she must, at this point, anything other than the hard triangle seat she was again perched upon sounded wonderful.

Finally, they made it back to the main bike path next to Highland Road. They turned east toward Clear Lake Township. The last of the high hills was just ahead. Bill and Jan picked up speed while racing to get to the hill first. Looking ahead, Anne could see they were a good distance in front of her, but she didn't mind. She thought she'd just take her time and enjoy the ride. As she crested the top of the last hill, she felt the wind behind her. The rest of the ride would be easy.

They had ridden on the north, or opposite side of the road on the way out to Bedford. Now while on the south side, they had a chance to ride past different things on the way back to Lancemen. Anne noticed that the sun wasn't beating down like it had earlier—maybe she could make it after all, she chuckled. Her speed picked up as she started down the steepest hill. A guard rail to her left protected the rider or walker on the path and kept them from going out onto the highway. The nearly perpendicular ravine at her right was a little discomforting, but the pathway was wide—and if she just stayed straight, which wasn't a problem, she'd be fine.

Suddenly, she noticed a wide dip at the base of the path running the entire width that had been shaded by the trees. She tried to slow down but the angle of the hill was too great to allow her to reduce her speed enough to glide over the dip. Seconds later, her front tire hit the ridge on the opposite side, full force. The front tire seemed to stop instantly, propelling her over the handlebars and onto the pavement face first. Her face felt numb, yet she could feel the blood oozing from her nose. She tried to sit up but her legs were tangled around the bike frame and would not move. This is not cool, was her first thought. I have to go to work tomorrow. Finally she was able to support herself sitting. Slowly she began pulling at her pant legs to move each leg from underneath the frame of the bike. Then she reached over and untied the bandana from the handle bar and held it against her nose to stop the bleeding. Her left cheek felt hot and swollen. Her arms and knees were abraded and felt like they were on fire.

Seconds later, she saw a silver toned pickup truck slow down as it drove past. The driver looked at her, then turned around to come back to where she was sitting on the ground; an angel of mercy, she thought. Then she heard the sound of gravel crunching underneath the tires of his truck when he pulled up behind her and then a squeak when he opened his door to step out. She turned around. He was about her age, mid-twenties, with dark wavy hair and a full beard. His brown eyes were filled with sorrow as he reached down to help her.

"Are you all right?" he asked.

"I think so. I was riding with my friends before I hit this dip."

"Where are they?"

"They can't be too far ahead."

"I think that I should take you over to the hospital."

"The closest hospital is in Lancemen. I can't ask you to do that."

"No, there's a hospital in Bedford."

"That's just a clinic. I don't want to go to a clinic. My friends are just up the road. If you take me that far, they can help me the rest of the way."

"Are you sure? I'll take you to the hospital. It's not a problem."

"Oh no, I'll be fine."

She watched as he ran his fingers through his hair. Guys always do that, she thought, when they're feeling beside themselves. I must really look terrible to him. I know he wants to help—but if I go to the clinic, they'll just call an ambulance to take me to the hospital anyway. I might as well let Bill and Jan call for someone to come and get me. I can't ride my bike, that's for sure. That thing's all twisted and bent. "Really, I'm sure I look worse than I am," she offered.

"All right. But I saw you go down. If you want me to take you to your friends, then I will. Just the same, I really think you need to go to the hospital."

Without another word he picked up her bike and put it in the bed of his truck, then helped her to her feet. While holding the bandana to her nose, she slowly walked to the passenger side and sat down. He watched every move she made while she buckled her seat belt. She wondered if he noticed her trying to hide the pain she felt in her face.

"It only hurts when I smile," she said, trying to ease his concern. But his expression didn't change. After checking his side mirror, he pulled out onto the road.

"How far up are they?" he asked.

"They shouldn't be too far. They weren't that far away when I fell, I don't think."

"Well if you change your mind, I'll be happy to take you to the hospital."

Poor guy, she thought. I'm probably making him a nervous wreck.

He drove so slow while watching the road and pathway for her friends, that it started to make her nervous. After driving a little further, she spotted them. "There they are," she pointed. "Sitting on the curb, in front of the fruit market." Bill stood up and put his hands on his hips when he saw her pulling up into the parking lot. As soon as the driver stopped the truck, she opened her door to get out. Bill and Jan walked toward her. It was clear from their expressions they didn't realize she'd been hurt. She could feel a scolding and a—I can't believe you're really getting a ride home, coming from Bill. Then, as she moved the bandana from in front of her face, he stopped dead in his tracks and stared at her for a moment before asking, "What happened to you?"

"I fell down, Bill."

"I guess," he chuckled.

Anne could sense the truck driver's anxiety growing at Bill's easy manner. "I really think that I should take you to the hospital," he insisted.

"No, really," she smiled, turning toward him. "It's all right. She's a nurse and he's a paramedic. In fact we're both paramedics." But somehow her reassuring words weren't very reassuring. In spite of his obvious reluctance he said nothing more when she slid off the seat and stood next to Jan and Bill. She thanked him while shutting her door, then watched as he sat unmoved—still hoping she'd change her mind, she supposed. Then he turned and opened his door. He got out of the truck and walked toward the back of the bed. Bill helped him lift her bike out and set it on the ground. Without another word, he got into his truck and drove off.

Bill went inside the store to use the phone while Jan waited with Anne.

"Anne, why don't you sit down on the curb until Bill comes back," Jan suggested.

"Sorry, Jan. I was doing good until I hit this ditch. It was right in the middle of the path. What a stupid place to put a drainage ditch. That thing must have been five or six feet wide!"

"I know, Bill and I hit the same thing. We almost dumped, too. Bill was ahead of me and warned me. Otherwise, I probably would have landed the same way you did."

"Geeze, I didn't even get that guy's name. Doesn't it just figure—some nice looking guy comes to my rescue, and I look like the 'wreck of the Hesperus'".

"You do look pretty bad," Jan teased. "But don't worry, we'll get you fixed up in no time."

The sunlight seemed so bright to Anne that her eyes began to water. She tried using the bandana and her hands as a shield. She guessed that her sunglasses were somewhere on the path behind her and probably smashed. Then she looked at her watch. It was still intact and working. The time was almost three thirty. Hopefully Jerry would be at home. Then she heard the sound of footsteps in the gravel behind her. It was probably Bill. She was too tired to look.

"Jerry's on the way. He's bringing the station wagon. Here's some ice for your face, Anne. It might smell a little like watermelon, but I didn't think you'd care."

"Thanks, Bill."

They passed the time while waiting for Jerry by talking about the bike ride—up until Anne's accident. Then they talked about the construction of the drainage ditch. And, of course, Bill had to demonstrate how he held his bike and lifted the front wheel to keep it from hitting the lip on the opposite side, which was exactly what Anne didn't do.

"Thanks for pointing that out, Bill," Jan teased. "We were going to wait for you, Anne, but we figured as slow as you were riding, you'd of been able to slow down enough to ride over it."

"Not when it's waiting at the bottom of the steepest hill of the highway! Man—I was flying when I hit that thing. I'm not blaming you guys. But if I ever find the guy who designed that ditch or whatever that thing is, I'm going to give him a piece of my mind, that's for sure."

"Well Jerry always has film in his camera. When we drop off the bikes, we'll have him take a couple of pictures, so you can show that guy what your face looked like when you fell," Bill offered.

"Speaking of Jerry, there he is," Jan said, pointing.

Bill stood up, then helped Anne to her feet. Jerry spotted them and waved. Once he'd pulled into the parking lot and stopped, Jan walked with Anne toward the station wagon. Jerry's girlfriend, Rhonda, was sitting in the front seat, Jack was sitting in the back. Anne tried to keep her head level while bending over to sit on the back seat, so her nose wouldn't start bleeding again. But as she moved, a sudden throbbing and a ringing echoed in her ears and for a second, she thought she was going to faint. The odor of alcohol came from Jack's direction.

"Jack, have you been drinking?" she asked.

"A little. But don't worry, Annie—Accident or no accident you still look good to me."

"That's nice, Jack, but right now I don't care." She was starting to feel woozy. If I could just lie down, I'd feel fine, she thought.

Jan got in and sat in the front with Rhonda. Bill helped Jerry load all three bikes in the back storage area of the car, then sat next to Anne on the back seat.

Jerry pulled out onto the main road and started toward his house to unload the bikes. Anne enjoyed the cool breeze against her face at first. Then her cheek began to feel dry, tighter and puffier. She closed her eyes, trying to ease the discomfort.

Jack placed his hand on her knee. "It's all right, kid, we're going to take good care of you. You know, I'll take good care of you."

She sighed silently. Clearly, something in his voice made her think that he was not talking medical take care of—but more of a Ooh baby, Ooh baby, take care of. "Jack, please," she grunted. "I really do have a headache."

"Just thought I'd offer," he smiled.

Listening to their conversation, Bill burst out laughing. "Geeze, Jack, leave her alone. This is not the time to go hitten on her, trust me."

Again, Anne closed her eyes. The bag of ice dripped and ran down her face and neck all the way to Jerry's house. As soon as they pulled in his driveway Bill hopped out and unloaded the bikes. After a few snapshots to back up Anne's proof of injury to show the builder of the ditch, they were on the way to the hospital. The ride there seemed quieter to Anne, for which she was grateful. She was about all talked out and just wanted to lie down. Jerry stopped at the ambulance entrance and waited while Bill and Jan helped Anne out of the back seat. The plan was, that after he dropped Anne and Jan off at the hospital, he would take Bill over to Anne's to pick up Bill's car. Then he, Jack and Rhonda would go back to his place.

Anne sat on the gurney in a room at the ER. Dr. Michael Dowell walked in. His expression when he saw her face was pitifully sad. She sensed the tenderness in his voice and fingertips as he touched the bridge of her nose and cheeks, feeling for broken bones.

"There's so much swelling. We need to get some x-rays of your face and spine. You must have hit the ground pretty hard, Anne. But you were never unconscious—not even for a few minutes?

"No. As soon as I hit the ground, I remember taking a mental inventory of my injuries."

He chuckled. "Sorry for laughing. That just sounded kind of funny."

"Here's a fresh bag of ice, Anne," Jan said when she walked into the room. Dr. Malley was right behind her. He stopped at the end of the gurney and stood poised in his famous, unto the crews at least, Dr. Malley—stance of ponder. Typically while in this position, the lower half of his left arm rested across his chest, with his left hand supporting his right elbow in order to steady the right hand as he held it against the side of his face. He tucked his right thumb under his chin and allowed the middle finger to rest above his upper lip. His baby and ring fingers were kept in a loose fist with the index finger on the right hand pointing up and held near his temple, all while giving full concentration to the matter at hand.

Anne sat quietly and waited. She didn't want to interrupt his silent assessment. Then without moving his hand he smiled and gently asked, "Your face—again?"

She knew he was referring to the steri strips he had put on her upper lip last spring, when the wind caught her car door and flipped it against her mouth. Then in the winter of 1979, she had to have a couple of stitches put in her forehead after a minor auto accident. That was the year her Duster bit the dust. Then in 1980, after another wintery accident, she had to have a couple of stitches sewn in, between her eyebrows after her sunglasses, that were still on the bridge of her nose, smashed against the steering wheel of her car.

Now after hearing his question, she was more curious than ever to see what her face looked like. She'd tried looking in Jerry's rear view mirror while riding to his house, but she couldn't lean over enough to see without getting too close to Jack; not that it really mattered, for as soon as Bill noticed what she was doing, he moved the mirror so she couldn't see.

"Wait until we get to the hospital, Anne."

"Is it that bad?" she asked.

"I've seen worse," he chuckled. "Just kidding. It's just a little swollen. Trust me. Just wait until one of the doc's takes a look at it."

Somehow his reassurance didn't stay with her as long as the—"I've seen worse," did. For she knew what he had seen—she'd seen it too. She could only guess by the way that it felt and from everyone's reaction, that it was probably worse than the small lacerations from her previous crashes. But she trusted Dr. Dowell and Dr. Malley, and was glad that everything outside of the swelling felt normal.

As soon as Dr. Dowell finished looking at the x-rays, he came in to tell Anne that she had a fractured left orbit. He said it looked like it would heal just fine without surgery, but he wanted her to stay in the hospital overnight for observation.

"Dr. Dowell, I don't want to stay in the hospital. I just want to go home. One of my brothers can come and pick me up. My aunt has taken care of me most of my life. I don't think she'll mind watching me for a few days. We have hospitals near Summerville too."

"That's up to you, Anne. Just as long as you're with someone for a few days and not home alone. We'll call your family and have them come to get you, if you're sure that's what you want to do."

"I'm sure."

A week and a half of Aunt Ruth's fussing was enough for Anne. Without a doubt, Aunt Ruth had been wonderful. She cut up Anne's food to make it easier for her to chew and brought her ice water and aspirin whenever she needed it. Anne was more than grateful, of course, but she had been living in her own apartment for a while and knew it was where she wanted to be. After a visit to their family doctor, who told her to stay out of the sun in addition to everything else she was already doing, he released her to go home. Aunt Ruth had never seen Anne's apartment and decided it was time she did. Anne welcomed the idea, then mentally raced through each room, as women do, making sure she'd have a clean place to show off to her aunt. The next day after breakfast, they headed for Lancemen.

After Anne gave Aunt Ruth a quick tour through her one bedroom abode, they sat down at the kitchen table and enjoyed a glass of tea. In no time Anne grew sleepy. Realizing the whole ordeal was still tiring to Anne, Aunt Ruth finished her drink, hugged her, then said good-bye. There is something restful about being in your own place. After a good nap, Anne got up and looked for something to eat. The milk had gone sour during her time away. A tall glass of milk sounded good to her. Finding an extra pair of sunglasses she slid them onto her bruised nose to hide the two black eyes that were starting to change from deep purple to yellow.

It'd been nearly two weeks since the accident and as much time since she'd worked. Fortunately, she had put some money away. It wasn't a lot—but when you live on your own, you learn how to get by with what you have. And she knew to look just for the items that she needed. After a short time of walking through the grocery store, once again she was tired and wanted to go home. It was hard to see in the store with her sunglasses on; but realizing that her battered face drew so many stares from the other shoppers, she left them in place.

Later on that day she grew restless again and decided to go to a movie. It would be dark in the theater. Surely, she'd be able to do that without drawing so much attention. While standing in line, she overheard a woman say that she looked like someone had beat her with a baseball bat. Feeling somewhat embarrassed, she took her ticket from the girl at the counter and walked straight to the cinema, without purchasing the pop or popcorn like she normally would.

The next day, Tracey and Roger stopped by Anne's to see if she wanted to go to a barbecue at Jeff's. Jeff was a medic and had worked at Mercy for a couple of years. He shared a house on the canal near Casey Lake with two other guys, Phil and Grant. There was always something fun going on at their place during the summer months. At least my face won't bother them, she reasoned. If I stay in the shade and keep my hat on while I'm in the sun, I should be okay. "Sure," she answered.

It was great seeing a lot of her coworkers at Jeff's and getting caught up on the latest events within the company. Hearing them talk about the calls they'd been on made Anne that much more eager to get back to work. She talked to Robbie's wife, Cathy, a nurse at LOH, who, after looking at Anne's face said she thought Anne could probably go back to work in a week if her doctor okayed it. At least by then her black eyes should be pretty well cleared up. After hearing that bit of encouraging news, Anne felt a sudden burst of energy. Just the mere thought of getting back into a normal pattern of life was like music to the soul for her.

Sipping on a bottle of root beer, she walked over to the shade of the huge weeping willow tree and sat on one of the lawn chairs. Minutes later another coworker Bob, came over on crutches and sat on a recliner that was next to her. She noticed his foot was in a post surgical boot and watched as he sat down, then as he tried to angle his foot just right. Once he had it set in a seemingly good position, he pulled out a silver flask from his shirt pocket. He held it up and bragged that it was full of ninety proof whiskey.

"This must be the gimp section," he chuckled.

"I guess so," she smiled. "When did you have your surgery, Bob?"

"A couple of days ago. But I'm doing all right. This is good stuff, Anne. Do you want to try some?"

"No thanks," she chuckled. "I'm taking pain medication."

"So am I," he laughed.

Shaking her head she scolded him halfheartedly. "Now I know you know better than that. You aren't supposed to mix alcohol with medication."

"So, then I guess it's true. Medical people do make the worst patients," he grinned.

It was fruitless to say anything else, she decided. If he got sick—what better—or worse place could he have picked, than to be with a bunch of other medical personnel who were also drinking. But Bob overdosing wasn't her first thought, she selfishly had to admit. Just the fact that he was drinking ninety proof anything and sitting next to her was unnerving in itself. While she'd never witnessed them, she'd certainly heard the stories of how—the more Bob drank—the more clothes he took off. And now he was sitting next to her in just a pair of shorts and an unbuttoned shirt. There really wasn't that much more to shed. But she decided she could always get up and move if he got frisky. For now he was just having fun watching Jeff's black lab, Roxanne, jump from a platform on the tree into the canal, diving for rocks.

It was Monday evening. Anne was feeling her best since the accident, well enough in fact, that she brought dinner in for the dispatchers at the main office. Buster, a dispatch supervisor now, was on the phone when she came into the radio center. She was quiet, at least until she realized that he was engaged in a personal conversation with one of the Townsdale medics. They were talking about a poker game that they had set up for later that night. They planned to hold it in the conference room just outside of the dispatch center in the main office, as it would be a central location for those who were playing. Ret, who was off the road and a full time dispatcher now, was scheduled to man the radio while the game was in progress.

"Hey, Anne, do you want to play poker with us?" Buster asked.

"Not really. That's gambling, isn't it?"

"We're not playing for high stakes. Just some pocket change—so we have an ante. Come on, it'll be fun."

"Well, I really don't know how to play," she confessed.

"We'll write everything out on the chalkboard for you. All you need is about six or seven dollars in change and a six pack, which in your case is optional."

"A six pack?"

"That's our high stakes ante. When we run out of money—we ante whatever beer is left."

"I don't know. I guess it'd be all right. I'll have to go to the store and get some change. When's the game?"

"Seven-thirty. Be there or be square."

Anne sat in her car in the parking lot of the main office, counting out the change she'd gotten at the drug store. Suddenly, a bad feeling surged through her. It was all the money she had left until payday, with the exception of what she had in her savings account. "Maybe I'll be lucky," she told herself, trying to dismiss the inner presaging tug. "After all it's just a game and I know these guys. They aren't going to cheat me. It's only seven bucks. If I lose, then it's my own fault for playing a game I know nothing about." Satisfied that she'd convinced herself, she grabbed the six pack of beer from the back seat, which she figured she could use to batter fish or as a hair rinse when the game was over, and got out of her car.

Ret was surprised when she came back to play cards with the boys. "Anne, you don't drink. And I bet you don't even know how to play. Are you sure you know what you're doing? Looks to me that maybe you hit your head harder than you thought."

"I'm just going to play for a little while—then I'm going to leave. It'll be all right," she smiled. "What else have I got to do?"

"Yeah? So, what's the beer for?"

"High stakes," she chuckled. "Wish me luck."

"You're going to need more than luck," he warned.

Buster had every type of hand, in descending order according to its value written on the chalkboard to make the game fair for Anne, just as he offered. She walked in and took her seat at the table. Reading over the board, she adjusted her straw hat which she wore just about everywhere since her accident. The atmosphere was light, as she and the guys joked about her hat and whether she had cards hidden in it like a magician. Larry, one of the Townsdale medics, began shuffling the cards. He offered the cut to Buster, then started dealing the cards. Buster twisted off the cap from a bottle of beer, then picked up his hand. Anne looked back and forth from her cards to the chalkboard, trying to get a match. She moved them and rearranged them a couple of times before Buster finally spoke up.

"Anne, what are you doing?"

"I'm trying to see if I have anything that looks like the board," she grinned shyly.

"Well, you get more cards, you know. You just don't play off of the first ones that are dealt. Save whatever looks good—like a pair, or anything of the same suit. Then when we tell you—throw what ever you don't want on the table.

"Sorry. I told you I didn't know how to play."

"Now see, that's another thing. When you play poker—you don't want everyone else at the table to know that. They'll take advantage and cheat you. Okay—now throw the cards on the table that you don't want."

Slowly and nervously Anne played through a couple of hands. The pot was only two dollars, but it may as well have been two hundred. She reached over and took a bottle of beer from the cardboard carrier and twisted off the cap. The vapor rose from the neck then disappeared. After bringing the top of the bottle to her lips, she took a drink. The liquid was cold and wet and pleasing at first. But after a few seconds it seemed bitter. She caught Buster watching her out of the corner of her eye, then without saying a word he looked back at his cards.

"The people on TV make this stuff sound like it tastes good. It's supposed to be smooth, they said. It doesn't taste smooth to me."

"You just have to acquire a taste for it," Larry said.

"You mean I have to learn to like something that I really don't like?"

"Something like that. You going to play cards—or are you going to talk?"

"Play cards."

"Okay then, chatty Cathy," Buster grinned. "Let's see what you got."

Anne laid her cards on the table. She had a pair of fours, a pair of tens and a queen of hearts. "Not bad," he smiled. "You beat me. I basically have nothing."

"Okay, Anne, you win," Larry said, sliding the pot toward her.

Unfortunately for Anne, it was the only pot she won. But even after losing the next hand, she was still five dollars ahead of her original purse. It was going on ten o'clock and she was starting to tire. Then a flush came over her face. After looking at the warm beer to her left, a nausea began churning. She knew it was time for her to go home.

"I'm going to call it a night, you guys. Thanks for letting me play."

"Sure, take our money and leave," Buster teased. "See you later."

It was mid-afternoon the following day. Anne was at home folding clothes when the phone rang.

"Hello," she answered.

"Hey, Anne, how you doing?"

She recognized Robbie's voice. "Good. I was just going to call you. The doctor said I can come back to work. My next normally scheduled shift is tomorrow."

"Well, that's good," he said somberly. "Listen, Merve wants to talk to you. He wants you to come down here at the main office."

"Right now?" she asked puzzled.

"Yeah, as soon as you can get here."

"Okay."

Something was wrong. She could tell by the tone in his voice. Her mind spun from one tragic thing to another. Maybe something happened to Roger or one of the other employees. Or maybe something happened to someone in her family. No, that couldn't be it. One of the her own family members would have called. She'd just have to wait. It was probably nothing. Why do people always jump to the worst thing, she wondered?

When she got to the main office and dispatch center, Robbie told her that Merve was waiting for her in his office. His expression was serious, but it offered no real explanation as to why she'd been asked to come so quickly. Now she was really puzzled. She walked toward Merve's office, then stood in the doorway. She saw Tom sitting next to the desk. Robbie was behind her. Merve asked her to take a seat and told Robbie to shut the door. This could not be good.

"Anne," Merve started. "Seems we had a little poker party in the conference room last night. Do you know anything about that?"

"Yes sir," she confessed. "I was there for a little while, but I left about ten."

"Well first I have to say that it didn't take a rocket scientist to figure out that the game had taken place. I mean there were beer bottles on the table and each card hand was written out on the chalkboard. You have to know that I was pretty mad when I saw that, but I wasn't really surprised—at least until I found out that Buster wrote that stuff out so you would know their value, which meant that you were playing—and you brought in some beer, too, I understand. Do you have something that you want say about this?" he asked.

"I didn't leave my beer bottles here, Merve—I took mine home. And I only really took one sip. I'm really sorry. I guess I should have known better."

Merve sighed. "You know that I can't let this go. I'm sorry, but I'm going to have to give you a day off with no pay."

"Merve—The doctor just cleared me to go back to work. I really need the money. Can't we work something else out?" She could feel the tears starting to well up in her eyes. She had never cried in front of any of these guys before. That was just something you never did. It was an agreed on rule, like an oath, that the girls had made.

Merve looked at Tom and then at Robbie. Neither of them said a word, or changed their grim mood. "All right. This is what I'm going to do. I want you to take a day off—and I'll pay you as if you were working. Then later when you get back on your feet, I'll deduct the money from your check. Of course you can't tell anyone that I did that for you, because you're not the only one on the chopping block. Agreed?"

"Yes sir," she softly answered, then asked. "Um—Merve? Do you want the money back that I won?"

"How much did you win?" he asked, surprised at her question.

"Five dollars," she shyly answered.

"No," he replied, trying to hide a smile. "You can keep it."

A knock on the office door drew Merve's attention. Tom opened the door. Shirley said that someone was there to see Merve. Both Tom and Merve left the room, leaving her alone with Robbie.

"Can I leave now?" she asked.

"In a minute. I just want to tell you that I was shocked when I heard that you were part of this. You know you can't do this kind of stuff on company property. In case you don't realize it, Anne, people look up to you, not that they've put you up on a pedestal—it's not like that at all. Let me put it this way. You aren't the one on the pedestal, Anne—you are the pedestal. I couldn't have been any more disappointed than if my own wife had been in that room." He sat for a second and looked at her, then got up and left.

If there was ever a time in her life when she felt lower, at that moment, she couldn't remember. Feeling numb and almost sedated, the words Robbie spoke echoed in her mind. "I couldn't have been any more disappointed than if my own wife had been in that room." Sadly, she reached under her chair for her purse then got up and walked out of the office. She didn't go and talk to Shirley or even stop to chat with the dispatchers—she walked straight to the door, went up the steps to the main level and stepped outside.

With her hand resting against her forehead, she sat behind the wheel of her car. Shame and remorse stirred within her. Merve certainly could have been harder on her, she knew that. While recapping the conversation in his office, she wondered who supplied the information as to what went on, but didn't blame them for the outcome. How could she? She was the one who had been on company property drinking beer and playing poker and she would have to deal with the resulting consequence. It wasn't the fact that she'd gotten caught that bothered her—she had that coming. Without a doubt, it was the fall that was upsetting to her. She had fallen in Robbie's eyes and to those who looked at her as the pedestal. Maybe she wasn't as strong as they thought. After all, she was just as human as they were. She understood that her faith set her apart from those who did not believe, yet she had given in to something that was clearly wrong and she knew it. She should have and could have left when her conscience surged through her while she was counting out the change in her car. And she should have left when Ret warned her—but she didn't.

Pulling her keys from her purse, she inserted a key into the ignition and watched as the angel on the attached chain swung and reflected the light from the sun. Instantly, a verse from the book of Romans entered her mind. "There is therefore now no condemnation to them which are in Christ Jesus…" She understood that God was bigger than her sin and that He had already seen her from the mercy seat. Even though she felt as if she had fallen from the cleft of the wall at The Ledge and landed in an abyss, she knew deep down inside that someday, this too would pass.

Then a song from her cassette player caught her attention. Reaching over, she turned up the volume as the voice of Keith Green, a Christian singer who died in a plane crash a month earlier, rang out and made her smile. As she listened to the words of a man who some called a prophet to his generation, Robbie's words seemed to fade greatly. "I know that I would surely fall away, except for grace by which I'm saved." Many times she had heard this song and listened to the words—but they never sounded as sweet to her as they did on that day. She stopped at the end of the parking lot, then sighed as an imprisoned tear escaped and ran down her cheek. Unquestionably she knew she had not fallen away, she had just stumbled and taken—a very big fall.

CHAPTER 27

THE LIFER

In the early years of EMS, the term lifer was an entitlement pinned to anyone who had worked the road for ten years or longer with no real plans of seeking a replacement trade. It was a term that was generally delivered in a respectful and lighthearted teasing manner by someone who by all definitions could have easily been described as a lifer himself—with the exception of one drawback. So far, the crews didn't know anyone who had worked in the field for ten years, much less longer. While indeed the EMT and Advance EMT profession had increased its pace, it still remained as a babe taking its first steps. Therefore, the term wasn't so much an earned degree at this point but really a sensed preemption, based on the titleholder's observed love for the profession.

To the crews it was an understood title that was only granted to those who were worthy. And while it had been passed on to Anne and a number of her colleagues, she alone carried the added christened appellation of—little mother. This endeared dubbing came about in response to the task she took on of blanket tucking and pillow fluffing, which she did on a regular basis in an unintentional motherly way to ensure the comfort of her patients. It was a task she did intuitively rather than like a chore, even from the first day that her feet graced the back of an ambulance. So while the EMS profession and her role in it had experienced many changes, some things remained the same—and in spite of the guys often teasing her with "Why do you always have to mother everyone," this was one of them.

Looking back to the mid-seventies when Anne first entered the world of EMS via the privately owned ambulance service, she, like some of the other EMT pioneers, viewed it as a stepping stone leading to other avenues in the growing business of emergency medicine—and for good reason. On the surface alone, there was the old mindset of the load and code, or the you call, we haul operation that was haunting and hard to shake. Although the crews understood it would take more than just training and an Emergency Medical Technician or Paramedic license to change this attitude, it was still bothersome to a degree; but that, in itself was not the robber of endurance. Nor was it the irksome feeling that came from dealing with the skeptics or the arrogant posture of some of the hospital and nursing home personnel. For that, even combined with the problems inside the political arena, still wasn't enough to lead the ground-breakers away. Simply—it was just the fact that the profession itself really had nothing long range to offer.

The earmark of the industry was a peculiar one; there was no doubt about that. For not only was the job literally back-breaking at times, but the lack of sleep at the busier stations in relation to the time frame of the crews' scheduled shifts was just plain crazy. Plus their meals were so sporadic, that sometimes their only hope for food came from being canceled on the way to a call in front of a fast food joint, or from sucking down a tube of instant glucose in the back of the rig. Subsequently on those busy days as an annotation, they often had to resort to the "pit check" method as their only means of determining whether or not they had recently showered, recollection alone wasn't enough.

In spite of the discomforts, they went on—sharpening their skills and intuitions on the way. One such learned craft was the developed ability of guessing a patient's weight like a carney at the fair, without even seeing them—just by counting the number of floors of the building. The higher number of floors most definitely formulated heavily, no pun intended, into the predicted weight of their patient; for without fail, for some unexplainable reason the heftiest patients always lived on the top floor and were always the best at getting themselves wedged between things, like the tub and the toilet, leaving the crew no choice but to call for a back up. And while initially, it was a different story for some of the outlying rural stations where apartment complexes were rare, the population growth in those areas soon reflected itself in their increased call volume as well. However sadly, the pay scale did not reflect the same image, for in spite of the training and license that was required to work as an EMT or paramedic, the hourly wage was still just a squeak and a hair over minimum wage.

While eventually the union groups were able to get better health care benefits for its members, they were still without a decent retirement package. This, however, was not the fault of the unions or the owners of the companies; but rather because most of the employees considered a retirement package a wasted item, since no one in their right mind would do this kind of work for twenty-five or thirty years anyway. Instead, they felt that having the extra cash in their pockets while they were still young enough to enjoy it was a better way to go. So with all of this in mind, a question arises. Why would anyone waste their time in such a profession, or even consider it as their sole livelihood? The answer to that could only be understood by those who truly felt the compelling desire to aid those who were hurting. And no doubt it was also those committed few who understood, while standing within its blood stained walls—that they were not in it for the money. Yes, there was a great deal of self-gratification that came with the position, but there was also something unexplainable—something that went beyond the glory and the adrenaline rush that everyone spoke of. It was more like a vocational summons that restlessly stirred, drawing them in, then holding them captive. They simply loved this job so much that they would have done it for free—and they practically did.

Anne's seventh year anniversary of working in the EMS profession had come and gone. During that time she stood well grounded in hope on the front row, patiently watching. Little by little, with the help of those who stayed to ride this bad boy out, she saw it clumsily evolve into a profession of longevity; not that she had forgotten her plan regarding the nursing program, that objective still held a place in her future. It was just that her love for the outdoors and her fondness of being on a one to one basis with her patients had grown over the years, and had unexpectedly created a struggle to join the rank and file of the nursing profession. Nevertheless, her postponement of a nursing career did not go un-rewarded; for now, as the summer of 1984 began, nearly two years after the famed bike ride and poker game incident, she became the first female supervisor at Mercy Medical Service. Even though it was only a part-time position, it was a start all the same if she was willing to pursue it—and if Merve was willing to let her go on.

Chuck, who had been working as a full-time supe, came up with the idea of having Anne cover for him whenever he was ill or on vacation. He felt her likable relationship with the other employees would make it easier for her to fill the uncovered shifts, plus he was confident she'd be able to handle any other small problems that might arise. Robbie, of course, would be available by phone to help out if she was really in a bind, but the aforementioned was pretty much the whole of her responsibilities. When it was laid out in front of her, she thought that it certainly sounded simple enough. And it probably would have been, if it had been set up within the time frame of a normal work day of people outside of the EMS business—but it wasn't. Instead, for the next two weeks she'd be on the clock, twenty-four hours a day, seven days a week, until Chuck returned from his vacation.

Initially, to no surprise, she felt the added responsibility was sort of difficult. Then after a few days, she got the hang of working her own shifts in addition to keeping pace with her new supervisory role. Right off, she realized that her least favorite thing was having the radio and phone next to her day and night like an adjacent limb. But then after following Chuck's advice, she found that the investment of a long phone cord to plug into the wall jack of her apartment was a great idea. At least now she could take the phone into the bathroom while she was in the shower. Next, she purchased an earplug for the hand held radio so she could be in contact with the dispatcher while grocery shopping or while doing her other chores. She was delighted to discover that by keeping the radio traffic for her ears only, it also was possible for her to attend church on Sunday morning. Sitting in the back pew for an easy exit, if need be, she could listen to the sermon with one ear and the radio traffic with the other. All it took was a few adjustments and she was able to carry out her temporary role while totally gaining a new perspective regarding Chuck's position, an aphoristic understanding of the expression "walk a mile in my shoes". Even though she took her new duty very seriously, she could see so reason that it should interfere with a friendly game of baseball with the crews.

It was Tuesday afternoon. The sun sat high in a cloudless sky offering little mercy to the thin brown grass that surrounded the baseball diamond. Anne stood in left field adjusting the glove she borrowed from Bill. The tiny feet of an insect on her bare calf drew a swat from her gloved hand, as she stomped her dusty shoe into the dry grass likening the horses on the farm. Jack walked up to the pitcher's mound and faced Buster who was up to bat and standing firm at home plate. They were in the bottom of the fifth inning. Every sport these guys played was normally as serious as a heart attack to them, but it did not retard their jeers and laughter during the game.

Jack eyed Buster while enfolding the ball in his glove. Buster leaned over the plate in a firm stance with bent knees while swinging the bat. "Come on, Jack. Put her here," he called. Seconds later, Jack pulled his arm back—then in one smooth motion whipped the ball forward and let it go. Buster's grip on the bat tightened as the ball spun toward him. His timing was right-on. While combining aim and force, he brought the bat around then connected ash and leather with a loud crack. The ball responded immediately and spun back toward Jack. But before the bat even hit the ground, the ball smashed into Jack's face bending and breaking his glasses.

Everyone jumped to the play. Randy ran from second base to third, Linda ran home. Anne's eyes followed the ball. She had a clear view of the incident. Fortunately for Jack, he saw the ball coming and reacted quickly by using his glove as a shield. Instead of his face taking the full force of the line drive, the ball deflected off the edge of his glove and hit the corner frame of his eyeglasses knocking them to the ground. Thank God for that, Anne thought. She was relieved to see that Jack wasn't hurt, not only for his sake but also for hers. She knew that if he couldn't work his shift the following day, she'd have to find someone to cover it—or work it herself. It was clearly understood that Merve would never let a car go down. So whatever she had to do to keep every station unit in full and running order, she did. If one of the road crews took a day off, she would offer that shift to another employee of the same level of licensor by playing let's make a deal. If you work this day, you can take off another day of your choice. Sometimes with Robbie's permission, of course, she'd even offer double or triple time. But that was only as a last resort, and only if she was already working.

Jack finished pitching the inning in spite of his broken glasses. He must be okay she thought, or he would have stepped back and let someone else throw the ball. Still to be on the safe side, she thought she better make sure. As they entered the top of the sixth inning, she quickly jogged up behind Jack and joined him as he sat on the bench behind the back stop.

"Hey Jack, you okay?" she asked.

"Yeah. It just broke my glasses. I've got a spare pair at home, but they aren't that good."

"Well the lens look okay—and it's still early. Maybe they have another frame like this at your eye doctor's. You can drop them off on the way home and pick them up tomorrow. I'll even hold over for you in the morning, while you go and get them."

"Hey—thanks, Anne. That's nice of you to offer. But then I guess it's easier to fill a couple hours, then it is the whole shift," he chuckled.

"You got that right," she smiled. "I might be new at this supervisory thing, but it didn't take me long to figure out that you don't use up all your resources of crews if you don't have to. People don't like being pestered—and if you ask too much of them, they generally burn out and aren't as willing to help out when you really need them. No, I'll just come in for you tomorrow myself. It'll be easier all the way around—plus you're working with Rod. He's a good guy to work with and I don't imagine it will take you that long."

"Probably not, but you never know."

The morning of Anne and Rod's shift had been slow. While driving back from their cover point, she watched as he leaned back in the driver's seat preparing his aim and eyeing the half inch slot in the window he had left, in which he would spit his gum through. This was an uncanny talent that she was sure no other person on the face of the earth possessed, or probably even wanted to; but still, it was fun to watch.

"All right," he began. "Do you think that I can get my gum through there?" he asked, pointing at the small opening between the glass and the inner edge of the door.

"Yeah, you probably can. But for kicks—why don't you close the window just a hair more."

"Oh, a challenge. I like a challenge," he smiled. After turning the handle to reduce the space of the slot even more, he asked, "How's that?"

"That's good," she nodded.

Satisfied with her interest, he rolled the wad of gum around in his mouth. There was no set consistency or exact shape that he tried for. It was just something that he knew was right. That was the only explanation he offered to describe the tiny canon that had spewed from his lips toward the window many times.

With the feeling of an expectant drum roll, Anne watched and waited silently as he continued to move the stick of gum around in his mouth. His concentration was acute and fixed. Then, after a few more seconds of rolling the wintergreen flavored wad between his cheeks and the roof of his mouth, he nodded that he was ready. After taking a deep breath, he leaned back in his seat while carefully eyeing his target. Then suddenly with an intended burst through his pursed lips, the hard little ball flew from his mouth, through the small crack of the window like rocket—and was gone. They both burst out laughing.

"Too bad there isn't a big call for gifted gum spitters," she cheered. "That was great!"

"Alpha 630. Radio calling Alpha 630." It was Ret's voice coming over the dispatch radio.

"Alpha 630, go ahead," Rod answered.

"Respond code three to Brandy Township for an unknown medical. Jump on the e-way in that direction, I'll get back to ya."

Rod reached up and flipped on the emergency lights. Now days they all were strobes. The spinning disks that used to twirl within the domed beacons on the hood of the rig were considered passé. The floor button for the Federal Q was gone as well. Plus the high-low tone on the siren had been replaced as a result of a number of complaints from the Jewish communities that the company served.

Ret's voice returned to the dispatch speaker grabbing Anne's attention as he gave the rest of the call information. It was for a man who was reported as not breathing at a group home in the north end of Brandy Township. The crew knew the township had a couple of group homes spaced a good distance apart but, unfortunately, the one they were responding to was the farthest away. The home, called Meadow Acres, was about ten miles from their initial starting point. It was a comfortable, clean place that sat neatly on a large grassy mead about a half mile or so down a long dirt road that quite often washed out during a good rain, making any driver or passenger of any vehicle traveling the rugged terrain grateful for the man who created cement.

Rod pushed the accelerator to the floor. They picked up speed while flying past the next exit ramp. Just eight more miles to go. Gazing through the window ahead, Anne thought about the volunteer fire station that was close to the scene. Generally, the fire stations were manned with one full time guy to respond, while the others were on call. Knowing that the first responders could at least provide a patent airway for their patient until she and Rod arrived with the ALS gear helped ease her anxiety.

They seemed to be making good time. Traffic was light and yielded the left lane, allowing them to keep up a good clip without interruption. The e-way and its roadside billboards were very familiar. As they flew past the next exit sign, the image of a past call at a nearby outdoor amphitheater off that adjacent road entered Anne's mind. It had been almost a year ago now. The weather had been very much like that of today's, warm and dry with a pleasant breeze. It was late in the evening when they received the call for an injured party. She remembered that a security person sat on a golf cart waiting at the amphitheater gate to take them back to where their patient, a girl in her mid teens, had fallen from the hood of a car and smashed her head on the paved parking lot.

The patient, named Melinda, and the group of teens she was with were there for a music concert. Whether they started drinking before they got there or whether they began drinking after they arrived, Anne never did find out; but they were indeed very intoxicated. Nor did she ever find out whose idea it was to ride across the parking lot on the hood of the car. She couldn't imagine what the driver was thinking as he reportedly whipped around in circles, apparently never anticipating that someone would fall off and get hurt. The whole scenario was beyond her comprehension, even though she knew that teens often view themselves as invincible. In addition to that, this group was probably too drunk to think straight or to assume any responsibility. The driver certainly fit into that category, for he was nowhere to be found when they arrived on the scene. As the image of that night reappeared in Anne's mind she supposed the reason that call had etched itself into her memory so well, while she'd forgotten so many others, was probably because of Melinda's assumed friend; a friend who stood alone in the dark next to the unconscious teen with a closed head injury, frantically weeping with her fists held tight toward the heavens as she yelled over and over again—"Why did God do this to us?"

As they turned onto the dirt road, Anne looked at her watch—they were almost there. The first hundred feet of the drive was smooth sailing. Then the ride became extremely rough due to a recent rainfall that eroded the road's graded surface, leaving a washboard covering in its place. Rod took his foot off the gas and braked at will to slow the rig before going over the next set of ruts in front of them. In spite of his effort to keep control, the tires bounced in a non-rhythmic syncopated reel over the corrugated roadway, causing the back of rig to sway from side to side as it went over the hard ripples of dirt before finally leveling out. The jostling eased for only a moment. Then without warning, the ambulance slid from the rugged roadway down into the ditch at their right before sliding onto someone's front yard. Rod tried to maintain his speed for fear that they'd get stuck on the soft sod while trying to keep the ambulance from flipping over. Looking ahead, Anne noticed a row of trees at the edge of the yard and knew that if Rod didn't stop the rig soon, they would hit them head on. In spite of the seriousness of the situation and while it seemed absurd, for some silly reason Anne started giggling. Then as suddenly as they went off the road, in a mysterious and dream like fashion, they like wise moved back onto the road maintaining their speed without falter. It was the wildest thing either of them had ever experienced and it all took place in what seemed like an instant. Rod burst out laughing. "Man, did you see that? If I wasn't here to see it—I wouldn't have believed it."

"No kidding," Anne chuckled. "It's like the big hand of God just reached right down and put us back on the road. That was something, all right!"

Finally, the group home was just ahead. Rod pulled in the driveway and parked behind the fire truck. Anne jumped out of the ambulance then stood at the side doors grabbing the orange box and the O2 bottle from the shelf. Rod took the drug box and cardiac monitor and followed her into the group home. The front door was open. Following the voices into the kitchen, they found their patient lying on the floor with two of the volunteers doing CPR, a sure sign that their patient was pulseless and not breathing. With that, Anne set the orange box on the floor then grabbed the intubation equipment and knelt next to the fireman who was squeezing the resusci-bag, while Rod reached into the box for an IV set up.

"The guy was already down when we got here," the fireman told Anne. "I'm really having a hard time getting any air in. There's a lot of resistance. But then with an entire cheese and baloney sandwich blocking his airway I'm not surprised." By the expression on his face, Anne knew he was serious and as dumbfounded at the thought as she was. Wasting no time, she unwrapped the airway equipment as she listened to the rest of his report. "I got out what I could, but it's really crammed in there; hopefully you'll have better luck than I did."

Kneeling at the top of the patient's head, Anne opened the package for the intubation tube then smeared the tip with a lubricating gel. After picking up the handle of the laryngoscope, she slid the clasp of the metal blade under the pin and flipped the blade down, locking it into place. The bulb at the end of the blade came on, providing the light she needed to see into the patient's oral pharynx. Crouching down, she carefully slid the blade into the patient's mouth. In a glance she realized yes indeed his entire airway was blocked with bread and lunch meat. Obtaining access to his trachea wasn't going to work unless she could clear his airway. Reaching toward the blue plastic and white gauze Chux pad that was on the floor next to her, she picked up the forceps to remove the obstruction. After a few tries she was able to get some of the sandwich out but still it wasn't enough to slip the endotracheal tube through. The bread was too soft, plus she was afraid that by probing or trying to insert the tube, the blockage would actually worsen. Time was running out. The longer it took to get an adequate airway, the more brain damage from a lack of oxygen would occur. She knew she had to move fast. "Ted," she called to the fireman behind her. "Go out to the rig and bring me the bio-phone and an OB kit."

He looked at her puzzled, but moved quickly to do what she asked.

Anne sighed while leaning over the patient with the laryngoscope. She couldn't just sit there. Maybe if she was real careful, she thought, she'd be able to peel at least some of the bread away from the patient's oral pharynx. Peering into the white glistening cavity, once again, she picked up the forceps next to her. Then, one of the group home staff members who had been standing in the doorway softly spoke up and said that the patient had a history of seizures and added that he was a ward of the state. The woman said he had lived at the group home for nearly two years and that he was sometimes difficult to control. During Anne's initial visual survey, she guessed the patient's age to be about forty-eight or so and wondered why someone that young was in a group home with elderly people. Now as she listened to the worker convey the information about the patient, she wondered what the woman meant by "difficult to control." Then she wondered how in the world he got what seemed like an entire baloney and cheese sandwich packed into his throat! She knew it was not her place to form any conclusions or allegations. That job would be left for the deputies who had arrived on the scene just prior to her and Rod. And then she wondered—where in the world was Ted? It seemed like an hour since he went out to get the OB kit—though she knew it was really just a mater of seconds. Still she could feel her own pulse start to quicken as a feeling of anxiousness rose and then she noticed that Rod had the IV going and was starting to push the first line meds for a cardiac arrest patient. As he grabbed a syringe from the shelf of the orange box, a large bore IV catheter on the shelf below it caught her eye. She reached for it, then began running her fingers over the patient's neck to find her land marks. Feeling the perspiration gathering across her forehead she looked down, then wiped the area with an iodine swab. While studying the area between the thyroid and the cricoid cartilage, she uncapped the catheter, then held the tip of the needle against the patient's throat. Taking a deep breath, she carefully steadied her hand, then pushed the tip of the needle into the skin, easing it into the membrane layer beneath. Once she felt the pop of the needle passing into the membrane itself, she stopped to remove it from inside the catheter. The needle was only used to gain access to the desired site. If it was pushed in too far, it could do more damage than good. Now with the needle out of the way, the hollow catheter could be used to get at least some air into the patient's lungs. Sighing, she continued to insert the catheter up to the hub, then had one of the firemen open a size three intubation tube. She knew that the connector end of that tube would fit into the hub of the catheter and would enable her to bag the patient. Here goes, she thought. Slowly and gently she tried to push air through the small hollow tube—but still—there was too much resistance. Ted came into the kitchen with the OB kit and the bio-phone.

"Thanks, Ted. Now can you get LOH on the line for me?"

Without a word Ted set the radio on the floor, opened the case, then moved the knob to the county frequency. In an effort to improve radio contact between the hospitals and the EMS providers, a multi-tower system was setup by the county throughout the county, enabling them to offer the best mode of transmission to the closest tower, from antenna to antenna. It sounded like a good plan—but how do you set up the closest tower for a moving vehicle? Plus there were so many dead zones throughout the county that the crews knew at best, they had a fifty-fifty chance of getting through. Because of that, it was understood that they might have to go outside of the pre-radio contact of their SOP's from time to time and act on their own. They also understood if they did, they needed to be prepared to deal with the consequences. And there would be consequences. If you stepped outside of the guidelines and your patient lived, you were a hero. If you performed the same act and your patient died, even if he probably would have anyway, you were at risk of losing your license.

Anne knew she had already stepped beyond the line by doing a crico-thyroid puncture; but that she could deal with. However, attempting a surgical cricothyreotomy without even trying to make radio contact was a little more than she dared to risk.

"LOH, this is Alpha 648, how do you copy?"

"Loud and clear, Alpha 648, go ahead."

"LOH, we have a male patient under CPR who has an obstructed airway. We have tried to unblock the airway without success and have even tried a cricothyroid puncture. I'd like to try a cricothyreotomy at this time."

"Alpha 648, how do you plan on doing this procedure?"

Instantly Anne recognized Dr. Malley's voice. Although he had always been an ally to the crews, she knew if he sensed even the slightest wavering in her voice, he'd never give his permission. "I can take the scapula from our OB kit to make the incision into the cricothyroid membrane," she said, confidently. "Then I can insert an intubation tube to accommodate the size of the incision and to bag the patient."

"What's your patient's down time, Alpha?"

"We aren't sure. Fire says the patient was down when they arrived about six or seven minutes ago. We have the line established and have the first line drugs on board."

"Very good, Alpha 648. What's your ETA here?"

"About twenty minutes," Rod answered.

"About twenty minutes, Dr. Malley."

"All right—then go ahead with the procedure, and watch for excessive bleeding. If you have any trouble, re-contact. Other than that, we'll see you in twenty minutes."

The second she heard the words "All right", Anne dropped the receiver. With a true unknown downtime and whatever small amount of air that the fire department was able to squeak through, she knew that their patient was beyond the golden time span. If she was going to make her move, she'd better do it quickly.

Rod had the OB kit opened and handed her the scalpel. She remembered there was bread packed down to where she had inserted the needle and knew she needed to go lower with the scalpel. Taking the tip of the unsheathed blade, she set it between the highest of the tracheal rings and made a small vertical incision from center to right. Immediately, blood ran from the laceration. Quickly, she held a sterile gauze dressing near the site, while pulling the blade straight up. Then she set the tip in the opposite direction to reinsert the blade to make the second incision, moving left. Using the handle of the scalpel, she then gently laid the end of it onto the edge of the surgical slot and applied enough pressure to carefully insert a size six endotracheal tube into the open area. Because the insertion point was at the throat rather then mouth, she kept a greater length of the tube out while taping it inplace. Rod held the bell of the stethoscope on the patient's chest and moved it from one side to the other, while Ted squeezed the resusci-bag. If air could be heard in the right side only, the tube was in too deep. She watched as he pulled the earpieces from his ears, then wrapped the stethoscope around his neck.

"Sounds good. You've got air going into both lungs. What do you say we get moving. You can do the rest en route."

"That's fine by me."

Ted and another fireman named Buck offered to ride in with Anne to do CPR and bag the patient while en route to the hospital. It was pretty much a standard curtesy and one that Anne was grateful for as it allowed her the needed time to keep a close eye on the EKG monitor and push the required medications per the countywide Standard Operating Procedures. After checking her watch, she reached for another syringe of sodium bicarbonate and epinephrine. Before inserting the needle of either drug into the hub, she felt for a pulse then looked at the monitor. The patient's heart rate still showed no sign of change. There wasn't much left to do. Releasing a sigh, she checked the placement of the ET tube making sure that it was still secure. From the moment they first hooked the patient up to the cardiac monitor at the group home, they saw that he was in a cardiac standstill rhythm or asystole, which meant there was absolutely no heart activity. Even though Anne and Rod had all but emptied the drug box, it just wasn't enough to jump start the man's heart.

Backing into the ambulance bay, Anne thought of the children's nursery rhyme of "Humpty Dumpty" and the phrase, "All the king's horses and all the king's men". While the end result of their call was not uncommon, it was still disappointing. At any rate, she couldn't help wonder if the patient's down time was longer than the people at the group home were willing to admit without sounding neglectful. Maybe they'd given him his lunch then got busy with something else before finding him at a later time than what they said. Or maybe he had a seizure. After all, he did have a history of seizures. Or—maybe he got "out of control," whatever that meant. Lord only knows what really happened, she thought. And more than likely, it would remain that way.

Hopping up onto the stretcher bar between two of the wheels, Anne leaned forward and began doing CPR while the guys rolled her and the patient into the emergency center. One of the orderlies waiting in the assigned room stepped in to relieve her. Then the respiratory therapist relieved Buck from bagging the patient's airway. They knew as well as Rod and Anne that the patient was pretty much dead. But the rule was, you continued CPR until the doc said to stop. Plus, they were curious to see Dr. Malley's response to Anne's tube.

"You did all right, Anne. Personally, I think it's better to make a horizontal cut and the incision's a little low—other than that, it looks perfect."

"Yeah? I was so nervous. But I made my incision lower on purpose—just so you know. When I pulled the catheter out that I inserted first, I noticed that it was clogged with bread and I knew that I'd have to go lower with the tube to get past it."

"Well in that case," he grinned. "It's perfect."

Anne looked around the large room that was usually reserved for trauma patients. She noticed that a couple of the interns and nurses had gathered bedside to see the infield surgical cricothyreotomy. They knew that even though she'd gotten permission first, and even though this procedure was part of the paramedic training, it was not the norm by any means and it could have gone either way as far as being positive or negative for her. So instead of talking or asking questions, they just smiled as they waited until Dr. Malley voiced his approval. Once that was done and out of the way, the small crowd clapped and offered their congratulations. Anne graciously accepted but thought as she glanced at the patient how odd it was that even while the man lay dead, everyone clapped and cheered her performance.

Clearly, if she had not been in the medical profession for as long as she had, the response from the group would have seemed monstrous and cruel. But she understood that their applause was a well meaning encouragement to her, and in no way was meant to show disrespect for the deceased man or lessen the tragedy surrounding it.

Heroism is short lived in this business—but to most it's not really the goal, for humility is by far more appreciated as it helps to keep one's focus on what's truly important. And without question, if there was anything that Dr. Malley could do—he could keep you focused. So of course Anne was not offended or surprised when she stood to leave the ER after finishing her run report, that he looked up from the x-ray he was reading behind her and said—"Now don't go getting cocky, Anne. It's just beginner's luck. You know this is the second patient you've brought in with a tube sticking out of his neck. Let's not make this a habit."

"There's no need to worry about that, Dr. Malley. There's not a whole lot that makes me nervous out there—but that kind of stuff does." she smiled. "And I promise—I won't let it go to my head."

Rod looked thoughtful while helping Anne load the stretcher into the rig. "I thought this was your first cric, " he said.

"It was. He's talking about that lady we brought in a few months ago that cut her own throat from stem to stern in the bathroom. Remember? The firemen dragged her out to the garage to have more room to work—and we didn't realize that she bled out until twenty minutes into the call, when they mentioned all the blood in the bathtub?"

"Oh yeah, the Pez lady with the flip top head."

"I don't know how you could forget that call. It was the easiest tube I ever had, even to this day. All I had to do was ease her head back and slide the tube into the opening that she made in her trachea. I knew I was in, there was no question about it." Then she paused for a second, thinking about something that was obviously on a whole different plane, as she began chuckling. "You know, Dr. Malley calls everything I do beginner's luck. That's the same thing he said to me when he taught me to do an intramyocardial injection. I don't think it's so much that I'm so good. It's more that I just listen—and I watch what people are showing me. That's all. You just have to pay attention and you can't be afraid to try the things that they're teaching you. Anyway, most of the stuff that I've learned so far has been pretty cool. And hopefully, the next time I do a cric it will actually benefit someone."

"Next time? Most people never even get to do one. You and Jack man, you guys really get the calls. Oh, I forgot! Ret said that Jack was back at the station. He called the hospital while you were exchanging the drug box. You know that was supposed to be Jack's call. And if his glasses hadn't of been broke, that would have been his tube. He's really going to be bummed."

"I don't think so, Rod. It was an eerie feeling putting a knife to someone's throat. I'm pretty sure he's not going to feel left out."

"I suppose you're right—and that's a good thing, seeing as we're both sleeping in the same room together," he smiled.

During the year or so that followed, Mercy Medical Service underwent a number of changes in order to keep up with the growing call volume throughout the expanding communities, county wide. In the earlier years, with the exception of the City of Lancemen, the numbers of calls that occurred during the night was much lower than the amount of calls that took place during the day. But slowly and more recently, the call volume at night had noticeably increased. As a result, the crews were up most of the night, which meant that they were all getting paid for twenty-four out of the twenty-four hour shift, rather than nineteen out of the twenty-four hours, which made Merve financially unhappy. So in the fall of 1985 the High Response Vehicles, or HRVs, were introduced as a new and proposed way of saving the worn and weary bodies of the company's crews, in addition to easing Merve's woes about money.

Initially the plan wasn't well received, but then change rarely is. Merve felt that he had to lighten the busy workload of the twenty-four hour cars and thought that by setting a few strategically placed rigs throughout the county at night, he could do that. Originally, the HRV system was set up with three, twelve hour cars starting at 20:00 and finishing at 8:00. After a month into the set up, Merve realized that two rigs would better suit the function of the design while meeting the overall cost. The idea was to run the HRVs first, from call to call while the other crews rested. When the call volume exceeded what the two cars could handle alone, the stationed crews would be called out to respond on the remaining runs in their own, or a nearby, area.

Certainly, there were pros and cons to the system and bugs that had to be worked out; but then that's what experiments are all about. What appealed to Anne was that the HRV schedule consisted of three twelve hour shifts one week and four the next, cutting the amount of hours from their normal twenty-four shift in half. After working the initial forty-eight hour shift, and then the twenty-four hour shift over the past nine years, she felt that testing out Merve's plan might be beneficial and wasted no time in joining the other eleven who were already on the list.

Of course, a higher pay scale was set up to make up the difference in the hourly rate which sounded great at first. But then they discovered that the HRV gross annual income would be five hundred dollars less a year in comparison to the twenty-four hour cars. While that was a big drawback to a lot of the crews, Anne quickly realized that she could easily make up the difference by simply picking up overtime—which would still amount to a total of fewer hours than if she had stayed on the twenty-four hour shift. So for her, the money and hours wasn't the problem. However, not having a station to call home was; not that they spent much time there anyway. Still, just knowing that their living quarters when time allowed would be solely within the confined area of the ambulance unless they decided to hang out at one of the hospitals, or at an all night restaurant, was a little hard to take.

Another item of discomfort that she realized on her first HRV shift was the lack of clean public bathrooms. Outside of the hospitals and restaurants, there just weren't any. And it was also during her first HRV shift while searching for a rest room, that she learned that the less attended facilities offered an education—in an unconventional sort of way. For it was there while visiting a gas station bathroom that she discovered a condom dispenser. The instant she turned on the light and looked around the unkempt room, the white dusty box positioned over the toilet drew her attention. She felt uncomfortable staring at the rows of different colored prophylactics with different tassely and bumpy adjuncts, yet there was a tinge of curiosity. What if a small child had to use the bathroom? she wondered. How would his parent explain them? As balloons? That wouldn't work. Certainly the child would want one of his own. But there they were all the same, hanging right there on the bathroom wall. Truly to her it seemed sad that anyone would feel the need to purchase such an item, but it was even sadder yet that it was in plain view for anyone to see—including children. Telling her partner what she saw, it came as no surprise, of course, when he responded with, "You don't get out much, do you?" She'd been around the guys enough to pretty much predict most of their ideals on such matters. And equally, they had been around her enough to know that she was not ashamed nor did she feel prudish when she smiled and said, "Not where I'd need something like that!"

Anne's new partner on the High Response Vehicle was fairly new to the company. His name was Edward Berry II. He was jolly most of the time and reminded her of Cubby in size and persona. While sitting at a donut place just outside of Lancemen, the two of them joked and talked as they sipped hot coffee from large mugs and munched on fresh fried cakes of sugar and cinnamon from napkins placed on the counter in front of them. The other HRV crew, Chary and Fred, offered to meet them when things slowed down, call wise. Chary was a stocky, yet feminine, young woman in her mid twenties who was very attentive to her shoulder length blonde curly locks—and, she loved chocolate. Fred reminded Anne of her cousin, Jacob, in build. He was sort of tall and strong looking, always clean shaven—plus he was just as fun and full of pranks.

Over the course of the last three months, the four of them had become very close; almost to the point that they were even maternal in the way they watched over each other. Part of the reason they felt so drawn together, they supposed, was probably because they rarely ever saw the twenty-four hour crews and therefore felt somewhat alienated from them. Another reason was that in the event of an odd interim with the stationed crews at the hospital, the HRV crews felt that they were perhaps even, treated differently, like now they were suddenly the redheaded step children. "Where's the HRVs," was the cry, or whine, that often came through the dispatch speaker whenever any of the twenty-four hour crews were pulled from their bed to pull any of the night calls that the HRVs couldn't pull, because they were already on a call.

"Cinderella, Cinderella," Chary mocked, while sitting on the stool next to Anne. Anytime they referenced the miffed voices that echoed through the dispatch radio speaker, they often chuckled lightheartedly, knowing that if the tables were turned, they'd probably respond the same way; although they'd never admit it.

"What do they think, that we're supposed to take all of the calls—and that dispatch is going to hold everything just so that they don't ever have to get up?"

"I'm sure that they would like that—but we're there to lighten the load, not do it all," Ed smiled.

It was one o'clock in the morning and the bars would be soon letting out. It had been a busy night so far but, thankfully, a lull in calls offered a chance for a quick bite to eat, a cup of coffee and time to exchange war stories. The waitress came around with a fresh pot of coffee to top off their mugs. Ed thanked her, then started to chuckle while remembering a call they had all been on earlier.

"I wonder how that guy's doing that I pinned to the footstool. I learned that move in wrestling, you know."

"That was so funny," Fred laughed. "When I was coming up the stairs into the house, all I could see was his legs and arms sticking out from between your butt and the foot stool. He looked like a turtle with a huge shell."

"Yeah?" Ed replied. His face blushed, embarrassed with the emphasized way Fred said the word huge. "Well, you saw how fast he gave up," he boasted in a quick recovery.

"You would too if you had two hundred and thirty pounds holding you down," Chary giggled.

"That was pretty funny. But if you think about it," Anne added, "That whole call could have gone bad. That guy wasn't trying to hurt me when he ran past me and slammed me against the wall. He was just trying to get out of there before the cops got there. A few years ago Dale and I had this call off of East Boulevard that came in as an unknown medical where we let ourselves inadvertently get trapped in the bedroom with this guy who had OD'd on something and I vowed on that day that I'd never let myself get in that situation again. When we first arrived on the scene of that call we were all alone—so we just walked in like we always do, thinking it was a typical sick party or something. One of the kids greeted us at the door and took us to the back bedroom where his dad was. Apparently one of them saw him swallow something, then called for help. We started to talk to the guy, asking him what was going on and if he was sick, you know. Then, without a word, he just stood up from where he'd been sitting on the edge of the bed and started to walk out of the room. The man was huge. I bet he was almost seven feet tall and he was built like a football player. Well, I didn't think too much about it—I mean, after all, we had three of his kids in the room with us. And I didn't even think too much about it when he stopped to reach in his back pocket. You know? My Uncle Henry carries a hanky in his back pocket—so I just thought the man was going to blow his nose or something. I never suspected that he was going to pull out a knife, but he did."

"You're kidding!" Chary exclaimed. "What'd you do?"

"We just watched him to see what he was going to do. Making a quick move at this point seemed like a bad idea with the kids there. And since we'd already let ourselves get pinned in—the next move was his. A second later, he unfolded the blade and held it to his own stomach. Then, right in front of his kids—he pushed it in."

"He stabbed himself?" Ed asked, making sure that he'd heard right.

"Right in front of his kids," Anne repeated. "I couldn't believe it. That's all I needed to see before I grabbed two of the kids and got them into the kitchen. Dale was trying to get the other kid out, a boy about eight, and throw me the radio to call for help at the same time. Within seconds of calling priority traffic, signal seven—two cops showed up and ran down the hall where the man was. It wasn't until then, that Dale was able to get the boy out. Poor thing, he was trying so hard to keep his daddy from killing himself that his own little hand got cut. So here I am standing in the kitchen, trying to calm these kids and wrap the eight year old's hand while Dale's standing in front of the bedroom watching the two cops try to subdue this guy. He told me later that the man looked just like Darth Vador when he stood up with one cop on each arm shaking them off like rag dolls. Seconds later, two more cops came and then two more after that. It wasn't until the last group showed up and held a shot gun on the man that he finally settled down—and still they had to pry the knife out of his hand. Even after we got the guy onto the stretcher, he was squirming and acting up. The cops already had him cuffed, of course, but we still had to tie his feet down to keep from getting kicked and to keep the kids from getting hurt. One of the cops rode in the back of the rig with me to the hospital while his partner followed with the kids. The entire way to the hospital this guy was spitting and yelling and fighting—right until we rolled up to the ER. Then as soon as the doors opened, he became the gentlest, most accommodating man that you'd ever want to meet. Now all of a sudden the nurses are looking at us like we're the bad guys. One of them even asked us why we tied him down, like we made the whole story up!"

"I hate when that happens," Ed smiled.

"Me, too," Anne grinned. "Ever since that call, I learned never to let myself get trapped like that again."

"Hey, that reminds me of an incident that Tom told me about just yesterday," Fred began. "You know how the state's always after us to keep the drug boxes locked up?"

"Yeah," Ed replied. "What a joke that is. That cage they bolted to the floor was a pain—literally. I was always banging my leg on that thing. The combination lock we have now is just as bad; trying to get that thing opened in a hurry is a cluster. That's why nobody uses it."

"And," Fred interjected, "The state guys know that. So to push the issue, this brownnoser from the state apparently tried to prove how easy it was to steal one of the boxes. So a few nights ago he walked up to a rig on an accident scene, hoping that no one would see him. Of course by then the crew was busy trying to backboard the patient and didn't see him. But one of the cops did. So the cop came up to the guy and asked him what he was doing. The guy told the cop, Martinet I think, that he was from the state and showed him his ID and everything. But Martinet didn't care about his ID and asked him if the drug box belonged to him. The guy said, 'Well, no it didn't'—so Martinet arrested him," he chuckled. "Tom said he cuffed him, then hauled him away. The guy didn't get released until morning when his boss came down to pay the bail."

"How funny," Chary laughed. "That guy should have known better than to mess around down here. You know how everybody watches everyone else's back."

"I don't think there's enough stuff in those drug boxes to satisfy any of the street junkies anyway," Anne offered. "Last summer we had so many people that we took to the hospital with huge ulcers on their arms from bad heroin it wasn't even funny. I remember one of the docs saying that it was crossed with some cheap, powdered cleanser."

"That's nuts. But then I'm sure the sellers don't care as long as they get their money," Fred stated. "I guess they figure they'll probably never see those people again anyway, so what difference does it make to them?"

"Well, Anne," Ed yawned. "I'm about all coffeed out. Looks like it might be a quiet night for a change. What do you say we go and find a nice dark place to catch a nap."

"Sure thing. I've got some reading to do anyway."

For a guy who weighs two hundred and thirty pounds and stands five foot eleven inches tall, the living space within an ambulance is a very cramped area to say the least. Even so, during the last four months, Ed had been quite pleasant and rarely complained. But he knew he needed more room. So when the new schedule bid came around, he opted to pick up a twenty-four hour shift at a station for the sake of comfort.

The other HRV personnel, however, decided to keep their slots and partners leaving Anne to work with a fairly new employee, Jason Collier. Jason received his medic training while in the service where he worked at different military hospitals. In addition to having a Paramedic license he was also Nationally Registered, which allowed him to work as a medic in any of the United States. He was stout in build and character with a known flare for the ladies and fashionable things like bracelets for men and popular colognes, which often entered the room before he did. While he and Anne shared different views on worldly things, they worked well together on a professional basis and made the best out of their mutual traits.

She learned that he was an avid supporter of the space program and often clipped out and saved any article she came across in the newspaper about the space shuttle missions for a scrap book he kept, beginning with Columbia which blasted off from Cape Canaveral on April 12, 1981. When it came to knowledge about the different types of shuttle missions, he was as thorough as Chuck regarding radio frequencies and Dan concerning fire-fighting. He was also very interested in the "Space Flight Participant" program and wanted nothing more himself than a chance to travel in space someday.

On January 28, 1986, an unusually cold day, the 10th launch of the space shuttle Challenger was scheduled. It would be the 25th space shuttle mission to leave earth. The crew aboard the Challenger was the mission commander Francis R. (Dick) Scobee, Gregory B. Jarvis, Ronald E. McNair, Ellison S. Onizuka, Judith A. Resnik, Michael J. Smith, a high-school teacher from New Hampshire Christa McAuliffe—and in spirit, Jason Collier.

As thousands upon thousands watched the event in person and on TV, it became a day they would never forget. For after only 73 seconds post liftoff, the Challenger disintegrated into a ball of fire. Everyone watched in disbelief as the mission and the lives of the crew, ended tragically at an altitude of 46,000 feet and at about twice the speed of sound. While Anne was not with Jason at the time of this calamity, she surmised he was probably devastated.

As spring turned into summer, Anne and Jason began their second schedule bid together. Earlier that week Anne had been over to visit the Johnstones' to help with a small vegetable garden in their back yard; the plan they once had of moving into a condo, had been put on hold for a few years. While she admitted she was nowhere close to being the farmer Uncle Henry was, she knew enough and was willing to do the tilling—which was the hard part. The Johnstones had a few gardening tools and a compost pile from grass clippings but no real way of moving it into the garden. So with that in mind, Anne was in need of a pitch fork. And since it was garage sale season, she figured there was no better place to find one at a good price.

"Yeah—I heard all about your garage saleing," Jason chuckled, as they pulled out of the Lakeview station. "I wondered when you were going to start with that stuff."

This was an overtime shift for both of them. The crew that normally worked the station was on a big fishing trip up north. Usually Jason and Anne liked to pick up an occasional eight hour, long distance transfer to the Cleveland or the Mayo Clinic in Ohio. For those trips, the company paid time and a half, plus picked up the cost of one meal. Working a twenty-four station was not their norm anymore, but overtime was over-time. Sometimes you just had to grab what was out there.

"Alpha 646," came the dispatcher's voice. It was Buster. He was a dispatch supervisor now. Most of the time he and Ret partnered up together;

and together, they could cook up a good portion of shenanigans—like sending a crew on a slow day to a deceased party call, non-emergency. The address would invariably be the address of a nearby cemetery, or they'd set up the coffee pot outside the dispatch door near the surveillance camera and act like it was a drive through restaurant. "That will be $2.50. Pull up to the next window, please," one of them would announce as the nearby rig approached.

"Alpha 646," go ahead, Anne replied.

"Get ready for a long one. You're responding to Oxthorn—to 57 Burgess. The company's name is Extel Molding. You got a man injured by a press."

"En route," she answered. She was glad that Jason was driving as it gave her a chance to watch for garage sale signs while passing through Lakeview on the way to Oxthorn. She'd have plenty of time to start filling in the run sheet once they were out of the township. For now, she'd concentrate on making a list of streets to shop at later.

Sliding the partially filled in run form back into the clipboard, Anne looked for the street address of the small factory as they pulled onto Burgess. "Fifty seven," she said. "There it is, up ahead on the right." A couple of the volunteer firemen were outside waiting to help carry in the equipment and direct them to the patient inside.

"We got a fifty year old man, hit in the abdomen with a large plate from a two ton press," one of the firemen began. He continued his report while grabbing the heart monitor from the shelf at the side door. "One of the bystanders said this guy just sold the place and came in to make sure everything was in good running order for the new owner. Apparently when he turned to leave, this plate let loose and knocked him down and the guy standing behind him. He's hurting pretty good. The other guy has a broken arm. I got a couple of my guys splint'en that. Both of the patients' families have been notified and are on the way to St. Luke's."

"We'll see. Chances are we'll have to go to LOH. St. Luke's isn't a trauma center," Anne advised.

Overhearing their conversation, Jason spoke up. "And it probably never will be. For most of their docs, the idea of treating trauma is IV and transport, anyway. It doesn't matter how critical the patient is, it's the same treatment no matter what."

The factory was well lit and both patients were easy to see from the doorway. They were about thirty feet in, lying on the cement floor. Surmising the man hit in the abdomen with the press plate probably had internal injuries, Jason quickly set up the IV while Anne examined him from head to toe. He was in so much pain he was doubled over. Sweat covered his skin and soaked through his clothes. He was pale and shocky.

"Dave," Anne said to one of the firemen. "Go out and get me the mast pants. They're in a plastic case under the bench seat."

With the mechanism of injury and with the man's blood pressure starting to bottom out, she knew the IV alone was not going to be enough. They needed to put pressure on the abdomen to control the bleeding. The pants would do that. Even though some of the docs didn't like the mast pants, she knew from experience that they worked. At least they had for a girl she and Max ran on some years ago with suicidal ideations, who stabbed herself in a park in Lancemen. The surgeon on that case told Max they had saved her life by using the mast pants on her. Hopefully they'd work as well for this man.

Jason finished taping the IV down then helped Anne slide the pants under the patient. Seconds later the matching color Velcro straps were in place. The yellow with the yellow and the red with the red. Slowly, Dave pushed on the rubber foot pad to inflate the pants, one compartment at a time. Within minutes, the patient's breathing slowed and his skin began to dry. Both patients were gently loaded into the back of the rig where a set of vitals was taken. The patient with the abdominal pain, Jim, insisted on being transported to St. Luke's. He didn't care if it was a trauma center or not. It was where his doctor was, and it was where his family was waiting. So the crew bypassed LOH against their better judgment and went to the patient's hospital of choice.

By the time they arrived at the ER doors, Jim was joking and looked good. His blood pressure was within normal limits and his heart rate was a regular sinus rhythm. The other patient with the fractured humerus was resting comfortably, but was glad that they had arrived just the same. One of the nurses and an orderly brought out a hospital cart and helped move him from the folding stretcher on the bench seat to the cart. Soon both patients were inside and in their assigned rooms.

"Now which patient is this?" Dr. Sands asked, walking into the room where Jim was. "Is he the one that was hit with the press? And who put these pants on him?" Without waiting for an answer he continued asking questions, then reached over and ripped the pants off without deflating them. Instantly, the patient sprang up from a comfortable, supine position into an agonizing sitting one, letting out the most horrifying painful scream Anne had ever heard.

"Dr. Sands," she started to say. But then she stopped herself. She knew there was no point in discussing the correct method of removing the pants.

She was sure that the good doctor knew but because he didn't like, nor give his approval for their use—off they came. The end result apparently didn't matter and it was too late now. Swallowing hard, Anne turned and walked out of the room. Anger surged through every vessel within her as she walked out to the ambulance. Jason jumped out of the patient compartment, gripping the pillow for the stretcher in his hand. He knew by her expression that something was very wrong.

"What happened?" he asked.

"He ripped the pants off," she answered soberly.

"Who did?"

"Dr. Sands."

"You're kidding!"

"I wish I was."

"I knew we shouldn't have come here."

"But the patient wanted to come here. They all think that just because their doctor works at whatever hospital they go to, that he's going to be standing at the door waiting to greet them or something. Man! I can't believe that he just walked over and undid the straps like that."

"Did the patient crash?"

"I'm sure he did. He sat up in writhing pain. There was nothing I could do, so I left."

"So what do you want to do now? Do you want to go over to LOH and talk to one of the docs? It's our base hospital—and a couple of the docs are on the Medical Control board."

"Doctor Corpuz is on the control board from St. Luke's. I wish he'd been working today. I know he'd never do anything like that. I don't know what to do Jason. What do ya say we go call Robbie and see what he wants us to do."

A meeting was set up for the following day with Robbie, Dr. Malley, Jason and Anne. If nothing else, talking it out might help ease the sick feeling Anne and Jason held. Until then, they'd just have to shake it off the best they could on their own. While driving through Lancemen toward Lakeview, Anne drove past the station where the volleyball games had taken place, in what seemed like a hundred years ago. A few feet beyond the station, she noticed old Barbara walking with another one of the regulars. Smiling, Anne tooted the siren and waved. Barbara stopped and put her hands on her hips while grinning her toothless grin.

"Looks like Barbara's got a boyfriend," Jason chuckled.

"Looks like," Anne smiled.

The day moved on without pause, offering little time for garage sale shopping. A small disappointment in comparison to the one they experienced earlier. But tomorrow there'd be time for that. With a box of chicken each, a diet soda and the fix'ens, Anne and Jason headed toward the station as the sun was setting in the west. After taking a sip from her glass of root beer, Anne put the glass back in the cup holder. As she looked up, she noticed something in the center lane up ahead.

"What's that in the road?" she asked. "See it in the center lane?"

"I'm not sure," Jason answered. "It's hard to make out."

"Oh my gosh," Anne squealed with delight. "It's my pitch fork."

"No way," Jason laughed. While realizing her excitement and sureness, he slowed the rig to take a better look. "Sure enough" he said soberly. "It's a pitch fork. Do you want me to stop?"

"Yes I want you to stop! That's my pitch fork!"

Jason pulled the rig into the center lane and flipped the emergency lights on. As soon as traffic allowed, he jumped from the driver's seat and ran to the tined object that was laying right in the middle of Dixie and picked it up. Smiling, he carried it back to the rig and carefully gave it to Anne who graciously took it from his hands, like a movie star who had just won an Oscar.

"Oh my gosh. Look Jason. It's perfect. I don't think it's even been run over. It's not bent or scratched. It's perfect. Thank you. Thank you. Thank you Lord, for my manna," she smiled.

"Manna? What's that?" he asked.

Hearing his question, she chuckled. "What's that?" she answered. "That's exactly what the word manna means. That's the same thing that the children of Israel said, when they saw it on the ground in the morning, once the dew was gone. What's that! Then they realized, that it was small round bread for them to eat. God has a way you know, of answering prayers differently than the way that we think He should. And sometimes, because the answer doesn't come the way that it was planned in our minds—we let it slip by. Or we sit around angry, because we think that God didn't hear us. Either way we miss out, because we see things in the natural order of our human minds, rather then in the spiritual way of God."

Shaking his head, Jason watched almost in disbelief as Anne examined what seemed like a gift from heaven.

"Do you know what else the Bible says?" she asked.

"No, what else, he replied."

"The Bible says that—'without faith, it is impossible to please God; for he that cometh to God must believe that God is, and that God is the rewarder of them who diligently seek Him.'"

"Man," he said, breaking his own silence. "I think I'm going to have to start going to church."

"Jason," she smiled. "You need to understand that's its not just going to church. It's a way of life. It's a journey. And it's not just believing that there is a God, but more the relationship that you have with God. Without getting too preachy, you generally lose people when you get too preachy; let me just say that I know that I'm far from being perfect but my desire is to be better. And with God's grace, I can be. Anyone can be. There's a verse in the Bible that talks about a peace that comes from God that is beyond understanding, meaning there are no human words to describe it because it's so wonderful. The only earthly thing that I've experienced that would even compare to that peace, at this point, is when I went skydiving. For the first few seconds of being aloft after my parachute opened, there was this unbelievable stillness, a peace, that to me was beyond words. But the peace from God is even better yet; and it never leaves. I know that, because as soon as I stop wrestling with difficulties in life that I come across, His stillness is there, waiting. Then I remember the verse, 'Be still and know that I am God.' I could not imagine my life without Him. These things are real to me not because I was raised in church but because I know them to be true. I'm in this for the long haul. No doubts. No regrets. I've come to accept that I've become a lifer here, in the world of EMS. But I was a lifer with God first and that will not change. With Him—I will always be a lifer."

CHAPTER 28

❦

AS THE BEACON TURNS

It was October 16, 1987, a day when the hearts and eyes of a nation were drawn to Midland Texas, where an eighteen month old baby girl named Jessica McClure had fallen into an abandoned well, two and a half days earlier. The hole that trapped Jessica was said to be eight inches wide and was surrounded by rock. She was reported to be twenty-two feet down. Her rescuers, the anchorman said, had to dig a parallel shaft before breaking into the well to reach her—but reach her they did. The dramatic moment of the rescue was covered live on TV where it brought tears of joy and a sigh of relief to many.

"Two and a half days," Anne said, thinking out loud. The group of nurses and medics that had gathered around the TV in the nurses' lounge at Lancemen General watched the event, while silently sipping their coffee. That was a long time to be on one call, she thought. The stress on those paramedics must be incredible. From her own experience, she knew that whenever kids were involved, there was always a different twist of emotion in the emergency.

As she watched the drama unfold on the TV screen, she thought of the EMS services within Lancemen County and surmised how they might handle a similar situation. She was sure that the full time fire departments within the county who had their own paramedics would act as the main rescue personnel in those areas. In the rural areas, where the fire departments were "on-call" with mostly Basic EMTs, that group would provide the protective gear, extra equipment and knowledge of its use, for there just wasn't enough space to store things like hydraulic tools or gas compressors on the ambulances. Still, it was Mercy who would supply the advanced medical care with their paramedics. In any event, she felt that the safety of the rescuers and the patient should always be the main objective. Unfortunately, though, she knew that wasn't always the case; for there were paramedics and EMTs in both the private ambulance sector and the fire departments where pride rather than common sense guided the thought process of some individuals.

Of course these folks were well known throughout the county's EMS system and were commonly referred to by the other firemen and paramedics as "para-gods." Everyone outside of their group dreaded working with them and most of the nurses, who labeled them differently using a number of adjectives, disliked even talking to them on the radio. Some nurses went to great lengths to look busy whenever they arrived in the ER with the patient, hoping that another nurse would listen to their report. These guys knew it all—or so they thought; not that there weren't egotistical, competitive mind sets in the early days of EMS. As long as people are people, the high-minded few will always challenge the wits of the remaining—at least until the problem is either worked through or squelched. Still, the difference between one persons way of thinking over another is not always the greatest challenge but more often the difficulty comes when one tries to avoid the trap of a self-serving deed, disguised as pragmatic behavior. Regrettably, even Anne fell into that snare a few times when she was a Basic EMT. In her case, it seemed that nearly every time she and her partner responded with a group of these self-inflated medics, they would deliberately fail to give a report of the patient's condition or vitals to them, as if it were privileged information, leaving her to re-ask the patient the same questions they had already asked, while en route to the hospital. This was frustrating not only to the patient but to her and her partner as well; for not only was the patient their responsibility, since the patient was in their rig, but they also needed to know what was wrong with the patient in the event that the malady worsened en route. What if the patient wasn't as stable as what the first group of medics thought, and the patient died? How would you explain that to the family or to a lawyer, if it got that far. What do you say? I'm very sorry that Mrs. Smith or whoever died. In spite of the fact that she was in the back of our ambulance, we really don't know what was wrong with her because the initial group of medics on the scene neglected to divulge that information. No—she knew that the dependency of each skill and the ability of every worker involved was too great for it to work any other way. Truly most of the medics throughout the county understood the concept of teamwork, and most of the medics and EMTs worked as a team.

As a ground breaker in EMS, Anne knew most of the firemen throughout the County of Lancemen. After all, many of them started out by working at Mercy Medical Service. Roger, Randy and of course Dan had all joined one of the nearby fire departments that ran with Mercy. The rest of the firefighters she got to know over the years in just simple conversation. On occasion, she and her partner would even slide over to the local fire station, at the invitation of the duty guys, for lunch or dinner. By chipping in two or three dollars they could grab a plate and eat to their heart's content.

But that wasn't the only time the crews visited the fire stations. There were other times when they were asked to cover incoming medicals for the different departments during a special fire training or if the department was tied up on a big structure fire. Plus, they always had a rig on standby at the fire scene. Most of them understood the relationship between the municipal fire departments and the private ambulance service was not only a fraternal one, it was also a kinship so to speak that had developed through the birthing canal of the EMS profession.

After refilling her Styrofoam cup with coffee, Anne reached into the basket on the counter for a couple packets of sugar and powdered creamer. Then while holding the packets between her thumb and index finger, she tapped them against her hand to move the contents to the bottom before tearing off the top edge. Held in thought, her mind began drifting to a conversation she'd had with Chief Blake and some of the other firemen from Lakeveiw Fire Department a few months earlier during lunch.

"So, Anne," she remembered Lieutenant Art Green asking. "Are you going to fill out an application? We're hiring, you know."

"Probably not. For one thing, I don't have any fire training. And to be honest, for another, I really don't have any desire to go into a burning building. Common sense tells me to leave a building that's on fire, not go into it. Plus, well not to be mean of course—but you do have some pretty big boys working here. If they got hurt, there's no way in the world I'd be able to pull them out."

"So what do you think—that just one of us alone is going to be able to drag Scotty or Moose out?" Art chuckled. "All you have to do is take a Fire One class—and we'll teach you the rest. You'd love it! Come on, Anne, we're going to have to hire a girl sooner or later; it might as well be you."

"Thanks, Art, I guess." She knew that coming from him, that was actually a compliment. "Tell you what. If Chief Blake grandfathers my seniority over, I'll go to every car crash and medical that comes in. You guys can go on all of the house fires and play to your hearts' content; and I'll stay here and cook up a really good meal for you to eat when you come back."

"Sounds good to me," Art smiled.

"Anne, you know I can't do that," Chief Blake said. "We're not a big city department. We don't have separate divisions. Firemen run on medicals and fires. You don't get to pick what you go on."

"Well that's my final offer," she grinned. "What I do now is dangerous enough. I hope to have a husband and kids someday. I'm sure if I was a firefighter, it would only complicate things."

Bringing the Styrofoam cup to her lips, she realized it was empty and that the group of TV viewers within the room were starting to break up to return to their duties. Paul, her partner of several months, stood up and threw his cup into the domed trash can that was at the end of the counter.

"Hey, Anne," he asked. "Did you let dispatch know we were available?"

"No, I thought you did. Oops," she smiled sheepishly. "Guess we better get on the air."

"Oh great! So what are you trying to do—get me in trouble?" he grinned. "What kind of training officer are you, anyway?"

"Hey, don't start with me," she teased.

Anne liked working as a training officer much more than she liked working as a fill in supervisor. Indeed, both positions had their challenges but working with the new employees kept her on the road full time. Plus, it paid five percent more an hour and she no longer had to make deals as far as covering open shifts. She'd always felt like a used car salesman when it came time to persuade the crew to work extra or switch scheduled days. No doubt, some folks are born salesmen, she however was not.

Her partner, Paul, was smart and a fine addition to the elite group of medics that were already working at Mercy. Without question, his previous experience as an on call fireman in Clear Lake Township would be to his advantage. In just the past few years alone, he had responded to a number of medicals with the fire department where Anne was called, making a workable foundation for them to build from now as partners. Thinking back, in spite of the many calls since then, Anne could still remember the first call they had together. Really it wasn't so much the call itself that she remember, but more of the grand way that he carried himself while on the scene. Even though he stood only about five foot, four inches tall, clearly from his commanding demeanor, his mental stature was at least six foot;

not that he was insecure about being short. Just by watching him, you knew that his mannerisms would have been the same at any height. He was no Napoleon Bonaparte—he was more of a Paul Bunyan. At least he fit the folklore character—in a fable like size, she thought. Nevertheless, neither he nor she were alone in this imagery, for the men that he worked with on the fire scene where she was "on stand-by" asked his opinion and took orders from him without hesitation. However, now that Anne was his training officer at Mercy, he was the one asking for her opinion and following her direction regarding medicals, all of which he seemed to do gladly.

Paul and Anne had a very good working partnership. It was like she was working with Dan or Dale again. In no time she and Paul were able to go through a call and do all that was needed with little conversation between them. They knew what the other would do and felt, by mere expression and intuition. She truly enjoyed his stories about his childhood, about hunting with his father and older brother, and about meeting his wife. He was the most animated person while telling a story that she'd ever seen. Sometimes he made her laugh so hard she could hardly catch her breath.

While she never said anything to Paul, she overheard him talking to another medic at Mercy one day when they first started working together. The medic asked Paul who he was working with. "I'm working with the legend," he answered proudly. She was so surprised to hear the title he used. She never thought that she was anything special, unless you consider the fact that she'd survived ten years of working with this wild bunch a spectacular feat. To that she'd have to credit a multitude of answered prayers for patience, being raised with the rascally brood on the farm and a little bit of attitude that she'd developed likening a suit of armor, perhaps large enough for King Kong at times.

"Alpha 630. Radio calling, Alpha 630." The dispatcher's voice echoed under the canopy at the ER entrance. The familiar sound grabbed Anne's attention as she exited through the electric doors. She dashed to the rig with Paul right behind her. He went toward the stretcher to heave it up into the patient compartment, while she reached for the radio mic up front.

"Alpha 630, go ahead."

"I've been trying to reach you for a call."

"Sorry, that's my fault," she replied. "Go ahead with the info."

"You're responding to 459 Talman, in Oakwood Hills for an overdose. Give me a TX for your times after the call."

"Ten-four."

Paul hopped up onto the driver's seat and flipped on the emergency lights. After checking the side mirror for oncoming traffic, he pulled out into the side street and turned right to head toward the main road. Several minutes had passed before they arrived at the residence of their patient. To their surprise, they were alone. Usually a police car or some of the volunteer fire department personnel were there.

"I'm sure somebody will show up soon. Let's go check it out," she said. While grabbing the equipment needed from the shelves at the side door, previous precarious situations ran through her mind. She knew to be cautious when entering the house.

After knocking on the front door with no response, she tried turning the knob. It was unlocked. "Hello," she called, while entering.

"Back here," the voice of a woman answered.

Following the direction of the sound she heard, Anne entered the bedroom but stayed in front of the doorway for the moment. A woman in her mid-fifties sat in her pajamas in bed. Her hair was uncombed but not mussed. The house was neat and comfortably furnished. There was no sound of a radio or TV playing.

"Are you alone?" Anne asked. After a quick overview of the bedroom, she felt it was probably safe and set the orange box down on the floor.

"Yes, dear, I am," the women said softly.

"Are you sick, Ma'am? Why did you call?"

"I've been feeling down for sometime. I haven't been sleeping well or eating much. My doctor gave me some sleeping pills—but you know, I really don't care if I sleep or not. I guess I really don't care much about anything—so I took the whole bottle of pills about a half hour ago. Now I'm thinking that probably was a bad idea."

"Where's the bottle now?" Anne asked. The woman moved her hand under the blanket and pulled out the orange plastic container. Anne walked closer to the bed and took the container from the woman's hand. "Diana Steele—is that you?" The patient nodded. "F—hydrochloride something. I can't make the name out, the label's smeared. Thirty milligrams," Anne continued. "It says there were thirty capsules prescribed a week ago. How many pills do you think you took?"

"I'm not sure. A handful, I guess. They were a red and an off white colored capsule."

Paul set up an IV of D5W while Anne wrapped the blood pressure cuff around the patient's arm. "Ma'am, exactly what do you mean by a handful?" Paul asked.

"Probably twenty or so, I suppose."

"Okay," Paul replied softly. "Now what I'm going to do is start an IV so we have an access to give you medication if we need to. Then we're going to call the hospital and give them a report of your condition and see if there is anything else that they want us to do. Now do you have any medical problems like cardiac or stomach problems and do you take any other medicine besides the sleeping pills?"

"No. I'm healthy, really. It sounds funny to say now, but I really don't like pills. I don't take anything else."

While Paul explained their treatment to the patient, Anne opened the drug box and took out a bottle of Ipecac syrup. "I'm going to pour some of this into this little cup and I want you to drink it. We'll have you drink three or four glasses of water afterwards. Just so you know ahead of time, it's going to make you sick and throw up—but that's want we want. We need to get those pills out of you as soon as possible."

"There's a glass for the water in the bathroom," Diana offered.

As soon as Paul had the IV taped in place, Anne handed the tiny cup of medication to Diana, then went toward the bathroom to get a glass of water. She noticed there were several photos on the hallway wall on her way back to the bedroom and asked Diana if they were pictures of her family. Diana started to answer while reaching for the glass of water in Anne's hand, then in mid sentence became unresponsive.

"Diana!" Anne said, patting the patient's face. Diana remained unmoved and speechless. "Well that wasn't supposed to happen," she sighed. "Okay, Paul, this is what we're going to do. She's breathing fine and we want to keep her that way, so we have to guard her airway. We can't lay her down, because as soon as that stuff kicks in she's going to start vomiting and we don't want her to drown in her own vomit. So we're going to put her on the stretcher with the back pulled up so she can sit up. And then we're going to strap her in place so if she does vomit, it will just go down the front of her pajamas. Then when we get in the rig, I'm going to set you up with a nasal gastric tube—and you're going to slide it into her stomach through her nose so I can lavage her while we're en route to the hospital."

"Okay. But you're going to have to help me with the tube. I've never done that before."

"No problem."

The crew moved quickly to package their still unresponsive patient. They were still alone, but wished at least one officer or volunteer would have shown up to offer a helping hand. Now with the patient in the back of the rig, Anne reached up into one of the top cabinets and pulled out a nasal gastric tube. After opening the sterile package she smeared the tip with a lubricating gel using her gloved hand, then handed the tube to Paul.

"Okay. You want to keep her head straight like this," she demonstrated. "You don't want the tube to go into her lungs. You want it to go into her stomach. So you're going to insert the tube into her nose through one of her nares. Now you might meet a little resistance at first, but you can usually get past that with some gentle pressure. Don't force it. I'll show you how to hold and angle the tube. Ready?"

"Sure."

Paul gripped the tube and gently inserted it into Diana's right nare. "It won't go any farther. And I don't want to push it too hard."

"Okay—so back out and try the other side."

Again, Paul inserted the tube into Diana's nose but on the left side this time. After meeting a little resistance, he was able to push the tube through the nasal pharynx and into the esophagus.

"Keep going. You should see gastric juice coming up the tube any second. As soon as you see that, insert the tube a hair more, then tape it in place so it doesn't slide up and down." Before Anne finished speaking a green liquid began to fill the tube. Paul was in.

"Good job. Now you can either drive, or lavage her. But either way we need to get going."

"Well I think I'd feel better about driving at this point—unless you want me to stay back here."

"It doesn't matter. I'm comfortable right now. I'll stay—you drive."

Paul looked up at the cardiac monitor that they had set up earlier. "She's still in a sinus rhythm."

"Thanks, Paul; as soon as I get some of this sterile water down her, I'll grab another set of vitals."

The side doors of the rig shut, one after the other. Seconds later, they drove out of the patient's driveway into the street, then were en route to the hospital. While tightly holding a bottle of sterile water between her knees, Anne inserted the long narrow end of the cath-tip syringe into the clear liquid, then pulled back on the plunger to fill the 60 cc reservoir. As the plastic, hollow barrel filled, she thought of the water fights that she and the other crews used to have when they used the syringes in place of a squirt gun in earlier years. They often joked that they were accurate up to fifty feet. But her objective and use of the syringe today was certainly different. Now, diluting and suctioning as much of the medication from the patient's stomach was its purpose.

After flushing the fluid from the syringe through the gastric tube, and into then into the patient's stomach, Anne pulled back on the plunger and repeated the process again and again. Each time that she drew the water back up through the tube and into the syringe, she squirted it into the large emesis basin that she had set on the bench beside her. Occasionally she'd look into the collected liquid to see how effective the procedure was. The mixture of water, gastric juices and tiny particles of the red and ivory capsules was a positive sign. "Eureka!" she said quietly to herself. Minutes after arriving at Lancemen General, she saw that the patient displayed brief moments of purposeful eye movements as the nurses and Doctor Bastein continued working at lavaging and neutralizing the stomach contents. While filling out her run form, Anne overheard the good doctor call for a room in the ICU. Once Diana was stable enough, his plan was to send her to the psych floor for treatment of depression and suicidal ideation.

Paul and Anne began working their last week together on a day shift in mid September in 1988. While Anne wasn't what you'd call a night person, she agreed to work a night car for one schedule bid. It was the only way that she and Paul would be able to remain as partners, due to a new addition that would soon be arriving at Paul and his wife, Michelle's home. Michelle was eight and a half months pregnant and looked like she was ready to burst at any moment. She was shorter than Paul, about five foot two, with blue eyes and light brown hair. Paul called her his best friend and treated her as if he meant it. He was excited about becoming a father and said he was concerned that he wouldn't be much help to Michelle during the night, as she planned on nursing the baby. So with that, he opted to work nights to be home during the day to help with laundry and such, while Michelle and the baby napped. Nicholas was the name they picked if the baby was a boy. It meant "victory of the people—triumphant spirit". A girl's name was still undecided for sure. Even though Paul had his heart set on a boy, he said either way he just prayed the baby would be healthy.

Anne enjoyed working with Paul enough that she gave up her training officer position to continue as his partner. This week they'd work out at the Clear Lake station and then start the next schedule bid by working nights at the Oakwood Hills station. Mercy still had a number of stations to work out of, at least for now. But rumor had it that was soon to change. And much to the union's initial objection, all the crews were now working twelve hour shifts. County wide, the company was just too busy to schedule any twenty-four hour shifts and have them be effective.

"Alpha 630."

"Go ahead for 630," Paul replied.

"Respond for a possible deceased party at 59 Jackson Lane. Time of call is 12:57."

"Ten four."

Paul opened the driver's door of the rig and yelled out to Anne in hopes to catch her before she walked into the local Chicken Shack. "Hey, Anne, we got a call!"

Turning around at the sound of his bellowing voice, she hurried to the passenger side of the ambulance and opened the door. "Always when it's time to eat. Did you ever notice that?"

"Relax," he said while flipping on the emergency lights. "We'll be just as hungry when the calls over. Besides, it's a possible deceased party. Usually when they say possible, there's a good chance they are."

"Shame on you, hoping that some poor person is dead, just so you can eat lunch," she teased.

"You know what I mean. Anyway, the call came through the sheriff's department. I wrote the info down on the envelope."

Picking up the map, Anne read the information, then looked for the street. Paul said he had a pretty good idea of where he was going; he just wanted to be sure. The address they were responding to was in a country like area near Bedford. Most of the neighborhoods in this part of the township were built in the early sixties on land where large farms had once graced the grassy fields.

As the ambulance screamed toward the given address on that Saturday afternoon, Paul was pleasantly surprised that the weekend travelers yielded so quickly to the sound of the siren—all with the exception of the one van.

"Come on, lady! Pull to the right and stop! Man, where's a cop when you need'em."

Paul moved in a little closer to the back of the van and slightly over the center line in an effort to get the driver's attention in her side mirror. Now he could just about see the woman's face. Seconds later, the van jerked to the right, then pulled over to the shoulder of the road. "Finally," he said. Pushing down on the accelerator, he sped up then swung back into his own lane as he passed the van.

Anne peered into the vehicle as they drove around it. "She's got a mitt full of kids in there. She probably couldn't even hear the siren over all that ruckus."

"I bet they're not seat belted either," Paul jumped in. "Now see, Michelle knows how I feel about that. She better never take our kids in the car and not seat belt 'em."

"Well I couldn't really tell for sure if they were or not. We went by her too fast."

As the crew pulled onto Jackson Lane, Anne looked to see which side had the odd numbered addresses and which side had the even.

"There's the deputy's car up on the left," she said.

Paul slowed down, then pulled into the driveway. "This house looks familiar," he whispered to himself.

Anne jumped out and opened the side doors of the rig. After grabbing the cardiac monitor and the orange box from the shelf, she hurried toward the front door of the residence. While she knew it seemed silly to rush to the aid of a deceased person, from experience she also knew that there was always the outside chance that the caller was wrong. Anyway, just the fact that they had screamed down the road and now that they were there they were just going to meander into the house, seemed rather contradictory. But at the same time, because she knew how graceful she wasn't, she knew that running was also a bad idea. Somehow, it doesn't look very good when the health care providers trip while coming to save someone else. With that in mind, she thought that a quick stride with her short little legs was good enough to get her where she was going.

The front door was ajar. After pushing it open the rest of the way, Anne walked into the house with Paul at her heels. There wasn't a foyer or even a coat closet. The front door opened right into the living room. Immediately upon entering the small ranch, Anne looked to her right and saw an older woman sitting on the couch, twisting her hands in her lap. Then, she noticed a deputy sitting at the dining room table at the opposite end of the open room, writing on a pad of paper. Another deputy came out from behind a partition that divided part of the kitchen from the other two rooms. As soon as he saw the crew walk in, he nodded to acknowledge their presence then pointed toward the kitchen floor.

"Looks like he's been gone for a few days," he informed them. "His wife said that she just came home from visiting her daughter up north and found him on the floor just like he is. She says that all those medications on the table are his. That's about as far as I've got with that." While listening to the deputy, who she knew as Officer Lane, Anne set the med box and monitor on the floor near the table then took the clipboard from Paul. It was common practice to let the new medic do the pronouncement of the deceased party, to give them more experience with the radio report to the hospital.

Leaning over, Paul opened the orange box then picked up the EKG cables from the top shelf. After putting on a pair of latex gloves, he grabbed a set of electrodes from the same shelf and walked toward the body. He knew to be careful while moving any article of clothing or anything else that could be useful in determining the cause of death. Throughout his visual exam, he made mental notes to offer to the hospital during his report. Right off he saw that the man's frame was slight and bony, giving notice to his hollow cheeks and barrel chest. Then he noticed that the deceased was still dressed in his light blue pajamas and a burgundy bathrobe that was undone and draped across the beige tiled floor. From any direction, it was hard to ignore the waxen glow that was cast by the light of the refrigerator's open door as it shown over the corpse in an insalubrious way; not that the dead should look healthy. But seeing a number of bodies in a number of different situations, after a while you unwittingly develop a sense of who was just dead and who was painfully dead; as if from the grave the deceased could tell their own story. Then Paul noticed that the man was clutching on to something in his right hand. Anne saw it too, but she couldn't make out what it was from her position at the table across from the deputy.

The scene was quiet but busy, with each person performing his or her role. Paul leaned over the body switching the knob on the cardiac monitor through all three leads as the paper strip recording of the lifeless rhythm rolled out onto the floor. Anne sat listing the name of each medication from the containers in front of her onto the run form. Deputy Doogan sat writing a report compiled of the information from the woman's statements and from his own observations. Deputy Lane had stepped outside to use his hand held radio to talk to the detective who was en route from the substation.

Periodically, while filling in her run form Anne looked over at the deceased's wife, who seemed a little odd to her in the way that she was handling the death of her husband. She looked nervous or distressed—but not in a mournful way. It was hard to pinpoint or explain. It just felt weird. Oh well, she concluded. I guess everyone deals with these things differently.

"Ma'am," she asked. "What kind of medical problems did your husband have? I see he was on a couple different heart pills. Did he have any breathing problems like emphysema or congestive heart failure?"

"I'm not sure. We didn't talk much," the woman replied. Her answers were short and to the point—she never moved. She just sat on the couch, staring ahead and wringing her hands. Deputy Lane walked back in through the front door toward Deputy Doogan. The phone that was on the end table near the couch started ringing. It was right next to the woman who seemed startled for a moment, then after the third ring she picked up the receiver.

"Hello," she said. Her face looked angry as she listened to the person at the other end. "No!" she belted. "I don't know what happened. I told you—he was on the floor when I walked in the door." Then as abruptly as the conversation began, it ended as she hung up the receiver.

Whoa, Anne thought. That was strange. She looked over at Paul to see his response noticing that the refrigerator door was still open. A sudden urge to get up and close it rushed through her but instead she fought the mental prodding and stayed seated. Like Pavlov's dog, she remembered while growing up that Uncle Henry barked nearly every time that she or the boys stood in front of the open refrigerator at home, gazing for something to eat. "There's nothing in there that wasn't in there the last time you looked ten minutes ago. Grab what you want—then shut the door," was just one of the lines they had heard many times. Of course they understood that he wasn't upset because they were hungry. It was just that with six kids, all taking turns at window shopping in front of the frig—it was hard to keep the cold things cold.

The phone rang again. The bell inside the black casement seemed to ring louder with each ring carrying an annoyed sounding tone throughout the room, as if bothered by so much activity—but it was clearly not as bothered as the victim's wife. After hastily grabbing the receiver, she gruffly answered. "Hello! No! Nobody killed nobody! I told you I just found him on the floor. They're here right now, working on him."

Anne looked over at the deputies. Deputy Doogan glanced back, but motioned with a slight movement of his hand for her to let it go for now. Paul stood over and straddled the deceased, while carefully unplugging the EKG cable. Anne finished filling in her portion of the run form as far as name, address, medical history and meds, then stood to help Paul pack up the equipment.

"I'll call the hospital and get a pronouncement time and the doctor's name," Paul offered.

"All right," Doogan replied. "I'll be out in a minute."

Anne handed the clipboard to Paul then carried the orange box and cardiac monitor out to the rig. Paul walked ahead to push the side doors of the ambulance open for Anne and to grab the apcor radio to contact the hospital. While sitting in the driver's seat, he jotted down a few points that he wanted to report to the hospital. Once he was set with that, he leaned to his right to grab the handle of the apcor radio that he'd set on the floor between the seats. After flipping the lid section of the radio case up, he took the receiver from the holder then turned the knob to the hospital's frequency. "LOH, this is Alpha 630 calling in with a signal six," he began.

"Alpha 630, this is LOH—go ahead with your traffic."

"LOH, we're at the home of a seventy year-old male who was found by his wife about an hour ago. According to the deputies on the scene, she stated that her husband was absent of a palpable pulse and was not breathing at that time. His wife stated that the last time she saw her husband alive was two days ago before she left to visit her daughter. At this time there is mottling and rigor mortis present throughout with no sign of injury. Unfortunately, the wife is a poor historian regarding her husband's past medical history; but, from the list of medications he was on, he was possibly a cardiac patient and maybe had some form of pulmonary disease like COPD. The EKG was an asytole rhythm in leads one, two and three. As I stated earlier, we have a couple of deputies from the sheriff's department on the scene and a detective en route at this time. I believe they're going to be contacting the ME shortly."

"Thank you for your report, Alpha 630. This is Doctor Kowinanski with a pronouncement time of 13:37. Feel free to re-contact if you need to, otherwise we'll be clear at this time."

"Ten-four, Doctor Kowinanski. I copy 13:37. Alpha 630 clear."

Paul moved the arm of the small antenna back in place, turned the radio off then closed the lid.

"Here comes Doogan," Anne announced. "That call was flipped out. If I didn't know better, I'd swear that old lady offed her husband."

"Hey, Officer Doogan," Paul smiled. "What's going on?"

"Sorry, Anne, I didn't mean to cut you off. This woman's a piece of work. As long as I can remember, she's been coming into the substation at least once a week, claiming that her husband's trying to kill her with this poison or some other thing. Just last week she came into the station carrying a plastic soap dish with a slice of bread covered in shoe polish or something."

"You're kidding," Paul broke in. "That guy's got a piece of bread in his hand right now!"

"Yeah? Well I hope it wasn't pumpernickel. I saw something in his hand—I figured Detective Oren could be the one to check it out. He got detained, but he should be here anytime."

"No kidding," Paul said, shaking his head. "Pumpernickel. That's wild. Anne and I were just saying that it looked like she did the old guy in."

"Well, I know it looks pretty suspicious.; but we won't know for sure until the autopsy comes back. Did you call the hospital?"

"Yeah. The doc's name is Doctor Kowinanski, common spelling—he called it at 13:37."

"LOH?"

"Yep."

"Okay. See you on the next one."

It was eight o'clock in the morning and the start of Paul and Anne's last day shift. Anne sat on the bench seat in the back of the rig, checking through the cabinets. She noticed a sudden darkness come and go as the sun hid behind a group of clouds, adding a colder feel to the crisp air. To her the dew seemed more like a frost and reminded her of many past autumns on the farm. Paul came out of the station carrying the orange box. His walk seemed somewhat urgent.

"Do we have a call?" she asked.

"Yeah. You riding or driving?"

"I'll ride," she replied.

While crawling through the narrow space that divided the patient and front compartments, Anne picked up the clipboard and the manila envelope that would hold their completed paperwork for that day. Paul hung up the radio mic after getting the call information, then snapped his seat belt in place. Anne finished writing in the normal data passed on by the dispatcher onto the run form, then in the blank area where she was to list the nature of the call, she wrote possible carbon monoxide poisoning.

The address of the call according to the dispatcher was in a new subdivision located off of Bristle Lake Road, called Provincial Estates. Anne remembered driving through the subdivision not long after the construction was completed during the summer. She was amazed at how large some of the homes were with their three car garages. And now as they neared the area, she thought about the nature of the call and hoped that their patient wasn't a suicide victim who had been sitting in a running parked car in one of those garages.

Carbon monoxide is a chemical asphyxiant that is colorless, tasteless and odorless. It is said to be the number one cause of death in house fires, as it saturates the body's hemoglobin which interferes with the normal oxygen absorption and CO disposing process. The early symptoms include nausea, vomiting and confusion but the most common complaint is head ache. Signs of prolonged exposure would be elevated temperature, facial twitching and of course "cherry red" skin color. While these indicators were well known facts to both Anne as an experienced paramedic and Paul as an on-call firefighter and paramedic, it was not uncommon to mentally review them in addition to the treatment while en route to the call.

Paul stopped for the red light at the intersection of Wise and Bristle Lake, then continued once he was sure that all lanes were clear or waiting.

"There's the entrance sign for the sub, Paul," Anne said, pointing.

"Thanks for the warning," he teased. "I just about flew past it."

"Oh you and Rod, you're such exaggerators. We had plenty of time. There's Washington Boulevard. According to Buster, our street is the fourth one on the right, off of Washington."

"Jackson, Roosevelt, Eisenhower and now Kennedy."

"That' it—216's our address. There's the fire department up ahead in the driveway. Looks like they've got a couple of people sitting on the porch at the front of the house. The garage doors are open, with two cars parked in the driveway and one bay's empty. That's a good sign."

Paul pulled up to the curb in front of the mansion like home and stopped. Anne hopped down from the passenger seat onto the newly laid sod, then opened the side doors of the rig. Grabbing the handle of the orange box, she slid it across the floor toward her. Paul came around with the clipboard tucked under his arm, to help with the other equipment. As soon as Anne was out of the way, he grabbed one of the smaller O2 tanks from the cabinet shelf then followed her up the long sidewalk toward the group just ahead.

While approaching the house, Anne glanced across the dew covered lawn and noticed a prism like effect from the streams of sunlight that had peeked through the soft gray clouds above. A gentle breeze, sweet with the crisp smell of fall picked up and carried part of the conversation between the firemen and the couple waiting on the stoop. Their chatter seemed easy—certainly there could be no urgency here, she thought.

Setting the orange box down on the sidewalk, Anne looked up at the firemen. "Hi, guys. What's going on?" she asked.

"Hi, Anne—Paul. This is Mr. and Mrs. Lausanne," one of the firemen replied. "They both woke up this morning complaining of a headache and some nausea. Last night was the first night they used their new furnace and thought that maybe there was a problem with it since they both felt fine before going to bed. I've got a couple of men inside with the gas man checking it."

"Hi," Anne began, looking at the couple. "How are you feeling now?"

"Pretty good," Mr. Lausanne answered. "We came out here and sat, right after we called the gas company. The fresh air has helped a lot. I didn't think that we needed to go to the hospital by ambulance but the gas man said we should let you check us out and then take it from there."

"Well sure. We can do that. Let me start by taking your blood pressure. My partner, Paul, will ask you a couple of questions, and if you check out okay and still don't want to go with us to the hospital—we'll just have you sign a release form."

"That's fine," Mrs. Lausanne said. "But I feel bad putting you through all this."

"It's no problem, ma'am," Paul smiled. "Why don't we star—." In mid sentence, he stopped. Startled by a thunderous banging thud behind him, he turned around. The firemen rushed to where Anne had left the orange box. Right away Paul saw that it was tipped over but it took a second look for his mind to register the two little feet that were sticking up in the air over the box. Using every bit of restraint not to laugh, he watched as the firemen helped her to her feet. "Oh my gosh, Anne, are you all right?" he finally asked.

Embarrassed by forgetting that she had set the box down right behind where she was standing, Anne quickly responded to the firemen who were aiding her. Brushing off her clothes, she answered. "Ya, I think so. Oh my word."

"You sure? Looks like your leg's bleeding a little," he said, in a forced concerned tone. Why don't you go back to the rig and take care of that—we'll finish up here."

"Geez. All right. Sorry, you guys," she sighed.

How humiliating, Anne thought, as she limped back to the ambulance. She was so shook by her tumble that she didn't even turn the box back over or pick up any of the gear or bandaging equipment that fell onto the grass. She knew Paul would never let her live this down—never! And not only would he tell everyone, but he'd tell it in such a way that even she'd have to laugh. Now that was something to look forward to. "Great," she whispered to herself. "Well at least I didn't break anything." After taking a couple of gauze four-by-fours out of the cabinet, she sat down on the bench seat and began rolling up her pant leg to assess the damage. It looked like an abrasion over her right shin was the worst of it. With the exception of that and ripping her uniform pants, she felt that she'd faired pretty good.

The sound of rustling grass came from outside through the side doors. Anne looked up. It was probably Paul, she figured. The doors opened wider. Sure enough, it was Paul gripping the handle of the orange box in his hand. Setting it on the floor of the patient compartment, he looked up at her and burst out laughing, reminding her of a whale spewing water from its blowhole.

"It wasn't that funny," she grinned.

"What are you talking about! That was the funniest thing I've ever seen. Here's this boom, boom thud—and then all I see is two little feet sticking straight up in the air. And that's not funny? Oh, my side's killing me!"

"You are so stupid," she teased. "Come on. I have to go back to the station and change my pants."

"You're going to have to go into central and fill out an on-the-job injury report too," he chuckled.

"Go ahead and laugh. Get it all out of your system."

After clearing the scene as SNR, services not rendered, Paul drove Anne to the station so she could change her clothes. With that out of the way and after a phone call to the road supervisor, they headed to the company's main headquarters. Central, as they called it, had changed locations a number of times since Anne first dispatched with Roman. While it was in a much larger building now, it was still the main facility for the dispatch center, all office personnel, maintenance, medical supply and of recent, their continuing education program. Even though Anne knew she'd have to put up with some guffawing from someone once they got there, she understood that it was all in fun and that it would only last a short time.

Hot dog day. As soon as Paul and Anne pulled into the garage of central, they could smell the yummy aroma of steamed hot dogs.

"I think the day just got better," she smiled. "I smell hot dogs."

"Cool," Paul grinned. "All that laughing made me hungry."

For most people, 10:30 in the morning is pretty early for chili hot dogs and the fix'ens. But then most people don't have iron clad stomachs like the crews at Mercy did. As soon as Paul and Anne walked into the bay area where the steam table was set up, Paul reached for a paper plate. Anne's growling tummy would have to wait. Before she could even think about the sweet juicy flavor of a chili dog with mustard and onions, she'd have to fill out an incident report about her fall. "Sure it's only an abrasion," Chuck agreed on the phone earlier; "but you still need to come in and fill out an incident report. What if it gets infected, or you start having back pain after a few days. You know it's for your own protection and it's not going to take you that long to fill out the form. Don't give me a hard time, Anne. You know the rules," he teased.

While Anne wouldn't admit it, it wasn't filling out the form that really bothered her. It was having to confess to the comical clumsiness that took place in front of the patients and the firemen that was disheartening. Without a doubt she knew that the story coming from her own lips would only be a catalyst for Paul's own animated version. Well, I might as well get it over with, she thought, as she walked into the supe's office. Expecting Paul to follow behind her, she was glad that he stayed back at the table to feed his face instead.

Chuck handed her the form. "I'll be back in a minute," he said, leaving the office. Taking a seat across from his desk, she took the pen from her shirt pocket and began recording the incident. The words were difficult to find at first. Everything sounded silly. Finally, they all came together and she was done. Getting up, she folded the paper in half then partially tucked it under the desk pad. I'm sure he'll see it, she thought. Walking out into the bay where the steam table was, she noticed that the area was vacant. "Good," she whispered. "Maybe I can eat in peace." Taking the thongs from a plate near the steamer, she opened the lid and picked out a soft warm bun and then a hot dog. Satisfied with her choice, her attention moved to the slow cooker that was filled with hot bubbling chili and then to another filled with nacho cheese for the corn chips. Her mouth watered while sprinkling a handful of onions over the concoction she'd assembled. Then she noticed a cooker filled with sauerkraut. "Oh man, this is going to be a yummy masterpiece," she smiled. After setting the chili, cheese, onion, sauerkraut hot dog down on her plate she scooped up a ladle full of baked beans then sat down to enjoy the first bite.

"Hey!" Paul said, as he came up behind her. "You really going to eat all that?"

"Yeah. As a matter of fact I am," she grinned. "And your sneaking up didn't scare me."

"Hey, Henry, look at this," he said. Henry, another medic, walked toward the table and leaned over her plate.

"Geez, Anne, no wonder you can't walk backwards without falling."

"Here we go," she chuckled. "I bet the news of my tripping over the orange box reached your ears with greater speed than that of Paul Revere during his famous midnight ride."

Henry laughed. "Hey, you still seeing Doctor Steward?"

"No. He's just in his internship. He had to go back to Kansas. So you see—since I don't have a boyfriend or a husband—I can eat anything I want."

"Yeah?" Henry chuckled. "Well did it ever occur to you, that maybe that's why—you don't have a boyfriend or a husband?"

Anne laughed, then took another bite of her hot dog.

Chuck walked up to the table. "Hey, Anne, we're starting to get busy. If you're done with the report, I need you and Paul on the air. Ohh," he sneered. "You weren't really going to eat that?"

"Not now," she groaned. "We're going out to get on the air."

After a quick wash of her hands, Anne went out to the rig where Paul was waiting.

"Get ready for a long one," he said. "We've got a call in Oxthorn for a possible deceased party."

After clipping her seat belt together, Anne filled in the top portion of the run form, then looked through the windshield at the road ahead. "Another deceased party." she said. "Man, they're dropping like flies. I'm glad we at least had a couple of good calls in between; where we were actually able to help someone. Nothing like a good diabetic or chest pain patient to lift your spirits."

"Yeah? Well after all those onions you just ate, it's a good thing that whoever it is, is already gone," he laughed.

"No kidding," she chuckled. "Those babies were strong. But I always carry mints. Want one?"

"Sure," he answered.

As the crew flew toward Oxthorn, the lights on the rig flashed and the siren blared, warning their approach like a warrior screaming his advance. Nearly fifteen minutes had gone by since they left Central. The mobile home park containing the requested address was just ahead. Paul turned onto their street then parked at the curb behind a sheriff deputy's car. Hopping out in her usual way, Anne opened the side doors of the rig and began reaching for the equipment. Suddenly, the front door of the residence flew open and a sheriff deputy ran down the porch steps.

"What's going on?" Paul called out. "We got this call as a deceased party."

"There's nobody dead here," the deputy yelled back. By his tone of voice, he was clearly angry.

"Great. Now what's going on," Anne mumbled to herself.

Carrying all the normal, portable equipment, the crew raced toward the residence. Glancing through the storm door as she closed it behind her, Anne noticed the deputy coming back toward the porch carrying a backboard. Then a ruckus in the room to the right of where they were standing drew her attention

"Hey, guys—what'a we got?" Paul called out.

"Come see for yourself," Lieutenant Klieg answered.

Without wasting anymore time, Paul and Anne walked toward the room and peered inside. The room, apparently a bathroom, was full of firemen and a very obese man in swimming trunks who was sitting in a bathtub full of pink water.

"This is Frank," Lieutenant Dave Klieg began. "He's alert and conscious. Seems he was trying to kill himself by way of electrocution. He said that after he got into the tub, he pulled a radio into the water not realizing that the plug unit was wired with a ground fault interrupter. Probably, as soon as the radio hit the water, it shut down. It was still floating in the tub when we got here. And then," Lieutenant Klieg sighed. "as a backup plan, Frank also cut his wrists; but, apparently after submerging his arms in the cool water for a while, the bleeding slowed down. The sheriff's department got the call from a relative. Deputy Hanna was the first on the scene. I think that he thought Frank was dead until he saw him turn his head to look at him. Must of gave him a start. He was pretty ticked when we got here."

"I can see that. So, Frank, all things considered, how are you doing?" Anne asked.

"Well I'm weak—and to be honest, disappointed. Plus, I feel like a prune."

"Well, let's get you out of the water and bandage up those arms."

"I had Deputy Hanna grab a backboard," Dave said. "I thought it might be the easiest way to get Frank out of the tub since he's such a big guy. We tried to help him stand up but his legs are as wobbly as a new calf."

As Dave talked, he motioned for one of his men to bring the backboard into the room. Anne couldn't see any reason not to use the backboard, if that was the most workable way for them. So with the plan laid out, she went to gather the bandaging equipment while a couple of the other firemen went out to bring the stretcher in from the sidewalk. Minutes later they returned, squeezing and angling the cot through the mobile home's narrow door. Now with the cot set up, they joined the others who were waiting in the bathroom for the raising of Frank Walker.

They say that many hands make light work—and after hearing all the huffing and puffing from Paul and the other guys, Anne was especially glad they were there. In minutes Frank was laying on the stretcher, dripping with water and blood. While using a couple of clean towels from the linen closet, Anne began drying his arms before dressing the large lacerations he'd made with a kitchen knife. Everyone else in the group used that time to catch their breath. Once she had finished the first aid portion of the job, she covered him with the paper sheet then unfolded the blanket to make it wide enough to cover him. Because the backboard was normally used for a suspected spine injury, a pillow wasn't part of its regimen. But in today's case, it was picked for the benefit of the EMS personnel. So with that, Anne grabbed the pillow and tucked it under Frank's head in her usual motherly way. Now he was ready to be transported to the rig. After twisting and pushing through the door, the guys worked together to carry him down the porch steps, then rolled the stretcher toward the rig.

Once the way was clear, Anne sped out to the rig with some of the equipment and hopped up into the patient compartment. In movements that were now second nature, she took a bag of IV solution and a tubing setup from the cabinet over the jump seat. In the time that it took her to put it all together, Paul and the firemen had rolled Frank into the patient compartment. After taking a blood pressure and feeling for a pulse, she jotted the information down on the run form. Then suddenly a gush of cold air whipped through the open back doors, widening the gap of the open side doors. Instantly Frank began to shiver.

"Hey," Anne called out. She could hear the guys just outside with the gear and looked to get their attention. "Sorry, Frank. It looked like it was going to be nice this morning. Guess that cold front the weatherman was predicting decided to move in." One of the firemen slid the equipment across the floor and into the cabinets but neglected to shut the doors.

"Good grief," she mumbled. As she got up to shut the side doors, she called out to a couple of the guys who were coming out of the residence. "Hey—could one of you shut the back doors? This guy's going to die from pneumonia." No sooner had the words left her lips then she realized they were probably not the best choice at this point.

Frank, after hearing them however, chuckled. "Now wouldn't that be a hoot."

"Well you still have a sense of humor, Frank; that's a good sign." Realizing that the firemen didn't hear her, she moved toward the back doors then heard Paul thanking them as he approached the rig. The doors swung open as he jumped inside, then slammed shut behind him.

"How you doing, Anne? What do you need me to do?"

"Well, I was just getting ready to start an IV. It's already set up. If you want to get the rest of the history and turn on the heat—that would be a good thing."

Frank seemed very comfortable with the crew. He answered each question with ease and eventually confessed that today was not his first attempt at ending his life.

"No," he said, sort of teary. "I tried to kill myself a few nights ago. I drank a bottle of whiskey then sat in my car with the engine running out in a field, with a hose going from the tail pipe to the back window. But that didn't work. Guess my car's too drafty. Then I tried it again the next night. I drank another bottle of whiskey hoping to get up the nerve to shoot myself—but I fell asleep and when I woke up I just couldn't do it. Then last night, I tried it again and you already know how that turned out."

"How long were you sitting in the tub, Frank?" Anne asked.

"Since about midnight."

"Oh geez, Frank," Paul gently teased. "You must be pretty waterlogged by now."

"Yeah," he chuckled. "I guess I am."

Anne finished tapping the IV in place, then tucked Frank's arm back under the blanket. The heat was well circulated and the rig toasty. Paul had crawled through to the front compartment and they were en route to St. Luke's, Frank's hospital of choice.

"You know, Frank," she began. "Seems to me that if you try to kill yourself that many times and it doesn't work—maybe it's not your time to go. Maybe your creator isn't finished with you yet and you still have things to do here, you know?" Noticing a tear run down his cheek, Anne reached for a tissue. "Granted, I don't know what's going on in your life or the circumstances that led you to these thoughts of suicide, but maybe you should reconsider your options."

Frank sighed, then began unfolding years of family problems. Anne listened and offered an occasional comment just to reassure him that she was truly interested. Before long, they were pulling into the driveway of the hospital where Frank agreed to get some help. While Anne knew that it wasn't a good idea to get involved with patients on a personal level, she wished that someday she and Frank would cross paths later on down the road just so she could see how he did with his treatment.

It was November 10, 1988. Throughout the country and probably the world, every newspaper's headline carried the announcement of the previous day's event, the fall of the Berlin Wall. Truly history was unfolding as the division of more than fifty years of communism in Eastern Europe and Germany had crumbled. But instead of joy, the promises of freedom and opportunity were met with unhappiness and unrest as one era gave birth to another. "I guess it's true, most people just don't like change," Anne said to herself, while reading the paper. "No doubt, it's uncomfortable to be taken from something that you're sure of, only to be moved to something that you're not. But then, that's life—its always full of changes and challenges. That's what stretches us and helps us grow. I wonder how long it will take for them to figure out that it's not even so much the challenges but more of the way that people deal with the challenges that makes the difference." After folding the newspaper in half, she slid it behind the seat in the ambulance, then said a quick prayer for the people and the leaders of Germany.

Peering into the party store window, she looked for her new partner, Tommy. Paul left in April to go work as a full-time fireman at Clear Lake Township. Since then, she and Tommy had become a team. Even though the onset of the partnership was awkward at first, those feelings soon passed. To her, Tommy seemed like an angry young man when he first hired on at Mercy. Then, little by little he began to open up. He had a twin brother Todd, who he resembled greatly; yet there were noticeable differences that set them apart.

Anne still remembered hearing about Tommy's first week as a paramedic. He was working with a seasoned medic then named Trevor. They were responding on an emergency call in the City of Lancemen for someone complaining of shortness of breath. As they neared the address, lit up and sirens blaring, a boy about ten years old ran out in front of them. The front grill of the rig slammed into the boy and killed him instantly. Later they found out that he'd been hiding in the bushes alongside the road. The kids in the neighborhood said that he liked to play chicken with the cars. "He was pretty fast," they said. Perhaps, but unfortunately he wasn't fast enough to get across the street unharmed that day.

As the year anniversary of that day approached, Anne sensed a tenseness in Tommy's behavior. He became almost philosophical as he tried to make sense of the incident, asking Anne a barrage of questions regarding her faith.

"God created you and everyone else with a free will," she answered. "It's just one of the many gifts He's given you. He is a gentleman. He doesn't force you to love Him. He wants you to make the choice. And, just like with every other choice or decision that we have the freedom to make, right or wrong, it will have a positive or negative effect, not only in our lives but also in the lives of those around us. The parables in the book of Matthew, for instance, exemplify good and bad choices. We need to think about what we are doing before we do it and the possible end result. You had no control over that boy's decision to dash across the road a year ago. Even though he probably never even thought he'd actually get hurt or be killed, it was his choice and now you have to live with the end result. We're taught that kids fall under the covering of other prayerful people until the age of accountability. While it seems to me that a lot of people who don't go to church, think that those who do view themselves as perfect. Well, I think that's really contrary to the truth. People who truly understand the reason they go to church, recognize that it's a hospital for sinners, so to speak—and no one is without sin. I don't have any special clearance or phone line to God, Tommy. You can talk to Him too if you want. So, quit beating yourself up over this. There's only one way to find peace with it—and you already know the answer."

"Alpha 648," Buster called over the radio.

"48," she answered.

"You still at the party store in Lakeview?"

"Yeah. Tommy's picked up the same bag of chips five times," she chuckled.

"Well, get him out of there. Clear Lake just went out on a medical—and you're the closest car I have. Let me know when you're ready to copy."

"Go ahead."

"You're responding to 57 Cleveland for a possible CVA. The incident number is 1542 at 14:12."

"Ten-four," she said. Before Anne even hung up the mic, she tooted the horn. Seconds later, Tommy came running out with a bag of chips and bottle of pop. As soon as his seat belt clicked, she flipped on the emergency lights and pulled out onto the main road. "Hang on," she teased.

Even though the roads throughout the west end of the county were full of curves and streets that started and stopped at different sections, the crew still made it to the scene in record time. There was no reason why they shouldn't, with Anne's knowledge of the area and the fact that Tommy had grown up in Clear Lake Township. As soon as Anne, had finished backing the rig into the driveway, she grabbed the clipboard from the floor and started toward the brown house with asbestos siding. Tommy pulled the equipment from the side doors, then followed behind her up the porch steps. The fire department was on the scene and had already taken a set of vitals. Anne was glad to see that her old partner, Paul, was there.

"Hi guys," Paul began. "This is Adeline March. She's seventy-two years old and apparently has a long medical history. Initially I thought that she presented like a stroke patient; then I noticed that there's no facial dropping or evidence of paralysis. I started making a list of her past medical problems through her husband here, who called. Russ is in the bathroom collecting her prescription bottles—he should be right out."

Within minutes of their arrival on the scene, the crew noticed that the fire department already had the patient on a couple liters of oxygen, via a nasal cannula. With that done, Tommy grabbed the EKG cables from the orange box, then hooked the patient to the cardiac monitor. Jim, one of the firemen, set up the IV while Anne examined the patient for grip strength. Loaded down with a shoe box full of prescription bottles, Russ emerged from the hallway. "Hi guys," he said. "I think I got'em all. Some are pretty old."

"Oh, she ain't taken all those," her husband sneered. "Just the ones on the kitchen table. I'm always gett'en after her about that dope! She doesn't know what she's doing half the time."

Anne listened to his statements while writing down the prescriptions from the containers on the table. "I think we might have something here," she said. "Mr. March—does your wife sometimes take more medicine than she should by mistake?"

"Oh, I don't know what she does. She could, I guess."

"What does she take the demerol for? It's a pain medicine."

"She has arthritis real bad. Maybe she takes it for that."

"Hey, Tommy, you about done with that IV?" she asked.

"I'm tapping it down right now," he answered.

"Good." After breaking off the plastic seal from the drug box, Anne reached for a vial of naloxone hydrochloride, then drew up zero point four milligrams. "Here ya go, Tommy, give her this."

Within seconds of the drug being pushed into the IV, she became conscious of the crew and fire department's presence. Her husband watched as she looked around the room.

"What was wrong with her?" he asked.

"I think she took too much of her medication by mistake. Basically, she was snowed," Anne smiled. "We'll run her over to the hospital and let them watch her for a while. She'll be fine."

As soon as Tommy and Anne left the new hospital in Bedford, they drove over to the fire station in Clear Lake to return the oxygen bottle that went with Adeline by mistake. Tommy was quiet during most of the trip. Sometimes he was just like that. As soon as Anne pulled in behind the fire station, Paul came out to retrieve the bottle.

"That call was interesting," he smiled. "Did you see the look on her face when she saw all of us standing around? Man, I've seen that look on the faces of druggies in Lancemen a thousand times, but never on an old lady before."

Tommy reached down to the floor between the seats and grabbed the O2 bottle, then handed it to Anne who relayed it to Paul through the driver's window.

"Sorry we stole your bottle," Anne teased. "Thanks for the help on that call."

"No problem," he grinned. "Hey, Anne, I noticed it's getting pretty cold these days. Probably before too long you're going to have to break out your wool hat."

"Funny," she chuckled. Waving goodbye, she pulled away before he had a chance to share his story.

After clearing the fire station, the crew was sent to cover in Lakeview near the area of their old "Fort Liz." After sitting there for a moment, Tommy grew quiet again, and after a few minutes he spoke up.

"Hey, did Paul know that lady overmedicated herself before you gave her that narcan?"

"Well, I can't say for sure—but I think he did. Why?"

"Man, how come I didn't see that."

"Maybe because you've only been doing this for less than a year? Tommy—I have never seen anybody so rough on himself as you are. What about all those cardiac arrest saves we had—and that letter of commendation that we got from St. Luke's for that kid with the messed up trach? You can't expect to know it all in the first year. Shoot, I've been doing this better than a dozen years and I'm still learning. That's the beauty of it all. Paul and I had worked together for quite a while. After so many days or months of running with one person, you just sort of develop this groove. You really need to loosen up, Tommy. This is a fun job. You get to see all kinds of things and meet all kinds of interesting people. Some you get to help—and some you don't." Chuckling, she continued. "Once, when I was working with this guy named Brian, we were transporting this psych patient. Everything was quiet. Brian was in the back with the patient, writing out his report. Then, out of the blue this guy yells out—'Well how do I get to Texas if I don't have a map?' Brian very nonchalantly answered, 'Don't worry about it, we'll stop at Triple A.' Seconds later, the guy decided he didn't want to go to Texas. So that was that."

Tommy smiled. "I remember Rod telling me about a psych patient that he and Bill were taking over to Eider Valley who decided to leap out through the back window half way there."

"Yeah—and fortunately they were stopped at an intersection," Anne chuckled. "Can you imagine being in the car behind them? That must have been a sight."

"Hey, so what was Paul talking about—with the wool hat?"

"Well, first let me say, that if Paul was telling the story you'd get a whole different, and I'm sure a more comical rendition. But here's the real story. See, we had this call in the middle of the night last winter for an old guy who fell in his apartment. He was legally blind and the group of old ladies next to his apartment heard the noise and called. When we got there he was sitting on his bed and he was fine, but we checked him out anyway to make sure. He said he didn't want to go to the hospital but I figured it might not be a bad idea; sometimes other things get missed, you know. But he was sure of what he wanted and even after a few minutes of trying to persuade him, he still didn't want to go. He said he could see just fine, in spite of his blind state, and that I shouldn't worry. So I asked him—well okay, then, if you can see so good, then what am I wearing? He looked me over, then started describing my clothes. 'Well you're wearing a blue jacket and dark pants—and you're wearing a wool cap.' Instantly, Paul and the patient's neighbors started to laugh. They could see that I wasn't wearing a hat at all. Of course Paul saw his chance. 'See, Anne,' he said. 'I told you to brush that mop before we came out.' Yep, Paul's a jokester all right. I remember last spring, when we were covering at the park and ride, at post seven. We used to always bring our lunch cause you never know when you're going to get to eat. So there I was, eating a sandwich when I noticed a patch of raspberries growing in a nearby thicket. Being a farm girl and everything, of course I went to investigate. They looked like really nice berries so I ate a few and then started filling up my empty sandwich bag. Well suddenly, while I was picking the berries I saw the bushes next to me move, so I stopped for a minute to see what it was. Then it stopped, so I continued. Then suddenly, the bushes moved again. So I figured, forget it—and backed out. Now with my few, fresh picked berries, I sadly walked back to the rig. As soon as I was a few feet away, I saw Paul sitting in the passenger seat, eating some of the grapes that he brought for lunch. First he ate some, then tossed a few into the brushes. Instantly I knew why the bushes were moving. He'd been tossing grapes in there. When he saw my face, he burst out laughing. Every time he tells that story he makes it sound like I ran from the bushes, like I was being chased by a bear."

"That's funny." Tommy said. "You know when they told me that I was going to have to work with you, I was so mad. I thought you were a witch," he chuckled. "Remember the first thing you said to me at LOH in the cafeteria?"

"Yeah," she grinned. "I asked you if you had an attitude yet. All you new people these days, come in with an attitude. I was just trying to see what you were made of."

"Whatever! Anyway, I was wrong. You're not a witch. But don't tell anybody I said that."

"What—that you thought I was a witch?"

"No, that I was wrong."

The months continued with Tommy and Anne as partners. And to no surprise, January of 1990 started out brisk to say the least. It was the second week into the year and all ready it'd been busy. After a few hours into their shift and after several minor car crashes, the crew left Lancemen General. They'd been cleared to attend a meeting that was being held in the banquet hall at the bowling alley a few miles away. Once the meeting agenda was covered, an awards ceremony was set to follow.

Robbie finished presenting the news about the new computerized dispatch system that the company was switching to, then turned the floor over to Doctor Malley.

"Well I wanted to start out by going over a few up and coming changes with the drug boxes; but Robbie reminded me that some of you are still in service for any call that might occur, so we'll save that for another meeting—fair enough? Now, even though the company has the Pro Club which was started a few years ago to let their people know when they're doing well—I'd like to go beyond that today. While we have a number of very good paramedics working for this company, I feel it's a great privilege to recognize one—who really stands out from the rest. As most of you know, I think that the medical field is too rough for most women. But once in a while—one or well maybe two," he smiled, "will prove me wrong."

As he continued speaking, Anne's mind began to drift. That's weird, she thought, I can't believe that he actually admitted to that. No doubt he's given me a pretty good lecture from time to time. I'll never forget the day that I was working a twenty-four hour shift and we had that chest pain patient who lived just a few miles from the hospital. I thought he'd have a stroke when we rolled that guy in without an IV. Well, really, I guess I had that coming.

"So today," she heard Doctor Malley say, "We're going to do something that we've never done before in this county. And while today's event only includes the paramedics that are within this company, I feel the end result would be the same whether it was the company—or county wide.

To the group of people who were asked to make the selection of our first paramedic of the year, it turned out to be an easy and unanimous one. I am proud to present this award to Angela Gates."

Anne was dumbfounded. Never for a moment did she think that he'd been talking about her. He said so many nice things—and she missed most of it by daydreaming. The medics around her pushed her up to the front. "Speech! Speech!" they cheered. As she looked over the crowd of beaming faces before her, for the first time in her life, at least the first time that she could remember, she couldn't think of a thing to say.

Then after releasing her biggest sigh ever, she smiled and in a warm shy voice said, "Thank you."

The crowd chuckled, then clapped as if the most elegant words were spoken. Then Merve came up and handed her a check for five hundred dollars. Wow, she thought. This is really something!

When the meeting was over, she and Tommy returned to the rig. Almost instantly, her mind wandered back to her first years of employment at Mercy. In those days, she was just a dispatcher in a man's world, waiting to become a nurse. But clearly, God had made other plans. Throughout her life, He had been the lamp unto her path. It was His light that had provided her sole guiding. While she knew not to search for earthly crowns, it was still nice to be appreciated. Thinking back, she remembered how the crews used to joke that the company was like a soap opera. The title they picked was, "As the Beacon Turns," which was an obvious, revised version of a real soap opera, changed to reflect the domed lights on the old rigs. But new or old, they were lights that pierced the night and glowed during the day to warn their approach and reassure the sick or injured that help was coming. At this time in her life, Anne entertained no question or doubt that she'd been led to a place of calling. And she knew there was no other place she'd rather be than in the light—As the Beacon Turns.

EPILOGUE

As The Beacon Turns was written in a fictional format but is based on real people, emergency and non-emergency calls, and true events. Most of the said characters within these pages, are still involved in the medical field in some aspect and have kept in fairly close contact with each other throughout the last twenty-six years. The author takes great pride in presenting this network of friends as life finds them, near present day.

Character name:

The characters of Roman and Roger are a mixture of several people of whom the author has lost contact. Cubby is a mix of two individuals; both, presently work as volunteer firemen, in addition to their full time jobs. Most of the nursing staff mentioned and others are still involved in their same careers in the Southeastern Michigan region.

Angela Naomi Gates:

The character of Angela or Anne, as her friends in the book call her, in real life is author of "As The Beacon Turns."

She has an Associate in Applied Science degree in Emergency Medical Technology. Her duties over the past twenty-eight years in the medical field include dispatching, EMT, paramedic, Training Officer, Fleet Ambulance/Paramed Inc., Patient Billing Services Coordinator and presently is the EC Coordinator of an area hospital. Proudly, she has completed the three-year Ministry Training Program at Mt Zion, where she sings with the church choir. In addition, she bravely has completed one sport parachute jump. She has two children Julie and Kelly and two grandchildren, Jamarl and Jannah.

Mr. Dewit:

Mr. Richard Osgood, was a well-liked EMS instructor at Oakland Community College for approximately twenty-five years. He strongly believed in the EMS system and spent many hours preparing a select group of medical personnel. Author's last contact with Dick, was at his retirement party where he planned to live in Arizona.

Chris:

Chris Stepleton and his wife Debbie, have been married for thirty-one years. He has worked in the EMS industry for thirty years. Debbie is employed at a local hospital as a cash analyst. They have three daughters. Beth lives in Tennessee where she teaches music at an elementary school. Erin is married and lives in Virginia where she works as International Consultant for a food company. Andrea lives in Florida where she works at Disney World in addition to studying fine arts at a Florida college.

Tom:

Tom Gahan has 33 years of working in the EMS profession and currently is living and working in Clearwather, Florida. His EMS career began as an ambulance driver while in high school. He started working at Fleet Ambulance in the early 1970's. Shortly afterwards, Tom received his EMT, and then paramedic license from the State of Michigan. Initially, he worked as supervisor then was given the position of Chief of Operations, Vice President and finally Company President. He and his wife Sue have been married fifteen years. Together they have five children, two grand-children, plus one the way.

Rick Stockwell:

Rick Stockton is presently a Safety Compliance Coordinator, OSHA instructor for SCI, Michigan Funeral Services and is an abduction prevention instructor, for Dignity Memorial Escape School. He worked at Fleet ambulance as an EMT starting around 1975, then left in 1985. In 1989 through 1990, he raced professionally with the International Motor Sports Association. He and his wife Lucy have been married for seven years and enjoy their blended family. They have a son Rich, daughters Angie and Elyse and a granddaughter Hailie.

Dan:

Daniel P. Delongchamp was seventeen when he began his career in EMS as a volunteer firefighter. In addition to the normal firefighter training, fire one and fire two, he is also skilled in Hazmat operations and extrication. He is an EMT/Specialist, has completed training for fire officer one, two and three and is presently a captain at Independence Fire Department. He has been involved in EMS for approximately thirty years, several of which were at Fleet ambulance. He and his wife Michele have been married eighteen years. They have two daughters, Nicole and Kristen.

Dr. Cupos:

Carlito C. Mojica M.D. was from Vegan, Philippines. He was born July 6,1942 and died December 18, 2001. He was Vice Chief of Emergency Services at St. Joseph Mercy Hospital in Pontiac and had practiced medicine for over thirty years. He was involved in the EMS community and was Charter President of Samahang ng. He enjoyed golf, playing the piano and was known for his uncanny wit. He was well respected and greatly appreciated by anyone who worked with him.

Merve:

Merve is a mixture of both of the original owners of Fleet Ambulance Service/Paramed Incorporated.

Floyd (Skip) Miles began his retirement almost nine years ago. He has a long history in the EMS profession, beginning as one of the original owners of Fleet Ambulance Service. Having the lead role in setting up the Michigan Ambulance Association, he went on as President of Michigan Association Ambulance Services, was Interim Chairman during its formation once incorporated, served twice as the Governor Advisor for the State of Michigan for Emergency Medical Services, was on Oakland County EMS Council, Predecessor to the Board of Commission and Coordinator of the NATI course a year before the Federal Government developed the EMT program. Wanting to fully understand what the EMTs under his employment were expected to know, he sat among them as a student attending the second EMT class offered at Oakland Community College. He is very proud of the fact that Fleet Ambulance was the first in the State of Michigan to operate with state licensed paramedics. Once retired, he enjoyed a great deal of time on his fifty-five foot boat where he journeyed to Maine, the Bahamas and along the coast of Western Florida. Finding he was not yet ready to fully retire from the EMS profession, he joined partnership with Bill in operating Star EMS. He and his wife Beverly, who he met on a blind date, have been married thirty-five years. They have two adult children, Doug, who is a paramedic and a daughter, Monica.

Dick Rudlaff, a co-owner of Fleet Ambulance, also began his retirement nearly nine years ago after being instrumental in many areas of the company's development. After retiring from the EMS industry in 1994,

Dick began a commercial real-estate business, building subdivision homes and condos in Northern Oakland County. Currently, he lives in Florida where he competes in saltwater fishing tournaments. He is a member of the Southern Kingfish Association, and has proudly won first prize in the World Tarpon Competition. For many years, Dick enjoyed flying hot air balloons. He and his wife Janis have been married for thirty-three years. They have two adult children, Sherry and Jeff.

Jenny:

The character known as Jenny, at last knowledge was living in California where she worked in the medical field.

Buster Johnson:

Joe Busto, started his EMS career in 1977 with Suburban Ambulance. He worked there for five years until Fleet Ambulance and Suburban became Paramed Incorporated. At that time, he moved into the dispatch center, a year later was promoted to supervisor. In 1996 he moved into the law enforcement arena as a dispatcher, then became a Sheriff Deputy in 2000. In 2001, while pursuing a life long dream, he moved to Southern California where he is presently employed at a privately owned EMS service.

Max:

AKA, Mike Hall, has worked full-time as a paramedic for twenty-five years. He completed his paramedic training at Oakland Community College in 1977 and was awarded his BGS from Oakland University in 1996. He was a former company union president, is a licensed builder, a private pilot and enjoys hunting. He has been married to his wife, Debbie, for nineteen years. They have four daughters.

Shirley:

Shirley Knebel, began working for Fleet Ambulance September 5, 1972. She hired in as the only office personnel and soon became "the-wearer-of many-hats." Her initial position(s) of running the office included billing, insurance, payroll assistant, normal secretarial jobs and janitorial duties. After a short time, she began dispatching midnights and during the day when needed. In 1979 she became a full-time dispatcher. Then in 1991 she began her EMD (emergency medical dispatch) training; currently she is EMD Certified as a 911 call-taker. Since then, she has trained many new dispatcher employees and created the company used training manuals for dispatching with the Computer Aided Dispatch system. Shirley celebrated her thirtieth year anniversary in EMS January of 2001. She has three children, Alicia, Tammy and Tim, and six beautiful grandchildren and one great grandchild. Shirley is also a cancer survivor.

Denny:

The character named Denny left the ambulance sector of EMS a number of years ago when she began working as a tech at an area hospital in the cardiac cath lab. Presently, she is living with her husband, two stepsons, and daughter in Southeastern Michigan. She is a successful entrepreneur. She and her husband own and operate a video production studio in Oakland County.

Linda:

Linda Honeycutt is still very much involved in the EMS arena. After leaving Fleet Ambulance, she acted as EMS Coordinator for a large Oakland County hospital. Currently, Elsevier (Mosby Jems) employs her as the Executive Editor for the EMS and Fire-rescue book division.

John:

John Haskin began his EMS career as a paramedic about nineteen years ago. He works full time as an ambulance paramedic and recently began working contingent at an area hospital in the Emergency Room. He proudly states that he and his beautiful wife, Nancy, have been happily married for eighteen years. They have two children, Samantha 14, and Ben 11. To all of this John gratefully says, Thank you Lord!

Robbie Thompson:

Tom Robinson worked in the ambulance profession from 1970 until 1996. He too was an EMT/paramedic student at Oakland Community College. Prior to that he spent four years in the Coast Guard, in the search and rescue division. Shortly after leaving Fleet/Paramed, he bought a marina and presently owns a classic boat deck and interior refurbishing company. Tom states that he and his wife Cathy, a registered nurse in the ER at a near-by hospital, have been married for twenty-five glorious years. They have two adult daughters and seven grandchildren ranging from three to thirteen years of age.

Officer Terrence Clark:

Vertis Clark served his community for twenty-five years as a well known and respected policeman. He was a marathon runner and after retiring and moving to Costa Rica, he ran in many international marathons in states and countries such as Hawaii, Boston, Germany and Australia. In the early part of September 2001, Veris passed away after finishing a jog near his home.

Chuck:

Michael J. Nutt received his EMT license from St. Clair County Community College in June of 1975. On August 18, 1977, he received his paramedic license from Madonna University in Livonia. After receiving his BS in Emergency Medical Technology and license as an EMS Instructor/ Coordinator he went on and graduated with a Master of Science as a Physician Assistant from the University of Detroit Mercy. In addition he worked as a member of the Michigan Disaster Medical Assistance Team, now part of the Department of Homeland Security. He has sailed in the Port Huron, Mackinaw boat races for many years. Both he and his wife Geri, of nearly eight years, are licensed pilots. Geri is a RN at a nearby hospital. Michael works as a PA in surgery at a different hospital than his wife. They have a daughter Kimberly and a golden retriever named Yeager. As an added note, Michael was second cousin to Pope John Paul I.

Big Rick:

Richard K. Schachern, much to the regret of all who knew and loved him, passed away May 5, 2003. Rick was a wonderful paramedic and was involved in the EMS profession for twenty-six years. He taught a number of paramedic classes during that time at Paramed's Training Institute, sharing his knowledge and EMS stories with EMTs in both the private ambulance sector, as well as the fire service. He was an avid outdoorsman who enjoyed hunting, fishing and bird watching. For a number of years he played his guitar and sang with an Irish band called the Gaels. He was well known for his unbelievable knowledge of trivia and dry sense of humor.

Ret:

Dan Ret is presently Chief Executive Officer of Bloomfield Farms Properties and Chief Executive Officer of Yellow Cab Service Corporation of Florida. His EMS career lasted twenty years, which he began as an EMT. After a short time he became a dispatcher then a dispatch supervisor. Gradually he headed up the executive ladder, as Communications Director, Information Technology Director, Vice President of Operations and finally Director of Operations for Michigan before taking a job a Metro Cars. He and his wife Diane, have been married twenty years and have two daughters.

Jerry:

Jerry Grubb enjoyed his career as a paramedic for 23 years and also served as Councilor to EMS Compliance. Presently, he and his wife of eighteen years, Rhonda, own and operate a large (approximately 120 children) day care center. They have two children, Jerrad and Caitlyn. Jerry also installs computer software, has coached football for eight years, been involved in chartable organizations for kids and enjoys deep-sea fishing.

Bill:

Bill Grubb moved from Texas and came to Michigan where he worked at a local newspaper before entering the EMT/Paramedic Program at Oakland Community College. He received his paramedic license in 1978. He is Jerry's younger brother (above) as well as good friend. Bill was an EMS Operation Manager at AMR of Michigan, before becoming a partner and co-owner of Star EMS with Skip. He and his wife Jan have been married for sixteen years. Jan is a RN at a nearby hospital. Bill and Jan have one cat Yoda, who is seventeen years old.

Randy:

Randy Callahan has been in the EMS field in some capacity for approximately twenty-seven years. Currently, he lives in Fort Collins Colorado where he is a full-time firefighter. He truly enjoys living in the foothills of the Rocky Mountains where he shares his life and love for the mountains, Irish music, and apple pie with three dogs, three horses, two cats and wife Patsy.

Dale:

Dan Marietta graduated as a paramedic from Lansing Community College. After working for several years in that capacity he left and entered the Detroit Police Academy and is currently a Grosse Point Woods, Public Safety Officer. In addition to his Public Safety Officer duties, he is also on the Swat Team. He and his wife Lisa have been married for eighteen years. They have two boys, Alex and Aaron.

Rod:

Rod Schlutow, also a paramedic student at OCC, began his career in EMS in the mid 1980's and is still going strong. In addition, he is a jack-of-all-trades and has a home-repairman business on the side. He and his wife Shannon, who is an ICU Nurse at a local hospital, have been married almost twenty years and together they have four children, Cianna, Allen, Alex and Emily Marie Schlutow, whose initials are EMS.

Jack:

Jack Bratun has been in the EMS profession twenty-six years. Now retired, he enjoys time with his three daughters, Tara, Trish and Tammy and his fourteen-year-old dog, Buddy.

Alex:

Eric Lutrell left the EMS profession approximately sixteen years ago to work in the cath lab at a nearby hospital. He and his wife, Gretchen, of twenty years moved to Florida for a short time but then returned to Michigan. Presently, he works in the cath lab of a Southern Oakland County hospital and runs a home repair business. Eric also studied auto design and worked as a draftsman for four years. They have five children, Amanda, Justine, Emma, Jacob and Alexa.

Ronny:

Rondale Parr studied for his paramedic license which he received in 1991, at Paramed Teaching Institute under Richard K. Schachern. He started working for Paramed in 1989 initially as support services, then became an EMT in 1990. Rondale also attended Specs Howard School of Broadcasting and was a freelance musician playing bass guitar in several bands for nearly twenty years. He has three children, two sons and a daughter.

Paul:

John Holland is a firefighter, engineer, arson investigator and paramedic. His arson investigation training was through the Michigan State Police and he attended the FBI academy in Quantico, Virginia for arson/crime scene investigation. Also, he received training in Socorro, New Mexico for incident response terrorist bombing, through the United States Justice Department. He and his wife Micki have been married for sixteen years. They have three active boys, Nick 14, who received football coaching from Jerry, Drew 11 and Noah 7. John is an avid hunter and outdoorsman, sharing his love for all with his family.

Dr. Big Dave Malley:

Dr. David Malickie DO, F.A.C.O.E.P., F.A.C.O.I., is currently practicing as a full-time Emergency Room Physician in Southeastern Michigan. He remains active as/with, the area's EMS Medical Control Authority, in addition to providing medical direction for the area fire department EMS systems and private EMS agencies. He has been married to his wife for thirty-four years. They have two sons in college; and yes, one of his sons in in pre-med to become an Emergency Medicine Physician.

Dr. Dowell:

Dr. Michael Q. Doyle, B.S. from University of Dayton and DO. from University For Health Sciences, Kansas City, Missouri. Doctor Doyle did his postgraduate training at Pontiac Osteopathic Hospital Medical Center. He is currently practicing as an Emergency Room Physician as he has for thirty years. He and his wife have been married for twenty-three years. They have two children, a son Brian and a daughter Megan.

Jason:

John Collins received his Paramedic Certification from the University of Texas which he attended from 1981-1982 and his National Certification in 1983. He joined the United States Air Force where he acted as an Air Force Medic. He also worked as a medic for San Antonio City Ambulance for a year and was a Basic EMT Instructor for the Air Force. After coming to Michigan, where he worked at Fleet Ambulance, he received an ADN from Oakland Community College and worked on the Critical Transport Unit for AMR of Michigan until he left in 1997. Currently, John works as an ICU nurse at a hospital in Mt. Clemens, Michigan. He and his wife, Robin, have been married for twelve years and have a six-month-old son, Nicholas.

Tommy:

Mike Chatterson began attending OCC right out of high school and received his EMT license in 1989. Soon afterwards, he attended the Paramed Training Institute under, Richard K. Schachern (Big Rick) and became a paramedic in June of 1990. Mike performed full-time as a paramedic until becoming an Operations Manager in 1998. In 1999, he left AMR to work in Genesee as a Genesee County Sheriff Deputy. He also works for Milford Police Department as a reserve officer. In addition, he is employed by Livingston County EMS and has attended classes in Tae Kwon Do for a number of years. He and his wife Karen, an emergency room RN at an outlying hospital, have been married almost nine years. They have two horses, Hobbes and Wizard, a miniature donkey, Sidney, and two dogs, Haley and Rolex.

ISBN 1-41204423-5